Sylvia

BRYCE COURTENAY

Sylvia

McArthur & Company
Toronto

First published in Canada in 2007 by
McArthur & Company
322 King St. West, Suite 402
Toronto, Ontario
M5V 1J2
www.mcarthur-co.com

Library and Archives Canada Cataloguing in Publication

Courtenay, Bryce, 1933-
Sylvia / Bryce Courtenay.

ISBN 978-1-55278-672-7

I. Title.
PR9619.3.C598S95 2007   823'.914   C2007-904189-2

Cover Photography:
        Woman – John Tziavis
        Vaulted ceiling over altar – Michael Gesigner / Getty Images
Original Cover © Penguin Group (Australia)

Printed and bound in Canada by *Friesens*

10 9 8 7 6 5 4 3 2 1

For Christine Gee,
my beloved partner

For Fiona McIntosh,
who gave me the concept for this book

PREFACE

The Jerusalem Fever

THIS WAS A STRANGE period, even for a time of civil war, when horrible surprise and uncertainty, sickness and blight upon the land seemed as commonplace as dogs barking in the night. People, sensible and devout, not given to open display and well knowing their lack of noteworthy lives, took to strange acts of sudden wilfulness. A vainglorious, corrupt and complacent Church, the only arbiter of right from wrong and well accustomed to owning all judgements, felt certain these signs and portents were visitations from the devil, while the ordinary folk clearly saw God's mysterious hand at work in their lives.

Though how God, one crisp March morning in the year of our Lord 1212, could cause two chaste women of Cologne to strip to public nakedness in the grey dawn light was a complex mystery even for those epochal times. That two fat women with no cause to want for anything, and at a time when to be rotund was a sign of contentment and privilege, took to behaving like drunken hussies seemed near impossible to explain as a divine manifestation.

These, you must understand, were enormous women, their pendulous breasts lifting and slapping against great wobbling stomachs, each milk-white thigh shifting its weight first to the left and then to the right as they trundled barefoot across the wet, cold earth.

The fact of the two fat women running was a near miracle in itself. But further to this, neither was known to the other – they came down different streets and it was well-known in their respective neighbourhoods that they would customarily walk only short distances before having to stop to recover their breath. But now they ran, if less the gazelle and more the hippopotamus, still it was running by any known description. They wept as they ran, constantly calling out the name of the most holy place in Christendom.

If this was a Satan-inspired early-morning madness, then it was also an infection that seemed to be carried within the stinking city not yet cleansed of winter ordure by the spring rains. At about the time the Angelus bell rang and even before the sun was to rise fully that morning, as if to some unspoken command, hundreds of pious women rose from their beds. The fortunate and the desperate poor, all keepers of the faith, sat bolt upright, then, as if possessed, stepped urgently from their beds and hastily drew their woollen nightgowns or the rags they slept in over their heads, casting them to the floor, and stood naked before their Creator.

To some further inward command, the women crept silently past sleeping husbands and children to emerge from the doorways of homes and hovels in every neighbourhood. That they regarded themselves as spiritually guided there is no doubt – foolishness and wanton display played no part in their chaste and pious thoughts. With their arms and faces raised to heaven, eyes tightly shut to the rising sun, they ran from every direction towards the square in front of the church of St Martin where from their collective lips issued the single chant, 'Our children in Jerusalem!'

The archbishop and his two attendant clerics, together with the small number of old women and a smattering of pilgrims seeking indulgences before the spring ploughing who were attending the early-morning mass, hearing the chanting that came from outside the church, hurried to the great doors. Some would later claim that at least a thousand women stood naked chanting in the church square. Later that day town officials would announce the figure at less than a hundred and then, as time wore on and at the insistence of the archbishop, it was further revised to a handful. Finally, when it came time to add the event to the pages of Church history, it was reduced to the original two fat women running, who, the Latin scribe was careful to add, were found dead, struck down by the hand of the Almighty.

History, when it is recorded from only one determining source, is usually as unreliable as it is self-serving. It consists, in the main, of what the Holy Father in Rome or the Princes of the Church, archbishops and proctors cared to acknowledge, and is usually rearranged to suit the political or doctrinal agenda of the day. The truth in those medieval times, as often as not, was placed in the custody of the eyewitness, where it too became degraded when carried forward in song and legend. This communal voice, if not entirely reliable, at least has the distinction of being neither politically inspired nor self-serving and therefore has no reason to conceal the facts.

Accepting that two people who witness the same event may see it quite differently and allowing for exaggeration and the usual ale-house talk, the layman's truth may yet be the more reliable of the two versions. The Church historian says two fat women possessed of a satanic frenzy entered the square where they were struck down for their sin of nakedness. The secular voice claims more, many more, naked women swept up in a common religious zeal inspired by the Holy Ghost gathered in the church square that early March day in the year 1212. We may choose to believe one or the other account, but the common voice possibly explains what the Church was never able to: how the Children's Crusade was initially inspired.

To continue the popular account, the congregation, watching from within the church, had barely sufficient time to gain a glimpse of the naked chanting women before the archbishop ordered them to return at once to kneel before the high altar. Whereupon the church doors were closed with a great banging and echoing and shooting of bolts into place by the two templars, who traditionally stood as the night watch for the few coins it earned. Alarmed by the echo of the doors, a blur of pigeons rose into the sky from the hundreds of carved and crenulated tucks, nesting nooks and crannies and from the snarling jaws of the granite gargoyles.

Inside the church the two ineffectual and near-hysterical clerics, shouting and wringing their hands, implored the morning congregation to stop their excited chattering and to kneel alongside four nuns at prayer in front of the great altar. These four devout figures, three nuns and a lay sister, oblivious of the events taking place outside the church, had remained steadfastly at prayer throughout.

With his flock finally gathered and silent at his feet, the archbishop reminded them that at the very moment Adam, tempted by a recalcitrant Eve, had taken a bite from the forbidden fruit, innocence in the world had ceased to exist. From that time, with the eviction from the Garden of Eden, public nakedness had become a mortal sin.

He informed them that, because they had been witnesses to this flagrant act of sinning, they too were no longer pure in spirit and therefore the wine of Christ's blood and bread of His flesh was withdrawn until they'd received confession. They would, the archbishop hastened to declare, be allowed to receive mass *only* if they confessed the sin of Eve and, as penance, purged their memories of the event they *henceforth imagined* their eyes had recently witnessed. This they all readily agreed to do; better to accept a Church-sanctioned lie than be forever damned by a satanic truth. The archbishop accepted their collective confession and pronounced them cleansed in sight, memory and mind.

In the re-telling of any event, a brief glimpse is far more dangerous to the truth than a good hard look, so that not everything 'apparently not seen' in the church square by the women attending mass that morning can be absolutely relied upon. What is certain – for it took place in front of their very eyes *and* after their minds had been cleansed, their memories expunged and their tongues hopefully silenced – was the subsequent behaviour of the three nuns and the lay sister kneeling in prayer.

Just as the archbishop pronounced the penance of compulsory

memory loss and began the final benediction, the four kneeling forms rose simultaneously to their feet and commenced to disrobe. In a matter of moments they stood naked with their eyes tightly closed, arms raised towards the statue of the crucified Christ and in clear voice simultaneously pronounced, 'Our children in Jerusalem!'

Outside the bolted church door the two old templars, setting aside their pikes, seated themselves on the topmost step. Slapping their knees in delight they cackled gleefully as they watched the curious proceedings in the square. They, who while twice serving as crusaders in the Holy Land believed they had witnessed every manifestation of the Christ passion, now found themselves confounded. They had seen pilgrims who had marched on their knees until the cobblestones ran red with blood; they had witnessed rape and pillage, mass hysteria, the eating of human flesh, ecstatic rending of garments, legions dressed in sackcloth and ashes, male nudity and self-mutilation, all in the name of the Christ figure. But now they merrily agreed that nothing they had hitherto seen compared to the situation evolving in front of their eyes on this early-spring morning. They proceeded to scan the chanting women for every lurid detail, knowing that for years to come no alehouse in the land would refuse to fill their tankards in return for their personal account of the onset of Jerusalem fever.

The two old soldiers watched as panting husbands, carrying garments of every description, some in possession of whips and stout sticks, began to arrive. Gesticulating wildly the husbands shouted out the names of their wives, while for the benefit of each other, they cursed the gullibility and hysteria of the weaker sex. But their presence did not diminish the spiritual exhilaration. Meek and untroublesome women, caught up in this moment of ecstasy, brushed their husbands aside as if they were beggar children tugging at their skirts.

Soon the homeless, mostly street urchins and cretinous youth, rapscallions all, sleeping under dirty rags in the dark, stinking narrow alleys that surrounded the church, wakened to the strange, high-pitched chant and descended upon the naked women like a pack of hungry wolves. Whooping and caterwauling they barged and darted among the frenzied gathering, groping unfamiliar parts, grinning lewdly for the joy of pawing and fondling female flesh while stealing bangles and beads from pliant wrists and necks. Husbands ceased from beating wives and fell instead upon the invaders from the alleyways. This seemed only to increase the fun for the errant halfwits and snot-nosed urchins who easily dodged their blows and were seen to lead the older men a merry dance. It was not long before their attackers grew short of breath and stood panting, stooped, with their hands upon their knees, whereupon the garments they clutched were ripped from their grasp as they now became the object of attack and robbery.

Yet the women remained oblivious to the mayhem surrounding them. No amount of promiscuous patting or licentious groping was to any avail; ignoring the errant hands, the thieving fingers, and the cajoling, cursing, bloody blows and cries from their anxious and angry menfolk, they chanted on and on, 'Our children in Jerusalem!'

CHAPTER ONE

Sylvia Honeyeater

I AM SYLVIA HONEYEATER. I came originally from Uedem, a village some distance from Cologne. This is the story of my life. I will relate it as honestly as I may, for they say confession is good for the soul and my soul, poor dead thing, is much in need of some good. If I should attempt to justify my deeds with the adage that the alley cat cannot choose the bowl from which it laps, you must accept that the truth is often painful.

To begin, I think myself born in 1196, whether at the beginning or the end I cannot say. It was an unpropitious year of great starvation when sickness and blight visited the land and half the village perished from the terrible epidemic that scourged Germany and all the lands surrounding. For the four years before, it had rained and flooded so much that the crops could not be harvested until late August when the seed had mostly rotted. Many folk, in an attempt to stay alive, ate the grass along the streams and the rotting flesh of dead animals, and if there were woods nearby they gathered acorns to grind into bread. It was also the year of recruitment for the German Crusade that failed in its attempt to get to Jerusalem.

I was the seed my father deposited in my poor mother's womb prior to his departure as a foot soldier and crusader for the Holy Land. He became a crusader not from any sense of piety, but to escape the sickness and in return for the promise by his Holiness the Pope that if he served in the attempt to regain the Holy Sepulchre from the vile hands of the infidels he would be forgiven his sins. It was a deal in which the Almighty most definitely got the worst of the bargain. My father was a drunk, a huge, bellicose brute, by trade a carpenter but one seldom seen to do an honest day's work. But then again, he was not alone. In order to escape from justice, many a layabout, drunkard and thief wore the Cross emblazoned upon his soldier's tunic. While playing the pious pilgrim my father was interested only in profit, in looting, the maddening frenzy of killing for Christ, rapine or some other nefarious mischief, with the forgiveness of his sins past being the glorious prize to be awarded at the conclusion of his pilgrimage.

True to my nation I was blonde and blue-eyed and later, as I grew into a woman and lost the starved look that comes with poverty, I was known to be of comely appearance and, more importantly, I knew from their constant flattery and attentions that men found me desirable. For all the advantage this was to give me I would have been better served with squint eyes and a harelip for I always find myself attracted to a rogue's bed. They say the nature of all humans is born within them, that what we are we cannot change. I am cursed as an optimist and a dreamer, a dangerous combination, for I seldom see the traps that men set for me and see only the excitement in the brute and the tedium in the good man.

If, as they say, I am as I was born, my social nature immutable, then my attraction to bastards is not something I may change, although my father, the first of many in my life, was one of the few not chosen by myself and also the first to cause me to commit the sin of hatred. As a child I grew to regard him with a great malevolence and in my thoughts he remains so to this day. May he rot in hell!

Let me begin with him then. A year after his departure my father returned from the siege of Toron in Galilee, which the crusader army abandoned in panic at the first news that the Muslim army of al-Aziz approached from Egypt. Despite this fiasco the Pope's promise of redemption carried a 'no cowards' clause and my father returned cleansed of all his past sins. With a clean slate and a missing right leg he claimed to have lost in the siege while demonstrating great valour, he took up the life of a wastrel. A carved wooden peg with a brass tip replaced his former leg and was further fitted with an embossed camel leather cup and straps decorated with small metal studs that bound it to a purple stump of scar tissue. Henceforth he was known as Brass Leg Peter the Forgiven Coward, a name he never saw for the cruel joke it was intended to be. He argued, too vehemently for credence, that due to his war wound and the courage he claimed had earned it, he was the exception, one of the few German crusaders to be forgiven of cowardice. I would later learn that he had lost his leg acting in a foolhardy manner while drunk when working on the construction of a siege engine.

Back home with the seasons back to normal he worked sufficiently at his carpenter's trade only so that he might drink and fornicate and be seen a generous fellow among the village men. He gave my mother none of his earnings but expected food on the table, a fire in the hearth and to receive all the attendant duties of an obedient and submissive wife. He was also a consummate liar and his outrageous tales of derring-do, if not for one minute true, were well told and worth the listening for the laughter and entertainment they brought. Is it not so that a coward's stories of heroism are always more valiant than those modestly related by a true hero?

Whereas the ale contained in my father's *krug* foamed with merriment among his drunken fellow villagers, the very same substance turned to bile in his stomach by the time he arrived home from the inn. My mother and I would hear him cursing and shouting abuse, sometimes crying out in pain as his peg leg jarred against a rut or entered into a hole in the uneven surface of the dark road. In the summer we would escape to the woods where we would pass the time singing.

We would return when the moon was halfway high in the summer sky, knowing that he would have collapsed into a drunken stupor, and we always drew comfort from the sound of snoring as we approached from the pigsty beside the cottage. But in the bitter winter snow there was no place to hide lest we freeze to death. While I cowered under the bed, my mother accepted an inevitable beating, dodging most of the clumsy blows my father, far from nimble on a wooden leg, aimed at her.

I was eight years old or thereabouts, in the winter of 1204, when at the age of twenty-eight my mother died of pleurisy. She was a woman of great character and resilience who took much pride in the fact that she came from free peasant stock and was not subject to tenure to the count who, together with the monastery, owned most of the land hereabouts. She was an only child and her parents, mindful of their precious daughter, had unknowingly caused her to be betrothed to a young carpenter, Peter of Pulheim, who was said to have excellent prospects. Thinking that his trade and diligence would allow their only child to prosper in her married life they were beguiled by his greedy parents and her father forewent the *munt*, the compensation due to him from the groom's parents, thinking that to have his daughter well matched and safe was sufficient reward. It was soon apparent that my father was indolent, a ne'er-do-well and a drunkard who spent his days fighting and carousing and who used what little money he earned to support a life of profligacy.

Those were, as they still are, hard times, but my mother was a woman proficient in most things concerning the peasant way of life. With the death of both her mother and father scarce three years after her marriage she inherited a small cottage and half an acre of land. The land she worked assiduously, growing corn and cabbages, onions and turnips for sale at the village market and a few vegetables for our own use. She also kept six hens and a rooster and three pigs of a good breed, a boar and two sows that grew fat on the spoilt cabbage leaves and turnip tops.

The black boar was a splendid animal and my mother took great pride in him as his seed was plentiful; both sows were good mothers and every teat was occupied with robust piglets that she would fatten and sell for a good price. She would always donate one piglet to the Church, which put her greatly into favour with the priest, Father Pietrus. If all she touched in husbandry was blessed with fecundity this was not true of herself, and like her own mother she too seemed barren in the first years of her marriage. This gave my father the right in the eyes of the Church to divorce her. But if he was a wastrel he was by no means stupid. She gave him a fire in the hearth, his food and a warm bed and even money for drink, and kept her thoughts to herself while demanding nothing in return. She was barren and therefore in the eyes of men, the law and the Church she was useless, an empty vessel. The shame of being known as a 'cast off' was a greater humiliation than the beatings and the scorn she received from him. But then, on the eve of my father's departure for Jerusalem came a late sowing of his seed that received God's blessing and I was born while he was away in the Holy Land.

As my father's drinking and bellicose behaviour grew he added infidelity to his list of public misdemeanours, taking up with wanton women and whores. He showed no improvement upon his return and would curse my mother for her girl child and her inability to give him a son and heir. Although she was often beaten, the shame his womanising brought her in the eyes of other married women was by far the worse punishment and increasingly she sought the solace of the Church. She possessed a natural and pleasant voice and took some pride in being allowed to sing a part of the Gregorian chant on her own when the convent choir was invited to perform before visiting ecclesiastics, a privilege usually only accorded a nun who possessed a sweet voice.

Eventually my father's dissolute life was beginning to attract the attention of the burgomaster. I well recall my mother's shame and relief when he would spend the night in the lockup. We would have the bed to ourselves and I loved these times when, snuggled into her arms, she would tell me stories and teach me the words and tunes of the many folksongs she knew.

But my mother was more, much more to me than these lovely nights spent together in bed. She would keep me constantly at her side while she worked, teaching me the ways of the seasons, of seeds, caring and harvesting of plants and the duties of animal husbandry. I'd accompany her to the markets where I soon learned how to sell and how to bargain.

We would spend hours together in the nearby woods where we would take her precious pigs to forage, until I knew all the wild herbs to be gathered for seasoning, the mushrooms that were good to eat and those to be left well alone. In the high summer we'd pick blackberries and wild strawberries and we'd laugh and sing until we'd quite forgotten the burdensome male in our lives.

She would often grow serious in the middle of laughter. It was as if she had suddenly experienced a strange prescience. Then she would bid me come to her and clutch me, as though desperate, to her bosom. 'My precious, I have long since forgiven every blow and bruise I have received from the drunken brute simply because his nascent seed finally brought my womb to life and God saw fit to give you to me.' Then kissing my golden curls she would add as if she knew that she would not be at my side much longer, 'Remember, Sylvia, you were late in coming into my life and so you have all the wisdom I have gained as I grew older. Whatever I know, you will know more abundantly and already your voice is sweeter and truer than my own. You are blessed with intelligence, a sweet nature and a lively character that will serve you well in life if you do not allow yourself to become too impetuous of spirit or let vanity at your coming beauty drain the charity from your soul. Hold your head high, my lovely child, let no one bring you down. A strong woman must be like the willow tree – while she bends to the wild and wicked winds of life she will endure.'

At the time I was too young to fully understand her words, nor did I think of myself as either pretty or tempestuous, though in the latter characteristic she has been proved to be right. In my younger years God blessed me with a certain beauty that proved as troublesome as it was an advantage. I loved and revered my mother with all my heart and while every child must try to honour and respect their father, he took such scant notice of me that I scarcely knew him when he was sober and feared and avoided him when he was drunk. Should he as much as touch me when he was in a drunken state my mother, who was otherwise compliant to all his wishes, would fly at him with a knife in her hand, eyes blazing. 'Touch my child, you bastard, and I will wait until you sleep and kill you!' she'd snarl.

Alas, with her death, I was now alone with my father who, no longer able to vent his anger on my mother and now free to do as he wished with me, would rape me when drunk. In one fell swoop I had gone from a loved, cherished and innocent child to becoming the victim of a wantonly cruel father who regularly slaked his lust on me. He would never rape me in the cottage, but instead drag me into the pigsty where he'd point to the black boar and in a slurred voice, he'd whine, 'Your mother loved that brute more than me!' Then he'd push me face down over a broken wine barrel. 'Let the bitch look now! See who has the last laugh!' He'd lift my shift and with his peg leg stuck out at an angle, its brass point buried in pig shit, he would take me, meanwhile grunting and snorting like the three pigs jostling alongside.

When it was over he'd grab me by the hair and jerk me to my feet, turning my head so that I looked directly into his broken face. A sour smell issued from a mouth possessed of yellow rotting teeth and blackened stumps. 'Sing! Sing for your papa,' he'd growl, releasing his hand. Fighting back my tears, I would sing a folksong my mother had taught me. When it was over he'd place his huge hand upon my head. 'Remember, it is *I* who have been forgiven past sins and will go on another crusade before I die to redeem myself for those I have since committed. It is *you* who are now the sinner condemned to hellfire.' Then tucking away his vileness, he'd add in what he thought an amusing tone, 'Never you mind, when you are older you too can be a pilgrim to the Holy Land, just like your brave papa who suffered so terribly in the name of the true Cross.' Pausing to cackle at such an amusing notion, he'd exclaim, 'Then, *abracadabra*, all your sins will be forgiven!' With his tunic and pouch adjusted and his peg leg upright he'd reach into his pocket to produce a lump of honeycomb wrapped in a twist of cloth. 'To sweeten you for the next time, *liebling*.'

There are few secrets in a small village and those who knew themselves my betters soon gave me the disparaging name Sylvia

Honeyeater. Why I have to this day retained it I simply cannot say. I have no cause to remember those days with fondness and have been given many more flattering names in life. Perhaps we come to think of ourselves in a certain way and by removing a childhood name, no matter how disparaging, we lose some small part of ourselves. Today most folk think 'Honeyeater' such a pleasantly amusing appendage that it must have come about because of my sunny disposition. I have long since learned that the hurt that we acquire in life can be disguised behind a smiling face.

I missed and mourned for my sainted mother with a terrible ache, and prayed every night to God that while I knew myself to be a sinner condemned to roast in hell, He would protect her in heaven from knowing what was happening to me. Knowing myself condemned, I grew silent and withdrawn and showed my face in the village as little as possible, only attending religious feast days or venturing in when I had something I might sell in the market. As my mother had taught me I attended Church on Sunday. I would hide in the graveyard until the last of the worshippers had entered the building before creeping silently into a back pew, seating myself convenient to the door so that the moment the service was completed I might escape the curious and accusing eyes of the pious parishioners. While in Church I remained mute, concentrating on the sounds of the Gloria, refining in my head the purity of the notes flattened and corrupted by the tuneless voices of many of the nuns. Later in the woods I would spend hours alone practising and bringing to life the various hymns.

Because of my silence and unobtrusive manner I became an acute observer of people and I also began to understand the lives of the birds and the small forest creatures. I would spend as much of my summer days as I could in the woods that covered the slopes of the surrounding hills. As I had done with my mother, I gathered herbs, wild strawberries, blackberries and field mushrooms and dug for roots and lily bulbs to feed the pigs. Here I would sing all day while fossicking, and spend hours alone practising the hymns I had memorised while in Church. I could recite the mass word for word, even though it was in Latin and beyond my comprehension, and would often remember an entire sermon.

Singing brought me closer to the memory of my mother, who had so often praised my voice. 'God,' she would also say, 'has lifted it from the soul of an angel who no longer sings in the heavenly choir and placed it as a precious instrument into your infant throat.' After her death I sang at first only to myself and later sometimes to the village children who would venture into the woods to play, and so I gave it no worth other than that it comforted me and brought me within her imagined presence. Despite the vicissitudes seemingly overwhelming me, my sainted mother had left me with a strong sense of my own worth. My father's vile and frightening actions condemning me to hellfire I locked away in a chamber within my heart. If I was denied the power to prevent him from harming me, then I told myself that within me remained someone uncorrupted and worthy of my mother's precious memory.

I was seldom miserable for the company of friends my own age. With my mother as my sole company I had not previously cultivated any friendships with other children and so knew nothing of child's play. To amuse myself I would have imaginary conversations out loud with various people I had observed or overheard in the village market. I would sit on the low wall of the pigsty and pretend the black boar was the village priest or the mayor or one or another of the more self-important town dignitaries, mimicking their voices as I conducted a conversation with them. I would use the sows to talk with the village women who loved to gossip and to condemn everyone or everything that didn't fit in with their own narrow views on piety and life. I loved especially to imitate one fat, large-breasted woman, Frau Anna, known in the village as the Gossip Queen. She was self-important, pompous and possessed a loud and vociferous voice that offered an opinion on everything, but seldom had a kind word to say about anyone. Generally speaking, if I may say so, she was a thoroughly nasty piece of work. In the process of this lonely children's game and unbeknownst to myself, I was becoming a very good mimic.

As a special treat to myself and after admonishing the black boar to be on his best behaviour I would turn him into the abbot at the nearby Monastery of St Thomas. The abbot, preaching as he sometimes did in the village church, would always delight me. While the village priest, Father Pietrus, intoned his message in a dogged and sonorous litany as if disinterested in the hallowed words of our Saviour and seeming anxious for his sermon to be over and done with, the abbot's were filled with the fire and brimstone of the Old Testament. At its crescendo he'd often draw a deep breath until he'd become scarlet-faced, when he'd commence to hiss as if adding vehemence to a word yet to be formed and which finally emerged in an expostulation of spittle and sound. These truncated and strangled words that hissed like a goose and fought for release before exploding from his mouth I would greatly enjoy imitating, holding my breath, then making them stop dead with a hiss, then leaping them forth at the command of my nimble tongue.

This gift for mimicry, though of course at the time I wasn't conscious that it was any more than the pastime of a lonely child, began at the age of seven or thereabouts when I began to imitate the calls and the songs of all the birds in the woods. The persistent call of the male cuckoo, the woodlark, redpoll, robin, hawfinch, flycatcher, the shy wood nuthatch, thrush and wren, the harsh caw of the crow, the chattering of a magpie and the assiduous *cookerooing* of the wood pigeon and the turtle-dove, even the woodpecker and many more were all grist for my mellifluous tongue. I was careful with the call of a raven or a jackdaw as they brought on evil omens. I learned to distinguish the mating calls of all the cock birds and soon enough I could draw them as well as the hens to my presence at will, until the trees above me trilled with the birdsong of courtship.

Then one indifferent autumn day when the sun seemed to be spending most of its time behind threatening storm clouds all this changed for me. I stood in my usual place in the market, my eyes downcast, hands folded at my waist, silently taking in the chatter around me when the Gossip Queen, Frau Anna, waddled up to me. She was one of three market women who seemed always to be together: the other two

I had nicknamed Frau Frogface and Frau Gooseneck. The first because her head seemed broader than it was high as if it had been placed in a clamp top and chin and squeezed causing her eyes to bulge and lips to protrude. The second for her small rounded head, sharp nose, beady eyes and long neck that constantly moved from side to side as if she was trying to locate a bad smell. Frau Anna was too well-known as the Gossip Queen to be renamed. Now she stood in front of me, her breasts heaving, her heavy leather-booted legs apart. She looked down at my naked feet in apparent distaste, then her eyes travelled across my ragged gown and still further up, lingering purse-lipped on my dirty face, runny nose and matted blonde hair. Whereupon she sniffed, jerked her chin in disapproval and pointed a fat finger at a small heap of field mushrooms, dropping a coin into the dirt at my feet. I bent down and silently scooped up the mushrooms and placed them carefully into her basket, then reached to retrieve the coin. 'Whore! Satan's child!' she hissed, whereupon I heard a sharp 'phfft' as she spat, a glob of spittle landing on the back of my neck.

I shall never know what possessed me; her insult was no worse than many others I had received at the hands of the self-righteous villagers. I would carry their cruel words home in silence where I'd crawl into a dark corner and weep for their reminder of the miserable sinner my wanton father had caused me to become. Barely conscious of my own voice or that the sun at that very moment had come out, bathing the corner in which I stood in bright sunlight, I commenced to sing the *Gloria Patri*, my voice rising above the noise of the marketplace. It is a short hymn, but well before I had come to the end a silence fell upon the market crowd who quickly gathered around me. Not knowing how to extract myself from the predicament in which I had so stupidly placed myself I followed this first hymn with a second longer one, the *Gloria in Excelsis*. Almost at the precise moment I'd completed the hymn, as suddenly as it had arrived the sun disappeared, followed shortly by a soft rumble of far-off thunder. To my consternation I saw that several of the more humble village folk had come to kneel at my dirty feet.

And so a different stage in my childhood had arrived. The incident at the market became known as the 'Miracle of the Gloria'. Those who boasted that they had been present that morning told how the general hubbub of the market stalls had suddenly ceased as a blindingly bright light appeared to surround me. They watched and saw my eyes take on a fiery red glow as the demon within me looked outwards and an expression of abject terror appeared on my face, contorting it horribly, so that they knew I was possessed by Beelzebub. As they drew back in fear, the glorious light began to enter my mouth and the demon's transmuted eyes immediately began to fade and mine return to a deep sublime blue. Whereupon my face softened to a beatific smile, as if I had just received a divine kiss from the Virgin Mary. At that precise moment my mouth opened and I commenced to sing the *Gloria Patri* in the voice of an angel, followed by the *Gloria in Excelsis*, causing many of those present to fall to their knees in prayer. As I came to the end of this second hymn of praise a great clap of thunder caused the earth to tremble around me.

From such small and unpropitious beginnings miracles are made. From that day on folk stopped disparaging me and bought my produce with a smile, placing their payment politely within my palm. The name Sylvia Honeyeater was no longer used and I was now known as Sylvia of the Gloria. The village folk would beg me to sing to them and I would do so, but only when all my produce had been sold. Nor would I again sing a hymn in a public place but only folksongs. In my usual pew at the back of the church on Sunday I reverted to my accustomed silence. I was now eleven years old or thereabouts and knew my mind, and while the village women begged me to sing in the church grounds after mass so that the priest, Father Pietrus, might hear my voice, I steadfastly refused. Despite my redemption in the inflamed imagination of the Christ-zealot villagers, I still knew myself to be a sinner unworthy of singing in or even near God's house.

My newfound public voice brought a reflected glory to Brass Leg Peter the Forgiven Coward, who now acted as if I was the result of his careful nurture, happily accepting the credit for my transformation into a songbird. He commanded me to appear at the inn to sing to his circle of drunken comrades. He would bask in their congratulations and when my singing brought tears to their eyes he would boast that my voice came from him. That he had once sung like a lark until the infidels had captured him. They'd poured lye down his throat when they'd caught him on his knees in his evil-smelling, rat-infested prison cell praising the Almighty in glorious song. This brought the usual derisive laughter from those who had known him as a young man. They claimed he had only ever been part of a drunken singsong and had never been heard to sing in praise to the Almighty. But others who knew him less well were quick to pat him on the back and refill his tankard. Nor was the innkeeper lacking in generosity; my singing attracted new customers and so he too saw to it that my father's tankard was always brimming with good cheer.

But idle tongues cannot easily be silenced and the news of the divine occurrence did not take long to reach Father Pietrus. The Miracle of the Gloria by this stage had increased even further in its lurid and improbable detail and it was now maintained that prior to the 'miracle' I had been a mute.

I have subsequently spent most of my life in the observation of people and know how they hunger for sacred manifestations, holy signs and wonders that they could perceive to be miraculous. Nor, at the time, was I willing to deny them. My newfound status was a great deal better than the one I had previously possessed and while I sometimes longed for my former privacy I confess I enjoyed the attention. Never having known anything but disparagement, the respect people now afforded me gave me my first small taste of power. My voice was the only thing I had ever possessed that was mine alone to control and I would often quietly refuse a request to sing. Refusal was a new experience for me. I had never possessed anything to withhold from anyone – even my body, that most sacred of female rights to refuse, had been taken without my consent. Curiously, refusal seemed only to enhance my status in the village and I soon learned that to give sparingly of my voice made it more valuable to those who hungered to hear me sing.

As I grew older it was a lesson I was to employ in other aspects of my life. As a woman I was to learn that the promise of something to come that must by degrees be earned is far more valuable to a man than a hasty, generous and wanton fulfilment. Despite this small sense of independence, I had some doubt that I possessed the courage to refuse the command of the village priest to sing, even though I thought myself a blasphemer should I be made to sing anywhere near the house of God.

I was to be escorted into the presence of Father Pietrus by Frau Anna and her two companions. The Gossip Queen had very conveniently forgotten the spittle and abuse she'd hurled at me. Now she boasted that she'd been the main presence at the moment Christ's spiritual light in the form of the Holy Ghost had entered to wrestle with and cast out the evil demon that had taken possession of me.

Ever since the 'miracle' she'd claimed certain privileges at my expense, the major one seeming to be the right to attach her presence to me whenever it was to her advantage. I have no doubt it was she who led the prattling contingent of old wives to the village priest to inform him of the miraculous event that had turned me from a deaf mute into a celestial singer.

I had been cleaning the pigsty, singing to myself, so that by the time I heard the three village women approaching it was too late to hide. Frau Anna was at the forefront followed by Frogface and Gooseneck, both carrying baskets. She came to a halt beside the pigsty. 'The priest wishes to see you, Sylvia,' she announced in a peremptory manner, then including the other women with a sideways nod of her head, added, 'but we have agreed thou art not in a fit state to see him.' I immediately thought she meant that as a sinner I was not fit to be in his holy presence. 'You will wash in the stream and then put on fresh linen,' she commanded.

I glanced shamefaced at my ragged gown. 'Frau Anna, I have only what I am wearing.'

'I know, child,' she said impatiently. 'We have brought a gown for you and shoes and a cap. They are not new but clean and well patched and the shoes are stout enough. Now hurry, we cannot keep the good father waiting.'

The stream, when I had earlier that morning gone to fetch water, had been covered in a thin layer of late-autumn ice. Though it was by now well past noon and the ice would have melted in the pale sunlight I knew it yet to be freezing. 'We will wash and prepare you,' Frau Anna announced firmly, then pointed to a basket one of the women carried. 'We have brought soap and a scrubber and some old linen to dry you.'

I was told to disrobe beside the stream where they sniffed in disgust at the ragged garment that fell to my feet to leave me standing naked, hugging myself and shivering in their presence. 'Look, she is still a child,' Frogface pronounced, pointing at my hairless crotch.

'Only in appearance,' Gooseneck said sardonically. This set both of them cackling.

'Shame on you!' Frau Anna chided. 'God has returned the child's virginity.' She turned to me. 'Has your bleeding come yet?'

'No, Frau Anna,' I replied.

'There, you see! She has been restored to a blameless innocent. Oh my God!' she suddenly exclaimed, visibly trembling, then grabbing me by my right shoulder and spinning me around so the other two might look at my back. 'See the fish!' she shouted out excitedly. 'It is the sign of Jesus the Saviour! The Son of God! The Fisher of Men!' Then in a tone of awe she suddenly whispered, 'Oh my God! He has marked her for Himself!'

I had never seen the small birthmark situated between my shoulder-blades and so had forgotten about it. I now remembered my mother saying it was in the perfect shape of a fish. She had joked that it was God's way of seeing to it that I would never drown. Now Frau Anna saw it for a part of the Miracle of the Gloria. I remained silent, too preoccupied with the cold, and besides, I saw no reason to tell her that I had been born with the mark upon my skin.

'There! I told you so!' Frau Anna, somewhat recovered from her initial shock, declared triumphantly. 'This is yet another confirmation that the Lord Jesus has personally blessed the child.' Not wishing to miss an opportunity to scold them she turned scornfully to her two companions. 'And you two see fit to mock God's special child! Shame on you both. I hope you will declare this sinful behaviour before next you accept the bread and the wine of redemption?'

Frau Anna's admonishment silenced them and somewhat resentfully they set about me with soap and wet rags, splashing me with jugs of freezing water until I gasped and turned blue from the cold, my teeth chattered furiously and I was unable to cease from trembling. They soaped my hair and then made me immerse my head in the freezing stream, Frau Anna's huge hand at the back of my neck forced my head below the water while one of the women rinsed my hair. At last, fussing and clucking, they dried me in the pale sunlight and dressed me in a woollen gown that fitted well enough and was clean and carefully patched. The wimple was almost new and wrapped snugly about my head, and though the shoes were too big and the wooden soles well worn they remained on my feet with only a little difficulty and were tolerably comfortable. One of the women produced a cloak to wrap around my shoulders.

And so we set off for the meeting with Father Pietrus, the three women excited by the further addition of a sacred fish, which added to my growing mystique. As we approached the village church Frau Anna turned to me. 'I will do the talking, Sylvia. You will be silent until the priest asks you to sing the Gloria. Say nothing, you hear? Nothing! Do you understand, child?'

I nodded, happy to comply with her request. I was anxious and frightened for I had never spoken to a priest and couldn't imagine ever doing so. Father Pietrus was busy and caused us to wait for some time before we were ushered into a draughty vestry by the old hausfrau who swept the church interior and cooked and cleaned for him. She bade us all to be seated in a pew too small to contain three fat women and myself, so I found myself squashed between the enormous buttocks of Frogface and Gooseneck.

The priest arrived and sat in a chair facing us; he seemed not to notice our discomfort, his hands spread on his lap and his head bowed as if he was about to pronounce a blessing, but no word came from his mouth. We waited for what seemed like ages until at last he sighed, raised his head and asked somewhat wearily, 'So, tell me about this so-called miracle I hear so much about?'

Frau Anna started to open her mouth when the priest's hand shot up. 'The child will speak of it first.' Shocked at this sudden command to speak I remained silent and terrified. 'Speak up, child!' Father Pietrus demanded impatiently. 'I do not have all day to listen to the prattle of three old women and a child.' He sighed again and then said in a mocking voice, 'It seems a month for miracles – last week an old crone visited me to say she'd seen the face of the Blessed Virgin appear on a piece of linen as the wind blew her washing on the line. She brought the rag to me and asked that I declare it sacred and pronounce it a relic!' He sighed and ran his hand over his bald pate. '"Use it to wipe the dishes, old frau, that way your food will be blessed," I advised her. She left well pleased.' He sighed. 'Is there no end to this nonsense of signs and portents?'

If Frau Anna was offended by the priest's cynicism she didn't show it, nor did she seem in the least put out. She nodded her head in my direction. 'She is a former mute, Father,' she said impassively, 'and has yet to learn how to talk.'

'A former mute that sings!' Father Pietrus yelled out. 'Did I not hear that she sang the *Gloria Patri* and the *Gloria in Excelsis* in the marketplace? Are they not formed by words of praise?'

'Ah! Now you begin to understand the gift from heaven, Father. But that is only a *part* of it,' she added mysteriously.

'There is more?'

'Oh yes, Father!' Frogface and Gooseneck exclaimed simultaneously, almost as if they'd been rehearsed in support of Frau Anna.

Frau Anna nodded, acknowledging them. Then, anxious to maintain her role as chief witness, she added primly, 'They are witnesses to the miracle and will confirm everything I have to say is the truth.'

'Of course,' Father Pietrus said wearily, 'of course they will.' He looked towards Frau Anna. 'So pray tell me more of this mute child bursting into hymns of praise. But do it quickly, woman, I have much to do.'

Frau Anna appeared not to notice the priest's mocking irony. '*Formerly* mute, now learning to talk, Father,' she corrected him, then she launched into the incident in the marketplace. She turned the coincidental sunlight into the spirit of the Holy Ghost descending from heaven to surround me in pure white light. She told of the demon's red eyes looking out of mine in fear and the look of terror on my face. Then how the light entered my mouth and my eyes turned to a heavenly blue and upon my face appeared a beatific smile. Pausing for effect she then explained how I commenced to sing the Gloria in the voice of an angel, whereupon God Himself was heard to send down his approval in the form of a mighty clap of thunder.

It was little wonder that Frau Anna was known as the Gossip Queen for she was a born storyteller. Well knowing the truth and despite myself I was impressed. On either side of me Gooseneck and Frogface had taken to their rosary beads and both were weeping softly, overcome by their leader's eloquence. Father Pietrus sighed, folding his hands across his chest and twiddling his thumbs. 'Well, I see the child has kept the blue eyes the Holy Ghost brought down from heaven in the glaring white light,' he observed. It was obvious that he remained unbelieving.

Frau Anna, who had up to this moment remained impassive to the priest's sarcasm, was now suddenly barely able to contain her fury. Father Pietrus hadn't, like everyone else, succumbed to her impassioned and detailed description of the miraculous event. Jumping from the pew she turned and grabbed me by the wrist, pulling me viciously to my feet. 'Look for yourself, Father!' she shouted. Then placing a hand on either shoulder she pulled, stripping the garment from my shoulders so that I stood half-naked. Then she turned me about so roughly that I staggered and would have fallen had she not held me. I now had my back to the priest. 'There, see the mark of the fish!' she exclaimed. 'She is among those chosen by the Lord Jesus Himself! *Come ye after me and I will make you to become fishers of men.*'

Father Pietrus rose from his chair and came to stand directly behind me so that I could smell the sour sacrament wine on his breath. 'Hmm . . . an interesting birthmark. You are right, it does closely resemble a fish.'

'It is the sign of Jesus the Holy Fisherman on the Sea of Galilee,' Frau Anna declared triumphantly, then added incredulously, 'It was not seen to be there before the miracle, Father.'

'Nonsense, woman! It is a simple birthmark.'

'The mark of Jesus our precious Saviour upon her frail flesh,' Frau Anna insisted, despite the priest's scornful opinion.

Father Pietrus suddenly threw his hands in the air. 'I have no more time or patience to waste on this blasphemy! Be off with you . . . all of you . . . out!'

'You have yet to hear her sing, Father!' Frau Anna said huffily, ignoring his scornful dismissal. She commenced to adjust my garment, pulling it back over my shoulders, whereupon she bade me turn to face Father Pietrus.

A look of exasperation crossed the priest's face. 'For God's sake, woman! Am I *really* to believe that the Holy Ghost has caused a mute child to sing?'

'Why, Father, I have twice already told you, the child cannot yet speak for lack of learning, but she *can* sing!' Frau Anna scolded. 'Sing to the glory of God! *That* is the Miracle of the Gloria! She will now demonstrate how the Lord has gifted this poor miserable mute.'

'Why has God punished me with the likes of you in my parish, Frau Anna?' Then, accepting the inevitable, Father Pietrus added, 'Yes, of course, it is not the child's own voice, it is the voice of an angel descended from heaven and placed into this dumb child's compliant throat.' The priest turned to me and with a degree of sarcasm commanded, 'Sing, child, let us hear the beatific voice within your recently mute throat.'

I had vowed, as an unworthy sinner, not to sing in the house of God. Besides, as I silently memorised all his deprecating words and angry gestures so that later in the woods I might reproduce the entire scene unfolding in the vestry, in the process I had completely lost my fear of Father Pietrus. Now I knew I had the strength within me to deny his demand to sing. There was plainly no point in continuing the farce – the priest had quite correctly concluded no miracle had taken place and I was about to be restored to my former status as Sylvia Honeyeater, the village outcast.

I'm not even sure if at the time I was disappointed at the prospect of returning to my previous life. Except for my father's drunken brutality, I had been left on my own to do as I wished since the death of my mother and as time went on, being the centre of attention and at everyone's beck and call was wearing thin and becoming most wearisome. I found myself escaping to the woods at every opportunity. But even there I wasn't always alone. The village children soon enough discovered my gift for mimicry and for storytelling and would frequently seek me out in the woods where they could have me to themselves. While I oft times enjoyed their company, there were increasingly frequent periods when I wished to be alone with only the birdsong surrounding me. Furthermore, it now occurred to me, if my voice should please the priest, while yet denying the miracle, he might force me to sing in church and by so doing increase my already heavy burden of guilt.

As I made no attempt to open my mouth, Father Pietrus repeated impatiently, 'Sing if you please, child!'

I looked up at the truculent face of Frau Anna and realised that if he should dismiss, as seemed certain, the Miracle of the Gloria, then Father Pietrus would cause her newfound status to be greatly diminished. I glanced at Frogface and Gooseneck and saw the gleeful look in their eyes as they too realised that Frau Anna, the bully and their constant tormentor, would become the laughing stock of the village.

I realised how desperately Frau Anna depended on my voice to save her from ultimate humiliation. In my mind I heard the 'phfft!' of her spittle and felt it land on the back of my neck, followed by the words, 'Whore! Satan's child!' She'd presented me to the priest as a near-mute and now she would have one. I remained silent.

'You will sing now! At once!' Frau Anna commanded.

I concentrated my eyes on the bridge of my nose so that they crossed alarmingly. It was an expression I sometimes used to delight the children when a *dummkopf* appeared as a character in one of my fairy stories.

The priest laughed scornfully. 'Ah, I see . . . the demon's eyes have reappeared!'

'Sing, child! I demand it!' Frau Anna screamed furiously.

I remained silent with my eyes crossed, the idiot's grin fixed to my face.

Father Pietrus rose from his chair and, with a dismissive wave of his hand, cried, 'Enough! The child is an imbecile and you are three foolish old women who have wasted the Church's time. Be gone . . . the lot of you!'

Outside the Church Frau Anna let fly with a cuff to the side of my head, knocking me to the ground. 'Whore! Satan's child!' she screamed, then one of her stout boots landed in my ribs. I scrambled to my feet and ran for my life, losing a borrowed shoe in the process and kicking the other free so that I might run the harder.

I hid in the woods until near darkness when the late-autumn cold caused me to return to the cottage. The moment I entered, I saw that the oil lamp had been lit: he was home. I was not quick enough to escape before my father, concealed behind the door, grabbed me. The pigs, grunting as they always did at my approach, had warned him of my arrival. 'Ha! The mute has returned!' he declared triumphantly. I could smell the grog on his breath as he held me to his chest, lifting my feet off the ground. 'You would deny the priest the pleasure of your angel's voice, would you? A mute, are you? An imbecile and a mute! You seek to shame me in the eyes of the Church, me, a Christ-forgiven crusader!'

I knew if I should struggle or shout out that he would crush the breath from me. I remained silent and unresisting with my head averted. He dropped me to the dirt floor where I landed on my bottom, then scrambled to my knees in an attempt to escape. Despite his peg leg and drunken state he was quick to grab me by the wrist and wrench me to my feet. 'What have you to say, slut?' His evil face and the wet shine of spittle on his broken teeth repulsed me, while his foul breath almost caused me to suffocate. Yet I remained silent. 'Speak or I shall beat you!' With this he twisted my arm around my back, pulling it upwards until I thought it must surely snap from my shoulder. The pain was so great I could only gasp. Somehow I managed to contain the agony, for I was prepared to die rather than to speak out.

Then, quite unexpectedly he released the pressure on my arm and started to chuckle, then to laugh uproariously. 'My little whore,' he gasped. 'I have just realised . . . you have done your papa a great favour!' He broke into renewed laughter. 'No more fucking piglet for the poxy priest! You are now an officially sanctioned mute and an imbecile. What I do to your body is of no concern to the Holy Church. You are possessed by an evil demon and as a child of Satan you do not have a soul that can be redeemed and so . . .' he giggled, 'I have no more need to waste a fat piglet on the priest.'

Let me explain the matter of my father, the priest and the piglet. With each new litter fattened, my father would sell them to the innkeeper for drink money but retain the fattest of the piglets and, as my mother had always done, gift it to the Church. It was, by the standards of the other peasants, a generous gift and one Father Pietrus could expect unfailingly. He would announce my father's beneficence from the pulpit, always careful to point out that as a crusader he was already granted a place in heaven by His Holiness the Pope. He would then add that such a valuable gift of pork came from a generous nature alone and not in the hope that it might win favour in the eyes of God. In God's eyes, the priest would point out, this made my redeemed father all the more worthy of his place in paradise.

The fact that my father was a drunkard and a child abuser I now saw counted for little in the eyes of Father Pietrus. In the first matter, did not Christ himself declare, 'A *little wine for thy stomach's sake*'? With the second matter, a child to be caused to suffer carnal knowledge was not uncommon among peasant behaviour. Besides, the matter had not been officially brought to the Church's attention and was in all likelihood simply the idle chatter of female busybodies and gossips. Moreover, my father must have known that as long as he continued his 'donation' the priest's fondness for suckling pig would override his ecclesiastic conscience. Though this was my own surmise, I felt sure at the time, and still do, that it comes close to the truth.

Moreover, if what I had concluded was true and Father Pietrus should accept the Miracle of the Gloria and take it to the bishop for ratification, things would be decidedly different. In the eyes of the congregation he would be forced to confront the issue of my father using his girl child wantonly for his own gratification and then there would be no more piglet for his table. This well explained the priest's indifference to the possibility of a miracle having occurred. Plainly, the certainty of the thrice-annual gift of a suckling pig was of much greater value to him than the unlikely miracle in the marketplace. Nor, I realised, would he give a tinker's cuss for the additional singing voice of a child who was one of his congregation, no matter how heavenly the sound.

My father still held my wrist in his giant paw. 'Come, *liebling*, we must celebrate!' he now declared gleefully. 'Merrily, merrily, to the pigsty we will go!' His enormous size and strength left me with no protection against him, and now, with my hand once again twisted behind my back, he forced me the short distance from the cottage to the pigsty.

It had been a long and eventful day that I'd started as a blessed and holy child and ended as one of Satan's children with my dress above my waist, bent over the old wine cask so that my father might take his grunting pleasure. I had found the strength to resist Frau Anna and the priest but had been rendered impotent by this brutish animal.

I have since in my adult life discovered that there are times when we must decide whether we will be crushed by the weight we carry or attempt to remove it whatever the cost. But I had never thought to resist my father, even though I knew that he had destroyed me. Behind me the cruel bastard was grunting and moaning when I suddenly decided I could take no more, even if it should cost me my life. I kicked out backwards, aiming the ball of my foot at his peg leg. I felt it slip then give way under his weight, sending him crashing onto his back into the pig shit.

Stricken with panic, without glancing back I clambered from the sty and fled into the nearby darkening woods. I knew that my escape was ultimately pointless, that I was only delaying the beating I would eventually receive. But I was beyond caring and vowed that he would never again take me to the pigsty. Within the safety of the woods I sought out the giant oak under which my mother and I would in times past sit. I wrapped my arms about the trunk and taking comfort from the rough reliable bark pressed against my cheek I started to sing, my voice choked with tears. I sang several Glorias and all the sad folksongs my mother had taught me until eventually I fell into a tearful and exhausted sleep.

I awoke the following morning and but for the warm shawl Gooseneck had wrapped around my shoulders when we had set out to see the priest I would have near frozen to death. Cramped and sore from sitting against the trunk of the oak I massaged my aching limbs to bring back the circulation. The sun was not yet up, although the dawn light had set the cock to crowing and the magpies, always the first of the bird calls, were chattering in the trees around me. I crept out of the woods towards the cottage, approaching the pigsty on my way. Pigs grunt in an unmistakable fashion when they are eating and as I approached I heard them carrying on as if they were at the trough. I crept up to take a closer look. Brass Leg Peter the Forgiven Coward lay on his back in the black, slimy mud, the clothes torn from his bloody carcass. The boar stood over him, a section of my father's gaping stomach hanging from the side of its mouth, its great pink snout covered in blood. The pigs had set about the softest parts first, going for the contents of his huge stomach, now a visceral hole where his intestines would once have curled and rumbled. In the process of tearing open his abdomen, the animals had also eaten the appendage that had caused me so much childhood suffering.

And so my childhood, both good and bad, was finally over. Several of the village men at the inn that night recalled that my father had left overcome with anger when Frau Anna's husband had brought him the news of my mute recalcitrance in front of the priest that had caused the Miracle of the Gloria to be rejected. The general conclusion was that he'd entered the pigsty for some reason and slipped, knocking his temple against its stone wall and falling unconscious to the ground where the pigs had viciously attacked and eaten him.

The three pigs were pronounced unclean and were summarily slaughtered and buried, the priest saying a prayer for the parts of my father that were missing from his body but refusing to bury the remaining parts in consecrated ground. As both the sows were pregnant at the time, with their disposal went any hope that I might survive the coming winter by selling the fattened piglets. Nor could I expect any local sympathy – the news that the priest had rejected the Miracle of the Gloria, together with Frau Anna's self-preserving description of my behaviour in the vestry and her conclusion that the demon had returned, meant that I was once again a miserable outcast.

While I had the means to survive the coming winter with turnips and onions stored and winter cabbage growing in the garden, I had not counted on the redoubtable Frau Anna. Together with a contingent of village women she arrived at the cottage a day after my father's burial. Indicating the women who accompanied her, Gooseneck and Frogface among them, she declared, 'We have had a meeting and have decided you may no longer remain in the village. It is clear to us all that the demon has returned to possess your soul and we are afraid that our sons and husbands will be tempted with a desire for Satan's flesh. You will soon be twelve years old and so no longer a child but a grown woman. We have declared you a wanton hussy and a whore and not a woman we want among us. You must leave this village forever!' At this a general murmur of approval came from the assembled fat and oh so self-righteous women. Frau Anna had not only regained her former status as Gossip Queen and leader in their eyes, but was now being hailed as the protector of the virtue of their husbands and sons. The eleven-year-old harlot possessed by the devil would, at twelve, no longer be forbidden fruit but instead become fair game for an adulterous husband or cock-randy son.

'This is my home, my cottage and my land,' I protested.

'Ha! You are possessed, your inheritance will be subsumed by the Holy Church, you have no soul and so no rights other than to become a ward of the Church.' She pointed her fat finger at me. 'But first it will be necessary for Father Pietrus to cast out the demon that now possesses you!' A general nodding of heads and murmuring of agreement followed.

I must say I couldn't blame them; after all, in their eyes I was Satan's child, a whore and, had they only known it, I was now guilty of murder as well. But of one thing I was certain: I was not possessed and would rather depart this wicked village than submit myself to Father Pietrus for the ritual of exorcism.

'You have a week to leave us, Sylvia Honeyeater!' Frau Anna said and then added with a final snort, 'Good riddance!' With this the women departed as though they were a gaggle of geese, well satisfied with their morning's work.

I felt myself to have no choice but to seek a new life elsewhere as my stay in the village was over. If I were to stay I would always be lesser than the rest of them, tainted by the demon's occupation and forever forlorn. So I took my only possessions, the hens and the rooster, together with my father's carpenter's tools, to the market hoping to sell them. But now people, seeming to enjoy my fall from grace, declared the hens not worth feeding and the tools no longer fit for use. One fat frau, whom I'd previously dubbed Frau Horse's Arse, sniffed at the hens and said, '*Ja*, maybe also these hens share the same food as the pigs?' This brought an all-round cackle and further discouraged any customers.

Having failed to sell anything at the market I decided to try the nearby Monastery of St Thomas, where the kitchen monk complained bitterly that the hens were aged and possessed no meat and were suitable only for the soup pot. It wasn't true – my hens were young, in good health and steady layers and the rooster was a lusty fellow. Greed, I was discovering, lives in every man, lacks a conscience and grows fat on the misfortunes of others. The whining monk was no different to the peasants at the market. Finally, complaining all the while, the monk exchanged the chickens for a small bag of corn, sufficient if I was careful to sustain me for no more than a week on the road.

The tools I took to the monastery carpenter's shop and foundry where the carpentry monk, an older and altogether kindlier person who introduced himself as Father John, examined them, then inquired closely why they were for sale, perhaps thinking I had stolen them. I told him of the death of my father and explained my circumstances.

He placed his hand on my head and sighed. '*Orphanus*,' he said, consoling me. 'We have heard of the Miracle of the Gloria. You are *that* blessed child?' he asked, surprised.

'It was not a miracle, Father, only some stupid villagers making up stuff they *think* they saw.'

'So you were not a mute who was gifted with an angel's voice?'

'I have sung to God's glory since I was a small child,' I replied.

'And now what will you do?'

I shrugged. 'Leave the village and go somewhere else . . . somewhere far away.'

'I see, a pilgrimage maybe?'

'If my sins may be forgiven I should like to do that, Father,' I answered, remembering my father's mocking words in the pigsty.

'Ah, yes . . . sins. We all have those. How old are you, child?'

'Eleven years . . . I think.'

'And what sins have you at such a tender age? Have you stolen? Have you used Christ's name in vain? Have you dishonoured the memory of your mother? What sins have you committed that would merit the trials and tribulations of a pilgrimage?'

'Sins of the flesh and sins of the spirit. I am condemned to the everlasting fires of hell,' I replied emphatically, wondering what he might say if I confessed to murdering my father.

'Oh dear, *that* bad, is it?' Father John seemed to be thinking for a moment. 'I am but a humble carpenter monk and so cannot take your confession, maybe you should see your village priest?'

'No!' I cried, suddenly afraid. 'Father Pietrus thinks me a mute and an imbecile and, because of the false miracle, claims I am possessed and have blasphemed in the eyes of God.'

The elderly monk shook his head sadly. '*Suffer little children to come unto me, and forbid them not; for of such is the kingdom of God,*' he quoted. Then he said quietly, 'The Lord Jesus does not *punish* children for sins of the flesh and of the spirit and they do not become possessed and are not blasphemers, but he does *forgive* them what small sins they have committed. From what I have heard of this so-called miracle, you have only used it as an opportunity to praise our Saviour in hymns to His glory.'

'Yes, but I may not sing anywhere near the Church as I am unclean and burdened with sinfulness.'

'Hmm . . . I see . . . awkward then.' He smiled. 'You would be a child sinner singing to the oh-so-pious peasants.' Father John seemed to think this notion quite amusing. 'Well if you can't confess you really are in a bit of pickle, are you not? You have been given a glorious voice to praise the Lord but now cannot use it near His temple.'

'Only alone in the woods,' I allowed.

He clapped his hands. 'Ah, such innocence! A child alone in the woods singing to the glory of God.'

I corrected my previous statement. 'No, never quite alone. I call the birds and we sing together and sometimes the village children are present.'

He looked doubtful. 'You call the birds?'

I nodded. 'They like to sing to the glory of God.'

He looked at me quizzically, then mocking me gently asked, 'Hymns . . . Gloria?'

'No, Father, birds have songs of praise of their own. We exchange hymns, theirs are much the sweeter sounding.'

He laughed. 'You have a lovely imagination, child.'

The carpentry shop together with a small casting foundry was set within the monastery garden and now after harvest, when the remaining fruit and corn were ripe, it was filled with birds. I stepped outside and listened, deciding on the nature of the birds I could hear. Then, taking a small handful of corn from the bag the kitchen monk had given me, I began to exchange their various calls using a pattern I had come to know through a process of trial and error and starting with the chattering magpie. The monk came to stand beside me and I bade him stretch his arms wide and open his palms to heaven whereupon I placed a little seed in each. As I continued the calls, birds began to gather in the tree above us. Quite soon the tree was filled with birdsong. Slowly, almost imperceptibly, I changed my voice from the carolling of a songbird into the first words of the *Gloria in Excelsis*, keeping it high and pure so that the birds above me continued in their own hymn of praise to Almighty God. A magpie, the cheekiest of all the birds, came to sit upon the monk's left hand, pecking at the corn. Soon a robin hopped from a branch and settled on the right, its breast scarlet in the autumn sunlight.

While I had often performed in the woods with the birds for the benefit of the village children, no adult had ever been a witness to the swapping of hymns of praise. In my experience, purity and innocence is soon sullied or exploited in the hands of adults. The false Miracle of the Gloria was just such an example: those who witnessed my singing in the marketplace could not accept it as a child with a pure, clear voice singing a hymn of praise, but must necessarily turn it into a miracle. Father John I hoped might be different. No adult had ever spoken to me in the compassionate and understanding manner he had adopted, nor treated me with such respect, and I thought him worthy to be the first adult to witness the Gloria of the Birds.

'Miraculous!' he exclaimed, at the conclusion of my singing, the sudden sound of his voice sending the birds in a wild flurry of wings from the tree and the robin and the magpie from his hands. 'I should not have believed it if I hadn't witnessed it with my own eyes,' he declared. 'You are truly blessed by God.'

I laughed, despite myself, having had my recent fill of being blessed I wished for no more such blessing. 'Oh, it is nothing, simply a trick the village children enjoy,' I replied trying to sound dismissive, though I was secretly proud of my prowess.

'It is a great deal more than that!' he said emphatically. 'Besides, you have a truly remarkable voice and a wonderful way with nature. Will you not let me intercede on your behalf with the abbot, and perhaps he might find you a place in a convent as a novice?'

'Nay! I cried out. 'If you please, Father, no!' In my imagination I saw the boar with its head over my father's stomach, a piece of his intestines hanging from the corner of its mouth, its great porcine snout covered in blood. I had used the boar too often to play the role of the abbot while I mimicked his furiously spitting sermons – now the prospect of being taken into his hallowed presence filled me with terror. As for becoming a novice nun, how could I ever entertain such an idea with the great burden of sin I carried upon my young shoulders?

'Ah, such a pity. Though, on second thoughts, burying you in a nunnery, while granting you salvation, would deny the world's children the benefit of your extraordinary talents.' He paused and smiled. 'Now you must tell me, what is it I can do to help you, child?'

I had never been spoken to with such generosity of spirit, but nonetheless I knew that I should not allow Father John's kindly words to seduce me into thinking I was more than a terrible sinner with the practical intent of escaping the environs of the village. 'You can give me a fair price for my father's carpentry tools,' I answered, in what I hoped was a businesslike voice. Then, rather cheekily, I held up the small bag of corn. 'The kitchen monk has dealt with me unfairly, Father. My six hens were plump and good layers and the rooster in his prime! Yet he claimed they were scraggy old boilers, fit only for soup, and gave me this small bag of corn in exchange for them.' Then, imitating the kitchen monk's voice, I mimicked his words to me: 'Child, be off! You are fortunate I feel generous today, the abbot will chastise me over the thin and watery taste of the soup these scraggly hens will make and the rooster is not worth fetching water from the well for the boiling pot. It has been a poor year and the corn crop has failed – you are well ahead in this exchange.'

Father John clapped his hands gleefully. 'Perfect! You have that miserable old fool down pat!' he chortled.

Anxious to press my advantage and desiring to stick to the subject of providing for my departure, I now said, 'Perhaps, in return for my father's carpentry tools you can arrange for a little more corn or even coin to purchase food on my journey, Father?'

Father John sighed. 'Alas, we are not allowed to handle money and only the kitchen monk has access to the corn bin.' He looked momentarily distraught, then suddenly brightened. 'A leather bag with straps for your back, a fine brass buckle I have recently forged to clasp it secure and a stout stave! If it should rain the bag of corn you carry will spoil! Yes, yes! A splendid idea!' he decided, and without consulting me further. 'A stave to protect you and help you over rocky ground when you embark upon your pilgrimage and a bag for your back so you have the means to carry what you gather on the way and protect it from the weather.'

'It is not a pilgrimage, Father,' I protested. 'I seek only to find somewhere else to go. Cologne perhaps, where I will find employment as a kitchen maid in a rich man's house.'

'Ah, yes, but that is no less a pilgrimage. We may not all reach Jerusalem, but we are all pilgrims and life itself is a rocky road with the promise of redemption at its end if we remain pure in spirit.'

I was not sure I understood him, thinking his words altogether too profound for such as me. Anyway, if I correctly understood him, it was a bit late for me to remain pure in spirit as the rocky road in life had long since stubbed my toes and skinned my knees and elbows and in the process, I felt sure, crushed my poor spirit. 'Thank you, Father, it is a generous exchange, the stave will protect me well and the bag is just what I need,' I said, wishing to be polite, although I would have much preferred a bigger bag of corn.

He seemed pleased. 'Come then, we must measure you for both, the bag must sit comfortably upon your back and the stave must not be too unwieldy for you to handle.'

Some hours later and after he had shared his midday meal with me, bread and wine and a bowl of boiled cabbage, he completed the bag and the stave. The leather satchel stoutly stitched and fitted with a strong brass clasp sat comfortably enough upon my back but Father John tut-tutted and fiddled, adjusting it carefully until he was satisfied that it was a perfect fit. Whereupon he reached for the stave, a lovely silvery colour that seemed cut from a yew tree, at its one end a metal tip and at the other, where I gripped, a cunning plaiting of leather most comfortable to my grip. The monk frowned, his head cast sideways to rest upon his neck. 'You are too young and, besides, too small to protect yourself by the defensive use of a stave. So I have fashioned it somewhat differently for your use. Use it only when you are threatened by the likes of knaves and robbers.' Whereupon he twisted the leather handle to the left and pulled from the top of the stave a dagger of sharpened bronze. 'I had forged it for a kitchen knife, but now have changed it to make a dagger. It is blessed by sprinkling with holy water and should not be put to flippant use. Each time you use it, when you place it back you must pray to our Saviour and thank Him for protecting your life.' Then he replaced the blade and putting his rough carpenter's hand upon my head pronounced, 'God be with you, my child. Remember always He has said, "*Suffer little children to come unto me . . . for such is the kingdom of God.*" Those are the words of Jesus who has seen that you have a way with children and with nature and He will ever guide and bless you.'

I was leaving a past I had no reason to remember and to which I had no wish ever to return. As I had told Father John, I vaguely thought that my journey to somewhere else might end up in the great city of Cologne, where I imagined myself indentured as a kitchen servant in the grand house of the *Richerzeche*, perhaps one of the *senatores*, in return for food and lodging. It would be a place where a fire kept me warm in winter, where plump round loaves, warm from the oven, were placed before me and a perpetual pot of soup simmered on the hearth. It is with such fairytales that poor motherless children remain hopeful and it just goes to show that, with the encouragement I had received from the kindly monk, even at this darkest moment I remained optimistic.

But for the chill in the air, travel wasn't difficult and the first two days passed without mishap. I would find a place in the woods and using the flint I had taken from home I would gather twigs and light a fire to cook my evening meal. I possessed only one blanket and after the fire died down it would grow bitterly cold at night, but I would soon grow warm with walking once the sun rose and I had regained the road. A few people passed me but they kept to themselves. There was no advantage to be gained from a passing acquaintance with a barefoot child in a patched gown; misery always begets more misery and an eleven-year-old girl has no amusing stories to tell to while away time spent on the road.

Even in late autumn there were still some green herbs to gather in the fields and lanes to supplement my small bag of corn and, while constantly hungry, I had sufficient gruel and green in my belly not to weaken my resolve to walk a hundred furlongs each day. On the fourth night my bag of corn was almost gone and I hadn't found anything to gather worth eating. Hungry and becoming concerned that no destination had yet presented itself, I crept within a wood for protection. I found a dry hollow deep within the roots of a giant oak tree, said my prayers, adding a despairing but not overly hopeful request for food, before wrapping myself in my blanket to slumber.

When I awoke, as if by a miracle, a dozen or so plump mushrooms had pushed up among the fallen leaves at my feet. I offered up my thanks at once to a merciful God, wondering meanwhile what it was I had done to persuade Him in His infinite mercy to come to my aid. I cooked and ate some of the mushrooms and saved what remained for a later time. With the rare pleasure of a full belly my spirits soared and my strength returned. I regained the road to continue my journey to the mythical blazing hearth, warm loaves and hot soup I had so set my mind upon.

By mid-morning it had begun to rain and the ruts in the road soon filled with muddy water. Soaked to the skin I lost my morning courage and became quite miserable, though I continued walking as the surrounding countryside consisted of open fields and rolling hills without a wood in which I might take shelter. I came at last upon a peasant farmer's cottage and knocked on the door.

The frau opened the door. 'Yes, what do you want?' she asked, looking at me suspiciously.

'I seek shelter from the rain this night, good mother. Perhaps in your cow shed?' I asked meekly.

'Ha! I knew it! You are looking for food without work.'

'No, mother, just shelter from the rain.'

'You lie, child, they all say that. God does not feed idlers or beggars and nor do I.'

Exasperated by her tone I foolishly pointed to my bag. 'I have food of my own, a little corn and some mushrooms.'

She looked me up and down, tight-lipped, one corner of her mouth turned down, as though examining a scrawny goose at the market. I was soaked through, so that my patched and mud-splashed dress clung to my ribs. With muddy feet, my hair wet and scraggly and me scrawny and dirty, I must have been a pathetic sight. 'Ha! In that bag you have food you have stolen! You are a thief and now you ask for charity?' she scolded.

'No, mother, only a place to shelter tonight from the rain. The food I came by honestly and I ask for no sustenance from you.'

She thought for a moment, then pointed a stubby finger at the splendid leather bag on my back that Father John had made for me and said slyly, 'If you give me that bag we will give you shelter.'

'Good dame,' I begged, 'I cannot part with it, it has been blessed with holy water and made by a kind monk to suit my needs on the road. Will you not show God's mercy? "*Suffer little children to come unto me,*"' I said rather pathetically, repeating the line I had learned from Father John in the vain hope it might soften her peasant heart.

'Ho! I am not so easily gulled. God has no time for vagabonds and children who carry expensive leather bags and steal corn from the pious poor. It is not yet winter and you are already wet. Be gone from my doorstep! Be on your way!' With this she slammed the door in my face.

'Bitch!' I shouted, much to my own surprise. Then, suddenly elated by my unexpected vehemence, declared further, 'May you ride in the night with the devil and may his vile seed give birth to a changeling!' It was the first time I had ever cursed anyone and it felt very good. I continued walking in the rain and it was true: the raindrops, heated by my anger, seemed no longer cold. As the evening progressed the rain turned to soft drizzle and towards the end of the twilight ceased altogether. I found a hedgerow thick enough to shelter me; wet and exhausted I fell asleep as only a child might in such an unforgiving clime.

I woke to a morning bathed in rare sunshine and my spirits rose, even though I could find no dry twigs to light a fire to break my fast and I had barely sufficient food to last two more days. This day, I knew, would be different. I had sometimes in the past experienced such days when I would remain clean and untouched. These were days when my voice would be purer in song and I was filled with a quiet merriment of the soul. It was on such days in particular when small children would follow or seek me out in the woods and beg for a story. They would laugh and clap and beg for more tales of ghosts, goblins, wights, elves, wicked witches, ogres, dwarfs and giants, as well as the well-known stories of Amazons who lacked breasts, snake-eating troglodytes, bearded women, Cyclops, pygmies, androgynous men, monstrous races and other netherworld creatures. Their eyes would grow large and frightened and they would clutch each other for reassurance when I told of the 'wild hunt' demons and spirits that invaded the air during the twelve days of Christmas. Often, to the delight of the children, with all the creatures and characters I created, I mimicked the voices and adopted the mannerisms of the more important and pompous people in the village. These were bewitching days when I had been blessed and this soft late-autumn morning, filled with sunshine and promise, on the road to somewhere else, I knew to be one of them.

I walked on until mid-morning when I came upon a stream running through a glade of oak and elm, the oak already almost bare of leaf and the elm ablaze with autumn colour. The banks of the stream were covered in moss and fern with bold, rounded rocks etched with lichen, the water running between them silver over bright black pebbles. I walked downstream until I was well away from the road and could not be observed, although I had seen no other traveller all morning. My garments had dried on my body in the sunshine, but the hem of my dress was stiff with mud and needed washing. If, perchance, I should arrive at Cologne, I told myself I would need to be clean and respectable-looking when I presented myself to the rich merchant's wife my imagination had now turned into existence.

I undressed and bathed in the icy water and then, as I stepped from the stream, I knew at once that I must pay penance for cursing the peasant woman who had denied me shelter from the rain. I had acted in haste brought on by my tempestuous nature and yet God, in His infinite mercy, had not punished me for my uncharitable words, but had sent me the gift of mushrooms to stave off my hunger. I would, I decided, remain naked until I could bear the cold no longer. Then I would attempt, in the spirit of repentance, to remain naked and still for the passage of five chants, *Kyrie, Gloria, Credo, Sanctus, Agnus Dei*, singing both the parts for the choir and the cantrix solo parts.

Who knows how the mind works? There I was, unclean from my father's wanton and vile attentions and guilty of his murder and also condemned by the Church as a blasphemer. Yet I was not about to do penance for these horrific sins of the flesh and the spirit, but only for a bitter and impetuous tongue, when it might all the while be justly claimed that I had every right to rebuke the mean and unpleasant peasant woman.

And so I sat upon a rock until the cold seeped into my bones and my lips grew numb and the skin felt as though it would peel from the roof of my mouth, until I knew I could bear it no longer. It was then that I attempted to sing, the words of the first hymn thin and only half pronounced from tremulous lips. But soon the Latin words began to flow easily from my tongue and I felt a warm glow within my bosom. It was when I had reached the *Agnus Dei* that I heard the notes of a flute, clear and clean as it accompanied my singing. My voice rose with the beauty of the music and I felt sure I had never sung as well to the glory of Christ Jesus. I came at last towards the end, singing the psalm verse as a solo, then on to the responsorial chants and the glorious solos to complete the melismatic chants, and all the while the flute played constant and most beautiful. Finally, aware for the first time that my fingers had grown stiff with the cold, I reached for my blanket and wrapped it about my body.

'Good day, young maid,' a male voice said behind me. Alarmed, I sprang to my feet clutching my blanket tightly as if it should protect me. I turned to face the intruder. A young man, perhaps twenty years old, stood with the sunlight behind him so that a halo seemed to appear behind his long dark hair. Tall and thin and most comely in appearance, he stood smiling at me, a flute held in his hand. 'Don't be alarmed,' he urged, a mischievous smile upon his lips. 'In my life I have yet to hear a voice as beautiful. Are you an angel descended from heaven?'

I did not possess the presence of mind to send him on his way, but stood open-mouthed staring at him. Then, gathering my wits somewhat I said as boldly as I could, 'You have spied on me!'

'Aye,' he replied unabashed. 'Would you not also do so if you had stopped by a brook in the middle of nowhere and in the morning sunlight heard the voice of an angel singing to the glory of God?'

'What have you seen?' I asked suspiciously.

'I have seen the sunlight on your hair and a fish,' he laughed.

'A fish? In the stream?'

'Nay, it sits most beauteous between your shoulderblades and is the sign of Jesus the Messiah.'

'It is simply a birthmark,' I snorted. Then growing bolder, 'You came too close then!' I accused.

He pointed to a small hawthorn bush that grew waist-high equidistant from where we each stood. 'You were seated, I saw only your back, part thereof – the sacred fish between your shoulderblades and the golden halo of your head.' He paused and grinned wickedly. 'The bush concealed the nether part.' Then looking at me, his head cocked slightly to the side, he asked my name.

'I am Sylvia Honeyeater.'

'A most comely name. Where do you journey, Sylvia Honeyeater?'

'To Cologne,' I told him. Not wishing him to think me some poor waif without a purpose, I added somewhat self-importantly, 'I have a position as a kitchen maid in a rich merchant's house.' So accustomed had I become to this fantasy that I was barely conscious that I was telling a lie. 'And pray tell, what is *your* name?' I asked with what small dignity I could still possess clutching an old blanket about my person.

He bowed slightly. 'I am Reinhardt of Hamelin. I think myself a musician.' He shrugged and tossing his head he gave a deprecating laugh. 'Alas, in truth, I am a ratcatcher.' He grinned. 'Though, if it will help you to think well of me, a most God-fearing ratcatcher who likes to play the flute!'

CHAPTER TWO

The Ratcatcher

REINHARDT THE RATCATCHER SUGGESTED that we wend our way together at least for a while and I readily agreed, for there seemed little about his manner that was fearful and his demeanour was most sweet and polite. He told me that Cologne was yet five days travel but that there were several villages on the way where we might find food.

'I have food only sufficient for two more days, or if I share it with you, only today,' I confessed, thus allowing him to think that I might be a burden and so decide to be on his way alone.

He laughed. 'Ah, Sylvia, the ratcatcher never goes hungry. Where there are folk there are rats and rats eat corn. So, you see, I am always welcome wherever I sojourn. We will eat well and sleep beside a warm hearth tonight.'

I looked at him fearfully. 'I will not bed with you!' I exclaimed. 'I am a good girl,' I lied.

He grinned. 'Aye! You are an angel who sings to the glory of God. I have seen your halo shining in the sunlight.' Then looking serious, he added gently, 'I solemnly promise you shall be safe with me, little sister. I shall play the pipe and you shall sing and folk will summon us not only for the rats but also for ourselves.'

'You played three discordant notes,' I accused.

'Only three?' he said teasingly. 'Out of the five Glorias we have done?'

I laughed. 'You are right, three is not many. In the congregation of St Thomas it is rare to hear a note well struck.'

'Then we may play together?'

'Only if you promise you will never touch me.'

He looked hurt and said quietly, 'I have already given you my word, Sylvia.'

I had seen that hurt look before and it is not uncommon in men and women who may the least be trusted. 'I have yet to learn if the word of a ratcatcher can be trusted, as I know the word of a wandering minstrel may not!' I said firmly.

'Ha! What know you of musicians then?'

'They are rapscallions and layabouts,' I replied, quoting my mother's caution to beware of the beguiling ways of itinerant men with little girls.

'I see no motley of red and yellow or tinkling bell cap on this fellow!' he rhymed cleverly. 'No pied piper am I, as you can see I wear the dull weed of a working man. So, for the purposes of trust, you may take me for a ratcatcher.' Laughing, he removed his broad felt hat and gave me a sweeping bow. 'Most reliable types, we ratcatchers. You may be sure you will be safe with me, Sylvia Honeyeater.'

He had a sweetness about him that I found compelling, yet I cautioned myself to be on my guard – he was a stranger and besides, I was not accustomed to folk approaching me in a friendly manner. 'I will walk with you a small way, then I shall decide,' I promised, my voice sounding brave while my heart was aflutter. Then pointing to a bend in the stream I said in as matter-of-fact voice as I could manage, 'Now, pray go beyond that bend and turn your back so that I may get myself attired.'

'Aye, and I shall keep my eye out for any wandering musicians, *especially* pipers wearing pied,' he grinned, turning to go.

I had tried to wash the mud from the hem of my dress but it remained somewhat stained. Once I had put it on I was wet from the knees down and most uncomfortable with the constant flapping of damp wool against my legs. I decided I would finally make up my mind whether to continue with Reinhardt the Ratcatcher by such time as my dress was fully dry.

However, by late afternoon and with night fast approaching, the bottom of my skirt was still damp. We'd reached the outskirts of a village that sat near the top of a small hill. On the downward slope beyond the village was a wood where I told myself I could rest for the night. By morning my skirt would be dry and then I could make up my mind whether to continue on my way with the ratcatcher. This was the first of many times to come when I was to let my heart rule my head in judging a man.

It had been such a merry day on the road with my new friend who told jokes and enchanting stories of times past, with no hint of lewdness contained in the telling. At times I sang and he played the pipes and there was nary a folksong or hymn that he could not further enchant with his music. I told myself that I had found a soul mate who, like myself, loved music and stories. In just a few hours on the road we'd forged a partnership of complementary gifts and I confess I hungered for more. I found myself resisting the return to loneliness, thinking I might tarry a mite longer while knowing full well that with the coming of nightfall the devil's imps come out to romp in the minds of men.

I was old enough to know that a warm bed shared with a young male on a cold night is a poor place for a maiden to guard her virtue. My mind harked back to a cautionary rhyme my mother taught me as a child. When, at the time, I asked its meaning, she'd laughed and said, 'It is not for now, my precious, it is for you to remember when you are a pretty young maid.'

When leaves turn gold
And acorns brown
Then skirts go up
And trousers down!

Despite my father having taken my chastity and by doing so condemning me to the eternal fires of hell, I tried always to remain pure in spirit. It was most wearisome to live with so large a burden of guilt when in my mind I had few sinful thoughts. It was as if there was contained in me both sin and innocence, the one a great weight placed upon my soul and the other a lightness of being that allowed me to sing to the glory of God and to call the birds from the trees.

So on the first morning of my journey to somewhere else, I decided to become two people at once. I would be 'Sylvia Then' – the sinner, and 'Sylvia Now' – the chaste. I had already experienced such a separation when I had been changed from Sylvia Honeyeater to Sylvia of the Gloria. I knew that until I could confess the sins my father had cast upon me and complete the terrible penance required for forgiveness, I would have to live with Sylvia Then. But with a fresh start in life, I could at the very least regard myself as Sylvia Now, the fine young maid my mother had hoped I might some day become.

This was to prove a most convenient though not always easy idea. It was not that I gave myself permission to sin and could blame it on my old self and so add to the load of the sins waiting for remission. But in making judgements I could clearly see which of me, sinner or chaste, was involved. Or so I thought, but I was to learn that conscience can be convenient to the moment and that we all have an infinite capacity to justify our actions.

Now, at the very beginning of my life as Sylvia Now, I knew that if I was to tarry with the ratcatcher and sojourn this night in his company I was placing myself in harm's way. Alas, as with all matters of conscience, I found myself in a dilemma. I much desired his pleasant company but knew it to be dangerous. I tried to convince myself that he had agreed solemnly not to touch me on three separate occasions, and that I could trust him. I argued inwardly that he appeared sweet in his ways and did not seem the type to harm a young maid. I trembled at the thought of continuing on my own along the lonely road to Cologne. I had laughed more in this single day than I had done since the death of my mother. I had sung in a voice pure and true to the glory of God when the lilt of his flute had carried my hymns up to heaven. Most of all, I had been utterly enchanted with his tales of olden times and he had promised more, many more, and all he claimed were true.

I recall that I had laughed, showing my doubt, when he had made this claim. 'Why do you laugh, Sylvia? Do you not believe me?'

'Your stories are well told and enchanting, what matters it if they lack truth,' I answered.

He frowned. 'A great deal. It matters a great deal!' he insisted.

'Oh, I fear I have hurt your feelings,' I said, attempting to console him. 'That was not my intention, your tales of yore are wonderful and exceedingly well told and I should like to hear them all,' I repeated vehemently.

'But to you they are *only* fairytales?'

I sighed, my mind casting back to the Miracle of the Gloria. 'Nay! It is only that I have seen people swear to a miraculous happening before the blessed Virgin when it was their imagination that blinded their eyes and closed their ears to the truth. Stories are no less worth hearing should they be imagined, but it is not wise to believe everything we see or hear.' I then told him about the so-called miracle that had taken place in the market. In an attempt to lighten his mood I laughingly said, 'All it would have taken was the priest's blessing and I would have been well on my way to sainthood! Saint Sylvia of Uedem.'

'Ah! I see why you doubt!' he cried, somewhat mollified. 'I hope later to prove the truth of each tale I relate to you. But if you will not accept my word, then if we should find a church I will swear it on the altar Bible.' He paused and looked at me, a small smile curled about his sweet lips. 'Will that suffice your doubting?'

'Hmm, we shall see,' I replied, still playing the doubting Thomas. 'The entire village was willing to swear in the name of the blessed Saviour Himself that they had seen a miracle, but that did not make it so.'

I could see that my reply did not fully satisfy him but yet he smiled.

He was a gifted teller of tales and no doubt well accustomed to an audience who listened without question, enchanted all the while by his silvered voice and the playing of his wondrous flute.

'Not a saint but still an angel, a chosen one?'

'Alas, neither! A poor peasant girl at very best.'

'And the fish?' he asked. 'What say you of that?'

I shrugged. 'A birthmark.'

'You doubt too much, my fair maid. You are yet a child and you possess the cynicism of an old frau.'

I could see I had asserted myself too much. I had yet to learn that the male ego is best puffed up by using my ears to pretend to listen, my mouth to smile approval and my eyes to express sincerity, even if I should think him speaking twaddle. 'I am sorry, I protest too much,' I exclaimed. 'It is just that I do not wish you to take me for a dullard or some skittish, wide-eyed maid. I have truly loved your tales and eagerly await more.' I smiled and then, adopting an expression of pleading, said, 'You promised to tell me of the first pilgrimage to the Holy Land? The trials and tribulations and the terrible things that happened?'

'And you will believe me?' he asked, teasing.

'Of course!' I said unstintingly.

He stopped in his tracks and frowned, seeming to be deciding. 'Although perhaps I should not.'

'Should not what?' I asked.

'I think you too young for those true and most horrific happenings.'

'No, please!' I begged, realising that now the game of doubt was his to play.

'Perforce, I must abstain from telling you this grand story. There are in it many parts to God's great glory but yet other bits too gruesome and too gory for sweet young ears.'

'Why?' I protested. 'I am old enough! Did you not just say I was cynical as an old frau?'

He shook his head vehemently. 'No, no . . . I dare not!'

'Oh, please, you must!'

'Look!' he commanded, pointing to his ears.

His ears began to move as if of their own accord. 'I once almost lost them!' he said, looking serious.

'Lost them? Your ears?' I asked, knowing it for a joke to come.

'The gruesome parts! The gory parts! When I first heard them my ears became so agitated that they jumped from my head to scurry into a dark corner where together they lay whimpering and cowering, trembling like butterfly wings!' He wiggled his ears once more. 'See, they are yet ever on the alert and ready to flee.'

'Aye, and how did you return them to your head?' I giggled, playing along.

'Well, alas I did not,' he said, giving me a look of mock concern. 'I kept them, both in my satchel, until this very morning.'

'And then what happened?'

'A miracle!' he exclaimed. 'I came across an angel sitting in the autumn sunlight beside a silver stream, a golden halo about her head and a pretty pink fish engraved between her shoulderblades. Alas, as I drew closer I could see her lovely mouth moving but could hear no sound coming from her sweet lips. Then, all at once I felt a great agitation within my satchel and I opened it to witness both ears leap from it and once again attach themselves to each side of my head.' He clapped his hands. 'Oh blessed miracle, from her lips I heard a hymn to the glory of God in a voice that only an angel could possess.'

Not accustomed to such flattery I blushed deeply and then, in an attempt to be dismissive of such a pleasing and romantic notion, replied, 'You play with me, Reinhardt the Ratcatcher! You cannot turn a crow into a peacock. Besides, I am a peasant and my ears are well seasoned with salty words.' In my mind I recalled the foul language my father used in the pigsty and told myself that if my ears had not then withered and dropped from my head, they would be safe with any tale told of Christian folk. 'You must tell me everything, leaving no detail out, or I shall be most unhappy,' I scolded, knowing that a story, like gossip, becomes a lesser tale with the juicy bits removed.

I knew myself defeated. The ratcatcher's way with words was well beyond my own. He was making me beg for his attentions and it was plain to me that he was now back in command. I was pleased that he no longer saw me as a challenge, although I did not suspect at the time that with his tomfoolery he was drawing me deeper and deeper into his company. Apart from the village children, it had never occurred to me that anyone would willingly seek my company for the pleasure it might bring, or that he hoped his stories would so enchant me that I would sojourn with him that night.

We had almost reached the edge of the village when the dogs came out to bark, closely followed by the children who stood shyly, kicking at the dust as we drew closer. 'Leave the talking to me,' Reinhardt instructed above the barking of the dogs, at the same time removing the flute from his leather belt. Placing it to his lips he blew a note so shrill that it was barely to be heard by human ears. Then he followed it with three less sharp, but still sufficiently high notes to rise above the barking. The dogs became at once silent and collapsed to the dirt with their noses placed upon their forepaws, eyes raised dotingly to the ratcatcher. Reinhardt approached each dog and touched it lightly on the forehead and as he did so it jumped to its feet, tail wagging, eager, friendly, as harmless as a dormouse.

The children, no longer shy, laughed and clapped at such a clever trick. 'Follow me!' Reinhardt called out gleefully. 'We shall march to the pipes and enter your fine village like soldiers returning to their loved ones from a great pilgrimage!' Placing the flute to his lips he commenced to play a merry tune and all the children fell into line behind him. They stood, their necks stiff, chins up, arms locked at the elbows. At his command, 'March on!', they started to march, their arms swinging straight as a walking stick, each little face as serious as a soldier's on the king's parade. I glanced back to see that the dogs had joined the throng and followed the children in single file, tongues lolling, tails wagging – they too were caught in the spell cast by the ratcatcher's magic flute.

It was just coming on dusk, the time of gloaming when the birds call out their evensong before finally nesting for the night. The peasants, returning from the surrounding fields with their scythes over stooped shoulders, trudged wearily up the hill and the shepherd boys brought in the ewes and goats for milking. Smoke rose from the chimneys of the cottages as women primed the hearth in preparation for the evening meal.

We came to a halt in a cobbled square at the top of which grew a large oak stripped of its summer garb and almost bare of leaf. We stood beside its massive trunk and Reinhardt continued to play. Some of the marching children ran off to fetch their mothers. Many of the village folk coming in from the fields entered the square to see what the commotion was all about. The ratcatcher now started to play another tune that set the young men and girls to dancing, and the older folk, despite their weariness, were soon tapping their toes and clapping to the rhythm.

Coming to the end of the jig and before commencing another, Reinhardt turned to me and said quietly, 'After the next I shall make a speech and then together we will perform.' It was growing exceedingly cold and I was not sure that I would be in good voice, but I nodded agreement. I confess to being cast under his spell, enchanted at what I had witnessed since reaching the village.

There had been much applause and Reinhardt was forced to hold up his hand for silence. When all was quiet he smiled. 'What a fine village!' he announced. 'We have wandered far and wide but have seen few finer. And such dancing! I think you a merry folk who enjoy music?' Smiles appeared all round with many a nod and 'Aye!' following. 'Then you must have more!' he promised. He turned to me and placed his hand upon my shoulder. 'With me is Sylvia Honeyeater, so named for her sweet and tender voice, sweet as the nectar from the honey bee and tender as the summer night.' The village folk commenced to clap but Reinhardt held up his hand again. 'But first there is a small price.'

A groan escaped from the assembled crowd. 'We are poor folk!' a male voice shouted.

'Who spoke of money?' Reinhardt shouted back. Then, in a gentler voice, he said, 'We ask only for shelter for the night and enough to fill our bellies, for we have not eaten since the sunrise of the day before this one.' It was a lie, for we had stopped at noon when I had prepared the last of my corn to make a meal.

'You may stay with us!' several voices called out. 'We have food enough for two more souls!'

'Thank you, thank you!' Reinhardt called, then placing his flute to his lips he blew a few bars. 'You are most generous and kind.' He paused. 'But there is one thing more.' He turned towards me. 'We are not brother and sister, nor are we betrothed. I must have a widow's bed for my partner to share, one who does not snore!' He looked back at the crowd and asked, 'Is there a widow who would share her bed with an angel?'

At this the crowd laughed and a woman stepped forward who seemed in good health and appeared no older than my mother when she'd passed away. 'She is welcome to share the bed with me and my three children – there are none among us old enough to snore!'

This caused more laughter and several of the women called out, 'We will bring food, Johanna!' I was thrilled at this prospect and smiled my gratitude to the widow. Reinhardt the Ratcatcher had kept his promise and I was to be safe this night.

Now he removed his broad-brimmed hat and bowed to the woman. 'Thank you, good dame, then it is settled. As for myself, I am happy with clean straw spread in the corner of a cowshed.'

'Nay, you may share with us – we all snore!' a man with a large belly, rubicund face and a wild bush of fiery red hair called out. 'There is cider and fresh ale. My wife is a most worthy cook!'

Under cover of the crowd's laughter I nudged the ratcatcher. 'Reinhardt, I am freezing, can we not start?' I whispered.

While my voice was affected by the cold and not at its best, we seemed to greatly please the villagers with the rendering of several folksongs. When we finally came to the end it was almost dark and Reinhardt addressed them I hoped for the last time, as the hem of my gown was not yet completely dry and I was truly cold.

'We will sing a Gloria in the name of Jesus Christ the Saviour, who has given us the ripened summer corn, the cow's milk, cheese from the sheep and the goats, pickled cabbage and turnips, the fare to see us through the darkest winter. We ask Him to cause the rats to be barren and to give the cats sharp claws and to keep them hungry.' With the mention of rats a cheer came from the crowd. It seemed clear the household corn bins must be greatly troubled by these wicked rodents. I hoped this mention of rats and cats to be the last of his speechifying, but alas, his gift for yapping was not yet done and I must shiver and shake with a grin fixed to my face yet a while longer. 'We thank you all for your welcome and for your hospitality, and if any of you return here at sunrise, then you will witness a scene so strange you will tell of it to your grandchildren and they to theirs forever and a day!' With this astonishing promise Reinhardt raised his flute and blew the opening notes, whereupon I sang the *Gloria Patri* while many of the village folk fell to their knees.

At this, the long day's journey had finally reached the night. My fears of being the object of the ratcatcher's desires had been in vain. So what is it about a woman with a man? That having maintained my chastity and remained pure in spirit, I felt somewhat discontented.

A night breeze had risen blowing cold. The villagers wished themselves beside their hearths and there was no time to ask Reinhardt what he meant by the invitation to sunrise in the square the following morning. The widow Johanna quickly gathered me up, while 'Red the Belly', as I had named the ratcatcher's fat host, bade Reinhardt follow him to a *krug* of ale or cider and a meal worthy of his wife's talent as a cook.

The widow Johanna, a slim and comely woman, reminded me somewhat of my mother; her house was well scrubbed and clean and a fire burned brightly on the hearth. All three children, daughters all, the youngest three and the eldest seven, were quiet and well behaved and the two older ones were much taken with the stories I told them. Several other children arrived with food delivered from their mothers.

One brought pork sidemeat, another the first of the salted fish for winter, a third, walking with care mindful of spilling it, a jug of ale, yet another goats' milk. Then arrived variously a loaf of white bread, cheese, pickled kraut, autumn pears, nuts and apples. At one stage the widow brought her hands to her head and cried, 'How shall we eat it all?'

'I will take some for tomorrow's journey if you will allow it?' I asked politely.

This she promised and more. Warmed at the hearth and well fed, with the children finally sent to bed, we sat a short while. She told me her husband had died during the spring when a ploughshare had severely cut his leg when he'd gone alone into their field to plough on St Peter's Day. He had bled to death while the remainder of the village prayed in the church situated in an adjacent village. 'Folks say it was God's wrath for working on a holy day that struck him down.' She paused. 'But I think no such thing. He was a clumsy oaf, lazy and too ignorant to take advice and always careless with the harnessing of the ox. He was ploughing too early in the spring and the plough jumped on the frozen soil, the harness broke loose and the plough severed an artery in his leg.'

'But who will plough for you next spring?' I asked.

'The cottage is mine and also three fields, six cows, five goats and a gaggle of geese. Most days there comes some greedy oaf knocking at my door, all toothless grin and promise of his fealty. I would rather share a portion of my barley or oat crop in return for work than take another such clodhopper to my bed.' She looked at me sternly. 'Your womanhood will soon ripen, Sylvia. How old are you?'

'Eleven,' I replied.

'Then next birthday you will be a woman and may be betrothed. When the time comes choose carefully. Men are for the most part poor company, dull lovers and wine-bibbers; you are better served remaining in the company of women.'

'I have no wish to be a nun,' I laughed.

'Nay, that's not what I meant,' she said. 'Do not rush to the altar, there is lots of time. Though the Church allows it, twelve is too young to become some brute's wife!'

'I would hope not to choose such a man,' I said quietly.

'My dear, at first we all think we have chosen well, but alas, we seldom do.' She reached out her hand to me. 'Come, it is time we went to bed.'

'I have no nightgown and the hem of my dress is damp,' I confessed.

The widow Johanna laughed. 'Goodness, Sylvia, we are five women, there are logs on the hearth to last the night and the bed is well covered and already warmed by the children. What care you for a nightgown? Why, I do not myself possess one.' She held out her hand. 'Come, give me your dress and we will hang it by the fire to dry.'

'I am not sure,' I said, hesitating.

'What is it child, are you bleeding?'

'No!' I said, alarmed. 'It is just that I have not been naked in the presence of women since my mother died near three years ago.' I decided the disrobing by the stream in front of Fraus Anna, Frogface and Gooseneck didn't count.

'What fear you then?'

Of course I couldn't say, and even now I hesitate. I had always feared that my father's brutal mounting would show that I was no longer a virgin, that his wanton thrusting had changed my woman's part. The three old fraus who had seen me naked knew of his wickedness and so would not have pointed out an alteration to my body, though what form such might take I had no idea. 'It is perhaps modesty,' I said shyly.

'Modesty is a luxury only afforded by knights and fair maidens, by my lords and their grand ladies. It is a dainty game they play in courtship, but it's not for such as us, Sylvia. We are peasants and our men know little of courtship and even less of gentleness – only of rough passage and grunting. They will pass by a rose and leave it unplucked, then bring you a pickled pig's trotter and not know the difference.' She gave a short laugh. 'Remember always, the one-eyed serpent overrides all sensibility! Men are pigs and so will treat you like a sow!' She looked at me steadily, then asked gently, 'Soon you will become a woman, what know you of your time of bleeding? If modesty forbids you asking, how will you manage these female matters?'

Frau Anna had also inquired about my bleeding but I was still not sure what it was. Only that it would soon occur and that it was a most frightening passage I must endure to become a woman, though I had no idea what I would need to do when it did. 'Since my mother's death there have been no women to tell me these things,' I confessed to Johanna.

'Aye, I thought as much. You poor child. Now, off with your dress, let me look at you,' she instructed in a no-nonsense manner.

I removed my dress standing within the warmth of the hearth, the fire and the pale lamplight revealing my naked body. I stood with my hands cupped between my thighs as Frau Johanna took a step towards me and stooped to pick up my dress and arranged it so that the wet portion around the hem lay nearest to the warmth. 'Your breasts are budding, it will not be long now, Sylvia,' she said in a matter-of-fact voice. 'Tomorrow I will show you how to prepare linen strips to make a pouch,' she said, 'but now it is to the bed,' she pointed to where I held my hands, 'where I will examine you.'

She had said all this in such a straightforward and womanly manner that I hadn't the words to object, and her promise of instruction in the morning I thought most generous. She would see that I was no longer a virgin and expose my shame, but if I must confess, I thought Frau Johanna, with her apparent repugnance for what men do to women, the one who might best understand. 'I would very much like instruction on the matter of this bleeding, but, perforce, I must be at the village square at sunrise,' I said.

Frau Johanna laughed. 'Be careful of that sweet youth, he is the type who will pluck the rose in passing,' she advised me. 'We will rise before sun-up and I will show you what is necessary.' Then without further ado she removed her dress and, turning down the lamp, she took me by the hand and led me to the bed where the three girls lay asleep, firelight playing across their faces, the youngest with her thumb stuck in her mouth.

The room was warm and it was most snug under the eiderdown, but my anxiety grew as Frau Johanna placed her hand upon my pubescent breasts. 'Sylvia, you will soon be a woman with all of a woman's needs. I will show you how to care for yourself without a man. It is something we can share for it is called "the widow's husband and the virgin's knight" but every maid and every woman needs to know it for the comfort it brings.'

'I'm not sure,' I said, my voice hesitant. I was about to be exposed; she would touch me down there and she would know immediately. 'Frau Johanna, I am not chaste . . . It . . . it . . . was my father!' Unable to contain myself I burst into tears. Frau Johanna took me into her arms. 'Shush, sweet Sylvia. Men are wanton pigs and if I should have a *pfennig* for every married man who this very night will "pluck the poulet" in his family then I should be the richest widow in Christendom. You should count your blessings that you were still too young and your belly isn't swollen with a child that, should you not abort, would bring yet another idiot into the world.' She kissed me lightly on my eyes. 'Dry your eyes, it is not a shame of your own making.' She reached over and took my right hand, and then my second finger. 'Have you found the way to please yourself, do you know the way of the virgin's knight?' she asked.

'No,' I replied, frightened.

She pressed my finger. 'This is the knight's dream rod and I will show you how to use it.' She released my finger and I felt her hand slip across my belly and soon her finger found a spot to rest. 'Here it is, know you this tender spot. I must needs touch softly, tell me if I rub too hard. Slowly, play slowly for there is no haste and the longer you tarry the better; there needs be time to linger, to think of loving things. Close your pretty eyes, relax, this is time well spent.' She fell silent, her finger gently working within me until I felt a pleasure grow such as I had never known. I began to pant and then to gasp. 'Feel you how good it is, this loving of a woman's own making,' she whispered, and kissed me lightly on the cheek. I had become wet and Frau Johanna's finger started to increase its rubbing until I could bear it no longer and cried out in ecstasy as an overwhelming joyousness filled my entire body. I lay panting, gasping, unable to speak when Frau Johanna said softly, 'Next time you will please yourself, Sylvia.' Then she took me into her arms and we lay still.

Perhaps I should confess that I cried out in alarm and pushed her away, but my body was so washed with a feeling of serenity that I simply let her be, thinking this new intimacy a lesson in womanly loving. No! That too is a lie. I hungered for more such caring. I had not been embraced in a loving way since I was a child, nor received a kiss or felt the soft touch of another woman. The widow Johanna who now held me to her breast caused me to sob softly for the memory of my mother and my lost childhood.

Some might say that I was still a child and that the widow Johanna had not the right to instruct me as she had done, and by touching me she had violated my body in a way no different to my father. Perhaps they are right: a woman's body is sacred unto herself and I had not given her permission to touch me in so intimate a manner. All I can say in defence of both of us is that at the age of eleven I did not see it as a violation. I now know that most young girls discover this pleasure without instruction, but I had not done so myself. That part of my body had been so crudely violated by my father that I saw it as unclean, forever changed and the cause of most of my subsequent misery and deep sense of having sinned. Now I had been shown that it could also be a source of personal pleasure, but of course, after my initial euphoria, my first concern was whether this too was a sin. I knew well that selfish pleasure is regarded as sinful.

'Is what we have done a sin, Frau Johanna?' I asked.

She gave a merry laugh then kissed me lightly on the cheek. 'No, I think not,' she replied, and then seemed to think for a moment. 'But then again, there is such a welter of sins, of mays and may nots, all the declarations of men, bishops and priests, holy men and hermits, clerics, clerks and lay preachers. They seem to all be vying with each other to proclaim new and better ways to accuse women of sinning. What know we of the latest declaration when today's blessing becomes tomorrow's sin? Methinks such womanly matters should not be left to a priest to decide upon. Sometimes we must go to our own conscience for confirmation. If what I have shown you is a sin, then every convent and nunnery has its share of sinners. But, if it is wrong to do as we have done, then it is I and not thou who is the sinner, for you came unknowingly to this bed with your thoughts chaste and pure. You must decide, as every woman must, if you wish to embrace the virgin's knight.'

'Why call they it the virgin's knight?' I asked.

'Ah, I cannot say for sure, but think it somewhat like this: the mounting of a woman by a man is seldom what a young maid hopes for in her imagination. She wishes a brave knight returned from a pilgrimage will come to "pluck the flower", but she gets instead a ploughboy who, drunk on cider, grunts and farts and groans and thrusts with only his own pleasure in mind, then rolls over, burps and sets to snoring. It is, for the most part, a great deal of noise from every orifice but in the sum of it there is little that might resound to please her.' She gave a short laugh. 'But, ah, when she chooses her own lover, even if it be only in her head, then she may have the shining knight himself.'

I laughed at her clever reply. I had seen it often in the village, a young maid, perhaps two years older than myself, her belly swollen with child, the result of a brief dalliance with some oaf met at a travelling fair and taken for a hasty rutting behind a haystack.

'Thank you, Johanna,' I said quietly, though I was yet very confused.

We lay still for some time but then she must have sensed my confusion because I heard her take an inward breath. 'You are still too young to know your own mind and have not yet been with a tender man you love or suckled at your breasts an infant of your own. Try to wait until you are sure you know what you want, Sylvia,' she cautioned me again. 'Randy young men will pester you and in their whingeing make you feel guilty, accusing you of hurting their feelings by showing no love for them. The urge you feel within you to lie with a man will often become very strong, the strongest emotion a woman, who deep within her desires offspring, can possibly feel. But a fatherless child on your hip when you yourself are not yet fully a grown woman will earn the scorn of others and destroy your life. Better the virgin's knight than such a calamity.' She paused, then said, 'Hear you what I say, Sylvia Honeyeater, that is what I mean by keeping to the company of women.'

'Aye, Frau Johanna, I thank you again.'

'Then it is goodnight.' She kissed me, then turned from me to slumber.

It had been a long day since I'd decided to wash the muddy hem of my dress by the side of the brook. I was beginning to discover that life can be a very confusing business and I was not at all sure whether I was Sylvia Now or Sylvia Then. But as sleep finally overcame me, what I did sense was that I had returned to my mother's world. I was to learn it was a country no male can occupy or ever comprehend, be he Pope or cardinal, abbot, bishop or priest or any man, even a ratcatcher who stills the barking dogs and marches children to the magic of his flute.

I awoke just as it was growing light outside. The widow Johanna was already up and dressed. A fire blazed on the hearth and the smell of cooking pervaded the cottage. The lamp had been trimmed as it was still near dark within the cottage. I glanced over at the three children who slept blissfully, too young to know how difficult a process life can be. Only yesterday I had arrived in this village more child than maid and today I would leave it knowing I was soon to become a woman. I walked over to where my dress lay together with my Father John bag and stout stave. Both his generous gifts had served me well and had, in the few days I'd possessed them, become a part of me.

'Good morrow, Sylvia,' Johanna said quietly, then reached out and picked up my dress. 'This is dry but the cloth is old and much patched and will not last much longer.' She pointed to the circle of light thrown by the lamp where I observed a fresh garment lay. 'You shall have one of my own that no longer fits me. It will be large on you but we can alter it to fit.' She indicated my old gown. 'This one we will use for your bleeding. Alas, I have no boots or clogs your size, but if you will tarry a little longer this morning we will inquire of the bootmaker who may have a second-hand pair that will fit you.'

I thanked her profusely for the dress but then said, 'The boots are of no concern. I have not owned a pair since I was seven and my feet are well accustomed to the cold.'

'Phfft! Will your young man not buy you boots? His own are stout enough and his clothes are of a good fit and not much worn.'

I had not told her that we had known each other but a day and were only travelling companions. Reinhardt the Ratcatcher and I had fitted so well together the previous night in the square that the widow Johanna must have taken us for a pair of wandering musicians well practised as a duo. Apart from cautioning me against his amorous intentions she had not seemed curious about our relationship, assuming by the ragged way I looked that he cared only for himself. It was a notion that fitted well enough with the opinion she seemed to have of men and was one most people would possess of a wandering minstrel.

'We only met yesterday, Frau Johanna,' I now told her.

'Oh, now I understand!' she exclaimed. 'I have misjudged you, Sylvia.'

'How may that be?' I asked, curious.

'When you told me of your father I believed you – it is as common as sunrise. But when I cautioned you against the piper it was because you are on the cusp of womanhood and if you are sleeping with him now you are yet safe from becoming pregnant, but when your bleeding comes, after that you will not be.'

'But he told you that I was chaste and asked last night that I might share a widow's bed?'

'Phfft! He is a minstrel and like his kind saw only what advantage there was for him in suggesting his piety and your chastity. I did not for one moment believe him. Now I see that you *are* chaste and had I not doubted it, I would not have instructed you as I did.'

'But I am grateful that you did!' I protested. 'For lack of a mother I know nought of such things.'

'Yours is a cautionary tale, Sylvia. I must make sure my own daughters are not so ignorant when the times comes.' She smiled. 'It is I who am now grateful to you. Come, let me show you how to make and fit the strips of cloth that will cope with your womanhood. But first you must have a slip so that you can attach them.' She reached over and handed me a linen undergarment. 'It is old, my own when I was your age, but the linen is still good and I shall give you pins to keep against the time.'

The three girls were up well before sunrise and we broke our fast on a bowl of gruel and pickled cabbage and made our way to the square. Frau Johanna asked me if I knew what the promised miracle might be, but I couldn't say. 'I do not think his flute, no matter how good the melody, will get me dancing in the morning cold,' she laughed.

'Oh we shall dance, Mama!' Gerta, the eldest of her children, cried, hopping ahead of us with her two sisters following and crying out in imitation of the older, 'We shall dance! We shall dance!'

'Nor will I be able to sing,' I replied. 'He has a silvered tongue and I hope only that what might happen will not disappoint and will be worth the early rising.' I clutched at the neck of my new second-hand dress with both my hands. 'Today is almost winter come,' I shivered.

Several dozen village folk were waiting at the oak tree, stamping their feet, their arms folded about their breasts, their vapoured breath rising in the morning cold. They nodded to the widow Johanna who seemed well respected, and also to me, but did not speak.

Reinhardt and Red the Belly had not yet arrived when the sun was past the rim of the hills. The birds in the nearby woods were well into their morning song and a large crowd had assembled when at last the two men came towards us. It was clear to see that both were the worse for wear, with Red the Belly's hair aflame and wilder than ever and his nose a bulbous lighted globe, while the ratcatcher's pretty face appeared a ghostly white, his hat askew upon his tousled head. Reinhardt came up to me, his eyes red-rimmed and raw, indicated the oak tree and in a whisper said, 'Come stand with me, Sylvia, the cider has destroyed me and my head throbs like the clappers of hell.'

Frau Johanna next to me cried out in a jolly voice for all to hear, 'Good morrow, young man! Is it not a perfect day for a miracle? We come with the greatest expectations!'

A murmur rose from the crowd and Reinhardt the Ratcatcher gave her a sour look. I followed him to the base of the tree. 'That one has a raspy tongue,' he growled, then groaned, 'Oh, my stomach is full of speck and cabbage that wishes to return to the cook!'

'We have come to witness a miracle!' a strident voice in the crowd complained. 'You said it would be at sunrise!'

'Aye!' several others called. 'The miracle at sunrise!'

'I think there will be worse than your sore head and regurgitating stomach to come if you don't do as you promised!' I whispered, then added, 'Nor do I look forward to my share of their wrath.'

'Can you not sing?' he begged.

'No! It is too cold, my voice is not yet warmed to the high notes. Anyway, singing is *not* a miracle!'

'I think I'm going to be sick,' he groaned again.

'Be sick then!' I cried, my voice trembling. 'That will finally do it! We shall be lucky to get out of this place alive!'

'Can you do nothing?' he begged plaintively. 'Something to calm them while I recover? My mouth is as dry as monk's parchment – I cannot play the flute!'

'It is not I who promised the miracle,' I protested.

'Oh sweet Jesus!' he exclaimed, bringing both hands up to his head.

'Do not blaspheme or we shall be the worse for it and more!' I hissed.

'Miracle! Miracle! Miracle!' the crowd began to chant.

'Come, lad, are you not made of stouter stuff?' Red the Belly called out. Then addressing the crowd, 'Last night when the cider talked, he promised to make puppy dogs fly and turn cats into tigers, turtles into turtle-doves!'

'Miracle! Miracle! Miracle!' the crowd continued to chant.

Reinhardt turned green before my eyes and rushing behind the oak tree brought up all of Frau Red the Belly's splendid repast, so that the men present clapped and cheered and the woman turned their heads away and cried out in disgust.

Then came the word 'Trickster!' followed by 'Buffoon!' – this from Red the Belly, now turned leader and the ratcatcher's tormentor.

The angry crowd started to draw closer. I could bear it no longer and as had happened with the Miracle of the Gloria I was not aware of my next action. Putting up my hand to command their silence I stepped forward and from my mouth came the coarse mating call of the jay; this I followed with all the mating calls of the birds I could so clearly hear in yonder woods. Soon enough they came in flocks, until the bare-leafed oak tree was clothed anew with the fresh colour and brightness of every bird that flew in the heavens. Some came to sit upon my head and shoulders, others perched along my outstretched arms, and all did sing so that no one in the crowd could hear themselves if they should speak. Then the miracle occurred. Reinhardt the Ratcatcher, all the better for the contents of his stomach missing, came to stand beside me, no doubt to accept some part of the unexpected glory of the birds. A crow flew down from a branch above and landed, wings flapping, upon his head and shat, crow shit running between his eyes and down his pretty nose. Whereupon I sang a single soprano note and the birds all rose to the sky in a vast cloud and flew away.

The shatting of the crow was a happy coincidence but the crowd immediately took it to be two miracles of my making. The summoning of the birds the first miracle, and the crow sent by God to demonstrate that pride comes before a fall and that vanity and vaingloriousness is a sin to be punished with the shame of humiliation the second one. There is more that I shall tell of later, but the telling of the two miracles was to spread from one village to another over the ensuing months, although this time no priest or bishop was asked to verify the miracle. The village shared a church with two nearby villages and there was a great deal of jealousy between them. The folk had seen with their own eyes the birds called from the woods to clothe the naked winter oak with bright new feathered raiment and they cared not to argue the veracity of the miracle with priests and bishops when there was no other simple explanation some doubting cleric might conjure up to thwart their miracle.

But now let me tell of the moments following the crow landing on the ratcatcher's head. It had the immediate result of causing laughter and ridicule among the more callow folk in the crowd and so divided their attention. But the widow Johanna, who I now perceived carried some influence in the village, spoke out. 'God has paid the piper for his male vanity! He wished to accept the credit for the miracle of the birds, when none was due to him! Let it be a lesson for all men to note that God rewards pious women with gifts of wonder just as he punishes the boastful and vainglorious man!' With this admonition to the men and lads present she looked sternly at Reinhardt the Ratcatcher, who had found a rag in his pocket and was attempting to wipe his face. To the delight of the crowd this served only to spread the bird droppings across his pale cheeks.

I approached her and said quietly, 'Frau Johanna, he is sufficiently humbled. Can we get water and a rag?'

She pointed to a woman in the crowd. 'Gilda, your house is nearest. Will you fetch a bowl of water and a rag for shitface?' With this the crowd roared with renewed laughter. The woman, grinning, nodded and left. Frau Johanna, enjoying the notoriety, held up her hand for silence. 'We have laughed enough! God has sent us a virgin maid who can charm the birds from the trees. I know her to be chosen by Jesus Christ as his special messenger, for I have with my own eyes seen the sign.' She paused and looked around the crowd, now grown completely silent. 'The holy sign of the early martyrs, the mark of Jesus, the fisher of men!' She drew breath and then shouting said, 'The Virgin Maid has the mark of the fish upon her back!'

I gasped, for she had not previously spoken of seeing the birthmark. 'Frau Johanna, it is only a birthmark – it means nothing!' I whispered urgently.

The widow ignored my plea. 'Ah, the bowl of water and a rag for the piper,' she exclaimed, as Frau Gilda broke through the crowd.

I was angry. I felt myself being used, though I was too young to understand why. Last night Johanna had talked of different things and I had seen her as a sensible woman, but not a pious one. My heart filled with fear, now she was taking control. I trembled to think I might be with another Frau Anna. I hurriedly took the small bowl of water and the rag and started to clean the ratcatcher's face, my own averted for the shame and humiliation I felt. 'We must away from here! We cannot tarry!' I whispered to him urgently, wiping the bird shit from his cheeks.

Now the crowd had started to chant, 'The fish! The fish! The fish!' Then Red the Belly's voice cut through the chanting. 'Strip her! Show us the fish!' The crowd took this up. 'Strip her! Show us the fish! Strip her! Show us the fish!' they chanted. I turned to see that they had started to move closer, those from the back of the square pushing forward so that the crowd began to surge towards us.

Suddenly Reinhardt stepped forward. 'Stand back!' he shouted, 'or you may harm the Virgin Maid! She has brought the birds from yonder woods to charm you, but should you touch her she will summon a jackdaw or a raven as an ill omen or else call a curse upon your homes and cause a plague of rats to destroy your summer harvest!'

But he had long since destroyed his credulity. 'Lies! Rapscallion! Whore's son! Devil! Let the Virgin Maid show us the fish! Fish! Fish! Fish!' they chanted, heedless of his warning.

Reinhardt the Ratcatcher drew the flute from his belt and blew a note so high and sharp that I dropped the bowl and brought my hands up to my ears to stop the pain. And then I saw that everyone in the crowd had done the same. He withdrew the flute and you could have heard a pin drop, so silent had the crowd become.

'They be in an ugly mood and want to see the fish, what say you?' he muttered from the corner of his mouth.

'Only if it will help us to be gone,' I replied, concerned for what might happen next.

He nodded his head and turned back to the silent crowd. 'Now hear me, all!' He paused so all could tune their ears. 'The Virgin Maid does not wish to show you the fish, we cannot tarry and must be away.'

'Charlatan!' Red the Belly boomed out suddenly, then turning and jabbing a fat finger at the ratcatcher yelled out, 'Turtles into turtle-doves! Cats into tigers! Flying puppy dogs! He would trick us once again!' He turned back to the crowd. 'What think you of rats? Maybe the cats turned to tigers will with their fierce roaring chase away this promised plague of rats!' The crowd broke into laughter at his taunt and Red the Belly waited for calm before continuing. 'Cup your ears against his flute, let not this boastful bounder gull us once again!' He looked directly at me, all wild, flamed hair, pink porcine eyes and great bulbous nose stuck luminous and veined within his brutal face. As he spoke, spittle bubbled at the corner of his mouth. 'If the maid be a virgin and a special child of Christ Jesus, then let her bear witness!' He turned to face the crowd once more and with his arms raised, bellowed, 'What say you? Let the maid show us the fish of Christ!' He placed both hands on his belt and made as if to take his trousers down. 'Or we must perforce see if she a virgin be?'

The crowd brayed their approval. 'Fish! Fish! Fish!' they called again and again, while some of the toothless youths unbuckled their belts, bottom lips dropped, leering.

Reinhardt turned to me, his eyebrows raised in alarm, as the widow Johanna cried out, 'The men have turned into wild creatures! You must show them the fish or we cannot contain them any longer!' With this she urgently pulled at the lacing at the front of my dress, then grabbed me by the shoulders and turned me fiercely around so that I was pulled against her bosom with my back to the crowd. She grabbed the neck of my garment from both sides and jerked it down to expose my shoulder-blades and so also the birthmark of the fish.

A sigh, as if all were transformed to one, rose from the crowd. While I could not see with my back turned, the ratcatcher would later tell me that the women fell silently to their knees and then Red the

Belly, his eyes grown fearful, lowered his great stomach and sank slowly to one knee to be closely followed by all the men. 'Praise be to the Lord God! Blessed be His name! Hallelujah! There is a child of Jesus among us! Glory to the Highest and hosanna to the King of Heaven! Christ Saviour, forgive our doubting!' they called out, a more pious lot of ne'er-do-wells you never did see.

So concerned were they in this lamentation that none had their eyes raised to see that Reinhardt the Ratcatcher had brought his pipe to his lips. He blew a note so high that it turned his pale face scarlet and caused his eyes to bulge, the sound pitched beyond the human ear. Soon rats were seen to emerge from everywhere – from the eves of houses, under floorboards, from ditches, drains, corn bins, stables, cowsheds, sheep pens. Behind rocks set upon the hill, abandoned foxes' dens and disused wells, all ran towards the kneeling crowd answering the irresistible but silent call of the magic flute.

The women commenced to scream and all the people rose, alarmed, as rats stumbled into ankles and bumped into calves, some running up the hairy legs of the men and straight up the skirts of the kneeling women. Helter-skelter, squeaking, hell-bent, they clambered, struggled, ran towards the piper, heedless and unafraid of the human presence.

The village folk beat at the rodents with their bare hands, crying out and running for dear life, stepping on rats that squealed and bit them as they fought to flee the scourge. The errant youths, who had previously unbuckled, were the first to turn and run, and in so doing they forgot their undone belts and stumbled, then fell, as their trousers descended to their ankles. The rats jumped and skipped and ran over them, biting as they went, so that many clutched their cods with one hand and trousers with the other, wailing as they ran.

The widow Johanna was soon among the fleeing crowd and in great haste I pulled my dress back up across my shoulders and tied the front. Reinhardt stopped blowing scarce a moment to call out, 'Come, stand by my side!' He turned and walked just as the rats arrived at his feet and still piping silent sound he moved among them towards the entrance to the square. The rats turned to follow us, remaining half a stave-length from our ankles, a wave of grey rodents ten wide and stretched along a line full eighty cubits long, obedient as pilgrims come to worship at a shrine.

And thus we did wend our way out of the square and past the cottages and up over the hill. When we reached the edge of the woods and were out of sight of the village folk, Reinhardt the Ratcatcher started to pipe a merry tune kindly to the human ear, whereupon the rats, as if of one mind, scattered and ran into the woods. Reinhardt ceased his piping and threw back his head and laughed. 'Aye, we will make a pretty penny from all these rotten rambling rodents, little sister.'

'How did you do this miracle?' I exclaimed. 'You have saved us from the wicked mob.'

'Ah! You did not tell me *your* miracle of the birds! Shall we each keep our own secret?'

I shrugged dismissively. 'Nay, mine is no secret nor miracle. The cock of each bird kind has a mating call that the hen cannot ignore and she comes, ever broody, to his tune, while the other cocks come also to see how bold a cock it is who calls. If he is yet young and lacks experience in cuckolding, they will compete for her attention.'

'And mine no less plain an explanation,' he assured me. 'The ratcatcher's flute is passed on each generation by the Guild of Ancient Ratcatchers to an apprentice who shows a talent to become a piper.' He tapped his flute. 'This ancient pipe is so contrived that there rests within it a certain pitch too high for human ears that nevertheless proves irresistible to rats. There is another for mice and yet another that will pacify the fiercest dog or cause a pack of dogs to whimper at my feet.'

'What of humans – can the pipes call them against their wills?'

He gave me a strange look. 'Why ask you me this, Sylvia?'

'Well, when we came here, I saw your way with the children, how quick they were to obey the tune played by your flute.'

He looked relieved. 'Ah, you well know how eager children are to join in any game.'

'Aye, they witnessed what you did to the village dogs and became themselves compliant?' I suggested.

He shrugged. 'They love to march, all children do, but the piping of children is not my calling. The containment of rats, mice and dogs within the municipality is my profession. Though I confess I have put much labour into new sounds for the ratcatcher's flute since I first obtained my commission from the Guild. I have worked arduously on the discovery of a pitch that will beckon cats and cause them to come running.' He sighed and gave me a wry grin. 'Alas! Cats, like women, obey only at their own convenience. I have yet to be successful in this new endeavour.'

I laughed. 'Cats in my village were for the most part strays, wild things, all skin and bone, who went about hunting mice within the eves. But there is a story told, where a call to summon cats such as you have tried to create would have been greatly cherished. It is of a nobleman, a great count who, returning from a crusade, brought for his fair lady a silver cat received as a gift from the Sultan of Babylon. She was well pleased and called the silver cat Princess Cardamom, being the name of the spice originally obtained from the East. The cat grew fat from eating tidbits all day long and did sleep a great deal on her lap but also, as cats do, sometimes in secret places. Often at nightfall Princess Cardamom couldn't be found and no amount of beckoning could rouse her to come to her mistress. Then all the servants in the castle would be summoned. They'd take lamps and led by stable boys and gardeners they'd scour the great estate, each bush or rock or nook or cranny, stable, oat house, rabbit hutch or folly, all examined to no avail. "I know it! She has been eaten by a fox!" her mistress wailed, wringing her hands and near tearing her pretty garments asunder in despair. But no amount of calling out the creature's name did in the least avail. Then, as if a miracle, a silver paw would reach out and touch the hem of her embroidered gown. All would be well in the castle again and the nobleman would sigh, but still happy he, for now he was assured of a sound night's sleep without his good lady wailing and bawling and striking her breast as she was overcome with woe. And in their rude beds the servants sighed and thought unkindly of the silver cat from Babylon.'

Reinhardt laughed. 'You have a goodly way with a children's tale. We will make a worthy pair, Sylvia Honeyeater.'

'What happens now?' I asked anxiously. 'We must needs travel back through the village to be on our way.'

'Of course, and we will profit by it,' he promised.

I grew alarmed, wanting to be well away from these cantankerous folk. 'I care only to be gone and do not wish to tarry,' I protested.

Reinhardt placed his hands upon my shoulders and looking into my eyes explained, 'Sylvia, these are peasants, mean as rat shit, who would rather cut off their wrists than give alms. But now we have them afraid and compliant. They believe by being scornful of your miracle and demanding its verification by the sign of the fish, they have earned God's retribution whereupon a plague of rats descended upon them. Now they have seen how the Virgin Maid, showing them great compassion and mercy, has led the rats safely away into the woods. They will see this as your warning that worse may come if they do not henceforth treat you as Christ's child. We may expect from this contrite mob some generosity.'

'But you did the rats,' I pointed out.

'Nay, the flute made no sound that they could hear. We walked together, they will think it was you who led the rats into the woods.'

'What do we do next?' I asked him.

'We will return and take our place in the square and I will play and you sing.'

'What, some of a Gloria?'

'No, that later, a folksong will do well enough.'

'Will they not be afraid to venture forth?'

'Some, yes, but they now have a need for contrition and to express their respect for the Virgin Maid lest she return the rats. First the bravest will come and then the more timid. But you may be sure they will all be there, for they may now speak of two miracles, the coming of the birds and the prophecy of the rats.' He gave a rueful chuckle. 'Three, if you count the crow shit!'

I giggled. 'If they persist with calling me the Virgin Maid then I have a folksong about a virgin maid who lost her chastity under a linden tree.'

'Ah, excellent! Is it named "Cursed be the Linden Trees"?'

'Aye, you know it?'

'I know the tune well. It is a minstrel's song and will serve as a cautionary tale to any village virgin who has thoughts of venturing down into the ripened corn, hand in hand with some randy clodpole.'

We walked back to the village, the piper playing a merry tune, along the main street and into the square. From all about fearful faces appeared at windows and through half-opened doorways.

Every once in a while the ratcatcher would pause from piping and call out. 'Fear not, good folk! The rats are gone! We will sing and play for your great entertainment and then give thanks to God for this fruitful day!'

Once back in the square he started to play, although I did not yet sing. At first came the children, small boys ever the bravest, then the men and finally the women and girls, until the square was full and it seemed the whole village had returned. Some knelt in contrition, others stood with their heads bowed, an altogether chastened and silent crowd.

Reinhardt stopped piping and addressed the assembled villagers. 'Good folk, you have seen what you have seen and now I ask you to pray privately for your own forgiveness. Let each bring his own conscience to God.' He grinned. 'Or perchance a crow descends and craps upon your head!' This brought the crowd to laughter and much altered the mood, so that people now stood happily, relieved that they were not going to be punished. 'As for the Virgin Maid, she has asked me to tell you that she bears no malice towards you, but cautions you to speak of the fish to no others. As for the rest, what you have seen with your own eyes cannot be denied. Now she craves your indulgence. There dwells a hermit, Wilfred of the Wilderness, in a cave near the great city of Cologne. He is the maid's teacher, a wise and holy man who preaches to the poor and succours the sick.' He removed his hat. 'I shall pass this hat around and ask that you give alms, not for the Virgin Maid, but for her teacher's cause. I must remind you that she has rid your village of rats that can as easily return at her beckoning, so give with a generous heart to God's poor and infirm. Now the Virgin Maid will sing a cautionary tale, a poem for all who may, like her, be a young maiden, pure in spirit and chaste but also aware that she might be tempted by the devil.'

He nodded to me and played the opening bars and I began to sing.

I was such a lovely girl
while I flourished as a virgin.
The whole world praised me,
everybody liked me.
Hoy and oe!
Cursed be the linden trees
planted by the way.

When I set out for the meadows
to pick flowers,
a crude fellow decided
to deflower me there.
Hoy and oe!
Cursed be the linden trees
planted by the way.

He took me by the white hand
but not indiscreetly;
he led me along the meadow
very deceitfully.
Hoy and oe!
Cursed be the linden trees
planted by the way.

He took me by the white dress
most indiscreetly;
he led me along by the hand,
very fiercely.
Hoy and oe!
Cursed be the linden trees
planted by the way.

He said, 'Maiden fair, let's go over there:
that grove is lonely.'
Woe betide that grove we took!
I had cause to lament it.
Hoy and oe!
Cursed be the linden trees
planted by the way.

'There stands a fine linden tree
not far from the path.
I've left my harp there,
my drum and lyre.'
Hoy and oe!
Cursed be the linden trees
planted by the way.

When he came to the linden tree,
he said, 'Let us sit down.'
Love really constrained him –
'Let's play a game!'
Hoy and oe!
Cursed be the linden trees
planted by the way.

He took me by the white body,
not without my trembling.
He said, 'I'll make you a woman –
your face is so pretty!'
Hoy and oe!
Cursed be the linden trees
planted by the way.

He pulled up my little shift,
leaving my body bare.
He broke into my little fortress
with his erect spear!
Hoy and oe!
Cursed be the linden trees
planted by the way.

He took the quiver and the bow.
Well he did his hunting!
That's how he betrayed me.
'End of game!'
Hoy and oe!
Cursed be the linden trees
planted by the way.

When it was completed and Reinhardt the Ratcatcher played the last sad note there was much cheering and clapping. Then the widow Johanna came to stand before me, the ratcatcher's hat held in both hands. 'Sylvia, I am truly sorry,' she said quietly, her voice penitent and her eyes lowered. 'I abused your sacred chastity and I beg forgiveness.' I saw then that the ratcatcher's hat was filled to overflowing with alms, more money than I had ever seen and such as might have been given to a visiting bishop or a cardinal or even perhaps the Pope himself!

'Frau Johanna, nothing is impure to the pure in heart,' I declared. It was a phrase I had learned from one of the abbot's strident sermons and had myself at the time taken courage from it. Although, since I was a sinner far more than she, I did not feel comfortable saying it so prudishly. I was later to learn that sometimes we say things that people hope to hear and that this is sufficient unto the moment. Priests do it all the time, laying their hands upon supplicant heads and giving out blessings, while wondering what's for dinner.

Then to close our sojourn at the village I sang the Gloria's *Laudamus Te* and the people knelt and praised God in their hearts. We thanked the good folk for their alms and with our back sacks filled with the finest provisions – wine, goat's cheese, loaves and pickles – we made our departure. The village folk, following us to the edge of the village, shouted to our future luck and good fortune as they wished our wending blessed. I had now learned that opportunity, when seemingly lost, is often at its ripest moment.

CHAPTER THREE

The Entertainers

WITH SOME RELIEF FOR having, in the end, fared handsomely at the hands of the villagers we once more set our path for Cologne. Now as we drew closer, but two days out, we came upon a group of pilgrims who told us they were bound for Cologne on a pilgrimage.

'Is Cologne a holy destination then?' I asked.

'It is the ancient churches there, St Mary's on the Kapitol and St Martin's, both most holy shrines,' the young cleric leading the group answered. Then anxious to tell me more, 'They are *quasi mater et matrona*, most holy places wherein reside numerous relics and in particular those of the Three Magi.' It was clear to see that he wished to impress upon us the earnest nature of the pilgrimage he led. This was spoilt somewhat when a simple member of his group added in a guileless voice, 'It is near enough for us to complete our pilgrimage and return home to our village before the winter snows claim the roads.'

The news that in Cologne I could take my confession and holy communion, then begin my penance, filled me with hope. Also, at the same time, I could be seen to embark upon a pilgrimage. Then, of course, I asked myself, if Cologne was already my destination, would this count as a pilgrimage in God's eyes? I thought probably not – there are always special conditions that apply and I was learning there are very few short cuts in life.

Later, when we'd moved away from the group, Reinhardt asked me if I knew the meaning of the Latin phrase the cleric had used to describe the cathedral.

'Nay, I am a peasant and know no Latin,' I replied.

'But you sing the Gloria, they are in Latin?'

'I have memorised the words of the chants but do not know their meaning, except that they be words to the glory of God.'

'That is enough, I daresay,' he replied.

'No! It is *not* enough!' I replied in frustration. 'I hunger for such knowledge, knowing I shall never possess it. It is like a glorious riddle that in knowing its meaning, you will become rich, but while you might recite it a thousand times, you cannot understand its secret.'

'The words mean "*like a mother and a matron*",' he replied simply.

'How know you this?' I asked, surprised.

He laughed. 'How does a humble ratcatcher know his Latin is what you mean to say, is it not?'

I did not deny this. 'Perhaps, yes.' Then added excitedly, 'When I sing the Gloria, do you know the words?'

'Aye.'

'And you will teach them to me?'

'You will sing them no better for the knowing,' he replied pompously.

'Yes I will!' I persisted. 'I shall, by knowing them, all the more worthily praise the Lord Jesus.' Then, remembering my question I inquired again, 'So? How know you Latin?'

'A fortuitous accident of birth. My father was the ratcatcher on the great estates of the Abbot Theodore of Hamelin and he befriended a priest, Father Eric, who taught the nuns in the Benedictine convent the abbot caused to be built. He would allow me, until I reached puberty, to sit silently in their classes with a slate and stylus. Here I learned to read and write Latin.' He shrugged. 'Thereafter I knew sufficient to learn more by later conversation with him.'

'You can read as well?' I asked, astonished.

'A little. Why? Do you think me a dunderhead?'

'Will you teach me?'

'And what good will that do you?'

'You mean because I am ignorant, a peasant?'

'Nay, because you are a woman,' he replied.

I did not know at first how to answer this as I knew it to be true. 'You said yourself there were nuns who learned to read.'

'Aye, they are women of noble birth.'

'And you, the son of a ratcatcher and one yourself, are entitled to learn and I, the daughter of a carpenter, am not?'

'Sylvia, you know what I mean. What enterprise can you, a peasant woman, embark upon that requires you to read Latin, or for that matter, to read at all?'

'I wish for more knowledge! I wish to know the truth! The abbot once read from the Holy Scriptures, "*The truth shall make you free*". I wish to read such words for myself!'

He laughed. 'What, so that you may argue the Bible with bishops? You are a brave soul, Sylvia, that I do discern, but alack, the Church will not allow it. You know as well as I do that God has preordained our character – it is immutable, unchangeable, what we are born we shall forever remain.' He smiled and gave me an apologetic look. 'You cannot change a crow into a falcon.'

'Are there no women who can speak and read Latin except nuns of noble birth?'

'Aye, perhaps some few noblewomen, though mostly nuns who do God's work, and so may learn to read the scriptures, some to also write, so that they can transcribe the works of the saints.'

'And this is the only way?'

'Unless, like me, you are fortunate and find a priest or perhaps a nun who will teach you and you discover that God has allowed learning to be contained within your own character.' He gave me a sorrowful look. 'Sylvia, we must all learn to accept God's will.'

'Ha! So it was God's will that you found your priest, was it? Or simply fortuitous that your father was the ratcatcher on the abbot's estate?'

He shrugged. 'The Lord works in mysterious ways,' he quipped, then added, 'It has always been possible for a peasant male to become a deacon or even a cleric, perhaps even a priest, but not so a female.'

'Aye, as Frau Johanna says, it is men, not God, who make the rules by which a woman must conduct her life. God's word is only their excuse.'

'You blaspheme, Sylvia! God is Himself a male! You are Eve incarnate and born evil so cannot expect the blessings of Adam,' he said, now visibly shocked.

I sighed. 'Well then, let it be.' I knew I was cutting too close to the bone. 'Will you at least teach me the meaning of words of the hymns I sing?'

'I think not. We are three days journey from Cologne where you would enter the employment of your rich merchant's wife. You cannot learn them all in this time!' Then he gave me a sly look. 'Unless?'

'Unless what?'

'Unless you care to stay with me a while longer?'

'And where shall we live – and no doubt you think it will be as husband and wife? No thank you, Reinhardt the Ratcatcher!'

'We have money, the alms we gathered from the village.' He grew excited and held my shoulders in both hands, his pretty face drawn close to mine. 'Sylvia, you and I, we are a blessed combination, you singing and I with the flute, your birdcalling and me with the rats! Ho-ah! We will make a pretty sum together!'

It was my turn to be shocked. 'The alms? But they be for the hermit! For Wilfred of the Wilderness? You told so yourself!'

'Oh him?' he said, looking vague, then grinning as he scratched his head. 'Well . . . er, yes and no.'

'There is no hermit, is there?' I asked, accusingly.

He spread his hands and said disarmingly, 'Little sister, they would not have given so generously or at all without a cause that would earn them grace in God's eyes.'

I pointed my finger, shaking it at him. 'And *you* accuse *me* of blasphemy!'

'Shhush! Not so fast!' he said, at once indignant. 'It was fair payment for getting rid of their rats!'

I stamped my staff upon the ground. 'No! We are stealing God's money! If you wished payment you should have asked a fee.'

'Oh, yes, sure! "Good people, as I stand before you covered in crow shit, I wish to make you a proposition concerning your rats!"' He gave me a scornful look. 'Remember, they thought the rats the work of the Virgin Maid. What do you think they would have thought if *you* should demand a ratcatcher's fee and thus broke the spell created by the miracle of the birds?'

It was a good point and I had no immediate answer. 'What would such a fee be?' I asked, my voice growing more accommodating. 'As much as we received in alms?'

'Perhaps,' he said.

'I think not!'

'You are right.' Scratching his chin he gave a rueful laugh. 'We are a *very* good combination, Sylvia.'

'Half as much?' I demanded to know.

'Aye . . . maybe.'

'I think much less, but let us say it's half. We must find a hermit and give him half our alms, the other half you may count as your ratcatcher's fee.'

'No! No . . . No!' he protested angrily. 'That is money hard earned and it is *mine* . . . ours.' He looked at me pleadingly. 'They say a Jew's money is glued to the inside of his pockets. That if, at the moment a Syrian infant comes from the womb, you should place a piastre in his hand, he will close his fingers about it and thereafter no might on earth can pry this tiny treasure from him. Be that as it may, it is my experience that the German peasant is the most rapacious of all the moneygrubbers and will make the meanest Israelite seem foolishly generous. We will not see such alms again. Believe me, it was the donation those peasants gave to the Virgin Maid that proved the true miracle!' He patted his satchel. 'This money was given because they greatly feared your powers, we will need every penny for the hard days ahead in Cologne.'

'Suit yourself, ratcatcher! Now I must bid you adieu.' I pointed down the road. 'Go on, be off with you, thief, rapscallion!'

'You don't mean that!' he protested. 'What of the words to the Gloria you sing, I know them all as well as the words to the *Kyrie*, *Credo*, *Sanctus* and *Agnus Dei*. If you will tarry I can tell you their meaning in but a few days.'

'Be off!' I cried. 'You said yourself I would sing no better for knowing them. Nor am I able to learn the Latin words for being created a peasant and ignorant. I am a sinner born, yes! But not one of my own true making. Now you would turn me into a thief and next thing . . . who knows . . . whore? A fine combination we'll be, you say, but only for your own profit and your terrible lust!'

While Sylvia Now spoke out thus, Sylvia Then was sorely tempted to accept his offer and take a chance on keeping my chastity. Why is it that the Christian conscience is always in turmoil? Is it that the devil is omnipresent? Lurking in the shadows of our minds? If I remained a pious maid, must I then remain ignorant? Or by wanting knowledge become corrupted? Was piety truly the greater of these two desires? Or dare I not ask such a question for fear of gaining the wrong answer?

Reinhardt the Ratcatcher raised his hand and pulled his arm back as if to strike me. 'You are a stubborn and churlish maid and I should beat you!' he cried out, his pretty face all a-pout, although I could see his eyes appeared more uncertain than angry.

'Go ahead!' I spat. 'If you should beat me and then rape me, will you then be satisfied? Ratcatcher, you will have changed nothing, you hear? It is as God wills, I shall remain a poor ignorant peasant and you a pretty ratcatcher!' I spoke boldly, while my heart was sorely afraid. When dealing with my drunken father I had long since learned that my voice should seem defiant, so that he would not perceive my fear and only feel my loathing.

'Rape you?' Reinhardt's expression was at first querulous then abundantly hurt. His arm fell to his side. 'Sylvia Honeyeater,' he cried, 'I have given you my word!'

'The widow Johanna says that you are just the type to pluck the rose,' I said accusingly.

He brought his hand up to cover his heart. 'No, I swear it. You are safe with me,' he repeated earnestly.

The knife was in, but I felt the need to twist it, even though I knew I had the measure of this flighty piper. 'You said that should we come across a Bible you'd swear upon it that the stories you tell of the pilgrimage to conquer the Holy Land were true. Would you also swear not to deflower me? Swear it before Almighty God?'

'That I shall, kneeling at any altar in Christendom,' he said, in an over-elaborate promise. 'Forsooth, did I not accommodate you with the widow in the village?'

'Ho! That well suited your cunning plan,' I accused.

'What plan? I had no plan. Only thought for food and lodging for the night and to keep you chaste.'

'Ha! On the morrow you planned that I would be seen the Virgin Maid and you would use me to trick those simple village folk.'

'Oh-ho! You think me too clever by half. I swear I simply kept my side of the bargain not to share your bed.'

'Why? Am I not attractive?' I asked perversely.

'No! Yes, of course! An angel and most amazing pretty. It's just that I don't care to . . . to . . . dance with Diana.'

'Huh?'

'Sleep with you!' he burst out. Then calmer, he looked at me and shrugged. 'So what now?'

'What do you mean?'

'Will we stay together?'

'Only if we give half the alms to a hermit!'

'But I don't *know* a hermit!' he cried.

'Then we will find one,' I said calmly.

I could see he was becoming exasperated. I had first belaboured the point of my chastity and now this. He fought to keep his voice calm. 'They are not that easily found and live mostly in the desert . . . alone! St Simeon Stylites who lived in Syria seven hundred years ago spent thirty years chained to the top of a column sixty cubits high so that he might be alone! That's why they're hermits! Don't you understand? They do not wish the company of men! They have no need for alms. Some eat only grass!'

'Grass?'

'Aye, and are said to lick the morning dew to quench their thirst.'

'Ha! What of Peter the Hermit, he was not alone?'

'Why? What do you know of him?'

'Everybody knows of him, even we peasants. He led tens of thousands of pilgrims against the infidel to capture Jerusalem and regain the Holy Sepulchre.'

'That was different, Peter the Hermit was called out of the desert by God to lead the People's Crusade.'

'And there are no hermits in the towns or in Cologne?'

'Sylvia, I have travelled far and wide and sometimes have seen men who wear the russet gown of wool and carry the crooked stick. But they are no more a hermit than I. They are men who prey upon the poor and the gullible but, in truth, are footpads and vagabonds. Some, I have observed, have wenches who follow behind and at night in the woods at the edge of towns and villages you may see their fires and their drunken dancing and fornicating. To give alms to such scallywags, reprobates and cullions is to do a great disservice to hard-working entertainers such as we.'

'Entertainers now, are we? What happened to the Guild of Ancient Ratcatchers?'

Reinhardt grinned. 'It is a vocation that is always there if we need it.' He clucked his tongue. 'But to tell the truth, catching rats is inglorious work. My flute and your singing will enchant the crowd and merriness is a far better pursuit than the rats that constantly remind me that they will be the certain cause of my death.'

'Why so?'

'The plague, it is the rat flea that carries it, when it strikes the ratcatcher is the first to die. My father and my grandfather both perished thus.'

I could see no point in arguing further as he had, after all, come around to all my expectations. Besides, I quite liked the idea of being an entertainer. If it was less about warm loaves, hot soup and the comfort of the kitchen hearth, singing for my supper seemed a better life than that of a humble kitchen maid answering to a bad-tempered cook and a scolding mistress in a rich merchant's house.

'If there are no true hermits to be found, then we must give half the alms to the poor,' I announced.

'But we *are* the poor!' he protested.

'You said yourself, the ratcatcher never goes hungry.'

'But we are entertainers now!'

I frowned. 'And *they* go hungry?'

'Very well, half to the poor,' he sighed. 'Then you will stay?'

'Let me count the money, the alms.'

He gave me a hurt look. 'You still don't trust me!'

'Aye, of the honesty of a ratcatcher I know nought, but you have acquired a minstrel's bad habits and his look of innocence when he plans to gull a peasant. It is this I do not trust.' I held out my hand. 'Give me your satchel.'

With a final sigh he unstrapped the satchel from his waist and handed it to me. I quickly counted the contents and divided the money, keeping half and handing back the remainder.

'I see the peasant is true to his calling,' he smirked, plainly upset with the loss of half the alms. 'She knows nothing of anything, but can count money more carefully than a Syrian Jew.'

I ignored this churlish observation and grinned at his cleverness in putting both the Jew and the Syrian together to emphasise a peasant's preoccupation with money. 'I will guard the purse we will from now on set aside for the poor and you shall keep the one that lets us eat.'

He looked at me first puzzled, then greatly alarmed. 'Purse for the poor? Is it not just this once we give alms to them?'

'You said yourself, we will be a goodly combination and make a pretty sum. From now on we will share our good fortune, half of all we earn we shall give to the less fortunate.'

If you think this showed some good in my character, then that was not how I saw it at the time. While I cared somewhat for the poor, for I was to be counted among them myself, in my mind I had formed a plan and was about to put a proposition to Almighty God. Later, when I had the time to pray in earnest, I would phrase it more carefully, but what it was, was this: if God had created me a peasant and a woman with an immutable character and therefore by divine design unable to learn to read and write Latin, then only He, in His infinite mercy, could change the preordained circumstances of my birth. If I gave alms to God's poor, then in return, I would be in a better position to ask Him to reconsider my destiny and to grant me the gift of learning.

In later years I would blush to think that I possessed such effrontery and dared to think that I might make a bargain with the Almighty. But the young do not see these things as cut and dried and all things become possible when we have faith and hope and act in ignorance of the impossible. I did, as I recall, allow God the right to refuse me. I decided it would be a test. If, despite my efforts, I proved unable to grasp the task of formal learning, then it would be God's indication that He had not changed His mind and that I was predestined to be ignorant. I told myself I would forever after accept His will and the lot in life chosen for me.

'Then you will teach me the meaning of the Latin words in the mass?'

Reinhardt nodded reluctantly. I then asked shyly and with my eyes lowered, for I had asserted myself overmuch to this point and it was time to assume a maidenly modesty so he might think himself back as the commanding male, 'If I learn these well, can we purchase a slate and stylus and then, if God permits, will you teach me more of Latin?'

'All I know myself,' he promised, his lovely brown eyes the picture of sincerity. But then he added a cautionary note that indicated the slippery, sly nature beneath his acquiesence. 'Rome was not built in a day. It will take time, much, much time, as learning is a difficult and tedious process and perhaps for you impossible, but it has always a slow beginning.'

'Thank you, you will find me patient and tireless,' I promised.

He laughed. 'It will go best if I be patient and you tireless, little sister.' Suddenly, all business over, he rubbed his hands together. 'Good! Now we must work out a way to best gull . . . er, set before the worthy citizens of Cologne a merry dish of entertainment so that we may profit from it.'

In the next two days as I sang the words to each of the hymns he would translate the meaning. I do not wish to sound immodest, but from childhood I had practised memorising the sermons of Father Pietrus and the abbot, the pronouncements of the mayor and village officials, the conversations of the village fräuleins and others at the markets, so that my memory for words was most finely tuned. I think Reinhardt the Ratcatcher found himself truly flabbergasted when in less than two days I could recite the meaning of every line in every hymn. He then promised to teach me the Latin alphabet in sounds, and when we should reach Cologne we would purchase a slate and stylus and I would learn to write.

So far I had not put God's will to the test, since repeating the recitation of others, as I was well accustomed to doing, did not count in my mind for true learning. But now I was about to learn the actual letters contained in the Bible and then to join them so that they formed silent words upon the slate. Words produced by my own mind and scratched with my own hand. If God permitted me to learn, then I knew this would be a true miracle and that I would give praise to Him ever after.

As we drew closer to Cologne the villages grew more frequent and the ox-drawn carts more numerous. Many contained winter produce for the great city – mostly cabbages, turnips and pumpkins ripened at the end of summer and stored for winter sale. Bark cages on the back of carts carried rabbits or pigs, ducks, geese and chickens. Often flocks of shorn sheep led by a shepherd boy blocked the road, withers all, destined for the butcher's block. Soon the wooded slopes ceased and no natural land existed. Fields stretching to the farthermost horizon now lay fallow, the summer wheat and barley crop they'd carried long since harvested. A few willows beside a crooked stream dotted the landscape, stripped as bare as witches' brooms. We heard no birds calling other than an occasional raven cawing mournfully against the lowering sky. But if the land lay empty and silent, not so the road. Here a great conglomeration of farmyard birds and beasts mixed their discordant cries with the creak of wagon wheels working through the muddy ruts to the urging curses of the peasant farmers.

And through this city-bound cacophony we rehearsed our act, a bit of everything for everyone, folksongs funny and sad, randified and of a sweet maiden plucking flowers in a field. Hymns for the pious, and always Reinhardt the Ratcatcher's flighty-flirty flute to cause the young to jump from their skin and the old and the infirm to do a merry jig and so remember days of yore when they too were young and bold-eyed lads and lasses.

At last, in the early morning light, we saw in the distance the ancient Roman city built in a crescent shape and enclosed by a huge rampart with walls and numerous gates. I was happy to see that to the eastern side of the city beyond the walls were wooded hills. 'There is a river that runs through the centre where I once piped rats to drown,' Reinhardt said a little boastfully.

'Did that not befoul the stream?' I asked.

He threw back his head and laughed. 'Your world of silver streams that tumble crystal clear o'er rocks and moss are over, Sylvia. This is a river most foul. It is called the *Blaubach*, but it has long since lost its colour blue. It is mainly used to carry the shit and piss from the open drains that run through the streets and the waste from the tanners' and dyers' vats, abattoirs, fishwife stalls, dog skinners and other foul and noxious wastemakers and to deposit the effluent into the Rhine. My rats caused to drown in it would not have made a scintilla of difference. If you should perchance swallow a thimbleful taken from its banks you would most surely perish.'

It was not long after the ringing of the Angelus bells on the third day after we'd agreed to stay together that we arrived at one of the city gates. We'd sojourned at a village inn an hour from the city the night before, where we'd slept together on a straw pallet, this being the cheapest accommodation. Reinhardt, true to his word, did not lay a finger upon me but lay with his back turned to me all night. I lay snug, wrapped in a fine sheepskin coat the ratcatcher had won for me at dice from a merchant who dealt in scissors and knives who was tarrying in the tavern where we had agreed to entertain in return for our supper and ale.

Mist hung over the great river Rhine as we crossed an ancient bridge Reinhardt said had been built by the Romans. We had left the village while it was yet dark to make an early start. It was market day and all the carts we'd passed the day before now stretched endlessly along the road to Cologne. 'They will be nose to back all the way to the city gates to await the ringing of the Angelus,' Reinhardt had explained. 'They must pay tax to the city before entering. Most pay in kind, a rabbit or a pair of chickens or a duck or half a sack of vegetables. It is a bargaining process and peasants, as you well know, do not part lightly with their property. Having waited all night they consider time well spent when arguing the price of entry. Those waiting behind them often grow angry and quarrel among themselves, afraid they'll miss the markets, but when their turn comes they bargain just as hard and long. Those on the very end will not gain the gates until noon and so must sell their produce cheaply before the markets close mid-afternoon. If, for want of time, they cannot sell their produce or their wares, then they must stay the night in the city to sell what they have left to poor widows and the infirmaries.' He laughed. 'This keeps the inns and taverns busy, which is good for us.' He then explained. 'The curfew is at nine of the clock when the church bells ring and the town crier comes to urge the city folk indoors. Only the homeless poor are left on the streets and they too must creep into dark alleys and corners safe from thieves. So, you see, there is sometimes work for entertainers in the taverns and inns where the merchants and peasants sojourn.'

I did not reply, but wondered how I might stay awake, much less sing, at such a late hour. As we approached the gates the ratcatcher stopped and pulled me aside and asked, 'Where keep you the alms purse?'

'Why do you want to know?' I replied, suspicious.

He sighed. 'Sylvia, we must learn to trust each other or we shall not survive.' He pointed to the leather bag Father John had made for me, which sat snug to my back. 'We are about to enter Cologne. If it is in there then you will be relieved of it ere we've walked two minutes into the markets – it is a place most wicked and thieves abound. There is a legend that goes thus: a man, entering an abbey, found many devils in the cloister but in the marketplace found only one alone on a high pillar. This filled him with wonder. But it was told him that in the cloister all is arranged to help souls to God, so many devils are required there to induce monks to be led astray, but in the marketplace, since each man is a devil to himself, only one other demon suffices.'

'Then should we venture there?' I asked.

'All do and are safe enough in person if one is not quarrelsome or foolishly inclined, but terrible close care must be taken with possessions for there be pickpockets not yet eight years old who will steal the wax from your ears. They will in a trice be gone with your alms purse,' he warned again.

'And you deem it safe in your possession?'

He shrugged. 'If I'd wished I could have taken it while you slept and claimed some thief must have stolen it in the night.'

I indicated the satchel with a backwards jerk of my head. 'That's why I use it as my pillow!'

'And sit bolt upright in your sleep three or four times each night and cry out,' he grinned. I knew this to be true for I had sometimes wakened sitting upright after dreaming that my father, returning from the tavern, had dragged me from the bed to the pigsty as he had often enough done. 'I could as easily have taken it then,' he added.

I removed the leather bag from my back and, opening it, handed him the alms money. 'I know the exact amount!' I warned.

'Aye, ever the peasant,' he replied, placing the money into the money satchel strung to the centre of his waist.

'And what is to stop some thief cutting the leather strap about your waist that holds your wallet and making off with it? Did not that merchant last night boast that his scissor blades from Ratingen would cut the stoutest leather as if it were butter?'

'Well said, Sylvia! You grow quickly accustomed to the ways of the city. The strap is leather plaited with wire so that a knife or shears cannot separate it.'

While I had yet to learn to fully trust the ratcatcher, it was comforting to know that I wasn't entering the city with some clodhopper or country bumpkin but instead someone who well knew the nefarious ways of city folk. I wondered how I could ever have considered coming here on my own and how I might have fared if I had so done.

We entered the gates of Cologne and I was much excited but also somewhat afraid by the prospect of so big a place. There was a great milling at the entrance of the gate and the street beyond was filled with carts and wagons, men on horseback, dogs, donkeys, mule carts, cattle, goats, pigs, herds of sheep and, of course, people. People everywhere bumped and pushed and acted most contrary and with the rudest mien. The noise was as if I'd found myself transported into hell itself. But my first impression was not just of the maddening throng, but of the smell! Never had my nose been so affronted by the noxious ordure to be found in the churned and muddy streets. At first I thought it must have rained the previous night and what I smelled was pig and sheep and cattle dung – these were smells familiar to me – but I soon realised this was not the stuff of barnyards. I then saw that on either side of the thoroughfare there ran the ditches of which the ratcatcher had spoken and where folk deposited their nightsoil.

I observed that the premises that opened to the street were mostly places of trade, shops, workshops and the like, while the city folk lived above them. The houses were so built that the top portion overhung and the house each side of the street was seen to nearly touch the other and so all but enclose the sky. Then I realised what caused the wetness: women simply emptied their night buckets of piss and shit into the road below, ostensibly aiming it to land within the ditch, but because of the overhang it mostly landed in the street itself. The mud that squelched between my toes was not the good clean earth of nature – nor was it mud at all!

'We must purchase boots – the earth is foul and my feet are soiled,' I said, when at last the crowd had thinned and the noise abated sufficiently to be heard.

'Aye, boots for the street and dainty slippers, petticoats, a pretty gown of velvet and a new white wimple,' he said, in a manner I took to be most flippant.

I pointed to my toes, then cried out, 'Don't you mock me, ratcatcher! I shall not walk in shit!'

He looked surprised. 'Nay, I do not mock you, Sylvia. When we perform and wish to attract the better folk with our entertainment we will need the right apparel. For you a pretty dress and slippers with a clean, starched wimple, and for me stockings bright and a velvet jacket and perhaps a cap adorned with a peacock's feather.' He looked down at his feet. 'These boots are well worn but I will cause a shoemaker to repair and stain them red so they may suffice a while longer and match my new red stockings.'

I looked at him incredulously. 'And how shall we come about such grand attire?'

'The Jew,' he answered, allowing no further explanation.

'The Jew? Is he a moneylender? Father Pietrus says all Jews are. That money once borrowed from a Jew grows quickly to a greater sum than that which has been borrowed. Is this true?'

'It is called interest and it is how the moneylender makes a profit on his loan. It is not cheating, Sylvia, unless the interest is too high. But for the most part this Jew is a tailor to the rich and a garment hirer to the not-so-rich and an occasional moneylender.'

'Garment hirer? He sells old clothes, you mean?'

'Nay, his garments are most prepossessing and fit for a rich merchant or a nobleman or town clerk or dignitary – someone who would wish to impress for some earnest or dishonest purpose. Perhaps someone who, previously of raised status, has come upon hard times and is now somewhat the ragamuffin but who wishes to attend the wedding of a rich relative or present a business proposition to a guild member or merchant of high repute.'

'But we are neither imposter nor of a raised status now or ever previously.'

'In all things there is a pecking order, even in the business of entertainment,' he explained. 'We must place ourselves above the jugglers, fire-eaters, acrobats, stilt walkers, buffoons and sword-swallowers, dancing bears and monkeys performing to the hurdy-gurdy, and alongside the troubadours, lute and harp players who might be employed at a wedding or a feast in the house of a rich merchant or nobleman. If we stay the way we are then we will have to work the streets or perform at the weekly markets, the cockfights, wrestling or dog baiting, where you know full well the peasant folk are not a generous lot. If we seek a venue better paid we must dress the part and so not disgrace the company we keep.'

'But even so, would not this Jew's finery be too grand?'

'Most of it, yes. But he has clothes suited for an entourage, should the hirer need to impress with servants or footmen who attend him. When this cloth is worn, the Jew will repair it well and hire it to a more impecunious person.'

'And we have money sufficient to pay him?'

Reinhardt shrugged. 'Maybe.'

I stopped and folded my arms across my chest. 'Do not think to use my alms purse, ratcatcher!'

He turned, his voice taking on a whine. 'Sylvia, think you a moment – if we should succeed with better folk, your alms purse will grow more quickly than if we must divide in half the pittance earned from gawking, mean-fisted peasants.'

'It is God's money . . . for God's poor!' I protested, knowing that what he said made sense and also knowing that once promised, alms may not be taken back and to do so would be stealing from God Himself and so put me in a poor light concerning the learning bargain I had made with the Almighty. Sensible as such a suggestion might be, I told myself that I must bear the sweet and light burden of Christ's yoke and sacrifice the advantage the alms money may perchance bring to us.

Observing my stubborn expression, he said as if to calm me, 'Let us wait and see, there may be another way – with a Jew you can always strike a bargain.'

'What is this Christ-killer's name?' I asked.

'Israel of Bonn – Tailor to the Aristocracy, a good, kind man,' Reinhardt assured me. I was shocked to hear a Jew described with virtue added to his name, but said nothing. 'Come, it is not far from here.'

He led me through a series of narrow, twisting streets and finally to a small shop where a man and a woman sat sewing, she a cape of rich red velvet and he the ruffle to the sleeve of a lady's blue gown. From the walls about them protruded rods and from these hung every imagined gown or form of grand attire so that the walls glowed with such a rich colour of cloth that I had never imagined existed.

Reinhardt bowed and swept his hat across his knees. 'Good morrow, Master Israel, sire,' he called out, an ingenuous smile upon his pretty face.

The Jew looked up at us, his flinty black eyes taking us in with a single glance, and then silently returned to his work. I had never seen a Jew before and was somewhat disappointed.

The tiny man seated before us grew a trim goat's beard and had an altogether neat and clean appearance about him, although a wild clump of frizzy grey hair grew on either side of his head, like two small bushes growing in the cleft above his ears. Otherwise he was smooth-skinned and shiny to the topmost part of his crown, upon the rear portion of which sat a small black cap no bigger than my fist. As there was no single hair present to pin this upturned cup of cloth to, I could not but wonder if he might have glued it to his pate so it wouldn't fly away against the slightest zephyr. His smooth pink face was most normal-looking, and while his eyes were sharp his mouth did not possess the cruel twist that, I had been taught, indicated a Jew's heart of stone. Moreover, I observed that his nimble fingers working needle and thread were blunt, with nails well cut and clean, not long and fiercely taloned, blackened underneath with the crusted blood of innocent children used in a terrible ritual named Passover. Nor was his nose bigger or shaped differently to any other and it was not, as I had been led to believe, large and hooked, resembling the curved beak of a great bird of prey.

'Do you not remember me, sire?' Reinhardt asked, unabashed that the Jew had not returned his greeting.

'Tush! Must I remember every ruffian who darkens my door? Can you not see I am a busy man? Who are you and what do you want?' He said all this without raising his eyes from his work, and while his words were brusque they did not in the way he pronounced them sound unkind, but seemed more a test of what the ratcatcher might say next.

'I take it then that your cousin, Solomon of Zülpich, is well content to have rats in his granary?' Reinhardt said, a smile playing at the corners of his mouth.

The Jew glanced up, a surprised expression upon his face. '*Mein Gott!* It is the ratcatcher returned. It is three years you are not coming!'

'And the rats are bad, eh?'

'Terrible . . . terrible!' He turned to the woman who had glanced up when we had first entered but then, disinterested, returned to her needlework. 'My dear, it is the ratcatcher.' The woman nodded but did not look up. 'Sarah, it is the ratcatcher with the flute! Remember? Solly's rats running down to the river and *kaplonk* they are drowned, one hundred, two hundred, maybe more, who is counting?'

'*Ja*, I can see, Israel. Ask what does he want.'

'Want? He wants to catch Solly's rats! What else?'

The woman Sarah sighed and put down the cloak she was mending and looked impatiently at Israel. 'Ask, is the girl for sale?'

'The girl? What girl?' The tailor looked puzzled, glancing up and noticing me for the first time. 'Ah, a girl!' he exclaimed, surprised.

'The *winkelhaus*,' Sarah said in an over-patient voice as if she should address a dull servant. 'When your brother-in-law Abraham borrowed money for extensions, do you not remember, we took a quarter share as security.'

'*Ja*, of course, but we are tailors, my dear.'

'So?'

'So of *winkelhäuser*, what do we know?' He spread his hands. 'Nothing!'

'What's to know? She is dirty and her gown is stained and old, but underneath the goy is very pretty and young enough to learn to please.'

'No! You make a mistake! She is not for sale!' Reinhardt called out in alarm.

The little tailor's shoulders visibly jumped at the sound of the ratcatcher's cry. 'For sale? This goyim girl is for sale? What for we are buying a girl?' He looked at his wife, confused.

'I merely asked,' Sarah answered, her right eyebrow arched and her lips pulled tight.

As for me, I was as much confused as the Jew. Someone wanted to buy me for a *winkelhäuser*, a slave in a *winkelhaus*! What was a *winkelhaus*? Why did it need slaves? Or was this just their derogatory name for a maidservant? If so it wasn't very nice to regard a person thus. I hoped that the ratcatcher might later have the answers to my questions. But now he asked one of his own. 'This *winkelhaus*, is it of good repute?'

Sarah looked him over, her expression close to a sneer. 'Why do you wish to know? It is too good for use by such as thee.' Then she smiled suddenly. 'Ah! I see! It is not the wench who is the pretty one for sale!' She laid aside her sewing and rose and came to stand beside him. 'Hmm . . . tall, pretty face, pretty nose, pretty eyes and when washed clean the skin will shine, smooth as Cathay silk,' she said, appraising all the while the ratcatcher as if he were an animal for sale. She then said, 'I do declare there is a secret accommodation in Master Abraham's *winkelhäuser* for those who prefer a *rear* entry.'

I could see from the ratcatcher's expression that whatever this meant he was not pleased but before he could open his mouth the tailor said in agitation, 'Sarah! What know you of this *winkelhaus*?'

'Enough to know that when you lend money and take a share as security, it is as well to know the investment is safely held,' she replied.

'But is that not your brother's concern? It is in the family?'

''Tis all the more reason to know how goes his business.'

'Business? Boy, girl, *winkelhäuser*, rats, musicians?' the little Semite shouted, raising his arms and flapping his hands above his head. Then he turned to Reinhardt and pointed angrily. 'What brings you here that concerns a *winkelhaus*? We are not that sort. You will at once answer or be gone, the both of you!'

'Why, sire, no *winkelhaus*. I told you afore, it be your cousin Solomon's rats.'

Israel turned to his wife. 'See, I told you so! It be about Solly's rats!' Then a thought occurred to him and he turned to Reinhardt. 'You know full well the place of my brother's granary beside the river. Why do you not go to him directly?'

Reinhardt shrugged his shoulders, spread his hands and answered most calmly, 'Because it is to you I wish to make a proposition, sire.'

The Jew's expression changed now to one of suspicion. 'Proposition? What proposition? I am a tailor, you are a ratcatcher. We have no rats here.' He thought a moment. 'Well, but a few. The alley cats do well enough to keep them down.'

'I am no longer a ratcatcher,' Reinhardt declared. 'Now I am a musician.' He turned to me and smiled. 'My partner is a singer of great talent and repute.'

The Jewess looked me over once again, this time her eyes travelling from head to foot in a way that reminded me of the time in the village market with Frau Anna. A look of distaste was clear to see upon her face, so that I drew back, thinking she might spit upon me. 'Oh, I can well see how you will succeed with such a stylish lady of repute at your side,' she said in a voice most disdainful, then turning away, returned to her seat.

'Ah! But good lady, you said yourself she is pretty and young enough to please.' Reinhardt looked down at his soiled clothes, spreading his hands. 'Pray, do not judge us thus for ragamuffins. We have travelled from afar and you know well how it is best to dress in a humble fashion to discourage footpads and the like. Then with the autumn rains the road was most muddy. We arrived but this very hour and came straight here.' He turned to the Jew. 'Sire, had we but known your good lady was so particular of the appearance of others, judging them for their dress and not character, we would have washed our attire and visited the public bathhouse first.'

'Would somebody tell me maybe also what is going on?' the tailor cried, bringing both hands to wrap around the tiny cap.

'A proposition, I have a proposition to make to you,' Reinhardt repeated.

'Tush! They are musicians!' the Jewess shrilled, stung by the ratcatcher's rejoinder and now dismissing us with a backward wave of her hand.

'Musicians, perditions!' Israel shouted, then glaring at us he cried out almost tearfully, 'What proposition you got, eh, Mr Ratcatcher now musician?'

Reinhardt gave me a quick glance then turned back to the Jew. 'First you must hear us perform, sire,' he said.

By now I knew him well enough to know this was an idea that only a few moments before had entered the ratcatcher's head.

'No! No!' Israel cried, his hands held up to heaven for mercy. 'I am a tailor, not a choirmaster!'

Reinhardt, ignoring his protest, removed his flute from his belt and commenced to play the opening bars to 'Cursed be the Linden Trees'. I had no idea where all this might be leading us, but forced to trust the ratcatcher, I began to sing.

If I may be forgiven my immodesty and if I may say so myself, my voice was sweet and pure that morning. My singing was most mellifluous and the high notes held firm and long as they danced along a single note held by the ratcatcher's wonderful flute, and when at last the flute could endure no more they flew *a cappella* off the end to rise yet higher still.

But after two verses the tailor shouted, 'Enough! Enough already!'

Reinhardt stopped abruptly and I ceased singing halfway through a verse.

'Shush, Israel! Be silent!' his wife remonstrated. 'Can't you let a person hear!' She laid aside her needlework and looked at us, placing her hands in her lap, and in a calmer voice instructed, 'Pray continue, but from the beginning, I must hear this voice in one piece.'

I became aware that a crowd now filled the doorway to the little tailor's shop and stretched along the narrow alleyway, folk pushing and jumping to their toes to catch a glimpse but silently, so they might more clearly hear us. I would later learn that we were in the Jewish Quarter and the crowd were mostly, if not all of them, Jews. When we had completed the song I turned to smile at the people gathered in the lane. This they repaid by clapping and shouting their approval, demanding more such gratuitous entertainment.

Throughout the song Israel had wrung his hands despairingly, frequently glancing at the crowd gathered outside the doorway to the shop and then back at his wife. It was plain to see he was afraid the street throng might enter the tailor shop, but he was even more afeard of his wife's wrath if he should cause us to cease once more. The moment we had completed the song he rushed to pull down the metal shutters. When the crowd saw his intention they commenced to whistle and shout abuse and some rushed forward to batter at the metal bars, cursing him in a strange argot, which I was later to learn was Yiddish.

'We don't want trouble,' Israel said, looking despairingly at his wife, then back at us. 'Why are you here? What do you want?' He pointed at the shutters. 'Now you bring thieves and robbers to my door!'

'Attire, sire.' Reinhardt pointed at me, indicating my metal merchant's sheepskin coat, somewhat soiled, and my gown from the widow Johanna, far from new, too large and fit only to be worn by a peasant and dirty also. Once again he indicated his own clothes. 'We have only these, they are not suitable for our new endeavour.'

Israel shrugged and with a sweep of his hand indicated the racks of hanging clothes. 'So, if you have money you can get.'

Reinhardt the Ratcatcher grinned and looked first down at his feet then slowly up at the Jew. 'Ah . . . that is the . . . er . . . problem, sire.'

'Then go, be off, already you have made enough trouble!'

'But your cousin, Solomon . . . the rats?' Reinhardt suggested again. 'I am prepared to do one last rat ridding.'

'Tush! Go see him. Let him pay you for his own rats. Then when you come back with the money we can do maybe some business.'

I confess I didn't understand what Reinhardt was conspiring to do. This suggestion by the Jew seemed to me the most likely manner in which to conduct ourselves.

A hurtful look appeared on the ratcatcher's face. 'This is not about money, sire. You may with my permission negotiate any sum you wish with your cousin Solomon for my services and then keep it for thyself.'

Israel the Jew appeared only to hear the first part when a look of incredulity appeared upon his face. 'Not about money? Let me tell you something for nothing, ratcatcher! Everything in the world is about money! There is only one certainty in life and it is common to both the prince and the peasant, the rich man and the pauper – neither the one nor the other will ever think they possess sufficient money.'

'Shush, Issy!' Sarah the Jewess cried out. 'Do you not hear what the boy is saying?'

Israel turned to look at his wife. 'Of course. It is about *geld!*'

'Of course not!' she retorted impatiently. 'He wants to make a gesture of mutual trust. He wants we should trust him. He makes us an offer, Solly's rat riddance, a reward for our trust.'

The little Jew looked incredulous. 'Trust? A Gentile offers a Jew a reward?'

'He wants us to go into the entertainment business.'

Israel, alarmed and astonished, looked at his wife. 'What for?'

I could see Sarah's patience with her husband was wearing to a final thread. 'Because we would be most suitable partners,' she explained, as if to a child. She looked at Reinhardt so that we should take good note of what she was saying to her husband as they were meant as sidelong words to us. 'They are good, *very* good, but who do they know? Let me tell you . . . nobody! They know nobody! We shall dress them and introduce them. In this place you have to know already people.' Playing to our attention she opened her left hand and with the forefinger of the right she touched each finger in turn as she spoke. 'We know and dress noblemen, their ladies, knights, fair maidens, judges,' then exhausting her left hand she flicked the fingers of her right to add, ' . . . guild merchants, mayors, important town officials, those who are rich and those who want to impress. They must needs be entertained and desire only the best musicians.' She turned and pointed to Reinhardt. 'The boy is no fool and, with my help, has a sound proposition.' Then turning back to the little Jew, 'Believe me, it fits like a glove. For the proper introductions and suitable attire, a percentage, what else?' She looked at Reinhardt for confirmation and he nodded his agreement. The Jewess, now playing once more to her husband, cocked her head to one side and with her forefinger lightly touching her lip appeared to be thinking, then as if tasting the words she said aloud, '"Israel of Bonn – Entertainments to the Aristocracy!" Hmm, it has a most pleasing sound. What think you, *liebling?*'

Israel sighed and looked wearily up at his wife. 'You ask me what I think? Of musicians let me tell you already. They are dirty, lazy, they smell, they eat all the food, they get drunk, fight, curse, fornicate and steal!' He spread his hands and shrugged. 'Otherwise, I have no problems with them!'

'Good! Thank you, *mein* husband,' she said, bowing her head slightly. 'They are no different to the nobility, we will make a nice business.' She turned to us, suddenly stern-faced. In a voice both businesslike and crisp, she commanded, 'Come, we talk.' She pointed to a doorway at the back of the shop, then suddenly turned back again to face us. 'Always you will call me Frau Sarah and you will deal *only* with me.' She looked directly at me. 'You will curtsy when you come into my presence,' she instructed. Then turning to Reinhardt, she added, 'And you will bow and remove your hat when you wish to speak to me. Now, what be your names?'

CHAPTER FOUR

The Petticoat Angel

FRAU SARAH TOOK FROM a hook one of the oil lamps that lit the shop and we crossed the room to reach the door at the far end where she bade Reinhardt tarry awhile and bade me enter. The room was the width of the outer one, though smaller in depth, with the earthen floor covered in strewing herbs. My nose was assailed with the fresh scent of both rosemary and sweet fennel, a most pleasant combination that reminded me of the woods. All about the walls were shelves from the floor to the ceiling that contained bolts of cloth of every colour and description, velvets and silks, cotton and wool, enough it seemed to make a thousand rich garments.

Frau Sarah, having learned our names on the way across the room, placed the lamp to hang on a hook from the centre of the ceiling and now inquired, 'Are you a virgin, Sylvia?'

'Aye, Frau Sarah, I am chaste and pious, a Christian child of Jesus Christ the Saviour,' I said with defiance. I had decided I would not kowtow to this Jewess and, as well, to take the widow Johanna's advice and not count my virginity stolen by my father's abuse (may he rot in hell). In my heart and soul I remained a virgin and felt sure that in this one thing I could with clear conscience create a lie, for God was well acquainted with my sins. I also told myself that if we were to work with this Jewess, then she must needs know that I was all the while a good girl and a devout child of Jesus.

'Child? You call yourself a child? How old are you, Sylvia?' she asked.

'We are all children of God,' I said sanctimoniously, then added, 'Eleven or perhaps twelve, I am not sure of the season I was born.'

'Well, do you bleed monthly?'

'Nay.' Ever since the widow Johanna had told me about the manner of the coming of my womanhood I had expected daily to find myself in a state of bleeding. Each morning in the four days that had elapsed I expected to wake transformed, no longer a child but somehow loftier of demeanour. The need for the strips of cloth she had torn from my old Frau Anna gown was more than just for blood of childhood past. It was a badge, though invisible, of the arrival of my maturity. Alas, while it had been a long time since I had felt myself a child, I still remained a child within my body.

'Can you feel your breasts tight and uncomfortable with swelling?'

'Aye,' I replied, 'for some time now.'

'It will come soon,' she assured me. 'If my brother, Herr Hermann, should ask, then you will tell him you are twelve years old . . . no, thirteen and already a woman. Do you understand me?'

'Yes, Frau Sarah . . . but . . . but I am not to be sold as a slave. I . . . I will not allow it,' I stammered.

Frau Sarah laughed and there was a pleasantness to the sound. 'No, that was my mistake. That was *before* I heard you sing. You are to be an entertainer now.'

'And a free woman?' I ventured.

'Do you answer to a nobleman from whence you came? Are you a serf? If so, then you must stay in Cologne one year and one day to be declared a free soul.'

'Nay, my family were free peasants.'

'Then you are as free here.' She sighed. 'That is to say, as much as any woman can be.'

I felt much relieved by this assurance and bold enough to ask, 'What be a *winkelhaus*?'

Frau Sarah looked momentarily surprised, but recovering quickly said, 'Why, a place men go to be entertained.'

I found myself puzzled. 'If I am to sing and Reinhardt play the flute and there are only men, how then will they dance? Men, I have observed, grow quickly impatient of just singing.'

'Oh, there are women also, that's why the men come. But do not concern yourself, the men will be otherwise well-occupied while you sing.'

She explained no further, so that I was none the wiser for her words. I am a person who is reluctant to leave a subject or a conversation in midair, but before I could ask her for further explanation she called out for Reinhardt to enter.

I have described my first reaction to Israel the Jew and expressed my disappointment that he did not fit the picture so often painted of the Semite. But while much was preached and told about the vile Jew, I had never heard expressed the dark and nefarious character of a Jewess. And so I brought no bias of forethought to my conception of Frau Sarah, who appeared to be of middle age, perhaps forty, but unlike most women of such advanced age, was thin and straight-backed and wore her gown well. She was firm of breast and still trim of waist and her body, what I could see of it, appeared quite young, though her face, well lined about her mouth and eyes, forbade the same description and seemed hardened by the vicissitudes of life and set distrustful in repose. This disdainful appearance was further aided by thin, straight lips and when she smiled she was somewhat gap-toothed. Her nose seemed long and thin but was perhaps no different to most, lengthened only in appearance by the manner she affected of looking down upon it with her lips pursed, as if in perpetual judgement of all she gazed upon. What hair poked from her wimple was dyed with henna root and did nothing to belie her age and shrewish appearance. She had nice eyes, tawny brown tinged with specks of green, sharp and birdlike, most intelligent and knowing.

When she laughed (a pleasant sound) they danced, transformed to an unexpected merriness that hinted of a past life more frivolous than the present. Perhaps her laughter told of a deep-held inward nature that was softer and more pleasant than her outward demeanour. I hoped that this might be so. In my mind I feared that she might turn into yet another Frau Anna.

Reinhardt entered and first removing his hat he bowed and swept it across his knees in a most exaggerated fashion. 'You called, Frau Sarah?' he said, smiling broadly, then glancing at me to indicate that all was going as he had planned. This I doubted, for he would have expected, if an arrangement was to be made, to deal with the Jew and not this shrewish woman who had I think his measure.

As she had done when I declared myself a Christian and a child of Jesus, Frau Sarah ignored his exaggerated greeting. '*Ja, gut,* you are here. Now I will talk and you will listen and do as I say.'

I did not reply but stood silently looking down at my dirty feet.

'*Jawohl,* Frau Sarah,' Reinhardt called out.

'Sylvia, do you understand?' she asked sharply.

'Aye, Frau Sarah, but only if what you ask of me does not betray my conscience.'

'Hurrph! Believe me, you will soon enough discover that conscience is a dish that does not fill the stomach.'

'As long as I suffer a hunger after righteousness,' I replied, although my heart beat fiercely at my gall.

Frau Sarah smiled and in a tone we had not heard previously, one softly spoken as if a compliment, she said, 'That is a reply well turned.' Then she cautioned me. 'You seem both clever and questioning, Sylvia Honeyeater. But alas, you are born a woman. My advice to you is to hide both these virtues well or they will most assuredly bring about your downfall.' Then she laughed, a tinkling, merry sound and again one contrary to the character I had at first supposed. 'Oh, perhaps not all at once. Cleaned up and in a fine gown that denies your humble status you will be very pretty and as you grow into a woman, men will think you beautiful and pay you much attention. Your beauty is your only weapon and you must learn to use it while it lasts, for beauty is a rose today and on the morrow scattered petals. If you learn the ways of a coquette and choose your bed carefully, then men will indulge your questing mind. That is, if you remember always to bow to their superiority, exclaim at their profundity, compliment their masculinity and sheath your sharpened tongue for use when later you are betrothed.'

Reinhardt laughed and clapped his hands. I could see that he too saw Frau Sarah for a different woman to the shrew we had both at first supposed, and besides, admired her wit and her insight into my contrary nature. We were to learn that she was a woman of both natures: shrewish, hard and difficult in the ways of business and demanding of our obedience and strict compliance while also not without kindness and concern for our welfare, especially my own.

'What would you tell us?' Reinhardt asked, now willing to listen without resentment or buffoonery.

'You will go to the bathhouse at once. You are to bathe from head to toe, pay the attendant for clean water not twice used and hot, not cold.' She turned to me. 'I shall give you a fresh petticoat to wear when once you are clean,' she pointed to my dress, 'so your skin is not tainted from that filthy garment. Also, a pair of slippers to keep your feet unsoiled when you return hence. Do you have oil of lavender for your skin and lye and rosemary wash to remove the dirt from your hair?' I shook my head. 'No, of course not, why do I ask such a silly question? I shall give you some of each to use, also for light hair such as thine a rinse of chamomile – it will not only clean and scent your hair but cause it to affect a glorious shine.' She reached out and with a look of distaste fingered my hair. 'When did you last wash this?' she asked, as if my hair were some unpleasant object to her touch.

'By a stream five days ago, but I had no lye.'

'It was not washed thoroughly, but there are no lice, that is something to be thankful for.' She bent forward and sniffed. 'You smell, Sylvia, but I have smelled much worse in women of nobility and of the exalted classes. You will need distilled water of the flowers of rosemary to gargle twice daily to curb the stench of your breath and to make your close conversation sweet to the senses as well as to make sense. A comely wench is placed lower in appreciation by a prince or knight or rich man if with each sweet kiss there comes a whiff of sow's breath.'

I confess to finding myself amazed at such careful attention to my body. Nor had I previously heard of any of these exotic preparations. 'How know you all this, Frau Sarah?'

'Ah, it is all a part of the business,' she said, happy that I should ask. 'I count myself a herbalist. It has been in my family for many generations. Many who come here wish to be seen to be more than they might otherwise be in life – their intention is to impress someone for some honest or dishonest purpose. While their attire or gown may be richly stitched, if they are ill-mannered, uncouth and carry a stench of body and breath, it poorly serves their chances of success.'

'Aye, you would turn a crow into a falcon – they are both birds of prey – but the one despised and the other exalted,' Reinhardt exclaimed, displaying his own clever turn of phrase.

'You would do the same for us then?' I asked.

'If in the end we are to share in a profitable business you will be a worthy cause. Though I do not believe it will prove a difficult task. You are both pretty and talented, which is more than may be said of most of our customers.' She now looked at us sternly. 'I ask only that you obey me implicitly – there are many traps for the unwary and the young and society is a prickly business with many a nose easily put out of joint. If we offend one, if they are of influence, then all will be offended. If in doubt how to comport yourself then you must consult me at once, do you understand?'

We both nodded our heads, then the ratcatcher spoke. 'We do not have the means for the public bathhouse, nor have we broken fast today.' He shrugged and glanced at me. 'I do not care for myself, but only for Sylvia who grows weak for want of sustenance.'

Frau Sarah sighed and shook her head. 'Already there are tricks.'

Reinhardt looked most hurt. 'It is God's truth, I swear it,' he lied.

Frau Sarah did not reply but looked directly into the ratcatcher's eyes and he in turn met hers so that they remained thus locked in defiance of each other.

'I have some coin, enough for the bathhouse!' I exclaimed. 'It is intended for another purpose but this one will suffice.' While I knew that I betrayed the ratcatcher with this admission, I simply could not stand by and allow him to take God's name in vain.

Frau Sarah turned. 'What purpose?'

'Alms, we will give half of what we earn to the poor.'

'But you *are* the poor,' Frau Sarah said, bemused.

'Yes. So I will pay for the bathhouse.'

'And to eat?'

'Today we will fast for a penance,' I said and looked at Reinhardt. 'That is why I shall pay *only* for the bathhouse.'

Frau Sarah turned to Reinhardt. 'There remains much of the rat still in you!' she snapped, her previous character now returned. She turned and left the room and returned shortly with a petticoat and slippers, both worn but clean and dainty, the first of each I had ever possessed. She also handed me the lye and two jars of herbal mixtures, then instructed me to wrap them within the petticoat and cautioned me against placing them in my Father John bag. 'You must hold them close in your possession for you will pass through the markets,' she warned. 'Leave your leather bag with me or all within it will be stolen as you press through the crowd. Nimble thieving fingers you cannot feel will empty your bag as you walk. Also your stave, you will find it awkward.'

'Nay, Frau Sarah, where I go, there goes also my stave.'

'But it marks you a peasant and is not comely,' she protested.

'It is a promise made that I shall always keep. I cannot part with it.'

'Very well, Sylvia,' she said, puce-lipped. 'I can see you are stubborn; in your very first lesson on comportment you have failed.'

It was but a tiny victory but it told her I would not be pushed about.

And so we made our way to the public bathhouse. I had not spoken to Reinhardt while Frau Sarah had been absent from the room and he was wise enough not to engage me in idle conversation. But once outside the tailor shop he advanced a tentative statement that did not require an answer. 'When we pass through the markets you will see where we have with great good fortune avoided working,' he said. I did not reply but walked steadfast and angry. We continued on a while, the silence between us growing until his garrulous self could no longer bear it. 'What think you of the Jewess?' he inquired.

I stopped and turned accusingly. 'Why?' I demanded.

'Why what?'

'Did you betray our trust, lie and then swear it was the truth on God's name?'

'Ah, Sylvia, you do not understand the Jew, they will cheat you and take advantage if they think you are honest. Now the Jewess knows we are up to her game and can match her cupidity.'

'Ha! You talk shit, ratcatcher!'

'No, it is true!' he asserted, raising his voice. 'I know these Jews, they are all the same!'

'And you'll swear it on God's name, I'll vouch?'

He ran several steps ahead of me and turned and spread his hands. 'Sylvia, she is rich. Did you not see the cloth in that room? Alone it is worth a king's ransom. They will make a pretty penny when they sell my rat-ridding services to the Jew's cousin and you can be sure the percentage she demands of our endeavour is nothing short of onerous. I asked but a pittance, the money so that we, for her benefit, might be clean and break our fast. Was that such a crime?'

That was the problem with the ratcatcher – he could well justify his most wicked actions and cause them to sound but a trifle, a mere indiscretion. 'Nay, but you blasphemed, you swore it on God's name. Don't you understand, that is a mortal sin!'

'Ha! Then all in the world is a sinner! We will shortly reach the markets and if you tarry at a stall but a few moments you will hear "My God!" this and "By God!" that, a thousand times each hour. This blasphemy you speak of, it is entwined within the language itself.'

'And God writes each utterance in the Book of Sin and appends the utterer's name to it.'

'Forsooth, Sylvia! Thou art impossible!' he cried. 'In all eternity there would be insufficient ink or goose quills or skins rendered to parchment for the names that must perforce be inscribed in such a sinful book!'

'Hence all the souls in purgatory and those that burn in hell!' I exclaimed. 'Frau Sarah told the truth when she named you yet a rat.'

'Aye, I am not struck low by her remark. Rats are self-employed, persistent, cunning and will survive when all else perishes.'

'To carry the plague,' I added tartly.

'Ha! What then of the Jewess naming thee contrary and cautioning you to sheath your sharpened tongue?'

I thought at once to say '*But only in the presence of a man*', but curbed myself just in time, for the hurt this would have caused him. 'And thou shalt pay for the bathhouse and our food today!' I said instead, knowing that to argue further would not be conducive to his better behaviour. But I was learning that he did not, as I had supposed, always get the better of me in argument.

'Very well, but I caution you, after the Jews have taken their percentage, there will be precious little left for alms to the poor and we, I guarantee, will not gain the larger share.'

'That's not what you said before,' I accused him. 'You said we would work with gentlefolk and sleep warmly and eat plentifully and not compete with jugglers and the monkey on the hurdy-gurdy.'

'Aye, that I did, but I did not then know of Sarah the Jewess, but thought only of doing business with the old man, a much gentler sort. She has the sharpness of a whip's crack and her sting may hurt as much.'

'Then should we continue with this dame?' I asked. 'Or perhaps persevere on our own?'

'Aye, let us try her for size. If she does not suit we will abandon her.' He grinned. 'At least you shall have a clean wimple and a becoming gown and slippers and I a handsome outfit and undarned hose.'

I shook my head. 'Nay, ratcatcher, there thou go'est again! We shall keep these clothes we now possess and if perchance we leave, then we shall return what is not ours to keep.'

'Sylvia, we will most surely perish with such Christian morality as our guide! Think Jew! They are not like us, but they survive through thick and thin.' Before I could think to make a suitable reply he said, 'Come now, we have reached the markets. Keep well thy vigilance, there are wicked folk abundant here.'

Yes, and Christians all I daresay, but I kept this thought to myself.

If I had hitherto thought the streets smelling of shit and piss and rotting garbage an affront to my senses, they were as a sylvan wood when compared to where we now entered. A miasma of evil-smelling stench hung at the height of the numerous stalls and tents, so that the morning sunlight could scarcely filter through and turned the air into layers of greenish, brown and dirty yellow effluvium that stretched in noxious strands as if the veils of hell itself. The vile smell of rotting meat and fish, mixed with pig shit, rancid fat, over-ripened cheeses and the stench of numerous substances that my nostrils had not before confronted sent me close to fainting. To add to this fetidity, the acrid smell of the smoke from charcoal fires further dimmed the air and made my eyes to water and caused my throat a raspy pain and my lungs to constrict and leave me short of breath. The noise of the stall-holders and the folk attending the market made conversation impossible and their pushing, bumping and elbowing left me feeling bruised and battered. I was not able to return the pushing or fend for myself as I held Frau Sarah's slippers and bath jars wrapped in the petticoat crooked in my left arm and my staff in the right. Thus, for lack of momentum, I could scarce follow the ratcatcher as he walked ahead amongst the motley throng.

Many of the stall-holders were peasant women of a type familiar to me, although the women selling wine and bread were from the town, a difference easy to discern from the colour of their cheeks and skin if not from the way they were dressed. The townsfolk were pale and sickly while the peasants of a much more robust hue. I thought to ask Reinhardt how anyone, a musician in particular, could entertain in such a place of ceaseless human babble and cries of sheep and goats and pigs and the barking of stray dogs.

The bathhouse, when we reached it, sat beside the river and was a building placed next to the communal bakehouse so that both might share the fire and thus reduce the cost of wood. Both were built on stilts against the flooding of the river. It was a wooden building with canvas flaps that fell from the roof on the riverside and when folded let the air in during the summer heat, but now, even though draped, they flapped in the breeze from the river and caused the enclosure to be most draughty.

We paid the female attendant, a thin and sickly looking woman with a harelip and face heavily pockmarked, who took our coin with a grunt and in a voice as coarse as a carpenter's rasp called over two young boys seated beside the bakehouse oven. She bade them each fetch two kettles of boiling water. Then she pointed to adjacent doors under which ran a set of six steps stretched across and under both doors, one the male, the other the female entrance. The bathhouse was separated down the centre with a wall of mud and reed, the floor covered with dried rushes, though dried only in the sense of being no longer green for they were wet from the previous bathers' muddy feet and the splashing from the tubs.

A dozen used wine barrels stood against the walls with three wooden steps beside them so that bathers could more easily enter these makeshift tubs. From three placed beside each other protruded the heads and shoulders of women. They seemed to be friends, as a rowdy cacophony ensued, with much laughter, interjection and shouting out, all talking simultaneously and none listening. They ignored me as I entered. I observed that there was a wooden peg placed on the wall above each barrel where I might hang my gown and sheepskin coat. I moved over to a barrel furthermost from the three bathers and waited, not knowing if I should undress the while.

The pockfaced woman entered carrying two large kettles, the steam still coming from their spouts. She seemed too frail to carry even one and I hurried to help her. 'Step back,' she rasped impatiently, 'or you will be scalded!' Then placing down one kettle and lifting the other effortlessly she poured it into the wooden barrel that I now realised already contained cold water. She added the second kettle and without another word departed.

I placed my stave against the wall, unwound the bundled petticoat and removed the two jars, hung the petticoat from the hook and placed the slippers, heel inwards, on two spare pegs. Then, first placing the small earthen jars upon the topmost step that led up to the top of the barrel I reached in to feel the temperature, but drew my fingers quickly back for it was exceeding hot. I decided I must wait a while or if the attendant should return, request she bring cold water to add to my bath.

'Hey, fräulein! Why do you wait?' one of the woman called out. 'Take off your gown and let us see your little titties and tight sweet cunny!'

There was a sudden cackling among them and then a quietness as they paused to see what I might do. I was unsure, not knowing whether to run, undress or stay and wait until the water grew sufficiently cool. I had stood naked twice before, in the presence of Frau Anna, Frau Gooseneck and Frau Frogface and, of course, the widow Johanna, but I knew they would not harm me. I watched, not moving, steam rising from the wine barrel.

'Come, pretty one, show us!' the same woman shouted out. Then with a great sucking sound she started to stand within her barrel and I saw that she was exceedingly fat and upon standing that her stomach seemed to fill the barrel as if she were its rightful plug. She gripped the sides and appealed to the other two to help her climb from it. Of a lesser stoutness, they stepped from their tubs and helped the huge fat frau from her own. She stood a moment panting, a gargantuan creature, bluish-white with rolls of lard that sat around her waist and hung like a heavy apron to her front and halfway to her knees. Her legs and arms were great pillars of dimpled fat, her arms alone thicker than my legs. She had three yellowed teeth, one of them at the bottom centre of her mouth, the two remaining at either side protruding crooked from her top gum. They seemed to frame a dark and threatening hole from the ugly face that leered at me. Then she commenced to walk towards me in a great menacing wobble. 'Take off thy gown, wench, or I shall do so for thee,' she commanded.

'Nay, frau, the water is yet too hot, I would wait awhile lest I scald myself.'

'Too hot is it?' She turned to the other two. 'Did you hear that? It is too hot for the dainty little virgin.' They laughed and she turned back to me. '*Jawohl!* Then I shall take it for myself. My own is now grown cold, perhaps you would prefer it, eh?'

'Nay, good frau, this is my bath, please will you leave me be,' I pleaded. Then seeing her almost upon me I slipped my arms from the sheepskin coat and let it drop to the floor. In haste I undid my bodice and pulled the widow Johanna's dress over my shoulders and waist and let it drop to the wet rushes before stepping quickly from it. Gripping the edge of the tub I lifted my leg to climb the wooden steps when her enormous arm closed about my neck from the rear.

'My bath!' she said and jerked me backwards, to send me sprawling onto my back, my legs flying apart. Before I could regain my balance her two naked companions fell upon me pinning me down. I cried out but felt a hand held to my mouth. 'A virgin is she, let's see!' one of the women cackled and a blunt finger stabbed down between my legs.

I bit as hard as I might and felt my teeth come down against the pink knuckle of the woman who had her hand to my mouth. She screamed and leapt from me. Then I kicked out and my right foot landed square into the stomach of the second woman, knocking the breath from her body so that she rolled away clutching at her stomach and gulping for breath, her eyes bulging.

The woman whose hand I had bitten turned and rushed to where her clothes hung from a peg and in a moment I saw that she carried a butcher's knife and turned to come towards me. 'Biting bitch!' she hissed. 'Taste this!'

'Cut her face!' the fat frau shouted from the barrel. 'The whore's cut! Under the eye down to the mouth, slice hard, so we ruin her prettiness!'

I had risen to my feet and was about to run for my life, but saw that the frau holding the knife stood between the doorway and me. I was also naked and there is no greater shame than for a woman to be seen naked in public. It was, I thought, better to die.

Then, as if my mind was possessed, my fear turned to fury and in a trice I had my stave. Twisting the leather handle I withdrew the dagger and turned to face my attacker. The woman who was winded had regained her breath and now stood to her feet and, seeing me with the dagger in my hand, turned and ran towards the other frau. Then, seeing the one with the knife advancing upon me, she turned again to face me. I saw at once that I might not be able to overcome them both and so I ran to the fat frau in the barrel who sat with her back to me but had turned her head to watch. A look of great surprise now replaced the sneer upon her face. I grabbed her by the back of the hair and pulled fiercely to jerk her head backwards and expose her throat, placing the point of my dagger to it. 'Touch me, and she dies!' I screamed at the other two, but then realised they stood behind me and could easily attack me.

I released the fat frau's hair and moved quickly to her front, placing the dagger to her heart so that I faced the other two. 'Out! Get out! Get out of my bath!' I screamed, my voice hysterical, my spittle landing in a spray upon the fat frau's frightened face.

The fat frau rose slowly, the rush of water falling from her in a sucking sound. Then turning to the other two I yelled again, 'Get out of here or I will kill her and then you, I swear it!' They hesitated a moment. 'Out!' I pushed the point of the dagger lightly into the soft blue-veined flesh, its point making a tiny prick to break the skin so that a thin trickle of blood ran quickly downwards over her nipple and onto her stomach and then rested in a crease created by a tube of fat that sat about her waist.

'She has stabbed me! Help!' the fat frau screamed. 'Murder! Murder!'

Without further ado the two women turned and ran naked and screaming from the bathhouse, the woman with the knife dropping it to the rushes as she reached the door. 'You! Get out!' I screamed again at the helpless frau in the tub.

'I cannot!' she cried in terror. 'I am stuck! Please do not kill me!' she sobbed.

A fear rose up within me and I thought I must faint from fright, and my hand began to shake so that I thought I must drop the knife. Then, as suddenly, the thought that this cruel woman, stuffed like a pickled porker in the barrel, would have caused me to be mutilated and then slept as easily in her bed at night caused me to regain my courage. My fear was now replaced by a cold anger. I had endured sufficient humiliation in my life. I would stand for no more.

But I had not seen her right hand pull free and suddenly it shot from the barrel and gripped my wrist and twisted so that the dagger flew from my hand. She was far too strong for me and holding me in a vicelike grip she attempted to throw me off my feet. I bit down hard into the soft underpart of her arm as she fought to pull her left hand from the barrel so that she could grab me about the throat. Still holding my wrist she screamed and pulled fiercely back in pain and her momentum, hard against the tub, overturned it. Feeling herself falling she released my wrist and landed in a great wash of water to the floor, spilling from it onto her back, her legs spread to reveal her dark and obscene hairiness. With amazing speed for one so large, she twisted about and was at once upon her hands and knees seeking the dagger. But I had reached it first. Seeing this and fearing for her life again she turned and snuffling like a sow fled across the rushes towards the bathhouse door, her great fat dimpled buttocks wobbling and emitting loud farts, then she shat herself and, still upon all fours, passed to the outside.

'Dear Jesus, forgive me, I have sinned in my heart.' I wept aloud, then sank to my knees and naked before my Creator I prayed for forgiveness.

Why then had I drawn the knife? Did I want to kill the fat one? For I knew in my heart that the mixture of fear and fury was sufficient to do so. I had also bitten the other's hand deeper than was necessary to make her remove it from my mouth. The harder I seemed to try to be pious the more I seemed to sin. Jesus instructs us to turn the other cheek and I had not done so when it would not have been difficult. All the fat frau wanted was my hot bath and the other two would, in the end, have done me little harm had I not so stubbornly resisted. I would have been humiliated and then forced to endure a cold bath in dirty water. It would not be the first time I had held my silence when I had been shamed. Why had I, by biting her, forced the woman to get her knife? Why had I drawn Father John's dagger this time, when in the past I had allowed Frau Anna to spit upon me in the market and then to humiliate me in front of Father Pietrus? I had allowed the priest to denigrate and insult me and had not so much as murmured in my own defence. I had taken a hundred insults from village folk and remained silent. I had meekly submitted to my father's wanton cruelty time after time.

Why now this terrible transgression? I had murdered my father, now this. My debts of sinning were accumulating to the point where I must surely be declared a lost soul. Why was it so hard to be good? It must be my contrary and vainglorious nature and the evil within me, for the devil was becoming my frequent tormentor and the godliness I thought I possessed when challenged was seen to constantly fail. And so I prayed for redemption, full knowing that I had little reason to expect God's tender mercy.

I was not aware how long I knelt beside the fallen tub before I heard a raspy voice command, 'Get up, fräulein!'

I rose slowly to my feet and wiped the tears from my face. The pockfaced attendant stood before me, a kettle of boiling water held in each hand, a smile upon her poor deformed lips. 'Come now, fräulein, it is time to bathe thyself,' she rasped.

'Nay! They will return!' I cried. 'I must away!'

'Forsooth, you have seen them off! Three caterwauling whores all a-wobble and in a frightful funk! They will not return,' she laughed.

I glanced over to the furthermost wall to see that their garments still hung from the wooden pegs. 'But they have left behind their gowns and slippers.'

'Aye, they ran naked through the market crying out that they had been attacked by a demon angel, an imp of Beelzebub!'

'Whatever shall I do?' I cried.

She pointed to the dagger I still held. 'You will place that back within the stave, for if it is known you possessed and used it, the bailiffs would arrest you. Then you shall have a bath,' she said firmly. 'If those three whores should concoct a tale to make trouble, I will bear witness for thee as I saw all that took place. Those three are well-known for their cantankerous natures and are not well liked.'

'But the dagger, they will tell of it?' I cried hastily, replacing it within my stave.

'What dagger? I saw no dagger. What be thy name, fräulein?'

'Sylvia . . . Sylvia Honeyeater.'

'I am Gilda.' She moved over to a barrel and commenced to add water to it from the steaming kettle.

'Nay, I think it best I should be gone,' I said, reaching down for my gown, only to discover it sodden from the contents of the fallen barrel. Then I saw the sheep's-wool interior of my coat carried puddled water and was soaked through to the leather outer skin.

Gilda placed the first kettle down and lifted the second to the tub. 'Folk are gathered at the door to see this demon angel. I have bolted it against their entry. If you should leave now, what then shall they see? A ragamuffin!' She lifted her hand to her head indicating the hair beneath her wimple and rasped, 'Your hair is all in rat's tails and your legs and feet are soiled. They will think you a common street brat who entered the bathhouse to rob those three fat whores while they soaked, and perchance believe their malevolent story.'

Still frightened at the prospect of the crowd outside and the return of the three women, I commenced to bathe. Gilda, as attentive as a mother, fussed over me, helping me to use Frau Sarah's rosemary wash and thereafter to rinse my hair in chamomile. She fetched a length of old linen from a locked box to dry me, then rubbed my back with oil of lavender.

I had not, since my mother's death, felt more cared for and clean, but remained all the while anxious, as the noise of the crowd outside the bathhouse seemed to be growing. Dressed only in the white petticoat and slippers, I went to place my soiled wimple upon my head when Gilda stayed me. 'Nay, Sylvia, thy hair shines golden, let your prettiness be seen by all.' Then she took my hand and led me to the door. 'Come, I am well-known here and while at your side no one will harm you. But now you must appear for all to see that you are but a slight and comely maiden, white and blushing, face fresh as an apple, with eyes the colour of the summer sky and hair of ripened corn, neither Beelzebub's imp nor demon angel.'

Trembling I allowed her to lead me to the door that she now unlocked and swung open so that we might stand on the topmost step to face the crowd. A great shout went up from the assemblage, a mob of at least a hundred market folk, while more still were coming. Standing on the steps above the crowd I could see them running from the street stalls, the cathedral and the riverbank.

A woman's voice shouted out, 'Demon!' and, at once, a male replied, 'Nay, Angel!' Then, as if by some silent instruction, they began to chant, 'Demon! Angel! Demon! Angel! Demon! Angel!' To my great relief, Reinhardt broke from the crowd and leaping up the steps came to stand beside me. He lifted his hand to command the crowd to silence.

As the noise abated he took from his belt his flute and, playing a mixture of softly sustained notes and dazzling roulades, finally found his way to a phrasal pattern I knew as the opening of the *Gloria in Excelsis*. With a nod of his head he bade me sing. I sang this hymn and then some plainsong and the crowd grew to complete silence and many of the women knelt.

'We are here not only to praise our Creator but on such a pretty day let us make merriment in praise of life!' Reinhardt shouted, smiling at the silent crowd. Then he lifted his flute and I sang several folksongs, ending some time later with a merry jig that set the older folk within the crowd to clapping and bakers' maids, wine sellers and many of the peasant lads and city wenches to dance together.

At last Reinhardt held up his hand. 'Now, who among you would call her "demon"?' he boldly challenged the crowd.

'Nay, none!' they chorused.

'And who would call her "angel"?' he shouted out triumphantly.

A roar of approval issued from the assembled folk. 'Angel! Angel! Angel!' they chanted.

And again the ratcatcher held up his hand calling for silence and when the crowd had finally ceased to chant he shouted out, 'Good folk of Cologne, I bring thee . . . the Petticoat Angel!'

A second roar rose, greater even than the first and it seemed quite certain that they much liked this name. 'Petticoat Angel! Petticoat Angel! Petticoat Angel!' they chanted. Eventually they grew still and Reinhardt addressed them for the final time. 'Good folk of Cologne, we cannot tarry now, but tomorrow afternoon at the ringing of the third bell we will entertain you in St Martin's square. Come all who would hear the divine and enchanted singing of the Petticoat Angel to be accompanied by the Pied Piper of Hamelin and his magic flute!'

When we returned to Frau Sarah, having tarried first to take sustenance, we told her the tale of the bathhouse. But to our surprise she knew it all.

'How know you so soon?' Reinhardt asked. 'Did thee follow us?'

Frau Sarah laughed. 'Do not flatter thyself, ratcatcher. I went to see a silk merchant who has his warehouse near the river and on my return I chanced among the throng gathered outside the bathhouse.' She looked at me. 'Sylvia, it is not in my nature to flatter, but your voice deserves a choir of angels – it has a quality of purity I have not previously heard. Where did you learn to sing?'

'At first my mother and then the birds,' I replied. 'I try to emulate their tone and pitch.'

She looked at me and frowned. 'The birds? But they have simple tones, straightforward, purposeful, they possess no clever tricks of sound.'

'Nay, you are wrong!' I laughed. 'Their tricks abound. Now listen to the nightingale.' Whereupon I emulated the song of this beautiful sounding bird. 'See how it challenges the human throat and requires practice to emulate. I do not have it yet, although I have worked to perfect it countless hours.'

'Aye, the flute, with all its cunning, cannot make so pure a sound,' Reinhardt added, then placing his flute to his mouth did a most amazing impression of the song of the nightingale.

'How good be that!' I exclaimed, clapping my hands together.

'You are a worthy duo,' Frau Sarah said crisply, though I felt her reluctant to praise the ratcatcher for fear that he would become too overweening. I smiled inwardly, for it was true and not in his nature to be modest, yet concerning music he was always humble. 'And what hear I of pied?' Frau Sarah said to change the subject. 'Would you then truly wish a suit of many colours?'

Reinhardt grew at once excited. 'Aye, stockings of the boldest-coloured diamond shapes and a coat of all the colours as you may, but with ruffs of velvet black with inserts of yellow and so also the cap, but black alone, this offset with a peacock's feather!'

Frau Sarah smiled. 'And you thought all this spontaneously,' she teased. 'Sylvia, how would you like your gown?'

'I have not thought upon it, Frau Sarah. I would accept your choice.'

'White!' Reinhardt cried, clapping his hands. 'She must have a gown of the purest white, no wimple to be worn, so her golden hair doth shine like a glorious halo, and dainty slippers, worked with silver thread so they will seem as if she is as an angel shod.'

'White?' Frau Sarah frowned. 'Nay, she is an entertainer in a *winkelhaus*; she must wear a gown bold and definite to the eye, so men are at all times aware of her presence. You in pied and she in crimson velvet or the like.'

'Nay, nay, nay!' Reinhardt insisted. 'Today she was named the Petticoat Angel and seen wearing a simple white petticoat, that is what folk will from her expect.'

'Folk! You mean commonfolk? Tut! They are of little concern. We wish to please a more worthy class and mostly men,' Frau Sarah insisted.

'It is but early afternoon and already you may wager that all the market folk know of the Petticoat Angel,' Reinhardt insisted. 'How she sent three notorious whores fleeing naked for their lives and then emerged from the bathhouse white and sprightly, a golden-haired angel to sing *Gloria in Excelsis*. You may be sure that the crowd will later tell how it was a voice that could only come from heaven and she an angel dressed in purest white. This will spread and grow and the gentlefolk will hear the tale and wish to see this vision. Men love such purity and women will protect it, thinking she has powers to cast out demons. But if she should wear some rich garment fit for a princess, men will wish to take her for themselves and ravish her and women bring her down and show her for a peasant, unworthy of their pleasant company.'

Frau Sarah nodded, no doubt thinking this reasoning sound. 'How did you put those whores to flight, Sylvia?' she now asked.

I was about to explain the dagger contained in the handle of my stave when Reinhardt once again took voice. 'It is a power she has contained within her that can summon the birds from the trees. But if she has been wronged, she will use it in a different way to strike the fear of God's wrath into the breasts of those who would do her harm,' he proclaimed, without a trace of shame and to my astonishment.

Frau Sarah looked doubtful. 'I am not a Christian, so am not so easily confounded by such augury.'

'Aye, but as a Jew you well know the power of an angry God. Would you doubt His wrath and so cause Sylvia to bring it down upon thee?' Before she could answer the ratcatcher, smiling, said, 'Nay, she would not do that to you who have shown us kindness. But if you wish to test her powers, we will go to the woods and you shall see the good side of her power. How she can charm the birds from the very trees.'

I did not know it then, but only later, that the Jews possess as many devils and demons in their religion as in the Christian and believe that some have supernatural powers. Also, that God's wrath is not to be provoked by mortals, and so his bluff was in good standing with her faith. Perhaps I should have chastised him for his lies, but knew that should Frau Sarah think I was of uncertain temperament and possessed a sharp dagger that might at some stage harm her, she would be reluctant to continue with our partnership. Also, Gilda, the bathhouse attendant, had warned me that such a weapon found in my possession might bring me swiftly to the attention of the city court. Prudence forbade me confess and I told myself that I would at some later time, if Frau Sarah proved a trustworthy partner, confess the truth to her.

'The songbirds in these woods are wary of being trapped by the street urchins who sell them to the merchants to hang in cages at their shopfronts,' Frau Sarah declared. 'Even the cathedral pigeons, knowing they may end their lives within a pie, are ever flighty.' She laughed. 'I know this because oft times when gathering herbs and mushrooms I come upon a sweet-singing bird trapped to a branch rubbed with a sticky substance and hasten to release it. I do not think the birds in yonder woods will come to thy beckoning, Sylvia.'

I felt she said this so that I might not be caught out for a fraud and must now concoct a reason to retract the ratcatcher's claim. 'Aye, perhaps not, it is but a trick of voice,' I replied. 'I have not yet encountered birds that dwell in woods adjacent to a city.'

Upon Frau Sarah's lips there played a knowing smile. 'Perhaps on the morrow in the morning when I go to gather herbs you will accompany me?'

'Thank you, I should like that,' I said, knowing at once that she wished to test me and that I should not avoid her challenge, even if she were proved correct about the city birds.

'Then it is a simple gown in white for tomorrow at St Martin's square?' Reinhardt asked.

Frau Sarah nodded her agreement. 'We shall see what we shall see.'

The Jewess was not a woman easily gulled and the ratcatcher would need to watch his slippery ways and forwardly tongue lest he trap us both within a nest of lies and deceit. Once again I found myself in a situation beyond my control and felt myself perplexed that I seemed to attract attention and trouble without having sought it in the first place.

Frau Sarah was now all of a business. 'Israel will measure you and cut a pattern and I shall sew a simple white gown for you to wear tomorrow, Sylvia.' Then she turned to Reinhardt. 'If we are to make you a suit of pied it will take a week, the hose alone will take a day, so while you wait we will dress you as a knave, but you shall have the velvet cap you so desire.'

'With a peacock feather?' Reinhardt asked anxiously. He was truly obsessed with his adornment and there was no modesty to his demeanour, except for his music, which, if the truth be told, was ever a more worthy reason to be vain.

Frau Sarah sighed. 'Aye, I will obtain one for thee.'

Reinhardt thanked her profusely but then added, 'Perhaps a pair of red hose to the knave's attire and bright buttons to the jerkin?'

Master Israel, as we grew to call him, measured me for a gown and informed the ratcatcher that a deal had been made with his cousin Solomon for a rat-riddance ceremony the following morning.

'He must be alone with no servants or workmen present and the path to the river clear with no people or impediment,' Reinhardt instructed. 'I wish no others to know I am returned or I shall be called upon for rat riddance by all the corn merchants on the river.'

'Nay, he will not talk of it. He will see the advantage to him of wheat and barley free of rat droppings. Also the greater share he will save of each commodity,' Master Israel declared.

'But you would make a pretty penny doing this for all the corn merchants?' Frau Sarah suggested.

'Aye, but who would wish a ratcatcher's flute to accompany the Petticoat Angel?' Reinhardt said. 'Folk would not perceive it well and we would be the lesser for it. I wish henceforth to be known *only* as a musician.'

For all his conceit Reinhardt was blessed with a shrewd head and I could see Frau Sarah thought the same but wished only to ensure our partnership was not sullied, as rats and music are not a pretty combination.

'Sylvia and I shall depart to the woods to gather herbs while you are at your final task as ratcatcher,' Frau Sarah decided. 'You with rats and she with the birds.' She grinned wickedly. 'I daresay, tomorrow morning both your reputations will be tested.' Then sensing my concern she added, 'Fear not, Sylvia, thy voice is not in dispute, nor is the ratcatcher's flute.'

With a small expulsion of air Reinhardt drew himself up to his full height. 'Frau Sarah, I beg you, call me Reinhardt and when in public, the Pied Piper of Hamelin.'

Frau Sarah laughed her nice laugh. 'Of all this pied I am not sure at all. Too much colour in a pretty lad's cloth doth cheapen the look, but then again thou art an entertainer where a suit of pied is not unusual.' She paused then, looking most sincerely into his eyes, she said, 'Reinhardt it shall be, the Pied Piper of Hamelin otherwise.'

Reinhardt, pleased, then turned to me. 'And thou, Sylvia, what say you?'

I laughed and thought a moment. 'No, I cannot promise. When I am angry with you I shall call you ratcatcher. Otherwise, I promise, it will be Reinhardt.'

'And with strangers?'

'Very well,' I sighed. 'The Pied Piper of Hamelin, even though I think it too toplofty.'

'Especially with a peacock's feather,' Frau Sarah added archly. But all this risibility had no sway with Reinhardt, who, I could see, delighted in this new appellation.

That night we sojourned with a good Christian woman of Frau Sarah's acquaintance who fed us well and gave us two pallets of clean straw to sleep on. 'It will be accounted and deducted from your earnings,' the

Jewess informed us. 'But she is a good, clean and honest woman who, I am told, keeps the rats and mice, fleas and lice mostly in control and who does not charge much. We cannot feed you here, as our food is kosher.' I would only later understand that a Jew could not partake of food prepared by a Christian or sup together with such as us.

Reinhardt grumbled that he must be up while the moon still shone and before dawn to expel Master Solomon's rats. Nor could I sleep late for shortly after the morning Angelus, Frau Sarah came to fetch me and I was surprised that she wore a veil to conceal her face. We commenced to walk through the early-morning city streets and up the hill towards the woods. My sheepskin coat had dried beside the fire and I felt warm, though I wore no wimple to my head. I had obtained a pair of stout oft-mended boots that once belonged to Master Israel, now kindly given to me by the Jewess. They fitted well and were most comfortable as we set off to climb the winding path up the steep slope behind the city.

Alas, we were not alone for long. Two street urchins, always early on the prowl, had seen me and both put their fingers to their lips and whistled a long, shrill note that echoed down into the wakening city below. In but a few minutes there were children coming from every direction, though most from the streets around St Martin's church.

I talked to one of these boys who told me his name was Nicholas and said his age was ten or thereabouts.

'And thy parents, they are dead?'

'My mother, yes.'

'And thy father?'

He frowned. 'He is a drunkard and beats me if I go home,' he said without self-pity. 'I prefer the streets.' He claimed he lived with lots of other children in one of the narrow alleys behind St Martin's and said that one day he wished to be a monk.

'You are pious then?' I asked him.

'Aye, as much as I may be, Fräulein Petticoat. It is not possible to live off one's wits and always follow the ways of God.'

'I know the problem well,' I laughed. I liked him instantly, not only because he too had endured a cruel father but also because he had a forthright and determined manner about him.

'I asked to be a choir boy in the church but they would not have it.'

'You like to sing?'

'Aye.'

'Then perhaps one day we can sing together,' I said.

'Will you sing for us?' he asked.

'Nay, not today, it is yet too cold.'

'But they will beg you.'

'They?'

'I . . . we have called the others, they will want you to sing.'

'Come, Sylvia, we mustn't tarry,' Frau Sarah called.

'They will want you to sing,' he repeated. 'All the city talks of the Petticoat Angel.'

'This afternoon, in St Martin's square,' I promised, then asked, 'Nicholas, can you sing and do you know the words to the Gloria?'

'Aye, some of it.'

'This afternoon come to St Martin's and we will sing together,' I promised.

'Yes, fräulein, we can try,' he said doubtfully. 'I am not much practised.'

'Come, Sylvia!' Frau Sarah called, all the while thinking me hindered by the boy.

I bade the boy Nicholas adieu. 'Until this afternoon then?'

'I will try, Fräulein Petticoat,' he replied.

By such time as we had scaled the hill and reached the woods there must have been fifty children, ragged, dirty and most cheeky, and as they followed they shouted out, 'Sing for us, Petticoat Angel!'

Frau Sarah pronounced herself puffed out and bade me wait while she caught her breath. We had reached a grassy glade on the edge of the woods where she rested on a large moss-covered rock. The children now stood at the edge of the glade shouting, 'Petticoat Angel, sing to us!'

'Be off!' Frau Sarah cried.

'Sing!' they chorused back.

'Nay, it is too early! I am unseemly puffed from climbing,' I called out yet smiling – anger has no place within the woods among the birdsong.

But they would have none of it. Persistence is the beggar's best attack. 'Sing, sing, sing! Petticoat Angel, sing to us!' they continued to cry out.

'Nay, I will not, but gather round and I shall tell you a story,' I declared, thinking this might please them just as well.

'Sing! Sing to us!' they chorused yet.

Then Nicholas shouted for them to cease their shouting and to my surprise they instantly obeyed. I could see then that he had something of the leader about him, for he spoke not in request but in command. 'The Petticoat Angel will *not* sing!' he announced. Then he turned to me. 'It will please us well if you should tell us a story, fräulein.'

The ways of children were familiar to me and a story doth often catch and hold their attention more than a song. So they gathered around and I waited until they were all seated in the sunny glade. I felt sure, like most city folk, they did not much notice the birds, but I was amazed at the birdsong coming from the wood and so thought to tell a story concerning these lovely flighty creatures.

'This is the sad tale of a land not so far away that contained only miserable and selfish people who decided they would banish all the birds so that they might keep every last grain of corn and barley for themselves. And so they sent the birds away across a dark, cold and bitter snow-capped mountain. The land grew silent from that moment on, as all the other animals refused to make their own particular sounds. All in nature is measured and there is a cadence all beasts understand and live by. So, with the banishing of the birds, the cow did not moo, the donkey heehaw or the mule bray, the horses neigh, the pigs snort, the sheep bleat or the dogs bark. Even the cats, of whom, it is well-known, never agree to do anything that others may agree upon, refused emphatically to miaow.

'There were no ducks or geese or chickens, for the stupid folk had forgotten they were birds and saw them only as possessions to pluck and eat and to lay their ever-willing eggs. Moreover, the knights and noblemen lost their falcons and could not hunt, and there were no owls to kill the mice, or eagles to take the rabbits now feasting on the young corn in broadest daylight. Soon the beasts could not be found, because their cries could not be heard. The dogs slept through the night so thieves came and no alert would sound, their owners snoring through the wicked plunder. Some fields remained unploughed – the ploughman, no longer waking to the sound of the birds, slept blissfully on and much of the land remained unsown by late November.

'That year, because the birds were gone, the insects had a merry time and devoured all the corn and barley long before it ripened. The whole land seemed filled with green- and yellow- and red-striped caterpillars arching their backs and making tracks and munching to their hearts' content. The greedy, selfish people were now starving and so cried out in despair, "Bring back the birds! *Please* bring back the birds!" But this could not be done unless they could find someone who could talk the language of the birds and cross the dark, cold, bitter snow-capped mountains to the neighbouring country where birds were still welcome and bid them return.

'Well, they searched and searched all over the land, but the country folk had long since forgotten the language of the birds, being too busy gossiping and meeting, quarrelling and cheating, and the city folk were even less inclined to listen to birdsong for the joy its presence brought. But one day they found a young maid who lived on the streets of the city near a great cathedral who was poor and humble and half-starved, but who oft visited the nearby woods and was said to have once upon a time talked to all the birds. They promised to make her a princess, to dress her in a velvet gown and adorn her with a precious crown of sea pearls and sparkling gems. Upon her dainty feet they'd place slippers spun from a spider's web. They'd feed her with cakes and ale and build her a castle of her own and seat her upon a golden throne and build her a carriage drawn by six white horses with fancy ostrich plumes like fountains spraying upwards from their heads. All this and more if only she would agree to make the arduous journey across the dark, black, silent, bitter, snow-capped mountains and, once arrived, persuade the birds to return.

'"I do not wish to be a princess and my jewels are dew drops poised upon the morning grass that sparkle just the same," she said. "How long do you think such silly slippers would last crossing the cold and bitter, silent, snow-capped mountains? You may keep your cakes and ale and I do not need a draughty castle or a lofty throne. As for a golden carriage and horses, white or not, I must needs sit behind their bums and watch them poo a lot? My wish is only that you provide food and warmth and laughter for all the children on the streets, now and forever after."

'This they agreed to do forever after and a day, or as long as they remembered, which wasn't very long, as is the human way. So she made the journey over the mountains and through the snow until she reached a great wood of oak and elm, fir and beech and yew that resounded with the most marvellous birdsong. And there she met with all the birds, among them the eagle and the robin, the owl and the talkative jay. Who, by the way, for all his chatter, had much to say and most of it quite wise, so that all the birds gathered there were quite pleasantly surprised.

'Then took place much parleying and a to-and-fro of arguing and sharpened point of view, with a snigger here and a yawn there and even a quarrel or two. For birds, as you well know, are talkative and simply must each have their say, and some will chat throughout the livelong day.

'Alas, there were times when the geese had to be hushed so that the proceedings might continue. The ducks and chickens were not far behind in their insistence to be heard all at once and at every moment speaking for their kind. What a mixture of cackling, quacking and a honking their concatenation proved to be.

'Finally the owl had cause to admonish them most severely. "You have lived too close and much too long with humans and have forgotten how to share a song and so constantly fight among yourselves. You have lost your pretty manners, but instead you strut and waddle like fat hausfraus who speak but never listen and don't know right from wrong! Would you kindly allow this small blue wren to have her say? She speaks more sense from her tiny beak than you lot from the farms and barns a-honking, a-quacking and a-cackling every moment of the day."

'There and then and on the spot the wren proposed that they adopt a proposition most seemed instantly to like a lot – to come back if they were guaranteed a fair share of the ripened grain and scattered seed. "In return and true to our belief, we will keep the insects down and snap up every caterpillar that dares to crawl upon a single ear of corn or eat a cabbage leaf," she added to the brief.

'"Aye, well and truly said, we birds of the air must earn our bread," the wise old owl remarked. "But, while I don't give a hoot for things that crawl, we must not really eat them all. It is my bird's eye view that insects too must lay their eggs and breed, for when you think it through, we'd find ourselves in the very same trouble as these silly humans do. Verily I must atone, birds cannot live by corn alone. I have long since learned to leave a mother mouse or two in every barn to breed, so that I might have a meal while passing through."

'And so they amended the proposition to allow some insects to be spared. The pretty butterfly in particular. Then, of course, the geese and ducks and chickens raised a last-minute objection and insisted that the words "birds of the air" be changed to "all the birds". "We birds who do not care to fly, who honk and quack and cackle and teach our young to cheep, are also worthy of our keep!" they honked and quacked and cackled most indignantly.

'And so as quick as an egg may be laid, a second amendment was duly made. And thus it was that they all finally agreed to return.'

I stood and addressed the children. 'Now would you like to see how it was when the birds returned?' I asked.

In one accord they shouted that they would. So I walked to the centre of where they all sat and cautioned them to be quiet as mice and then I began to call. The blue jay, always inquisitive, was the first to arrive and sit upon my shoulder. Then a chattering magpie came and landed upon my outstretched hand. As each mating call went out, birds of lovely twittering, raucous chatter, soft cooing, sharp tapping, hooting, chirping, warbling, piping, clacking, trilling, tweeting, cackling and screeching, even the mournful cawing crow came flying in to share in this tumultuous and most glorious din. I saved to beckon the raven, for its appearance is said to bring ill fortune, though I doubt this true, even though it is a sooty-black and beady bird and its cawing can be often heard. Then to complete the glory of the coming of the birds, I sent out the mating call of the nightingale. Now hundreds of birds sat upon the shoulders, hands and heads of every street child but none upon Frau Sarah who looked somewhat forlorn. Then last of all, two nightingales came to flutter above and then to land upon her outstretched hands and then to sing the song of the rising sun and the coming of the dawn.

After I had sent the birds away to brighten up this lovely day, I asked Nicholas if he would persuade the children to leave. 'We will tell folk to come this afternoon, Fräulein Petticoat,' he promised.

And so the children left to find a way to break their fast, as children hate to delay a rumbling stomach. Frau Sarah sat silently a while upon the rock. Finally she spoke. 'Sylvia, I have today witnessed a miracle and I am a Jew and do not believe in such phantasmagoria. Now I well see how you learned to sing such notes with glorious clarity and pitch. But the calling of birds confounds me. Whether a Christian or Jew, it is a God-sent gift.'

'Nay, I told thee once before, there is a natural cause – their mating call cannot be resisted,' I protested. But I could see she did not believe me and thought it modesty or a way I had to deny my power so that she refrained from questioning me too closely. And so I learned the Jew is just as superstitious as we Christian folk. And that all the world would rather have a great wonder than a simple explanation.

Much to my dismay Frau Sarah now declared, 'Sylvia, methinks thou art a *wunderkind*. I am not sure that what is planned for you in a *winkelhaus* is in thy best endeavour. What is it that I might better do for thee?'

'Oh, nay, Frau Sarah! I love to sing and I will do my best to please you,' I cried.

'Is that then enough for thee?'

I had never been asked such a question and knew not how I might answer her. 'Frau Sarah, I hunger to learn,' I said at last, 'to read and then to write in Latin. Alas, I am a peasant and have been told by the priest that it is written that God has made me as I am and that I must be content with my lot. Learning, the Holy Church has proclaimed, is not for such as me – my peasant sensibility and reason cannot tolerate it and I will find myself confounded with every conundrum and so will end in madness. If this be true, then I pray to God that he expunge my name from this Holy writ and grant me His precious gift of knowledge.'

'Latin, not German? You wish to be a scholar?'

'Aye, there is much I ask myself about God's word and think perchance the answers have been written down in Latin.'

'Aye, so they might, but they were writ in Hebrew first.'

'Nay, in Latin! I must learn the language of God's Holy Word and that is most *definitely* in Latin!' I insisted.

'Sylvia, God's word was first writ in Hebrew and thereafter Greek and then it was translated into Latin.'

'Are you sure?' I asked, confused, thinking she must surely be wrong. *How might a Jewess know such a thing?* I asked myself.

'Aye, my husband Israel is a scholar of all three, Hebrew, Greek and Latin, and speaks as well the Arabian tongue, for he was born and raised in Jerusalem where all are needed.'

I could not believe my ears. 'Frau Sarah, if it is discovered that God has granted me permission to learn, will Master Israel teach me Latin?'

'I will ask him, but I cannot say how he will feel about teaching you.'

'Why? Because I am a Christian?'

'Nay, because you are a woman.'

It was the same reply as the ratcatcher had given me. 'But will you ask him, please, Frau Sarah?' I begged.

'Of course.'

'But what if I should fail him?'

Frau Sarah laughed. 'Then, as you say, it will be God's will. But I would be most surprised if God doth not grant thee permission to learn, Sylvia. Do you play chess?' she asked suddenly.

'Nay, "six, two and one" is the only game I know, it is played with dice,' I explained.

'He will teach you chess and if you prove a sprightly opponent, quick to grasp the game and show a natural cunning and a love to conquer him, then I feel sure he will agree to teach you Latin.'

'But he is a male and you have said he must not be seen to be conquered?'

She laughed her merry laugh. 'You are a quick learner, Sylvia, but chess has no gender.'

'Perhaps I shall fail, I know little of games.'

'Aye, to a Jew chess is not just a game. It is the very game of life. If you fail, then you must accept, once again, it may be God's will.'

I was constantly surprised that she so often talked of God as if He was to her, a Jew, as close as He was to me, a Christian. Had I not been taught by the priest that Jews were Christ killers? If this were so, why then did they worship the same God the Father but crucified His son? It was to this kind of question I longed to find the answer. 'Has Master Israel taught thee to play chess?'

'Nay, I have not felt the need and am, besides, not gifted.' She held up both her hands. 'Perhaps a small gift with these and another with herbs. Israel says I am nimble with needle and thread and I can count and write numbers and add and subtract and multiply, so I do the business and that is as well. Israel is a fine tailor and a scholar, but does not much care for numbers and has a muddled head for money.'

I did not think that it might be possible to find a Jew who did not care about money. 'Are all Jewish tailors also scholars?' I asked.

'Nay, but every Jew may study to be one. It is our tradition. Knowledge, we are taught, is power, and ignorance enslavement. Here in

Cologne we have a great rabbinical teacher, Rabbi Brasch the Good. He would have every Jewish boy a scholar.'

'And female?'

'Alas, no. It is not forbidden to a woman to have knowledge. In our past there has also been many a wise prophetess, but women may not be taught with men in the synagogue and it is there that knowledge is given out.'

'Then how shall she learn?'

'Alas, she must garner what she may from her father or her husband or even her brother. But not all men, like Israel, are forthcoming. We Jewish women have a saying: "Honey obtained without a sting is not as sweet. Knowledge has a price and is capital hard-gained, so we must spend it wisely."'

And so I understood that chess was to be the sting I must feel if I was to be granted the sweet gift of learning. *Did God play chess?* I asked myself. *Who better than He knew the game of life?* I knew I must pray to Him to grant me yet another opportunity. My requests were piling up and I had yet done nought to earn His grace and knew that I must soon prove a worthy penitent or He might forsake me, thinking me only an asker and not a giver.

We began to gather herbs and Frau Sarah was surprised that I knew them all by name and also their cooking uses and those that brought a balance of humours in the body and those for melancholia or bilious upset and other maladies.

'You must teach me what you know, Sylvia,' she said.

'Nay, I know only a little and of most of it, I caution, thou should be most wary. It is peasant lore where herbs and maladies are as often mixed with superstition.'

'Tell me of such as you know – the herbalist within me grows most curious.'

'Well, if a woman is pregnant and four or five months gone, and she eats nuts or acorns or any fresh fruits, then it frequently happens that the child is silly.'

Frau Sarah laughed. 'And another?'

'Again there is a matter concerning the pregnant woman. If she eats bull's meat, or ram's or buck's, or boar's or cock's or gander's flesh or that of any begetting animal, then it sometimes happens that the child is humpbacked and ruptured.'

'Sometimes? That is most convenient. Not *all* the time as might be true if the meat of the male beast or bird were the cause of this deformity.'

'Aye, it is this "sometimes" and this "frequently" that causes me to doubt. While acorns eaten green are known to contain some little poison and will cause stomach cramps, fruit and nuts, if fresh and brown, methinks cannot create a silliness in children born.'

'And of beauty? Is there peasant herbal lore of this? Or how to keep the body fresh?'

She laughed when I confessed I knew nought about their uses to make a woman comely and a man cease to stink. 'We peasants have little time for vanity and think that stench is a natural part of men, nay, women also, for we work upon the land and with domestic beasts, the cow, pig, goat and sheep – all have their own peculiar smell and each night they share our dwelling.' I laughed. 'If all smell the same then none shall stink.'

We came suddenly upon a cluster of mushrooms and as she rushed to pick them I quickly stayed her hand. 'They are poison!' I cried alarmed. 'You cannot eat them!'

Frau Sarah ignored me and took a small linen bag from her basket and, plucking each one, carefully placed them within the bag. 'Ah, glory be, today has been most propitious. Look, we have come upon a cluster of Ruth's Truth!' she exclaimed excitedly.

'Nay! Beware!' I cried again. 'They are poisonous and you name them wrongly, they are Satan's Shadow!'

Frau Sarah laughed. 'We call them Ruth's Truth. I will show you how to use them and by their use how you can confound the mind.' Then she turned and placed her hand upon my shoulder and looked into my eyes and spoke sincerely. 'Sylvia, you have shown me your Miracle of the Birds when I did challenge you. You did so in the nicest way, so that I did not feel ashamed for doubting you. Instead, you told a story to the street children and so most gently overcame my doubting. Now I shall share with you the secrets of this magic mushroom discovered by the wise and faithful Ruth, the great Hebrew prophetess. Its secrets have been passed on by countless generations of Jewish women herbalists. But you must tell no male of it, or use this mushroom's magic power without first careful thought. It has strength to possess another's mind, especially to capture a man's and turn it to your own design. If men know you possess such power they will call you a sorceress. If in Christian company, beware! For the priest will name thee "witch". I warn you, if taken yourself, you will behold visions beyond this earth, sometimes of heaven and sometimes of a darker place. Try it *only* once when you are alone and in a safe place, then save it for when you will most need it.'

'But it *is* Satan's Shadow! I know it well and may not touch it lest I will be harmed in body and soul!' I cried, alarmed.

'Satan's Shadow, is it? Is this also peasant lore? Who called it that? Men, you may be sure. Your priests perhaps? Then you should know that Satan strives to make us ignorant while God seeks to make us wise. I can but show you how to use this magic mushroom and then you must yourself decide if it is Satan's hand that guides you or that of the wise and gentle Ruth, worthiest of all Hebrew women.'

'Oh no, Frau Sarah!' I cried. 'The worthiest of all Hebrew women is the Virgin Mary, the Mother of God!'

'Ah, Sylvia, we Jews have strange superstitions of our own, but none as unlikely as a virgin birth. Our prophets and rabbis and, let me assure you, all Jewish men are far too arrogant to think that we women might conceive without their noble intervention.'

And so, with these disquieting words, we returned to the Jewish Quarter where Frau Sarah was to do the final fitting for the white gown I would wear in St Martin's square that afternoon.

There, outside the great church, we would test the ratcatcher's doubtful notion that busy folk would gather to hear him play and me to sing. Despite my fear of this encounter with the people of Cologne, I could barely contain my excitement that Master Israel might agree to teach me Latin if at first I could master chess, the game of life. I would then know if God had granted me, a peasant sinner and not yet a confessed and worthy penitent, the true gift I desired most of all.

CHAPTER FIVE

Blood on the Rose

I MUST SAY THAT Reinhardt in his new guise as the Pied Piper of Hamelin was a real pain. Even in the fitting of the knave's outfit, a used but well-kept garment, he strutted and fussed like a peacock, asking for it to be taken in here and made looser there and tucked and puckered. He was determined to turn a sow's ear into a silk purse. A *cotehardie* such as worn by a knave, a mere servant, does not have the affectation of buttons. But, ah, buttons he must have, six in all of carved amber, carefully matched each for its reddish-brown glow. He clapped his hands in glee at the new hose, not red as he'd supposed, but yellow, Frau Sarah explaining that the red dye was wont to run in the rain and that yellow was fast and true and much more dependable. As for the black velvet cap with peacock feather, he fussed a good hour, pushing and pulling it to every angle with a right eyebrow slightly cocked and head to one side, a vanity that sent me almost to puke. With all this fuss over a mere knave's garment, I vowed to make certain I would not be present when his suit of pied was fitted. As for my gown, it fitted well and Frau Sarah declared it most satisfactory and even admitted, for all his foppish behaviour, Reinhardt had been right about it being made of white linen.

All the while Frau Sarah fitted me and attended to Reinhardt I had grown quite contrary as the hour of departure for St Martin's square drew closer.

'What happened yesterday at the bathhouse will be forgotten by now and we are fools to think otherwise,' I said to Reinhardt.

'But you spoke this morning of the street brats following you to the woods and naming you Petticoat Angel – *they* have not forgotten.'

'Ha! Urchins have nothing better to do,' I replied. 'A few dozen ragamuffins present will not do anything to serve our cause.'

'Three women running naked through the markets and the making of an angel, this does not happen every day, Sylvia. To ordinary folk, even city folk, it was a most momentous experience.'

'Nay, folk came from a curiosity of the moment. Why should they come again?' I persisted.

'Aye, curiosity is what brought them there, I well admit. But thy singing, that is what kept them. They will come, you will see,' Reinhardt said, his voice ringing certain.

I turned to Frau Sarah. 'What think thee, Frau Sarah?'

She shrugged. 'It is hard to say, city folk be most fickle, yet yesterday when you sang they were most attentive and cried for more.'

'Will you come, Frau Sarah?' I asked, not knowing in my mind whether I wished her to be present or not.

'Nay, Sylvia, I have work to do and I am a Jewess and so wear a veil when I am outside the house. Some may think I blaspheme by being present in the church square when you sing.'

'Then I will not sing hymns,' I promised. 'Besides, I do not think there will be many people present.'

'If you sing only folksongs then it will be thee that is named blasphemer. St Martin's is one of the great churches of Cologne and the square outside is not well-chosen for folk dancing. Moreover, the fewer people present the greater chance that I am recognised, and some will take exception to my presence, of that you may be sure.'

All my life I had heard Father Pietrus and sometimes the abbot chastise the Jews and name them Christ-killers. But until now I had never met a Jew or thought about a Jewess and I was slowly beginning to understand that the Jew must be cautious in everything they do for fear of the Christian's wrath. I thought it strange that I, who possessed no power, was yet someone a Jew might be afraid of simply because I was a Christian.

We made ready to leave for St Martin's square. Reinhardt in his tricked-up knave's outfit of bright amber buttons, yellow hose and velvet cap with the ridiculous peacock feather bobbing as he walked. Me, without a wimple, hair well-brushed and shining in the rare early-winter sun that had persisted all day, dressed in a simple white gown that could well pass for a petticoat but made of a finer weave of linen. It was not unshapely as an undergarment might be, for Master Israel had cut it to suit my body well and Frau Sarah had stitched it with great care.

Reinhardt's vanity forbade his wearing his ratcatcher's cloak, which he pronounced too worn and soiled for the occasion. 'You will not die of some rat disease but of pleurisy,' I warned him. But methought he would rather perish with this infection than be seen less the fop for our debut.

A woman feels the cold more than does a man and I was not content to freeze to death and so wore my sheepskin coat and the boots Master Israel had given me and took up my stave as we prepared for our departure.

Reinhardt, who had previously pronounced himself most pleased with my appearance, now grew most unhappy. He insisted that I remove the sheepskin coat and my boots and wear the dainty slippers I carried under my arm, and also to leave my stave as it was not prepossessing and did not serve me well. 'How can an angel be seen wearing heavy boots, a dirty sheepskin coat and carrying a stout stave!' he exclaimed, his voice near hysterical.

'This particular angel is exceedingly cold,' I replied, 'and the streets are full of shit! My stave goes with me everywhere!'

'A prophet or a hermit or perhaps a wandering monk, but a stave is ridiculous for an angel!' he insisted.

'My stave is no more ridiculous than thy bouncing peacock's feather,' I responded in a snappish way.

'Thou art a dainty maid and with the light upon your hair and wearing thy white dress you look as if you are made of gossamer and sunlight, the Petticoat Angel most perfect. Now all that is gone and here appears the peasant in heavy boots, dirty coat and stave, *galumph, thump, galumph, thump, galumph, thump*! It upsets the whole effect! You are not upon a pilgrimage, Sylvia!'

'Nay, thou art wrong – that I truly am. Mine shall be a Christian life and that is a pilgrimage, thus said Father John who bade me take his stout stave wherever I go and never be without it. It is blessed with holy water and will protect me as it did yesterday in the bathhouse.'

'It is simply not seemly,' he grumbled, but said no more and we departed, him in a great huff, so that he walked ahead of me to show his pique. As we drew closer to St Martin's the crowd increased and his bouncing peacock feather with its gaudy pinnate eye above the heads of the crowd became a useful beacon for me to follow. Moreover, I blended well within the crowd, though not so Reinhardt. I could hear folk calling out, 'Who's the pretty boy then!' and suchlike remarks. While he would take delight in their japing, I was grateful for the anonymity my coat and stave afforded. A maid in a plain white dress without a wimple on a cold winter's afternoon might have attracted some attention and so, apart from the increasing crush, I was carried along with the general throng.

I thought the folk that pressed around us the usual street crowd, the same as we had endured walking through the markets the previous morning. A city, I was learning, was always busy and its narrow streets congested. But as we drew closer to the church square the street seemed all the deeper thronged with folk. 'You see, I told you!' Reinhardt called back, grinning. It was then that I realised all these city folk were walking towards St Martin's square.

The square was already half full with folk and as we entered I glanced behind me to see the alley leading to the church thronged as far as I could see. Then suddenly Nicholas, the lad who wished to be a monk, the leader of the street children in the woods, came up to me and proffered a white rose. 'For you, Sylvia,' he said smiling.

'A rose! Thank you, Nicholas,' I exclaimed. 'From whence comes this lovely blossom?'

'From the cloisters at St Mary's on the Kapitol,' he replied, then added, 'From the blessed Father Hermann Joseph's rose garden.'

'Will he not be angry to lose such a beautiful bloom?' I asked, naturally assuming he had stolen it. The white rose was as large as my hand and was cut with sufficient stem and leaf and the thorns removed so that I might easily hold it.

'Nay, he bade me give it to you. It is a holy white rose and comes from one that was once given to him by the Virgin Mary,' he said solemnly. 'I told him of the birds in the woods and he plucked the rose and said I must give it to you and if he could find the time he might come to St Martin's to hear you sing.'

'Oh dear, I hope not,' I replied. 'I shall be nervous if so famous a monk should be present.'

Nicholas laughed. 'He is not a priest like any other and refuses a horse or wagon and goes on foot everywhere. He cares for the common people such as us. Come, Sylvia, we have kept a place on the church steps for you. Follow me, there is a back way so we can avoid the pressing crowd.'

He led Reinhardt and myself into a side street beside the church that seemed a dead end, and when we reached the end he opened a small door in the wall of the church and we found ourselves within the refectory. 'Are we permitted here, Nicholas?' I asked in a low voice.

Not answering my question, he said briskly, 'Follow me.'

We soon found ourselves within the baptistry and then shortly after walking down the centre aisle, our footsteps seeming to echo through the empty church so that I felt sure they would summon someone in authority. Then Nicholas opened a small door beside the main doors leading out into the square and there, standing on the topmost step well above the crowd, stood twenty or more street children in a row with their arms locked so that none might attain the top step. 'Take off thy coat and give me the stave and I will look after both,' Nicholas, ever the leader, instructed.

I did as he bade me and then put on my lovely slippers. The urchins parted to make a place for us to stand. It was then that some in the crowd must have seen me, for a roar went up that was soon followed by another as more people looked up to see us. Reinhardt, ever the showman, removed his hat and held it aloft until the crowd consisting of perhaps five hundred souls grew silent.

'Thank you for coming,' he cried. 'Draw closer, brothers and sisters, and be seated on this fine sunny winter's day so that you may keep warm, the one against the other!' The crowd surged closer, then seated themselves and remained all well behaved. By now they filled a goodly portion of the square.

Reinhardt raised his feathered hat once more and they drew to silence. 'May I present to you, the good citizens of Cologne, the remarkable voice of the Petticoat Angel!' he shouted down to them. There was much cheering from the crowd and I grew afraid that I would disappoint them so that they might grow angry at coming to the square for no good reason. 'We will sing first in praise of God and thank him for His glorious presence in our lives!' the ratcatcher called out. 'Then we shall sing in praise of life itself!' he shouted to a murmur of laughter from the crowd.

'Call the birds!' someone from the crowd shouted out. There followed another murmur from the folk below the steps, not knowing what he meant by this. The man stood to his feet and turned to the crowd. 'I hear say the Petticoat Angel can charm the birds from the trees!' he explained.

'There are no trees here and the birds in this square are only pigeons, rooks and sparrows,' Reinhardt called down to him.

'Call the birds!' several more people now shouted.

'Pigeons and sparrows need no calling, they are always at our feet,' Reinhardt replied, a tincture of anger added to his voice.

'What about the rooks?' the man, still standing, cried, pointing to the belltower.

Reinhardt, ignoring him, lifted his flute to his mouth to sound an opening note.

'The rooks! Call the rooks!' the section of the crowd below the steps began to chant.

Reinhardt removed the flute from his mouth and, somewhat exasperated, shrugged and turned to me. I nodded and the crowd grew still. I began to call and soon enough a pair of rooks came to sit upon my shoulder, and then shortly after, a dozen, then more until there seemed to be rooks hopping everywhere making their not so pretty chirping. The crowd sat silent, marvelling at the sight of the dark birds clustered about me until with a single sound I sent them away, black wings filling the air with their noisy fluttering. The crowd began to cheer and then to chant, 'Petticoat Angel! A miracle! Petticoat Angel! Show us another!'

Reinhardt waited, then raised his hand and brought them to silence, and this time when he brought his flute to his mouth all were attentive. I sang several hymns from the mass, a motet, plainsong and Gloria, then followed with folksongs, though none that were bawdy or suggestive, only those that might be sung in any company.

As I had promised him, I called Nicholas to sing with me, a simple folksong often sung to children and well-known to all. He sang in a young boy's voice, though slightly out of tune and seemed relieved when it was over. The crowd liked his inclusion and whistled and clapped at the end. Each song upon completion was greeted with the greatest applause, people springing to their feet and surging forward. Had it not been for the street urchins who fought to hold them back, they would have overcome me in their anxiety to touch me.

But then as we neared the end a most calamitous happening occurred. While I was in mid-song a strange feeling of warmth occurred between my legs and glancing down I saw a spot of blood upon my dress. How I maintained my voice I cannot say for I knew at once that my womanhood was upon me. I quickly brought the rose I held to cover the spot as if it were a natural pose and somehow managed to complete the song. Whereupon I turned to Reinhardt. 'We must end now!' I whispered urgently.

Reinhardt nodded but ever the showman must have felt the end too sudden, for he stopped and held his hand up for the applause to die and then announced, 'We will end as we began, in praise of God!' Then he blew the first notes to a hymn of praise. How I completed this I shall never know for I could feel the flow between my legs increasing and dared not look down upon my gown.

By the time we had completed this last rendition it was growing dark and I hoped those seated on the steps directly below me had not looked upon my dress. Reinhardt thanked the ecstatic crowd, for it was clear to see we had been a great success. They cheered us loudly and continuously, chanting 'Petticoat Angel!' as they left the square for the warmth of their homes, for piety may burn within the saints but it does nothing to warm the commonfolk on a winter's night.

'My coat, Nicholas!' I cried urgently. When he brought it, together with my stave, I turned away from him and handed him the rose and placed my stave against the wall, turning my back to all so that none might see the bloodstain at the front of my dress. I hastily put the coat on, buttoning the wooden toggles as quickly as I could to hide my shame.

I turned to see that a priest had come from within St Martin's and now stood with Nicholas at the small doorway to the church by which we had first emerged. 'Good evening, fräulein,' he said. 'I come to ring the Angelus, but no bell, if it should toll from heaven, will sound as glorious as thy voice.'

Before I could thank him, Nicholas suddenly began to shake and then cried out, 'Look! The rose cries tears of blood!' He held up his forefinger on the tip of which it was easy to see the wet bloodstain. My woman's blood must have covered the underside of the rose petals.

He held the rose out to the priest who turned it upside down and I saw the red stains upon the underside of the white petals. 'Glory to God, this is a miracle!' he exclaimed and handing the rose back to Nicholas he clasped his hands in prayer and fell to his knees. 'We must take it to the bishop at once!' he cried out.

'Nay, to the blessed Father Hermann Joseph!' Nicholas shouted. 'It is his Holy Virgin white rose and he must bear witness to this miracle!'

The priest rose to his feet. 'Blessed be to God, I am witness to a miracle,' he sighed, then clasped both my hands and turning my palms upwards brought his lips to them.

Without waiting a moment longer, Nicholas jumped down the steps two at a time, closely followed by his entourage of ragged urchins yelling at the top of their voices, 'Miracle! Miracle!' I watched in consternation as they ran across the square to disappear in the growing dark within the departing crowd.

'How shall I find thee, Petticoat Angel?' the priest asked.

'Ah . . . er . . . there is . . . er, an explanation, Father,' I stammered.

'Come, we must away,' Reinhardt said, shivering from the cold, not at all sure what was going on. 'We must hurry, Frau Sarah will be waiting.' He took me by the arm and I had just sufficient time to grab my stave when he pulled me away.

'Nicholas will find me!' I called.

'The urchin with the rose?' the priest asked.

'Aye, he lives hereabouts. Good night, Father!'

'Father Paulus! Paulus the scribe!' he shouted down at us.

'Shit! I am freezing cold and must get my cloak!' Reinhardt called, half running ahead of me.

'There has been an accident, please, I cannot walk so fast!' I cried.

He stopped. 'Accident?'

'My bleeding. It has come.'

'Bleeding?' His eyebrows shot up. 'The rose?' he suddenly exclaimed. 'The blood on the rose?'

'Aye, my womanhood.' I felt myself close to tears.

At once he understood and his eyes lit up. 'A miracle! The rose cries tears of human blood?' he exclaimed, delighted. 'Holy Jesus! What have we here?'

'Do not blaspheme!' I shouted, upset, angry and humiliated. Then in a sudden fit of frustration I brought my stave down hard upon his toe.

'Ouch!' he yelled and commenced to hop on one leg in a circle, clutching at his toe and sucking in his breath.

'See! My stave is the instrument of God's wrath!' I pronounced, feeling a whole lot better.

When he had recovered and still limping he attempted to explain himself. 'Sylvia, see you not? Look what we have here to our advantage. Yesterday you sent the three whores a-caterwauling naked from the bathhouse and you were pronounced the Petticoat Angel. This morning you did call the birds in the wood in front of the street urchins, who, judging from the crowd this afternoon, spoke much of this. Then you caused the rooks to fly onto your shoulders from their rookery in the belltower of St Martin's. Thereafter your angelic singing in praise of our Saviour caused the rose you held to shed tears of blood, the very rose given thee by the blessed Father Hermann Joseph, of whom it is known was once given a white rose by the carving of the Blessed Virgin and grew it as a cutting to create holy blooms, this white rose one of such!'

I felt miserable – the flow between my legs made me anxious and I was most worried about my dress. We were to be at the tailor's shop in an hour where Frau Sarah was to take us to her brother's *winkelhaus*. What would she say about the bloodstain to the front of my dress? I felt sure that she would be very angry. 'You know what your trouble is?' I replied, frustrated at his absurd outburst. 'You have too much imagination. You talk utter shit, Reinhardt!'

At our lodgings I undressed and washed carefully and tied the rags I'd kept all the while in my leather satchel in the way the widow Johanna had shown me in the village. Then I changed into the dress she had given me and asked the old woman if I might soak my new linen dress in cold water in the hope that I might somewhat remove the bloodstains from it. She was immediately most consolatory and took the dress from me and examined it. 'It is not yet dry, that is good,' she declared. 'I think we may well remove this stain. My husband was a wrestler and I was well accustomed to removing bloodstains,' she explained, 'although white linen be a veritable challenge to my skills.' I said I would pay her for her trouble but she would not hear of it. 'This blood, when it comes, is a mark of thy womanhood, Sylvia. I am glad that I may help you bear this burden.'

But Frau Sarah was not as forgiving. 'That was good new linen,' she cried, 'and most expensive. You will pay me from your earnings!'

'I did not do it deliberately,' I protested, feeling she was being unfair. 'It was an accident, Frau Sarah.'

'You should have worn your rags all the while, you knew your bleeding to be close!' she scolded.

There is a peasant saying: If hindsight is to be avoided then the eye in the centre of the arse would not be blind. But I did not have the courage to quote it to her.

Frau Sarah took a red gown from a hook and took in the side seams and tucked the bodice smaller and hemmed furiously, and in a surprisingly short time her fingers, most nimble with a needle and thread, had this pretty garment fitting me amazingly well.

'A scarlet woman, eh?' Reinhardt said, one eyebrow slightly raised.

'Don't talk nonsense, Reinhardt!' Frau Sarah said impatiently, placing a dark veil over her wimple. 'Come, we are late, Abraham will be angry and I cannot bear his yapping.'

But yapping she must bear because her brother Abraham greeted our arrival without cordiality. 'You are late!' he barked. 'Do you think so little of me that you arrive at your own convenience? I have patrons arriving soon and there is yet no music!'

'Hush! They come soon but are not already here. There is yet time to get ready,' Frau Sarah soothed him.

'Ha! I must hear them first. What if they do not suit?'

'Then you would have a lute player standing by – I know you to be a cautious man, Abraham. But these two will not cause you trouble,' Frau Sarah replied calmly.

Well that truly set Abraham off. 'What know you of trouble? The cook is sick, the wine is sour, the linen not yet dry, the bed maids are careless in their work, the courtesans all quarrel, my nightingales purchased at great expense do not sing! And you dare talk of lute players who stand by yet want to be paid – you bring me German flute and song that comes here late!' He said all this as if in one breath and at an astonishing speed, each word rising higher and bumping into the other from behind his flibbertigibbeting tongue.

Frau Sarah sighed and spread her hands. 'But the good news is that now we are here,' she said, smiling sweetly.

Abraham's *winkelhaus* was known as Ali Baba's and appeared to me to be like a sultan's cave, the whole place created as a potentate's harem with cushions in great numbers laid on silk carpets from far-off Cathay. There were low ebony tables inlaid with mother-of-pearl and ivory. Upon them rested silver bowls of nuts and dried fruits, figs, apricots and dates, almonds, balls of honeycomb covered with sesame seed so the fingers are not left sticky, walnuts, the shells carefully cracked so they might open at a touch to reveal the rich, sweet nut within. Silver flagons of wine stood on every table surrounded by goblets made of glass. The walls and ceiling were scalloped with richly dyed drapes of damask and silk in saffron, scarlet and azure blue. In the corners stood huge burnished copper jars as tall almost as myself and from each a hundred or more peacock feathers plumed. Above these jars hung elaborate golden cages wrought in marvellous patterns of wire and each contained a nightingale. In the centre of the room was a canopied platform of polished walnut that stood waist-high with drapes of rich red velvet pulled to each of the four posts and tied by silken tassels of a silver hue. From either side of the canopy there hung a chandelier on a chain made from links of burnished copper and each contained a hundred candles, so that the room seemed a great luminous wonder. Unbeknownst at first sight, the damask curtains that fell around the walls concealed short corridors that led to the courtesans' booths. There were eighteen in all, each heavily curtained and private, and they contained a broad couch resplendent in silk cushions and most inviting to the reclining figure. Each served two courtesans, though not at the same time. Even though no people were within this richly draped and cushioned room where the courtesans met their patrons, it gave off the effect of romantic wickedness, so that I gasped as I entered, afraid at once for my mortal soul.

Master Abraham seemed to ill suit this Ali Baba's cave of shimmering silk and brilliant light. He was a tiny man dressed in plain cloth, brown and black, not as a peasant nor yet a rich merchant, perhaps in the manner of an important servant or scribe in a noble house. Unlike Master Israel he did not wear a yarmulke or about his waist the *tzitziyot* tassels of the Jew. He had the look of someone who would go unnoticed in any company and was so thin, sallow and hollow-cheeked that he gave the effect of a skeleton only just sufficiently stretched with bluish skin to yet be on this mortal coil. I was to learn that despite his appearance, he possessed great energy and seemed to be everywhere at once. His eyes, black as obsidian, bright as beads, saw everything. No detail of error escaped his closest attention. A dish of nuts half empty would be instantly refilled; sticky fingers would bring a finger bowl and towel at once. When he laughed, which was seldom with those he paid and often with those who paid him, he screeched like a cantankerous parrot. When angry, which was often, though never to his patrons to whom he acted most obsequious, his voice took on a yapping note so like a dog that he was secretly known among those who worked at Ali Baba's as Master Yap.

The raised platform with the tasselled canopy that stood in the centre of the Courtesans' Room, as it was named, was for the musicians, usually a lute player or a minstrel from France who were known to be the best. Master Yap was most apprehensive that his sister's share of the *winkelhaus* had caused him to be saddled with two musicians who were German and so would lack musical refinement and besmirch his reputation, though I think his reputation had nothing whatsoever to do with the music he played. I was soon to learn that the patrons were, for the most part, stout burghers who would prefer the tooting of a trumpet and the thumping of a drum to my dulcet tones. I sang as best I might but I doubt that they took much notice, being in other ways preoccupied.

Of course it didn't take long for me to understand that I was working in a brothel and while I was most shocked at first I soon learned to enjoy it for, as Frau Sarah often said, 'Sylvia, you are safer in a high-class brothel than a noble's castle. Abraham has been told that you are not to be touched or he must answer to me. You are to tell me if he makes any lewd suggestions to you.'

Master Yap's courtesans were the envy of the *winkelhäuser* in Cologne and also the most expensive. They came from all over the known world: tall, elegant Nubians, sultry Turks and other Oriental damsels, Slavs, Danes with hair whiter and eyes bluer than mine, sloe-eyed Chinese from Cathay, Syrians, Egyptians, Persians and, of course, German, English, Italian, Sicilian and French. They were not slaves, as in many other brothels, but worked willingly, each vying for patronage as Master Yap worked on a system of percentages. He took a half share in their earnings and if they did not attract patrons and earn sufficient they were soon parted from his company and replaced by others anxious to join. Although a great deal of squabbling took place among them they were, for the most part, contented with their lot. Many had been slaves, ill-fed and badly treated, and life as a free courtesan, for the words 'whore' or 'harlot' were never mentioned, was easy by comparison providing they made their quota each week. They were well fed, with warm accommodations, and made good money that they were not forced to give to pimps or ne'er-do-wells.

The first night in Master Yap's *winkelhaus* came as a surprise, not only because it turned out to be what it was, but also because of my singing. I had all the while thought of myself as a modest person as I saw little in me of particular note and was aware that as a peasant I had no learning or importance. But ever since the Miracle of the Gloria I had grown accustomed to folk being in praise of my voice and without thinking about it must have all the while grown quite vainglorious. The very afternoon prior to arriving at Master Yap's the people in the church square had cheered and clapped and wished to touch me. Now Reinhardt and I stood within the canopy in Ali Baba's Courtesans' Room and my singing and his playing went completely unnoticed. It was as if we were invisible and after each folksong there was silence from the patrons. When it was all done I expected Master Yap to show his displeasure and to inform us that we would not be needed on the morrow. But instead, while not over-generous with his praise, he told us that we had performed satisfactorily and that he would no longer cause a French lute player to stand by. That night I went to bed at the widow's lodging exhausted. It had been a very long day, from the visit to the woods in the morning to bed well past the midnight hour. Reinhardt, as exhausted as I, grumbled that the rat-ridding at Master Solomon's had caused him to have little sleep.

'If you'd been wearing thy cloak and peacock feather cap, the rats would have scurried off in amazement without you playing your flute,' I teased. But I do not think he was amused.

You might imagine my consternation, then, when the widow woke me with the news that an urchin had come to fetch me to go to St Mary's on the Kapitol. It was Nicholas, who by some mysterious way only known to street children, knew where I lived and came to summon me to an examination by the blessed Father Hermann Joseph and Father Paulus. It was no more than an hour after the ringing of the Angelus.

'Come, Sylvia, the blessed Father has set aside an hour from his prayers, and Father Paulus, the scribe from St Martin's, is with him.'

'Nicholas, there is an explanation,' I cried, but then realised I could explain no further to a ten-year-old boy.

'They will see the bishop if it turns out well,' Nicholas said enthusiastically. 'Already the people in the market know and marvel about the white rose you held that wept tears of blood.'

'How can that be? It was nigh dark and not long before the ringing of the curfew bell that we departed from St Martin's.'

'Street children rise early,' he said simply.

'And are tattletales!' I exclaimed.

Nicholas looked at me, astonished. 'But we have witnessed a miracle! Do you think we would keep this a secret?'

'It is *not* a miracle, Nicholas!' I scolded.

'That's not for you to say, Fräulein Petticoat,' he retorted.

'Call me Sylvia!' I demanded, feeling both guilty and frustrated. 'Nicholas, you must not believe everything you see to be true. There may be yet another explanation.'

'As you wish, Fräulein Petticoat,' he said, not believing me. 'Can you please hurry – they are awaiting your attendance at St Mary's on the Kapitol.'

I had always been forthright about the events in my life, even though I seemed to be one of those people who was constantly misconstrued and seemed always to be explaining or denying. How then was I going to explain the blood on the Virgin's rose? I would have to admit that I had stained my white gown with my woman's blood in front of perhaps five hundred people. Already the street children had spread the news of the latest miracle, who knows how far and wide. The commonfolk were always receptive to gossip and no doubt anxious to hear more of the Petticoat Angel, who, judging from my reception in St Martin's square, seemed to them to be touched by a divine hand. Now I must confront two priests and my shame and their piety made it impossible to admit the truth.

Perhaps the matter of the blood on the rose would soon be forgotten. Until now all the misconstruction placed upon events in my life had been witnessed by ordinary folk, who are always on the lookout for signs and portents and cry 'miracle' at the flapping of a bird's wing. On only one occasion had the scrutiny of a priest been involved and Father Pietrus had summarily dismissed the Miracle of the Gloria. I felt sure these two priests would do the same. Walking towards St Mary's on the Kapitol with Nicholas I prepared myself for the humiliation I was about to face.

But I had not reckoned on the blessed Father Hermann Joseph who, since childhood, had been devoted to the Virgin. It was known he spent countless hours kneeling before her image in ecstatic raptures. Miracles and visions were commonplace to him so that he was no Doubting Thomas to begin with. His life since childhood was so blameless that his fellow priests dubbed him Joseph, a nickname he would not in all humility accept until he had a vision where he was mystically espoused to Mary with a ring and so became Joseph her earthly husband.

As a child of seven he was already enraptured with the Virgin and the Child and would occupy every moment he possessed kneeling before the blessed stone carving of Mary and the infant Jesus at St Mary's on the Kapitol. The best-told story of him was when as a hungry child he had been given a precious apple and instead of eating it he had presented it to the Christ Child recumbent on the Virgin's lap. Jesus had reached out, accepting it. Thereafter, Mary helped him to climb over the choir screen to play with the baby Jesus in the presence of Joseph and John the Evangelist.

Of course I knew none of this at the time. As we walked Nicholas told me what had occurred the previous evening when he'd taken the rose to the two priests.

Nicholas and his street urchins had run all the way to St Mary's on the Kapitol and trembling with faith asked to see Father Hermann Joseph who had just gone in to prayers after the ringing of the Angelus. Nicholas, unwilling to wait, brushed aside the monk on duty and entered the church, running down the aisle to confront the priest as he knelt in his accustomed place before the statue of the Virgin and Child.

'Father! Father! There has been a miracle!' he cried, still trembling.

Father Hermann, deep within his devotion to the Virgin, at first ignored Nicholas, until the boy grabbed him by the cord of his cassock and pulled, demanding his attention. The priest, who had worked all his life so that he might be sanctified, had never been known to show anger, but he would later confess that the boy's rude interruption to his devotions had tested his spirit sorely. Containing his vexation he rose to his feet. 'What is it, Nicholas? Can you not wait?' he asked the agitated urchin.

Wide-eyed and trembling, Nicholas held out the white rose now stained with blood. 'A miracle, Father, we have seen a miracle. Your Virgin's rose has wept blood as the Petticoat Angel sang to the glory of our Saviour!'

'Blood? The Virgin's rose? What mean you, Nicholas?'

'A miracle, Father, ask anyone!' He turned to the urchins who now stood behind him. 'They saw it!'

'Yes, Father!' several chorused while others nodded their heads in confirmation.

The priest now took the rose and examined it carefully. 'Aye, I do not deny this is blood, perhaps a thorn upon the stem?'

'Nay, Father, you did yourself remove the thorns,' Nicholas said.

'Perhaps one I missed?' Father Hermann said gently. 'My eyes are not as good as they once were.'

'Then it would be present now,' Nicholas protested.

'Or removed?'

'Nay, Father, look, all the petals to the underside are stained but not the stem.' Nicholas was close to tears knowing the priest doubted his word.

Father Hermann, ever gentle, then explained, 'A miracle must have verification, Nicholas.'

'But . . . but we all saw it!' Nicholas cried again.

'A priest or someone whose truth cannot be denied must be a witness. While I truly believe you *think* you saw a miracle and speak the truth, Nicholas,' Father Hermann said gently, 'alas, the bishop will not accept the word of a street child or the verification of his companions.'

'Father Paulus saw it!' Nicholas exclaimed. 'He called it a miracle and fell to his knees and kissed the Petticoat Angel's hands.'

'Paulus the scribe? I know him well!' the priest said, surprised. 'I will call upon him at St Martin's tomorrow.'

But there was no necessity for this, because, almost as he spoke, Father Paulus arrived, much agitated and puffed from hurrying through the streets. He seated himself to recover his breath and in a halting voice exclaimed, 'A wondrous happening . . . the rose.' He saw the rose in Father Hermann's hand. 'See, it bleeds!'

'Aye, I have explained to Nicholas here, a thorn perhaps to the finger of the maiden?'

'Nay, I clasped her hands and turned them palm upwards to examine them more closely, and there was no blood, nor single wound or prick to her fingers!'

'Are you sure, Father?'

'I swear it upon my life, Father Hermann! You know me well enough to know that I am not, as thou art, blessed with holy visions. I am but a humble scribe and scholar trained to tell things as they are. I came to ring the Angelus and heard this maiden sing. It was as if the heavens had opened and she was the solo voice to that celestial choir.' He pointed to the white rose. 'Then I saw the bleeding to the underside of the petals with mine own eyes and will verify it to the bishop or any other without fear or contradiction.'

'Nicholas, come here,' Father Hermann commanded suddenly. Nicholas stepped forward to stand in front of the priest. 'Spread your hands.' The boy spread his hands and Father Hermann examined them closely. 'Now the underside, your palms, show me.' Nicholas turned his hands so that his palms faced upwards and the big priest examined each finger individually for the slightest sign of a cut. 'No cuts. There are no cuts!' he exclaimed. Now greatly excited, he cried, 'The white rose of Mary, the mystical rose Herself! We must jointly confront this maiden they name the Petticoat Angel and examine her before we go to the bishop. We must be quite sure.' He turned to Nicholas. 'You shall bring her here tomorrow, Nicholas. I will pray to the blessed Virgin for forgiveness that I doubted you and as penance I will wear a garland of the Virgin's rose thorns about my neck for a week.'

Nicholas, delighted that Father Paulus had verified his word, promised he would seek me out. 'She can call the birds from the trees to sit upon her hand, ask anyone, Father,' he said.

'We saw it ourselves!' some of the urchins chorused.

'Aye, and the rooks to come down from the belltower,' Father Paulus added, then he smacked his hand to the side of my head. 'Oh, glory be! I have forgot to ring the Angelus.'

With all the questioning on thorns and pricks to my fingers, I thought that Father Hermann would be most wary and demand an explanation. Father Paulus, as a scribe, would be even more particular with his questions. Priestly scribes, I had often heard, were both a cynical and doubting breed. But when Nicholas told of Father Paulus's emphatic insistence that no coincidence of thorns was possible and then further, how Father Hermann had promised to wear a necklace of rose thorns in contrition for his doubting the boy's word, my heart sank.

It was only then, with Nicholas at my side, that I thought to withdraw Father John's dagger from my stave and cut my finger, but it was too late and I recalled how Father Paulus had looked carefully when he kissed my palms.

By the time we reached St Mary's on the Kapitol I was in a state of near terror that I must either be seen a liar within the sanctity of the Church or tell a truth that would shame me forever. Worse still, upon our arrival, we were taken to stand outside the open door to the sacristy where the reliquary and vestments were kept and through the doorway I glimpsed a small carving of the Virgin clasping to her bosom a rose. The two priests waited in front of the door, in view of the figure. I felt that I must turn and run for my life, for if I should tell a lie in such a place I felt sure God would strike me dead right there where I stood in front of the Holy Mother.

Father Hermann was an elderly man, perhaps over sixty years. He was big-boned and must once have been powerful in his physique but now was thin and sallow in his face, the hair surrounding his cleric's bald pate grown white. Around his neck was a garland of rose thorns and already several sharp pricks marked the skin on his neck. I felt terribly ashamed that I should be the cause of his penance and his pain.

Father Paulus, who I remembered from the previous day, was the younger of the two, aged forty or so, small in stature, not much bigger than myself. His red hair was speckled with grey, his eyes a pale washed blue. But it was his nose that was most unprepossessing. It dominated all his other features and was so straight and long it seemed falsely appended to his tiny face. It was as if it was intended for someone else and God, momentarily distracted when in the process of His creation, had affixed it to the wrong visage. It extended beyond his bottom lip and cast a shadow upon his chin.

Both greeted me most courteously and in the manner of an equal so that I grew even further afraid in their presence.

'Please, fräulein, show me your hands,' Father Hermann asked. I held out my hands. 'No, turn them over,' he instructed. I did as he asked and from his cassock he produced a round magnifying glass such as scribes use to do illumination and brought it down to my hands, his eye up against it, examining every part of the palms and fingers. Then he turned to Father Paulus. 'Praise be to God, there are no cuts!'

My mind raced. What would I say when they questioned me? How could I tell these two holy men that it was my menstrual blood? Frau Sarah had told me that when it occurs in Jewish women their priest, the rabbi, pronounces a woman during this time as unclean and that the woman must attend a ritual bath she named the *mikvah*. If the Jews thought this time in a woman was unclean then how much more so would a Christian, I reasoned. To admit my parlous state to the two priests was unthinkable.

But to my surprise they did not question me, thinking no doubt that a miracle is a matter for a priest and God and that I was merely His instrument. So it was the instrument they were interested in as they had a duty to perform by informing the bishop and they must be sure that they could well explain my nature.

'Nicholas says you called the birds from the trees in the woods above the city?' Father Hermann said, then not waiting for my answer turned to Father Paulus. 'And you spoke of the rooks called from the belltower, did you not, Father?'

'Aye, it was most remarkable,' the little priest said.

'Perhaps we should witness this for ourselves?' Father Hermann suggested, looking directly at me. 'Can you take us to the woods and show us, Sylvia?'

I agreed and once more we climbed the hill to the woods. I asked that they remain still and silent and I demonstrated calling the birds, causing a robin to sit upon Father Hermann's hand and a chaffinch to alight on the shoulder of Father Paulus. I made a cry and the birds surrounding us rose in the usual lovely flutter and departed.

Able to talk, Father Hermann cried in a most excited voice,

'Remarkable! Glory to God, this is yet another miracle!' He turned to the other priest. 'What say you, Father Paulus?'

Father Paulus nodded his head and seemed at first speechless, then finally said, 'I am not a man of visions, signs, portents, auspicious comet happenings in the night skies or even much taken with miracles, but I am this day and yesterday convinced.'

At last I was back on safe ground. 'Nay! Please! This is not a miracle. As I child I practised every birdsong – it is nothing but the mating calls imitated. The hens must come and cocks cannot resist and must examine the competition of the other cocks and they too come flying in to see if they might match the calling male in courting the hen bird.' The two priests looked at each other and I could see they thought I was talking gibberish.

'Come, we must return to St Mary's, there is a great deal to do,' Father Paulus said.

'You must leave these affairs to us, my child,' Father Hermann added gently, placing his hand on my shoulder as we walked down the hill. 'You must understand, it is up to the Church to decide these things.'

'Yes, there are a great many documents to prepare for the bishop,' Father Paulus said importantly, and I could not help but feel that he looked forward to creating these.

'Ah, how fortunate that you are a scribe of high standing *and* a clerk, Father Paulus. I myself was not good at school, a poor student though I could understand the workings of timepieces,' Father Hermann admitted. Then turning to me, he asked, 'How long is it since you have been to confession, my child?'

'Never, Father,' I admitted shamefully.

I expected him to show surprise, but he smiled and asked instead, 'How old are you, Sylvia?'

'Now almost twelve.'

'A good time to confess – at twelve you are a woman and I think our Saviour may have some very special task for you.'

'I have much to confess, Father,' I said.

'Then come tomorrow and I will hear your confession.' He turned to Father Paulus. 'After this we will begin to put our case together.'

Father Paulus nodded. 'I shall write what we have seen today and also yesterday. Will you keep the rose safe?'

Father Hermann answered him as if I wasn't present. 'Last night after I had talked with the boy I placed it between two pages and put them under a parchment press when the blood was still wet upon the petals. This morning I examined it and the bloodstains have dried on the page and the petals are pressed, the stains show clearly upon them.'

When we reached St Mary's, Father Paulus took leave from us and I asked Father Hermann when I should attend for confession. 'Immediately after the Angelus tomorrow morning, my child. I do not suppose it will take long. I shall set aside ten minutes from my devotions,' he instructed.

'Father, I have much to confess, it will take more than ten minutes.'

I thought how I would need to confess the blood on the white cloth. It was the last time I would be permitted to wear white as the Church henceforth forbade it to mature women. To have stained the virgin white of childhood with the red blood of womanhood was a sin. Not only must I confess the blood on the rose but also this, and the prospect filled me with terror.

He smiled. 'Then however long it takes, but God is generous with those he loves and has set aside for a special purpose, you must not fret too much, Sylvia.'

The following morning I arrived at St Mary's as the Angelus rang and stood outside the church in the bitter cold for some time before entering. Shortly afterwards Father Hermann arrived and bade me take my seat in the confessional, then moments later he entered his side. He left the screen between the two sides open so I could see his face and commenced with a short prayer and then asked me to proceed.

I had decided to make a clean slate of all my sins. Whatever the penance, no matter how hard, I would carry it with great joy knowing my terrible life of deception would finally be over. I would confess everything no matter how difficult this proved to be. My father's wanton abuse, my acceptance of the Miracle of the Gloria when I knew it to be nothing of the sort, the abuse I had hurled at the peasant woman on the road when I had been denied shelter, the gulling of the village folk concerning the banishment of the rats and the Virgin Maid. I would tell him of the incident in the bathhouse with the three whores and how I was not worthy of the name Petticoat Angel. Then finally, I would have to admit for the sake of my immortal soul the true reason for the blood on the rose.

However, this did not turn out to be the usual confession where the priest listens without comment and then at the end pronounces the penance. With each incident Father Hermann made a fairly detailed comment.

With my father's abuse: 'You poor child, do not fret. If I have heard this incident in confession once I have heard it a thousand times. You are free of sin – God does not blame children for the wrongdoing of their parents.'

With the Miracle of the Gloria: 'That priest was much too impatient!' he exclaimed. 'I am sure there is more to this than you claim with your own simple explanation. Those who witnessed what happened saw what you could not see. Demons and devils are everywhere and one had come to rest in thy soul from your father's wantonness. Others saw how it was cast out and the light of heaven descended and the thunder of God's word that followed. I cannot accept thine explanation and do not regard you as having sinned.'

With the peasant woman's abuse: 'God places the charity of love above all things and when we show it to strangers we are especially blessed. He will be angry at her response to a child in need of shelter. But, nevertheless, you were wrong to abuse her and I will take note of this in pronouncing your penance.'

With the village people: 'I have witnessed the Miracle of the Birds and think you were gulled by this ratcatcher who claims these extraordinary powers. You said his flute was silent – how may a rat respond to a silent flute? I pronounce you mistaken, my child. The rats following you to the woods was yet another miracle. I see all the signs of God working within you.'

I tried to protest, to tell him this was not so, but he gently pointed out that I was in the confessional and must *only* answer his questions.

The incident at the bathhouse: 'While our Saviour commands us to turn the other cheek, the good Father John who created the stave for your protection blessed it in holy water and advised that you were to use the dagger if in danger. I have no doubt that the woman who attacked you would have cut your face in a most severe manner. Therefore I must pronounce your actions as both very brave and appropriate to the circumstances. You committed the sin of stubbornness, in that you did not forego your bath. It is a minor sin, my child. As for thy being named the Petticoat Angel, it was in response to your singing and a most pleasing compliment.'

When I reached the confession involving the blood on the rose I began, 'Father, I must explain the blood on the rose.'

But he bade me be silent. 'Sylvia, this is not a matter for the confessional. Two priests are involved, one of whom is a noted scribe and clerk and was present when the blood appeared. Both have witnessed the Miracle of the Birds. It may take a while to prepare this matter for examination by the bishop and the archbishop, then beyond to the Ecclesiastical Council in Rome for a decision to be made. This matter will take a great deal of time. I forbid you to talk any further on the subject. Nicholas tells me that already people in the market are talking about the blood on the Virgin's white rose, which is most difficult, as these things are soon taken over by the commonfolk and reinterpreted by means of rumour and hearsay. I am now convinced God is working through you for a higher purpose that we do not yet understand.'

Finally he pronounced my penance. 'You have sinned in chastising the peasant woman and you sinned with your stubbornness in the bathhouse: you are to say twenty Hail Marys and ask for forgiveness. You may now commence the study and preparations for your first communion and in three months time you may partake of the bread and the wine, the body and the spirit of our blessed Lord.' He smiled. 'As further penance you are required to sing a solo Gloria after mass. Let us pray.'

Afterwards, as Father Hermann was about to take his leave he stopped and asked, 'Can you read Latin, Sylvia?'

'Nay, Father, but I am most anxious to learn.'

He seemed only to hear my denial. 'How long does it take you to learn a part of the mass, a Gloria?'

'If it is sung or said twice,' I replied.

'Then would you this Sunday sing what I have composed, *Summi Regis cor aveto*, the first hymn to the Sacred Heart?' he asked shyly.

'I would be honoured, Father.'

'Good, I will make a time for you to rehearse after you have come for your first confirmation lesson.'

The next three months were taken up with learning my catechisms, the Scriptures and duties required for my confirmation. I was greatly excited when the time came for the bishop to accept me into God's Holy Church and so allow me to participate in my first mass. It was for me a most auspicious and exciting occasion as Reinhardt and the girls in Ali Baba's who belonged to the Church of Rome all attended. Afterwards they threw a grand party in my honour with all the courtesans of every nation and religion at Ali Baba's joining in. Master Yap, to our great surprise, supplied the food and drink without a single grumble at the extravagance. In a short speech he said anyone who could make the nightingales sing was truly blessed by God.

It was a momentous afternoon during which there was a great deal of giggling as we, who had attended church, all recognised the bishop as a regular patron at Ali Baba's who was known to have a very funny proclivity. He required honey to be spread on the lips, breasts, stomach and to the one-eyed dragon's cave of the courtesan he chose, whereupon he would proceed to feast upon her, to his ultimate satisfaction.

I did not mention this in my prayers that night, as God must have had a very good reason to create him a bishop, though I couldn't think what this might be.

CHAPTER SIX

Of Whores and Heretics

WITH FEW EXCEPTIONS I grew most fond of the courtesans at Ali Baba's and they of me, and soon I knew a great deal about pleasing a man even though I had never laid my hand upon one in a gesture of pleasuring.

Each had her secrets, the Nubians, the Slavs, Greeks, Egyptians and Chinese as well as all the others, and while they guarded their special talents for male arousal from each other, they told me willingly of their various wiles and the ways and means of pleasing a man. Some men when drunk cannot raise the sword of honour and they told me how this might be done. Other men are old but have not lost their appetite, yet cannot reach arousal, and they instructed me how such may be truly satisfied and leave with their manliness intact. They showed me how to prolong a young man who pleasures too soon and then how to bring him to frequent pleasure until he cries for mercy so that he may brag to his friends of his achievements and so bring them to taste the courtesan's delights. Demonstrating on a small marrow they taught me how to use my mouth to best effect. How to enchant a man by touching him in various places and how to massage him so that he becomes so soothed and satisfied that he returns another night for this alone.

All this was done with much giggling and laughter so that I became the most knowledgeable courtesan of all but had yet to bed a man.

I learned from the Nubian girls how to assuage the pains a man may have to his back or legs and how to soothe the brow or rub the neck to remove a headache.

And to please the girls in return I had them teach me the songs of their native lands. These lovely melodies I would sing and Reinhardt play when we weren't busy, or late at night when the drunks snored and the girls could relax a while. It is strange that the lute and the harp and many of the other musical instruments only know some languages, but the flute knows them all. Often there would be tears among the courtesans as they forgot how cruel their earlier lives had been and remembered loved ones in far-off lands.

I also learned the art of utmost discretion: that unwritten law that whosoever entered Ali Baba's left it yet a stranger. Should the Pope himself (God forbid) visit, when he left it would be as if he had never been. I was witness to the presence of many of the most noble, rich and important men of Cologne and beyond, bishops and judges, counts and knights, guildmen and rich corn and silk merchants, lawyers, princes and traders from across the seas. What was said or done within was, as if by magic, evaporated in the air once they'd returned to the outside world. If one were to meet them on the street there would not be the merest flicker of recognition.

It was here also that I learned what everybody seemed to know already: that Reinhardt did not care for a woman's love. When, afterwards, I thought upon the matter, there seemed a thousand instances when it should have been plain as the nose on my face to see his proclivity. But in my naivety I had thought him ever gallant, true to his promise that he would not attempt to seduce me, when all the while he had no such inclination and it was my own vanity that blinded me. I had often enough suffered through many a lugubrious sermon, delivered from the pulpit of Father Pietrus, that the sin of sodomy was one of the greatest in God's eyes; that he who loves men in the way that men love women was possessed by demons and would burn in eternal hellfire.

Jew and sodomite, both were thought to be evil incarnate. Yet I had found Master Israel and Frau Sarah more kind to me than any mortal being other than my own mother and, of course, Reinhardt. Master Yap, another Semite, while snappy and unhappy was a fair man and if he did not treat us with affection we were no exception. Affection was not within his nature and he was born a pessimist, forever waiting for the sky to fall down. Although perhaps I judge him too harshly, for the night I made his nightingales sing he placed a gold coin in my hand. If I was not mistaken, his dark eyes wore a sudden mistiness and he clasped my hand to his chest a little longer than he might otherwise.

I knew Reinhardt for my fosterer and friend who only wished for our success. He had never harmed me in the least and taught me all he knew of Latin and told me grand stories of olden times and always used his cunning and contrivance in our mutual interest. He was no angel, a consummate liar and ever on the lookout for some advantage to himself with little thought of conscience. But no sister could possess a better and more faithful brother and I would still honour him, even if he should be named a sodomite in public and ridiculed by all. Even, I told myself, if the Church condemned me for it. But every night from that time on I prayed that God would forgive him and show him his errant ways, for I told the good Lord that the heavenly choir would possess an even sweeter sound with the accompaniment of Reinhardt's wondrous flighty flute.

More and more I was beginning to ask questions of the Holy Church. If Jews who showed Christians kindness, and the sirrah (which was another name used to describe someone of Reinhardt proclivity) proved my valued friends, and both were condemned to Satan's furious fires, what then of he who fornicates with little girls? Was he not the greater sinner? It seemed not. Father Pietrus never spoke of this infamy as sin. But for his untimely death and the lack of time to make his confession and receive a suitable penance, upon embarking on a crusade the Church had decreed my father's sins forgiven and he would now rest in paradise. God's laws, I was discovering, are sometimes difficult to understand.

I was not alone in my high regard for the Pied Piper of Hamelin. The girls at Ali Baba's treated him as if he were one of them. They would spend hours with him on their presentation and manner of dressing so they would appear the more comely. They consulted him on the tone they chose to colour their lips or prepare their eyes or what style their hair or what gown to wear so that they would seem all the more alluring. He became the authority on their every beauty concern and they faithfully followed his every whim, even though sometimes I would think he had gone too far with his outrageousness.

He made them to walk with their shoulders thrown back and to bounce off their toes, heels slightly raised so their hips swung provocatively. 'Thy arse must move as two round river stones set to grinding corn!' he'd shout out. 'It should be the promise of the rich treasure that lies buried in thy pussy cave that the one-eyed dragon must, at any cost, hasten to enter and so save the maiden in distress! Look at the Nubian, she can do it without thinking!' The girls would squeal with laughter and do as he bade, practising for hours with the courtesan from Africa showing them how to drive men crazy by viewing from behind.

They loved, admired and respected him and took his advice in other matters concerning their health – some small blemish to the skin or the misconduct of their bowels or bladders or the sweetness of their breath. He would obtain herbs and cures from Frau Sarah and claim them as his own, Reinhardt the good doctor in attendance. He patched their quarrels, made them laugh when they were sad and told them outrageous stories that set them to giggling until they couldn't stop. I had never seen him happier and Master Yap, despite his pessimistic disposition, respected him.

But, oh dear! When his pied suit was finally ready what a to-do this caused at Ali Baba's. With the courtesans all watching, Reinhardt commenced the grand parade. He had them all clapping and giggling and 'oohing' and 'aahing' as he played the part of musician-extraordinaire with the greatest style and a little playful buffoonery. His new mincing step was a wonder to behold for he had caused heels to be placed on his pointy boots so when he walked it gave a haughty and most provocative look. Soon he contrived new suits even more extravagant and outrageous than his pied one, so that most of what he earned was paid back at once to Master Israel since the Pied Piper of Hamelin's taste in apparel fell well beyond our clothing contract with Frau Sarah.

Frau Sarah had been right about featuring us in Master Yap's *winkelhaus*. I had always supposed that the men who visited had no ear for music. I had grown accustomed to our receiving no applause as they sat unresponsive among the cushions, drinking wine and listening to the courtesans whispering sweet nothings in their ears. But it seemed I was quite wrong. We were soon invited to noble houses and rich men's homes as the musical entertainment and we commanded the highest fees. Other musicians of a high quality, mostly French and Italian, soon heard of the Jewess Sarah's fame and contacted her, requesting that they be placed under her care. Frau Sarah kept to the same strict rules and chose only the best of their kind. This suited some and others not and those who would not abide by her dictates – no drunkenness, theft, dalliance or loud and boastful behaviour – were soon sent on their way.

By the end of one year she had built a thriving business and Master Israel was also obliged to expand his tailoring shop. This came about not only because Frau Sarah dressed all her entertainers but also from Reinhardt's foppish style of dressing being noted by young noblemen who flocked to the little Jewish tailor so they might be attired with the same design, cut and fit. Soon Master Israel had six good women doing his needlework and another tailor and apprentice working for him. Frau Sarah appointed a cousin who was a bootmaker and Reinhardt designed boots of every colour for him to make with heels the height of her forefinger. These came to be called 'Hamelin heels' and were soon all the rage among the best-dressed young nobles and knights. Frau Sarah ran all these businesses and seemed all the happier for it. 'My most cherished hope is that I never again have cause to thread a needle other than when it brings me joy, such as making a garment for you, Sylvia,' she had once said.

Her reputation for the quality, discretion, courtly manners, cleanliness and suitable attire of her musicians soon spread in Cologne and Bonn and at castles in the nearby countryside. No event of importance, christening, wedding feast or any other celebration among the high society, was complete without her furnishing the means of musical entertainment.

In the matter of courtly manners I was of course greatly lacking. Peasants are not shown how to behave in polite company and I was to discover that chastity and modesty were not enough in the complexities of modern society, in particular my table manners. Frau Sarah approached me on the matter the first time when we were to visit the home of a rich merchant to entertain, and I was confounded at how complex the simple matter of eating could become.

'Men shall want you as their pretty daughter,' she declared, 'and so you will need to mind your manners well when eating, for it is here that most are first judged and if found wanting it is difficult to recover the initial advantage you possessed from your appearance.'

'But I know nought of manners,' I cried, alarmed. In the *winkelhaus* we ate our evening meal in the kitchen and so no mannerly ways were required, as all within ate in the same accustomed way.

'Thou art such a pretty one and sprightly and quick of mind that I constantly place you beyond your station and forget you are a peasant girl but lately arrived in the city,' she said.

'How does one learn manners?' I asked. 'For I would greatly desire to have them for myself, Frau Sarah.'

And so began a lesson that would continue for many months. As she pinned and tucked and stitched my gowns she made me learn a list of what to do when I supped with a man, or a lady or anyone from that time on. 'Manners,' she explained, 'are not for parading, but must instead be a natural part of your demeanour, so you do not ever have to think upon them in company and you affect them unknowingly in private.'

I was amazed how complex these mannerisms were. While sitting at a table, no elbow to lean upon it, hands scrubbed and nails well groomed and clean. Food to be plucked from the bowl with only the forefinger and thumb, and if a lady, the remaining three fingers extended so they do not touch the food. If your hands cannot wait until the water bowl and cloth are brought at the conclusion of the feast then the underpart of thy garment sleeves must be used to wipe them. The salt is not to be touched with the food where it sits in the salt dish. This instruction I found most curious, for I had never encountered salt but knew it only for a precious commodity and should I come upon it, then I would know myself to be in the grandest company. Moreover, I would not touch it at all, not knowing what quantities to be used.

There was one instruction I already understood: if you can, please refrain from belching at the table. Never start to eat before all are ready to partake. Strangest of all, if thine own bowl, and perchance the contents is soup or curds, the bowl is not to be brought up to the mouth and supped, but the contents taken up with a spoon, scoop by scoop. This is a mannerism most inconvenient, for the soup may well be cold by the time thy bowl is emptied by such laborious means and is easily spilled when carried the journey from bowl to mouth. Nor must thou, under any circumstances, gnaw a bone with thy teeth.

These were but the barest necessities to good manners and there were many other rules of behaviour that I would learn so I could pass for a respectable and respectful maiden. My good fortune was that, while a Jew and kosher and therefore not able to attend a feast or dine with Gentiles, Frau Sarah, who had once been a serving maid in a noble house, knew all the courtly ways and rehearsed me in these social niceties. She seemed to very much enjoy this teaching.

In the months that followed she would often regale me with pieces of advice that were always cogent to the time of my development as a woman and the experience I underwent in our partnership. For instance, she might say things such as, 'They say you cannot turn a crow into a falcon, but we shall prove them wrong, Sylvia. A pretty woman may happily slip between the sheets of an emperor's bed providing her manners are correct, her body clean, her breath sweet and her mind nimble. But most of all, if she can curry favour with his courtiers and win their trust.

'It is seldom the king who is the high-lofty, but those that fawn in his service and are protective of their own position and puffed-up with self-importance. The Jew knows that the biggest bribe is not always to the master, but most often to those who guard access to him. If the servant's right hand is held open and the left is a fist, the right will close when gold is placed upon it and the left open to reveal the key to his master's presence. Always look where the bribe is best placed. Even when there is more than sufficient and there is no need for further gain, greed is never satisfied and lies in almost every heart, curled as a serpent, ready to strike.'

'And what if I should meet one who cannot be bribed?' I asked, thinking all the while of saints.

'Then add more gold to his palm.'

'And if still they are not tempted?'

'Then run for thy dear life, for they are not to be trusted and will betray you for the greedy need they have for their own self-righteousness.'

'But what of myself? May I be bought in this same manner?'

'Of course! But never cheaply, a pretty woman must not be deemed an easy purchase. Sylvia, thou must always behave as if thy favours are most difficult to earn and cannot be given up without a struggle. Men treasure most what they cannot obtain. The purse between thy legs must prove most difficult to open and it must only be spent on merchandise that will bring you a rich return. But, know also this, when refusal seems to your disadvantage, think if you abstain a little longer, is there more to gain? If there is, then it is well to remember thy mouth has three amorous uses beside the art of kissing. It can enchant with thy singing, charm with thy sensibility and wit or be used to satisfy a begetting male without yet the need to open your precious purse. Once you have caused him satisfaction, his sword will droop and you may live another day to keep him at bay and so, in the end, gain the greater advantage.'

I did not tell her that I had already learned this third use of my mouth, if only on a marrow. 'But what of love?' I asked. 'If my heart is plundered by some poor but handsome knave, how then will I resist?'

'Knave!' she spat, her eyes grown wide. 'A knave is a servant, a lackey, a monk's donkey and a kitchen maid's snatchy catch! No knave should ever be found within your menagerie of men. It is unworthy to marry simply for money, but it is a sensible wench who tarries *only* where riches may be found and so chances upon her true love. The company you keep should never be cheap and thy dainty lady's hand must be welcome within your lover's overflowing and always generous purse.'

'But what if I am deceived and he, like Reinhardt, outwardly struts the peacock in his finery but his pocket is as bare as a widow's pantry?'

'Ah!' she replied. 'There are two empty-pocket types you must avoid when speculating upon your future: those who have a full vault and an empty house and those who have a house resplendent in every furnishing but an empty vault. The first is by nature mean, perhaps a miser. And miserly and misery are words that walk hand in hand. The second is a spendthrift and, while often artful and beguiling and always self-indulgent, they are not to be trusted with your love.'

'Like Reinhardt?'

'Aye! You learn quickly, Sylvia,' she laughed, 'although his affliction is vanity and his amorism lies elsewhere than to capture and then break the heart of a pretty maid.'

'How then shall I know these two empty-pocket types before they deceive me?' I asked, thinking meanwhile that my future life was unlikely to encounter either type, or, for that matter, require any of the precautionary 'purse lessons' she gave me.

'Visit their parents,' she replied. 'The miser man or woman is over-cautious and frugal, a pessimist by nature, thinking only of the blight brought by ill winds and for their own future safety. The portions on thy plate will be small, the meat, if any, of a middle quality and the wine sour to the taste. If it is the mother who is miser she will look upon you with a wary eye. She will ask the cost of everything you wear and be critical of your shoes that yet wear the soles they carried when first bought. Then she will point to her own, you may be sure they have been to the bootmender so often that they can lead her there while she is blindfolded. If the father he will ask you what goods and gold you bring into the marriage.

'The other empty-pocket's offending parent is almost always his mother, who is besotted with her son and will laugh at his merry jakes and indulge him, cajoling her husband to give their son whatsoever he wants, while scolding her scion for his extravagance. He can, in her eyes, do nothing wrong and so she will forgive him his every transgression, though they be constant.'

If I should give the impression that Frau Sarah wished only to turn me into a hard-faced coquette then that would be quite wrong. I was much too young to put any of her tuition into practice. These were simply her beginner's lessons and, to wit, only a few small stitches in the tapestry of a woman's life. There was much more of richer weaving to be garnered from her instruction. While she showed me kindness she was also very strict and expected in all things to be obeyed. As I grew more knowledgeable of life and also wilful, I confess I often found her ways constricting and her control to be most arduous. Had it not been for Master Israel and his learning I would much sooner have snapped the reins and spat the bit and as a young filly galloped away, though I now know that had I done so this would have proved to my disadvantage.

Fully a month passed before Master Israel called me to his side and bade me be seated, a chessboard placed between us. 'Frau Sarah tells me you wish to learn chess, *ja*?'

'Yes, Master Israel, I should like that very much.'

'You are a Gentile and I am a Jew. How does a Jew play chess with a Gentile, fräulein?'

'Master Israel, I am Sylvia, if you please?'

'Sylvia If-you-please,' he said, as though 'If-you-please' was a portion of my name, 'you do not answer my question.'

'Because there is no answer, Master Israel. You only speculate whether a Gentile plays chess differently to a Jew. How can I know until you teach me how to play? Then, perchance, as a Gentile I may answer your question.' I said all this in a most demure tone so that he did not think me forward.

'Aha, that is *gut*! Sylvia doth answer a question with another better question. That is bold. *Ja, gut*, at once you are learning the first lesson in chess. "Boldness, will you be my friend?" you are asking when always you open against your opponent. But to know *when* to be bold, that is the real question.'

'What be the answer to the question you asked yourself, Master Israel?' I now asked.

'What question?'

'How does a Jew play chess with a Gentile?'

'Carefully, lest he win,' he chuckled, then seeing my bemused expression added, 'This is a Jewish joke.'

I half-laughed, but it would be some time before I understood its meaning. 'Will you teach me? Frau Sarah says chess be the game of life.'

'Nay, it is much more, Sylvia. In the game of life we all cheat. In chess, never! You hear, *never*! To cheat in chess is to defile thy soul.'

'But you just said a Jew must be careful lest he win against a Gentile. Is that not cheating?'

'Aye, you are right, it is only a joke, but it is not a joke concerning chess, but of other things between Jew and Gentile. When you are older you will understand.' He picked up the king. 'This be the king and he is the all-powerful one.' Then he picked up the queen. 'This is the queen. She can be a lover, a witch, a sorceress, a whore, a prophetess or a tender mother. Which of the two do you think is the more powerful, Sylvia?'

'The queen?'

'*Ja, gut*, excellent! So, now we can begin.'

One afternoon shortly after he began to teach me chess we commenced lessons in Latin, and then again shortly after this, he said, 'Tush! You are quick to learn, we will try you on Hebrew as well. In this way you have the text of the Christian and the text of the Jew and so may inquire in both to find the truth.'

But if both languages came easily to my ear, then chess remained a challenge to my mind. It would take me close to a year before I took a game from Master Israel. It was then that I understood the joke. Only now it was transposed, it was I who should have been careful not to win because winning at chess was something beyond triumph and losing beyond disaster.

Master Israel sat upon his stool all morning, both his hands held to his head, his gaze fixed upon the chessboard with my checkmate displayed before him. 'Witchery!' he cried every so often, though this was not intended in my praise but said sincerely. Then he became silent and would not speak to me or Frau Sarah or even an important customer. He remained thus for an entire week and Frau Sarah informed me he only picked at his food and lay awake in bed at night. She took me aside. 'Sylvia, I beseech thee, contest him once more, but I pray most earnestly you lose, because if you win again I fear he will never agree to continue to teach you Latin and Hebrew.'

I well remembered her words on being a woman and how I should regard a man once conquered, 'to bow to their superiority, exclaim at their profundity and compliment their masculinity'. Her threat that Master Israel might not continue my lessons made me greatly afraid. I was learning so that I might know the truth and so act with integrity to all and not be deceived by others who claimed it without foundation. But if I should betray Master Israel's trust and allow him to win when the game was mine to take, I would be denying the very truth and integrity I hoped to gain from knowledge. It was thus with a beating heart that I replied, 'Nay, Frau Sarah, I cannot do that or I betray all that Master Israel hath taught me about chess.'

Frau Sarah became angry, for she had expected me, as I always did, to comply with her wish. 'For God's sake, Sylvia! He is only a man!' she exclaimed. 'Must I then live with him in this foul humour of thy making?' She said this puce-lipped and with her eyes grown flinty sharp and, as well, with her peering down the bridge of her nose. I could see she would not accept my refusal.

'Frau Sarah, please do not fret, we have played a hundred games or more and each time I have lost. That I won one game is nought but a fluke. If we play another Master Israel will most assuredly win it. But I cannot cheat, or he will know himself betrayed and I the same, for I cannot abuse his trust!'

Frau Sylvia jerked her shoulders, then stamped her foot. 'Get on with it, Sylvia. You are a pretty woman and may betray a man whenever you wish! I have told thee what to do and you will do as I say!' she shouted angrily.

And so I went to Master Israel. 'I should much like another match,' I suggested.

'Nay! Go away!' he said, his chin tucked to his chest, all the while the sulky child.

'Please?'

'Nay! Nay! Nay! Be off!' he cried.

'I will sing your favourite Hebrew song?'

'Go!'

I did not depart, but began instead to sing the beautiful song of praise from ancient times when the children of Israel were released as slaves and Moses led them out of Egypt. When I reached the part where God parts the Red Sea to let the Jews pass through while drowning the pursuing Egyptian soldiers, Master Israel's chin rose from his breast and he looked at me. By the time his people had entered Canaan, the land of milk and honey, I had won his heart and he began to weep.

Alas, it was the best game of chess I had ever played and yet again I won. As quietly as my excitement would allow I said, 'Checkmate!', then looked up fearfully. Master Israel clapped his hands. '*Wunderlich!*' he cried, a look of great delight upon his face. 'The Jew is well beaten! But he is *not* betrayed!'

That afternoon he said to me, 'Sylvia, you have almost a year of Latin and speak and comprehend it surprising well and also you speak

Hebrew without an accent and you have quickly picked up Yiddish. I have seen you learn more of these languages in months than others have learned in full five years. Your gift of singing and mimicking aids your exceptional ear and your mind is as sharp as a bootmender's tack. I cannot continue to instruct you in written Latin as you will soon be beyond my knowledge. What say you we teach you Greek and, if you can manage the extra burden of learning, also Aramaic?'

I think perhaps that single moment was the happiest of my life. I knew then that God, in His infinite mercy, had expunged my name from the Book of the Stupid and granted me permission to learn. Moreover, if Master Israel's praise seemed heaped upon me, it was the first I had received from him and I oft doubted that I pleased him and would sometimes cry at night that on the morrow he might proclaim me not sufficient unto the task of learning. I would cry out in despair to Reinhardt, but he could not help me, as I was now beyond his own knowledge of Latin.

'If it pleases you, Master Israel, I would very much like to try these two other languages.'

But it was Latin that I must know above all else and I had yet much to learn. Master Israel had taught me to translate what testaments he could obtain, but they were few and when I had completed them he told me that I must henceforth go to the Church, as only the Church possessed the Latin library I would require in the future.

The matter of the blood and the rose was already close to a year past in presentation, first the bishop who took several months to respond and then the archbishop who might take even longer and then, Father Paulus said, perhaps to Rome. 'Heaven alone knows how long!' he cried, exasperated, as I knew his ambition was attached to his concern. For my part I hoped it might take forever and then just fade away, even though this would disappoint the two priests a great deal, for they had both worked exceedingly hard to bring the 'miracle' to the attention of the Church hierarchy.

However, the whole matter of the Virgin's white rose and my blood upon it had greatly benefited me. The blessed Father Hermann Joseph had accepted me into his charity work and I now spent every morning among the street children and the desperate poor, with young Nicholas constantly at my side. This work brought me great satisfaction but it also had a disadvantage, for the name Petticoat Angel became one the poor folk and the street children thought of as blessed. It caused me great vexation when they would often kneel in my presence and ask to kiss my hand or that I should give them a blessing. I finally took the matter to Father Hermann.

'My child, I too felt the same when younger even than you; the acceptance of the apple by the infant Jesus became known and folk would fall to their knees at my approach. You must not see it as a reflection of yourself, but only as God's work. If piety is the reward for your name and presence, then God is well served.'

'But I have no right, I feel I blaspheme, Father.'

'Blaspheme? I think not! What right have you to question God's word? In thy first confession you persisted with worldly explanations of your past deeds and did not consider that it was your heavenly Saviour who brought these circumstances about. Your blasphemy lies in your refusal to accept His will and not that people recognise in you the hand of God at work!'

'But I am not a worthy vessel, Father,' I persisted.

'There are none worthy, but some are called despite our sinfulness. Sylvia, I watch your work among the children and the poor and how what you earn is spent on feeding them and it is exceeding good.' He paused, then said, 'But it is not sufficient, you must do more.'

'More, Father? I would willingly, if you show me how.'

'You must become a nun!' he said emphatically. 'God's work is not just mornings spent with the street children and the poor, it is every moment of thy being.'

I was deeply shocked and had no immediate reply except to say, 'Father, I am not yet ready for a nun's habit.'

'Think upon it, my child. Do not kick against the thorns of righteousness. God's work is never easy, but His will is a divine instruction and *must* be obeyed.'

'I have tried to do as much as I can, Father,' I said, a little hurt. From the day when he first had me sing the solo part in mass as part penance, I had attended every morning afterwards to do the same. I had been called upon to sing before the bishop on several occasions and sang again at Sunday worship. Every morning after mass I devoted to working among the street children and the poor. There were to my observation very few nuns who contributed as much as I did. I simply could not see myself cloistered in a convent with my every movement and thought controlled by an abbess who thought me all the while a peasant and used me for kitchen and garden duties.

I could not bring myself to decide upon Father Hermann's instructions, even though they had been couched as God's own word. If Father Hermann knew of my thirst for knowledge he had not taken this into consideration when asking me to become a novice in a nunnery. Learning was not his inclination and he admitted to being a poor student. I had never seen him with a book. Although he had composed the hymn *Summi Regis cor aveto*, which I sang constantly for his pleasure and whenever he presided as the priest who delivered the morning sermon, he had, he told me, received a great deal of help with its Latin transcription. His poems, though numerous, were simple in composition and mostly not written down and all in endless praise of Mary. While I would not say so to anyone, I thought they were simplistic and Reinhardt would have composed them a great deal better.

Master Israel had commenced to teach me Greek and Aramaic and I was greatly taken up with learning these two languages. While my work with Frau Sarah was of the least concern, I enjoyed it and it paid for food for the poor. It was all very well for Father Hermann to speak as he had. He had been ecstatically connected with the Virgin and the Church since the age of seven. At the age of twelve he had offered himself to the Premonstratensian monastery, but was too young to be accepted as a monk. Nevertheless he used his every available moment in prayer to Mary (whom he called 'The mystical rose'), until he was ordained and could devote himself entirely to the cause of our Saviour and his beloved Virgin. Apart from being a very good repairer of clocks, he knew no other vocation. I did not see myself doing God's work wearing the habiliment of a nun and so I tried, though always gently but with no less determination, to resist what Father Hermann referred to as 'Your divine calling'.

But now, with Master Israel having exhausted his knowledge of Latin and lacking any Latin text to take me further, I would have to choose to curtail my studies except for what I might find to read outside the libraries of the Church. The alternative was to take the chance that by becoming a novice in a nunnery I might be allowed access to a library.

Reinhardt frequently announced that I was lucky and that by remaining with me he shared in my luck. Now he too was in a dilemma. He had found a lute player, Jacques, a Frenchman of exceeding skill and great beauty, and was much in love. But the lute player wished to return home and the ratcatcher was most distraught.

'But if he loves you, why would he wish to return home?' I asked.

'He is contracted to the noble Count St Gilles as musician and if he does not return his reputation will be destroyed in France. He begs me to go with him and swears his love for me is the equal of my own for him and that they will equally applaud me for my flute in France,' Reinhardt lamented.

The thought of losing my beloved ratcatcher, rapscallion though he might be and foppish, deceitful, boastful and often blasphemous, but always cheerful and clever and concerned for my wellbeing, was too awful to contemplate. But it must be admitted that my work with Father Hermann and Nicholas among the poor every morning and my study each afternoon meant that I only saw him when at night he played and I sang.

'I pray for your redemption every day, Reinhardt, but if you love Jacques with all thy heart then you must go to France with him, though I shall miss you more than I can possibly say.'

'Sylvia, you are my talisman, since meeting you beside the brook my life has been most fortunate. All my life I have wanted to be a musician but lacked the courage. As a ratcatcher my vocation fed and clothed me well enough and I never wanted for anything. If I say so myself, I was amongst the best of my kind, possibly the best, for I have never met another who with his pipe can call so many rats to their doom. To be the best at something is better than being only among those who do something well enough. I was most afraid that as a musician I would only amuse others, a wandering minstrel of no great importance or respect. Since we have worked together I now know myself elevated to be among the best with my instrument in Germany. It is you I must thank for this.'

'Nay, thank Frau Sarah!' I protested. 'It was she who has given us both the opportunity.'

'Aye, but you, Sylvia Honeyeater, supplied the inspiration.'

And so now, aged almost fourteen, I was once again at a crossroads in my life. I had performed often enough to know that I did not depend on Reinhardt, even though we fitted hand in glove and no other musician would suit as well. Frau Sarah would not like his departure, because between us we had made her a pretty penny and still commanded a greater fee than any other musicians or entertainers under her management. But she would not be destitute without him or, for that matter, myself, and she would know we had served her well and with loyalty. Several Christian folk, seeing the success of the Jewess, had attempted to do the same thing and in the process attracted four of Frau Sarah's entertainers. But all the rest stayed and the four who had left were for the most part malcontents or thought their talents greater than she saw them to be. Her judgement was seldom wrong and her business would continue to prosper.

So with Father Hermann almost daily exhorting me to become a novice nun, and Master Israel, my beloved teacher, unable to take my Latin studies any further, and with Reinhardt likely to depart with his French lover, I found myself confused and undecided. It was then that I was summoned to see Father Paulus at St Martin's church.

I had seen him from time to time since the inquiry into the blood on the rose. But he was by nature withdrawn, and had quickly seen that Father Hermann saw me as his protégé, and had stayed away so we had not cultivated a deep friendship, remaining all the while most cordial towards each other. He would sometimes ask if I would sing at St Martin's, once or twice over Lent or on a holy feast day. If I appear to be familiar with them, or speak as if I now saw myself on equal terms with the two priests, this would not be true. I was ever the sprat and they the big fish in the sea.

Upon my arrival at St Martin's Father Paulus led me into the baptistry and when we were seated he took my hand and looked most sincerely into my eyes. 'Sylvia, the blessed Father Hermann Joseph has asked me to talk with you about entering a convent.' I dropped my eyes and he must have seen that I seemed immediately disconsolate. 'Nay, please look at me, child. What I have to say is, I think, important.'

'Yes, Father,' I said meekly, looking into his pale blue eyes, their whites reddened from working late under candlelight.

'Sylvia, you know that we, Father Hermann and myself, think you are divinely blessed, and so it is not unexpected that he should want you to devote your life to the work of our Saviour. There is, after all, no greater calling.'

'But, Father . . .' I began to protest.

'No, pray hear me out, my child. What I have to say may yet surprise you. I have also had a visit from the Jew, Israel of Bonn.'

'Master Israel! He came to visit you?' I exclaimed, surprised.

'Aye, in a matter concerning you.'

'But he is a Jew! As a priest do you not think him Satan's child?'

Father Paulus laughed. 'I am a scribe and a scholar and do not always agree with every doctrinal *veritas* of the Holy Roman Church. Master

Israel, as you call him, is a good man and God looks first into a man's heart before he passes judgement on his faith.'

'And what of the infidel?' I asked, knowing I should not be arguing, but it was Master Israel himself who taught me that good argument is the pathway to truth and in discussion lies the seeds of the resolution to most human problems.

'It is the same with the infidel, Jew, Gentile, Muslim – we share the one God. Christians do not always behave well and there are both Jews and infidels who have shown us charity in the past when we Christians have shown them none. "Judge not lest thee be judged," saith the Lord.' He smiled. 'We talked about chess.'

'Chess?'

'Aye, he claims you are very good.'

I blushed furiously. 'Nay, Father, I know only what he has taught me.'

'Chess is an easy game to teach and a very difficult one to play. The teacher, while important if he is a master, is only one part; the quality of mind and the courage of the heart are the others.'

'Do you play chess, Father?'

'Since I was a child. I should like to play you, Sylvia.' He rose and walked over to a curtained partition and parting the curtains withdrew a chessboard already set up and placed it on the bench between us.

'Now? You wish us to play now?' I asked, surprised.

'Aye, there is much resting on this contest,' he warned with a smile.

By warning me that more than the game rested on the result, he had already made his first move and I mine, for I recognised this ploy to divide my concentration, thinking I must win as failure would not be to my advantage. *Thank you, Master Israel*, I said silently.

I would like to say I lost and then returned another day to win, or even that we reached a stalemate as it would make for a better telling. But hallelujah! I trounced him within the hour. Male, vanity is thy name. He had thought himself against a peasant girl but did not realise that I had been well tutored by a Jew. They are a people who are taught in their cradle to read a Gentile's mind and to use their brains to ward off the blows of those who would do harm to them.

Father Paulus was wrong. It is not *only* the quality of mind and the courage of the heart that is required in playing chess – understanding the innermost nature of your opponent is the essential difference. Master Israel had taught me to watch every mannerism, the eyes, hands, gestures, movements, sweat, rapidity of blinking and breathing, then, if possible to touch, seemingly by accident, an opponent's skin and read its temperature. Chess is always won narrowly by one of two equally competent players. But it is not always the grand and bold advance or the superior intelligence, but often the smallest observation that accounts for the winning move. That is why it is more than the game of life. It is also the answer to the question, 'How must a Jew play chess with a Gentile?' If the Jew wins then the Gentile will know that the Jew understands his nature, both his weaknesses and his strengths, and will use both well when they do business together.

Father Paulus remained silent for fully a minute as he examined the chessboard, then he shook his head. 'My arrogance has brought me undone, I must pray for humility.' He looked up. 'I confess you continue to surprise me, my child.' Then, suddenly brusque, he said, 'Chess was not why Israel of Bonn came to see me. He asked if I could make the church library available to you. He admitted that he could no longer teach you as you have reached the extent of his own knowledge of Latin text and he lacks books and manuscript. It was both a brave and worthy thing for him to do as it is not easy for a Jew to ask such a favour from a priest. He must have a great regard for you, Sylvia.'

'Thank you, Father, for telling me this. I too have a great love for him.'

Father Paulus cleared his throat. 'I would caution you to be careful to talk about a Jew in this familiar way. With myself it matters little, but others may not view it the same.' He glanced down at the chessboard and shook his head ruefully, then without looking up from the board he said somewhat shyly, 'I agree with Israel of Bonn – you are sufficiently intelligent and worthy to learn more of Latin.' He looked up at me. 'I have decided I shall be your tutor.'

He must have seen my expression of delight because I could see from the shine to his pale eyes that he was pleased. 'Thank you, Father, I shall not let you down and pray only that I may please you.'

'I am told that your language is already well advanced, but that you lack skill with a quill and with the nature of the alphabet and the art of spelling. We will work assiduously on these.'

'Thank you, Father,' I replied again. I should have liked to kiss him if he hadn't been a priest.

'Do not thank me so quickly, my child. There is a condition.'

My heart stood still. Frau Sarah had been through the various conditions males impose on the prettier of the opposite sex and I had heard of errant priests who break their vow of chastity. *Please, God, let it not be that*, I prayed silently.

'After a few months at the age of fourteen you must enter a convent as a novice in order to undertake religious orders. Father Hermann and I both agree that God has a special calling for you, Sylvia.'

I felt at once ashamed that I might think of Father Paulus as I had just done. It was a sin to think evil in anticipation. I would ask God for forgiveness. Then I realised that the blessed Father Hermann Joseph with his constant nagging that I enter a convent had won with this new promise of Latin instruction. Father Paulus, it was now obvious, had consulted with him after Master Israel's visit and he, as the senior cleric, had placed this condition on my opportunity of further learning.

I needed now to decide if the terms were acceptable, although I knew immediately in my heart that to be able to search out the word of God myself from Latin text was priceless and that I would accept. But I could hear Master Israel's words as if he was standing at my side. 'Never accept the first price, there is always a little more to be gained. If not, you have lost nothing.'

'But what of my Latin, Father? After but a few months there will still be a great deal to learn and I cannot continue my study as a novice in a nunnery where they will regard me as a peasant and set me to work in the kitchen and the vegetable garden.'

'Humility, my child. To work in a kitchen and a garden is also God's work,' he chided.

'Then I have been doing God's work since I was seven years old and mark Him pleased with me, for He has given me the gift of learning and placed it in thy hands, Father.'

Father Paulus laughed. 'I begin to see why I lost to you at chess, my child. We will find a convent where the facilities exist and the abbess agrees that you may learn further in order that you become a scribe.'

'And only perform the duties of a scribe and not a peasant?' I pushed him.

'Sylvia, what is this about a peasant? Can you not see, you are far from this humble station in life, even though to be born of humble lineage is no disgrace. Your manners are courtly. You have the appearance and the voice of an angel. I am told you speak Hebrew and the dreadful patois of the German Jew, Yiddish. That this year, under the Jew's tutelage, you undertake to learn Greek and Aramaic and if you learn them as well as you did Hebrew then you will be quadlingual without counting your native tongue. Father Hermann and I have with our own eyes seen you perform two miracles, the one of the birds and the other of the Virgin's rose. There is also talk of others we have not witnessed. Do you think that an abbess, accepting you into her convent, would want to use thee for a scullery maid to stir the soup or pull turnips from the garden?'

'Will you tell Mother Superior all this, please, Father? Discounting the miracles, for I do not claim them.'

'Yes, willingly,' he said, a little impatiently. 'I do not think it will be necessary – whether you disagree we all know of the blood on the rose, the birds and of thy miraculous appearance in the bathhouse as an angel to castigate the three harlots for their sins.'

'What!' I cried, astonished. 'Nay, Father, I went there to take a bath! You may ask the attendant! Her name is Gilda. She saw me well.'

'Aye, we have interviewed her and the three sinful women who have repented and vow to henceforth live chaste lives. Gilda of the Bathhouse says she heard them screaming and then saw them run naked from the bathhouse. When she entered she saw an angel naked with the sign of the fish on her back. She swears she had never set eyes upon you before that moment and that no person may enter the bathhouse without her knowing or paying the bath fee.'

'They are not being truthful, Father. Gilda, perhaps to protect me, for she proved a goodly woman and took good care of me when the three whores . . . er, women, threatened me. As for them, I know not why they would want to tell such a confounding and preposterous tale.'

Father Paulus seemed unimpressed with my explanation. 'Sylvia, the woman Gilda claims she gave you a petticoat to cover your nakedness and to hide the holy sign of the fish upon your back.' He paused for breath and looked at me steadily. 'The bathhouse woman's veracity is soon determined. Sylvia, is there the fish sign of the apostles on your back?

'It is a birthmark, Father.'

'Do you know that it is a mark of our Saviour and His apostles?'

'Father, I beg you, it is but a mark I was born with, the shape is happenstance.'

There was a silence now between us, then Father Paulus looked up at me, his washed-out blue eyes appealing and sincere. 'Sylvia, I do not wish you to take this in the wrong manner for I am a priest and sworn to celibacy. But could you turn your back towards me and show me this sign?'

Sighing deeply, I replied, 'Father, I cannot disobey you, but it is of no importance. My greatest wish is that it never was.' I turned so that my back faced the little priest and pulled at my gown until it was halfway down towards my waist, sufficient to reveal the birthmark.

'Glory be to God!' he exclaimed, and I heard a slight thump and looked back over my shoulder and down to see him on his knees, his hands clasped in prayer. 'Though art truly blessed!' he exclaimed. 'Why did you not tell us of this before? It would count greatly in the favour of the Miracle of the Blood on the Rose if the bishop should know that God has singled you out with the sign of Jesus and His apostles.'

'Father, you must please rise!' I cried in impatience and despair. 'I am no more blessed than any other and count this sufficient in God's eyes.'

Father Paulus rose to his feet. 'The three harlots were right to come to Father Hermann and tell him of the vision.'

'Nay, Father, there was no vision!' I said, now close to tears.

Father Paulus shook his head in wonder, seeming not to hear my outcry. 'Father Hermann agreed to hear their confessions but asked what the vision might be. It is not unusual for simple folk to think they have witnessed a miracle and it is every priest's task to examine them. Many miracles are claimed, but few of them go beyond the initial questioning of the village priest.' I recalled Father Pietrus talking about the woman who had seen the face of the Virgin on a piece of cloth that hung from her washing line.

'When was this, Father?' I asked, thinking by questioning him I might bring him to his senses.

My question seemed to work and he paused to think. 'I am not exactly sure, a day or two after the blood on the Virgin's rose, perhaps?'

'Ha! When Nicholas and his urchins had already spread the rumour of the rose.'

'That I daresay, but how does this affect their testimony? Oh, I see. You mean the three women named it a vision to explain their shame at running naked from the bathhouse. Is that it?'

'Aye.'

But the scribe in him was now back and the bewildered priest quite gone. 'But what else might have caused them to run unclad from the bathhouse? If you were there and not as an angel, then you must know this!'

I was placed in a predicament, not knowing how to answer this question without telling of the dagger. 'They ran from me . . . there was a fight,' I explained, somewhat lamely. Father Hermann had obviously honoured the confidentiality of my confession and not told Father Paulus the details of what had happened in the bathhouse. If I now explained the incident to the little priest, what would he think of me when he knew of my violent nature? Would he yet agree to teach me Latin?

Father Paulus looked at me somewhat askance. 'Do you expect me to believe that three large and rough women known to be of a violent disposition were sufficiently terrorised by a young girl to flee naked from the bathhouse?'

There seemed no point in explaining any further. Even the correct explanation now seemed improbable and with the addition of Gilda revealing the so-called sign of the fish and thinking to protect me by saying she hadn't seen me enter the bathhouse, I wasn't going to be believed, no matter what I said.

'Yes, Father, that was what happened.'

Father Paulus was silent for several moments, seeming to be thinking. 'Sylvia, what know you of the nature of visions?'

'Nothing, Father, other than that saints appear to have them and Father Hermann claims them numerously in his childhood and often enough as an adult with the Virgin Mary.'

'Did he tell you what happens when one has a vision?'

'Nay, Father, he has not talked to me about them. What I know is only hearsay, as any Christian might hear from the pulpit about a saint or one that is blessed.'

'Well, a vision is what is known as an out-of-body experience. We see it and we are immersed in it, but we are not necessarily a physical part of it, experiencing it *not* with our body, but in our hearts and minds. A child, in his innocence, will speak of a vision quite ingenuously. A man of God, such as a priest, will speak of it from knowing it to be a spiritual experience. But others, commonfolk, who count themselves both sensible and sane, will think it but a dream or some peculiar and sudden alteration of the mind and will either remain silent or seek a simple explanation such as the one you have just given me. I put it to you that God used you to appear in a vision to these three sinful women, and that not understanding why they fled, you thought it was because of your rebuke. There is clear evidence from witnesses that when you appeared on the steps of the bathhouse people could see that you had about you the touch of the divine hand and they pronounced you there and then the Petticoat Angel.'

Father Paulus seemed well pleased with this explanation. He had stated it with such cogent authority that, for several moments, I felt myself taken up with its possibility, which goes to show that belief is not always fostered in *what* is said, but in who it is that pronounces it. Such an explanation from Reinhardt would have set me to laughter and ridicule.

Realising that by accepting his ecclesiastical sophistry I might bring an end to this discussion, I answered meekly, 'Yes, thank you, Father, I can see what you mean.'

It was an answer meant to satisfy him but he must have sensed the doubt in my acceptance, for he declared, 'Father Hermann and I have decided that the Miracle of the Blood on the Rose taken together with your summoning of the birds is sufficient evidence for the bishop to peruse and we have not included the vision of the Petticoat Angel in the bathhouse.' I was most relieved to hear this, but then Father Paulus added, 'We may need it as evidence at a later time, and I will notify Father Hermann of the blessed sign of the fish. I know he will be most excited.'

I confess I felt much safer in the pragmatic hands of the Christ-doubting Jews, Frau Sarah and Master Israel, than ever I did in the hands of the two priests bent on proving that I was touched by a divine authority. And I longed to be back in the reasoned and secular presence of Master Israel.

As I walked home from St Martin's much pleased that my Latin studies were to be continued, I could not help but wonder what the two priests would think if they knew that I spent my free time in a whorehouse laughing among the courtesans, or that they told me of the strange proclivities of their patrons or that I knew the most delicate and intimate information about the mayor, the bishop, many nobles and notables.

Then, again, these two were of different ambitions, Father Hermann in his extreme naivety would regard this fraternisation as a manifestation of my saintliness: that in the mornings I worked among the street children and the poor and then at other times among the harlots to cause them to repent and so bring them the comfort of Jesus Christ our Lord. I could also understand the motives of Father Paulus, a scribe, cloistered and all but chained to his desk, suddenly presented with tears of blood on a pure white rose that had no explanation other than a divine one. Of course, he wasn't stupid and he'd examined my hands and no doubt also the boy's, but the advent of my woman's blood would have been beyond his imagination or perhaps even his secular knowledge. It was not only the common people who were constantly on the lookout for signs and portents and he would be overcome with joy that he had been privileged to witness a miracle.

If I appeared to have changed in how I perceived my faith, it was not that I had forsaken my love for Christ Jesus or my belief in a merciful, all-powerful and loving God, but only that Master Israel was teaching me to think for myself, to always closely question how I interpreted what I saw or thought was the truth. 'The mind is conditioned early and prejudice is often bred in the cradle,' he'd once said. 'Do not deny your own experience or belittle it for what may be a common though false belief. To thine own self be true.' Furthermore, my increasing knowledge of God's word in the Latin text often gave me a greater insight into His truth and its meaning, so that I was less reliant on the words of priests who, it seemed to me, often quoted text from habit and by rote, long after they had forgotten the true, blessed and proper meaning of the Scriptures.

In teaching me more than one language Master Israel would say, 'As a Jew I know who I am and I know what it is to be Jewish: the culture, the God I worship, the laws I follow, the food I eat. What I teach my children is the righteous way and also what is wrong. I observe the laws regarding my wife and my marriage duties. As a Gentile it is the same with you, Sylvia. But when we learn another's language we begin to understand how we differ from others and, more importantly, how we are the same. Their language teaches us how they think, how their culture works, how they use their religion in their daily life and what makes them laugh and what makes them cry.

'When you learn another language you change your own and understand it better. You see its beauty and ugliness, its wisdom and its foolishness. It is possible to hate a Jew if you cannot speak Hebrew. A Greek if you cannot understand Greek. Or call an Arab an infidel and he calls you one, if you each do not speak the other's tongue.

'But when you speak someone else's language and may thus get to know them first, it is far more difficult to despise them or to believe what is said about them. Keep thy mind open and thy thoughts clear when the oracles in the temple declare upon the villainy of other nations. Ask always, "Do they know these people? Do they speak their tongue?" If you want to make a man your enemy when he has done you no harm, then know nothing about him, his language, religion or nation so that you may call him infidel and vile with impunity.'

'But we know why we call them infidels, they killed our Saviour!' I protested.

'Did you know that they recognise your saviour, the Jew you name Jesus?'

'Nay!' I declared, shocked.

'They declare him a great prophet within their own religion.'

'But not the Son of God?'

Master Israel shrugged. 'They honour him nevertheless, whereas you do not honour Mohammed, the Arab's intermediary to the same God.'

I was shocked that Master Israel would think of Jesus our Lord as a pathway and intermediary to God and not as God Himself. 'But you are a Jew and do not honour Christ Jesus, so how can you speak of Him thus?' I cried.

'We honour him as a Jew and a Jew has only one path to God, to Jehovah.'

'But you crucified Him! You nailed Jesus to the cross!' I shouted, close to tears.

He spread his hands. 'To us he was a heretic.' He sighed. 'If only we had known. It was a great mistake and we have suffered ever since.'

'Mistake! You killed the Son of God by mistake!'

'Shush! Be calm, Sylvia. The Christian faith has killed many a heretic by burning them at the stake. I ask you, did they ask each time, "Is this the Son of God?" Nay, they did not. They burned him, or perhaps it was a witch, because they thought they did not accept the tenets of your faith and were heretics and blasphemers.' He shrugged. 'We Jews did the same. If only we had known of the calamity this would cause to our people we would not have been so stupid and the Nazarene carpenter would have lived and died and, like all mortal beings, soon been forgotten.'

'If I should tell a priest of what you have just said to me, what then?' I cried.

Master Israel looked suddenly afraid and to my shame I felt a great sense of power rise within me. 'Then you would burn me as you do a heretic, but with less ceremony, for I am *only* a Jew.'

CHAPTER SEVEN

The Shrine of Bread and Fish

WITH MY BELOVED REINHARDT gone to his French lover (oh dear, I had not thought I would miss him as much), Frau Sarah had teamed me with a lute player of competence by the name of Klaus of Koblenz. Klaus was a man of perhaps thirty-five years, short, fat and morose. No matter how carefully dressed by Frau Sarah, he always looked untidy, as if he had but moments before risen from his bed. His breath smelled constantly of ale when mixed with the slops from a pigsty, and whereas Germans were for the most part clean-shaven, in the manner of the Frank, he wore a beard as untidy and rank as himself. He played tolerably well, although he lacked imagination and, I admit to my disappointment, made no comment on my singing. Whether thinking it good or bad, or, alas, anything at all, except as a partnership that was his way of earning bread and ale, I couldn't say. While I had learned to accept praise for my voice with due modesty, I was secretly angry at his indifference to it and felt I deserved better than this fat and foul-smelling fool. Being accustomed to Reinhardt who carried his every mood on the surface of his face and from whom praise came easily, being partnered with Klaus the Louse was like being dunked in the Rhine on a bitter winter's morning.

Frau Sarah was aware that I was not happy. I could find no real fault in Klaus the Louse's lute playing other than that it lacked surprise or inspiration, both so very much a feature of Reinhardt's playing. The ratcatcher would play tricks with his flute, so that my voice was constantly challenged and I could never take him for granted.

'Sylvia, Klaus is good with his instrument and we must be thankful for this,' Frau Sarah said. 'But if a happier musician of similar competence should be forthcoming I promise I shall make the change.' I knew that as long as the bookings continued and provided Klaus the Louse behaved by not turning up drunk and disorderly, she would be content with the arrangement. Proof of this came when she told me, 'With an older man at your side I will know you are safe from those who would wish to seduce you, Sylvia.'

'Have you smelled his breath?' I cried, indignantly. 'It is shield sufficient! No knight or paramour may venture close enough to touch me!'

However, she knew that I would do nothing to create a disruption because of my learning Greek and Arabic from Master Israel. As with music, I found language came naturally to me. If others (I speak mostly of Father Paulus and occasionally Master Israel) pronounced me clever, I did not think this of myself. Sounds, whether the notes to a song, the mimicking of another's voice, bird calls or the pronunciation of words in a language other than my own, I found most easy to retain and once told, or in some cases with Arabic, perhaps twice, I could remember them. This facility was a gift from God and while I constantly thanked Him for it, I did not have the right to boast of it. Moreover, I had the advantage of constant practice, as I could converse with the Greek and Arab girls at Ali Baba's. I soon learned all the tribal and regional accents as well, for the Egyptians, though similar, do not speak the same as the Syrians or the Persians or the Arabic spoken in Jerusalem that Master Israel was wont to teach me.

With the written word I was less sure. Mastering the quill and the letters to the Latin and German alphabet was not as easily undertaken. I needed much more practice, and so there was mounting pressure placed upon me to enter a nunnery where I might completely learn calligraphy.

Father Paulus would laugh at my efforts. 'Sylvia, in the matter of the goose quill, thou art the goose!' I think he was secretly pleased that this did not come to me as effortlessly as Latin verbs or, for that matter, chess. At that game I was now often the winner and he increasingly the pupil. This was not the same with Master Israel, who had a cunning and a guile when playing that was beyond my years and experience and he often left me floundering and totally bemused.

And so the time drew near when I was to meet Father Hermann and Father Paulus together. These combined meetings did not occur often although I saw both almost daily – Father Hermann with the street poor and, of course, Father Paulus for my Latin lessons. I was certain that now I was almost fourteen they were meeting with me to discuss my entering a convent, and though they seemed sure that this was the best next step for me I was far from decided on this course. The idea of being shut up in a cell to rise each morning not long after the midnight hour to pray, and then to be cut off from the world around me, did not serve my needs. I had grown fond of the city where I was free to be myself and now I must once again be subject to the will of others. I was doing God's work every morning among the destitute children and could not see why I would serve Him better in a cloister. The only temptation lay in the promise of learning, so I needed to decide whether the sacrifice of my freedom was a worthy price. No, I do not tell the truth, there was within me a hunger for the touch of a man. I knew all there was to pleasing a male yet I had never even kissed one. The girls at the *winkelhaus* laughed when I said I felt a strange stirring and that when a pretty knight approached me I felt a melting in my thighs. 'Sylvia, we will find the right one for you, gentle and kind, but knowing well how to please a woman.'

'You mean men must also know these pleasuring things you have taught me?' I asked, amazed.

'Aye, there are some few that give as much as they get – they know a woman's needs and give great pleasure – but they are rare and you must be patient. You are a great prize and we do not wish you to give of yourself lightly. Also, it must coincide with your periods so that you do not become pregnant.'

'But I cannot while . . . you know, when they are upon me?'

'Nay, but just after, you must let us know.'

Of course, the girls had taught me the various new ways I might pleasure myself other than that shown to me by the widow Johanna. Some of the courtesans preferred each other for their pleasure and they regarded men simply as a means of gain. They offered to pleasure me thus, but while I judge them not, this was not for such as me. In my heart I knew it was not the same, that I hungered for the hardness of a man. I was aware that my thoughts were sinful and that God did not wish me to give my body to another simply for the experience of knowing a man. If I should take a partner then God required that I did so in order to produce offspring. I was not ready to take this course or to become a bride of Christ and never taste the physical love of a man. So I was caught between the devil and the deep blue sea.

Therefore, you see, I was miserable and weak and not worthy and, moreover, not ready to take the vow of chastity. How might I tell the two priests of my dilemma? These were two holy men sworn to celibacy and most anxious to help a young peasant girl who, unbeknownst to them, woke up wet between her thighs most mornings, then pleasured herself, writhing and moaning, as she imagined the arms of a man about her and his glorious rod within her. This was a maid who they thought was innocent of the ways of the world but, in truth, knew every manner there was to pleasure a man. They saw me as a gifted and specially blessed instrument of God, a child chosen by Jesus the Saviour unto His calling and, woe is me, I knew myself for what I was.

And now I must make yet another confession, whether good or bad at the beginning I cannot say. If I am to suffer guilt for my conduct in the matter, this was only to happen at a much later time. I can now say the ultimate result was a great disaster and I will do penance for the remainder of my life in an effort to obtain forgiveness for the part I played in it. Whether it all came from this incident I cannot be sure, but it concerns Nicholas and myself and Ruth's Truth, Frau Sarah's magic mushrooms.

Although two years younger than me, there was much of the natural leader about Nicholas, and the other street children would do his bidding without question whereas they would obey no one else. With Reinhardt departed, Nicholas now became my friend and sometime confidant, although a young boy, no matter how trustworthy, cannot grasp the complexity of a woman's life or understand her innermost feelings, so that only the simple things could be shared: attending morning mass together; working with the street children; begging for food to give to the poor from the market stall-holders. We would laugh secretly together at Father Hermann's thinking himself the Virgin's husband and when asked a question to which he knew not the answer he would say, 'I must ask my wife, she will know.' Or once when he said, 'Our child Jesus cried all night from teething, but by the morning all His teeth had appeared neatly in a row, top and bottom, so that He could eat the toughest meat for dinner that very same night!' We suited each other well in friendship, for as it turned out, although he had been a street child from the age of six, he had a father living in Cologne, who, like my own, was a drunk and a ne'er-do-well who possessed a reputation for thuggery and violence. Nicholas preferred living on the streets to the unhappy and violent hovel his father provided as his home. Like me, he also wanted to know more of the workings of God's word, although, unlike me, he thought that he might do this by becoming a priest, though he was not yet old enough to enter a monastery, whereas I did not wish to become a nun other than to learn Latin calligraphy.

Frau Sarah had on more than one occasion told me that the mushroom was best used to look inward to see what it might be that caused us to think as we did and to reveal to us the unknown parts to our hidden and secret selves. 'If taken, it will often show you a path you have not previously considered that, if followed, may bring you reward,' she'd once said.

With the constant urging from the two priests to enter a holy order and my wicked morning writhings, my desire to learn and the meeting coming up, I was in a quandary over what I should do. I finally decided that I would try Ruth's Truth, the magic mushrooms, to see if they could clarify my mind. Frau Sarah had long since shown me the amount and how to prepare the mushroom, although she had advised me that someone should be present during its taking. 'You will see strange things, some even fearful,' she had cautioned me. So I asked her if she would be the one to stay with me while I was in the trance. 'Sylvia, the trance may last a full day or beyond or only an hour. It will have to wait until I have a day available. Perhaps when Israel travels on business or to visit his cousin, the silk merchant in Bonn, otherwise I must be here with him or he will give away the shop. You know how hopeless he is with money.'

It was as good as saying she did not possess the time. Master Israel seldom travelled beyond Cologne these days and besides, Frau Sarah was ever the busy one, whether he was present or not, and of late it was she who travelled quite often to Bonn. I hadn't ever told Reinhardt about Ruth's Truth as I knew he would not be able to resist the temptation to partake of the mushroom and would almost certainly use the knowledge unwisely. But now with him gone, I decided to ask Nicholas if he would tarry with me.

'Aye, Sylvia,' he agreed, then naturally asked, 'This mushroom, what does it do?'

'There is little I may tell you other than what I have myself been told,' I replied. 'I will go into a trance that may last an hour or half a day and then experience visions inwardly.'

'Like Father Hermann and the Virgin?'

'Nay, this is not come about from piety. At least I think not.'

'What then?'

'I know not, some substance contained in the mushroom.'

'Will it harm you?'

'Not if it is taken in the correct dose and manner.'

'But, if it should last half a day, where will we do this? In the church after morning mass?'

'Nay, the woods. It is summer and we can leave early and hope to find the mushroom and then tarry in some safe place. I know a small cave beside a great beech tree where no soul will disturb us. I will bring food and drink, bread and perhaps a smoked trout and a jug so that we can get fresh water from a stream. I have been cautioned not to partake of wine.'

And so, two days later Nicholas and I set off at dawn for the woods. Daylight came as we climbed the hill and we were well searching for the mushroom when we heard the Angelus ring. Although we found various kinds, even some we could eat, we found not a single one of Ruth's Truth. We would do this three times and with the meeting with my two priests drawing closer I was becoming most anxious. Then on the fourth morning we finally found what we were looking for and repaired to the small cave I had discovered while exploring in the woods.

'Nicholas, there is a special way to prepare this and I regret I cannot show you how it is done.'

Like all boys he asked, 'Why?'

'I have sworn to keep this as women's knowledge, it is a secret ancient and profound.' Then I asked him to return in about half an hour and to call out as he approached. I handed him the black earthenware jug and pointed deeper into the woods. 'Will you fill this from the spring we passed and bring it back with you? If I am already in a trance, place it beside the food to my front so that I may use it should I become thirsty,' I instructed.

But Nicholas, accepting the jug, was not yet ready to depart. 'What mean you by women's knowledge, Sylvia? Cooking is women's knowledge, but it is not secret and a man may know it if he wishes.'

'Ah, but sometimes the herbs used in flavouring, they may be a woman's secret. Or other herbs used to heal, their nature and uses *only* women know about. This mushroom and its preparation has been known *only* to women healers for hundreds of years and they have sworn not to reveal its secret except to women who they consider appropriate to the knowledge.' I knew that if I told him this was knowledge possessed by

Jewish women herbalists he would think I was partaking of the devil's work. In fact, I was not altogether certain of this myself. In Christian terms, that is, to the Christian peasant, this mushroom was named Satan's Shadow. I was placing my faith in Frau Sarah and not in the folklore of my own people.

'Aye, healing is a woman's work. That I well understand. I have seen you use unguents and medicine of your own making on all of us. But this is not some cut or bruise, festering ulcer or stomach ache. It is not the same and inward visions do not heal.'

I had learned a great deal about herbal mixtures from Frau Sarah and now used them to help the people of the street. Nicholas's question was a good one. All I could think to say was, 'Ah, but what of the spirit? It may heal the spirit. Take prayer, is it not healing? Is it not inward vision? We are not all, like Father Hermann, blessed with holy visions we can clearly see, but we know they exist and feel them naturally as they heal our spirit while we pray. This, you may say, is just as natural, for a mushroom is also God's work. If He has caused it to induce visions that are safe and heal the spirit and instruct the mind, are they not to be tried?'

Nicholas looked doubtful and I knew my logic faulty. 'Sylvia, I ask only because I don't want anything to harm you,' he said, somewhat tremulously, and I saw, to my surprise, that he loved me.

'Nicholas, I have chosen you above any to be my guardian. Will you do it for me? Please?'

'Aye, I have said I would.' He hesitated, then stammered, 'But if it should not turn out well I will call Father Hermann, he knows much of visions.'

'Aye, if you must.' I could not tell him to call Frau Sarah, for the reasons I have already stated, and thinking I would not come to any harm I agreed that he could call the priest.

'Then one more thing,' Nicholas asked. 'If all goes well with you, will you let me take the mushroom?'

I nodded. 'If all goes well, yes. But you may tell none. Not even

Father Hermann, unless you have cause to call him. It *must* be our secret. Do you understand?'

'Aye,' he said.

'Nay! Nay! Nicholas! You *must* swear it on your life!'

He placed his hand to his heart. 'I swear it on my life,' he said.

'Before Almighty God.'

Nicholas looked hurt. 'You know you can trust me, Sylvia.'

'Before Almighty God!' I repeated. 'Swear it, Nicholas!'

'Before Almighty God,' he proclaimed loudly, smiling the while at my insistence.

'In four hours you must give me food and water if I do not ask for sustenance myself,' I instructed. 'If the vision persists beyond daylight, then you must lead me home by the hand. Only call Father Hermann if I do not prove compliant.'

'But you said only half a day?'

'Aye, perhaps not even that. But just in case, eh?'

He nodded. 'Now be off and return as I asked. Don't forget the water,' I said, smiling. As he walked away I cried, 'Nicholas, I care greatly that you are my friend!' I felt that he would have wished me to say that I loved him. But there was about him much of the zealot and once said he might dwell on it in a mawkish manner, and I would lose him as a friend as he sought to occupy a greater place in my heart than I could bring myself to feel. Nicholas did not turn about but threw both his hands above his head, the black jug in one of them glinting in the sunlight, whether pleased or upset I couldn't say.

I began to prepare the mushroom as Frau Sarah had instructed. The method I may not reveal here as it does not deny my original promise to tell the whole truth about my life. A secret held a thousand years or more by women of one religious persuasion is not to be summarily revealed by women of another. There is an instinctive trust among good women that men may never understand.

Nicholas returned soon after I had consumed a portion of the prepared mushroom and placed the jug next to the food in front of me and then went to sit on an adjacent rock. I did not speak with him as already I began to feel light-headed. I tried to focus on a root from the beech tree that had grown across the surface of the rock he sat upon and then entered the ground on the other side, as if it was a rope binding the rock to the ground. Nicholas had chosen the spot well as he could observe me seated cross-legged at the entrance to the small cave without disturbing me. I had sat in this position a thousand times in the woods at home when I had practised imitating the bird calls, and found it most comfortable and conducive to concentration, more so even than when one kneels in prayer. Although I don't suppose kneeling before God is supposed to be comfortable.

For some time nothing seemed to happen and then to my surprise, for I did not see it occurring, the trees about me had turned a brilliant purple and their trunks bright yellow. The cave sat at the edge of a small clearing so that the sun shone brightly onto the part of the grass the shade from the tree failed to reach. The grass had now turned light blue, the shaded parts a deeper hue, and the patch of sky showing above me had taken on a pale green colour, like the green of a daffodil shoot. In my mind all seemed perfectly natural and I wasn't in the least disturbed by the recolouration of the world around me, except that Nicholas had disappeared, although the rock upon which he sat was still there but now appeared transparent as if made of glass. Embedded within it I saw a silver object and I rose, or in my vision I rose (in fact, throughout the trance I remained seated), and with my stave in hand approached the object set in the rock.

As I drew closer I saw that it was a large fish, perhaps half the length of my arm. I recall thinking that with all else recoloured why did the fish remain silver as any fish might be? But there was one feature to it I had not seen before. The fish possessed a brilliant blue eye that seemed to be watching me. I touched the rock with my stave and at once it shattered into a million particles that fell around the fish to form a pillow on which it now rested. The pillow, light as a dandelion, rose before my eyes until it sat in the air above me like a small cloud, though growing all the while bigger, with the fish also increasing in size. The cloud containing the fish continued to rise into the green sky directly above the clearing. I watched, standing on the blue grass, as the cloud rose to the height of the steeple of St Mary's on the Kapitol, and was now grown sufficiently for the fish upon it to be the size of a horse, its great blue eye never for one moment leaving me.

Two dark shadows, which I then saw were great hands with their fingers spread, appeared above the cloud. Moments later the fish opened its mouth and from it issued in pairs, male and female, every bird of the air from the blue tit and the robin to the eagle and the albatross, each pair calling out until the air was filled with such a cacophony that I must perforce drop my stave and place my hands to my ears or be driven mad by the pitch and screeching.

The dark hands disappeared and birds now circled the cloud and began to peck at the fish until they had devoured it, leaving only the head and the tail, then the birds commenced to peck at the cloud until finally only a wisp remained. Then this too was gone and the fish skeleton hung but a moment longer, then plunged to the earth, and even in the plunging the eye watched me steadfastly. It fell at my feet now no larger than when I had first seen it within the rock and bouncing landed back again, balanced on its tail. In an instant wings grew from its gills and its fishy skeletal bones, still intact, began to turn to flesh and then skin black as ink. Its tail divided to form two legs with dreadful claws for feet and then arms appeared. Suddenly there stood a winged imp, bold as brass, with its arms bent and hands held to its waist, its dark and wicked wings flapping with evil intent.

The creature stood no higher than my knees, black with no hair to its shiny burnished skull and a tail that stretched to a fleshy arrowhead many times as long as the creature itself. Only the blue eyes of the fish remained within its wicked-looking face that possessed no nose, but for two pumping holes and a bony fish's mouth of tiny needle-sharp bloodstained teeth. And all the while the screeching of the birds continued and the air around me vibrated with the fluttering of their wings.

The creature's long tail began to thrash like a whip upon the blue grass, raising small puffs of bright pink dust, its mouth opening and closing as if it would talk with me, but with the bird cries I could not hear its voice. Then, fast as lightning, the tail came round and wound tight about my ankles several times and the tiny hands of the devilkin grabbed at its own extended tailpiece and jerked me off my feet. I lay hard against the ground, though strangely I felt no impact as I fell. I looked up and saw the tiny devil standing over me and from his front protruded a monstrous blue-veined hardened penis I knew at once to be my father's vile protruberant. Then the devil, his long tail unwinding about my ankles, his dark wings spread wide, lowered himself upon me and I knew he would surely enter me. I reached for where my stave had fallen to retrieve the dagger from its top but grasped instead its end that turned into a serpent that I now held by the tail. Afraid to release it, I aimed it to strike in the manner of a whip at the creature. The great snake rose high into the air and arched, then struck deeply into the flesh of the imp and as it did the creature turned back into the fish that now lay harmless between my legs, its fishy eye gone cold and dead.

'Sylvia! Sylvia!' I heard calling in the distance, then closer and closer as my name was called again and again and slowly I began to feel someone tugging at me. Then, quite suddenly, I was out of the trance and staring into Nicholas's frightened face. He knelt in front of me with his eyes grown wide and his hands upon my shoulders shaking me. I still sat cross-legged as before but now I held my stave poised in one hand above my head. I was also aware that my clothes were soaked with sweat and my face wet from weeping. I felt something upon my lap and saw that the smoked trout I had brought for our sustenance now lay head and tail alone connected with its bones stripped bare of flesh. In front of me the loaf of bread was missing from where I had placed it upon a small rock with only a few crusts and crumbs on the ground next to the black water jug that now lay smashed into several pieces.

I had experienced my first mushroom trance and now Nicholas explained what he had seen me do during the course of it. 'Sylvia, all went well at first and you smiled and laughed and clapped your hands and it seemed you were having a right merry time. Then you reached for your stave and commenced to strike the end into the loaf of bread until it broke into several pieces. It was then that I was myself distracted for the birds in the woods were screeching and I glanced to the sky to see two falcons looking for prey. When I looked back you held your hands to your ears and the expression on your face was as if the anxiety of the birds and their urgent screeching hurt your ears. Then you uttered the cry of the falcon and the two circling above immediately flew away and you commenced to call all the birds unto you as if you wished to calm them. They soon surrounded you as I have previously seen them do and now commenced to eat the broken loaf and pick with their beaks at the trout, feasting on the bread and the fish as you watched. Then when they had eaten the bread and removed the flesh from the fish, a large black crow came flying in and scattered them and then attempted to lift the remains of the fish from the ground. But as you well know the sudden arrival of a crow means bad luck and I thought it time to wake you. Then the crow holding in its beak the fish with head and tail and bones observed my approach and flapping its wings it lifted the carcass into the air above your head. But the fish proved too weighty and fell back onto your lap. Whereupon I saw you reach for your stave and strike at the water jug and smash it asunder. You were crying out in terror, gasping and weeping, and so I thought to wake you if I could.'

When I had recovered sufficiently to be about my wits, I found myself bitterly disappointed. I had received no insights into my mind, no vision of eternal truth and no guidance. To my dismay the explanation for everything seemed simple enough.

The mushrooms had caused me to hallucinate so that one thing became another and it did not take me long to work out how each of the objects had caused the vision to come about. The rock that became translucent was either the small rock on which I had placed the bread and beside it the trout to keep them from the dirt or, alternatively, it was the rock upon which Nicholas sat, although I think the former for in the vision he did not appear seated upon it. This explained my striking the bread that then turned into a pillow on which the trout lay and this then became a rising cloud with the fish upon it. The two falcons, which I had seen as two great dark hands above the cloud and the screeching of the birds alarmed at the presence of the birds of prey, became the birds fleeing from out of the fish's mouth.

Then, according to Nicholas, I had caused the falcons to fly away and the birds to calm by calling them to me. They had landed all about me, hence the fluttering of the wings and, naturally enough, they had devoured the bread and the fish, in other words the cloud and the fish upon it, squabbling all the while to continue the cacophony I had first heard.

The crow arriving to stand in front of me became the imp, or perhaps part of it, its wings and feet, the black earthenware jar with its two handles on either side making his arms and the fish its visage. Together they gave the tiny demon wings, arms, legs, a fish's nostrils and mouth with sharp teeth and the eyes of either the crow or the fish. My stave became a serpent and I had struck the black jar, thinking it the devilkin. The wetness I had supposed was sweat was in fact the water from the jar that had splashed over me when I had broken it.

It all fitted neatly except the tail the tiny devil carried. This too I solved soon enough. It was the beech-tree root that crossed the rock upon which Nicholas sat. The only thing I couldn't solve was the huge blue-veined and bone-white appendage between the cacodemon's legs that I knew to belong to my father. But when I cogitated I could see that it was the fish possibly held by the tail in the beak of the crow as it attempted to escape, its head and skeleton making my father's appendage. His wanton actions and the birthmark on my back had possessed my spirit since childhood and were ever-present in my mind. These two things had been the cause of everything that had happened to me, and so I was forced to conclude they had naturally emerged as the most apprehensive components in my hallucinatory state.

I told Nicholas the sequence of events throughout the trance that had, I discovered to my surprise, occurred over a period of four hours, although I did not mention the final aspect concerning my father. He listened wide-eyed and amazed, then said, 'And all this happened in your mind! Just think, you are now a receiver of visions, Sylvia.'

'Nay, Nicholas, think upon it a moment. They were not visions such as experienced by Father Hermann or, in the past, by the saints. What I saw were merely objects that lay in front of my eyes that became changed in my imagination. This is not of the spirit but of the mind and seems to me to contain no value or even serve as a useful insight. I carry no wisdom from it, except the appearance of the crow as an omen of bad luck, and I cannot bring myself to think as others do that the appearance of a crow or jackdaw is the harbinger of misfortune. All birds live in God's world and only man is capable of original sin. As for myself, I shall not hurry to repeat this experience, as I was greatly frightened at the latter stages.'

'But you came to no harm from this tiny winged devil?'

'Aye, but it frightened me.'

'But no harm,' he insisted.

'Aye, no harm, it was only the fabric of my imagination, objects changed to other things.'

'Then I must have some of this mushroom for myself.'

'Nay, Nicholas, it was not a pretty experience.'

'What of the colours, the trees, grass and the green sky – I have never seen a green sky or blue grass or trees the colour you describe except near enough in autumn.'

'They are no prettier in the new colours, in fact not pretty at all. God made them the right colours from the start and gave them new colours in the autumn to satisfy all our needs.'

'You promised that if you came to no harm I might try the mushrooms for myself,' he insisted, now all young-boy sulk. 'If you break your promise I will not trust you again, Sylvia,' he threatened.

'Very well, but it is almost noon. I have a Latin lesson with Father Paulus at two o'clock and then Greek later. Perhaps we may do it tomorrow morning, eh?'

'Nay, we do not know if the mushrooms act the same if they are not freshly picked. What if we cannot find others on the morrow?' He looked at me, pleading. 'It took us three days to find the ones this morning. Please, can we do it now, Sylvia? There is time. I promise. I am younger than you, my trance will be over the sooner!'

But it wasn't. Nicholas finally came out of his trance at sunset when we barely had time to get back to Cologne to change for the evening where I had to perform at a rich merchant's birthday party. After my trance that morning and waiting all the afternoon for Nicholas to come out of his, I wasn't much looking forward to the evening spent with Klaus the Louse and a roomful of noisy drunken burghers and their wives.

Nicholas hadn't moved during the entire afternoon and now said almost nothing on the way home, but instead kept repeating, 'Yes, Lord! Yes, Jesus!' in a most fervent and ecstatic voice, his eyes turned heavenwards. Every once in a while he'd suddenly exclaim, 'Jerusalem!', just the one word. I could see his eyes were strange as if not focused, his face wore a look I had not seen before and he seemed to barely notice my presence beside him.

'Are you all right?' I asked him. He nodded but did not speak. 'What did you see, Nicholas?' I asked.

'Jerusalem.'

'Jerusalem? You saw Jerusalem?'

'Yes, Lord. Yes, Jesus,' he answered or repeated, I cannot say, for his eyes were cast heavenwards.

He lived behind St Mary's on the Kapitol and I stayed with him until we reached the church to be sure he was safely home. But instead of joining the other street children in the alley where they slept he entered the church. I followed and he walked up to the high altar where he collapsed to his knees, then prostrated himself, all the while calling out, 'Jerusalem!' I knew him to be safe within the church and so made my departure as I was already late and would barely have time to change my clothes before Frau Sarah sent the horse and cart to fetch me to the merchant's house.

Though I am a peasant born, it is ill-fitting when a peasant gains great wealth but with it gains no knowledge or self-improvement. Master Wilhelm, whose birthday party I attended, had made a great fortune when he'd started importing muslin from Egypt and then it was other cloth – damask and silk and, most curious of all, at the most humble end of weaving, hessian for grain bags. In the process he had gained great wealth and could now command the respect of the nobility and claimed a worthy place in the society of Cologne. If ever there was an illustration that money does not purchase manners, it was the goings-on at his birthday party.

If you think because I'd had a few lessons in deportment and good manners and the advantage of seeing how manners work in society that I am coming the high lofty, this was not the case. There were both nobility and old acquaintances at the party and both behaved as badly as the other did. It was just that the peasant does not perceive the grossness he allows and thinks it natural that all should become drunk – the women loud and brazen and the men groping and licentious.

While none took notice of my singing, this was the least of it. Soon there was coupling to be seen in every dark corner and in some places not so dark. As it grew to a later hour both men and women took to spewing out of windows and on several occasions the servants were summoned to clean the floor. I was groped in passing by leering and drunken burghers with Klaus the Louse, drunk himself, unable to, or uninterested in, protecting me. So much for Frau Sarah's older man ever at my side to keep me safe.

Finally, Master Wilhelm, the birthday boy, grabbed me to his vile breast. He was a grossly fat man with his hose near down to his plump knees and his tunic only half covering his huge belly, though fortunately this vile flesh overhung and successfully concealed his one-eyed snake. He pushed me against the wall and tore my gown from my shoulders and started trying to hump me, kissing and covering my breasts with his drunken slobbering, his fat fingers groping my bottom. This was much to the amusement of the other drunks who, both male and female, screamed and clapped in huge delight, egging him on with cries of encouragement.

By this time I had had enough – I was entertainer and not hired whore – and I tore at his face with my nails. 'Bitch!' he screamed, releasing me and grabbing at his jowl. If his previous fondling was considered amusing, then my scratching became the highest humour of the night and the guests howled and fell about with laughter as the fat bastard withdrew his hand to reveal the blood that now flowed from his puffed and purple-spotted peasant's cheek.

Grabbing my stave I ran from the house where fortuitously our cart and driver waited outside. 'Klaus will not be coming back with us,' I said, hurriedly jumping into the back. He must have noted my dishevelment, but as with all cart drivers, he customarily saw and knew nothing, having known and seen every form of human bad behaviour worth the knowing and seeing.

'Home is it then, Miss?' he asked nonchalantly. Then geeing his horse we set off for my lodgings, well past the midnight hour.

The next morning I arrived at St Mary's on the Kapitol where Nicholas and I would attend mass together and afterwards meet Father Hermann prior to working among the street children. We would distribute bread among them and tend to some of their other needs, both spiritual and physical. In the summer they did suffer much from ulcers to their legs and arms and Frau Sarah had shown me a preparation that contained the jelly of the African aloe that did help exceedingly to diminish their suffering. You may imagine my surprise to find Father Hermann and Nicholas on the church steps with maybe two hundred children gathered about them. Moreover, Nicholas stood on the uppermost step, and as I drew closer I realised that he was preaching and that the children cried ecstatically at his every word.

Father Hermann brought a finger to his lips, cautioning me to be quiet as I came to stand beside him. It took but a few moments to realise that the sermon Nicholas preached was both simple and profound and greatly affected the children kneeling below him. I have said before that he was a natural leader, but he had never been one to preach and led mostly by example or direct command. But now he had about him a compelling attraction – it was as though the zealot I had sensed in him now fully possessed his character. Whatever he had seen in his mushroom trance, it had affected him greatly and now his eyes blazed with a burning faith.

Nicholas's sermon came to an end shortly afterwards and Father Hermann could not contain himself. 'Nicholas, what has happened? You have found God today in a different way from yesterday! You seem profoundly blessed, how came this about?' he cried out.

'I have seen our Lord, Jesus Christ, in a vision,' Nicholas said simply.

My heart sank. He had promised on his life and sworn in God's name not to tell about the magic mushrooms. Now, the very next day, he was about to confess all to a priest. With his newfound possession of a vision of Christ Jesus, if questioned further he would be compelled to reveal what had happened. I dared not interrupt to stop his confession by announcing that we ought to be going, that it was getting too late to beg from the market people the food we needed to distribute to the poor, that once the markets get started the stall-holders will not stop to sort out the poor-quality produce for alms giving.

'You have seen the Christ figure? Where? You have both been absent for three mornings and I did not see you at mass yesterday or the day before or even the day before that. Did you look into the sacristy where the small Virgin and Child stands and here receive your vision of Christ Jesus?'

Nicholas pointed upwards to the hills where the woods lay. 'Nay, in the woods. I found a small cave I had not seen before and did stop to pray, as it seemed a quiet and untroubled place.' Nicholas then looked directly at Father Hermann. 'Then Jesus of Nazareth appeared to me in a vision.'

'This cave? Could you find it again, Nicholas?' I said, feigning excitement. Then turning to Father Hermann, I asked, 'Would not such a quiet and untroubled place where our Saviour appeared to Nicholas be regarded as holy?'

'Aye, even a place of pilgrimage,' the priest replied excitedly. 'Will you take us to this holy cave, Nicholas?'

I had prevented Nicholas from telling Father Hermann about the magic mushrooms and so also saved myself from discovery.

'You would go now, Father?' Nicholas asked.

'Aye, God's work cannot wait. We must go there at once. You said you could find it again?'

'Aye, I think easily enough. It has pieces from a broken jug lying at its entrance and a rock beside it with the root of a tree growing over it as if the root is a rope that doth hold it fast to the ground,' Nicholas said, taking my own description for himself.

So, alas, that morning the children of the street would go unattended as the three of us climbed the hill behind the city and repaired once more to the tiny cave that now held a spiritual significance to the good priest. Father Hermann fell to his knees as we reached the cave and we were forced to do the same. Nicholas now seemed himself to be in earnest prayer, as if it was indeed a place where a great vision had taken place and deserved the sanctity the priest now allowed it. Two zealots on their knees and me, in this instance, turned unbeliever. '*To thine own self be true*' – Master Israel's words rang clearly in my mind.

Rising at last from his knees Father Hermann turned to say something and then his eyes grew wide. 'Look!' he exclaimed, pointing to the ground at his feet where the skeleton of yesterday's fish lay. 'And there!' he exclaimed again, pointing this time to a crust of bread that remained uneaten by the birds. 'Christ's loaves and fishes!' He stared incredulously at Nicholas and I at him, amazed at his naivety. 'You have seen Jesus and have eaten miraculously of the food He prepared when He preached to the multitudes in the desert!'

I could not tell him it was the loaf and the trout I had brought for our own sustenance, as I wasn't supposed to know about the cave. I waited for Nicholas to explain but he remained silent. Then the priest took us by our shoulders and bade us fall to our knees once more while he prayed. He thanked the precious Saviour again for His appearance to the child, Nicholas of Cologne, and then for giving him to eat of the bread of heaven and the fish from the Sea of Galilee. Then he promised Christ Jesus that the cave would henceforth be known as 'The Shrine of Bread and Fish'. Which was how it was known henceforth and until a few years later when it became a place of pilgrimage for children and was renamed among the populace of Cologne as 'The Children's Shrine', this for reasons I will tell about at a later time.

The afternoon of the day following our visit to the cave with the priest I was to meet him and Father Paulus at St Martin's for our discussion. I wakened early that morning, still undecided about entering a nunnery. I dressed and made ready to set out for early-morning mass when the old widow came upstairs to my tiny alcove room to say a small boy had arrived with a message from Frau Sarah and waited at the door of the street.

'Frau Sarah asks that you attend her, Fräulein Sylvia,' the boy informed me.

'What, I must go now? But I must go to mass,' I protested.

'She says it is urgent.'

'Urgent?' I became concerned. 'Is it Master Israel? Has something happened to him?'

'I know not,' the small boy said, his dark eyes earnest. 'It may be, yes.'

I ran all the way through the dirty streets and alleys, my boots splashing through the puddles of freshly thrown nightsoil and urine and the other filth that lay about. I reached the tailor shop blowing like an old carthorse. Banging on the door, I shouted out, 'Frau Sarah! I am here! Open up!'

I could hear her coming from above and then a rattle of chains followed and the door opened. 'Sylvia, what's all the fuss?' she asked calmly.

'Master Israel . . . is he all right?' I panted.

'Of course! Hear for yourself, he still snores blissfully upstairs.'

'A small boy came . . .' I gasped.

'Oh, him. I told him to tell you to come by some time this morning.'

'He said it was urgent, that it was Master Israel.'

'Nay, Sylvia, it is Klaus of Koblenz, he is no longer your lute player.'

'Why? What happened?' I asked, relieved at both pieces of news.

'He was murdered in a low-class *winkelhaus* in the late hours last night,' she said calmly.

'Murdered! But the Angelus has just rung. How know you this already?'

She spread her hands. 'It is my own. I have purchased it recently, a low-class and foul dive, but I have promised the guild I shall attend to it.' She placed her arm about my shoulders. 'Come in, Sylvia, let us be seated, I wish to talk to you.' Then she pointed to my filthy boots. 'You will take them off, please.'

'You have found another lute player?' I asked, as I slipped my boots from my feet.

'Nay, it is more important than that.' She smiled. 'When you and the Pied Piper came to see Master Israel two years ago it changed our fortunes. Sylvia, I want you to know I am grateful.'

When we were seated Frau Sarah once again explained how they had loaned Master Yap money to refurbish Ali Baba's, and then the ratcatcher and I had come along and she'd gone into the entertainment business. 'We have done well together, Sylvia, but it is hard work and not all musicians are like yourself – they are a fickle lot, and even Reinhardt has since departed.'

'Aye, I miss him greatly, it is not the same without him,' I said wistfully.

'Yes, I know. Hence what I have to say to you.' She drew breath and then seemed to think a moment. 'In the past two years I have learned a great deal about the entertainment business, which, as I have just explained, has many ups and downs, though one part within it remains always the same and all the while profitable.'

'The *winkelhaus*?' I asked.

Frau Sarah nodded. 'Master Israel always says you have a quick mind. Yes, it is the only consistent business. The one-eyed snake is king and will forever reign in his palace,' she laughed. 'So I have purchased this new one with my brother, Master Abraham,' she smiled. 'You will see, we will make it even better than Ali Baba's.'

'And of your entertainment business, what?'

'Titch! It has served me well, but I have had enough of recalcitrant lutes and prancing fruits,' she said, no doubt referring to Reinhardt.

'You would forsake it?'

'Aye, but not you, Sylvia. We, my brother and I, have also purchased a licence for a *winkelhaus* in Bonn and this one will be most splendid and of the highest class in the land. In Cologne you are known as the Petticoat Angel and are much taken up with priests and the poor. In Bonn you are known only for your wonderful voice. If you will agree to be the singer in the new *winkelhaus* there, we will give you a quarter share of the brothel we have purchased in Cologne.'

'Where Klaus was murdered?'

'Aye, but it is but a small thing – murder happens all the time as you well know and he was a man of little worth and no character. We will soon change it to be a high-class establishment and most profitable.' She smiled. 'My brother says that you have a way with the courtesans and they happily do your bidding. I know that you speak most of their languages. We will teach you the business in Bonn, so that when you are older and no longer wish to sing you will always be well provided for by running and owning a part of the *winkelhaus* in Cologne.'

It was an astonishing and generous offer and brought me immediately to tears. If Frau Sarah had gained from my singing, I had received much more from Master Israel and from her wages sufficient to eat and help the poor. If I received nothing else from them I had been generously, even lovingly, compensated. Now she had made me an offer that exceeded the bounds of generosity.

However, as so often seemed to happen in my life, I was forced to choose between the spirit and the flesh – bride of Christ or brothel-keeper? This then was the question I needed to ask myself. Alas, I wish I could say the choice was simple and that God's calling to serve Him as a nun was of paramount importance. But I had much to consider. You may ask how a child of God could also be a brothel-keeper? I must reply that if a bishop and an archbishop could attend a place such as this then why would it be thought a godless and wicked vocation?

I did not feel I had the fortitude to be a nun, although I greatly desired to do God's work among the poor. Father Hermann preached that the spiritual need of the poor was far greater than their need for food and care, that with their souls once prepared for paradise where they would never know hunger, it was far better for them to die. 'They are no different to mangy bare-ribbed dogs that scavenge in the gutters, Sylvia. But their souls, once saved, are eternal,' he'd piously explained. 'For them to continue to live is only to perpetuate their misery. When they die they enter paradise!'

But, while I could not argue with a priest, I also could not accept his sanctimonious logic. Children with their bellies empty, their tiny mouths covered with blisters and sores, with suppurating ulcers on their legs and arms, were in my opinion ill-equipped to accept God's promise of eternal life. They beheld only greed and the devil's work around them and saw no sudden virtue in the promise that the hunger in their souls would be satisfied while they continued to suffer empty bellies and abject misery. As a nun I would be cloistered in a convent and, while hopefully studying, would have no access to the street children I truly loved, whereas, if I should prosper in business, I would have the means to feed and care for the poor and also have access as the rich do to further learning.

'I am grateful for all you and Master Israel have done for me, Frau Sarah,' I said, tearfully. 'This new thing is most tempting, but I must pray upon it.'

Frau Sarah sighed. 'I told my husband it would be thus. Why will you never learn that God helps those who help themselves, Sylvia? We have learned that others, the priest that teaches you and the other one with whom you work, wish you to become a nun. Master Israel and I, who seldom agree on much, are both agreed that to shut a mind such as you possess in a cloister is a sin against God.'

'Hush, Frau Sarah, that is blasphemy!' I cried, alarmed.

'Not to a Jew, Sylvia. To a Jew, to squander the talents God has given you, *that* is blasphemy!'

'To be the bride of Jesus Christ is not a waste of my life!' I exclaimed.

'Aye, exactly what Master Israel said you would say. "Sylvia is of a brilliance seldom encountered, but she will waste it on God and the poor. Both of whom will always be with us, but, alas, she will not," he lamented.' Frau Sarah pulled herself up so that she sat straight-shouldered and stiff-necked. 'Sylvia, I beseech you, *please* think upon this carefully. What you decide will change your life forever. Do not lock all the glory that is thy God-given talent away in a convent.'

'But if it is God-given, then should I not return it?' I asked.

'Titch, you know what your trouble is, Sylvia Honeyeater? You have spent too much time with my husband! Few things in this world are wrought by logic alone and you begin to think like a man! It is men who want to incarcerate you in a convent, not God! Are women not put upon sufficiently by men and are we not prey to their many vicissitudes? Can you not then be a torchbearer for us? Can you not be your own self? Or must you always be servant to the whims of men?'

'Is not running a brothel being servant to the whims of men?' I asked quietly.

'Nay! It is simply profiting from their weakness! This is every woman's given right,' she shouted, her hands flying above her head in exasperation at my foolishness.

'I will think about it, Frau Sarah,' I said softly.

CHAPTER EIGHT

The Reluctant Bride of Christ

IF YOU CAN, IMAGINE my confusion and trepidation when I met with the two priests, the zealot and the scribe. Neither knew my true nature with all its faults but thought me halfway to being a celestial creature. To them I was the Petticoat Angel and they had witnessed the Miracle of the Birds (so-called) and the Miracle of the Blood on the Virgin's Rose (also so-called) and they were quite certain that I was intended as a bride of Christ. Moreover, that I should have an opinion on the matter did not even occur to them.

The meeting took place in a room beside the sacristy of St Martin's and I arrived a few minutes before Father Hermann so that I might apologise for missing my Latin lesson the previous day, when Nicholas had stayed so long in his mushroom trance. Father Paulus laughed instead of chiding me. 'Thank you, my child. I confess I took the opportunity to sleep and dreamed of bells, accursed bells! I hope only that there are no bells in heaven.'

Father Hermann arrived and Father Paulus opened the proceedings, his voice quiet and pitched low. 'Sylvia, we have consulted the bishop in the matter of the convent where you will become a novice and he has personally instructed us that it is to be the Benedictine convent, which stands close to the monastery.'

Father Hermann clapped his hands. 'How fortunate you are, Sylvia,' he boomed. I could see Father Paulus wince, for his was a confidential tone, whereas Father Hermann's peasant voice could easily be heard in the furthermost pew in the main church. 'The convent has a large garden and its woods abut the monastery's grounds and the nuns are, for the most part, fine women of noble birth.'

Ha! I thought to myself. *Who do not dirty their hands with work.*

'The monastery has the finest library in Germany,' Father Paulus continued. 'While you are yet a novice and must endure what all who take the vow must undergo, the abbess will welcome you. The abbot has received a letter from the bishop himself asking that you be given special dispensation to receive the finest tuition available at the hands of Brother Dominic, who is a famous scribe and scholar known to prepare missives for the Pope in Rome. He will put this before the abbess. I have also written to the abbess extolling your virtues. It is in the name of Father Hermann and myself and doth inform the abbess of the convent of your proclivities.'

I was at once overwhelmed. 'Did you not tell the bishop I was but a peasant maid, Father?' I asked, all the while hoping that their letter to the abbess was plainly put and without embellishment.

'Aye and no,' Father Paulus replied. 'It is not usual for the Church to regard a woman as worthy of scholarship but we told the archbishop that we believed you would become another Abbess Hildegard, a female scholar of great note. In the matter of learning you can no longer count yourself a peasant. Besides, the bishop has been told of the sign of the fish, and says he has heard you sing, and has been told by many of the rich burghers and nobles in Cologne who have also heard you that they would welcome you into their homes as a guest. Sylvia, you are known to have dainty manners and to converse on topics in a modest, though by no means superficial, way. You now speak well enough three Bible languages, Latin, Greek and Hebrew, and also the language of the infidel. There are only a few scholars within the Church who can match this. Perhaps the time has come to eschew your peasant beginnings and assume the mantle of a young scholar who has no social position but, if proof is given that they have the proclivity and the intellect, may eventually move freely among all, from peasant to Pope.'

Father Hermann, perhaps feeling himself as the senior priest unable to contribute to this soliloquy, quite suddenly and unexpectedly protested. 'My learned friend Father Paulus forgets that our Lord was a carpenter from common stock. It is no shame to be a peasant. I myself have little learning but move, as did our Lord, with equanimity among all,' he growled.

Father Paulus seemed almost physically struck by his rebuke. 'No shame, Father. Only for the most part a lack of opportunity, many a fine mind may have been lost to us,' he explained in a voice all but disappeared.

'Ha! I have not found the lack of learning a hindrance! Fine minds do not need learning unless they crave it, and in my experience few women, even those of noble birth, put much store in books and are better for it. I grew up in poverty but was afforded instruction by the monks. I hated school and found it a waste of God's time and desired only the consolation of the Virgin Mary. Am I then lost?' Father Hermann asked rhetorically.

'No, no, of course not, you have a fine and pious mind,' Father Paulus replied, anxious not to aggravate the senior cleric any further.

'Perhaps Father Paulus means that a peasant, should he be most gifted, has a difficult path if he does not possess the good fortune to receive the guidance that thee and he do provide for me? Though I do not think myself worthy – without your help I could achieve nothing,' I said as quickly as I might to forestall a further quarrel between the two of them. It was, of course, not true – it was Master Israel who had guided my tender and hungry mind and set it upon the path of learning.

'Hurumph! Thou didst perform two most worthy miracles! That is why you go to do God's work in a convent. The truly blessed of God are of the spirit, *not* the mind.'

'Aye, it is truly thus with thee, Father. Did not the Christ Child receive an apple from thy hands and was there not an annunciation from the Virgin to name you Joseph, her earthly husband?' I said in a further attempt at amelioration.

'Ha! True my child! That did not require me to be learned.' Then he added sanctimoniously, 'Blessed are the pure in heart: for they shall see God.'

I glanced over to Father Paulus who looked mortified for the upset he had caused. I turned and smiled sweetly at Father Hermann. 'Father, though you are indeed a man of the spirit, I think you are over-modest. If you lack so much of learning as you claim, how then could you write the magnificent hymn '*Summi Regis cor aveto*', the first hymn to the Sacred Heart?' I did not allow him to reply but began immediately to sing this somewhat indifferent hymn until it was completed. By which time he had calmed down and wore a smile upon his formerly frosted face.

'Aye, you are a sly one, Sylvia,' he declared, suddenly laughing. Then turning to Father Paulus, 'And I am stubborn as an ox led to the plough on a late-autumn morning. You are right, my brother in Christ, this one must have every opportunity, both of the spirit and then also of the mind. Although I fear too much learning may rob her of her innocence. Yet she has humility and a reconciling tongue and this may be enough to save her from the scribes who have no faith in Jesus and would compose the world out of facts alone. How do facts explain the scarlet blood on the Virgin's snow-white rose? How do they explain the charming of the birds from the trees or the appearance of an angel to the three whores?'

Father Hermann was back in his stride and I thought of Frau Sarah's lessons in pandering to the male: '*Remember always to bow to their superiority, exclaim at their profundity, compliment their masculinity and sheath your sharpened tongue.*' How could I possibly tell the two priests that I might prefer to run a brothel than enter a convent? I had all but made up my mind to accept Frau Sarah's offer, but now the opening words from Father Paulus had left me confounded. To receive tuition from a famous scholar was an opportunity I would be incredibly foolish to miss.

And so the decision was made, not I fear for the gentle and precious love of Jesus, but for the curiosity of learning and the ability to reason. Already I had acquired sufficient learning to know that I did not want to be told what I should believe. All my life I had been instructed in what was sinful and false and what was true and glorifying when my heart and mind often told me this was not true. My mind craved reason and not Father Hermann's trust in faith alone and I could not see why this should confound my faith in Jesus. I told myself that I believed in miracles as the true manifestation of God's divine presence, but unlike Father Hermann, they must first defy explanation. They must be subject to the most rigorous examination of the mind.

I was beginning to discover that few things in the world I lived in were as I was told they were, or I saw with my own eyes their contradiction. In my own small world, the birds charmed from the trees, the rats in the village, the scene with the three whores in the bathhouse, the blood on the rose, Nicholas and the magic mushrooms and the shrine of bread and fish all possessed logical explanations. Even the coincidence of the birthmark on my back, all were too quickly and with a lack of intellectual examination declared as signs and miracles and all because of ignorance and superstition.

I had come to understand that those who have power invent those truths that will sustain their power and suppress any truth that would destroy it. The examples of this were all about me, yet my ignorance had blinded me. For instance, the hate we have in our hearts for someone not of our own society or nation is inculcated within us in childhood, so that we will know only the perverted version of the truth those in power would want us to possess. Jews are vermin and Christ-killers and may not be trusted as they will lie and cheat and steal your infant and use its blood for their Passover ritual. To hate the Jews who killed our Lord and Saviour is a conviction that pervades Christianity. These are the 'truths' with which we are born. But, if the Jews had not killed Jesus, how then could there be Christianity? If there was no Christian faith, how then would our souls be granted eternal life? Should we not then be grateful to the Jews for giving us our faith and our God? Again, if Christ's death was preordained by God the Father, how then are the Jews guilty if they were merely following His instructions for the salvation of mankind? How do I explain, as Master Israel pointed out to me, that we burn heretics and that to the Jews of that time Christ was seen as a heretic and thus, using our own spiritual logic, was worthy of crucifixion? How do I explain the kindness Frau Sarah and Master Israel showed to me if all Jews are vile, greedy child-killers? Why is it that we may with impunity murder the infidel's women and children without guilt or fear of God's retribution, for they have no soul and so, we are told, are not in God's eyes human. How is it then that the Syrian, Persian and Egyptian courtesans in Ali Baba's are most loving, kind and generous and care greatly for my welfare? Must I believe they are animals without a soul, a dog that, even though kicked by its master, returns to lick his hand?

Master Israel told how, before the First Crusade, when the Christians conquered Jerusalem and slaughtered all the infidels until the alleys ran to the conquerors' knees with the blood, the Christian, Jew and Muslim lived peaceably together, that all religions were free to worship without hindrance. The Holy Sepulchre was open to any Christian pilgrim who wished to sojourn and worship there.

Was the Holy Sepulchre more holy because it was drenched with the blood of Christian revenge? Is it now less holy because it is once more under the guardianship of the infidel? Is God's mercy best illustrated when the Pope announces that a crusade endured in an attempt to regain the Holy Sepulchre will lead to the forgiveness by God of all our past sins? Is it not a denial of God's mercy that, with their sins forgiven, men such as my father return to their villages to commit even greater evil in His sight? Yet with a further crusade completed they may be once again forgiven?

It was the Lord Jesus Himself who said, 'The truth shall make thee free.' Realising that our true enslavement was ignorance I decided I would dedicate my life to finding the truth. Power, I could clearly see, feeds on ignorance and the truth is nourished by minds that are open to enlightenment. In the end, the price I would pay by being a nun cloistered in a convent was a small one if I should know the truth. It would be a truth not gained by reason alone, for reason cannot explain the infinite nature of God or the nature of truth or the truly miraculous. I would use reason guided by the hand of God Almighty to find the truth. I was not to know at the time that in the name of God's truth, I would help to commit a disaster of such unconscionable ignorance that I would suffer its awful guilt for the remainder of my life.

So it was with these high-minded ideals and, looking back upon it, not a small measure of sanctimonious virtue, that I entered the Benedictine convent.

However, before doing so, the girls at Ali Baba's wished to give me a grand farewell party that, they said, they had been forced to delay some days, because a delegation from Munich on business had booked the *winkelhaus* for its exclusive use while in Cologne. So I was forced to plead five extra days in the city from Father Hermann, who was to be my escort to the nunnery.

Frau Sarah insisted that I wear a gown she'd made of peacock-blue Shantung silk obtained from Cathay, the most expensive in her collection. To this she added pretty slippers of a matching colour with a clutch of violets embroidered on the toe of each. She had fussed and tucked until the beautiful gown fitted every curve of my body most seductively. 'You are a beautiful young woman and ripe for plucking, Sylvia,' she sighed, then added, 'Alas, no man will possess this treasure now.' Then she stood aside and looked at me and declared my hair needed further attention and so she treated it with chamomile, then taking up a brush she brushed until it was as burnished as the morning sunlight. Very much pleased with the result she stood back to examine me, then she asked, 'Now Sylvia, I beseech you, you are as pretty as an angel. Just this once, do not take your stave.'

I froze. The stave was my talisman, my protector, almost my Holy Grail. It lay beside my pallet when I slept. It was with me when I attended mass, and always within arm's length when I sang or took my lessons. It was in my right hand when I walked. Father John's stave had become a part of me, as if an additional limb – without it I was naked in spirit and vulnerable. Frau Sarah saw my shock at her suggestion but persisted still.

'Sylvia, tonight there be no maid in Germany more beautiful or better dressed than thee. You are a princess and if I should have had a daughter I would pray to God that she looked as you do now. I fear if my breathing should increase but a little it would see you rise as some lovely ephemeral creature into the air. I have asked a hundred times or even more in the years past that you leave your stave behind and so announce your lightness and beauty, but you have ever resisted and denied me. Now, just this once, this last time I may ever see you and as a departing gift to me, I beg you, do not take that ugly stick tonight.'

'Aye, if you wish,' I said in a whisper. Frau Sarah had done so much for me and I simply couldn't refuse her request, though my heart beat furiously.

The courtesans loved my gown and the three girls from Cathay simultaneously burst into tears as they stroked its beautiful silk. The party was in its nature both merry and sad, for there was much crying and carrying on as we women are wont to do when, as I knew myself to be, a much-loved friend departs. As the midnight hour approached we had drunk much of good wine supplied by Master Yap and all were very merry of spirit. Then Marlena, one of the girls, called out and asked that I should sing 'Cursed be the Linden Trees'. There was much nodding and clapping and cries of approval as it was a favourite at Ali Baba's.

You will remember this song, I feel sure. I shall sing the first two verses to remind you.

I was such a lovely girl
while I flourished as a virgin.
The whole world praised me,
everybody liked me.
Hoy and oe!

Cursed be the linden trees
planted by the way.

When I set out for the meadows
to pick flowers,
a crude fellow decided
to deflower me there.
Hoy and oe!
Cursed be the linden trees
planted by the way.

I began to sing *a cappella* but to my surprise, almost immediately, the beautiful sounds of a lute accompanied me, its player most accomplished. I glanced in the direction of its sound to see a lute held in the playing manner by two male arms that extended from behind a set of drapes that hung from the wall concealing one of the passages that led to the client boudoirs.

All about me the girls could barely contain their giggling, so that I struggled at first to concentrate on the song, wishing all the while to give them of my best voice, as I would never again return to sing for them. Besides, the lute player was better even than I had at first supposed and he challenged my voice and lifted it as Reinhardt had so often done in the past. By the time I approached the last verse all was still but for the two of us. The courtesans, though loose with the wine they had consumed, had grown quiet as they realised the character of the playing and my joyous response to it.

Perchance it was the wine, but I had already fallen in love with the hands that plucked at the beautiful-sounding lute. *What if it is some old codger, slack of limb, his only strident instrument his lute?* I thought to myself. *Such masterful playing is not often found in a young musician.*

The giggling had commenced once again and all eyes were turned on the muslin drapes. Then the lute commenced to play once more, though it was a tune I did not know. At first soft yet loving and then in parts strident, then anxious, and within it I could hear the maiden's plaintive cry. Then followed her delight as her lover held her to his breast, then at last painfully sad, so that to my ear it was the music to a most beautiful love song I would have longed to sing.

I braced myself for a disappointment for I felt myself wet with desire. Then the curtains parted to squeals of delight by the girls who could contain themselves no longer. There stood a young knight perhaps twenty years of age, so beautiful that he took my breath away. The sun had stroked his skin the colour of the finest young leather, his eyes were as blue as mine but the hair that fell to his shoulders was black as a Sicilian's, his lips well fleshed but manly and his nose straight and just a trifle arrogant. He was tall and strong of stature and as he played he walked towards me and smiled, his teeth good and straight and white enough to dazzle. He was perhaps twenty steps away from me, time sufficient for me to note he wore a black velvet tunic with silver buttons to the front, scarlet hose and pointed black leather slippers, and I saw that his codpiece bulged as it constrained the one-eyed snake within.

And now came various girlie cries: 'He's yours, Sylvia!' 'We found him at last and just in time!' 'May we share him, *please*!' 'It is safe – you are five days past the blood!' 'Enjoy, our lovely one!' 'That codpiece doth not lie!' 'Go to thy handsome lover, Sylvia!' 'Time to use what we have taught you!' (Laughter.) And then in Arabic a spate of rapid words from Fatima that cut through all the others: 'Take him as if it will never happen again, love him, possess him, stroke him, bite him, lick him, soothe him, suck him, ride him from the top. Make love to him the way we have taught you until he comes gloriously. Then massage him and sing to him to bring him back to desire. Then scorn him with a brazen voice and challenge him to do for you what you hath done for him. My precious jewel, if you are to be loved by a man but once, let him prove himself worthy, let him break his back for you. Go well, my pretty one!'

By this time the lute player stood in front of me and, still playing, raised his right eyebrow in a query, and then gave the slightest jerk of his head in the direction of the drapes and turned and walked away from me.

'Go, Sylvia! Go, thou! Go now, my lovely! Go!' the girls called out, some clapping their hands at the wonderful mischief unfolding in front of their eyes. I could feel their happiness for me and the delight that all their careful plans were about to be brought to fruition, even to delaying the time for my deflowering until it was safe for me to be loved by a man.

I should like to say I hesitated, overcome by modesty. But I did not. Instead, so as not to interrupt his playing, I ran ahead and opened the drapes for him to enter the passageway where I would for the last time wear my maidenhood. Then to their cheering and laughter I passed through the curtains myself and followed the handsome lute player.

We entered a boudoir specially prepared with the finest silks and draped with flowers such as might be readied for a prince or archbishop. On a small table beside the lovers' couch stood wine and cakes and freshly picked grapes and dried fruits and nuts and with it all a bottle of the finest arousing oil.

The young knight set aside his lute and took me in his arms and kissed me tenderly, his breath free of any rancidity. I thought I would swoon for the feeling to my entire being was more even than I had ever imagined. That so slight a thing, my body held thus by a pair of male arms, should so affect me left me bewildered. 'You are such a pretty maid,' he whispered, 'such a pretty, pretty maid for me to plunder.'

There was no threat contained in this plundering word, only promise, and my desire was for him to take me in any way he wished and urgently. I thought not of Frau Sarah's precious purse and how it should not be opened with impunity. But now I would, without a moment's thought, have opened it, my legs clasped about his back. I was overcome by desire and panting. I craved the divine rod of Eros – my most ardent wish was that it be plunged deep within me, my purse plundered to this sweet knight's heart's desire.

But then Fatima's voice came to me. Above all she had been my most skilful teacher, as she had learned her amorous craft in a sultan's harem and knew every way there was to please a man. 'Sylvia, men are animals who when their blood is up will kill or rape. Even at their tender moments, violence still lingers in their blood. When first they come to you they hunger for thy pussy and think not of you, but only of themselves. Their needs are simple and their pussy plunder is hard and quick and over before there is any benefit for thee. You are left bereft while he is sated, his breathing heavy and his breast content, between his legs his useless rod lies soft and spent.' When she had first told me all this I had thought it very funny and ran to compose a song that they all thought was great fun. I called it 'My Pretty Maid'.

Now, such are the words a maiden doth hear
When a randy knight errant whispers into her ear.

'Come, my pretty maid, feel my true affection,
Take in thy snow-white hand my fine erection.'

For thee, for thee, my pretty maid, for thee.
How happy you must be, I come for thee.

'Prithee, will you remove thy offending dress
To let my pulsing rod thy lovely nest possess.'

For thee, for thee, my pretty maid, for thee.
How happy you must be, I come for thee.

'Let your pretty mouth play on my throbbing prong
And your sweet lips sing the siren's song.'

For thee, for thee, my pretty maid, for thee.
How happy you must be, I come for thee.

'Now let me plant within thee my virile seed.
Through thy gate of Eros comes my prancing steed.'

For thee, for thee, my pretty maid, for thee.
How happy you must be, I come for thee.

Then hear now how fair maid to herself replies
As he groans and grunts and pummels her poor thighs.

Soon now he'll hear my plaintive maiden's cry:
'Enough, kind Sir, enough, enough, you satisfy!'

For thee, for thee, my pretty maid, for thee.
How happy you must be, I come for thee.

Then with an anguished shout I'll feel him come
And then a moan and with a final thrusting it is done.

For thee, for thee, my pretty maid, for thee.
How happy you must be, I come for thee.

As he lays his head upon my heaving breast
He boasts that I've been mounted by the very best.

For thee, for thee, my pretty maid, for thee.
How happy you must be, I come for thee.

This rigid rod he likened to a mighty steed
Lies atrophied and twitches like a centipede.

For thee, for thee, my pretty maid, for thee.
How happy you must be. I come for thee.

If my loving has brought about his flaccid worm
Alas, I cry, why is it never then the maiden's turn?

For thee, for thee, my pretty maid, for thee.
How happy you must be, I come for thee.

Now snoring lies this knight in deep repose.
He . . . happy that he's come. I . . . anxious that he goes.

I must quickly add that this was not my experience with the lute player for his love was long and tender. While I seized upon Fatima's advice to love him first and well, he needed no chastisement to return his amorous attention to me. After I had oiled him and with my lips rekindled his desire, he laid me down upon my stomach and starting at my neck he smoothed the fragrant oil along my back and buttocks and legs to my ankles. Then he commenced to massage me, his pliant hands seeming to know the nature of every muscle in my body. As he traversed over my buttocks it was as if he plucked a single note upon his lute string, his finger slipped within me and played that sweet erectile organ only the briefest moment before it was gone again. So that each time his hands returned to my neck and began the slow slide down my back the promise of the loving finger caused me to gasp as I anticipated his lovely pluck. When it came at last, I moaned with pleasure.

I had learned well the gasps and moans and sounds of mock arousal from the courtesans, but now my cries came uncontrolled until I could bear it no longer and thought I must surely burst asunder from desire. I begged for him to enter me but still he lingered. Then he lifted and placed me on my back. Gently parting my legs he crouched within them and but a moment later his tongue entered me and unerringly found the little rod and played upon this loving flute until the flood within me finally burst and I screamed out in ecstasy. Only then did he mount me. Like waves rolling continuously into shore, I came and came and came.

Then long did he linger with kisses and caresses and sweet talk, before once more he turned me on my stomach and oiled and stroked my back, but this time more tenderly and sans his plucking finger for I was wondrously wet and ready. Then he mounted me from behind, stroking softly at first and then harder and harder until my gasping was beyond mere gathering of broken breath and then together we reached that vortex of extreme and unrelenting loving, that marvellous indescribable moment of coupling when two people do come together.

If I appear the hussy I deny it not. But if you do not judge this the devil's work and me his evil instrument, I ask that you forgive my wantonness, knowing as I did at the time that this was the first and also the last time I would know a man with intimacy. I too was ashamed at the urgent need within me to act as I did and if it seemed impulsive that I went so willingly, it was not. I have spoken before of my hunger and I can only say that I felt fortunate that this was now replete and that, unlike my song where the lover cares only for himself, this lute player had been my most tender and concerned lover. I could not have asked for more. I knew, though it was sinful and I guilty, I would savour this first loving forever, knowing that I had experienced the eternal mystery of creation.

More so now than ever I felt myself the reluctant nun. I knew in the pantheon of nuns that loved Jesus as their betrothed and He them as His faithful and devoted wives that He would place me last. All-knowing, He knew that I came to the holy altar for selfish reasons and, moreover, had indulged myself up to the very last moment and not delivered myself up unto Him unsullied and virginal before pledging my troth and accepting His sacred ring.

But I confess as I lay supine with the arm of my lover about me I did not think even a moment on this consequence. In truth I felt cleansed and consummated and filled with the wonder of the creation of loving. Then came the first blush of guilt, for I realised that I did not know my lover's name and in my haste to abandon myself to him had not even thought to ask it.

I turned and resting on my elbow I looked at him and asked, 'What is your name, my lovely lute player?'

He smiled a quiet smile. 'Ah, that is the joy of it, Sylvia. You know it not and are much the better for it.'

'Pray tell, how am I better for it?' I asked, grinning stupidly to hide my shame.

'I have been told that you are about to enter a nunnery?'

'Aye. Do you think me shameful?'

He laughed. 'Do you think you are?'

'Perhaps . . . Aye, I confess, it is, but I truly loved it.'

'Then how may it be shameful?'

'I go to be God's bride,' I said, suddenly shamefaced, these words summoning the awful truth of what I'd done.

He thought a moment then turned to me. 'Sylvia, I am well accustomed to loving women. I count myself most fortunate – my lute attracts them like a bee to summer blossoms and I confess I seldom sleep alone. If this seems boastful then take it as you may. But this I say to thee. I am told, though you did not bleed, that I am the first man you have known and I am truly grateful to have been so chosen. You are an exceptional lover and as pretty as a maid might ever be. How learned you such loving ways and kept your virgin's mantle I cannot say, but the pity is that such joyous coupling will now be lost to all who may have been fortunate enough to pluck this lovely rose. What would be shameful is if you possessed my name and forever after thought only that it was I you loved and not what you *truly* loved, which was the act of loving. When this is felt and it is rarely so the first time for a maid, then it is the mystery of life and is created by God. Only He can create perfection and only His name may be used when thinking of it.'

With these lovely words, which did both forgive my sinning and flatter me immensely, he rose and quietly dressed and then he kissed me. 'Farewell, Sylvia, I must leave you, but will cherish you for what you brought to me.'

'Nay! Lute player, I thank you for your tender loving, but I wish but one more thing from you.'

'What is it, Sylvia?'

'The words to the love song you played when you came for me.'

To my surprise he threw back his head and laughed. 'Nay, you do not want them.'

'Please, I must!' I begged.

'Nay, they are foolish. A joke before I truly knew you.'

'I *must* have them, or else they will haunt me forever.' I hummed the first few bars. 'See, I have the tune already, now I *must* have the words.'

'I fear you will think less of me for telling you.'

'Nay, I will not. Please?' I begged again.

But still he seemed reluctant and looked at me somewhat shamefaced. 'It is a song composed by a young novice nun who finds herself bemoaning her new life in a convent. I thought it a joke most private when I played it. But now I fear this feeble jape turns on me, nor will it serve you well to know the words.'

'Lute player, I am not easily made churlish, but if you do not tell me I will scream and tear my gown and beat myself to bruising and gouge my eye, then swear that I came about this state by thy cruel hand,' I laughingly threatened him.

'Very well, Sylvia, but know you that it was you who persisted. It is called "The Reluctant Bride".'

Whereupon he sat and taking up his lute he sang to me while I memorised the words. And when he was done and I had this song in my head, I could feel my courage begin to fail me.

The following morning, shortly after the ringing of the Angelus, Father Hermann and I departed for the long day's walk to the Benedictine convent at Mount Disibodenberg. St Mary's on the Kapitol possessed a horse and cart for the transporting of priests but he refused to use it. 'We shall walk as do all commonfolk,' he informed me. Then he added in his usual critical manner, 'Not like other members of the clergy that arrive seated on a cart with their feet clean and the hem of their cassocks free of dust or mud.'

'I would much prefer to walk, Father,' I replied. This was true, as I knew I might not appear back in the outside world for four years or even longer. It was late summer and the wheat and barley were being brought in from the fields, always a happy time in the countryside.

'Our Lord did only once ride upon a donkey when he entered Jerusalem for Passover, which is what we now call Lent,' he reminded me. 'But at every other time he walked with His disciples. Tush! We priests have forgotten that we are called in His name to follow in His footsteps. Footsteps, you hear, Sylvia! Not cart wheels or mule hooves, footsteps! Only *once* a donkey! But oh no! Now we would raise ourselves to some lofty status that denies our vows of humility. Now we travel high-seated above the crowd, waving a blessing to those who acknowledge us, our chins and stomachs bouncing and a fat basket filled with bread, smoked fish and wine recumbent at our feet.'

'I have a little money for food, Father,' I replied.

'Nay, child, it is but a long day's journey. We shall trust in the Lord and if He doesn't provide, it can only be that our precious Saviour means us to fast this day.'

I felt sure that the other priests thus constantly regaled by Father Hermann's sanctimonious piety regarded him as a tiresome and self-righteous bully. I thought of poor Father Paulus, a recent victim of his brusque, disapproving and forthright scolding, although, I felt sure, all the while Father Hermann simply sought to conceal his lack of learning by seeming more pious, humble and worthy, proving himself to be a more conscientious disciple than his more learned brethren. This practised humility was simply another form of arrogance, in its own way just as vainglorious as the priest who rode high-handed on a mule or travelled contented in a cart. Humility does in silence; it does not constantly remind others what it does.

The prospect of not eating all day was not a pleasant one. For just a few small coins, food in the countryside was abundant and to a priest more likely given freely without payment. The bread would be baked with new-harvested corn and the wine would be young and sweet. Besides, to stop for a short repast would break the tedium of the long journey to the convent. I had not eaten before our departure and slept little as it was well after midnight when Master Yap's night watchman escorted me home. Once abed I lay awake for the remainder of the night, at alternate times savouring the moment then feeling guilt-ridden, at once knowing myself wicked and then altogether fulfilled as a woman.

The Benedictine buildings on Mount Disibodenberg were far more formidable-looking establishments than the Monastery of St Thomas. As we approached the high walls and massive wooden gates reinforced with iron bars and studs that enclosed the first building, I thought little more than two years had passed since I had left the carpentry shop of the sainted Father John. So much had changed from the little girl who had felt Frau Anna's spittle landing on the back of her neck. Now, God willing, I would become a scholar in search of the truth and perhaps some day I might return to the village of Uedem where even the abbot of St Thomas would treat me, a famous woman scholar, with due respect.

Father Hermann rang the rope that hung from a belltower on the wall full thirty cubits above us. In the stillness of the late afternoon the sound of the bell clanging seemed far too intrusive for announcing someone of such small importance as me. Presently a door not much larger than a man's face opened in the lower region of the great gate and a monk's head inquired as to our business.

'I bring a novice for instruction!' Father Hermann boomed, even though the monk's head was but two cubits from where we stood. It was as if the size of everything confounded the priest and he must match it with the stridence of his voice.

The monk winced at Father Hermann's barking. 'Nay, not here. The convent is the next building. Go to the side . . . there is a gate.' Whereupon his head withdrew abruptly and the tiny door closed.

'What side, left or right?' Father Hermann bellowed, perhaps to hide his discomfiture at mistakenly approaching the wrong entrance.

There followed a pause before the door opened again and the monk looked at us bemused. 'Er . . . the side with the mole on the ear, ' he said, and then once again quickly slammed the door shut.

'It's to the right, Father,' I grinned, realising the monk had not known his right from his left, but had spotted the large mole on the priest's ear.

'What mole?' Father Hermann demanded to know, then turned and examined both my ears. 'Rubbish, there is no mole on your right ear, Sylvia.'

We walked quite some distance beside the massive monastery walls and once when I made some small remark Father Hermann, lost in thought, impatiently replied, 'Shush, Sylvia, I am preparing our announcing!' We walked in silence until we came upon a small door set into the stone wall, the bell above it much smaller and its clang polite enough. We waited some time and Father Hermann, ever impatient, moved to ring a second time when a small peephole opened in the gate and a female eye asked, 'Who is it?'

'I bring you Sylvia Honeyeater, the blessed child of God, known to folk in Cologne as the Petticoat Angel. It is she who doth charm the birds from the trees, has caused the Virgin's rose to bleed and sings with the voice of an angel. Her miracles are, as I speak, with the bishop himself. How fortunate you are to have her in your nunnery!' Father Hermann stentorously announced. It was immediately apparent that his words were much rehearsed and I blushed to the point where I did not know where to hide my head.

'Oh, the novice,' the eye said, staring. 'She is five days late!'

'But I sent a message!' Father Hermann protested, taken aback at this accusing and unexpected reply from the single staring eye.

'We did not get it,' the eye said firmly.

'Perchance it went to the monastery?' Father Hermann suggested, his voice surprisingly intimidated.

'Men!' the eye exclaimed. 'They never do things right.' There followed a pause and I looked up at Father Hermann to see that he seemed lost for words. Even a humble disciple of Jesus who walked everywhere and was the earthly husband of the Virgin Mary and a giver of rosy red apples to the baby Jesus was still a priest and so was unaccustomed to any woman speaking to him in such an abrupt and contemptuous manner. But even before he had sufficiently recovered, the eye launched yet another tirade. 'Well the abbess is not pleased! Five days is a terrible long time to be late! Terrible! Terrible!' she scolded further. Then still not yet completed added, 'We'll have to have reasons.' The eye seemed to be looking directly at me. 'Lots and lots of reasons and explaining! Our plans are spoiled for this extreme tardiness of time, this coming, then not coming and now coming! We must know the reasons or it will not bode well for this untimely novice!'

My heart started to beat furiously – I wasn't even within the gates of the convent and already I must tell a big fat lie. What could I possibly give as reasons to the abbess? *I am delayed because the whores in Cologne's most famous brothel did wait the five days after my monthly bleeding to be sure that I was safe from becoming pregnant. This they did because they had procured for me a handsome young knight who played the lute wondrously well and possessed violet eyes and dark hair and lips that seemed dipped in nectar, and with his cunning finger, pliant tongue and lovely rod did fulfil my every desire. Of all the young maids in Cologne I am the rose best plucked. This is why I am five days late, Abbess.*

But now Father Hermann seemed at last to recover his equanimity. 'Learning!' he said emphatically. 'Lots and lots of learning. This blessed child of Jesus who has two miracles for the bishop's appraisal doth study the testaments in Latin, Greek and Hebrew under the great scribe Paulus of St Martin's. Her curriculum did require five more days to be completed.'

'Never heard of him,' the eye replied.

'Well, he's famous and was the first cleric to witness the Miracle of the Blood on the Rose,' Father Hermann said, vastly exaggerating the status of Father Paulus. Which was in fact somewhat lowly, a scribe who lived in the belltower and rang the bell at the approved times and was steadily going deaf as a consequence. Besides, he seemed to have forgotten Father Paulus taught me only Latin.

'Bleeding rose? A rose bleeding! Never heard of that either and I'm a gardener and should know,' the eye remarked flatly.

Father Hermann had finally had enough of the accusing eye and, realising she was *only* a gardener and probably a lay sister, rose to his full indignation. 'Why are we waiting, Sister? Will you open the door at once,' he demanded.

'Yes, Father, of course, welcome to the convent of Disibodenberg, known to the blessed St Hildegard, the great scholar.'

'Yes, yes, we know all that! Open up!' Father Hermann replied irritably, now fully back into his stride and his usual bombastic self.

The gate opened and a small, rotund woman in a rough habit soiled with dirt stood before us smiling. Then she bowed her head to Father Hermann. 'I am Rosa,' she said quietly, all the boldness from the prying eye now disappeared.

'To the abbess, at once!' the priest demanded. 'We have walked all day and have not eaten since dawn and then only a single crust and water!'

My stomach rumbled for lack of food and I dearly wished that I had shared his crust.

'I shall inform the kitcheness, but first must tell the cellaress – it is she who must decide who eats and who does not,' Rosa said, regaining some of the confidence formerly possessed by her single eye.

Father Hermann ignored this remark. 'The abbess! Where do we find this dame?' he asked again.

To our surprise Rosa brought two fingers to her lips and whistled. A shrill sharp sound I could myself perform, but knew it for the skill possessed by a peasant, a countryman, usually a goatherd. Moments later a nun appeared from what I would later learn was the entrance to the chapter house.

'Come, Sylvia,' Father Hermann said, walking to meet her, Rosa following us.

'Welcome, Father!' the nun called out as we approached.

'The novice, Sister. The one that is late!' Rosa called from behind us.

'Thank you, Rosa, that will be all, you may go,' the nun said sharply, then added, 'I have told you not to whistle!' Then, turning, she smiled sweetly at Father Hermann. 'I am Sister Angelica, the novice mistress.' She turned to me with a slight frown. 'You are Sylvia Honeyeater?'

I curtsied, lowering my eyes. 'Aye, Sister.'

'We had expected you sooner,' Sister Angelica said, perhaps a little archly.

'She had first to complete her curriculum, Latin, Greek and Hebrew,' Father Hermann repeated. 'It was the bishop's wish,' he then declared, further embroidering this spurious reason for my delay.

'Oh? That doesn't sound like my brother the bishop, who cares little for learning, hated Latin as a child and to my knowledge knows nothing of Greek and even less of Hebrew.' Sister Angelica looked at me sharply. 'Nor cares he much for miracles to roses or the summoning of tweeting birds.'

Whatever Father Hermann had caused Father Paulus to write about me to the abbess was clearly now well distributed amongst the nuns or, at the very least, shown to Sister Angelica. If it contained anything like the verbose introduction he had given at the gate to Rosa, I knew I was in trouble. The letter concerning me had obviously not been well received. Like most nuns, Sister Angelica was highborn, the sister of the bishop and therefore a member of the nobility. She would regard me with disdain, and she would not be in the least beholden to the priest.

'I, myself, was a poor student,' Father Hermann said, 'but I was witness to both miracles,' he added, though his voice was too soft to be called defiant.

Please say no more, Father! I begged him silently.

'Ah, that is helpful to know, Father,' Sister Angelica said sweetly, then turned and smiled at me. 'To have a novice of such *superior* intelligence and then also *spiritually* blessed is indeed a great privilege. Come now, we must see the abbess, she has been awaiting your arrival most anxiously these five days.' There was no mistaking the sarcasm to her voice. Tired and hungry, I trembled at the thought of what lay ahead of me.

'They have not eaten!' Rosa called out. She had retired when asked to leave our presence, but still remained within earshot, settled on her haunches a little way down the path pretending to pluck out weeds.

'Rosa!' Sister Angelica called sternly, the single sounding of her name her shrill admonishment.

Sister Angelica led us to the chapter house and bade me to be seated on a bench outside the door. Then she turned to Father Hermann. 'It will not be necessary for you to tarry any longer, Father. The novice is now with us and we thank thee for her safe delivery.' She pointed to several buildings some distance away and higher up the mount. 'It is now almost sunset. You may, I feel sure, sojourn this night at the monastery.'

There was no offer of sustenance, as Rosa had suggested, and it was clear Sister Angelica considered Father Hermann dismissed. I could see that he felt humiliated, but lacked the courage to demand food from so imperious a person as the sister of the bishop. God, it seemed, had granted him his wish and given us a fast day. I wondered how I would last until the bread and wine of breakfast yet twelve hours hence.

Father Hermann placed his hand upon my head and said a short prayer, while Sister Angelica stood aside, impatient for him to be gone. 'Bless you, my child. May the Lord be with you as you continue His wondrous works to perform,' he prayed. Then looking down at me said in a voice I felt was close to tears, 'Farewell, Sylvia. We, Father Paulus, Nicholas and myself, will greatly miss thy presence in our lives.'

'Farewell, Father, I too shall miss you and will try to do God's bidding,' I said, softly sobbing. I knew I would greatly miss his presence in my life. He had been kind and generous to me and despite his failings I loved him dearly, for I knew that underneath he was no different to me, very afraid. I watched as he walked away, his tall figure slightly bowed. The Virgin Mary had chosen her earthly husband well, for there was no badness in him.

'Stop crying at once, Sylvia, you are not a child!' Sister Angelica demanded. Then she pointed to my stave and the leather bag on my back. 'No, no, you cannot bring those with you,' she said, shaking her finger.

'But I must!' I cried. 'They are ever with me!'

'Nay, no earthly goods may thou possess, they must go at once!' Then turning she shouted, 'Come here, Rosa!'

Rosa came at her bidding. 'What is it, Sister?'

Sister Angelica pointed. 'The stick and the bag, take them and burn them.'

'Nay!' I screamed. 'They are holy, blessed with holy water, the gift of a priest!'

Sister Angelica looked scornful. 'If they were gifts from His Holiness the Pope you may still not possess them.'

I was suddenly in a blind panic. 'Father Hermann,' I yelled at the top of my voice. 'Father, please come back! Please!'

Rosa, seeing my distress, said quickly, 'I'll fetch him.'

'No, Rosa!' Sister Angelica called, but Rosa had already turned and was running towards the gate.

'Really, this is too much! I shall have to tell of this! You are hardly arrived and already you are a troublemaker!' the novice mistress chided angrily.

Rosa soon returned with Father Hermann and I ran to meet them and fell to my knees clutching my precious stave to my breast. 'Father, tell her, tell her I *must* have my stave!' I wept.

'What is this, Sylvia?' he asked.

'We can possess nothing here, Father. Ours is a vow of poverty,' Rosa explained.

'But a stave, our Lord Jesus Himself possessed one?' he said, bemused.

Sister Angelica had by this time approached us. 'Tush!' She pointed to the stave clasped to my bosom. 'It is wordly goods and we have forsaken any such,' she scolded.

Father Hermann tried to assert his priestly authority. 'It is a stick that grows upon a tree, God's tree, God's stick, Christ Himself carried such a stave.'

Sister Angelica gave him a small, triumphant smile. 'This is a convent where a woman doth preside who has within these bounds the absolute authority. No stick, no stave, no anything! I go at once to fetch the abbess,' she threatened.

'No, please don't,' I begged. 'I had not thought to cause trouble.' Turning to Father Hermann I asked, 'Father, will you take my stave and keep it safe? And my bag, will you give it to Nicholas? They are from the Monastery of St Thomas, the work of Father John, and are blessed with holy water from the Pope.'

Father Hermann looked straight at Sister Angelica and slowly shook his head, then he looked down at me. 'Of course, Sylvia, I shall keep the stave in the sacristy of St Mary's.' He grinned. 'Pilgrims will think it a relic of some past prophet or holy monk.' He looked pointedly at Sister Angelica. 'And perhaps it will turn out that they are not far wrong.' With this he reached out and took my hand and raised me to my feet. Then he took possession of my precious stave and leather bag.

'Please go now!' Sister Angelica said, deliberately not appending 'Father' to her dismissal.

When Father Hermann had once again departed, Rosa escorting him as far as the gate, I stood miserable and forlorn, sniffing and wiping the tears from my face with the back of my hand. Once they were beyond hearing, Sister Angelica turned to me. 'Tears are of no avail here, you stupid girl. So stop crying and pull yourself together. We go now to see the abbess, who you will, at all times, refer to as Magistra, both to her face and otherwise, do you understand?'

'Yes, Sister,' I said, sniffing back my tears.

'Yes, Sister Angelica! I am your teacher and must be obeyed,' she commanded.

'Yes, thank you, Sister Angelica.'

I followed her to the chapter room where she bade me wait, then departed, leaving me alone on the bench outside. The sun was beginning to set and I was dog-tired, hungry and thoroughly miserable and thought that I might escape at the first opportunity. I felt weak for lack of food but with darkness approaching I knew if I bolted now I would have to sleep in the woods and it would be too late to forage for wild strawberries, blackberries and the like, all abundant at this time of the year. I decided I'd wait until morning. I would have slept and eaten and then I could all the better make a run for it.

'Psst!' A voice sounded behind me. I turned to see Rosa. 'Take this, but eat it quickly,' she said urgently, thrusting a thick crust of bread in my direction. I grabbed the bread and hid it in the fold of my dress. 'No! Eat it now or else they'll confiscate it!' she hissed.

'Thank you,' I said softly.

'Come and see me when you can,' she said in a loud whisper and then was gone.

I devoured the bread hungrily, hastily swallowing half-chewed chunks, the crusty rinds rasping at the lining of my throat, terrified that Sister Angelica or the abbess would come upon me chewing. But I need not have worried. The sun was well set before they approached, Sister Angelica walking beside a tall, thin woman who carried a lantern in her left hand and a testament in her right.

I stood and curtsied as they came to a halt in front of me. 'This is her,' Sister Angelica announced, then sneeringly added, 'our little miracle worker who would carry a stave and begging bag as if a little prophetess.'

'Thank you, Sister Angelica. It is late. You must attend the other novices at Vespers. I will take over from here, then send her to the lavatorium to thee to have her head shaved and be given a nightgown.' Without further word Sister Angelica departed, though I sensed she would have wished to stay. Whereupon the abbess turned to me. 'Welcome, Sylvia Honeyeater,' she said.

'Thank you, Magistra,' I answered softly.

Then, as if that was the end to her pleasantries, 'Follow me,' she commanded. I followed as she mounted the five steps into the chapter room and walked over and placed the lantern on a table behind which stood a single chair. To the front of the table were several rows of wooden benches. A coloured statue of the Virgin and child hung from the wall behind the chair. I took a seat on the front bench. In the half-dark the room appeared most gloomy.

'So you have come at last,' the abbess said crisply, while turning the pages of the testament.

'Yes, Magistra,' I replied meekly.

'And why is it so?' She did not look up from the book.

'Excuse me, I don't understand, Magistra?'

'Understand what? I ask you, why are *you* arrived late?'

'We . . . Father Hermann and I walked from Cologne, we left as the Angelus rang.'

She looked up, exasperated. 'No, stupid girl! You are five days late! *Five days!* The other novices were all here at the required time. Why-were-you-late?' she scolded, her patience worn thin.

'I . . . I had to complete my curri . . . culum,' I stammered, repeating the explanation Father Hermann had given to Sister Angelica.

'Ah, yes, the bishop's wish,' she said, returning to the testament, so that I knew Sister Angelica had instructed her of Father Hermann's conversation.

'Read this,' she demanded suddenly, looking up and pushing the testament towards me.

I rose and approached the table and then saw that the book was not turned about. I had often faced this problem with both Father Paulus and Master Israel. They would read to me aloud, facing me, and anxious to see how the letters were formed I had from the very beginning watched the words on the page, so when I learned to read I could as easily read words upside down as the right way up. Fortuitously the lamp threw sufficient light for me to see the Latin words quite clearly.

The passage I was to read was from a text by St Benedict of Nursia written some six hundred years previously. It was upon this text that the order I was to enter was based. I began to read aloud and read for some time before the abbess demanded that I cease.

'Where have you learned this text, Sylvia?' she demanded.

'I have not, Magistra. I come to it for the first time now.'

'Nonsense! You are reciting it!'

'Nay!' I protested, forgetting to add the word 'Magistra'.

'Ha!' She turned the book the right way so that the letters faced me correctly. 'See, it was upside down, you are reciting it, you know it off by heart, you cheat!' she accused.

'Nay, if it pleases you I can read it just as well if it be upside down or the right way up, Magistra.'

I could see she did not believe me, and turning the book towards the end of its text some many pages forward, she turned it again so the letters faced me upside down. 'Read!' she commanded.

I read the text as well as I did the former.

'Remarkable!' she said at last. 'Do you know of St Hildegard?' she asked.

'Aye, Magistra, she is the greatest woman scholar who ever was.'

'And was a nun and then an abbess,' the abbess boasted. 'The letter from Father Paulus says that you may be another such as she. What say you to this?'

I was truly astonished – neither priest had told me what the letter contained. Now my fears, which had begun with the ridiculous eulogy at the gate with Rosa, were totally confirmed. 'Nay, never! I could never dream of such, Magistra. You must believe me. I know not what the letter contained, but such aspirations are impossible! I hope to learn from those who are much more learned than me and to gain a small portion of their vast knowledge. If I can do this, I shall be well satisfied with my life.'

But my outburst seemed to fuel her contempt. 'You are of peasant birth and bring us no dowry to stake your claim to learning or your right to be here! You think to further your knowledge by becoming a nun, a single peasant present who wears our habit where all the other nuns are of noble birth. I no longer doubt that you are as clever as they say. But you will never be another Abbess Hildegard! How will you take your place in manners and deportment among those of us who are more civilised than thee?'

'I will try to learn thy ways, Magistra,' I replied, looking down at my feet.

'Nobility is not learned, it is born! You will forever be a peasant,' she spat.

And so that night, still hungry and miserable, I started my life in a convent. After my interview with the abbess she summoned a servant, a lay sister who cleaned the lavatorium, to take me to Sister Angelica to have my head shaved.

My hair, like my voice, had often caused people to comment and I had not until that moment realised how much a part of me it had become. Frau Sarah would wash it with chamomile and brush it at every opportunity and so would the girls at Ali Baba's. It was truly my crowning glory and if I was known to be pretty to look upon, it was as much my hair and eyes that accounted for this advantage not of my making.

Sister Angelica waited for me with the shears. 'Ah, all is vanity, my little novice, and we must all learn to be humble and not prideful,' she smirked. 'You did not create this crown of gold and now God wants it back.' I could feel the pleasure she took in saying this.

I was determined I would not cry and choked back the tears as my hair fell in strands to the floor, a golden mat at my feet for me to contemplate one last time. I thought of the ratcatcher who had first remarked upon it when he'd found me by the stream; Frau Sarah as she fingered it and looked for lice, then gave me sweet herbs to wash it at the bathhouse and then loved to attend to it; of Fatima who had once asked me if she might have a golden lock to plait into her own beautiful hair, which shone as a raven's wing and needed no adornment. Now it was gone forever, an untidy mat that lay on the dark wet floor of a lavatorium in a convent.

'Look now for the last time with your beautiful blue eyes,' Sister Angelica said, pointing to the golden locks upon the floor.

And if thou could you'd pluck them out as well, you bitch, I thought, and it was this that kept me from bursting into tears. Sister Angelica was envious, not only of my looks but of my intelligence as well. It was a small comfort as she bade me wash and then put on the coarse and prickly woollen nightdress I must wear to bed.

I lay on a straw pallet with the other novices, all gently bred, who had come from their prayers of Compline and gone to bed in the dorter without saying a single word to me. But if I hoped, despite my tears, for a long night's sleep I was about to be initiated into the ways of nuns and the monastic timetable or Horarium.

This daily and nightly routine of nuns began at midnight, but three hours after we had gone to sleep, with Matins. We were barely back an hour when we rose again at three of the clock for the Office of Lauds, which occurred in the dark and required us to memorise a chant, three antiphons, three psalms and three lessons. The novices had been here but five days and had not yet learned the recitations, but knelt in the dark alongside the nuns and tried not to fall asleep. I confess I failed to remain awake and would later be punished. Then back to bed once more for two hours sleep until the Office of Prime at six of the clock when we rose and washed, then gathered at the chapter house for the day's instructions and to attend to any judicial business. Judicial hearings were when those who had been discovered to have fallen asleep during one or another of the offices or had committed the sin of disobedience or some other transgression were subjected to the rod. This was often a caning of harsh severity by the Magistra. I had been at the convent but one night and part of a morning when I received the first of many thrashings. Then came breakfast, bread and beer, followed by private mass and spiritual reading until nine of the clock in the morning, then followed the Office of Tierce, then high mass. At noon came the Office of Sext and the midday meal, vegetables and fish, salted herring or cod fresh from the sea, served with wine and sometimes bread. Meat was only served to those who ailed and had been sent to the infirmary.

After lunch we had a period of recreation, a walk in the gardens, or for me a visit to the nearby woods to sit alone and call the birds to share this precious time with me or sometimes to sing a song that was not a hymn. Then back to the dorter to rest until the Office of Nones at three of the clock in the afternoon. Then we worked at whatever we might do, embroidery, delicate spinning, the illumination of manuscripts and in my instance, because I had been granted special dispensation, study at the monastery with Brother Dominic, the great scholar and scribe. This we did until Vespers at six of the clock. Then the evening meal, broth and bread and cheese with wine or beer, eaten in silence with only gestures allowed. If milk was required then one must imitate the milking of an udder, or for broth the lifting and scooping of a ladle. Then after supper an hour to ourselves for doing mending and the like, before once again the prayers of Compline and to bed at nine of the clock.

It was for a poor sinner such as me a miserable life. Too much praising the Lord with little that was praiseworthy in our thoughts. If one must worship God so many times each day, then worship soon loses its piety and simply becomes a mumbling of memorised Latin words no longer meaningful or even thought about. I found myself far closer to God in the brief moments I was spared to tarry in the woods with the birds than I did on my knees half dead with fatigue at the Office of Lauds at three in the morning.

And then there was the great disappointment of my learning. It was only after the Office of Nones at three of the clock in the afternoon that I was allowed to study with Brother Dominic, who was too frail leave the monastery. I would run all the way and could get there in fifteen minutes. Then back before Vespers at six of the clock, another fifteen minutes spent, so that at best he would give me an hour and a half of instruction each day. It was not sufficient and I craved more learning. Nor was I allowed to read in what free time I could find within the day and if caught, as I often was, I would be thrashed severely by the abbess.

'I shall beat the peasant breeding from you!' Whack! 'Do you not have enough of books?' Whack! 'Gentlefolk do not spend their time with

Latin.' Whack! 'Or is it Greek or Hebrew?' Whack! 'You will never be another Hildegard!' Whack! 'This for the sin of disobedience!' Whack!

I endured the first month as I served my postulancy, my introduction to serve in the order of the Benedictines, then finally somehow reached the end of my novitiate year and took the Benedictine vows of stability, obedience and *conversatio morum*. Brother Dominic had made repeated attempts to have me for longer periods of study but while I was a novice the abbess had complete control and she would not allow it. But when my first year was over and I must serve three more years before I could take the nun's vows, he went to the abbot and asked that he intervene on my behalf with the abbess. The abbot was a kindly monk who claimed he had once heard me sing when he attended mass on a visit to St Mary's on the Kapitol. He asked the abbess that I might come to sing each day at the high mass in the monastery after the Office of Tierce. While couched as a request, the abbess could not refuse him and so I would take my midday meal, under supervision, with Brother Dominic and then study the entire afternoon in return for singing. At last I was getting the true benefits of study and felt that I could happily endure the harsh treatment I seemed to endlessly attract from the abbess, and the scorn of the nuns, still led in my chastisement by Sister Angelica. While she was no longer my novice mistress, she remained the thorough bitch.

If the abbess had thought that she would show me for the peasant I was in the way I comported myself and with my table manners, she was to be disappointed. I had been well trained by Frau Sarah and had entertained in a great many noble palaces and houses of the rich burghers. I had learned the ways of comportment required of a gentle lady perhaps even better than the abbess herself and was the equal in all the niceties of behaviour of any nun, no matter how highborn. I fear that with this opportunity to chastise me denied, the abbess was even further angered.

I was the first and the quickest to learn the rule of St Benedict, a text that was read to the novices each day and was in length thought impossible to learn in recitation. This reading was traditionally the sternest test for the novices, who, while highborn, knew only a little Latin and struggled greatly, while I was by now fluent and found the text quite easily absorbed. This did not help the abbess's quick temper and she would usually find reason to put me before her at the Judiciary. Yet I had refused to become compliant and to remain silent and felt that if I should do so I was denying the truth I had come to learn. She even required that I stop singing in the abbey as my voice showed up the voices of the nuns. 'God does not want to hear thy voice as if there is no other to be heard,' she castigated me in front of all the others. 'He wishes to hear all our praises sung to Him. You will remain silent as a punishment for such arrogance. It is enough that you sing daily at the monastery.'

My only friend was Rosa, who would often comfort me while we worked in the vegetable garden together. This was not compulsory and put a sneer upon the faces of the nuns as it clearly indicated my peasant past. But I enjoyed her company and down-to-earth nature. She was a cheerful soul and seemed to know everyone's business, and in particular their nasty little secrets, and kept me well informed on all that happened in the convent. Sometimes she would join me in the woods and I would show her how to gather herbs and make the various unguents and ointments taught me by Frau Sarah. Alas, these soon gave her an added importance and she was appointed to the infirmary and so I sadly lost her as my regular companion, although she would come to see me whenever she could. It was difficult after the courtesans and Frau Sarah to have no other female company I could trust. Gossip is a natural part of being a woman and its absence dries up the very soul. If a woman should have to choose between prayers and gossip God would be poorly served.

I have also not spoken of the urges burning within me since entering the convent. If I had thought that the night with the lute player would satisfy forever I was quite wrong. My body ached constantly for the need

of a man's touch and I imagined much how I would like to repeat the
lute player's night with someone else, though I knew not who. Rosa
said that the miller and his son who brought grain to the convent were
happy to accommodate a randy nun and named several sisters who were
regularly serviced. But I had looked upon them both and heard them
in conversation with the kitcheness and in my mind declared them fat,
churlish fellows, thick as a pair of oxen and possessed of a sly leering.
Their vacant faces were dusted with flour and a mucoid runnel ran from
their broken noses cutting through to the rubescent skin below. I decided
that the pleasure of my finger was, while far from satisfactory, still much
the preferable way of sublimation.

It was a most curious thing that the words of the song the lute
player had given me, which had at first brought me great consternation,
now brought me some consolation. I would go into the woods when I
could endure my longing no longer and would pleasure myself as the
widow Johanna had taught me in the village that first night on the
day I had met the ratcatcher. Of course the courtesans had taught me
more sophisticated ways of self-pleasuring, but somehow the widow's
way seemed still innocent and was a lonely woman's given right and
therefore not a sin. As I went about this female right I would, feeling
very sorry for myself, sing the lute player's song, 'The Reluctant Bride
of Christ'.

A young nun is crying,
weeping inexpressibly,
accompanying her lamentations
with groans.
Oh poor me!
Nothing is worse
than such a life,
for someone sexy and lusty
like me.

I ring the bell,
repeat the psalms,
have to leave pleasant dreams
when I'd like to sleep.
Oh poor me!
I have to do a vigil all night
when I don't want to.
How glad I'd be
to put my arms around a young man!

I can't take pleasure in jewellery,
I'll never wear a wedding veil,
I'd like to put on a headdress,
a fine diadem.
Oh poor me!
I'd steal a necklace
if I could.
It would be nice to wear
furs and ermine.

I walk round and round the floor,
trace my steps in a circle,
bow my head in prayer,
never get outside.
Oh poor me!
I stretch out my hands in appeal,
break my heart in my breast,
bite my tongue with my teeth
as I utter these words.

My bed is a black hole;
it's made of felt, not rich fabrics,
with a hard pillow

and underneath a filling of straw.
Oh poor me!
The food I eat is wretched
and bitter;
it tastes only of flour
and cheese.

My tunic is filthy.
My underwear stinks;
it's coarse and rough.
I'm in a foul prison.
Oh poor me!
There is smelly dirt
in my pretty hair,
and I have to endure lice
scratching my skin.

Young man, don't wait!
I'll do what you ask.
Sleep with me! If you don't want to,
there's no point in saying more.
Oh poor me!
No use doing more,
wasting my life.
But at least
I can kill myself!

Then when the song was ended I would reach the point of private pleasure and thereafter I would weep with a longing for the lute player. Knowing all the while that if my thoughts were impure and I was sinning, I could not help myself and knew I would return to do so again and again.

How I longed for the company of the courtesans at Ali Baba's who seemed to me far nicer than the nuns of Disibodenberg. While the girls quarrelled constantly among themselves, they were far less spiteful, secretive and cruel than the noble and holy sisters who were now my sisters in Christ. I greatly missed Master Israel and his corny Jewish jokes and gentle wisdom, and Frau Sarah with her up-and-down moods and plans, her scheming and herbal secrets passed on to me so that the street children would benefit.

I missed dear Father Paulus who was going deaf in the belltower of St Martin's as penance for sins he thought about but could never do, even if he should have the opportunity to do them. And Father Hermann also, so full of bombast and secret low esteem but also love and compassion for the poor. I much longed for his daily company and also that of young Nicholas, who since the occasion of the magic mushrooms possessed the fire of salvation in his belly and a compelling voice for the poor and hungry starvelings of the street. But most of all I missed the ratcatcher and the life he and I had led together.

I had lost all this and more in order that I might seek the truth. While I gained knowledge where I now found myself, I gained no wisdom. I would grow old incarcerated in a convent, old and bitter. I knew that as I grew older and gained more knowledge (more truth), I might well compose religious texts and essays and even sermons that others might read or preach. But I knew already that if my writing told the truth as I hoped it might, it would be too controversial. A complacent Church of Rome would burn or bury it in some dusty archive. Or, if what I had discovered was, at the very least, worthy of debate, then it would be condemned as the ranting of a female scribe, therefore of no possible importance to God's work.

Brother Dominic constantly pronounced me brilliant and talked of sending me to Rome when I had taken the nun's vow. But more and more I thought myself entirely stupid. Why had I locked myself away where I could do no good in a world that needed both nurturing and enlightenment? If this was the only way to gain true knowledge, then I was beginning to understand that the price of learning was going to prove too high. I had worked long enough among the street children in Cologne to know where a nun's work needs to be. Yet I was languishing in a convent where the holy sisters, all born into privilege, spent their twittering lives mumbling prayers they did not feel and did not understand and looked upon the poor with undisguised disgust.

Then, just when I had reached the point of despair, the archbishop came to visit the monastery and while celebrating high mass heard me sing. Afterwards he declared that a cart would be sent for me and that once a week, accompanied by two nuns, I must sing at the morning mass he conducted at St Mary's on the Kapitol. I was to be allowed out and would stay at the cloisters of St Mary's overnight. This meant that we would need to leave the convent in the morning of the day before and I would have the pleasures of the countryside to enjoy and even perchance the opportunity to speak occasionally to the peasant folk. I might also, perhaps through Nicholas, find a way to see Master Israel and Frau Sarah and even on occasion the girls from Ali Baba's.

I was not to know that this self-serving decision by the archbishop to have me sing at his mass was to be the beginning of the greatest tragedy the Church has ever committed upon the lives of children. Moreover, I would be one of the main perpetrators of this terrible crime, all the while thinking I had at last found both a truth *and* a miracle that confounded me, a truth brought about by the faith and purity of the hearts of children and a miracle sent by the precious Saviour to guide and to instruct it. At last I would achieve my desire to become a true and humble instrument of God.

CHAPTER NINE

Suffer Little Children

REGARDLESS OF HOW WELL I comported myself, and despite having completed my novice year, my peasant birth was not to be forgiven and, in addition, my aptitude to learning was deeply resented. I was still given every onerous task the abbess could think of to consume my time at the convent so as to prevent me reading. I would be made to empty the bedpans as penance for misdemeanours I did not commit, or made to knead dough until my arms felt as if they would drop off. I would chop and carry wood for the kitchen fire and on my knees clean the floor of the lavatorium. These were all tasks usually given to the lay sisters, but the abbess taunted me by saying, 'You think yourself high and mighty from all your learning, Sylvia. You will never be likened to the blessed Hildegard. I must protect her from your insidious ambitions. It is my God-given task to teach you humility and grace!'

The tasks the abbess gave me were of little concern and I suffered them gladly for the opportunity it gave me to have Brother Dominic as my tutor. Despite her constant ridicule and attempts to disparage me in the eyes of the nuns, I loved the convent for the learning I was receiving. The long afternoons of study always seemed to pass too quickly. Then, glory be! Praise to the archbishop! Each Sunday I found myself in Cologne singing at his early-morning mass at St Mary's on the

Kapitol, or at St Martin's where he would conduct mass every alternate Sunday.

I was escorted to Cologne from the convent by two nuns, a task that was much cherished among the sisters of Christ who were always eager to accompany me. A great deal of bickering and bargaining took place in order to be chosen as my escorts, though I hasten to say this was not for the honour of my company. They were women of noble birth and always knew someone in Cologne they could visit after attending mass and the Sunday morning service. It was a rare opportunity to socialise and they knew I would not talk of it to the abbess.

We would spend Saturday and Sunday nights in the cloisters of St Mary's and return to the convent the following Monday morning, departing Cologne immediately after the Angelus was rung. That is, we were supposed to sojourn at the cloisters but we were directly under the orders of the archbishop who, apart from allowing us to stay in the nuns' dorter, left no instructions as to our hours of prayer or our containment. Moreover, the prioress of St Mary's had no authority over us and so we were free to spend the Sunday afternoon much as we wished. It was not infrequent that one or another or both nuns came back to the cloisters just in time for the Angelus and our departure on Monday morning. They'd be escorted back to the church in a nobleman's fancy carriage and would wear a smug look to their faces on the long day's journey home.

These indiscreet visits by my two escorts suited me as perfectly as it did them. I would sneak away to visit Master Israel and Frau Sarah, as their Sabbath was completed the previous day, and they always welcomed me. The *winkelhaus* was closed for Sunday, so it was the girls' day off and we were free to spend time together. They were delighted to see me and I them, for there was no better source of gossip and laughter. When I returned to the convent Rosa would badger me for details and she longed to accompany me on one such trip to Cologne. 'We will hatch a plan,' I promised. 'Something will come up.'

Of course I also spent time with Father Hermann, Father Paulus and

Nicholas, who was becoming famous for his preaching to the children and always waited to greet me when the cart from the convent arrived. I had become increasingly concerned over Nicholas's behaviour. Sometimes he was the firebrand who swept thousands of children off their feet with his preaching, and at other times he was bereft of enthusiasm and hardly spoke, his mercurial tongue slurred and his famous energy forsaken. In the summer, if he was in fine fettle, we would spend Sunday afternoon in the woods where one Sunday he confessed he frequently used magic mushrooms.

'But you don't know how they are prepared!' I exclaimed, dismayed.

He laughed. 'I do now.'

'What do you mean?' Frau Sarah had told me that if not prepared in a certain way and taken in the correct amount they could lead to dangerous visions or other manifestations. *Perhaps this accounted for his different moods*, I thought. 'Did you skin them? How many did you take?'

'Nay, not at first and I took four, then three the next time and then two thereafter. Each time I thought I was going to die.'

'Half of one, Nicholas! That is the correct amount. Half of one and skinned! But why then did you persist?'

'Voices. I hear bad voices,' he said.

'Huh? You hear bad voices when you take them?'

'Nay, when I don't.'

'When you don't? What sort of voices?'

'Satan's voices,' he said, looking at me tearfully.

'Bad?'

He nodded.

'And when you take the mushroom?'

'Jesus returns.'

'What? His voice, Christ's voice?'

'Aye.'

'And that's what makes you preach to the children?'

'Aye. "*Suffer little children to come unto me.*" It is His command and I *must* follow it. But when the bad voices come I can't.'

'Nicholas, for how long after you take the mushroom does the voice of Jesus come to you?'

'Sometimes a week, sometimes three weeks, even more.'

'And then it goes?'

'No, it changes.'

'Changes how?'

'I feel a great torpor descend upon me and then it is not the Saviour's voice any more. It is evil. It is Satan. Satan speaks to me.' He started to cry and I held him to my breast. 'I don't want to hear those other voices, Sylvia! Only Jesus! Jesus is my Saviour! I only want to hear Jesus!' he now wept like a small boy.

After a while he calmed down and I continued to question him. 'But the magic mushrooms are not always easy to be found. What do you do when there are none?' Frau Sarah had always stressed that they must be picked and used fresh.

'Aye, you are right.' His hand went to the inside of his tunic and produced a small linen bag and loosening the drawstring he removed a dried mushroom. 'They are dried and then I soak them in water and soon they are plump again. Although I must use three times as much – the magic is not as strong when they have been dried,' he explained.

'Nicholas, listen to me, this is *not* magic!' I cried.

'What then?' he asked.

'There is something in them that turns the mind, it is not good to take them all the time!'

'Sylvia, you said yourself that they were of God's creation.' He then repeated the conversation we had had in the woods the first time we had found the magic mushrooms. 'You said the mushroom was like praying, which you said was inward healing. "Prayer heals our spirit while we pray," you said. You also said a mushroom is God's own work.' He quoted me again. '"If He has caused it to induce visions that are safe and heal the spirit and instruct the mind, are they not to be tried?"' He looked at me accusingly. 'That's what you said, Sylvia.'

His sharp mind had not diminished with his taking the mushroom and I felt myself unable to answer other than to say, 'Nicholas, I, like you, have taken the mushroom and now know its efficacy. It *only* alters the perception of what we see. It distorts our concept of things – trees and grass and sky change colour. Everything is exaggerated: water jugs, ravens and tree roots become a winged demon with a long tail, the bread we took to eat becomes a rising cloud, and the fish changes to play a different part in this mushroom-induced vision. Don't you see?' I pleaded. 'It is simply a thing of the mind! It is *not* a miracle *or* a message from God.'

But Nicholas remained unconvinced. 'Sylvia, you saw only coloured trees and well explain the reason for the devilkin, but it was not the same with me. I witnessed a miracle. Christ Jesus appeared before my very eyes. "*Suffer little children to come unto me,*" He commanded, then told me to preach, to lead the children to salvation. If it was only a trance then why could I afterwards find words in my mouth I'd never summoned before? Words such as "Jerusalem", words of God and the way of repentance and salvation, words that children can understand, when previously they've ignored the sermons and the threat of hellfire and eternal condemnation when these words are spoken by a priest or bishop or even archbishop?'

I thought for a moment, trying to find another way to explain what had happened to Nicholas. 'Nicholas, you have *always* been a leader. The street children have *always* done your bidding when they would heed no other person. It is something you have within your character. Moreover, you wish to become a priest and have heard a thousand sermons, priestly words planted in your mind. The trance that first time, it may well have moved a block in your mind. Now all those priestly words and God's messages that snuggled, hidden in your head since childhood, are made available and are on your own tongue with your particular translation and expression. That is what the magic mushroom *can* do! Sometimes they remove these blocks, these fears that we cannot do what we wish to do.' In the end I was well pleased with this explanation. The lessons in reasoning I was receiving from Brother Dominic were, I felt, beginning to work.

Nicholas, as he always did, dwelt upon my words for several moments before answering. 'Then why do I hear Satan's voice when I wish only to listen to the words of Jesus?' He did not wait for me to reply. 'Why when I take the mushroom does the voice of Jesus return to guide me?'

My confidence in reason and the manner in which I had established my previous explanation now found no answers – I had no way of explaining why taking the mushroom would banish the devil and restore the voice of Jesus. 'I don't know,' I said, my voice flat. 'But I feel sure there is some simple explanation. Perhaps it is your expectation, something your mind wants to hear.' But I could see he remained unconvinced, as I was myself.

'Verily there is an explanation, Sylvia,' he said, looking directly at me. 'I am chosen to greatness by Jesus and the devil would tempt me. It is as simple as that. Satan is sent by God to test my faith. To see if I am worthy or not. When I wish to know what Jesus wishes me to do He has given me the magic mushrooms to chase away the devil and his attendant demons and to restore His presence.'

'Nay, Nicholas, it was I who showed you them.'

'Aye, but God who used them not on thee, but on me!' he replied emphatically. 'You saw coloured trees and created from one thing another in your mind, but I came face to face with our Saviour.'

'Who have you told of this?'

'Thou art the first and only.'

'Not Father Hermann?'

'Nay!'

'Have you prayed upon it?'

'Often.'

'Nicholas, you are fourteen and may do as you have always wished.' I placed my forefinger under his nose and rubbed. 'There is some evidence of hair under your nose, a sometime moustache!' I laughed, attempting to lighten the conversation. 'You are now a man. Will you now enter a monastery and prepare to take holy orders?'

'If that is God's wish,' he said seriously, not smiling at my little joke. 'But I think not. Our Lord has even greater plans for me.'

'Greater? What could be greater than serving Him? A priest, a servant of God?' I asked, slightly shocked, thinking perhaps that my stories of my treatment at Disibodenberg may have caused him to change his mind.

He looked at me steadily, then shrugged. 'I am *already* a servant of God, Sylvia. I preach to more children than may be contained in St Mary's and St Martin's together. Jesus has plans greater, then . . .' He did not explain further.

'Greater, then what?'

'Never mind, you'll see when the time comes,' he said, dismissing my question.

'Will you continue to preach to children?'

'That is my calling,' he replied. '"*Suffer little children to come unto me.*"'

That was the trouble with me. I simply couldn't accept that Nicholas was truly blessed, a child prophet or mystic with a purpose ordained by Jesus Himself. Father Hermann would have no trouble accepting this evidence. Given half the chance I knew that the good priest would equally embrace the mushroom and name it Christ's glorious potion or some such thing in order to accommodate it within his faith. Without even knowing about the magic mushrooms he had declared the tiny cave where Nicholas's vision had taken place a holy shrine. I was told that people were already visiting it. Why was I consumed by doubt when others were so eager to believe? *Just one miracle, Lord, show me just one miracle*, I begged daily while praying.

I wanted so badly to believe, to renounce doubt and to embrace faith, to accept as others did without questioning. But my mind refused. It was I who had the block that must be removed but I knew it would not come about by taking the magic mushrooms. They could only create distortion – objects and things seen otherwise than the way they truly were. Whereas what I needed was the opposite – things seen otherwise that were shown to be the truth. I wanted a miracle shown to me that I could not explain.

I set myself conundrums that I tried to solve. For instance, when a ploughman is struck by lightning the people cry out that it is the wrath of God, that His fiery hand has descended from heaven to punish the ploughman who has dared to blaspheme. But when the ploughman's ox is struck by lightning, how may a beast become guilty of blasphemy? Does God punish an ox for resisting the yoke? Or if a tree is struck, is this because the tree did not render shelter to a weary pilgrim? What if I rush out into the field while the storm rages and shout profanities and curse the name of the Father, the Son and the Holy Ghost, then challenge Him to strike me dead? If no sudden bolt from heaven strikes me down, is this then the result of His everlasting mercy? My mind was becoming plagued with questions to which I could find no answers.

If I have not spoken much about Brother Dominic, my tutor, it is not that he was unworthy of mention, far from it, he was the most learned soul I had ever met, more even than Master Israel and Father Paulus put together. He lived only for learning and was over seventy years old and dry as an old stick with joints that ached constantly, so that he seldom moved from his cell. He did not taste the food he ate, nor seemed he ever to know if it was sunrise or sunset and only set his time by my arrival. 'Oh, you have come, Sylvia? It must be afternoon. Let us begin then.'

His interest in me was only to see if I was worthy of receiving knowledge. His hands were too crippled to continue as a scribe and the thoughts and ideas that came to him he could no longer write down. By this time my calligraphy was passable, though I would never conquer this skill well enough to write and illuminate manuscripts. So, in his mind I became neither male nor female, nun, monk, peasant or noble, not even a scholar, but simply a container, an empty vessel that he must fill and which he must make sure does not leak, so that what he knew might be passed on accurately. And what he knew most about was the power of reason. He would say to me, 'Child, understand, the ability to doubt and to question is what makes us divine. The ability to reason, to find an explanation for why things are, this is God's greatest gift to us.'

Sometimes, when he became lost in thought, I would sing to him and while he never remarked upon my voice, tears would begin to flow from his rheumy eyes and so I had this small consolation that I was, in some meagre way, paying for my lessons. On other occasions I would tidy his cell, as he would not allow anyone other than me to enter it, not even the monk who was supposed to supervise our time together, though if truth be told the monk soon became so bored with my regular tuition that he went about other duties. Food would be left at the door and I would make him eat. If I did not fetch it, it would remain uneaten. It was customary for me to fetch his noonday meal upon arrival at the monastery. Often the food to break his fast in the morning would still be untouched when I brought his midday repast. I would make him take sustenance, then wash his face and hands before we would begin my learning.

My lessons always began with the same injunction. 'They would kill my knowledge!' he'd exclaim, pointing to the dusty manuscripts that lay piled beside his bed and along the walls and in towers on the floor. 'So, we will prevent them, eh, Sylvia? They cannot crawl within thy head.' Then he'd cackle, 'Come, child, let me fill your empty vessel!'

He'd send me to the library to fetch a text and when I returned he'd grab it and hug it to his chest. 'It must never again leave here, we must keep it safe, nobody must take it, they will destroy it, burn it, the words, my words, will be consumed in the devil's fire!'

'But you allow me to take them to the convent,' I'd once teased him. 'What if I should not return them?'

'Nay, child, you do not take them *out*, you take them *in*. What goes into the mind is never lost. You shall be my vessel, my repository. But *they* will take them and without reading what they contain they will burn or bury them as they did in Rome to all my work.'

The first time he talked of the treatment of his work by Rome, I protested. 'But, Father, are you not known to be one of the wisest scribes in Christendom? You have written missives for His Holiness. Why would they burn or bury your work?'

He gave me a wry smile. 'Aye, my importance to the Pope is so great that he banishes me to a tiny cell in a Benedictine monastery in Germany and declares my penance is that I should never leave this place. Do you see his papal couriers hastening to deliver his instructions? Or the horse champing at the bit as his rider waits to take my missives to Rome? I am known in Rome as Doubting Dominic. What I have written about is the right of all Christians to doubt. Alas, the Church in Rome cannot tolerate the right to doubt. It insists that all things are achieved by faith and all God's truth is unequivocal.'

'But, Father, is it not so? God's truth *is* unequivocal!'

'Aye, child, and we must accept this on faith, but the very essence of faith is doubt. Faith can only exist if there is first doubt – the one cannot exist without the other. It is this that most turns Rome against me. They would treat religious faith as if it is beyond doubt. They teach that faith is knowledge when it is *only* belief.'

'So what you are saying, Father, is that faith, not reason, makes us believe that as Christians we have an immortal soul?'

'Ah, the immortal soul? Well done, my child, it is this concept of the immortal soul that has corrupted the word of God and causes us to embark upon these endless holy wars. The word of God tells us we shall not kill – "*Vengeance is mine . . . saith the Lord*". So that we may justify a crusade and still obey the word of God, the Church declares that the infidel does not possess a soul. Now we may with impunity and in God's name kill anyone without a soul – they are, after all, no different to animals.' He leaned back and spread his hands. 'But I most sincerely doubt that this is the will of God.'

Much of what Brother Dominic said in these lessons was to take me many years to absorb. I was young and he beyond seventy, and his reasoning often left me confused and not a little shocked. The idea of the crusades, a holy war that we had waged upon the infidel for the past hundred years, not being God's will was incomprehensible. Or the notion that we may doubt and still be Christians was, at that age, not possible for me to accept. So much of what I heard him say seemed heretical and I dared not speak of it to anyone else. I recall on one occasion the subject of miracles came up.

'But what of miracles?' I asked. 'Are they acts of reasoning or of faith and belief?'

'Aye, miracles, the sop to the people. Give them a nice miracle and they will no longer question, eh?'

'You do not believe in miracles, Father?' I asked, astonished. 'I confess I have a great need to witness one.'

He laughed, an old man's cackle. 'You are trying to trap me, Sylvia. I did not say that. When I watch a bird fly I do not know how it does so, it is certainly one of God's miracles, but I do not declare it a miracle and so worship a bird's flight. I will accept a miracle only when I cannot find an explanation for it, but at the same time know it to be God's doing and His instruction that I become worshipful because of the lesson delivered to me through the advent of the miracle.'

'What if I could summon the birds that fly outside to your presence here, Father? Would you name that a miracle?' I challenged, feeling for once that I might confound him as I had done so many others.

'I should like to see you do so first,' he said. 'Then I would question how it was done. Only when I could find no explanation would I accept that, having seen it with my own eyes, I must declare it true. But if this appearance of birds lacked a purpose and contained no spiritual instruction, no message I could understand, I would not declare it a miracle. I would exercise doubt and then name it only as a strange occurrence for which I have no explanation.'

I worked my way around the piles of manuscripts and parchments towards the small window of his cell and began to call. At first two sparrows, then a lark, a blue tit and a magpie came. Soon the windowsill became crowded with their barging, fluttering and twittering as birds of every description began to arrive. They entered the cell and sat upon the texts and on Brother Dominic's shoulder and landed on his gnarled hands. He watched, smiling, as the cheeky magpie began to peck at a crust left over from his noon meal.

But after a short while the tiny cell became too crowded and I sent the birds away and when the last had gone (the ever-greedy magpie, of course) and the cell was once again silent, I waited for his response. He smiled and shook his head. 'It has been nigh fifty years since last I heard these calls in concert; it was when I was a small boy and with my nurse did often walk in the woods. You did give several repetitions and in all sixteen different calls. Reasoning tells me that if each bird hears its own call and comes to the source of this beckoning, then there must be a good reason. Now all the birds possessed male plumage did they not? Brightly coloured some.' He thought a moment longer. 'Perhaps it is a female mating call and cannot be resisted?'

I clapped my hands in glee. 'Yes! You are correct. It is no miracle and only a trick I learned as a child.'

'It seldom is a miracle, my child,' he said quietly. Then smilingly added, 'But it is a very clever trick and I have seen miracles proclaimed not half as cleverly disguised. Talking of birds, I have recently heard from a wandering monk I knew in Rome who sojourned here one night and came to see me in my cell. He told me of a new religious order, the Order of the Lesser Brothers, founded by a deacon of the Church named Francis of Assisi. This fellow is sworn to poverty and is said to preach to the birds.'

'Assisi, where is that?' I asked.

'It is in Italy,' Brother Dominic explained.

'Does he preach *only* to birds?' I asked, thinking that if he did so, he would need plenty of grain to keep their attention, as believe me, birds know only two things: food and mating. Nor could I see any advantage the birds might possess once they had embraced the Christian faith. Rather than have them follow us and become Christians, had not the Lord Jesus extolled us to follow the example of the birds of the air, '*for they sow not, neither do they reap*'? Other people might think this Francis fellow, deacon, lay preacher, whatever he called himself, was blessed of God for his sermonising to our winged friends, but I did not. I loved birds and sought their company often, but I couldn't help feeling that anyone preaching to them must be some sort of half-wit or idiot.

Brother Dominic, seeing my expression, cackled. 'Nay, not only to birds. It seems Francis of Assisi is a fine preacher, he wears tattered beggars' garments and is said to emulate the ways of Christ the Saviour even though untrained and not a priest. The commonfolk do flock to hear him preach.' Then he added cleverly, 'As it seems, do the birds.'

I could not help myself and started to giggle, then ventured, 'As you have seen, I know somewhat of birds, Father. I should very much like to see how he does this preaching.'

'Ah, you are learning fast, my child, ever doubting while seeking the truth. I asked the same question. "How do you preach to birds?" I asked the monk, thinking he would not be able to answer. But he claimed to know, having heard the story on good authority.' Brother Dominic paused and glanced up at me. 'Always be suspicious of good authority,' he warned. 'It is a term usually used when there is little proof available. Anyway, this is what the monk claimed.

'The incident occurred about four hours walk from Assisi at a place named Bevagna. The birds had all gathered at the sowing of the new corn. But the peasants, well accustomed to the scavenging of birds at sowing time, noted that this particular spring many of the birds were of a kind they had never seen before. Moreover, they all sat and waited without attempting to dive for a single grain of spilled corn, nor did they scratch among the turned clods for barley seed. It seemed they waited patiently in rows as neat as church pews for the preacher Francis to arrive.'

Brother Dominic cackled, both amused and doubtful. Then he drew breath before expostulating. 'And *what* a sermon lay-preacher Francis delivered that morning! He, Francis, commenced by saluting the birds as brothers and told them to praise and always love their Creator. He then reminded them that they had good cause to love God as it was He who had bestowed manifold blessings upon them – feathers for their clothing and wings for their flight and they had also been given a safe home in the purity of the air. He pointed to the peasants toiling in the sun, their weary feet dragging in the dirt, reminding the birds that unlike the poor farmers they neither sowed nor reaped but were still protected.'

'Ha!' I exclaimed. 'What think the quail or pheasant, pigeon or blackbird of this? Who protects them, eh? They must look sharp or they are sure to end up on some nobleman's table or on some pastrycook's Sunday pie cart!'

Brother Dominic smiled at my interjection, but continued. 'The birds, it is claimed, rejoiced in his sermon by extending their wings, stretching their necks and opening their mouths, meanwhile gazing in complete adoration at this Francis of Assisi. He then blessed them and gave them permission to fly elsewhere. Afterwards he castigated himself, calling himself Brother Ass. This, for not preaching to the birds sooner, as they had listened to the word of God with such reverence.'

'He would be better named Brother Cuckoo!' I said. 'If I should ever meet this Francis of Assisi, I'll tell him a thing or two about birds!'

'Ah! You make an admirable student, my child,' Brother Dominic said, pleased.

'Father, may I ask you one more question concerning miracles or the lack?'

He nodded. 'What is it, Sylvia?'

'Well, it's just . . . well, you did so quickly work out the true meaning of my beckoning of the birds and I have one other thing that does constantly create worshipful astonishment in people. I should very much like to reveal it to you, so that you might give it, once and for all time, a natural explanation.'

Brother Dominic looked curious. 'Tell of it, Sylvia.'

'Nay, I must show it. I ask that you forgive my immodesty as it is upon my back.'

'Your back?'

'A birthmark, Father.'

'So? What is so strange about a birthmark – they are commonly found. Why should I wish to see a birthmark?'

'May I show it?' I pleaded.

'Aye, child. A young woman showing her naked back is a small immodesty and I am too old to be affected,' he cackled.

I turned my back to him and arranged my habit so that it fell from my shoulders to halfway down my back. To my surprise I heard him gasp and looking over my shoulder saw that he had fallen to his knees and now he prayed aloud.

Adoramus te. Glorificamus te.
Gratiam agimus tibi propter magnam gloriam tuam.
Domine Deus, Rex coelestis, Deus Pater omnipotens.
Domine Fili unigenite, Jesu Christe.
(*We worship You. We glorify You. Lord God, Heavenly King,*
God the Father Almighty, Lord Jesus Christ.)

I hastily rearranged my garment so that the fish was once again concealed and then turned to help Brother Dominic's creaking frame up from his knees and back onto his chair. But he rose promptly by himself and then, seated, appeared somewhat dazed. 'Father, it is but a birthmark, think you not?' I asked, shocked at his unexpected reaction.

He shook his head, a slow movement back and forth three times. 'Aye, it is a mark. A fish clearly imaged upon thy skin that may well have been there at thy birth.' He looked directly at me. 'But it is *not* a birthmark!' he insisted.

'What then?' I cried.

He shook his head again. 'I know not. It is a holy sign, the sign of the fish.' He shrugged, then bowed his head as if thinking, then raised it again and spoke slowly, carefully. 'It is in my nature and my training to seek the truth. To doubt before accepting. To constantly challenge my faith until at last I am convinced. I am old and weak, my bones creak and it doth take several minutes for me to fall to my knees. I have begged God's forgiveness that I now pray mostly seated in my chair. I know I should glory in such pain and embrace it willingly, but it is too great to concentrate and I feel that our Saviour does not need me to carry this penance of pain when it denies the possibility of prayer.'

He paused and shook his head as if doubting his sensibility and then pointed to the floor. 'When this fish upon your back was revealed to me I found myself at once upon my knees and know not how I got there. I felt no pain, nor do I now.' He lifted his arms, his hands open, palms facing me. Then he balled both hands tightly into fists. 'I have not closed my hands in ten years. See, my fingers bend and there is no pain.'

He seemed for several moments lost in thought, his head bowed, his pliant fingers curled about his knees. 'This fish is no birthmark, Sylvia.' Brother Dominic now looked directly at me. 'I am confused. I know not what I must now think of thee or it, but know it for a sign,' he said softly.

But for all Brother Dominic's erudition and wisdom, and then the admission when he saw the fish that he was at last confounded, I remained young and confused and very much in doubt. I obeyed his principles of learning by constantly asking questions, but despaired when no answers, reasoned or otherwise, came to me. He was an old man and I was yet a young woman and doubts, so easily resolved in his mind, were not my doubts and not my solutions. I still doubted the symbol upon my back and the way folk declared it sacred – even a man as wise and doubting as Brother Dominic saw in its coincidence a holy sign.

While I could not explain his loss of pain and the return of the movement to his hands and knees, faith-healing was a common occurrence and was often witnessed among sick pilgrims touching relics or visiting holy places. I did not doubt the power of his faith, or that a relief to his aching joints might be brought about by his seeing the birthmark on my back. But I knew it to be no miracle, but instead something of the mind. So that my own faith might be restored, I hungered for a miracle that bore no possible explanation.

And then it came without any warning one Sunday in Cologne. It was no different to any other Sunday except that this Sunday there were three others who accompanied me. The usual two nuns and, as well, I had found a suitable excuse for the indefatigable Rosa to come to Cologne.

I must explain Rosa's presence. On my frequent Sunday visits to play chess with Master Israel, Frau Sarah had continued to instruct me in the various herbs and unguents used for medicinal purposes. I would take these recipes back to the convent and with Rosa gather the necessary herbs in the woods and beside the streams. Rosa no longer worked in the garden but resided permanently in the infirmary where she was achieving a reputation for her remarkable knowledge as a herbalist and was given the title of Adjutrix Infirmaress.

If the abbess knew where Rosa's newfound expertise came from she did not say. But she caused to be set up a small dispensary where the medicines were prepared. The convent was soon achieving notoriety by preparing these medicinal herbs and syrups for the monks in the monastery and pilgrims who would sojourn overnight. All spoke highly of the efficacy of the convent medicine and the abbess received a lot of praise, and it was soon apparent that she gloried in the attention. So Rosa, in order to gain more importance in the eyes of the monks and outsiders, was permitted to wear some of the accoutrements of a nun's garb.

Rosa still longed to visit Cologne with me and then an opportunity eventually came when she received a message from the monastery of a most delicate matter. It was a request from the abbot and was delivered by a young monk who wrung his hands and blushed scarlet, but eventually stammered out his requirement. Rosa came to see me, as she had no idea how she might comply. I saw it immediately as the opportunity for her to visit Cologne that we had been waiting for. And so she requested an interview with the abbess.

She had knocked on the door of the chapter room one morning after the abbess had whipped the day's miscreant novices and was writing their names in the book of punishment. 'Come!' the abbess called. Then looking up and seeing Rosa, 'What is it, Rosa?' she asked impatiently. 'I am busy, so be quick!'

'Magistra, there is a need for me to go to Cologne,' Rosa said directly.

'Need? What need?'

'An urgent need, Magistra.'

'This is a convent, we do not have urgent needs, Rosa. We contemplate the blessed Saviour and conduct ourselves in prayerful repose as the Virgin Mother Herself has taught us.'

'Yes, Magistra. Then it is a reposeful and contemplative urgent need,' Rosa insisted.

'Don't talk nonsense, Rosa! What is it you want? I don't have all day. No, you may *not* go to Cologne!' All this said in a single breath.

'Not even for the abbot's piles?' Rosa asked, all of an innocent expression.

'Piles? Abbot! What of the abbot's piles?'

'The monastery has asked if we have an unguent for such a malady, as the poor abbot suffers mightily.'

'And do we?' the abbess asked primly, looking down her nose.

'Nay, but we may get one,' Rosa replied.

'Where? How?'

'In Cologne, Magistra.'

'How know you this?' the abbess demanded to know.

'Little Sister Sylvia, Magistra.'

'Ha! Her! How?'

'She knows a famous herbalist who is an expert in this malady, Magistra.'

'Methinks that one thinks she knows all there is to know. How doth a young woman know of such a treatment? It is a thing of old men.'

'A past tutor, Father Paulus, did suffer much and she did find this unguent that relieved it and brought him much comfort,' Rosa said inventively.

'With her it's all about knowing. Her head is empty of common women's things and filled with ointments for piles!'

'Yes, Magistra, she is very clever.'

'Clever! I think not. She knows not how to starch a wimple, but everything there is to know about men's bottoms! You may ask her to fetch this ointment for the abbot herself.'

'Nay, Magistra, she has her vow of silence to the outside world. As you know she may not leave the cloister of St Mary's where she spends her time in *contemplation* and *reposeful* prayer to the Virgin,' Rosa lied, her expression remaining earnest and sincere.

'Tush! Very well then, you may go. But I warn you not to spend time with that one. She will corrupt thy peasant innocence!' Then to Rosa's astonishment she added archly, 'It would not surprise me if the archbishop required her presence for reasons other than her singing.'

'Thank you, Magistra,' Rosa said, curtsying to the abbess. But then, as she turned to leave, her sense of fairness prevailed and she said, 'Little Sister Sylvia knows well how to starch a wimple or knead dough or chop wood and scrub floors, Magistra.'

And so that is how Rosa was in Cologne with me when my faith was at last confirmed and I witnessed the mysterious hand of God at work in a way that confounded reason and had no explanation. This was to take place during mass at St Martin's on the Sunday.

The previous day's journey to Cologne from the convent had been one of mixed pleasure, the pleasure of Rosa's company on the one hand and the odium of Sister Angelica on the other. The two nuns sent along to supervise me would usually chatter all day during the course of the journey while generally not saying a word to me. But on this occasion it was the dreaded Sister Angelica and a nun, Sister Freda, whom I did not know well. During the cart ride Sister Angelica took great delight in enumerating my shortcomings to the other nun, who soon joined in this spirit of general bitchiness, until Rosa could contain herself no longer.

'I am not a nun and I know myself to be your inferior, but if you continue to chastise Little Sister Sylvia thus I shall report you to Magistra!' she threatened.

This sent Sister Angelica into gales of laughter. 'And you think you will prevail? Ha! Magistra thinks less of the archbishop's little singing whore than do I.'

'Whore?' I said, confounded. 'Who do you call a whore?'

Sister Angelica ignored me and spoke directly to the other nun. 'This little peasant wants us to believe that it is her singing that doth attract the archbishop. But we know hers is a voice that is forbidden by Magistra for its raucousness. My brother, the bishop, tells how the archbishop is a randy sort and has a gleaming eye for a comely wench.' She paused and sniffed, 'Although what he sees in her I cannot imagine!'

'Your brother would know, of course,' I spat. 'He who is a frequent visitor to Ali Baba's, the well-known Cologne *winkelhaus!*'

I wished I'd swallowed my tongue instead, as the moment I said these words I regretted them. If I expected Sister Angelica to seem rebuffed I was to be disappointed.

'Aha!' She turned to Sister Freda triumphantly, barely able to contain her laughter. 'And how would *you* know this?' she asked. Then together they screamed with laughter. 'The little whore who sees my brother in the whorehouse!' she spluttered through her mirth. 'Did he like you? I think he told me you were his favourite,' she lied. 'Is that why he so readily agreed that you might join us at the convent? A reward for favours past, eh?' This brought fresh gales of laughter.

'I was the singer there!' I shouted. But I knew she had beaten me all hands down.

Sister Angelica clapped her hands. 'Magistra will be delighted to hear of this! The clever one who thinks herself the next Hildegard is nothing but a little whore! The archbishop's little whore!' Then she asked, 'Does he hear your confession afterwards, my little songbird?' More laughter followed and I could see how Sister Freda admired her companion's clever serpent's tongue.

It was well-known among the girls that the bishop was a most wearisome and messy task to service. He had great difficulty 'rising to the occasion' and Fatima, his favourite courtesan, would have to scold him severely and whip him until his holy bottom was ruby red, and then he'd beg for forgiveness and ask if he might be permitted to sweeten her. Then with his soft bishop's hands he would spread her with honey over her breasts and stomach and the other lower part and proceed to feast upon her. It was all very tame by many standards but also very messy as the bishop lay on large silk cushions, which could not be used again. Nor did he pay for her services or for the wine he drank. Fatima would complain and say the task should be shared among the girls. 'Why must I be the one to spend two hours cleaning myself afterwards?' she'd protest. 'For days, no matter how hard I scrub, I stink of honey!' Master Yap would pat her on the shoulder and chuckle. 'Never mind, darlink, zat Jesus man is not so stupid, eh? If he vants he can choose from all in Christendom, but the infidel's pussy is still always most definitely the sweetest!' Then he'd place a silver coin into her hand. 'Buy some of zat nice smellink from roses you can get from Frau Sarah.'

Despite my anger, of course I could not say this to Sister Angelica. I had already said far too much and if the nun should talk to her brother, Master Yap's *winkelhaus* would soon enough cease to exist. Instead I bit my lip and remained silent, fighting to contain my tears, when I felt Rosa's arm about me. 'Take no notice of them, Sylvia,' she said quietly. 'They have no manners.'

Rosa had never been to Cologne and was as astonished as I had been when I had first arrived with the ratcatcher. She marvelled at the houses and streets filled with milling crowds, carts creaking, beasts of every domestic kind – goats, sheep, pigs, donkey's mules, horses – a-neighing and braying, baaing and snorting, cackling and crowing, and all the while the almost deafening hum of people everywhere. She sniffed and coughed, holding her nose at the festering alleyways, then threw back her head to wonder at the lopsided and precarious upper parts of the houses that touched and seemed to hold each other up like wrestlers bent each to the other and so preventing both from crashing to the street below. As we passed through the markets many of the women recognised me as the Petticoat Angel and placed bread and sausage and wine, cabbages and cheeses in the cart, calling out their blessings to me.

I had not mentioned this weekly occurrence to Rosa, as it never failed to mortify the nuns who were meant to be my supervising superiors. But on this occasion and after the chastisement from Sister Angelica, I confess I played the part to the full. I laid my hands on the heads of several women who rushed to fill the cart and then to touch me. The two noble bitches watched as the women turned tearful, grateful for the Petticoat Angel's doubtful blessing.

'They treat you like a saint,' Rosa exclaimed, awe-struck.

'The food is for the street children. We are blessed at such generosity,' I said, more than a little sanctimoniously, raising my voice so that the two nuns, who glared silent and truculent, could hear.

Sister Angelica still attempted to have the last word. 'Only the cretinous peasant may turn a whore into a saint,' she smirked.

But this time Rosa was her equal. 'Ha!' she spat. 'Only a person of noble birth would be so overwhelmingly possessed by the devil as to make such an ignorant remark!'

I had not previously denied myself this ritual blessing in the marketplace as perhaps I should have, for I told myself I had no right to such attention. But it meant that when Nicholas met the cart at St Mary's it would be near filled with food for his hungry street-children followers. Father Hermann named this weekly bounty 'Sylvia's Saturday Loaves and Fishes'. When I mentioned to him that I was unworthy of this adoration and felt myself a hypocrite, he'd chided me, 'Sylvia, the Lord works in mysterious ways, His wonders to perform and He has placed His hand upon thy head. Do not now wish His blessed touch be denied to you.'

So, if in the end Sister Angelica had won the contest of the cart to Cologne, then it was not by much. The following morning the mass was to be held at St Martin's and we had arrived before the Angelus bell to prepare for it. The square outside was empty as the sun was not yet up and the dawn light was only just penetrating the dark interior of the church as we knelt in front of the altar to say our personal prayers for the opening day. Soon the worshippers began to arrive; as usual they were the old women and some old men and a smattering of pilgrims. The spectre of death hovers over the old and they are conscious that opportunities to confess their sins and prepare for their entrance to the Gates of St Peter must be grasped at every opportunity, while the young, with lots of time to spare before facing their Redeemer, snuggled impiously in their beds against the early-morning blush of the departing winter.

The mass commenced and I had just completed singing my part in the *Gloria in Excelsis Deo* directly after the Kyrie and the archbishop had started to intone the opening prayer to the mass when the chanting outside first caused some disturbance. It soon grew so loud that the archbishop's voice could no longer be heard and the congregation began to murmur. Still on our knees in front of the altar, I opened my eyes and looked back to see that many of the old women present had risen and now moved as quickly as they might to the doors of the church to see what was causing the disturbance outside. The archbishop seemed still to be mouthing his praying and the two officiating clerics, waving their arms, yelled at the top of their voices for the congregation to keep calm and remain at prayer. It was obvious that they themselves were beginning to panic, and soon the entire congregation was heading willy-nilly towards the doors. Meanwhile, the four of us from the convent remained on our knees, afraid to offend the furious archbishop, although, I confess, I had to resist the temptation to jump to my feet and join the curious throng.

The archbishop, suddenly grown impatient at his helpless clerics, forsook his praying and with his shepherd's crook in his right hand strode towards the door where a great confusion reigned. In his absence we ceased our praying and turned to watch the milling mayhem as the clerics tried to stop the congregation from leaving the church. Three dozen determined old women were more than a match for the two aging clerics and they were soon brushed aside. After some minutes, with the help of the castigating and belaying archbishop who, using his crook, rained impious blows upon the backs and shoulders of his clerics, some semblance of order was restored. The church doors finally clanged to a close to deny the congregation any further knowledge of whatever was happening in the square.

The chanting outside now became muffled as the congregation was once more restored to their seats. It became possible for the archbishop to be heard. And heard he was! He commenced to deliver a furious sermon on the evils of Eve who forced Adam to take a bite from the forbidden fruit, and with their eviction from the Garden of Eden, public nakedness had become a mortal sin. Whereupon he made the congregation swear a denial of all they'd seen under the threat of forbidding them to ever again partake in mass or to receive the holy oil if they should mention to any person outside the walls of the church what they had now *definitely not* seen. He then commenced to pray.

The four of us from the convent who had remained within the church had no notion of the goings-on outside. I grew wretched for a lack of knowing and my curiosity could scarcely be contained. The archbishop's sermon, so clearly directed at what was going on in the square, remained a complete mystery. We did not know that a thousand women stood naked outside, as he did not say as much, but simply preached of the perfidious Eve and her wickedness and referred to an uncleanliness and abomination that the congregation recently thought they'd witnessed but hadn't, since their memories had been purged. Even the chanting was distorted and it was impossible to interpret the words, so that there were no clues to help me comprehend.

It was all very confusing and I confess that when he proceeded to read the prayer of the day, my mind was not possessed of piety but otherwise engaged in the thought of Brother Dominic's expulsion from Rome for his writings on the subject of reason and truth. I clearly understood that I had just witnessed the monumental hubris of the archbishop when he had simply expunged what the congregation had just witnessed, denying them the divine unction and the bread and wine of forgiveness if they should persist with what they knew to be the truth. Thus I had not heard a single word of the archbishop's prayers when quite suddenly I felt myself possessed of an urgent need to remove my habit. I did not for one moment think that my naked form would be unseemly in the church, or even bring me or others shame. Within me I had a sense of absolution and purity, as if at that moment I was purged of all wickedness. I could feel the burning light of the Holy Spirit descended upon me. From my lips, without reason or forethought, came the shouted chant, 'Our children in Jerusalem!'

It evidently took some time to bring me out of the trance I had fallen into. I hadn't felt the urgent and persistent shaking of the two clerics, both mortified and weeping at the sight of my nudity, nor had I felt the archbishop's blows as he used his shepherd's crook to beat furiously upon my shoulders and my naked back, so that now his stave lay broken in three pieces at the foot of the altar. As my eyes cleared, I saw that I was not alone in my trance: Sisters Angelica and Freda as well as Rosa knelt naked before the altar with their eyes closed and their sensibilities not yet returned. They too chanted the words, 'Our children in Jerusalem.'

The two clerics, whimpering and fearful, held our habits as the archbishop, his eyes near popping from his head, shouted at them to cover our nudity. They had no idea how this might be done. As they tried to gather up a habit and place it over the head of one of the three naked forms still in a trance, the nuns grabbed at it and impetuously thrust it away, their eyes yet closed and their chanting continuing. The archbishop became so angry that he picked up the longest part of his broken crook and now commenced to beat the clerics. They cowered at his feet and, first casting aside the habits, brought their arms up to protect their heads against his furious blows. 'Dress them, you fools!' he shouted, his mouth spit-flecked and his face grown purple.

I hastily moved to the garments, anxious to find my own. As I crouched to where the clerics cowered with the archbishop standing over them, one of them suddenly shouted, 'Look! Look at her back, your Grace!'

The archbishop paused and turned to look where I crouched, the broken stave still raised. I glanced back, fearful that he might strike me, only to see that he seemed struck by some invisible force. He stood a moment perfectly still, his mouth half opened as if about to speak. The broken stick dropped from his grasp and clattered to the flagstones. I watched, fearful, as he clutched at his heart, then his great bulk descended slowly to his knees as he collapsed, his head crashing to the flagstone floor, his eyes turned back into his head, his mouth gone slack. He gave a small convulsive jerk and then lay still.

I found my habit and my boots and dressed as quickly as I might with the two clerics kneeling in prayer over the dead archbishop, hysterically reciting the last rites. I looked about and saw that the church was empty, although in my trance I had not heard the congregation depart. Beset by a terrible fear, I had no idea what to do next. Then, as I had done in the marketplace in Uedem when Frau Anna had spat upon me, I began to sing. Almost immediately the two nuns and Rosa emerged from their trance.

But I had scarce time to see them rise and, gasping at the sight of their own nudity, hurriedly reach for their habits when my feet seemed turned of their own accord. I started to walk down the long flagstone aisle towards the two great doors at its end as if I possessed no will of my own. At that very moment Nicholas entered the church through the small side door we had used when, as the Petticoat Angel, I had first come to sing to a crowd gathered in the square. He took one look at me in my dishevelled state and gasped at my shaven head, then turning, quickly darted back through the side door. Moments later, the two templars swung open the great doors to the church and I walked through to stand beside Nicholas on the top step looking down into the square at what seemed to be utter confusion.

Below me street children darted in among the chanting women chased by angry husbands who did not seem to be getting the better of the feral urchins. Some of the older men lay sprawled and beaten on the ground, others were bent over panting and clutching their knees while the children danced gleefully about them, snatching at the garments they held. All the while the naked women, pushed and jolted by pursuing urchins and roughly shaken by castigating husbands, seemed heedless of the mayhem that surrounded them and continued to chant words that I could now clearly hear, the same as those I'd spoken in the church: 'Our children in Jerusalem!'

I continued to sing and Nicholas beside me held up his hand. It seemed impossible that I could be heard, but surprisingly the chanting started to abate. Several older children ran up the steps to Nicholas who gave them orders to stop the harassment by the children and to return the clothes they'd stolen. Then I started to sing the *Gloria in Excelsis Deo* with the words:

Glory to God in the highest,
and on earth peace to men of good will.
We praise Thee.
We bless Thee.
We adore Thee.
We glorify Thee.
O God, heavenly King,
God the Father almighty!

As I completed it, the chanting stopped dead.

A low moan rose from the square and then followed a thousand cries of despair. The street urchins threw the garments they had stolen to the ground and started to run away. Women snatched up what apparel lay nearest to them to cover their shame. The square became filled with the sound of sobbing women, some of whom had found husbands who still carried their clothes and began to dress hastily. Then the battered and angry men began to beat their wives as if to alleviate their own frustration. Some women remained unclothed, walking in circles, wailing in confusion, their hands covering their most private part.

I turned to Nicholas and was astonished at what I now saw. He trembled as though in a trance and his eyes possessed a glow I had not seen in a human face before. I knew at once that it was he who was now possessed. It was as if all the power that had driven the women into the square had now entered him. He began to shout, his voice astonishingly loud, as if that of a large man, a giant, someone who might be accustomed to shouting at a host of soldiers in the course of battle.

'SUFFER LITTLE CHILDREN TO COME UNTO ME AND I WILL SHOW THEM THE GLORY OF JERUSALEM!' he shouted.

From every corner of the square the street children turned and started to run towards him. Then he collapsed upon the steps beside me and fell into a trance so that none could contain his jerking.

CHAPTER TEN

The Cross and the Fish

THE DEATH OF THE archbishop caused a great deal of ecclesiastical fuss and it was scarce two weeks after the funeral that the four of us from the convent were quietly excommunicated by the bishop. The Church, initially calling what happened in the square the work of Satan, tried to cover up the incident at the altar. It used the one event (the archbishop's death) to eliminate the other (the nude nuns in the church), hoping that the pomp and circumstance of the burial ceremony and our quiet excommunication would settle the affair once and for all. The public, the Church reasoned, given a good burial and the appointment of a new archbishop, would soon forget the little problem of the three nuns and lay sister disrobing at the high altar in front of the image of Christ.

But it had misjudged the tittle-tattling tongues of the old women in the congregation. The dead archbishop's injunction to them that they had *not* witnessed the event in the square was no longer valid. If God had erased their earlier memories of the outside event, then He had not done so for the incident within the church. They now had no need to talk of what they'd been forbidden to say. They'd been amply rewarded with all the juicy details while within the church itself.

These interior events soon gained credence among the population and served to convince the folk of Cologne that, rather than Satan's dark work, the event in the square was the hand of God. How else, they asked, if not His glorious work, would the nudity have simultaneously occurred within the church to four women, four servants of God, among them the Petticoat Angel? If the bishop was right and it was the work of Satan, then surely on that Sunday the church of St Martin's must have been host to the devil?

While this 'people's logic' could not be easily refuted, the bishop, never popular with the people of Cologne and well-known to be a philanderer, stubbornly resisted these arguments and persisted with the idea that Satan had conspired to create the incident in the square. He could no longer keep our excommunication quiet and issued a missive to say that the nuns had brought the evil with them into St Martin's from the square and that their blasphemy was the power of Satan that lurked within their hearts.

However, the old women present at the mass that morning would have none of this Church dogmatism and readily took the side of the nuns and the lay sister. Satan, they insisted, had *not* entered the four women, but possessed the archbishop, who, cursing the congregation, had chased them from the church with eyes bulging while visibly frothing from the mouth – this bulging and frothing being a detail added afterwards as the telling grew.

There were rumours that the Pope had asked the bishop to remove his ring until he adequately explained the striking down of the archbishop. Of course, such an assertion was preposterous, the Pope being too far away for the news to have reached Rome and for a reply to come back.

Having, for once in their uneventful lives, captured the attention of everyone the old fraus now lavished the incident with detail. Inventions and exaggerations seemed added every day. While keeping more or less to the facts they were now given metaphysical meanings. The archbishop, upon seeing the nuns disrobe, bellowed with rage and brought his holy bishop's crook down to strike the Petticoat Angel twice across the back. At the first blow the crook broke but the archbishop persisted, so that at the second blow another piece of the holy stave broke off, whereupon

the archbishop discarded the piece he held and it clattered to the floor
to join the others at the foot of the high altar. It was only moments later
that the women saw the shape of a perfect cross on my back and at its
centre sat a fish, the holy symbol of Jesus the Saviour and Fisher of Men.
They pointed to the significance of the shepherd's crook breaking into
three pieces that lay at the feet of the crucified Christ, each piece, they
suggested, represented a part of the Holy Trinity: God the Father, God
the Son and God the Holy Ghost.

The old women then insisted that the sudden appearance of the
cross and the fish upon my back was the precise moment the devil was
seen to enter the archbishop. They told how he turned to face them, his
eyes demonic and likened to red-hot coals. Then, with a stygian roar,
he'd sent them screaming from the church.

The people of Cologne now talked openly of the Miracle at St
Martin's and railed against the bishop, demanding that the Petticoat
Angel be restored to her former sanctity and that my excommunication
along with the other three be rescinded.

The funeral procession of the archbishop and his internment in a
vault at St Mary's would normally have attracted several thousand people
and would have filled the church and the square beyond it. But apart from
the usual town dignitaries, nobles and church officials, the great church
of St Mary's on the Kapitol resembled a morgue. The pews set aside for
the poor were empty and the square held no more than a couple of dozen
people, mostly out-of-town pilgrims. Earlier, as the procession moved
through the almost deserted streets, the few people present registered
their disapproval by turning their backs on the funeral cortege.

The month following the incident of the chanting women and
the death of the archbishop was a difficult one for me as the people
of Cologne insisted that it was me who had been blessed and cast the
devil from the Church. When I protested they pointed out that it was I
who had come out of the trance after receiving the anointment of the
cross; that with the archbishop possessed by the devil I had been guided
by God to restore the sanctity of the Church and to still the chanting

and chase the thieving street children from the square. The other nuns had meanwhile remained in a trance and had not witnessed any of the events directly after the archbishop expunged the congregation's collective memory and driven the congregation from the Church. This, they maintained, was evidence that I had been chosen by God.

I had unfortunately brought much of this upon myself by telling Father Hermann and Nicholas what had happened in the Church after the archbishop had driven out the congregation. I should have known that neither would be able to contain themselves and they spread the story freely, with Nicholas including the entire incident in a subsequent sermon to many hundreds of children.

The only true witnesses, apart from myself, were the two clerics who, throughout the inquiry by the bishop and despite his efforts to get them to modify their viewpoint, had unfortunately remained obdurate. The archbishop, they maintained, had seemed truly possessed, if not by the devil, then certainly by an evil spirit. They described how he had taken to beating them severely with a section of his broken shepherd's crook. How in the process of this uncalled-for beating, one of them had seen me stoop to regain my habit and had seen the cross and fish symbol suddenly materialise on my back. He'd pointed and shouted out the single urgent word, 'Look!'

Whereupon, he claimed, the archbishop ceased beating them and turned to see the crucified fish and the cross on the back of the nun they named the Petticoat Angel. They then both witnessed that his eyes filled with fear and, dropping the broken crook, he'd clutched at his heart with both hands. Moments later he crashed with a groan to the flagstones. The two clerics, rather vaingloriously, told how they'd immediately administered the last rites but feared the archbishop was already struck dead. Asked if they believed the archbishop had been struck by the Almighty or by Satan, they wisely agreed they could not say. They proved to be loose-tongued and instead of keeping what they'd seen to themselves they'd told the two templars, Father Paulus and, it seemed, the three old women who cleaned the church. So that what had occurred when I'd come out of my trance was soon the subject of general gossip. It further confirmed my status as the one chosen to chase the devil from the church and to reduce the mayhem in the square.

Of course, I had not been present when the two clerics appeared at the bishop's inquiry. The bishop, aware that I had become a central figure in the incident and, also through Fathers Hermann and Paulus, knowing of the matters of the birds and the blood on the rose, called them as witnesses to my character. It was Fathers Hermann and Paulus who later told me of the evidence given by the two clerics, and unfortunately Father Hermann had once again told others of the inquiry, so that the evidence of the two clerics served only to confirm the earlier version of what had happened in the Church.

This, as might be expected, fired the brouhaha anew and there seemed some evidence that someone somewhere in the Church was taking note since the bishop, who might normally have been consecrated as the new archbishop, was passed over by Rome. A new archbishop who was unknown to the local population was duly appointed. Anxious to settle the matter of the death of his predecessor and to calm the people of Cologne, he called for a second inquiry to examine what he described as 'new evidence'.

It was to this inquiry that I was summoned and fetched by a standard-bearing troop of six of the archbishop's splendidly uniformed soldiers on horseback and with a pretty mare bearing a side-saddle brought for me. On the route to the archbishop's palace we travelled along the banks of the Rhine and through the busy markets. By honouring a peasant in such a grand manner the archbishop was desirous of letting the people of Cologne know that he was attending to their urgent concerns.

It must be said that the new Prince of the Church faced a difficult task. The pious people of Cologne were already predisposed to think me sanctified. In their minds they believed they possessed four previous reasons for this without adding the recent incident in the church and the square. They talked of my miraculous appearance in the bathhouse in front of the three whores that had caused them to flee nude and to forsake their wicked past; the symbol of the fish, the mark of Christ, the three women swore they'd seen upon my back and its further existence also confirmed by the bathhouse attendant; my calling of the birds in St Martin's square; and, on that same occasion, the blood on the Virgin's pure white rose was now well-known and accepted. All four incidents had combined to convince them of my spiritual significance. And now, not only the fish symbol previously upon my back, but added to it the miraculous sign of the cross.

The bishop, by excommunicating me, had, they asserted, denied the Petticoat Angel the comfort and sanctuary of the Church. They claimed that I was being sacrificed in order to exonerate the devil-incarnate archbishop. The appearance of the cross embracing the fish taking place in front of the high altar clearly indicated that God had chosen me and not the dead archbishop as the one who was innocent and His beloved servant. Moreover, further proof of this blessed approval was my singing the *Gloria in Excelsis Deo* on the steps of St Martin's that caused the chanting in the square to finally cease.

Added to all this, another complication had arisen for the new archbishop. With the blessing and encouragement of Father Hermann, known as a greatly respected and visionary priest at St Mary's on the Kapitol, a youth from the streets who called himself Nicholas of Cologne, also well-known by the city's population, was preaching daily to a thousand or more children. He had also been present with the Petticoat Angel at the chanting in the square, where it was said the Holy Spirit had descended upon him and witnessed through him that he should lead a Children's Crusade to Jerusalem.

To even further complicate the situation, the Pope was at that very moment calling for pilgrims and recruiting soldiers to embark on a new crusade against the infidel in Egypt. Now the people of Cologne were saying it was clear that God had ordained that this crusade should be composed entirely of children; that not Egypt but Jerusalem should be its destination, with the purpose of regaining the Holy Sepulchre. This notion gained even further credence when news arrived that a boy preacher known as Stephen of Cloyes had presented a letter, said to be from Christ, to the king of France. He too preached about a crusade to Jerusalem led by children and, like Nicholas of Cologne, it was claimed that tens of thousands of French children were being swept up in the movement. The assertion was that the advent of the two movements started simultaneously and at too great a distance apart to be a coordinated effort and, too strange an occurrence to be a mere coincidence, was clearly the work of God.

Upon my grand arrival at the archbishop's palace the four of us who had been excommunicated met again. Sister Angelica, now Lady Angelica von Essen, appeared gorgeously attired in the very latest and most expensive gown and high, feathered hat accompanied by her personal maid. Lady Freda, less ostentatious, but well attired as a minor noblewoman, stood with her, while Rosa, in the brown linen shift and heavy boots of a peasant, stood apart and was ignored until I joined her.

I was dressed by Frau Sarah who had insisted that I should be able to hold my own with anyone and be seen as the proper lady I had become. In deference to the Petticoat Angel my gown was of a simple design and made of purest linen dyed as blue as a cloudless summer sky and I wore white, calfskin pointed slippers slightly splayed at the ankles. It was the cut of the gown that made the whole difference and it showed off my slim figure to the utmost. 'Even an archbishop must admire a beautiful young woman,' Frau Sarah had said, well pleased with the result. As always I wore no wimple and my hair had grown a little. She'd tut-tutted about the crude act of shaving it, despite her own religion requiring that her head be shaved in marriage. She'd cut and snipped and shaped my hair so that it sat in a soft bowl about my head and then she'd brushed it until it shone like the morning sun.

We were ushered into an anteroom leading from the great hall and asked to wait. Upon first seeing me a smug-looking Lady Angelica turned to Lady Freda and sniffed, 'You may dress a peasant in finery but she remains yet a peasant underneath.'

No longer subject to the restrictions imposed on me by my inferior position at the convent I was free to answer back. 'Ah, Lady Angelica, you may well speak of underneath. For try as you might to cover up with silks and bows, I have seen your own underneath and thy tits, poor empty sacks, do sag halfway to thy waist, while thy bum is much too large and wobbles deeply dimpled!' In truth, I had barely noticed their nudity in the church, being much too upset and preoccupied with regaining my habit and boots. My wimple I never found.

Lady Freda and Lady Angelica's personal maid gasped at my temerity while Rosa, wide-eyed, brought her hand up to her mouth to conceal her delight. 'You'll pay for this, you bitch! I shall speak to my brother,' the former tormentor hissed.

I shrugged. 'What else can he do? We are already by his hand disowned by the Church and all of us condemned to hell.'

'You'll soon see!' she spat.

The hearing took place in the great hall of the archbishop's castle, and despite the early summer sunshine it was a cold and draughty place of flagstones, flags and stone-carved saints. Lady Angelica's brother, the bishop who had expelled us from the Church, Fathers Hermann and Paulus and at least twenty other ecclesiastics were present. The archbishop, in a high-backed chair that carried his noble crest, sat at the centre of a long banquet table while the priests, clerks and scribes were seated at either side of him. We stood at its centre on the opposite side facing the Lord Archbishop.

Like his late predecessor, who despite being under his patronage I had scarcely known beyond a curtsy given and a grunt returned, the new archbishop was a very large man. His enormous head carried a face of almost perfect circumference, its roundness spoiled only by dewlapped cheeks that hung a good thumb-notch beyond his jawbone on either side of a small petulant mouth. His small dark eyes were set into bruised sockets under coarse, untidy, salt-and-peppery eyebrows. His nose, a twin-burrowed bump, seemed hardly noticed in so large a face. Whether bald atop or not I couldn't say, for his mitre sat resplendent and seemed raised from his brow almost to touch the soot-darkened beams that spanned the underside of the roof. The overall effect was a face of gravitas that, in repose, seemed to disapprove of all it saw.

He began with a short prayer, mumbled and unintelligible. Then he looked up sternly, his bruised eyes sweeping across our faces. 'You well know why you are here,' he said in a stentorian voice, then turning first to each side of his chair declared, 'We, the bishops and servants of Christ are gathered today to do Christ's bidding in the matter of the excommunication of these four women who stand before us. We must decide if they may regain a state of grace within the Holy Church of Rome.' With this frightening prologue concluded he leaned back, his hands clasped about his enormous belly. In an avuncular tone, different and surprisingly unaffected, he asked, 'Now, what have you to say for yourselves, eh?'

I was completely taken aback, expecting some long and ecclesiastical diatribe and not this almost fatherly voice. There is always a pecking order in these things and I waited for Lady Angelica to speak or even Lady Freda, though I expected it would be the opinionated former Sister Angelica. But none spoke.

'Hmm? The devil take your tongue? What say you now – speak up, someone!' the archbishop said, though still in a pleasant and inquiring tone.

Whereupon Lady Angelica suddenly burst into tears, all the while crying out that she was deeply sorry. 'My Lord, I am sorry, deeply sorry,' she wept copiously, 'deeply, deeply sorry!' Then she began to howl her misery in a most undignified and childish manner, her head thrown back and her lungs pumping out her wailing. Lady Freda, affected by this spectacular lachrymal display, immediately joined in, the two noble ladies wringing their penitent hands and wailing at the top of their voices. Rosa simply bent her head and sniffed, and I remained mute, though thankfully free of tears.

'Tut, tut . . . we cannot have a hearing if there is only weeping and wailing,' he called out. He looked at me. 'You, what say you? What's your name?' he shouted.

'Sylvia Honeyeater, my Lord Archbishop,' I said, my voice drowned in the howling.

'Eh?' He brought his hand to his ear.

'Sylvia Honeyeater!' I shouted out.

'Well then, Sylvia Honeyeater, speak up at once!' Then before I could answer he threw up his hands. 'Will someone throw those wailing women out!' Then turning back to me, commanded, 'You wait there!'

The two women had now commenced to weep at a slightly lower tone. A porter approached and Rosa looked up at me. 'Go,' I whispered, raising my eyebrow in his direction. With Angelica and Freda still sobbing and gulping and crying out that they were 'terribly, terribly sorry', the porter led them back to the anteroom followed by Rosa, who kept looking behind as if undecided. With a backward flick of my hand, I encouraged her to continue. Perhaps it was arrogant of me, but I felt that Rosa could add nothing to the proceedings and in her peasant garb seemed totally ill at ease and overcome by the awesome gathering of priests and scribes. I was, of course, delighted at the archbishop's dismissal of the other two.

I cannot claim I wasn't terrified, because that wouldn't be true, but I knew that now I alone would be responsible for what was said. If condemned a second time, it would be after a defence constructed by myself and I hoped that some of Brother Dominic's lessons on reasoning might be used in our defence. With the other two, especially with Lady Angelica's arrogance a component, the result, had they been permitted to stay, could easily have been disaster. Or so I reasoned. But then I recalled the spiteful 'You'll soon see!' she had spat at me in the anteroom. Did this suggest that she'd spoken with her brother the bishop? In any noble family would it not be a natural thing to do? It suddenly occurred to me that her tears might well be at the bishop's direction to show extreme contrition in front of the new archbishop. She was by nature a hard-faced bitch and, now that I thought of it, her dramatic tearfulness seemed odd in one with such an acerbic and spiteful tongue. Thinking further upon it, Lady Freda's eyes had splashed sudden tears as if only waiting for the right moment to begin.

Brother Dominic's words when we had been discussing the nature of the Church in Rome now returned to me. 'Sylvia, *things are seldom what they seem to be. It is a foolish body who holds an inquiry when it doesn't already know the outcome. Even if it hasn't decided in advance, it is careful to place people on the inquiry who have a dependable point of view. If you want a judgement against a cat then you would do well to place a majority of mice on the committee.*' I told myself I must be careful, this was nobility versus the peasants and the peasants had never been known to win. While I knew I could depend on Fathers Hermann and Paulus, I must assume the remainder of my judges on the other side of the table were mice. This might also explain the archbishop's initially friendly method of inquiry.

With the hall once again silent the archbishop cleared his throat. 'Hurrumph! Well now, where were we?'

'My Lord, you asked me why, in my opinion, we were being brought in front of this august assembly.'

The archbishop's bushy eyebrows shot up and he turned to the bishop. 'Didn't you say she was a peasant?' he asked.

'An educated peasant, Archbishop.' Both men spoke as if I was not present.

'*Educated* peasant? What mean you by that?' This was said in a tone that suggested no such person existed.

'She speaks four languages, five if you count our own. She has studied under Father Paulus, the scribe of St Martin's who is here today, and under Brother Dominic of the monastery of Disibodenberg,' the bishop answered.

The archbishop, ignoring the presence of Father Paulus, cackled, 'Doubting Dominic, eh? I thought him long dead. Troublemaker, always asking awkward questions.' He looked up at me suspiciously. 'You're not going to give us any trouble, are you?'

'No, Lord Archbishop,' I replied softly, looking down at my feet.

'Good! Then let's begin again. Why are you here?'

It seemed a strange question. He had already told us all why we were there. I answered as obviously as I could. 'We are condemned for the sin of nudity in a holy place and have been excommunicated, my Lord Archbishop.'

'Yes, yes, we know all that! But what have *you* to say about it? That's what we want to hear.' Then before I could begin he suddenly brightened and turned once more to the bishop. 'Aha! She's the one they call the Petticoat Angel, eh?'

The bishop nodded. 'Yes, my Lord.'

He turned back to me. 'Crosses and fishes, isn't it?'

'I can explain, my Lord,' I said softly.

'Explain? This whole business is about crosses and fishes and nude women chanting and the archbishop dropping dead!' He snapped his fingers. 'Now, abracadabra, you would explain it all to us. Just like that?'

'Not all, not the nude chanting or the archbishop's death, my Lord, just the cross and the fish.'

'But you witnessed the death?'

'Yes, my Lord.'

'And the nude chanting?'

'Yes, some, my Lord.'

'And the cross and fish?'

'No, my Lord.'

'No?'

'The cross and fish was on my back, my Lord.'

'Yes, yes, of course, but you can, you say . . . explain them.'

'Yes, my Lord.'

'Are they still there?'

'Nay, I'm not sure, perhaps only the fish, my Lord.'

'How do you explain the disappearance of the cross then?' he demanded. 'Did it go, disappear . . . when you were excommunicated?'

'Nay, my Lord,'

'Then when?'

'Perchance some slight mark still remains, my Lord.' I had asked Rosa to look at my back two days previously and she'd said that the scabs from the twin marks made by the dead archbishop's blows had almost healed but could still be observed as a cross bisecting the fish.

The archbishop straightened in his chair and then looked to his left and then right. 'This fish and cross, has anyone here seen it?'

There was a silence as all at the table shook their heads. 'But we na-na-na-know the f-f-f-fish is t-t-t-true, my Lord,' Father Hermann stammered, indicating his overpowering nervousness.

'Oh? You have seen it, Father?'

'Nay . . . others,' Father Hermann said softly, forgetting to add the 'my Lord'.

'Others? What others? Who are these others?'

'Three prostitutes . . . the b-b-b-bathhouse attendant,' Father Hermann managed. This produced a great roar of laughter. Mortified, the big priest turned scarlet, his eyes tightly closed and his chin tucked into his hunched shoulder. It was as if he had just received a violent slap to his face.

'If my Lord Archbishop agrees I will show it . . . the fish,' I ventured, when the laughter had almost ceased.

A sudden silence ensued. Then the archbishop exclaimed, 'What? You would undress in public . . . once again?'

'Nay, my Lord!' I protested. 'Let shears be brought and a window cut to the back of my gown.' I looked up at the archbishop, my expression most demure. 'If this is not thought to be too immodest?'

Father Hermann looked up slowly and gave me a grateful look.

'Where exactly is this fish and cross?' the archbishop enquired.

'Between my shoulderblades, my Lord.'

The archbishop turned to his chief clerk. 'Shoulders. Are shoulders and their blades allowed in public?'

The clerk thought for a moment, then said, 'I believe it is among the many fashions, my Lord.'

'Then they may be exposed?'

'I think my Lord may permit it,' the clerk answered.

'With shears or rolled down?'

'Rolled down, if judiciously done, my Lord,' the clerk suggested.

'Who will do this rolling down?' the archbishop asked.

'My Lord, my friend Rosa waits in the anteroom, she will do it,' I said quickly.

'And she won't cry?'

'Nay, she was the one who *didn't* cry, my Lord.' I was delighted that they were not going to cut my beautiful dress and momentarily imagined the horror on Frau Sarah's face if she should see it damaged.

'Very well, then.' The archbishop turned to the porter and called out, 'Fetch this Rosa woman!'

During all his questioning I had been waiting for an opportunity to explain that the fish was simply a birthmark, that the two lashes administered to my back by the archbishop by sheer coincidence bisected the fish to form the shape of a cross. But now I realised that so much had been made of the fish and the cross that I must make the most of the disrobing opportunity.

I had learned in Ali Baba's that men like nothing better than that they be present when one courtesan undresses another. I knew that I could as easily and with due modesty draw my gown over my shoulders to reveal the fish, but that this would spoil the anticipation. I could almost hear Fatima saying, '*Sylvia, the movement of a woman, it is this that stirs the male's imagination and awakens the one-eyed snake. Her hips, how she uses her hands, her mouth, her eyes, the shrug of a shoulder, a sideways glance. When one woman removes the clothes of another, it is as if he possesses them both and also, at the same time, watches them making love to each other. Two women making love to each other is every man's fantasy.*'

While Rosa was neither comely nor artful, with a peasant woman in an unshapely brown linen shift undressing a comely and shapely lady there nevertheless existed a certain drama for the male imagination. At the same time, it would be seen to be done with due decorum. The porter returned with Rosa and, in a low voice, I briefly explained that I would turn my back and undo my bodice whereupon she must pull down the back of my dress to reveal the fish.

'I crave your indulgence, I must turn my back to you, my Lord,' I explained.

'She has nice manners for a peasant,' he announced to nobody in particular and then nodded his acquiescence. 'Only shoulders and their blades,' he added as an afterthought.

Complete silence fell over the assembly as I turned my back and, unseen by them, undid the ties to my bodice, my movements slow with my elbows raised and pushed outwards so they might see the movement of my arms. When my arms finally fell to my side in repose, Rosa stepped behind me and lifted my dress slightly by taking hold of the top of both sleeves. Then she proceeded to pull downwards slowly. I moved my shoulders as if to ease the passing of the cloth knowing that it would look pretty and provocative. Rosa being somewhat shorter than me meant they could now see the top part of my shoulders while her body and head covered the area between my shoulderblades. She waited until the fish was fully revealed before she stepped aside.

A collective gasp rose from the assembled church dignitaries. Then followed a frantic scraping of feet and the sound of benches pushed backwards. Moments later the archbishop's voice rose in prayer.

With the help of the astonished Rosa I hastily pulled my gown back over my shoulders and retied the laces to my bodice before cautiously turning to face the table. The churchmen knelt and the archbishop stood with his hands clasped. Praying in Latin he glorified God for showing them the path of righteous judgement in the matter before them. Anticipating the end of the prayer I whispered to Rosa to quickly turn her back to them again. Then bowing our heads, and with hands clasped in the humble and pious position, we waited for the collective 'Amen'.

When it came, there was at first silence, then followed the archbishop's injunction for them to be seated. A second scraping of benches and legs occurred while Rosa and I stood silently, not moving a muscle. Later Rosa would tell me that the scabs had all rubbed off the mark of the cross but that a bright pink scar remained where the skin had not yet returned to its normal colour and that the fish was still neatly bisected by it.

'You may turn around, Sylvia Honeyeater,' the archbishop said in a modified and respectful voice.

'Thank you, my Lord Archbishop,' I said softly, trying to hide my anxiety and surprise that the sighting of the fish had affected the priests and scribes and others present in the same way as it had Brother Dominic. I confess I had no idea what might happen next.

Then the archbishop rose and left his chair and proceeded along the table to its end, and then turned and came over to where Rosa and I stood. Towering beside us, he turned to the gathering at the table. 'The Church has erred in this matter and we will immediately start proceedings to bring this precious child of God back to a state of grace.' He turned to the senior clerk. 'You will attend to this matter, Monsignor Strauss.' The clerk who had allowed that shoulders might be seen in public nodded and, dipping his quill in blacking, wrote on parchment in front of him. 'Now, Sylvia, we would like your opinion of what occurred in St Martin's square and in the Church,' the archbishop said, looking down at me from his lofty height.

I told the gathered assembly as best I could what had occurred in the Church, up to and including the death of the archbishop and the fact that I had felt impelled to walk out to the square while singing a Gloria.

'It is witnessed that the archbishop struck you, that his first blows were directed at you?' the bishop now said. It was the first time he had spoken.

'I cannot say, my Lord. If it was so then I did not feel it.'

The bishop rose to his feet, clearly pleased with my answer. 'Then he may *not* have struck you?' he asked.

I was placed in a quandary. They had accepted the cross on my back as a holy sign placed by the hand of God and had been brought to prayer on witnessing it. How could I now diminish its importance? I decided to tell a cautious truth. 'It is said that the two marks on my back are the result of his blows,' I said.

The archbishop interrupted. 'Blows you did not feel? How very strange. Yet if they were blows the marks remain still,' he exclaimed. Then turning to the bishop who was once again seated, he said, 'We must accept that there were blows. But holy blows. God caused the archbishop to use his crook to place the sign of the cross upon the back of His child. A cross upon which He placed the holy fish, the sign of His precious Son and our Saviour and Redeemer, Jesus Christ. If they had been blows with harmful . . . with devilish intent, then they would have been felt. But miraculously there was no pain.' He turned to me. 'Is that not the truth, Sylvia? You felt no pain?'

'Aye, my Lord Archbishop, it is the truth.' I did not say that later I had well and truly felt the severity of the blows to my back. It was clear he was building a theory for what occurred in the Church. It was certainly not my place to contradict him.

'Good! That's good.' He turned to the bishop. 'Do you accept this is what happened?' he asked.

The bishop nodded. 'Yes, my Lord.'

'Good! Now let us get on with it.' He turned back to me. 'Tell us about the death of the archbishop. Do you believe he was struck dead by the hand of God?'

'Nay, my Lord,' I exclaimed in a shocked voice. 'It was a heart attack.'

'A heart attack? Are you sure?'

I had witnessed five heart attacks at the *winkelhaus*. It was Master Yap's greatest concern when a client who was over-corpulent visited. The girls spoke often of how a very fat male, if over-excited, might at any moment while he is pumping have a heart attack and fall dead to almost smother them under his weight. 'Yes, he was greatly vexed at what had happened in the square and then in the church and the Lord God chose that moment to transport him to heaven,' I said piously, my voice on the edge of tears.

I could see the archbishop very much liked this explanation. 'And you're sure he wasn't possessed? Struck down because he was possessed?'

'Nay, my Lord, it was his heart, I am sure of it.'

'But he struck the two clerics wantonly, or so they claimed.'

'I cannot contradict the two priests, my Lord. But they had become panic-stricken. It is a state often stopped with a severe slap to the face. The blows may have been intended for this purpose?' I suggested, then added, 'The archbishop was trying to restore order and was himself very agitated at the behaviour of the clerics.'

'Perfect! Restore order!' he shouted, clapping his hands, clearly pleased with the two words I'd used. He turned to the table. 'Note this! The archbishop was attempting to *restore order* when he died of a *heart attack*. The Lord God, who sees everything, knew that the time had come to take our dear brother in Christ away from us. So, He placed the sign of the cross on the back of this pious child. By so doing, He delegated her, in the absence of the archbishop and because of the panic of the two clerics, to *restore order*! *Restore order* in the Church and then later in the square outside!'

I don't think the archbishop's reasoning would have passed a Brother Dominic test but no one present appeared to be sufficiently brave to challenge it and Father Hermann positively beamed at me.

The bishop, knowing that with my sudden sanctification his own judgement was to be questioned, rose and pointed his finger at me, his bejewelled bishop's ring catching the light. With his voice raised, he accused, 'There is still the matter of the nudity. Do you have an explanation for why you felt compelled to remove your habit? Do you not think this the work of the devil?'

'Nay, my Lord, it occurred in the midst of the first prayer of the mass when I had just completed singing the *Gloria in Excelsis Deo*, a most pious moment. In truth, I felt the presence of the Lord protecting me.' I was telling the truth but it nevertheless proved quite the wrong thing to say.

'The Lord does not condone nakedness in His church!' the archbishop said severely. Then turning to the bishop, he said, 'Thank you for your point, my Lord Bishop.' The angry bishop reluctantly resumed his seat. 'Does anyone here have anything to say on this matter? The people are,

I believe, calling this reprehensible behaviour a miracle – what say you, eh?' the archbishop challenged.

A moment's silence ensued and then, to my surprise, it was Father Paulus who rose to his feet. 'Perhaps a contagion, my Lord Archbishop,' he said nervously.

The archbishop whirled around to face where Father Paulus stood at the very end of the banquet table. 'Contagion! Who said that?' Pointing his finger at Father Paulus, he demanded, 'Who are you?'

'I am Paulus, scribe at St Martin's church, my Lord,' Father Paulus answered, plainly terrified at the great man's sudden attention.

'Explain! What mean you by *contagion*, Father Paulus?' the archbishop demanded.

'It is of the mob, my Lord. A mass hysteria, when hundreds of people find themselves taken up with a cause and an invisible excitement – a spirit miasma seems to possess them so they will do what they would not normally do on their own. It is commonly seen with pilgrims at shrines and I have read that it also occurs during crusades . . . in battles and the like,' he ended lamely.

'But that is the work of God! The spirit, the Holy Spirit descends unto them, moving them to praise, I have seen it in Rome many times,' the archbishop stated. 'But this is not the same. This chanting we are told was the work of the devil.'

'Aye, my Lord. But it is not always done for God's purpose. When, for example, a mob might rampage against a moneylender, perhaps a Jew who is said to have cheated. Not all have been cheated, perhaps only one or two, but a thousand may soon be gathered at the Jew's door and demand that the offender be dragged out, and they, the mob, will do so and may kick him to death or hang or burn him.' It was a very brave statement and I felt proud that Father Paulus showed the courage to make it.

The archbishop sighed. 'Aye, I know it happens. The mob, eh? Contagion.' He seemed to be savouring the word, saying it quietly as if testing its veracity. 'But how might this spread from the square into the church to affect four women kneeling in prayer at the altar?' he now asked.

'It may have been brought in by members of the congregation, perhaps those who first rushed to witness the chanting in the square outside,' Father Hermann piped up, no longer intimidated. He had not been in St Martin's that Sunday but had heard all about it from me.

But the bishop was not yet silenced. 'Then why did the congregation not suffer from this *contagion*, only the women who did not see the chanting?' he shouted.

It was a good question and it was obvious Father Hermann didn't have the answer. I looked over at Father Paulus but could see he too had no answer. 'They were past the age of child-bearing, my Lord Archbishop,' I said, trying to sound convincing.

This brought a string of titters from the table. 'What mean you by that?' the archbishop asked.

'The chant, my Lord. "Our children in Jerusalem" concerned women who have or may still have children.'

'Ah! Contagion! It *only* affected women who have or may still bear children,' the archbishop repeated, suddenly delighted. Curiously this seemed to be true. It had been remarked on several times in the past that there had been no old women in the square. The archbishop returned to his chair and sat pensive, his ringed finger touching his small mouth that was pulled tight so that it resembled another orifice lower down and at the back of his corpulence.

'The nuns! They are forbidden child-bearing!' the bishop sneered. 'Why then were they possessed of this contagion?'

There followed a hum of acquiescence from the table. I waited until silence had resumed. '"*Suffer little children to come unto me,*" saith the Lord,' I quoted. Then added, 'They are brides of Christ and therefore beholden to His word in this matter concerning children, my Lord Bishop. It is a thing of the mind *and* the spirit.' I then lowered my head and looked down so as not to seem too forward with this response.

'Aha!' the bishop replied, triumphant. 'Did we not declare the women's nakedness a sin and the chanting the work of the devil? Now you say the nuns obeyed the word of God!'

Again there was a general murmuring at the table.

'We have not yet addressed the matter of the words they were chanting, my Lord Bishop,' the archbishop said sharply. He was plainly upset with the bishop for poking a stick in the spokes of his hitherto well-trundling argument.

The mice sat silent. I thought of how Brother Dominic might conduct the argument. He would take each separate piece of evidence, each finding, and relate it to another, thus revealing either its falsehood or veracity. 'May I speak, my Lord Archbishop?' I said, thinking all the while that perhaps I had already said too much.

'Aye, it seems no other is willing. What say you on this matter of the chanting and the nakedness, Sylvia Honeyeater? I must warn you that we may not condone nakedness in public and as the bishop has said, it is declared a sin!'

'My Lord, it is the bishop who hath declared this gathering a sin and not the people of Cologne.'

'The bishop speaks for God and the Holy Scriptures and the people of Cologne for themselves!' the archbishop chastised.

'Yes, my Lord, but in the Holy Scriptures there are several instances when God's children did rent their clothes in worshipful and praiseworthy distress. The sudden loss of a child to a woman is the greatest distress she may bear, and when the word of God came to the two women who first came naked to the square commanding that their children depart for Jerusalem it is quite possible that they were so distressed that they rent their clothes and ran to the church for succour. Others by means of contagion, hearing the words of God, "Our children in Jerusalem", all those women who have children did, as the first two had done, rent their clothes and hasten to the square of St Martin's beseeching the Almighty to spare them this terrible sacrifice.' A stunned silence ensued to which I added softly, 'A man may also feel this terrible travail, as did Abraham, when God commanded that he sacrifice his beloved first-born son, Isaac.'

'Four languages, eh . . . and I'll vouch she reasons as well in all four. Meanwhile we know her to be specially blessed of God, or why else would she be allowed to bear witness at this hearing? It is no different to the incident in the church, where our Saviour did command her to restore order when our dear brother in Christ was taken away from us. Now she brings this blessed explanation that every woman, every mother in the land would understand.' The archbishop turned to the bishop and demanded, 'What say you now, my Lord Bishop? The nakedness was neither the work of God nor Satan, but the manifested love of a woman for her children brought about by contagion?'

'And the chant?' the bishop asked sourly, silently rebuking me with his look.

'Ah, the chant, we must now declare it the word of God.' The archbishop turned from us and walked slowly back to his chair, panting slightly at the effort. Had he ever visited Ali Baba's, Master Yap would have persuaded him to return home, whereupon he would have sent a courtesan secretly to his bedchamber. A dead archbishop in his *winkelhaus* could very easily invoke the mass hysteria or contagion Father Paulus talked of when he produced the example of the Jewish moneylender. It would certainly mean the closing of his premises. 'Does anyone have anything to say?' the archbishop said, looking first to his left then his right and then directly at the bishop. But the mice remained silent and it became clear from the tone of his voice that the archbishop did not expect nor would he welcome a challenge, as the matter was now neatly wrapped and tied to his satisfaction.

He turned to me. 'You may go, Sylvia Honeyeater. If I am not mistaken we shall hear more of you,' he said. He extended his hand and I moved forward and knelt to kiss his ring, but the table was too broad and I was too short to reach him on my knees and so was forced to lean across it to kiss the bright stone. Rosa went to do the same but the archbishop withdrew his hand. He had not for one moment indicated during the inquiry that he had seen Rosa's presence at my side. She was a peasant and therefore rendered invisible.

'Thank you, my Lord Archbishop,' I replied. I was suddenly aware that I had, whether well or badly, reasoned our way out of our predicament and the thought of my own impetuosity now almost overwhelmed me. How had I dared to have an opinion and to sound it well, when my duty as a woman was to remain silent in the company of a man as high-lofty as a bishop much less an archbishop? Gulping down my fear I said, half in a whisper, 'There is one more thing, my Lord.'

'One more thing? What is it?' he asked impatiently.

'My Lord, the two nuns,' I indicated Rosa at my side, 'and Rosa, they are innocent – like me they suffered only from the effects of the contagion.'

'Yes, yes, I suppose so.' He turned to the clerk. 'Prepare the papers.' He pointed at Rosa. 'Her and the two who weep so hysterically.'

The bishop then spoke up. 'My Lord, with your permission the two noble women would like to return to the convent of Disibodenberg.'

Ha! I thought. *He wants that female viper back behind the convent walls for his own comfort.*

'How know you of this desire?' the archbishop shot back.

'They have dedicated their lives to be brides of Christ; the Lady Angelica is my sister.'

The archbishop sighed. 'Very well, you may give the directive yourself.' He turned to me. 'What about you, my child?'

'I think not, my Lord,' I said quietly.

'Why, when God has so blessed you with signs, would you not become a nun?' the archbishop questioned.

'I wish to work among the poor children, my Lord. Prayer and contemplation in a convent is ill-suited to my temperament. I have worked with Father Hermann and Nicholas of Cologne among the street children. I would like to return to this work.'

'Nicholas, the boy preacher?'

'Aye, my Lord.'

'He is not serious about a Children's Crusade, is he?'

'I do not know, my Lord.'

'May God have mercy on your soul, Sylvia Honeyeater. Like the poor it is not an endeavour that in the end will bring you much profit. What of your study?'

'I will miss it greatly, my Lord.'

'Four languages, that is quite enough! It does not serve a woman well to know too much lest her head grows too large and her paps shrink for lack of womanliness. You are a comely wench and my advice to you is to find a rich man to marry and then to please him well.'

'Yes, my Lord, I will pray upon it and ask for guidance,' I answered.

'Yes, do that, it is God's wish for every woman,' he said absently. With Rosa at my side we turned to go and as we reached the door to the anteroom I heard him call, 'Bring wine and food. It has been a busy and well-concluded day, and just as women must weep so men must eat.' Laughter followed from the mice.

The following day I took up my Father John bag and my beloved stave, now restored to me, and made the journey on foot to the monastery at Disibodenberg to report to Brother Dominic. I would, I told myself, tell him all about the inquiry and what each person had said. I confess in retrospect to being somewhat pleased with my performance and wanted him to know that he hadn't wasted his time by tutoring me. It was vainglorious and unworthy but at the time it seemed appropriate, couched as I intended in the context where I would be crediting him for my precocious performance.

But my tutor was not as easily gulled as the archbishop and his council. 'Aye, child, you have learned your lessons well, but you are nevertheless most fortunate to have answered to a pair of dunderheads and a committee of mice. The present bishop of Cologne is well-known for a philanderer and when it comes to ideas has a thinly populated mind. Your new archbishop, Count Leonardo of Mentz, I knew in Rome where he spent his time with horses, arms, soldiery and banqueting and is more taken up with sophistry than earnest inquiry. He and his family are good friends of Pope Gregory, that ambitious lawyer who cares little for matters spiritual and even less for intellect, who now demands a crusade to Egypt from the Emperor for his own nefarious reasons. It is fortunate that the archbishop thinks so well of you and you would do well to keep his lordship on your side. Like all men of power who seek only solutions, whether righteous or wrongful, that further their ambitions, he makes a good friend and a bad enemy. Although they are birds of a feather, that poltroon bishop who excommunicated you would do well to guard his back.'

I then told him of my decision not to return to the convent and thanked him for his generosity and his teaching. 'Father, you have shown me the path to wisdom and I will strive to keep my feet upon it all my life.'

The old man shook his weary head. 'Sylvia, you have traversed wisdom's rocky road with a sureness of foot and it is I who must thank you. Before you came I had sunk into a well of deep despondency and your presence has kept me from total despair. There will come a time when men will once again think for themselves, but in these dark times it is such as thee who must carry the torch of reason and burn the true light of our Christian belief. I am old and will soon die, but I am content to leave this mortal coil knowing that you are among the few who may carry our faith forward, constantly seeking the truth no matter what the cost. If we are blessed with the unremitting mercy and compassion of Christ, then our belief in His true teaching must constantly be tested and tempered by reason. The word of God rests separately in the heart of every man. Each must consciously decide what His will is for himself and not blindly accept the dogma of the Church. True faith is not for the lazy and compliant – it is a vigorous and strengthening habit practised by a thinking mind, nourished by the heart and tempered by the spirit.'

Knowing myself unworthy of his lavish praises, I wept. As I departed the monastery of Disibodenberg I knew that I might never again meet another such as the beloved Doubting Dominic. He had taught me so much of how the rich and vainglorious think and had, at the same time, managed to instil in me a little wisdom and a small courage in the extent of my mind. I grinned through my tears. He had also helped me develop some perspicacity as well as cunning. I also now wrote fluently in Latin.

Two weeks later I was to hear of my blessed tutor's passing, that he had died in his sleep with a manuscript, one of his own, clasped to his chest, after the previous evening calling for the last rites. The following day with my bag and stave I left Cologne as soon as the gates to the city opened to walk back to the monastery to pray at Brother Dominic's grave. Arriving at the great wooden gates in the late afternoon I rang the clangorous bell. The same little monk who had appeared at the peeping window when Father Hermann had first brought me by mistake to the gate appeared almost at once, his tiny face seeming even more grumpy and stupid.

Seeing I was female he sighed heavily. 'What do you want?' he demanded.

Adopting a suitably supplicating tone I answered, 'Good Brother, I wish to pray at the grave of Brother Dominic.'

'Who?'

I realised that even tiny men can bully. 'Brother Dominic, the great scribe and scholar from Rome, who died here four days ago,' I answered.

'Never heard of him, go away!' he said in a peremptory voice, withdrawing his shiny, fat little face and slamming shut the peeping window.

I slept that night in the woods and in the morning drank from and then washed my face in the stream, and soon after found a few early berries, not yet summer-sweet but not entirely unpleasant. It was a lovely late-spring day when I stood once again at the giant wooden gates. But this time I called the birds until several hundred flocked about me. I reasoned that if that Italian deacon, Francis of Assisi, could impress by preaching to the birds, maybe it would also work for me. I did not ring the bell but simply waited directly opposite the little window set into the gate. It opened soon enough and a different gatekeeper's face, surprised to see me, appeared. 'Good morrow! What is it you want?' the monk shouted above the bird cries, pulling back in fright when a magpie landed on the ledge in front of him.

I indicated the birds. 'We have been sent to pray at the grave of Brother Dominic. He was a great friend of the birds and they have come to sing a Gloria of their own at his graveside.'

'We saw them coming,' he exclaimed. 'They came from everywhere – the sky was filled with their cries. I am sent to inquire,' he shouted in a friendly voice. I made a mental note to think a little better of this bird preacher, Francis of Assisi. Perhaps he wasn't as stupid as he seemed.

'Well then, you are to let us in, we do God's bidding,' I shouted back.

One of the great doors swung open and with the birds hovering above me in an avian cloud we followed him. But with the monastery already alerted by the gathering of the birds and with their noise in the air above me, by the time we reached St Michael's Chapel, which served as the monks' burial ground, a hundred monks had gathered and soon even the abbot arrived. I was led to the grave of Brother Dominic where I let the birds sing a little longer before letting them be gone, and then I asked permission of the abbot to sing a Gloria I knew to be my tutor's favourite.

The abbot then intoned a short prayer and thanked me for coming. 'We have heard much about you, Little Sister Sylvia. It seems God has blessed you in Cologne and you have made a powerful friend in the new archbishop.'

'Father, I am no longer at the nunnery and am now plain Sylvia Honeyeater, and as for the archbishop, I have met him but the once.'

'But well met it seems. He has visited and speaks mostly highly of you and claims you have great sensibilities for a woman and are gifted with four languages. I know Brother Dominic greatly loved you and you brought him great joy with your questioning mind. He thought us all not worth the time to tutor and claimed you would one day be another Hildegard von Bingen.'

I blushed. 'Nay, Father!' I protested. 'Brother Dominic was always over-lavish in his praise.'

'I think not,' he replied quietly. 'Perhaps you will tarry sufficiently to take some repast?' Then he added, 'I would greatly like to hear the story of the archbishop's inquiry. We get scarce any news here and the archbishop on his visit told that you did play a surprisingly relevant part in the hearing and greatly helped his deliberations, though he didn't tell us more of the proceedings.'

'Did Brother Dominic not tell you? I told him all of it.'

'Nay, he was old and felt himself betrayed by Rome.' The abbot sighed. 'He trusted no one in the priesthood and in the end, perhaps only thee.'

I would not have found myself able to accept the abbot's hospitality knowing that news of my coming would reach the abbess and that this might prove awkward for him. It was he who had originally urged her, to her fury, to free me for the afternoons so that I might study with Brother Dominic. I did not wish to make further trouble between them. But now, by telling the abbot of the archbishop's inquiry, I would justly earn the food he offered and so I readily agreed. Besides, with only a few half-ripe berries in my stomach I felt myself famished. 'Thank you, Father, you are most kind and I cannot refuse. I have not eaten since the morning of yesterday and the return to Cologne is long and without sustenance would prove arduous.'

'Then you are welcome and you must have bread and wine to take with you.'

He led me to the guest room near the kitchen where the smell of newly baked bread from the nearby ovens caused me to salivate. He bade me be seated though he continued to stand beside me. Soon fresh bread still warm from the oven and cheese and a little smoked fish with a jug of ale was brought to me. 'Will you not sit, Father? It is a long story and you will be more comfortable.' It was then that I suddenly remembered. 'Oh dear, please forgive me, Father. I have brought you a small gift that I hope you will accept.' I removed my Father John satchel from my back and from it took a large jar. 'It is ointment. I am told it is most efficacious and will bring you some comfort.'

The abbot took the jar of ointment for his piles without a change of expression. 'Thank you, it is most thoughtful of you, Little Sister Sylvia. The abbess has closed the dispensary at the convent and we greatly miss the many efficacious items she prepared for us.' Then, to indicate that he understood the nature of the ointment, 'Though an ointment such as this, though promised, was never obtained.'

'Father, the woman Rosa, it was she who prepared these medicines at the convent but she has since departed. I know her whereabouts in Cologne.' I hesitated a moment, drawing a breath. 'Perhaps she might bring the unguents and ointments you need from time to time, her payment being perhaps in wine and grain?' I knew that Frau Sarah would be happy with this arrangement – she had taken a liking to Rosa and enjoyed her cheeky peasant wit. Whenever she had an early morning free they would spend time gathering herbs in the woods.

'Ah, that is an excellent solution. We have always paid the abbess in wine and wheat or barley and sometimes smoked fish – it will be no greater burden to pay this woman, Rosa.'

I then commenced to eat and all the while to tell the abbot the story of the naked women chanting in the square right through to the end of the inquiry when we were once again restored to the bosom of the Church.

The abbot, still standing, looked pensive. 'This boy, Nicholas of Cologne, you know him well?'

'Aye, I have known him since I first came to Cologne.'

'And is he blessed?'

'Yes, Father. On the days he preaches his sermons are filled with the glory of our Saviour and his message is most inspiring. He now preaches to over a thousand children and each time still more come. Some have travelled for days to hear him,' I added.

'And this Children's Crusade, what think you of it?'

'It is a miracle, Father. A miracle I have been waiting for all my life.'

'Miracle? Has it guided you? Is there a message?'

'Aye, God has bade the children to march to Jerusalem to take the Holy Sepulchre back from the infidel.'

'And you would go?' he asked, surprised.

'I must answer God's command and do His bidding.'

'You have prayed? Sought guidance? After all, you are no longer yourself a child.'

'Aye, but I work among street children and know their natures well. I must go to care for them.'

'Oh, Little Sister Sylvia, will you not think carefully upon this!' he cried in a tone of great alarm. 'Jerusalem, it is a year's walk if you are fortunate. How will you cross the sea? Who will provision you? There are perilous climbs and dangerous places, mountains and snows and deserts, brigandry is everywhere and you will have no arms or knights to protect you.'

'I cannot deny God's command to me, Father,' I replied softly. 'I have seen this miracle and I must now test my faith.'

CHAPTER ELEVEN

The Cross of Crows

I ARRIVED BACK IN Cologne from the monastery of Disibodenberg on the 25th of April in the year of our Lord 1212 to find Nicholas in the highest of preaching spirits with energy that could not be contained. This was to continue for the next ten days and both Father Hermann and myself were run off our feet. Halfway through this period, the good priest was heard to declare, 'I cannot keep up with him, Sylvia. He preaches daily, recruiting for his crusade, and each day the children attending increase in number and come from everywhere. Only yesterday I met boys from Liège and Floreffe and they told of others from Marbach, Neresheim and Zwiefaltern. I came across a group of young girls from Schäftlarn in the east! I told them to return home, that embarking on a crusade was hard and dangerous and no place for girls.' He laughed wearily. 'One of them looked at me and said, "Who then will do the cooking, Father?" It was a good point, we have not thought of this.'

In fact we had not thought of very much. Nicholas had insisted that on his latest visitation the voice of Jesus had instructed him that he must leave on the day of Pentecost, just sixteen days after I'd returned from the visit to Brother Dominic's grave. When I pointed out that we couldn't possibly be ready he shrugged. 'I cannot disobey my Saviour!' And that was the end of it. Which was all very well, but it left Father

Hermann and myself shaking our heads in dismay.

Father Hermann had set up an alms box near the sacristy of St Mary's on the Kapitol and the people of Cologne gave generously at first. While they had given the Children's Crusade a nod, thinking it the natural outcome of the Miracle of St Martin's, they were being called upon to feed several thousand children each day and things were slowly turning sour. Some grumbling in the markets could be heard when our collection carts went round. Peasants are steady grumblers and not a naturally generous lot, but it must be said in fairness that with so many hungry mouths to feed and with very few children possessing any means of their own, they were beginning to have good reasons to complain. Moreover, the country folk coming into Cologne with produce, who camped outside the city gates waiting for them to open when the Angelus rang, now found their passage hindered by the hundreds of children arriving overnight.

The churches of St Martin's and St Mary's on the Kapitol possessed four horsedrawn carts that the bishop, thinking to regain the people's confidence by supporting the Children's Crusade, had allowed us to use. We would visit the markets daily with them, two of the carts to the produce market, one each to the fish and butchers' markets. Every day the carts, fitted with special harnesses, would be manned by volunteers among the children who did not see this as arduous work but simply fun, and there was always a rush in the morning to occupy a harness. Pulling the carts made them feel important and a part of the coming crusade and it was often difficult to keep at an even pace. Young boys are naturally competitive and they were always trying to race each other.

Father Hermann and I would take turns in manning one of the carts and upon arrival at the market I would sing, and he would give a short sermon and then take confessions, and thereafter conduct mass. Country folk, unless they live in a large village, seldom enjoy the services of a priest and so have few opportunities to confess and thereafter partake of the blessed bread and the wine, the body and blood of Jesus Christ. Having been given the opportunity for confession and mass they gave generously. It was thereafter, when their consciences were once again clear, that they were heard to grumble.

Both church squares were now filled with child pilgrims and the older women worshippers of both St Mary's and St Martin's did the cooking, feeling themselves an essential and cheerful part of the impending crusade. We also gathered together a couple of hundred of the children, some girls but mostly boys, who were given lessons in rudimentary cooking.

If all this sounds well thought out, it wasn't – chaos abounded and then the alms box was stolen from near the sacristy of St Mary's on the Kapitol. It was a large sum of money, almost sufficient to purchase an ox wagon to carry the portable altar the archbishop had donated as well as the huge cauldrons needed for making soup and the bags of flour donated for baking bread on the journey to Jerusalem. Father Hermann was deeply anguished by the crime, as he felt personally responsible, it being his church, the alms box having been taken in front of his beloved Virgin's eyes. He thought this a particularly bad omen. But Nicholas seemed infuriatingly unconcerned.

'Nicholas, don't you understand? We are done for!' I yelled at him.

He smiled. It was a smile he was increasingly seen to wear, halfway between saint and precocious brat, and I was beginning to hate it. 'Nay, Sylvia, God wishes us to have faith. When the time comes He will provide.'

'Horseshit!' I yelled angrily. 'What? Manna from heaven?'

Nicholas shrugged, ignoring the expletive. 'He has done so once before,' he said disingenuously. 'Are we not *also* departing for the Promised Land?'

My nerves were already frayed, beside me Father Hermann was wringing his hands and bemoaning our fate and this stupid boy was looking at me smug as a bug in a sacristy rug. 'God requires us to plough the field and plant the seed before he does the growing!' I yelled. Then, looking at the priest's anguished and helpless demeanour and Nicholas with his superior little smile, I could contain myself no longer. 'For

God's sake, do something!' I cried. It was the first time in my life I had blasphemed and I crossed myself immediately.

But neither seemed to have noticed, too amazed at my anger to register. 'What can we do?' Nicholas said, with another infuriating shrug, although for the first time slightly on the defensive.

'There are at least a thousand children in the square outside this church,' I yelled. 'The alms box was large and sealed and not broken into but taken – the coin slot is too small even for a child's hand. Someone must have seen the thief carrying it out of the church!'

'Good idea!' Nicholas said, then added pompously, 'Why didn't I think of that?'

Father Hermann visibly brightened. 'Ah, such a good mind!' he exclaimed, clapping his hands.

Ever since the archbishop's inquiry he had gained a respect for me that at times proved highly embarrassing, often deferring to me in front of others. A woman's opinion, apart from that on domestic matters, was seldom if ever sought, and I would note the look of surprise, even disbelief, on people's faces when he asked me to pronounce on some secular or religious matter.

That afternoon Nicholas was due to preach in the Church square. 'I'll ask,' he promised.

There would be a number of incidents that I would deeply regret in the months to come, but this request to get the children to find the thief was to be the first of them. At the appointed time the Church square was packed with children so that all had to stand to hear Nicholas. His sermon was as fiery and inspiring as ever we'd come to expect and the spirit of the Lord Jesus seemed to invade the square. I sang as usual and, carried away in the euphoria, had entirely forgotten about my request to ask if anyone had seen the thief. Then I saw Father Hermann urgently whispering into Nicholas's ear and his nod in reply. Turning to the crowd, he held up his hands for silence.

He then explained the theft and in conclusion shouted, 'This money belongs to Jesus! It has been stolen from Him! To steal from God's pocket is a mortal sin! I bid you to go out and find the thief and hang him in God's name and in the name of the Children's Crusade!'

A great roar rose from the crowd. My heart sank and I rushed over to where Nicholas stood. 'Nay, Nicholas! Tell them they must bring the thief to us!'

'I just did!' he protested in a querulous voice.

'No, you said they must *hang* him . . . the thief!' I cried.

'Well, yes, he has stolen from God!' Then, as if not understanding my concern, 'What else? Hanging is the normal punishment for theft from the Church.'

'Aye . . . the authorities, with the bishop's consent, not us.' I pointed down at the square. 'Look at them, they are already a mob.' The compulsive feeling in the air was palpable. I had never seen a mob formed, but it was done almost in an instant. Filled with the spirit of redemption by Nicholas's sermon, they now had a God-given purpose. 'Contagion', Father Paulus's word for it, was a perfectly apt description. As if one entity the children rushed into the two streets leading from the square. 'Thief! Thief! Thief!' they chanted.

The evening meal was about to be served to a thousand hungry children, the only meal they received all day, yet heedless of their growling stomachs they felt compelled to find the thief. It was, I now realised, ridiculous – an angry mob crying out wildly was unlikely to flush out a lone thief hiding in the city, a veritable needle in a haystack.

With this notion I became calmer and said to Nicholas, 'If they find him you *must* promise that he will be brought to justice by the authorities.'

'Why?' he asked insouciantly. 'He stole from us. May we not judge him ourselves in the name of Jesus our Lord?'

'Nicholas, don't be stupid! Listen to me. There are several thousand children in Cologne sleeping in the streets, and with more arriving each day we are trying the patience of the city. Already there are complaints of theft from the market stalls and shops. Now, what will they think of this rampaging, angry mob? If we should catch this thief and hang him that will be the end of it for the Children's Crusade. No one will feel safe and we will not have the archbishop's blessing or the cooperation of the city.'

He seemed to suddenly make up his mind. 'I should be leading them!' he cried out urgently.

I grabbed him about the waist. 'Nay, don't, Nicholas!'

'Leave me alone!' he lashed out angrily with his arms. 'I know what I'm doing! Jesus tells me!'

Father Hermann now had him in a neck-lock. 'No!' he said. 'No, you're not going, Nicholas!'

The resistance suddenly left his body and he collapsed on the steps and commenced to weep. 'Nobody cares!' he sobbed, and his eyes seemed to go vacant, the almost supernatural energy of the previous days gone. In front of our eyes Nicholas had sunk back into one of his states of despondency.

I tell you this because it is always made out that Nicholas of Cologne, while only fourteen years old, was a strong and charismatic leader. And it was true, when the spirit of the Lord possessed him he was irrepressible and irresistible. But when, as he put it, the devil visited him, he was listless and possessed of a constantly despairing mood. We had learned that no amount of cajoling would restore him to his previous self and that it must come about in his own time.

When these despairing turns occurred, Father Hermann would allow him to stay in a small cell in the crypt of St Mary's that was occasionally used by priests to rest during the day or by a visiting monk. It contained a bed, a small table and an oil lamp, and we would bring Nicholas his food, and a clay pan so that he might defecate. After a few days of solitude he would ask me to obtain a magic mushroom and then, emerging from its trance, he would slowly regain his energy until he was once again the fiery leader.

A part of our consternation at the theft of the alms box was that we proposed to build a dark, covered section on the ox wagon we hoped to purchase so when these so-called 'devil moods' possessed Nicholas he might be spared from the children who constantly sought him out. Now, without at least one wagon where he might rest during these periods of despondency, I was at a loss to know what we'd do when his zeal failed. For now we could explain his absence by saying that he had gone to pray for God's guidance on the forthcoming Children's Crusade. These periods free of his preaching were even useful as they freed us to make the countless arrangements needed for the departure to Jerusalem.

Alas, I had been wrong about the ability of the mob to find the thief. The eyes of children are everywhere and I should have known that street children, as a matter of survival, see everything. One of the children, a boy named Stefan, returning from the woods where he had been setting traps for songbirds, came across a man with only one good eye; the other a white sightless ball rolled back into his head. The man carried a box on his shoulder with the symbol of the cross painted on the side. A leather strap across his left shoulder was attached to a wineskin resting on his right hip. The boy was thirsty and hoped to beg a free tipple. With the box so marked he thought the man might be a pilgrim, perhaps a country bumpkin and so an easy mark. Ever artful at coercion Stefan had suggested that the box looked heavy and asked politely what it might contain. The man halted and then sighed and explained that his woman had lost a child and that the box had been intended as its cradle, that it now contained the dead child wrapped in swaddling cloth and he wished to bury it in the woods as it had been born prematurely and did not yet possess a soul.

The boy was curious why the man didn't simply throw the stillborn child into the Rhine or, as was more often the case, into the fetid and stinking waters of the *Blaubach*. I am reminded that this former method of disposal was so common that there exists a child's rhyme that goes:

Dead children
not yet consecrated,
hang on hooks
the devil's baited.

Make them dust.
Make them ashes.
Turn them into
muddy splashes!
A child thus born
with Satan's kiss
must needs be food
for hungry fish!

The boy Stefan, pointing once more to the box, asked, 'If it is not baptised why not throw it in the river? Why bury it in a box with the holy cross upon it?'

'Ah! A worthy question,' the man replied, then shaking his head sadly, he said, 'This is the fourth child we have lost stillborn and by painting a cross upon its cradle my good frau and I hoped that God, in His infinite mercy, would this time bless us with a healthy infant.'

Seeing an opportunity the boy replied in a consoling voice, 'Aye, my good and pious friend, you may be sure that God will hear your prayers next time.' Then he added, as if a mere afterthought, 'Come, let us drink to the health of your next child!' He smiled disarmingly and pointed to the wineskin. 'A prayer to God and a drink to ward off the devil's evil eye. What say you, eh?'

The one-eyed man shook his head. 'Nay, I regret I cannot tarry and the wine is for another; my master will be angry if I am not soon returned.' With a hasty farewell he'd continued up the hill towards the woods. The speed of his departure and the incline was such that it caused the contents of the box to rattle. While Stefan would later remember that the man had said the dead child lay swaddled within the coffin, at the time he was too chagrined at missing out on a drink to question the contradiction of a rattling coffin. It was only when Nicholas told of the stolen alms box that he realised that the rattle would have been coins and the coffin the alms box stolen from St Mary's church.

The mob rushed up the hill into the woods and did not have to go far before they found the alms box broken open and empty. And so the search began in every tavern, every brothel, every place a man might drink a wineskin on his own. A thousand children asking: 'Have you seen a one-eyed man? A one-eyed man carrying a wineskin at his waist? A drunken one-eyed man? A one-eyed man with lots of coin in his pocket? A one-eyed man buying wine for others? A drunk with one good eye?' They woke a hundred men asleep in the dark alleyways of the city and examined their eyes. Three one-eyed men were found and brought to Stefan, but they proved not to be the culprit and were released, fleeing for their lives. By the time the nine o'clock curfew bell rang, the children, tired and hungry, returned to St Martin's square where they ate the half-burned stew and gruel and the coarse bread cut for an earlier meal and now dried out.

While I feared the children rampaging through the city would have caused a high degree of consternation among the citizens of Cologne, at least no public lynching had taken place. There would be gossip and people prophesying no good would come of it, but no harm had come to the prospect of the crusade.

However, I had not reckoned on our own street children, those who had grown up with Nicholas in the area around St Martin's church. They proved far more careful and patient in their search for the alms thief and most had not returned the previous night but had stationed themselves at the various city gates and at the river dockside and any other place where a person might leave the city. They reasoned that with the hue and cry and hullabaloo of the previous afternoon and evening every citizen would be alerted and on the lookout for a man with only one eye. Stealing the alms box from a church was a heinous crime and none would show the culprit pity or keep him hidden. His only chance was to escape the city, otherwise it became only a matter of time before he would be apprehended.

Our own street children found him early the next morning down by the river docks. He was a merchant sailor and had slept on a vessel that carried roof tiles to the cities and towns along the Rhine. The boat was moored to a jetty and he had come bare-waisted from below decks to vomit into the water, no doubt carrying a severe hangover. A sharp-eyed street child had seen him as he turned and wiped his mouth with the back of his hand and then reached for the goatskin waterbag hanging from the centre mast. A sharp whistle and a few moments later a dozen boys had swarmed aboard and dragged him onto the shore. Soon their shrill whistling was heard all over the city as the street children started to converge on the docks. They were joined by the Crusade Children and in less than an hour, a thousand children congregated in the docks area.

The tragedy was that the city gallows stood close by and after Stefan positively identified the sailor, everything quickly got out of hand and the alms thief hung kicking from the gallows. It was the first public execution by children in Germany, and the Church and the city guilds and authorities would not be pleased.

All this had taken place without my knowing. I had left very early for the woods to find mushrooms for Nicholas. Fortunately the spring weather for the last two days had been mostly overcast and humid, ideal conditions for magic mushrooms and, for once, they were plentiful. Had I only needed one to bring Nicholas out of his slough of despondency, though it was too early for this to happen, I would have been back down the hill perhaps in time to prevent the tragedy. Mindful of the long journey ahead I'd been collecting the mushrooms at every opportunity and drying them. I didn't know if the same mushrooms grew in other places but knew there would be many times on the journey to Jerusalem that they would be needed.

It was nearly nine o'clock when I returned, by which time the thief had been dead an hour or more and the news was already known in the marketplace, where many of the peasants had rushed to witness the lynching. It would be only a matter of time before the news reached the bishop and the guild masters and whoever else in the city in authority would regard the lynching as a major misdemeanour.

Father Hermann and Father Paulus were waiting for me at the gallows where the children still milled about, shouting and singing snatches of hymns as though it was a religious gathering. Stefan pushed through the crowd and handed me a leather bag. 'It is nearly full and must be the coins that came from the alms box, Sylvia,' he said happily.

I took the bag and handed it to Father Paulus as Father Hermann was forbidden to handle money. 'Stefan, we are in big trouble and if the authorities come and ask who is responsible you must say you don't know, then send them to me, you hear?'

Stefan looked puzzled. 'But he is a thief and he stole from the Church. Is it not right to hang him?'

'Only with the bishop's permission and also that of the guild masters – we may not take it into our own hands. Now *promise* me! If they ask, no names should be given, just say, "The mob did it". They will be looking for the main culprits to make an example, but they cannot punish a thousand children. Now hurry! Spread the word.' Stefan nodded and turned to leave. 'Wait, Stefan!' I called out, and turning to Father Paulus asked for the moneybag I'd given him. 'Stefan, go to the markets and purchase a coffin, the cheapest you can find, and bring it here.'

'Aye, Sylvia, I will hire it,' he grinned. 'One with a sliding bottom.'

I made a mental note that he would be a worthy helper on the crusade, then turned to the two priests, both looking doleful and concerned. They seemed at a complete loss as to how to control so great a crowd of children. I pointed to the gallows. 'We must cut him down and you must give him the last rites and then I want you to preach from the gallows platform.'

Father Hermann looked shocked. 'The rites, yes . . . b-b-b-but I have n-n-n-no words for a sermon on a gallows platform,' he stuttered. With Father Hermann, when facing an awkward situation it was either bombast or faint-heartedness. I would need him on the crusade but knew he would prove hopeless in any crisis.

I looked at Father Paulus who, calling upon his deafness, pretended not to hear. 'Eh?' he yelled.

'You must talk, preach,' I pointed at the crowd, 'to them!' I shouted.

His hands shot up in protest and he shook his head vigorously. 'Nay, I am but a scribe, Sylvia!' he shouted, as if I too was deaf.

I turned back to the Virgin's earthly husband. 'Father Hermann, listen to me! The bishop will demand an explanation and will chastise you severely and who knows what else. We are in trouble and must try to make some good come from this disaster. We will cut this fellow down and you will administer the last rites. Yes, I know he is already dead and his soul departed, but we will be seen to be doing the right thing. I will sing a Miserere and you will give a short sermon!'

'Sylvia, I am bedazed and have no words within me,' he whined.

'Then hear this!' I exclaimed, impatient with the milksop priest. 'Was it not a thief who was crucified at Christ's side at Calvary and did not the Son of God say, "Today shalt thou be with me in paradise"? This, Father, will be your theme today, the thief on the cross beside Christ. Then you will say that we of the Children's Crusade do, in the name of the Lord Jesus Christ, forgive this thief who stole alms from the church and ask God to have mercy on his everlasting soul.'

Father Hermann perked up immediately. 'A grand theme, we will be remembered for our compassion,' he said, forgetting his reluctance of but a few moments ago, or that all of this had been brought about because the children in our charge had just brutally murdered a man.

The thief, still shirtless, was cut down from the gallows and placed in the reusable coffin Stefan had obtained from the coffinmaker's shop near the markets. I then stood on the gallows platform and addressed the children, explaining that we were formed to be a crusade in Christ's name and under His protection and must forgive those who have sinned against us. That we must now give thanks to God and ask His forgiveness. That Father Hermann would conduct the last rites and commit the soul of the thief to God's mercy and then he would follow it with a short sermon and general absolution, whereupon all must disperse. I said it as much for Father Hermann's instruction as for the children. The message was passed on from mouth to mouth until the children stood solemnly and well-contained within a sombre mood of piety that prevailed as the priest delivered the last rites.

I must say, with the corpse no longer dangling from a rope and safely hidden from view within the wooden box, Father Hermann did great justice to the event and his sermon was soundly evoked and most moving. Moments after its commencement and with the coffin at his feet, a carriage arrived containing several of the city's guild masters followed by a troop of soldiers on horseback. They had no doubt heard of or seen the rampaging mob of children the previous day and the news that they had now found and hanged the thief without trial or official permission must have reached them.

The children silently and politely watched as the good burghers stepped from the carriage, then stood aside to allow the group to come right up to the gallows followed by the troop of soldiers still on horseback. They stood at the foot of the platform somewhat bemused, not quite knowing what to think. With two priests and myself on the platform, and Father Hermann, who was well-known to them, conducting what in every respect purported to be a formal funeral service, this was a long way from the scene they'd envisaged of savage and maniacal children gleefully hanging a miscreant.

Father Hermann then bade the children kneel and ask forgiveness. 'Say after me, "Forgive me, Lord, for I have sinned,"' he demanded. Whereupon a thousand or more children's voices repeated the words, and then, as penance, he most ingeniously committed them to visit the Holy Sepulchre in Jerusalem. I then sang a Gloria and the children rose from where they knelt in the dirt and dispersed to look, no doubt, for some way to fill their rumbling stomachs.

But if we had managed to mollify the town fathers, this was not true of the bishop. We had transgressed the laws of the Church and hanged the alms thief without his permission. He demanded that the two priests and myself be summoned to his presence at the bishop's palace at seven of the clock the following morning.

This proved very unlike the occasion with the archbishop's inquiry. The palace was two hours walk from Cologne so we had to persuade the city gatekeeper to let us out before the ringing of the Angelus. It was hot enough to be a summer's day and the new-sown fields of barley on the bishop's estate were green against a cloudless sky, with the mournful cawing of the crows adding a cautionary note to this perfect but for us unlucky day. When we arrived at the palace we were made to wait outside the gates, fortunately under a spreading elm already sufficiently in new leaf to provide good shade. It was mid-afternoon when we were told the bishop had completed tending to his other more important duties, one of which we'd witnessed when he'd ridden imperiously past us on horseback and into the nearby woods with a falcon sitting on his wrist. I was very tempted to cause it to flap, cry out and attempt to break its chain. The bishop had glanced down at us without a word as he passed. We had not been offered water or any sustenance and weary of waiting and thirsty we were at last ushered into the palace entrance hall. I was told to wait while both priests, escorted by a porter, were taken into the chapel.

What transpired with the two of them I would only learn much later but an hour passed before they emerged from the chapel and I could see at once that they had been severely chastened. Father Hermann visibly shook and Father Paulus was red-eyed from weeping. I stood up as they approached but the porter led them straight past me to the door and I could hear him instructing them to return to Cologne without waiting for me. 'Those are the bishop's strict orders,' I heard him say, and my heart beat faster at such unpropitious news.

I waited perhaps another hour before a page, a boy nine or ten years old, came to fetch me and bade me follow. He led me up a broad stairway and along a wide passageway and then turned into a narrower one and opened the door to a small stone-walled bedchamber not much bigger than a monk's cell. A narrow window high up near the ceiling let in the only light and air, so that the room seemed cast in shadow.

'Water? I must have water,' I said. Without a word he pointed to a small table on which stood a jug of wine and a plate of figs and small cakes. 'Nay, water!' I demanded, not intimidated by this silent boy.

'I will ask,' he said hesitatingly, then turned and left.

I looked about me but there was little or nothing more to take in than I had seen at first glance. The bed contained a blanket but no cushion, the floor was tiled but without even a small prayer mat upon it, the small table with the wine, an earthenware mug, cakes and figs the only objects to suggest this wasn't a punishment cell. I could just make out a snatch of blue sky at the topmost right corner of the window.

The page returned shortly with an earthenware jug and mug, stepping mindfully and watching the surface of the water in the jug so as not to spill its contents. I poured and drank greedily while he stood waiting. Handing him back the jug and cup, I asked, 'What is your name?'

'Matthew,' he replied. 'I am named after the first apostle.'

I was trying to contain my anxiety at having been taken into this bedchamber, and talking to the boy Matthew was helping to calm me. 'Where are you from, Matthew?' I asked him.

'The monastery at Disibodenberg,' he replied. 'I am a foundling and will one day become a monk,' he said proudly.

'Disibodenberg!' I exclaimed. 'I know it well. How long have you been in the bishop's service? A page here at the palace?'

'I am an acolyte,' he corrected, then added, 'Only a week.'

'A week! Do you like it?' He did not reply but looked down at his feet. 'Oh dear, you miss the monastery, is that it?' I asked kindly.

He looked up slowly, not answering my question, but then said, 'You are Little Sister Sylvia and you brought the birds to the old monk's grave.'

'You knew Brother Dominic?' I asked.

'Nay, only that he died, but we know of thee – you are the Petticoat Angel and have a fish and a cross on your back,' he said ingenuously, then added, his little face serious still, 'And you brought medicine for the abbot's piles.'

I laughed. 'I hope it brought him some comfort. Nay, I have no cross on my back – it has gone and the fish is a birthmark – nor am I Little Sister Sylvia any longer. My name is just Sylvia or, if you like, Sylvia Honeyeater. There, now you know everything, but you have not answered my question, Matthew.'

'What question?'

'Do you like it here?' He lowered his head and remained silent. I had spent too much time with street children of his age not to know he was saddened and hiding something. 'What is it? Tell me, Matthew.'

'Nay, I may not.'

'Yes, you may. I won't tell.' His lips started to tremble. 'Is it the bishop? What does he do to you?'

'He . . . he touches me.'

'Where?' He pointed to the bed. 'There, in that bed.'

'Nay, where does he touch you?'

'In the bed,' he repeated.

'You are naked?'

His bottom lip began to tremble.

'What happens in the bed, Matthew? Tell me!' I said, my voice raised to push him further.

'He snores,' he said tearfully.

'Nay, answer properly, does he get hard?'

'Aye, he just likes to stroke me.'

'Stroke you? Does he kiss you?'

'Sometimes.'

'He doesn't hurt you?'

'Nay, I must hurt him,' he said sniffing, then knuckling his eyes.

'How?'

'He lies on his stomach.'

'Yes?'

'I must beat him with a switch to his arse.'

'Then what happens? Does he cry out?'

'He shouts "*Suffer little children to come unto me*".'

'Then?'

'He jerks and moans.'

I reached forward and drew him to my bosom and kissed him. It was probably the first time in his life that he'd consciously felt a woman's arms about him or knowingly received a kiss from one. With street children it was the single most powerful thing you could do to comfort them. 'You'd better go, Matthew,' I said softly. 'I'll see what I can do.'

He pulled back. 'Nay, I will be beaten,' he said, alarmed. 'It is only two months, then I return to the monastery and will be safe.'

I smiled. 'You'd better go now,' I said, knowing there was very little, in fact nothing, I could do. He was a foundling and belonged to a monastery, a place where the abuse of children was well-known and whispered about but never documented. The vow of chastity, it seemed, did not always include little boys, although it seemed from what Matthew said, this did not happen at the present time at Disibodenberg. The foundling children from all the monasteries surrounding Cologne were under the bishop's ultimate jurisdiction and if by his own promiscuity he covertly sanctioned this behaviour, the poor children had no further recourse to justice.

Nor could Matthew hope to escape by running away. In a monastery he could justify the food he ate by working in one of the minor orders such as a porter, lector, exorcist or, as he did, as an acolyte, with the hope of some day becoming a priest or monk. But to run away never having known the city streets he wouldn't last a week before the sodomites who preyed on street children discovered him. Unless he lived within a gang, such as the one Nicholas had formed when I first met him, he would soon enough be found sodomised then murdered.

Matthew had not been gone ten minutes when two men entered the room. I drew back frightened, for it was at once obvious that they meant me harm. One of them carried a scourge while the other stood with his arms folded across his chest with a rope attached to his belt. 'Take off thy garment,' the one who carried the whip instructed.

'Nay!' I cried, moving backwards and away from them so that I felt the back of my thighs bump against the bed.

The knave holding the whip smiled – he lacked teeth and the left side of his crooked mouth was shiny with fresh spittle. His nose had been broken frequently and a valley dipped between the top and tip so that it appeared as two separate lumps upon his fleshy and sanguineous face. A deep purple scar tracked from the edge of his half-closed left eye in a jagged curve to the corner of his mouth where his lip was slightly raised and the skin puckered upwards. It was from here that the wetness leaked. 'You may choose, fräulein, to have the cloth torn from your body.' He glanced at his partner. 'We would greatly enjoy doing this, or you may undress for us. What say you now?'

'She has nice tits,' the second knave said, licking his lips. He was less ugly, but hard-faced and pockmarked, his eyes cruel and the way his tongue now stroked along his top lip I knew was intended to frighten me. He unfolded his arms and brought his left hand down to grasp his codpiece, which he commenced to slowly rub with the ball of his thumb, his obsidian eyes never leaving my face. The forefinger of the hand so employed with caressing his wakening erection was missing, as was the tip of the second finger, and a white scar ran diagonally across the back of his hand. It was a common scar among fighting men and came about when warding off a blow from a sword with the naked hand. Scarface had not been as quick as Pockface and he forever wore the keloidal disfigurement to his face.

I raised my stave as if to hit out and both men laughed. 'Drop it, fräulein, or it will be to thy cost if you attempt to use it,' Scarface said. I dropped my stave and it clattered to the floor and rolled under the bed.

I was breathing heavily, trying to contain my fear. 'What are you going to do to me?' I asked.

'Ah, if you do as you are told then you shall only get a beating,' Scarface replied. He tested the scourge in the air. 'The bishop requires lots of little crosses placed upon thy back.' He shrugged and giggled lewdly. '"Not strips, lots and lots of little crosses," those were his very words. But if you resist us, then you will have the selfsame but we also have permission to rape you.'

'She is a dainty dish,' Pockface smirked and I now saw that he had gained an erection, his cock straining at the coarse weave of his stockings. There was no escape – they were both big men and stood with their backs to the door. Now that I knew my fate I remained very frightened but knew I could endure the beating but not the rape. In my mind's eye I was back in the darkened pigsty with the two sows and the boar snuffling and grunting in the corner. I was bent over the broken wine barrel holding grimly to the cold metal hoop where two oak panels had broken away. My father stood behind me, his peg leg pushed out at an angle to gain a firmer purchase in the wet pig shit so that he could, with his own porcine grunts, penetrate me all the harder. I had sworn to myself that I would rather die than have my body so violated by a man again.

I looked at both vile creatures and shouted to gain courage, 'I shall take the bishop's beating, though I wish he were man sufficient to do it himself. If I am to be punished let it be at the hand of God's earthly servant!' As I said this I saw both their eyes shift involuntarily above my head to the ceiling. *Ah! I am being watched! My Lord Bishop is watching this and no doubt has his consecrated cock held in his bejewelled and priestly hand.* I did not turn to look for the peephole in the roof that I knew must be there, but looked instead at the two brutes, no longer afraid of them. 'In God's name I promise, if I am raped by either of you then you will have to kill me or I will not rest until I have destroyed you both.'

Scarface looked at me and must have seen something in my eyes that bade him hold his tongue. But Pockface was too stupid and lacked the other's imagination, thinking me only a silly young cow mooing empty threats to hide my own fear. 'And how will you do this, pretty wench? Will you send me fleeing like you did the three old whores?' He laughed. 'I must warn you I am not so easily frightened by angels in petticoats.' So, they knew who I was.

'Aye, perhaps you have heard of what happened at the gallows yesterday?'

'So?' Pockface said, his smile evil. 'Must I be afraid?'

'Not if you have made your peace with God,' I said slowly, surprised at the coldness in my voice. 'With you the children will not cut you down and bury you in consecrated ground but leave you hanging for the crows to pick your eyes out, then feast upon your brains. That is, if they may find any within thy stupid skull!' Then, as if suddenly possessed, I began to caw, calling as a crow might for his female mate. The unexpected presence of a crow is known by all to be an omen of bad luck; crows are carrion birds and always present at the gallows. I saw the sudden surprise in their eyes. My mournful and repeated caws were as if a crow was already present in the small bedchamber. I commenced to slowly remove my clothes, uttering a silent inward prayer that God would protect me from these two, continuing to call the birds of misfortune so that the two men might be distracted from my undressing.

'Stop!' Scarface cried. 'Stop that calling out!' He lashed at me with his whip and I felt its sharp sting across my thighs but forced myself not to react and looking directly at him called once more, the sound mournful and threatening, filling the shadowy space around us.

Although I should with due modesty have turned my back to them, my every instinct told me to continue to look them in the eyes, to lock their eyes to mine so that they might see my defiance and think carefully of my threat. The news of the hanging of the alms thief I felt sure would have reached the servants' quarters in the bishop's palace or why else were we summoned? Pockface, I surmised, had spoken unthinkingly or from plain stupidity.

I stood naked and defiant in front of the two brutish oafs and willed myself to keep my hands to my side, my feet slightly apart and not to turn my shoulder and cover my breasts and crotch as any maid might do. And then a sudden flutter and a crow landed upon the outside sill of the small window, and then a second. Their heads pulled to one wing then the other in the familiar way of carrion birds, then their sharp black beaks poked inquisitively through the window bars, their red eyes, often called Satan's eyes, fixed on the two men.

'If you touch me again I promise you will not tomorrow see the sun rise. If you are not already dead, then you will have two blood-spilled holes for eyes!' Another crow arrived, pushing the first two into the room where they beat the air with their wings looking for a place to land. Then more, each arrival pushing the others inwards until twenty or more were contained within the bedchamber, with Scarface beating at the air in panic with his scourge. 'See! They come for thee!' I cried out, as more and more crows entered the room, their wings battering against the walls, and attempted to land upon the shoulders and heads of the two terrified men. I dressed hastily, pulling my peasant's shift over my head and slipping on my boots, still calling all the while to the invading birds.

The two brutes could contain their fear no longer. Scarface was the first to turn and flee, closely followed by the pockfaced braggart. Changing my call slightly I sent the crows after them as they fled down the corridor, their arms flailing the air about their heads. I ran out to watch as the big black birds fluttered above them, darting in to attack them, landing momentarily upon their shoulders and pecking at their cheeks and necks, and all the while a terrible cacophony of cawing filled the palace.

'Run! Run for your life, it is the devil coming to get you!' I shouted, as they reached the stairs and leapt down two steps at a time into the hall. I now stood at the top of the stairs. 'Bastards! Pig shit!' I screamed down at them, then turned and quickly ran back to the bedchamber and knelt beside the bed to retrieve my stave. Crows were still coming through the tiny window and so I placed the stave across my back to rest behind my neck and on both shoulders. The birds quickly came to sit upon its length. Unbeknownst to me at the time, to an observer it appeared as if my body was the mainstay and the stave with the large black birds perched along it the cross-stay, so that together we formed an avian cross. This would later become known as 'The Cross of Crows', and would be another item added to the gossip of old women in the church and among the peasants at the markets in Cologne.

'Thank you, Lord Jesus,' I prayed aloud and then walked, turning sideways to go through the narrow door, along the small corridor, then turned frontwards when into the bigger passage and then down the broad stairs.

I began to sing a Gregorian chant, my voice echoing into the great beams of the entrance hall, punctuated by the lugubrious cawing of the crows seated on the cross and others whirling around the ceiling. Servants came running and stopped in their tracks when they saw the cross of crows. Some fell to their knees and made the sign as I walked unhindered out of the bishop's palace. I could feel the eyes of the awed and frightened servants upon my departing back as I walked, my footsteps making a crunching sound on the gravel path leading to the gate. Still singing I passed the sheltering elm tree. When I was well clear and some distance down the road, I stopped and sent the crows up into the sky and fell to my knees and thanked my precious Saviour for my rescue.

Two hours later as the sun was setting, turning the Rhine into a sheet of burnished copper and the fetid *Blaubach*, struck at a different angle, into a river of gold, I arrived back in Cologne, weary and hungry. After eating bread and smoked fish and drinking a little summer wine, I went to St Mary's on the Kapitol to see if I might find Father Hermann and to visit Nicholas. I had cried most of the way back to the city and wished only to return to my quarters with the wrestler's widow to hide my head and to sleep. I knew myself emotionally exhausted but was aware that I must first seek out the two priests and hear how they had fared with the bishop and, as well, look in to see Nicholas.

Arriving at the church I peeped in the door and saw Father Hermann in the sacristy praying to the figurine of the Virgin, so I went first to visit Nicholas in the crypt, to try to persuade him to come up and breathe the evening air. I found him listless and moribund and not to be encouraged. To every positive suggestion I made came a negative and despondent reply. I lacked the strength to persist. It was then that he told me the news of both priests and how they had fared with the bishop. Father Hermann had been to see him to ask him to pray for my safety and told him what had occurred at their interview.

'Father Hermann can't come,' Nicholas began in a toneless voice.

'Can't come where?' I asked.

'The crusade. The bishop has forbidden him.'

'But we *must* have a priest,' I exclaimed, alarmed. 'A priest carries the authority and respect we need!' I was depending on Father Hermann, an imposing figure of a man, just the sort to approach town dignitaries and their like when beseeching alms or help along the way. His bombast and forthcoming nature would impress any town or village priest we met and press him into service on our behalf. 'What of Father Paulus?' I asked.

'I cannot say, I haven't seen him, he must have gone directly back to St Martin's.'

I had never thought that Father Paulus would accompany us and he had never indicated that he wished to do so. He would be a poor substitute for Father Hermann, being small, mousy and much too timid of life. He didn't preach, was half deaf and not the sort who could cajole or intimidate a local priest. I had seen him after they'd been with the bishop and it was plain that he'd been reduced to tears. He was not the type we'd need for our spiritual authority or guidance.

'We go without the blessing of the Church,' Nicholas said with a hopeless shrug.

There was no point in even talking to him when he was down like this. While his moods varied when he was in his despondency, some, as was now the case, were worse than others. One of the grandmothers who helped with the feeding in the square brought him his evening meal and I left soon afterwards. I would usually stay with him and encourage him to eat and try to restore him to a lighter mood, but now knew myself too weary and anxious and also discouraged by the latest news.

My stomach began to knot and I felt quite ill as I thought about the task that lay ahead. Two thousand children waited for our departure, with more arriving every day. We had no priest as our spiritual guide, a leader who sat all day in a monk's cell staring at the wall, no carts to transport the few bags of flour and smoked fish we had stored, and a vengeful bishop who would, if he could, destroy our every endeavour.

I began to doubt that this crusade was the result of a miracle I had myself witnessed and been a part of, or that God had so clearly spoken to me and told me that I must be beside Nicholas as he led us to Jerusalem. Perhaps others, such as the abbot who had begged me to have no part in this 'absurdity' of a children's pilgrimage, were correct in their advice that we should abandon this crazy idea of a Children's Crusade. Who then would send these children home? How would they respond to the news, their faith in Christ's word forever after questioned as they returned disillusioned to their homes or hovels or the dark alleys of the city?

I looked in at the sacristy to see that Father Hermann was still at it, moaning and mumbling, sighing, crying and praising. When he went into one of his ecstatic sessions with his beloved Virgin Mary he would only rise at Matins. There would often be two red patches where his white habit was bloodstained at the knees, caused by the all-night vigils spent with the Mother of God in prayer.

I knew that I myself should pray for guidance. It was not in my nature to despair, but the day had been an anxious and traumatic one and Nicholas and his news had added to my depression. I could not clear my head of the sudden and terrible fear I had felt at the threat the two brutes had made to rape me. The image of my snorting, pumping father persisted in my head. This interchanged with the perfidy of a bishop of the Church who would allow these oafs to violate a young maid's virtue for his own carnal satisfaction or revenge and to corrupt a small child whose only earthly desire was to work in praise of God.

Evensong was over and the church was deserted. The faint and familiar smell of incense reached my nostrils. Dipping my fingers absently into the holy-water font I crossed myself and then began to walk down the centre aisle, my footsteps on the marble flagstones causing a hollow sound that matched my sense of all-aloneness. I knelt before the statue of our Lord, intending to pray for guidance. But no words came. Not even the familiar Latin prefaces to praising God that little children can recite with alacrity. It was as if I was suddenly struck dumb, all sensibility having deserted. My spirit emptied. Then rising from deep within me, as if the first trickle of a stream or drops of sudden rain, rose the notion of a song. At first, it was only the tremulous sounds where I didn't recognise words. Then, all at once, they flooded into my mind and possessed my heart. It was a hymn composed by the Abbess Hildegard, whose beautiful

Gloria I had been forbidden to sing while at the convent, but which I had stored silently contained within my very being. As the folded song arrived and opened upon my tongue I felt myself lifted from my knees and looking into Christ's glorious face, my hands clasped in prayer to glorify His image, I stood before His holy presence and began to sing.

I cannot say how long I stood and sang in praise, but only that I was transported and, as if imagined, I could clearly hear the sound of a heavenly flute, more beautiful than ever I had heard before. It lifted my voice and carried the notes forward and each phrase seemed to accentuate the beauty of the hymn. When at last I could sing no more I opened my eyes and turned to see that the entire church was now filled with children and that the Pied Piper of Hamelin, the erstwhile ratcatcher, stood directly to my front. He smiled and brought his pipe to his lips, turned and with a cheeky nod bade me follow him. Then he piped a tune I did not know, no doubt one he'd learned in France, most beauteous and haunting in its sound. As we passed each pew the children rose and followed us silently into the square outside, enchanted by the ratcatcher's magic flute.

All the doubts in my heart and mind disappeared. Christ Jesus, the blessed Saviour of mankind, had answered my silent cry of despair. I now knew that He intended that there should be a Children's Crusade and, moreover, I knew as well its sacred purpose. With children there would not be slaughter, greed or avarice, no jealousy, nor rape or pillage justified in the name of a God who watched and wept for man's inhumanity to man. Not even the vainglorious and presumptuous papal promise of sins forgiven would be needed to set our feet and will our hearts for the Holy Land. Only the true spirit of love, as only a child may love, without guile or thought of gain or promise of redemption.

With Reinhardt back I no longer felt alone and my spirits soared. He was a great organiser and fell to the task with alacrity. I had no need to ask him to accompany us, for he seemed immediately to act as if such an event as a crusade would be impossible to accomplish without his presence. When I asked him about his French lover he shrugged. 'C'est la *vie*, it lasted long enough so that I might take lessons on the flute with his elderly uncle, a grand master of France, and, as well, learn their mannered ways. Their court is influenced by the Italian way,' he explained. 'In decorum it contains many niceties I shall teach you. My dear, you shall be as well tutored in the ways of society as any princess in Germany.'

I laughed, glancing down at my coarsely woven linen shift and rough boots. 'I doubt I'll need these dainty manners where we're going, ratcatcher. I see you still wear high heels?'

'I confess, you look frightful, Sylvia. What on earth have you done to your hair! Rats' tails and knots and dull as dishwater!' he exclaimed, then added gallantly, 'But still somehow you remain the very prettiest of maids. To answer your question, heels were my contribution to the French culture and with them buckles.' He pointed to his pointy-toed boots. 'See!' I saw that they each contained a square silver buckle. 'They are all the rage in the court of France and I am much admired there and nicknamed "The Royal Boots 'n' Buckles",' he boasted, then laughed as if at this absurdity.

'If you are not careful, they will soon enough be admired equally here and you will promptly be up-ended in a muddy street in Cologne and your pretty boots with silver buckles stolen from your feet while you rub your silly ratcatcher's head. If you were so well regarded by the King of France, why then did you come back to Germany?' Nothing had changed, it was still the old ratcatcher, ever posing as the pretty knight or attempting to seem a high-lofty, someone of a status birth had not granted him, yet all the while still capable of laughing at himself.

He looked suddenly serious, a very serious condition for someone who seldom looked serious. 'Not Germany, Sylvia. I came back to you. I love you the most of all. Now that you are no longer Christ's bride I have returned to be at your side. My flute has never played as well as it did in St Martin's square. Without your voice it lacks the magic touch.'

It was my turn to be serious. 'Reinhardt, we do not share the same proclivity. I cannot be your mistress when you have no need for one.' I smiled. 'I am now grown up and I have needs of my own.'

'Nay, nay, nay! You get me wrong, my dear,' he cried out in alarm. 'I am much too much the scallywag and not to be trusted in such connubial matters. Every day I see a new bottom and think it tops.'

'On tops!' I corrected, laughing.

He clapped his hands in delight. 'See! That's just it! With you I am myself. It is you, our music and the comfort of your company I crave. Oh, how very much I have missed these three things.'

'Then you may have them with pleasure,' I said laughing, knowing that I had greatly missed the same three things. 'I too have missed you, ratcatcher. Missed you very much.'

'Then you will let me come?'

'To Jerusalem?'

'Aye, my faith is poor but my flute is rich with the encouragement of hymns of praise, and my tongue is no less lively and can tell a tale that will soften any heart and open the most reluctant purse on behalf of this holy venture.'

'Thank you. I need you for more than just piping as right now we're in a dreadful mess,' I confessed. 'The bishop hates us. Nicholas, our fiery leader, sits helpless and forlorn staring at the wall. Father Hermann is forbidden to accompany us. We lack the two wagons we must have for transport, the food we have will last less than two days and more children are arriving every day from all over Germany.'

'Hmm! My instinct tells me to run away at once.' He smiled. 'I can see I have arrived just in time. May I sojourn with you tonight? Do you still stay with the wrestler's widow?'

'Aye, there is room enough.'

'Then let us depart and on the morrow, I promise, things will be better and we shall, as of old, begin together to untie the calamitous knots in this hangman's rope of circumstance.'

I sighed. 'If this is how the French speak, can you not simply say in the plain-speaking German way, tomorrow will be better?'

But the following day proved, if anything, to be worse. I awoke well rested and with my spirits lifted. With the Pied Piper of Hamelin (as Reinhardt again insisted he be termed) at my side I felt much more confident. It was wonderful to have someone whom I could trust and talk to. For all his frippery, buckled boots and nonsense, he was a born organiser and never short of ideas. On the way to St Mary's to meet Father Hermann and get the carts, I informed him of our progress. Or perhaps – a better description – our lack thereof, showing him the few bags of corn and racks of salted fish and a small pile of blankets we'd been given and had stored for us in a pious merchant's yard. 'It is not enough to feed them for a single day,' I said, laughing to hide my anxiety.

'Sylvia, there are twenty granaries along the Rhine, all within this city. If each give six bags of corn or barley . . .?'

'And why would they do that?' I asked.

'Simple. Rats!'

'You would return to being ratcatcher?' I asked, amazed.

'For thee, my pretty maid, for thee!' he laughed. 'In a few days it will be done and my noble flute can then return to better things.'

I did not tell him they were among the words for a song I'd written, but knew that at some later time I would sing it for him. I did a quick calculation. 'That's one hundred and twenty bags of corn and barley! But we shall have no wagons to transport it!'

Reinhardt shrugged. 'None needed,' he replied. 'Each child shall carry their own, perhaps two weeks supply with a little dried or smoked fish. The rest of their food we, they, will have to beg or scavenge.'

So that he didn't think me entirely senseless, I laughingly said, 'Ah, I had already thought of doing that! But thinking, as there would not be enough to give every child a portion it would cause great resentment among those who went without. It would also encourage bullying, the strong taking from the weak. That will still remain a problem for us. Street children do not show charity towards each other and they will be constantly hungry. I fear for the smaller ones.'

I then told Reinhardt about Nicholas's moods and the need from time to time for him to be alone. 'We must have one wagon – there is almost half enough saved from the alms box. Master Israel has promised me canvas for a canopy where Nicholas may go when his moods overtake him.' I mimicked the voice of the wonderful old man I so loved. '"I am *meshugga!* If the rabbi knows of this donation,"' – I slapped my forehead as he would do, '"*Oi vey!* I should be expelled from the synagogue."' Then waving my arms in the air, '"You know nussing from Jerusalem. Listen to me, Sylvia. From Jerusalem children should be goink out, not goink in!"'

We arrived at St Mary's at the usual time, half an hour after the Angelus and Lauds, to wait for Father Hermann. The four church carts stood ready in the square to do the rounds of the markets, the children harnessed and chattering happily among themselves. Then a cleric I had not seen before came out of the church and walked towards us. He didn't offer his name or even greet us and sought no introduction. 'Father Hermann has been forbidden to see you and has already left for the Cistercian convent at Hoven where he is to be the priest.'

'Did he not leave a message?' I asked, shocked. 'This is his church, his beloved Virgin Mary and her Child Jesus live here! He is Father Hermann *Joseph*, her earthly husband!' I cried out.

'It is at the instruction of the bishop and you are forbidden to contact him at the convent,' the cleric said spitefully, clearly enjoying the task of bearing bad tidings.

'And you're absolutely sure he left no message?' I asked once again, still shocked. I simply could not believe Father Hermann would leave without some sort of explanation or attempt to contact me.

'None. It was expressly forbidden.' The cleric's chin lifted indignantly and his small mouth pulled into a rosebud of pique. He handed me a small brass key. 'It is the key to the alms box. You may have what it contains, but from today it is no longer for your benefit. Please leave the key near the screen to the chancel, place it under the alms box.' He pointed to the carts. 'They may not be used – it is forbidden, Church property. You must ask the children to take them back to the stables at once.'

'But how will the children eat? We must have them! The carts are needed to collect our food!'

The cleric shrugged. 'I am only following orders.' He turned and walked away, then stopped as if suddenly remembering, and turning to face me he said, 'Oh, and you will no longer sing at Holy Communion, Sylvia Honeyeater.' Why is it that some people seem to take great pleasure in the discomforting of others?

We watched silently as the cleric walked back into the church. 'Well!' Reinhardt exclaimed, then drew a deep breath before expostulating, 'Well, well, well! Now the cat is truly set among the pigeons!'

I started to cry as I watched the chastened, silent children begin to pull the carts back to the church stables. 'Whatever will become of us?' I wept.

CHAPTER TWELVE

The Rock of God's Wrath

REINHARDT AND I SCROUNGED all morning for food for the children, having persuaded a peasant to lend us the use of his cart for a few hours. The ratcatcher played and I sang, but without a priest to lend us authority or to shame the peasants and townsfolk into donating in the form of a tithe, it proved a difficult task. Most would simply shrug and say, 'I gave last week,' or more shamelessly, 'What's in it for me?' Some of the men leered at me, their randy looks suggesting that a quick knee-trembler behind a stall would soon enough open their hearts. Folk were growing weary of the constant need to give, and with the fear of God removed were now openly reluctant. It was rapidly becoming time to move on, but Nicholas still sat staring at the wall waiting for the world to end. By mid-afternoon, when we needed to return the cart, we had not near sufficient food to feed the multitudinous children.

'We leave on the day of Pentecost yet ten days hence and even then it will depend if Nicholas is no longer beset. Whatever shall we do?' I said disconsolately.

Reinhardt, new to the unrewarding task of gathering food, smiled. 'Tomorrow I shall visit Master Solomon – his rats will once again be numerous. I shall make him an offer too good to refuse. On the morrow he will deliver six bags of corn, three to St Martin's square, the other three to St Mary's, in return for a rat-ridding.'

'But he is a Jew! He will not aid a Christian crusade,' I said, thoroughly down-hearted. We had played and sung our hearts out and yet our flock would go hungry.

'Well, did not Master Israel give you canvas for a cart we don't have?'

'He is my friend.'

'He is *also* a Jew. Cheer up, Sylvia, let us have faith one day at a time, eh? I am not sufficient Christian to think beyond one small step in the many that will take us to Jerusalem. The reason Master Solomon will agree and, as well, the city's corn merchants is that it is a bargain. A thousand rats will eat a bag of corn a day. The value of a merchant's conscience is always negotiable and a bag of corn lost to rats each day is a solid reason to discount its value.'

'You would rid the city of twenty thousand rats?' I asked, amazed.

'Aye, there are many more than that – for every person dwelling in a city there be ten rats. Of mice,' he gave a low whistle, 'a great many more and only fleas and lice surpass the number.' He took up his flute and played a silly little nonsense song children sing when they skip or play 'Hop-along Tom'.

Rats and mice
and fleas and lice
We wish them all
gone in a trice.
But if we didn't
itch and scratch
We'd use our hands
to steal and snatch.
If rats and mice
were never born
How fat we'd grow
on all that corn.

Reinhardt's promise to see Master Israel's cousin on the morrow considerably cheered me. We would at least have gruel to give the children, if not tonight, then tomorrow. His advice that we have faith only unto the day was well reminded. I recalled Brother Dominic's words: *'If we attempt to understand God's glory all at once, we will be blinded by His infinite light and so see nothing. But taken one sunrise at a time, by sunset our eyes will have been opened to all things wise and wonderful.'* It was a reminder to regard each day as a small part of His glory, a task given to me, so that I might earn my faith and know a small portion of His love.

It was near sunset and we were in St Martin's square to apportion half of the meagre rations we had gathered to the good, pious, ever-cheerful waiting cooks, when a horseman arrived, his mount carrying a saddlecloth showing the bishop's colours with the mitre embroidered upon it. He dismounted and walked over to where we were standing and drew me aside.

'Fräulein Sylvia, His Lordship the Bishop summons you to his palace. We have a cart standing by.'

'Nay, I will not go!' I protested.

Reinhardt, watching, came over. 'What is it, Sylvia?'

'The bishop. He wishes me to return to his palace.'

Reinhardt looked at the horseman, who was a small thickset man of mid-years, judging from his good hose and neat dress perhaps a trusted manservant. 'Do you know what happened to her yesterday?' the ratcatcher asked.

'Aye, it was a mistake. His Lordship meant only to frighten her. No harm was to come of it.'

'Then you may tell the bishop he succeeded exceedingly well,' I interjected.

He shook his head and smiled, speaking softly, 'Nay, nay, fräulein. His Lordship apologises and wishes me to tell you he meant you no harm. It will be to your great advantage if you should come.'

'And if I don't?'

He smiled again. He had been well chosen for this task and would not easily be drawn to anger. 'It is not a consequence we have contemplated,' he said calmly. We both knew that I had no choice – a peasant and at that a woman might not disobey a Prince of the Church and hope to survive the experience. The very least I might expect was a public flogging and it could be worse – he could declare me a heretic.

As if he read my thoughts, not smiling, he said, 'The cross of crows, might that not easily be seen as the work of a witch?'

'But it is the raven and the jackdaw, not the crow, that are the devil's birds,' Reinhardt exclaimed. 'Sylvia's way with birds is well-known to all! The bishop has already been petitioned by two priests and asked to pronounce this gift of summoning the birds of the air as an act divinely inspired.'

'Aye, but not the crow! The crows of Cologne are long known for their satanic powers. They are the third of the devil's birds, the carrion bird that eats gallows' flesh and, like the raven and the jackdaw, is a harbinger of misfortune. To cause one of these satanic birds to fashion the holy cross, the very birds that were present with the Jews at Golgotha when they crucified our Saviour, is that not the work of a witch? What think you if a bishop should call a convocation of priests to bear judgement upon this heinous cross of crows?'

I looked at him in astonishment. It was obvious this was no humble manservant. I had never thought the bishop a man sufficiently intelligent to serve his holy vocation, and Brother Dominic had often pronounced him a bumbling, garrulous fool. I now saw whence came his counsel on those rare occasions when it proved to be sound. I did not for one moment think that he believed this artifice of crows contrived into a cross was witchery, but, instead, was well aware how it might be made to look thus to the commonfolk.

'How then must I be punished a second time? Was the bishop's frightening not sufficient?' I asked, trembling inwardly.

'Punished?' he asked, surprised. 'I did not speak of punishment, only of consequence.'

'You play with words, sire,' I said softly.

'And for a woman you have far too many,' he said, for a moment losing his patience and indicating quite another character concealed within. 'Come, I have a cart waiting.'

'But it is near Evensong, may I not go in the morning?' I cried. 'I shall leave with the ringing of the Angelus.'

'Nay, you are needed in the palace at first light.'

'Where will I sojourn?' I glanced at Reinhardt. 'May I bring my friend?'

'With the servants, and nay! You *must* be alone,' he said firmly.

'I will follow, Sylvia, and will wait outside the gates, under the elm,' Reinhardt said. I had told him of our previously being made to wait at the gates and of the elm tree.

'Do not try to enter the bishop's palace,' the envoy said sharply. 'I will not tolerate it.'

It was now certain that he was the high-lofty among the bishop's retainers. We had arrived at the bishop's palace when it was yet twilight and the horseman, who had ridden just ahead of the trundling cart as if to ensure that I made no attempt to escape, now rode up, the animal's hooves crunching on the gravelled forecourt. He still had not introduced himself, and the cart driver had simply grunted when I'd asked him if he knew the name of the bishop's envoy. He had clearly been told not to speak to me and, despite several attempts at conversation, remained silent. Looking down at me from his horse with an expression of disinterest, his formerly patient and equitable demeanour absent, the envoy said abruptly, 'A servant will take you to your lodgings. He has been told not to speak to you.'

'I have not eaten today,' I said to the manservant who accompanied me. He merely grunted and soon we arrived at a small stone building that stood on its own near the stables where he unbolted the door and with a nod indicated that I should enter. 'Will you arrange for some sustenance?' I asked again but still he made no answer.

'Lodgings', as I'd been promised, is a word that usually contains some sense of comfort. It was a small room, bare but for a pallet with a sacking mattress stuffed with straw. Discarded in a corner lay a dirty blanket. In the middle of the floor stood a small wooden stool and upon it a clay dish that contained the pooled wax of a spent candle, a finger-prick of burned wick frozen in its near-translucent centre. In the corner nearest the door was a wooden bucket, its purpose made clear by the smell that came from it. The room had a tiny window near the roof, not sufficient to cleanse the air of the sour smell of ale and gruel mixed with the sharper tang of urine. It was little more than a prison cell.

The manservant closed the door behind me and I heard the rattle of the bolt sliding into place. It was dark and damp within the rough stone-walled room and, despite my sheepskin coat, I was cold. The lice and bugs within the foul woollen blanket would be abundant, also the mattress would be infested and I would touch neither. I fell to my knees and began to pray. How long I prayed I cannot say but these precious words rose up in my throat so that I sang out the beautiful *Angele Dei*.

Angele Dei,
qui custos es mei,
Me tibi commissum pietate superna;
Hac nocte, illumina, custodi, rege, et guberna.
Amen.

Angel of God,
my guardian dear,
To whom His love commits me here;
Ever this night be at my side,
To light and guard, to rule and guide.
Amen.

I continued to sing, for how long I cannot say, except that I could see the stars in the night sky through the small window. I sang to these heavenly pricks of light, the discarded souls of angels who, already contained within the glory of heaven, had no further need for them, as they waited to be gifted to newly baptised children. Then, quite suddenly, came the rattle of the door bolt as it was drawn back and the door swung open with a soft creaking to reveal the shape of a small person dimly silhouetted against the dark night.

'Little Sister Sylvia, it is Matthew,' the figure said in a low voice.

'Matthew!'

'Shush!' he cautioned. 'I am not allowed to be here. I've brought you some bread and ale.'

'Thank you,' I whispered back.

'Where are you, I cannot see you?' he asked.

'Wait, I will come to the door.'

'Please don't escape or I shall be beaten.'

'Nay, it's all right,' I assured him. Then to put him at ease, 'You're a lovely boy.'

'You must drink the ale now, quickly,' he said anxiously. 'If the jug is found, they'll know I've been here.'

I reached for the loaf of coarse bread I could now dimly see in his hand and tucked it into a fold of my skirt locked between my knees. Then I took the small jug of ale he held out and swallowed greedily, knowing that I would have to use the foul bucket quite soon, but my thirst overcame my repulsion at the thought. I drank nearly half the contents of the jug before handing it back. 'Thank you, Matthew, I cannot drink it all so quickly.'

'I must go,' he whispered anxiously.

'Nay, tarry just a moment. Put down the jug and let me give you a hug.' I hugged him to my breast and kissed his cheek, then pushed him gently away from me. 'Do you know why I have been brought back?' I asked. But he was already shutting the door.

'Crows!' he whispered loudly, and then I heard the bolt slide back into place.

It was too dark to see in the room and I edged across the wall furthermost from the pallet until my toe touched the dirty blanket, and then drew back sufficiently so that I thought myself between it and the bucket. I sat with my back against the wall and chewed on the small dry loaf, soon wishing I possessed the jug of ale to wash it down. When I could eat no more I rose and found the blanket and concealed the remainder of the bread within it in case someone in the morning came upon it and somehow traced it back to Matthew.

I returned to sit against the wall and attempted to make sense of what I knew, which wasn't much. I felt fairly sure that the bishop had remained hidden behind the peephole in the roof of the room from which I had escaped, which meant he could not have been present in the great hall to see the effect the crows perched upon my stave had on his servants. The term 'The Cross of Crows' had surfaced in the markets this morning and by late afternoon I had been summoned by the bishop's horseman to come to the palace. The term could only have come from a palace servant visiting Cologne this morning. If the bishop thought it blasphemy, then the cross could only be hearsay. Perhaps I was being punished to quieten the servants who might, as the horseman suggested, have seen the cross of crows as the work of a witch or the devil? I soon convinced myself that this was the case and I sang a Gloria as loudly as I could, so any person listening would think of me differently, knowing I was a child of Jesus Christ the Saviour and singing His praise into the night. Finally, exhausted, I fell asleep still seated with my back against the wall.

I was wakened at dawn by the sound of the bolt being drawn back. The door opened and Scarface stood in the doorway. The shock of seeing him was too great and I screamed and jumped to my feet. Moments later I felt a warm trickle run down my legs. I drew back whimpering and cringing into the corner, stepping on the blanket, as the warm piss ran into the tops of my boots and between them, soaking into the dirty wool at my feet.

'Hush, fräulein!' Scarface said, a frightened expression upon his face. Then, in a most supplicating voice, he declared, 'We are blamed and have been beaten for the curse you have set upon us. I plead your forgiveness and beg your mercy.' His eyes were lowered to look down at his feet, unaware that I was in the process of spilling my bladder. I was still too shocked to react to anything he said. 'I am sent to fetch you,' he said again, then added, 'You will not be harmed.' He gave a small involuntary jerk as he saw me reach down for my stave. It was as if he now saw it for an object other than for what it plainly was. I walked stiffly towards him, the inside of my thighs stinging and uncomfortable, hoping no wetness showed through and grateful that I wore my long sheepskin coat to conceal my shame.

We walked the short distance to the side of the bishop's palace and entered through a side door situated close to the stables. The door opened to a narrow passage that ended at a stout, oaken door reinforced with heavy metal plates and studs. Almost beside it and to my left was another small door set into the wall of the passageway. I took the passageway with its heavily reinforced door to be a means of escape should the palace come under attack. Scarface stopped outside the smaller door and knocked. 'Stay here,' he whispered, then turned and walked quickly back down the way we had come and out into the stable yard. I heard the outside door creak and then close and the sound of the bolt being slid into place. If I'd had any thought to escape it was now too late.

'Enter!' a voice called.

I pushed at the door and it opened to my touch and I was surprised to see the bishop seated on a large leather chair covered by loose sheepskins. A jug of wine, a half-eaten loaf of bread, a small haunch of meat and a knife sat on a large earthen platter on a low table beside him. To his right stood the horseman who had fetched me the previous evening. I took the few paces towards the chair and knelt and kissed the proffered ring, hoping the smell of urine wouldn't reach him. If it did, then he did not remark on it but simply grunted, withdrawing his fat hand after my lips had touched the ruby.

'Stand up, Sylvia Honeyeater,' the bishop's man demanded. Though it was a command, it was not said over-harshly. I stood with my hands folded to my front and my eyes downcast. 'You will only talk when His Lordship permits. If you do as you are told you will not come to any harm. My name is Master Nicodemus and you know well how to address His Lordship.'

'The accommodation!' the bishop called out, turning to look impatiently at Master Nicodemus.

'Oh yes,' Master Nicodemus said, slightly flustered. 'The bishop regrets that you were not better accommodated last night, but the palace is vacated and all the out-buildings occupied. His Lordship was himself *forced* to sleep in the wine cellar where the rats kept him awake all night.' Master Nicodemus said this to suggest the bishop's uncomfortable night was my fault, but spoke in such a carefully rehearsed and contumelious manner that it was meant more to satisfy the bishop's self-sorrow than intended for my ears. I glanced up at him in surprise.

'Well?' the bishop said, glaring directly at me.

I was completely lost for words.

'Speak, woman!'

I opened my mouth but no words came. I had been commanded to speak without knowing what I was expected to say.

'The curse!' the bishop shouted.

'Curse, my Lord?'

'You will remove it at once!'

'It?'

'What is this? Can't you speak? Yes, you can! You twisted us around your little finger at the archbishop's damned inquiry! Jabbering like a magpie! Now will you, or won't you?'

'Is it about the Cross of Crows, your Lordship?' I asked querulously.

'Cross of Crows? What on earth are you talking about, woman? The only cross I have to bear is your stubborn insolence!'

So, he has not been told of the cross, I thought. The threat of me being pronounced a witch had been of Master Nicodemus's own invention. If it was not the Cross of Crows, then what was the bishop going on about?

'Perhaps I may explain, my Lord Bishop?' Master Nicodemus suggested.

'Nay, you may not!' the bishop shouted, his furious face near-apoplectic. 'This tweeting bird who has conveniently lost all her jabber will do all the explaining.' He stabbed a fat finger at me. 'You will stop the invasion at once!'

'As God is my witness, my Lord, I know of no invasion,' I said, now close to tears.

'Crows! Crows! Crows!' the bishop shouted, thumping the arm of his chair, a spray of spittle issuing from his lips. 'I *will* have an end to crows!'

I looked at Master Nicodemus and shrugged, appealing to him for an explanation. 'Crows have invaded the palace in great numbers – we ask that you rid us of them,' he said, disobeying the bishop's earlier instruction not to speak.

'That's what I told the stupid girl! Get rid of them at once, you hear? Or you will be flogged or much worse!' The bishop turned to Master Nicodemus. 'Take her away!' he said, pointing to the door.

Matthew's single word 'Crows' now made sense. 'Come, fräulein,' Master Nicodemus commanded. I followed him out of the small windowless room and, closing the door behind him, we walked the few steps to the larger door but he made no attempt to open it. 'I must warn you, Sylvia Honeyeater, if you fail in this task it will be not too difficult to persuade the bishop that this is a case of witchcraft.'

'You made that stuff up . . . about witches and the cross,' I said, knowing I should remain silent but unable to do so.

He looked at me, one eyebrow raised. 'Well, as a matter of fact, I am not at all sure that this isn't witchcraft. A case may be easily made that this invasion of the crows is revenge for your excommunication by His Lordship. Then, of course, there is the hanging by the children – your hand in that is well-known.' He shrugged. 'It won't be difficult to have you named a witch – crows do not invade palaces unless a spell, a witch's spell, or some such evil, has been cast.' Then he looked at me sternly. 'And you well know what the Church does with witches.'

'Why am I blamed for this, Master Nicodemus? I am not evil!' I cried.

'We have it from the two men who were sent to frighten you that the crows came to your summoning when you were here the day before yesterday. They are still coming. Every hour brings more, the palace rooms are now infested. There are hundreds, nay a thousand or even more. The beams, walls, floor, the furniture, beds, carpets are all covered in crow shit.' He pointed at the door of the little room we'd just left. 'This passage and that room are the only place in the palace where there are no windows they may enter to torment us. They show no fear of man and will attack six or eight at a time, so that we have all been driven from the palace.'

I now realised that what he accused me of doing was possibly true. I had walked out of the palace with perhaps a dozen crows perched on my stave but others had already entered and I had sent them after Scarface and Pockface, then I had left the palace without calling the crows away or withdrawing the call that set them on the attack. The ones upon the stave I had set loose when I had been well down the road.

I had never before been faced with such a problem and had no idea whether a thousand crows or more would heed or even hear my calls to vacate the palace. I knew at once that if I failed the consequences would be horrendous. I remembered Brother Dominic's advice that from the darkest moment the light begins: '*Panic is the harbinger of disaster, to think when you are mortally afraid is the beginning of the solution. It is from the darkest moment that the light begins.*'

'If I fail you have warned me of the consequences. But if I succeed, is there no reward?' I asked, my heart thumping like a sultan's drum.

Master Nicodemus grinned. 'Only a small, inconsequential one – your life.'

'My life is in God's hands. It will end when it is time,' I heard myself saying in a surprisingly even voice. 'But the bishop's palace is in mine.'

'What mean you by that?'

I shrugged. 'The crows will *never* go away.'

His head jerked backwards. 'You would threaten us, fräulein?'

'Nay, it is you, not I, who do the threatening, Master Nicodemus. I simply point out that the bishop will lose his palace and be the laughing stock of Cologne, chased from his palace by a flock of cawing crows. If the Church would condemn me as a witch, then the people would, with the naming, expect the curse of the crows to be lifted.' I paused. 'But think now . . . it won't be. It will remain forever and my guilt will soon enough be questioned and His Lordship blamed for falsely condemning me of witchcraft.' I attempted to smile. 'What is to be gained if you kill me?'

Master Nicodemus seemed to think for a moment. Then to my surprise he smiled and slowly shook his head. 'I have heard of your silver tongue, Sylvia.' He spread his hands. 'What is it you want?'

'A donation.'

'A donation? To you?'

'Nay, to the Children's Crusade.'

'And what shall it be?'

'A wagon and four mules with harness.'

He gave a low whistle. 'I see . . . for the Children's Crusade?'

'Aye, a donation from the bishop.' I added quickly, 'It will enhance his reputation for generosity and folk will regard it well. He has been previously seen to support this holy cause, permitting us to use the church carts, but has now withdrawn his permission. This will restore his generosity and show he bears no malice towards the Children's Crusade the common people of Cologne so eagerly support.'

He grunted, as if to suggest that the bishop did not have a reputation for generosity that might be enhanced or restored. 'I will need to ask him.' He retraced the few steps to the small door and knocked, then opened it without waiting for permission to enter.

I moved silently over to the door and placed my ear up to it. 'What now?' I heard the bishop yell.

Then Master Nicodemus, with an even voice, said, 'Your Lordship, the Crow woman wishes us . . . you . . . to make a donation.'

'What for?' the bishop shouted.

'The Children's Crusade, my Lord.'

'No!'

'The crows, my Lord. The donation is in return for ridding us of the crows.'

There followed a moment's silence and then came the expostulation. 'What! This mangy bitch, this tweeting little whore would threaten me? Take her out and flog her! That will change her mind soon enough. A good flogging! Who does she think she is that she would threaten the bishop of Cologne?'

'She does not fear for her life and says she places it in God's hands. She is very popular with the common people, my Lord. A flogging will not serve your reputation well.'

'Peasants, fools! I have no need of their approbation!'

'I do not think a flogging will cause her to send the crows away, my Lord. Perhaps she will cause more to appear,' he warned. There was no doubt that Master Nicodemus knew his mark.

There was a silence, then the bishop's voice, this time somewhat mollified, 'What does this wretched woman want? This donation to that damnable crusade, what is it?'

'A wagon and four mules, my Lord. With harness.'

'What?' the bishop exploded. 'Is she mad? Nay! Over my dead body!'

'The crows, my Lord,' Master Nicodemus said in a soothing voice.

More silence. Then, 'When she has done the deed, give her an old cart and a donkey.' The bishop chuckled. 'Yes, excellent! An old cart and a donkey. Do we also have an old donkey?'

Silence. Then from Master Nicodemus, spoken carefully, 'My Lord, this is a stubborn wench. I fear she will simply bring back the crows, perhaps ravens and jackdaws as well,' he cleverly suggested.

Silence. Then, 'Must I do all the thinking? When she has rid us of the crows, kill her. Let us see how she calls their return from the grave, eh?'

'My Lord?'

'Kill her!'

'My Lord, I most humbly beg you to reconsider. This is no ordinary peasant maid, but is known among the people as the Petticoat Angel. They believe she has performed several miracles and even the good Abbot of Disibodenberg speaks of one such at the funeral of Brother Dominic.'

'That old fool!' the bishop interrupted. 'What would he know? He speaks through his arse and his thoughts are so puerile he is punished with piles!'

Master Nicodemus ignored the bishop's humour, though perhaps smiling, then continued, 'Now she helps to lead the Children's Crusade with the boy Nicholas. This is a most popular cause and has great support among the commonfolk, more so because she helps to lead it. This incident of crows they may well see as God's punishment on thee, and see her as His instrument of its deliverance. It will sit badly with the people if you harm her as she is most popular and some think her already a saint. There is also the matter of your excommunication of the four women and her restoration by the archbishop at the inquiry. If you should be known to be her murderer, you will have to answer to him as well.'

It was most bravely spoken and I waited with my heart pounding. 'Bah! I slept not a wink last night!' the bishop complained. 'It is her fault that I am not now archbishop and she must pay! What use is it to be bishop when I cannot do as I wish?'

'May I make a suggestion, my Lord?'

'What?'

'We will give her the wagon, mules and harness and send her away with your blessing and a prayer for the safe keeping of the Children's Crusade. You will sprinkle holy water upon the wagon and the mules. All the servants will be present to see your piety and benevolence. Then I shall send two gossips, two scouring women from the kitchen, who will spread this tale to your benefit among the people of the markets and then, soon enough, the simple folk of Cologne will speak of it to thy glory.'

'But . . . but I shall have lost a good wagon and four mules and she shall escape punishment!' the bishop protested. 'I like it not, Master Nicodemus. I like it not at all. They will think her gain of a wagon and mules a triumph of her own clever contrivance. Bishops do not give wagons and mules to peasants.'

'Ah, I have not yet cracked to the kernel of this nut, my Lord. Sad news follows. Brigands come upon this wagon driven by a lone young maid. Alas, she is killed, the wagon purloined.'

'Raped and killed!' the bishop demanded, his voice suddenly excited.

'Aye, if you wish, my Lord. The rape is clever – she is a comely wench – and when the corpse is found it will add more veracity to this sad tale.'

'Ah, but how will my wagon and mules be returned to me without it being seen as complicity?'

Silence followed. Then Master Nicodemus said, 'Two of your soldiers on horseback, well-armed, will come upon the wagon and, recognising it to be yours, will set upon the two brigands, who unfortunately will flee for their lives before they can be apprehended. Alas, they will find the raped and battered body lying at the roadside and bring it hence together with the wagon, all the while appearing innocent of the plot. The soldiers and the brigands, they are, of course, the selfsame two!' he explained, in case the bishop had missed the point.

'Ah, neatly done! Who can you trust among my men not to talk? They are a lazy, good-for-nothing lot,' the bishop grumbled.

'The pocked and the scarred, the two you sent to frighten her when she came with the priests. Pockmark Hans and Scarface Kurt, both are seasoned soldiers and crusaders and well accustomed to killing. Both have good reason not to love this wench and to undertake both tasks. They are lewd and will rape her, then kill her with alacrity and can be trusted to shut their gobs.'

'Excellent! You are a worthy man, Master Nicodemus,' the bishop exclaimed.

'Then you will give the poor wretch the last rites posthumously and cause her to be buried at St Mary's with a great outpouring of grief. Her burial must be a most public affair, with your solemn promise that her many "miracles" will be most conscientiously investigated by the Church.' Master Nicodemus said all this with a voice rising to a conspiratorial giggle. He was plainly delighted with this neat solution to my ultimate demise.

'These brigands waiting in ambush who turn into soldiers, is there yet time to set up this cunning plot?'

'I shall send them ahead within the hour on some good pretext. It will be noon before the crows are cleared from the palace and the wagon ready to depart. There is time sufficient, my Lord.'

'Go to it, Master Nicodemus, I can see your guile is well up to this task. See that I am not disturbed until the wagon departs. Send the boy Matthew to me.'

'You do not wish to witness the departure of the crows, my Lord?'

'Nay, I must not be present – there must be no record that I bore witness. When the crows are departed we will make light of it, a few stray crows nesting in the beams she incidentally called away when she visited the palace to ask for a donation of a wagon and mules.'

'Which, naturally, you gave without thought for the expense and with a full heart and your blessing.'

'Precisely! You are not the only one around here who has a modicum of guile, Master Nicodemus. I shall bless this purely "temporary departure" of my wagon and mules when it is time. It will be we who do the ultimate crowing, eh, Master Nicodemus?' he chortled.

'Very clever, my Lord. I am humbled by your intelligence,' the servant said, licking the bishop's fat arse.

I retreated from the door and went to stand beside the large door where I had been previously left. I was concerned for poor little Matthew but knew I must put him from my mind, as I would need all my wits about me to survive this day. Master Nicodemus soon appeared. There was a smile upon his face when he spoke. 'I am happy to say the bishop has agreed and is pleased at the prospect of a donation to the Children's

Crusade. He wishes also to bless your departure.' He paused and looked at me sternly. 'That is, of course, if the crows are seen to depart from the palace.'

I looked suitably relieved. 'Thank you, thank you, Master Nicodemus.' I then paused and said, 'Alas, you did not tell me the nature of my task before I came, or I would have told you that I would need help, sire.'

'Help? You did not need help to summon the birds?' he said suspiciously.

'Nay, a ridding is different. If I am to cast the crows from the palace then I must end as I began. The two men who were sent to frighten me in the bedchamber, the one with the scars to his face and the other pockmarked, must be by my side throughout so that the crows will know they may no longer be attacked by them nor by any other person who may enter the palace. This is an essential part of the ridding.'

'I think they have both been sent on an errand,' he said quickly.

I took on an expression of the utmost concern. 'Alas! Then we are forced to await their return. Their presence is essential!' I cried. It was as if I heard Master Israel's voice: '*If you know the plot then it is soon undone, the trick is to undo it so that it appears as if it failed due to unforeseen circumstances and not at your own hand. In this way you may escape, then when you strike back, it is in your own good time and your enemy is taken completely by surprise.*'

'I will see, perchance they have not yet left,' Master Nicodemus now said.

'There is one more thing, Master Nicodemus. If I may say so, a most fortunate coincidence and greatly in favour of this ridding. Beneath the elm tree by the palace gate waits my friend, who you would not allow to accompany me last night. He is a piper and has special gifts. I shall need his flute to calm these angry birds before I send them away. The crow, as you are aware, is a bird of prey and so naturally bold, and in such great numbers may well attack the two men and pluck out their eyes. I must have the Pied Piper of Hamelin with his calming flute beside me.'

'Very well,' he said stiffly. He then stepped forward and made to open the door.

I placed my hand upon his arm. 'Nay, tarry! Where does it lead?' I asked.

'To the main hall. You must go in.'

'And you also? Will you come?'

He drew back, startled. 'Nay!'

I grinned. 'Then neither shall I. It is *much* too dangerous. We must first be well prepared and I must go through the front door, the same way as I formerly left the palace. But I must assure you,' I emphasised once again, 'I may only do so with your two men and the piper at my side.'

He cleared his throat. 'Hurrumph! As you wish, Fräulein Sylvia.' It was said with a tincture of respect. Perhaps, with his plot so soon beginning to unravel, he was less pleased with himself, though I knew myself still to be in mortal danger and must not be seen to overplay my hand. This was a very clever man with a quick mind and not to be trusted. Every step I took with him must help to assure my safety.

We walked back to the stables where Master Nicodemus instructed a stable hand to, as he put it, 'See if Hans and Kurt have not yet left and fetch them to me at the front of the palace.'

'Nay, they have not left. I have not been asked to harness their horses, Master,' the lad replied.

'Good. Find them and send them to me immediately.'

A stable boy was also sent to bring Reinhardt to the front of the palace. My earnest hope, for much rested upon it, was that he'd made good his word and followed me. A night spent in the open under the elm tree would not be much to his liking and with his new French manners he might have sought shelter on the way, planning to arrive later in the morning. Reinhardt wasn't one for roughing it and I had previously wondered how he would endure when once we were on the crusade. But, true to his word, he soon stood at my side, though looking somewhat bedraggled and not his usually spruced-up self. I had also told Master Nicodemus to summon all the servants and peasants from the bishop's estate. He had departed to give instructions, so that the ratcatcher and I stood alone. I quickly explained what had happened with the crows.

'Aye, the gatekeeper has told me,' he replied. 'They speak of it as a curse upon the bishop by "the angel". They think of you as near a saint, Sylvia, and your miracles are well-known among the bishop's women servants.'

'You must have been most uncomfortable sleeping in the open, I know it is not to your liking,' I said in an attempt to change the subject away from myself.

Reinhardt gave a short laugh. 'Nay, I shared the gatekeeper's fire and his broth last night and slept in the gatekeeper's hut. He gave me a sheepskin so that I might keep warm.'

'Lucky you,' I said. As usual he had landed on his feet.

He sniffed. 'You smell terrible, Sylvia! Did it not go well with you?'

'I pissed myself and, nay, I was locked in a prison cell,' I replied, perhaps a little over-dramatically. 'I will explain later.'

'Hmm . . . Nice people, so much for the adoring servants,' he said, one eyebrow raised.

'Reinhardt, you must do exactly as I ask – we are in mortal danger and we risk our very lives.'

'What? Is it the crows? The ridding?'

'Nay, the bishop wishes me, us, killed when the ridding is done.' Servants were beginning to gather and, as quickly as I might, I explained the situation, the donation of the wagon and the later ambush planned to kill me.

He gave a low whistle. 'I should have stayed in France, you're nothing but trouble, Sylvia,' he grinned.

'Please, be serious, ratcatcher! You must do as I say,' I said in an urgent whisper, as Master Nicodemus was seen to approach with the two soldiers, Hans and Kurt, at his side. I must say, for fierce soldiers who had embarked upon a crusade, their ugly faces wore an expression of utmost apprehension. I looked directly at them as they approached and both lowered their eyes.

'I have told them they must enter with you,' Master Nicodemus said as he drew up. He nodded at Reinhardt.

'Good morrow, sire, we meet again,' Reinhardt said cheerily, so that I was forced to chasten him with an angry look. The bishop's man simply grunted, thinking, no doubt, that this piper fellow was yet another unexpected knot he must untie in the plot to kill me.

'Hans and Kurt, is it?' I asked in a friendly voice. 'Who is Kurt?'

'I am Kurt, fräulein.' It was Scarface who answered, though without looking at me. Both stood with their shoulders hunched, looking down at their feet, their hands clasped behind their backs. And then I saw the peck marks to their necks received when they had attempted to escape – angry red marks where the beaks had struck at them, as if they were infected with the pox.

'The first thing I wish you both to know is that I bear you no malice – what happened is in the past. I truly regret that you must now accompany me into the bishop's palace.' I shrugged. 'But alas, there isn't any other way. What began in one way must end in the same manner. Birds are easily confused,' I explained. 'And crows very dangerous when they become so. If they attack you, cover your eyes, and even if they peck your fingers to the very bone do not take them away. Better a crippled claw that may eventually heal than blindness, eh?' I said, hoping I was not spreading the gory details too thickly for credence.

I glanced up at Master Nicodemus and saw from the look in his eyes that he took this instruction to the two men and the possibility that they would be severely injured for a known fact. He too must have seen where the crows had previously pecked them. I touched my neck to indicate their peck marks. 'You have been punished sufficiently as it is,' I said sympathetically. 'Now, you must each stand to the side of me while the piper with his calming tune will be two steps ahead. We are now in God's hands. Let us pray silently to our Saviour that we are spared and come out of this ordeal no worse than when we went into it.'

I could see as they came to stand beside me that they were truly afraid – big, burly men with great barrel chests shaking like a leaf.

Reinhardt then took up his place in front of me and started to play a dirge that would well suit a funeral procession. We arrived at the great door to the front of the palace and Reinhardt halted and continued to play as I moved forward. Then with my stave I tapped, as might the prophet Elijah have done upon the rock that brought forth water in the desert, three times for the effect it would have on the servants and serfs who watched. Then I lifted the latch and pushed at one of the doors, but it didn't budge. I turned to Kurt and indicated he should open it, but he shook his head furiously, refusing. Then to Hans, who did the same, both men fearful and drawing back, afraid to open the door lest the crows within attack them. Placing my stave to lean against the door to the left, I pushed the other, using both hands to swing it open. A murmur rose from the servants watching.

Though I had seen the crows flying in and out of palace windows all the while we'd stood outside, and heard their cawing through the stout door and thick stone walls, I was not prepared for the noise that met us. A mighty roar issued from the interior, from the entrance chamber and from the great hall beyond it, so that I knew my voice would not be heard. Even if I should scream it would be drowned in this furious cacophony of beating wings and bird cries. A thousand, nay five thousand, even more, the concatenation of cawing crows seemed to boil the thickened air above me, and they were so numerous they appeared as one great whirling creature. I knew as I stepped into the entrance hall that we were done for, that there could be no ridding of these birds. The sharp stink of bird shit assaulted my nostrils and I thought I must choke.

I retreated back to Reinhardt and shrugged. 'We are done for!' I shouted. But so great had the noise become that I could no longer hear his flute, even though he stood before me. Whether he read my lips or possibly heard me I cannot say, but he nodded and his eyes closed, his cheeks puffed out and he began to turn scarlet as he blew upon his pipe. I had seen him do this once before, when he'd summoned the rats in the village on the first night we had been together. Then, as I now supposed, the notes he played were well beyond a pitch that might be heard by the human ear.

Quite suddenly only the sound of beating wings persisted. This in itself was a roar but a different sort of noise so that I could call out for the crows to leave the palace. I kept calling, and then had the presence of mind to push open the remaining door, and walked back towards Reinhardt who was now at the entrance to the great hall, when all at once a mighty roaring sound came towards us. 'Drop!' I screamed to Reinhardt and fell to the floor myself, my stave sent flying. I pulled my sheepskin coat over my head to protect it and lay on my stomach frightened out of my wits.

It took five minutes or so for all the birds to depart the palace. We would both wear bruises to our backs and he some cuts to his hands and back for weeks to come, although I had been the more fortunate of the two of us. The full force of the leading birds had not been low to the floor, the birds naturally seeking the sky they could see through the open doorway. The leather of my long sheepskin coat pulled over my head had protected me. Similarly, Reinhardt had pulled his broad-brimmed felt hat over his head and down to protect the sides of his face. His back and hands were bleeding and the rear part of his tunic hung in strips, but in outward appearance at least, I seemed unscathed.

I stumbled to my feet and stood over Reinhardt who lay still. 'Oh my God!' I said, unknowingly blaspheming as I saw his torn and bleeding back and then his hands. 'Are you all right?' I cried.

'Sweet Jesus!' he cried, lifting the hat from his face and looking up at me. 'What was that?'

'Don't blaspheme!' I cried, not thinking.

'You just did!' he accused, pushing his arms up from the flagstones and rising shakily to his feet.

'No I did not!' I protested, still taken aback by the shock. Then we both began to laugh, although perhaps a little hysterically.

But not for long, for in the doorway lay Hans and Kurt. I would later realise that they had not dropped to the floor, but instead had turned, attempting to flee out of the palace only to be hit by a vortex of several thousand crows. All around them lay dozens of dying crows, some on their backs still jerking, their wings flapping, others attempting to fly turning in circles, a broken wing extended with the tip feathers touching the bloodied flagstones. Others lay quite still upon their backs, their claws curled with their legs in the air, while others shuddered in final death.

We ran the few steps to where the two men lay, kicking aside the dead and dying crows. The men's tunics and hose were ripped but there was only a little blood to be seen on their backs and the backs of their legs. Both their heads lay at a peculiar angle, although it was the colour of the skin to the entire back part of their bodies that caught our immediate attention. It was as purple as a ripened plum where the pounding of several thousand crows had brought the blood under the skin to form a total bruising to the back of their bodies. Then we saw that it was not this that had killed them, though it might well have proved a later, slower cause of death, for their necks had been snapped by the impact. It was as if they had been struck with a blunt instrument to the nape of the neck and back of the head.

We rose and walked through the great doorway. 'Reinhardt, can you play?' I asked.

'I think so,' he said, working his hands to see if he'd broken any fingers. 'Aye, they seem all right, what do you wish?'

'To sing the *Tantum Ergo*.' He nodded and we stood at the doorway, then slowly sank to our knees.

Tantum ergo Sacramentum
Veneremur cernui:
Et antiquum documentum
Novo cedat ritui:
Praestet fides supplementum
Sensuum defectui.

Down in adoration falling,
Lo! the sacred host we hail,
Lo! oe'r ancient forms departing
Newer rites of grace prevail;
Faith for all defects supplying,
Where the feeble senses fail.

I had barely commenced to sing this hymn when all the bishop's servants and serfs fell to their knees, their hands clasped in prayer. Even Master Nicodemus went to ground and I saw that he crossed himself as he rose after I had completed singing and the last beautiful strains of Reinhardt's flute had died away.

Of course, the servants and serfs who witnessed the event clearly saw God's hand in all of it and were quick to make yet another miracle of the incident. They told how I walked from the palace without a mark upon me while the two soldiers, Hans and Kurt, lay dead at the entrance to the doorway. God had punished them for their sins against the Petticoat Angel. It was, they said, as if the birds had been a great rock hurled through the air to strike them both down, a rock thrown by the hand of an angry God. Quite soon the story had further changed. The bishop's servants swore that as they watched, the birds had been transformed into a great black rock that contained an angry roar. Many years later I would hear tell of this miracle, but by then a round, dark-coloured rock with reddish stains, the blood of the two men, had been found upon a hillside near the bishop's palace. It was named 'The Rock of God's Wrath' and it had become a sacred place.

Master Nicodemus approached us and it was clear to see that he was overcome by emotion. He saw Reinhardt's bleeding back and called out to a woman to bring clean water and rags to cleanse the wounds and ointment to soothe them, then said he would cause to be fetched a fresh linen tunic and hose for him to wear. Then, almost as an afterthought he called for the two bodies to be moved.

Death on the streets of Cologne was a commonplace event. As Father

Hermann, Nicholas and I worked among the poor, it was to be witnessed most days. Sometimes it was by violence, but mostly from slow starvation or sickness. Father Hermann would often sigh and say, 'I give the last rites as often as we give out bread.' Yet the death of the two soldiers, Kurt and Hans, was so immediate that I could not yet comprehend it. They were alive and stood fearful at my side, then moments later lay dead. If it had not been for Brother Dominic's teaching, I would myself have thought, as the serfs and servants did, that they had been smitten by God's hand.

Master Nicodemus, other than to instruct that they be removed, seemed unconcerned. A cold fish this one, to be sure. 'You would break your fast, I shall arrange food to be brought,' he said in a newly acquired unctuous voice. 'I will then see that your wagon and mules are made ready.'

He turned to go and I said, 'Oh, Master Nicodemus, I have a favour to ask now that we are rid of the crows.'

Despite seeming overwhelmed by the nature of the crow ridding, I knew this might not be how he would come to think when, in a calmer frame, he reported the incident to the querulous and ever-cantankerous bishop. They would, I felt sure, agree that I had brought this curse upon them in the first place, that I was ever dangerous and that to be rid of me, and also now of Reinhardt, was the better solution.

'What is it, Sylvia?' he said in his new and respectful voice.

'We ask that there is an escort back to Cologne, perhaps you and six soldiers, to protect us? The road to Cologne is dangerous and we would not otherwise be safe with such a splendid wagon and four mules.'

He looked surprised but, quickly recovering, frowned. 'Six soldiers? I am not at all sure I could persuade His Lordship. On the morrow he is to undertake a journey to Bonn and I must be at his side and he will need his troop to ride with him.'

'Perhaps you could point out to His Lordship that such a grand escort would do much to restore his reputation in Cologne and would serve to emphasise the generous nature of his donation to our crusade?'

'Ah! While the bishop is ever mindful of his duties to his flock, he is a man of God and leaves the final judgement of his nature not to the people of Cologne, but to our heavenly Father.'

The silver tongue was back. I looked down into the palms of my hands and spoke hesitatingly. 'Master Nicodemus, I ask not for my sake, but for thine own.'

'What mean you by this?' he asked, again surprised. 'We will keep our part of the bargain. A wagon and four mules?'

'With full harness,' I added quickly.

'Well then?'

I took a deep breath. 'All is not as it seems with a ridding. If any harm should come to us, then the crows will return threefold by the ringing of the Angelus tomorrow.' I wore a most innocent and wide-eyed expression but held my gaze steady, then gave a small shrug. 'You have seen yourself how dangerous it is to perform this ritual and how the wrath of God punished two sinners who, I fear, bore malice in their hearts from the previous occasion when I was summoned by His Lordship. If harm should come to us I greatly fear the consequences, the return of the crows being perhaps the smallest part of it. I implore you, for the sake of the safety of the bishop and yourself, to ensure our safety back to Cologne.'

Despite his silver tongue and high-lofty manner, this man, like me, was a peasant and I had seen the look of fear upon his face when he had knelt then later crossed himself. I was almost sure I had my man well fathomed, but he nevertheless had a slyness about him that was hard to read. Moreover, the bishop was likely to prove stubborn, having made up his mind to kill me – the addition of Reinhardt as another victim would not bother him unduly. He had not witnessed the ridding of the crows and lacked imagination and was also undeniably stupid. Like any member of the nobility, he would place the value of a pig, much less a wagon and four mules, well above that of a peasant's life and in particular that of a woman. I knew it would be up to Master Nicodemus to convince him otherwise. It was important that he knew the threat concerned him as well as his master.

'I must consult His Lordship, it is beyond my authority to grant your wish,' Master Nicodemus said, spreading his hands. If he was frightened by my threat, his fear was now well contained, so I wasn't at all sure whether my attempt to gull him had been successful.

I told myself if he returned from the bishop with a refusal to accompany us to Cologne, it could only mean that they didn't believe the crows would return and had called my bluff. It would also mean the bishop still wanted to go through with the plan to kill us.

An old woman arrived with water and cloth and a jar of unguent to attend to Reinhardt's cuts. I sniffed at the jar – it was mostly sulphur and a herb I didn't know. 'What herb is this?' I asked her.

'St John's Wort,' she replied. 'Have you any cuts I can attend to?'

'Thank you, no,' I said, then added, 'Poor Reinhardt has enough for both of us.'

'Of course you don't, I should not have doubted. An angel does not cut or bleed or bruise except to stain with Christ's precious blood the petals of the Virgin's pure white rose.'

I laughed and shook my head – this woman knew and believed all the market gossip. 'Frau, I am no angel and I bleed like any other.' I wondered what she might think if I told her that I'd earlier wet myself.

'They say that you always deny your wondrous works. Is it true you have the sign of the fish upon your back?'

'A birthmark,' I replied dismissively.

'Aye,' she said, not believing me, smiling and nodding her head in silent wonder. I had long since given up arguing with folk, for the more I protested the more convinced they became.

After the woman had left, a kitchen maid brought over a meal of bread and wine. We sat under a linden tree where a bench and table had been placed not far from where an outdoor kitchen had been created, convenient to the stables, bread oven, granary and the nearby stream. I now told Reinhardt in more detail of the overheard conversation between the bishop and his servant. 'Ratcatcher, you are not in this, you could leave now and be safely in Cologne before noon and I would think no less of you,' I said.

Reinhardt jumped to his feet. 'Then I must be off at once,' he said. 'You have been nothing but a burden since I returned! I was free as a bird and now I am nearly killed by ten thousand such. I can barely feed myself and now must help to feed thousands of children every day. I have, I swear in God's name, not a single enemy, but now I am about to be murdered by a bishop!' He smiled and threw up his hands, then did a little jig. 'Oh, how very much I have missed you, Sylvia Honeyeater. My dear, it will be a pleasure to die in your arms with my head against your delightful breast.'

'Reinhardt! We are in terrible danger and you may yet escape!' I cried.

'Sylvia, every breath we take is one more towards the last one. We will think of something, I know it. If God had meant you to die he would not have placed this terrible burden of a crusade for guttersnipes upon your shoulders! Our luck is forged together, but, alas, must we have this damned wagon? Without it we would walk freely from this place.'

'Ratcatcher, be serious! Yes, the wagon is essential! Thank you,' I cried, trying to rebuke him, answer his question and show him I was pleased he would stay with me, all at the same time. I had, of course, thought of forgoing the wagon and mules, but Master Israel's advice, that I could win by knowing the plot, persisted. Besides, I knew myself to be stubborn and not easily persuaded if I should have a cause I believed was God's divine will. It was, I knew, a dangerous trait in a woman and I knew it might yet bring me undone.

'You have a plan, I know it!' Reinhardt exclaimed. 'Or why else would you have warmed him up as you did with a most thinly concealed threat?' he asked, picking up his wine and once again coming to sit beside me.

'I didn't think it was that apparent,' I replied, slightly miffed, then shook my head and sighed. 'Nay, alas, ratcatcher, *that* was the plan. If he sees through the bluff we are done for.'

He shrugged. 'God did not bring us together so that we might die in each other's arms,' he said, attempting to comfort me. 'In any event, we shall soon know how goes this plot – here comes the bishop's little arse-licker.'

Master Nicodemus approached carrying a garment over his arm that I took to be a tunic for Reinhardt. This proved to be correct, and with it hose. 'You have eaten well, I hope, though I regret only bread and wine?'

'Aye, we thank you, sire,' Reinhardt said, putting down his wine and jumping to his feet. 'Both were excellent, the wine young yet the grape plucked sweet enough, the summer sun its sugar brought to bear, bread still warm-baked from the oven, we may ask no more!' Reinhardt replied in his cultured Frenchified voice, speaking of the wine as if he possessed knowledge gained in a more refined society. His posing sat awkwardly with his disarray, torn tunic and hose and the sticky yellow ointment smeared across his back and hands.

Master Nicodemus laughed. 'A good summer, yes, for both wine and grain. Both the cellar and the granary are full and we thank our Saviour for His bountiful blessings. It was also most fortunate that the bread oven, granary and the wine cellar are outside the palace building and so we have not gone hungry while held hostage by the crows.' His manner was relaxed and friendly and there was no hint of the decision the bishop had made concerning our lives. He handed the tunic and hose to Reinhardt. 'I regret they are not new, but clean and in good repair, the cloth still has some wear in it and the hose no holes. You may keep them,' he said generously. I could not help but wonder if they were meant to be his death shroud.

'Thank you, I shall go down to the stream to wash so they are not stained.' Reinhardt left us to walk down to the nearby stream and I watched as he walked behind the large granary that was as big as any such as were to be found in Cologne. In this alone the bishop was a very rich man.

Master Nicodemus waited until the ratcatcher was out of sight before he spoke. 'Alas, Fräulein Sylvia, the bishop's business in Bonn is of great importance to the Church and must proceed. He greatly regrets that he cannot give you protection as he needs his escort and myself to be fresh for the journey.' He gave me a deeply sincere look. 'We will pray for your safe return to Cologne.'

I shook my head sadly, still playing the bluff even after it had been called. 'Thank you, Master Nicodemus, I understand. His Lordship's prayers for our safety are greatly appreciated.' I looked up to see that a small smile played at the corners of his mouth and hoped that, from the look of my eyes, he did not sense the despair contained within my heart.

'I have seen to the wagon and mules, they are nearly harnessed and will be brought to the front of the palace.'

I fought to keep the note of desperation from my voice knowing this conniving Nicodemus, servant and chief bishop's bum-licker, missed very little. 'May we at least have a muleteer, since neither Reinhardt nor I know nought of mules or wagons?' I pleaded.

He shook his head slowly. 'Regrettably the mule driver is employed with ploughing, we cannot spare him,' he replied, the smug little smile still hiding at the corners of his mouth. He must have momentarily forgotten that I was a peasant and would know that ploughing takes place in October and not in May. I would have liked to play this perfidious bastard at chess. He had just the mind for it to be a good contest, that is, if he was not tempted to cheat as I thought he would be.

'Shall we wait at the front of the palace? I must see to it that the cleaning is underway. The wagon will soon be here and the bishop himself will bless you and it and send you on your way wishing you Godspeed,' Master Nicodemus said in a benign voice.

We walked to the front of the palace where numerous servants with buckets and mops and ladders and long brushes hurried through the doors. I walked inside with Master Nicodemus and was astonished at what I saw. The interior of the great hall was thick with bird droppings and the great beams caked and whitened. The sharp smell was, as before, quite overpowering, so that I held my hand to my nose and mouth. The servants busy at cleaning wore rags tied across their mouths and a great coughing was heard from one and all. None could tarry long and rushed past us with half a bucketful of bird shit, not able to endure long enough to fill it. We both quickly retreated, coughing and gulping as we hurried back through the doors and into the fresh air beyond.

It was then that I noticed Reinhardt coming from the direction of the granary and that he was piping with no sound. As he drew closer I saw the rats following him and then the rats within the palace started to rush past our feet to join the mighty rush of rodents. Soon we saw that they came from every direction until the ground swarmed with the vile brown creatures. Reinhardt drew ever nearer to us. I looked at Master Nicodemus who stood pop-eyed beside me, unable to believe what he was seeing.

'Ah, here they are, come to replace the crows,' I said in a most natural voice, as if we had both been expecting this pestilence to arrive all along.

'Nay! No, please no!' he cried out, bringing his hands to his face. 'Please, I beseech you! Oh my God!'

'A troop of soldiers and thyself and a muleteer, the one that is ploughing in May?' I said, then shouted to Reinhardt, 'Bring the rats into the palace where they might have a long and happy home!' By this time the rodents must have numbered several thousand and there were still others coming, running and jumping over small rocks and other obstacles to join the swirling throng. 'What say you?' I now asked the distressed Master Nicodemus.

Servants were fleeing for their lives, the women screaming out as rats dodged and ran through and around their legs. Discarded buckets and mops, ladders and brushes lay in their wake. And then I saw that the bishop, who must have come unobserved around the corner of the palace, stood close to us, terrified and dressed in full regalia. His back and palms were hard-pressed against the palace wall, with Reinhardt, who must have seen him, turning slightly and silently piping, commencing to walk directly towards him. 'Your Master is here to do the blessing of the wagon,' I said, pointing to the bishop who had now sunk to his knees in the gravel, blubbing and pleading in terror. 'Do you need to ask his permission?' I asked politely.

I would beat this man at chess, I thought to myself.

CHAPTER THIRTEEN

On the Road to Jerusalem

WE HAD DEPARTED THE bishop's palace without receiving a blessing, as His Lordship had not been in a state to perform even the smallest task. Shaking and sobbing like a small child he had been quite convinced that he was about to be devoured by the rats, and was eventually carried sniffing and blubbing to the safety of the little room to the side of the passageway. On the surface all seemed well, although I wasn't fool enough to think that the bishop would forgive me.

The gossips among his servants would no doubt tell this story of the crows and the rats to all and sundry and so further damage would be done to what small reputation he had left with the people of Cologne. I had been the instrument of his previous mortification with the rescinding of our excommunication. Now I'd brought him undone once again. What had happened to him with the rats did not serve him well as either man or bishop and, unlike Master Nicodemus, it had shown him up to be a coward. Although the bishop's servant stood quaking in his boots, in contrast to the other servants he had stood his ground while Reinhardt piped the rats through the great doors. With the rampaging rats in the palace, the bishop collapsed and lay sobbing near the palace doorway. Master Nicodemus had hastened to lift his master to his feet, but the bishop had brushed his arm aside with a petulant cry, unwilling to rise.

Reinhardt returned and bolted the doors behind him and I stepped forward and solemnly tapped thrice on the oak panels with Father John's stave. Whereupon I recited a hastily composed incantation that, I confess, was not near good enough to meet the exacting standards of the dear departed Brother Dominic. But in the prevailing atmosphere the words seemed sufficient to cause Master Nicodemus to fall to his knees beside the inert form of the bishop. I spoke out so that they could clearly hear me.

> *These are the fierce avenging rats!*
> *A curse to show God's discontent.*
> *He who protects all pious children*
> *has caused them hither to be sent!*
> *Now we journey to the Holy Land,*
> *God's true cross we hope to gain.*
> *Children who carry a burning faith*
> *to the glory of His precious name!*
> *If you should seek to do us harm,*
> *hear now what we as pilgrims say:*
> *'May this plague of vicious rodents*
> *be with you forever from this day!'*
> *Confess now the evil in thy heart.*
> *Ask for forgiveness in God's name.*
> *Then vow to give us thy protection*
> *and we will bring you peace again.*

By the end of my recitation the bishop had half risen to sit with his back against the wall and his knees pulled up against his large belly, his mitre tumbled from his balding head. Spent tears glistened down the cheeks of his near-scarlet face and a stream of yellow mucus spilled from his warty winebibber's nose. Every few moments he'd sniff or a loud hiccup would issue from his heaving chest.

I had spoken as loudly as I might so that the bishop would hear the full extent of my 'jabbering' tongue. But it is well-known that fear often blocks out every sensibility and it was quite possible he had not heard a single word. Rats are vile creatures to be sure, but I had never seen anyone as frightened by them as this gibbering Prince of the Church.

Master Nicodemus rose from his knees and standing in front of the bishop waited silently for permission to help him to his feet. Then as if his servant had spoken, which he had not, the sobbing bishop cried, 'Yes, yes! (sob) Give them all they ask. Anything! Anything! If they (sob) rid us of the (sob) rats and go away!'

'Eighteen bags of corn!' Reinhardt shouted out, to my astonishment.

'Yes, yes, take them, and go!' came the tearful response.

Reinhardt duly opened the palace doors and piped the rats into the nearby stream to drown. Whereupon, with the bishop sufficiently recovered to be carried away on a stretcher, we were soon on our way with a wagonload of corn, four frisky mules, a troop of soldiers and a very quiet and much chastened Master Nicodemus as our escort.

Reinhardt was well puffed up that he had saved the day with the piping of the rats and I was pleased for him. I recalled Frau Johanna's words – that men are simple creatures and so must be seen to be the leaders in all things and are in need of constant praise. So I did not tell him that he had done exactly as I had known he would when he'd made the excuse to go down to the stream to wash. If, previous to this, I had prompted him to pipe in the rats should the news from the bishop's servant turn out to be bad, then he would have had to share the glory and success with me. He would not have been the sole and all-conquering hero who had the pleasure of his remarkable forethought all to himself. It was a small enough reward and one he richly deserved. Without him the day could not have been won.

I was surprised that he hadn't waited for the bishop's decision before going to the stream on the pretence of washing, a contradictory act that would have removed all the carefully applied ointment to his back. I had, of course, expected him to wait and see whether Master Nicodemus brought good or bad tidings. But I then realised that Reinhardt might not be given any future opportunity to slip away unnoticed to pipe the rats from the granary and stables. Reinhardt had sensibly decided that if the news had been good, then we would be seen to have conducted a ridding of the rats as a gesture of goodwill, one made to thank His Lordship for his kind donation and the protection he had provided for our return to Cologne.

Sitting atop the bags of corn on the wagon on our way back to Cologne, as grand and happy as can be, I paid due tribute to the ratcatcher. 'Reinhardt, you have saved us this day and your clever wit has given us sufficient corn to embark with confidence on our crusade. I am forever in your debt and have no way to repay you.'

How true, I thought, the notion that from the darkest moment begins the light. Brother Dominic and Master Israel's advice had prevailed, and together with Reinhardt, Father Hermann and Father Paulus, I felt most fortunate that I had such good men, each in his own way, to guide me.

Before we'd departed and as he was being placed onto a stretcher I thanked the bishop for his donation. Then, knowing I must grasp the moment or I would never get another chance, I asked him to allow Father Hermann to come back to his beloved St Mary's on the Kapitol and Father Paulus to the bells of St Martin's, also that they be allowed to administer the oath of allegiance to the cross that the pilgrim children would be required by the Church to take if they were to embark on a true crusade. I could not possibly have hoped to gain his permission at any other time nor dared even to ask. Still tearful, to my astonishment he agreed, and I sensed that he was afraid of me. Moreover, so anxious was he to see us gone that if I had asked His Lordship to give me his mitre for a basket then I feel sure he would have readily agreed.

Sitting in high glory Reinhardt laughed. 'Today I have been more afraid than any in my life and I shall wear the marks to remind me of it forever.' He grinned. 'How shall I tell a future lover, when he remarks upon the myriad tiny scars upon my back that they were made by the flying feet of a thousand crows? No other soul alive in Christendom will be so uniquely marked. Think you, Sylvia. I shall be a goodly part of the miracle folk will create out of what happened today. Moreover for once you will not, as you always do, be able to deny it. I have my back to verify its truth. Hey, I have an idea!' he suddenly cried out. 'We should together make an entertainment, a pious play composed around the miracle of the ridding of the rats and crows from the wicked bishop's palace. I think such a performance would be well attended and much enjoyed by commonfolk.'

'Don't you start,' I snorted. 'We have nonsense enough with miracles and all they do is lead to trouble.'

'Aye, but with you, Sylvia, it is always something that may be given a strange interpretation. It is why I love to be with you – every day brings a new surprise.'

'Hmmph, the true miracle today was that you managed to stop the cawing of the crows so that I might call to them to depart the palace. How did you know to do this?'

He laughed. 'Just another small miracle from the Pied Piper of Hamelin. Nay, it was too easy and I cannot take the credit. You may thank the cackling geese and my lazy nature.' I waited for him to explain. 'Geese, as you know, rise before dawn and so none may sleep a further wink once they start their rackety cackling. When as a child I was learning the ratcatcher's flute, my father would make me rise each morning to let the geese out to graze. So I practised until I found the note that piped them silent. With their first raucous cry I would awake and quickly silence them two hours or more and so gain the extra sleep.'

'But how did you know it would work on crows?'

He grinned sheepishly. 'God is kind to those He loves and I borrowed some of your faith.'

'You mean you didn't know?'

'Aye.'

News of our arrival back in Cologne had somehow preceded us. By the time we passed through the city gates several thousand children, and many of the citizens, filled the square at the entrance and continued well into the streets beyond. The troop of soldiers and Master Nicodemus on horseback, together with the bishop's gift of a splendid mule wagon loaded with the eighteen bags of corn, was an affirmation to everyone that the Church had given its blessing to the Children's Crusade.

Then to my surprise Master Nicodemus came to bid us farewell, though what he had to say seemed addressed for the most part to me. 'Sylvia Honeyeater, much has come to pass since we met and I can hardly believe but a night and now only today have passed. You,' he nodded to Reinhardt to include him, 'have taught me much and with it renewed my faith. Whereas, when we first met I spoke of a witch who would soon be led to the flames, now I speak of one who I know has been truly blessed by our Lord.' He turned to one of the soldiers. 'Bring it,' he commanded. The soldier rode up and we saw that he carried a cross about as high as a tall man's arm, not a common Latin cross, but the more unusual Greek tau variety. 'It is said to have been forged in Antioch where the Holy Lance was found and brought hence by a crusader returning from the First Crusade, who was perhaps a member of my family, for it has always been with us. I beg that you accept it to guide you on your Children's Crusade.' He sighed. 'Alas, the bishop was in no fit state to bless it, or the wagon and the mules.' He made the sign of the cross upon his chest. 'His Lordship and I have much to confess and then penance to be undertaken and it would be better if it was blessed elsewhere. Perhaps your leader may carry it to Jerusalem?' He held the cross out to me.

I accepted it and, suddenly overcome, thanked him somewhat tearfully and also for our safe deliverance, greatly relieved that we had not made an enemy of this clever man. 'I promise we shall carry it always and I shall have it blessed when we reach the Holy Sepulchre and then some day I shall return it to you,' I said in an emotional voice.

When, to the continual cheering from the vast multitude of children following the wagon, we arrived at last at the square outside St Martin's, to my surprise there stood Nicholas to welcome us. He embraced me as if a hero returning from a crusade and also Reinhardt, exclaiming all the while at the wagon, the mules and the bags of corn.

I handed him the tau cross. 'It is from the First Crusade,' I said, stressing its importance.

He examined the cross, weighing it in his hands. 'It is different and will serve us well as a holy symbol. I shall carry it with me to Jerusalem,' he declared.

'You are well again, Nicholas, I am glad,' I said, much relieved that the boy I loved was returned to me.

'The devil has departed and Jesus our Saviour is again with us and I am ready to depart on the day of Pentecost,' he said excitedly. Then he announced, 'We have no time to lose – we must have banners with an icon and brass trumpets to carry and everyone must sign themselves with a cross and wear it on their tunic. They must carry a pilgrim's stave and leather pouches for alms.' He said this as if all in one breath, then taking another said, 'Of the utmost importance, all must take a sacred oath of allegiance to the cross, to me and to the Children's Crusade. Father Hermann must perform the ceremony!'

Bewildered by all these requests at once I took the easiest. 'We have no icon for the banners,' I protested.

'Then we must find one,' he said, with a wave of the hand. 'Must I do all the thinking?'

'Perhaps a crow?' Reinhardt said sardonically. 'They have been much in our mind of late.' I could see he was appalled at Nicholas's presumption.

'Crow? Why yes! Excellent!' Nicholas cried, clapping his hands. 'We have the cross, now we may place a crow as the icon on our banners.'

'I do not think this a good emblem, Nicholas,' I said, having had enough of crows to last me a while.

'Nay, you are wrong, Sylvia. Think now, people will ask us, "Why is your emblem the crow?" "Oh," we will reply, "we go to find the true cross. Our crusade will not stop to wage war or conquer the lands of the infidel as others did. As Christ's children we carry no weapons and seek no wealth, but we journey to the Holy Land and to God as *straight as the crow flies!*" Do you not think this a good rejoinder?'

'And what of the sea?' Reinhardt asked with a superior smile. 'It is in the direct way, methinks.' I could see he was taken aback by Nicholas's exuberance and utter conviction and determined to put him in his place. It was a task I knew to be futile – Nicholas was blessed and the children would have no other leader but him. If the ratcatcher was to come with us he must accept that God had chosen this vainglorious child to lead us to Jerusalem.

'It will be as it was for Moses when he fled the land of Egypt,' Nicholas said, his eyes burning with conviction. 'We will cross as if it were dry land, our feet upon the water as were the footsteps of Christ when he walked upon the sea. I have had this vision and know it to be a promise from Christ Jesus Himself.' Whereupon Nicholas called out that he would preach at this very moment to the multitude.

Reinhardt glanced at me and placed his forefinger to the side of his head. Then he shook his head slowly and I could see he was even less impressed with this bumptious child.

The children had not heard Nicholas preach during the time he had been in the monk's cell and others, newly arrived, not at all. There was enormous excitement as he mounted the steps of St Martin's. 'Come, Sylvia, you must sing to His praise as always,' he called.

'Nicholas, I am weary. It has truthfully been a very long day for us.'

'But you *always* sing before I preach in the square!' he cried, alarmed at my refusal and not prepared to accept it. 'What shame is this?' he asked scornfully. 'You would end this day without singing to the glory of the Lord? Come now, be quick, it will soon be time for the sun to set and I wish to preach about the parting of the seas.'

The ratcatcher looked at me and shook his head, unable to believe the boy's tone of voice. But as always, since Nicholas had been called by God to lead the Children's Crusade, I was completely beguiled by him. I believed with every fibre in my body that he was God's purest instrument. I knew him as often churlish, and much taken up by sombre and brooding moods that often lasted days and increasingly even longer. Also, when, as now, he was approaching his charismatic state, he was utterly selfish and self-involved and could not be contradicted or he would fly into a towering rage. This was not a fit of temper as one might expect from a young boy denied his own way, but an outpouring of God's condemnation and wrath. His words burned to the very core of one's being and it seemed they came from elsewhere and were not to be found in his normal vocabulary. Reinhardt had not yet heard him preach, which was when all fell under his spell and seemed never to recover from the effect it had upon them. Nicholas of Cologne could not be resisted and when God was not at his side, even the devil waited, ever eager for his company.

And so I sang a Gloria but Reinhardt did not accompany me. 'I will not be taken in by this young whippersnapper! Sylvia, you pay him far too much attention!' he chided.

While I knew that this was a fair comment and my intelligence told me that my behaviour was not what it ought to be and that a crusade involving children who were poverty-stricken, immature and unprepared was not likely to succeed, my faith told me to persist. I knew in my soul that this was God's will and my given task was to be with this blessed and difficult child no matter what should come to pass. Nicholas of Cologne was to be the cross I would have to bear.

It was customary when he preached for me to sing at the commencement and the end. I sang the first Gloria well enough but somewhat lacking in spirit. The absent Father Hermann would then say a prayer to bless the message to come. Now, in his absence, Nicholas waited, fidgeting and impatient for the Gloria to end, and then launched immediately into his sermon as if the words were rioting within him and demanding to come out. When he preached, he was as a being completely possessed and none could resist his voice in which he had that same power to throw to the multitude that I had first heard on the occasion of the Miracle at St Martin's square.

His message was the story of the escape of the children of Israel from the land of Egypt. He began to paint a picture of the pursuing Egyptians, the devil's infidels, that was so awesome that the children shook in fright. 'The faces of the enemies of God,' Nicholas cried, 'were smeared with the blood of Israelite children taken for sacrifice, then too, each deadly spear they carried they'd dipped in infant blood so it would know the taste and hunger for more of this flesh of children!' Then he went on to describe how when Moses reached the Red Sea, the children of Israel turned to see the dust clouds of the pursuing Egyptians on the horizon and cried out in mortal fear, 'Today this water runs with our blood!' How Moses held his mighty stave aloft and called out to God to save the children of Israel. The gathered children in the square cried out in ecstasy when Nicholas told how God's hand pushed through the rolling clouds and with His forefinger dipped into the incarnadine sea and drew it across the breadth of the great waters. They gasped as he told how the waves reared up behind God's rippling finger, hanging motionless as they towered a full league up into the heavens.

His voice gathering in speed and urgency, Nicholas continued. 'And ever closer came the infidel hordes while the children of Israel began to cross the dry seabed. Then a mighty roaring and thunder of hooves was heard as the chariots drew nearer and nearer, ten thousand entering that same God-drawn road across the gaping waters before the fleeing Israelites had a chance to entirely reach the other side. With cries of triumph and blood-curdling yells, the Egyptians, whipping their horses so that they foamed at the mouth, began closing in. The hapless children of God ran and stumbled, shouting in terrible anguish as the thundering war chariots were now near close enough to throw the deadly spears that hungered for more of the flesh of little children. The snorting of the wild-eyed horses was clearly to be heard when the last Israelite, a lame shepherd boy, limped exhausted to the far shore.' Nicholas stopped and his eyes travelled across the heads of the awed and silent children in the square. Then in a voice slowed and deepened he all but growled, 'Then came the roar of doomsday as God's finger again appeared and touched the towering edge of the dreadful hovering waves. The earth shook so that the sound of it was heard across the great desert, carried by the howling wind to faraway Jerusalem. Whereupon the waters thundered to earth to fill that divinely created path of escape with the terrible judgement of God's awful wrath.'

The gathered children now roared their approval. These were not the children of Israel that Nicholas preached about, but they imagined themselves as holy pilgrims voyaging to the Promised Land. This was confirmed in their minds when Nicholas reached out and took up the tau cross Master Nicodemus had given me and held it above his head. 'Hear ye, all!' he shouted. 'Just as Almighty God parted the waters for Moses, so also will He make a dry path on the stilled and adamantine waves for Nicholas of Cologne and those pious Christian children who go with me to Jerusalem. With one heart and one voice we shall pass through the seas on dry land to recover the Holy Land and Jerusalem, where we will kneel within the Holy Sepulchre and pray in the presence of the true cross!'

If, from my telling of this sermon, you think me a bystander looking on, then I have misled you. I was as much awed and taken with his words as the smallest child listening and I had not the slightest doubt that the Holy Spirit was present, for we all felt as one being, cleansed and renewed in the spirit and glory of the Lord. No priest alive or dead – by this I mean also my beloved Brother Dominic – could have persuaded me otherwise. I glanced at Reinhardt and I could see that his once-suspicious eyes now burned with a newfound faith and that he too had fallen under the spell of the preaching of Nicholas of Cologne.

And so began the last of the preparations for our departure. Father Hermann returned from the Cistercian convent at Hoven surprisingly cheerful and perhaps less grateful to be rescued than I had supposed. 'I am well-liked by the nuns and they wish me to return as a part of my ministry,' he declared.

'Does that mean you will not be coming on the Children's Crusade?' I asked.

He nodded his head and was slow to reply, this to indicate that he had given the matter a great deal of thought. 'I have prayed to the Virgin for guidance and she has forbidden it. She says my health will not survive the journey, and besides, she needs her earthly husband by her side as the Christ child is going through a difficult stage. Also, the nuns at the convent now need my ministrations as their priest has recently passed away.'

'Then will you administer the oath of allegiance to the true cross so that the children may be permitted to wear the cross emblazoned upon their chests?'

He looked doubtful. 'Sylvia, they are for the most part penniless and have not yet reached their majority and so are not old enough to be accepted to the true cross.' He cleared his throat a little guiltily, then said, 'I must have the permission of the bishop.'

I was right – Father Hermann, for all his goodness and faith, was not a character independent of mind and would always be subservient to any authority placed above him. He had been an eager participant before he had been sent to the Cistercian convent and had now returned doubting our cause. This served to confirm my previous suspicion that he was not of a suitable nature for the large and forbidding needs of a crusade. The Virgin Mary is always shown as a strong woman and I thought to myself, though somewhat amusingly, perhaps she had chosen him as her earthly husband for his ready and unquestioning compliance to her every demand, that in his mind this sojourn with the Cistercian nuns had been a respite both from a nagging wife and her precocious Child. I thought this not as blasphemy, but because in Father Hermann's frequent conversations he spoke of Mary as his earthly wife as any husband might and of the Christ Child as if still in His infancy. He saw no contradiction in the fact that Christ had grown to manhood, been crucified, risen from the dead and ascended to heaven. Instead, in Father Hermann's mind he was still a mewling infant at Mary's breast who had teethed but one day before receiving all His teeth. Perhaps this miracle of sudden teeth had caused an equally sudden and painful consternation at His mother's breast.

'I have gained the bishop's permission for you and Father Paulus to administer the blessing and the oath,' I replied. Then, perhaps a little cruelly, added, 'I promise you won't get into trouble this time, Father.'

My sarcasm was lost on Father Hermann, who immediately brightened. 'If you have His Lordship's permission then you have mine. I shall be glad to accept the children's oaths.'

Father Paulus had also returned from the monastery at Disibodenberg, which I must say came as a surprise. I had expected Father Hermann to return to his beloved St Mary's and his Holy Virgin wife with tearful gratitude, whereas I was sure that Father Paulus would wish to remain at the monastery where he would continue in the footsteps of the great Brother Dominic. After all, at the monastery he had a warm and comfortable cell, good food, solitude and silence; at St Martin's he lived in a cramped cell within the belltower where the constant clanging was making him deaf.

In the next three days, in batches of fifty at a time, the two priests officiated at the oath of allegiance to the cross and the children were given a cross to wear on their tunics. Initially this presented a problem as we had no red cloth available and no money to buy any. So I had made both priests declare that the cross each child wore was forbidden to be bigger than the hand of the wearer, this as a symbol that they, by their own hand, placed their faith in God and agreed to become a part of the Children's Crusade. The cross was to be placed over their hearts so that they might renew their faith by placing their hands to cover the cross and know that they, the children of the Crusade, were of one heart and one cross.

As no red cloth was available, in fact no cloth of any colour of the large quantity required, we were reluctantly forced to use the green canvas Master Israel had given me to cover the wagon ready for when Nicholas sank into his moods of despair. Each child received a square of green canvas no bigger than his hand and from this the cross was cut. Of course I never mentioned that the cloth had been a gift from a Jew. This is the first time I have ever spoken of it to anyone. If it was to prove an evil portent, which I think not, then no harm came to my beloved Master Israel for his generosity. I recall his lamentation when I went to fetch the cloth that he had sent to Bonn to get.

'My dearest Sylvia, I am a Jew and so cursed to remember that in the name of your Jesus my people have been killed in great numbers in your past crusades. In the Third Crusade King Philip cancelled all debts that were owed to Jews and many Jews were killed and others driven out of Spain. Already your Church in Rome talks of a badge of shame we are soon to carry, a yellow patch, that folk may use to identify us wherever we go. No matter how honourable and chaste our lives, now we may be chastised and persecuted by any Christian, be he of the lowest rank, a thief, vagabond or worthless scoundrel, he will feel himself more important than a dirty Jew.' There were tears in his eyes as he looked up at me. 'Sylvia, Frau Sarah and I have learned to love you – to us you are neither Jew nor Gentile but a person of rare worth and to us always a devoted daughter. If I could persuade you, though I know I cannot, to abandon this Children's Crusade I would do it with joy in my heart, for I would know I had saved your life. I cannot refuse you this gift of cloth, though my greatest hope is that it is not used as your shroud. I shall weep and pray each day for you until we meet again.'

All I could think to say in reply was, 'Master Israel, I solemnly promise, no Jew will suffer or die in the Children's Crusade as long as I remain alive.'

When Nicholas had been presented with his green cross he had cried out, 'But the crusader's cross is *always* red!'

I had anticipated his objection and had my reply prepared. 'Stay a moment your opinion, Nicholas, and hear me out. No colour of blood spilled in Christ's name must tarnish the Children's Crusade. There is a good reason for this green cross. Think you now, all the other crusades are drenched in blood. This wilful killing that included women and children was always justified by the scarlet of the cross they wore on their tunics. But we are not as they were and go in peace and love and not to despoil the lands of the Saracen. The earth will remain green and bountiful after we have passed by and not be razed to the torch and desolated as our forebears were wont to do. We shall spill no blood upon this journey to Jerusalem! Our cross is green, the colour of verdancy and new growth and the sign of God's peace and goodwill.'

Nicholas clapped his hands, delighted with this new notion. 'I shall make the cross of green, the green cross, a part of my sermon today. I shall explain how I have chosen green so we may rejoice in our intention and be ever mindful that we go in peace and joy; this cross shall be the symbol of the true nature of our divine intention.'

As in all other things, the idea of the green cross was appropriated by Nicholas to become his own inspiration. In his sermon, his reasons given were more eloquent and better explained than mine, so that the children rejoiced in this new green cross and knew themselves to be elevated in God's eyes by its symbolism. How, I wondered to myself, would Nicholas have felt had he known whence came the cloth that made the crosses? I still pray that Master Israel, now long dead, never knew how the canvas came to be used. At the time I comforted myself with the thought that, along with all the Jews of Cologne, on our day of departure he would have remained behind locked doors, so was unlikely to know about the crosses.

So taken was Nicholas by this colour green that when a rich burgher's wife, who was entranced by his preaching and the Children's Crusade, begged what she might do for him, he had asked for a monk's robe and cowl to be made in green wool. He now wore this garment when he preached at night and the effect was most prepossessing. With the cowl extended to the front his face was almost completely hidden in the dark interior. When he preached with his face in deep shadow he appeared much the mysterious messenger of an awesome God and the children waiting to hear him shivered in ecstatic anticipation.

We would eventually make the cover to the wagon with the hessian from the bags that had contained the bishop's corn and it served our purpose, though proved a miserable shelter in the wet. As for the banners, children are ever inventive in their scavenging and soon enough banners appeared everywhere with crude crow shapes stitched upon them. I later heard say that the women of Cologne, many of them the wives of rich burghers, had stitched them and given them as a contribution to the Children's Crusade. Many of them had seen their own children join, and our departure would prove both joyous and sad as parents bade them farewell not knowing if they would ever see them again.

To pay these parents homage I had arranged for those children from Cologne to lead us through the city gates with the Pied Piper of Hamelin piping them out, the ratcatcher having composed a special tune to pipe us from the city. The remainder of the children held back so the Cologne children might be the first to march away. How proud these children seemed as they passed the people who thronged the streets, many women weeping to see them go, though nothing would have prevented them from doing so as each one burned with the true faith. In the years to come and perhaps forever more, folk will tell of the Pied Piper of Hamelin's piping of the children.

We had taken the first steps to the Holy Land, and as we passed through the city gates folk called out as the naked women had first done that early spring morning in the square of St Martin's: 'Our children in Jerusalem!' And now we understood the meaning of their nakedness, for we had departed for the Holy Land without money or weapons or armour, scarce any food or any means of protecting ourselves or of surviving. We had entered this crusade as naked babes, trusting only in God to deliver us to the gates of Jerusalem.

The ecstatic children blew on brass trumpets and carried their banners aloft and every child who didn't have a trumpet or a banner carried a wooden cross. All sang in praise of the heavenly Father as we departed during Pentecost on the eleventh hour of the thirteenth day of May in the year of our Lord 1212. In all, four thousand passed through the city gates and it was well into the afternoon before the last of the marching children left Cologne.

On that day we had risen long before first light and Nicholas, wearing his new green monk's robe and cowl, had delivered a final sermon lit

with a flaming torch on the steps of St Martin's. We had partaken of
our last meal, a feast of bread, gruel and ale, though we soon ran out
of ale. Then Father Hermann conducted a final mass and often but a
single crumb of bread was placed upon the tongue of a child who was old
enough to partake of Holy Communion. The younger children, many of
them no more than the age of six, received a blessing, and so it was close
to the eleventh hour before we were ready to leave.

Of great concern to me was that with Father Hermann's decision
to stay at St Mary's we had no priest to attend to us on our journey.
Apart from conducting mass, there was much a priest would be required
to do, not the least of which was performing the last rites. I was not so
naive as to think that none would perish on the way. Already there were
a number of sick who had joined us, among them adults and women
with small children, even some with babes at the breast. Whenever
I came across the sick or those with children not old enough to take
care of themselves I would exhort them to remain behind, explaining
that even with God's blessing the journey would be long and hard to
endure. But they were blinded by their faith, expecting that they would
be miraculously cured when they reached the Holy Land. As for their
children, had not Nicholas of Cologne preached that on the journey to
Jerusalem their children would feast on manna from heaven cast to their
feet by God with the morning dew? Moreover, even though we would
soon find the Church turned against us, it was unseemly that a crusade
should depart for Jerusalem without a priest in attendance.

Then, as the wagon passed through the city gates with much
shouting out and singing and trumpets blaring, I saw that Father Paulus
walked beside it. Hurrying towards him I shouted to make myself heard,
'Do you journey a small way with us, Father?'

He cupped his ear. 'Eh?' Then he shrugged and shook his head,
indicating that there was too much noise for him to hear. I walked beside
him and it was not until we were well clear of the city that we could
converse. 'How far do you journey with us, Father?' I asked a second
time, my mouth held close to his ear.

'How far?' he asked, bemused. 'Why, to Jerusalem, of course! I shall enter the Holy Sepulchre with you, Sylvia,' he said, his pale blue eyes shining with conviction. He reached down and took up the small wooden cross that hung suspended on twine from his neck and kissed it. 'Then, for Father Hermann I have promised I shall say a prayer at the crypt of the church near Gethsemane.' I could see that he was as excited as any child, in fact, himself in this matter a small child, convinced that everything will happen exactly as he imagined.

Hallelujah! We now have our priest! I thought joyously, though perhaps not the one I had supposed we would need. Despite his timorous demeanour in the face of senior Church authority, Father Hermann would have been ideal. He was a hearty type who could be somewhat the gentle bully while capable of cajoling and also disciplining the wayward. He was an imposing size and a respected man of God with a reputation for holiness and visions and would not have been afraid to face the town councillors and priests in the towns and villages we would enter. Alternatively, Father Paulus seemed the least likely to succeed at these tasks imagined for our crusade priest to perform. He was near deaf, did not preach, was reluctant to officiate at mass, and seemed confused by children and unable to converse with them or, for that matter, most adults. But for the study of Latin and his ability as a scribe he was completely lacking in persuasion, and his personality, if described, might be said to be washed out and ineffectual. I loved him dearly but expected little of practical help from him.

However, I reminded myself that it was Father Paulus among the mice at the archbishop's inquiry who had stood up to suggest that the naked women were overcome by a contagion. This single word, 'contagion', and the subsequent illustration he had given concerning a mob attacking a Jewish moneylender, had turned the inquiry in our favour. Perhaps there was more to this little man than I thought, though my commonsense told me I was clutching at straws; his faded blue eyes, pale freckled skin and sparse ginger hair peppered with grey formed a physiognomy that seemed to replicate almost exactly his character. At best Father Paulus was a shy, loyal and unworldly priest who craved isolation and peace and who wished the egregious babble around him to be drowned out by the clanging of church bells.

On the first day we walked only a few hours until sunset and camped in a field on the outskirts of a small village the name of which, for the life of me, I cannot remember, even though it was important being our first place of sojourn for the night. Many of the smaller children were overcome with exhaustion and slept where they'd halted, on the side of the road beside the field, too weary to crawl the smallest distance into it.

Before we'd left Cologne I had bade the sick come to the wagon each evening as I had stored large quantities of herbal remedies and ointment for use on the journey to Jerusalem. But on the first day away and just three hours journey from Cologne, my heart sank when I beheld the extent of the children that needed attention. We had barely left and already there were several dozen who had some complaint. I knew we would be on the road for at least half a year and now, but one day out, we were already busy with the sick. My only hope was that this was a hardening process, that the children would soon be calloused to the blisters and their stomachs grow accustomed to the conditions so that they were no longer possessed by the need for frequent evacuation of their bowels or given to vomiting.

Previous to leaving I had created a group of young girls and taught them what herbs to gather and then how to make the basic unguents and ointments and the various medications for the stomach and ailments of the bowel. I don't know how we would have managed without the knowledge Frau Sarah had taught me and I thanked her daily in my prayers. The girls were much taken by our secret women's knowledge and soon proved most proficient in the basics of efficacious remedies and eventually became the very backbone to the task of treating the sick. They took great pride in the name Father Paulus gave them, for he called them the 'healing angels'. Each morning before we left and again at night it was to become customary to treat the sick. And while I knew that this would be a busy time, I had no idea that we would soon come to call it 'The Hospice of the Dying' where, too often, we were required to act as the angels of death.

I recall that first morning how the villagers arrived to wonder at so large a throng, some bearing food and all curious and much overcome with the sacred nature of the journey. Alas, the following morning they would lose all their children, the ploughboy and the shepherd, the goatherd and the goosegirl, the milkmaid, the swineherd and the children who laboured in the fields. All would forsake their homes to join the crusade. It was the first indication of things to come.

Before departing Nicholas preached what for him was a short sermon. A mist hung over the field and the children's clothes were drenched with the morning dew as we departed, the children singing hymns and blowing their trumpets to the glory of God.

Nicholas was on fire with his message of hope and his energy knew no bounds. He had spent the night praying and possessed less than three hours sleep, yet seemed the most refreshed of all of us. There was no containing him as he walked among groups of children on the road who would burst into praising and song as he approached. The fever (or was it a contagion?) swept over all of us as we marched that first full day.

We had received a gift of four bags of corn from the village to replenish what we'd used, as sustenance for the smallest children and to feed the mothers with babies to keep the milk at their breasts. But 'gift' was a relative word. It had been a hard bargaining process aimed at their collective conscience and it was Reinhardt, by piping the rats from their precious stores of grain, who would eventually shame them into giving.

This reluctance to give was in part due to the weather. The rains had not come and the late spring weather was exceedingly hot for the time of year, so that the newly planted corn had not progressed well and stood less than two hands high. These were peasants and they knew the signs of a coming hardship and were aware that if a summer of drought was to follow, even four bags of corn might prove the difference between survival and starvation. 'You will save more than four bags if you are rid of your rats,' Reinhardt had pointed out. In the end, it was this reasoning that had finally persuaded them to part with their precious corn.

As summer advanced and the drought continued, the ratcatcher was to strike his rat-ridding bargain on more than one occasion, though not always successfully. He would rid a place of rats and then the townspeople would go back on their promise of grain, often using the scurrilous excuse that his magic flute was stealing their children away from them. In fact, the children could not be prevented from joining us and I despaired as their numbers increased with each new town or city we visited. It was soon obvious that we could not hope to feed the multitude or even the smaller children or mothers with infants and that each must fend for himself.

Soon enough we were joined by the *ribaldi*, unarmed scavengers and hangers-on, the dregs of society who stole what little the children possessed causing great consternation and grief. Yet Nicholas was oblivious to all of this and his message prevailed so that the children continued to believe with a passionate certainty that they would reach Jerusalem. When asked by the unbelievers how they could expect to do what kings, dukes and so many others, well armed and wealthy, had failed to do they replied, 'We go with God. We will bear with a willing spirit whatever God places upon us.' These were words constantly pronounced by Nicholas in his sermons and by now had become the common litany.

I go ahead of myself. Everywhere we arrived in the first few weeks of the Children's Crusade we were welcomed by the common people as a holy congregation and equally rejected by the Church as if a throng sent from the devil. But despite this early approval by simple folk I was often disconcerted by what we witnessed in the towns and cities and prayed that God would send me explanations. It was common to be met by naked women who ran ahead of us crying out, 'Our children in Jerusalem!' At first we thought this a reaffirmation of God's message first heard in St Martin's square, but soon it seemed only a kind of madness in the air that was difficult to understand and did not have a feeling of God's divine intention. Often people watching us started to foam at the mouth and throw fits. Others rent their clothes or beat themselves with whips or cut their arms and chests with knives. In one town an old man, well-dressed and from his plump appearance and well-barbered head not in need or taken up with any bewilderment of mind, fell to his knees in front of our procession and slit his own throat with a butcher's knife. People would constantly throw themselves under the wagon wheels and some who were not pulled clear in time were injured.

It seemed that the coming of the Children's Crusade into a town or city had become a device for people to indulge themselves in a kind of temporary insanity, and witnessing all this, increasingly my faith was being tested. We had come in peace and everywhere we went we seemed to cause some kind of violence.

It was in the town of Koblenz where an incident occurred that will forever haunt me. A priest, wild-eyed in appearance, spumed spittle about his mouth, began to shout at us, rushing back and forth and pointing, 'You are the devil's children and will all go to hell! Repent now and leave this unholy throng! Repent! Repent! Repent and be saved or all go to be consumed in hellfire everlasting!' He continued yelling out at the children who marched behind the wagon, his arms flying wildly above his head, and repeatedly running up to the front of the wagon where Nicholas stood in his green robe with the cowl over his head, his tau cross raised. This was the manner we always chose to enter a new town or city, although it was usually Father Paulus and not me who stood beside Nicholas. But on this day the good father must have been delayed somewhere in the procession, which now stretched four furlongs, and I found myself standing in his place.

'Nicholas of Cologne, you are the devil incarnate!' the priest shouted, standing half-crouched in front of the slowly moving wagon, pointing at Nicholas and running backwards just beyond the front hooves of the mules. Then he'd turn to the crowd who watched and yell, 'This is the devil come into your midst! You must hang him! Hang him or put him to the flames!' He kept repeating this procedure, running up and down, exhorting the children to repent and then returning to Nicholas and accusing him of being the devil and demanding his death.

I stood beside Nicholas and each time the priest approached I urged Nicholas to remain silent. 'It will not profit us to rebuke him,' I said softly. 'He is a priest and we must show respect, even if he does not deserve it.'

'But he wishes me dead!' Nicholas hissed.

'Nay, say nought, Nicholas, or this crowd may turn. Let them see by his own actions that the priest is mad and that we come in peace with goodwill.'

'I shall cast out the devil within him,' Nicholas declared.

'Nay, don't! You have not the gift of miracles,' I said urgently.

'But the people who watch will see it as a worthy and Christlike act,' he asserted.

I was shocked. 'Nay, I beg you, shut your gob! If you fail to quieten him they will see it as proof that you are not God's messenger.'

The priest returned once more and shouted as before. But this time he added, 'You say you go to Jerusalem, Nicholas of Cologne? I say you go to hell, and all these children with you, where you will burn, burn, burn!' And then the priest began to laugh, with a mad cackling and a-slapping of knees and throwing his head back and laughing and gulping and snorting and snotting, and saying in between this insane caterwauling, 'Burn! Burn! Burn! Hell! Hell! Hell! Ha-ha-ha-hah! Ha-ha-ha-hah!'

Nicholas could contain himself no longer and he shouted out, 'No, Father, we children go to God!'

The priest stopped as if frozen to the spot, one arm still raised above his head so that the boy driving the wagon was forced to draw the mules to a halt lest they trample him. The crowd lining the street was hushed as the priest's arm descended slowly from above his head and pointed at Nicholas. 'You say you go to God? These children go to God?' He smiled and turned to the watching crowd. 'Then let me be the instrument to send them to their heavenly Father!'

He rushed past the mules to the back of the wagon where a fourteen-year-old named Katrina sat nursing her baby, born two days previously. I turned to see the priest rip the child from its mother's arms, then grabbing it in one hand by both tiny ankles he stood to my side of the wagon. The baby now swung in a circle above his head. 'I send this child to God!' People broke from the crowd and ran towards him and I jumped, screaming from the wagon, but not in time, as he dashed the child to the cobblestones, its soft baby's head striking the road to split open and spill its brains. I landed on the priest, knocking him onto his back while yet straddling him and beating at his chest. Then I was pulled away from him, my teeth bared and snarling. The priest lay still, not moving.

Reinhardt rushed up to comfort me and several of the women in the crowd did the same. Four men in the crowd rushed up and began to kick the unconscious priest, just as Father Paulus arrived and quickly stepped in and bade them stop, while I was lifted, sobbing, back on the wagon where I lay weeping. Then two clerics pushed through the crowd and thanked Father Paulus for preventing the mad priest from being killed by the mob and carried the still-unconscious man away.

All this I was later told, as I was in too great a state of shock to be aware of what was happening around me. It seemed that throughout the ordeal Nicholas had remained standing motionless, his face hidden deep within his cowl and with the tau cross held to his front. If this seems unworthy of him, it was to prove most fortunate. The townsfolk then told how the mad priest had come among them several days before and had been tormenting their children. They had reported him to their own priest and then to the abbot at the nearby monastery but neither would take responsibility, saying he was an itinerant and a prophet and would move on.

The mood of the crowd remained hushed as Father Paulus said a prayer over the dead infant and a piece of sackcloth was found to wrap the tiny corpse and this was placed next to Katrina who sat, blank-faced and dry-eyed as if uncomprehending, her naked breast exposed. Her milk had only that very morning arrived and her swollen pink nipple where the tiny urgent mouth had suckled, now dripped wet.

Reinhardt, it seemed, was the only one to keep his wits active. Even Father Paulus, having prayed for the infant, was in no further state to respond to the crowd. While he had every day been surrounded by the dead and dying, it was the manner of the infant's death at the hands of a priest, albeit a mad one, that now brought him undone and he too climbed onto the wagon and wept softly to himself.

'Good people of Koblenz!' Reinhardt shouted. 'Come now in God's name to hear our prophet preach!' He pointed to the motionless Nicholas. 'There is war and evil in our land and God is angry! Our crops shrivel and death and pestilence abound. Come, let us gather in God's name to bury this murdered infant and hear God's verdict pronounced so that we may all beg for His forgiveness!' Whereupon he motioned to the mule driver to proceed and for those of our children who stood close to sing as he piped.

We were eventually to find ourselves on the outskirts of the town in a small valley nestled between wooded hills, one of these slightly taller with a rocky cluster extended above the trees. Below it, almost halfway up the valley lay a great flat rock large enough to carry more than twenty or thirty people, with one side sloped so that it was easy to climb upon. It must at some time past have separated from the cluster that had crashed down into the valley below and was an ideal platform from which Nicholas could preach as it stood well above the heads of the crowd. We made this rock the centre of our camp, preparing a gravesite on the leeward side for the dead infant.

Reinhardt now stood with me by the grave of Katrina's child, the poor girl herself still too shocked to weep for her lost baby, and with me shivering and shaking and not yet fully in control, though I had by now ceased my sobbing. The ratcatcher placed his arm around my shoulders to comfort me, while Father Paulus conducted the funeral surrounded by our own Crusade Children and many of the townsfolk.

From the first day after we'd left Cologne we had every morning conducted burials of small children who had died during the night. It was impossible for Father Paulus to pay due ceremony to these as there was scarcely time to say a hurried prayer, committing the infant souls to God's mercy. Then, at best, a shallow grave of scraped earth covered the tiny body with perhaps, should a weeping mother or one of my healing group think to provide it, a single blossom, usually a wild poppy plucked from a field, placed upon the hump of dirt. Now this child, least known of all the dead, not yet baptised and sans a soul, was to receive a burial attended by a vast multitude of mourners.

Still shaking, I said to Reinhardt, 'We must sing a requiem, *Libera Me*.'

'You are too weepy and upset,' he replied in a consoling voice.

'Nay, I will try. It is the least we may do to bring comfort to the poor mother.' He nodded and withdrew his arm from about me and took up his flute. People would later declare that my voice was as if an angel of God had come down from heaven to sing to the dead child and Reinhardt's flute an instrument played in some celestial choir. Many knelt in prayer. Then we followed with a second hymn, one that was well-known. This time the voices of several thousand children sang with us and now all fell to their knees as God's glory shone down upon the unnamed baby's grave.

Then Nicholas preached what would become one of his most famous sermons. He spoke of peace and love and of God's desire that this time children should journey to the Holy Land. He stressed that there was no papal promise of our sins redeemed and that the only purity to be gained was on the pilgrimage to Calvary and then to enter the tomb of Christ Jesus. He told how the almond trees would blossom in the coming spring and at summer's end the ripened corn would neither be stolen nor be put to the avenging torch. Nicholas then promised that in return our glorious heavenly Father would grant us the keys to the gates of Jerusalem and allow us to climb, unhindered and unopposed, the sacred steps to enter the Holy Sepulchre. Whereupon the Sultan of all the Saracens would be so confounded with the piety and peace that prevailed in this joyous throng of Christian children that he would return the true cross to us.

Nicholas, then concluding, stood on the great rock and raised his cross to a cloudless pewter-coloured sky and promised that God would soon send rain to nourish their failing crops. He followed this improbable pronouncement with a blessing to the town and its people and commended them for their piety while, at the same time, softening them up for what he hoped would prove a demonstration of their charity. He asked that they, in God's name, feed the children. It was during this sermon that the exhortation, 'In every home one extra mouth for God,' was first created, which was to become our future plea to townsfolk in an attempt to feed the children of the crusade.

At the end of the sermon from the rock, with the people of Koblenz rejoicing in the Lord and praising the precious name of Jesus, it seemed that we had recovered well from the calamity in town. I too was by now somewhat better in my disposition. It was then, with the townsfolk each choosing a Crusade Child to take home to feed, that we heard the thunder of hooves. Soon a troop of soldiers on horseback appeared, carrying swords and urging their beasts into the milling crowd and moving at a canter towards the rock. People scattered in every direction trying to avoid the charging, snorting horses, though two of our children were knocked over, one to receive a broken arm, the other later to die from bruising to his chest. The soldiers drew up to the rock and their captain urged his horse up its sloped portion to stand with his sword drawn, huge and menacing atop. Then we saw that his saddlecloth bore the cross and the mitre of a bishop and the colours and coat of arms of a noble house.

'We come for the priest's murderer!' he shouted down at the crowd. 'Deliver her and none will be harmed!' He waited but no answer came. The other horsemen were now moving among the crowd with their swords drawn, all intending to intimidate in case the people would grow angry. I felt the children start to close in around me as if they would protect me. With Reinhardt I stood not too far from the edge of the rock within plain hearing of the troop leader.

And then I saw Father Paulus approach the base of the rock and climb up to stand in front of the captain on horseback, the soldier and his horse towering above the little priest. 'We come in God's name and there is no murderer here, captain! The priest fell backwards and was unconscious, two clerics then took him away!' he shouted.

'He is dead, that's all I know,' the captain said. 'She attacked him and now he is dead, that is murder!'

'Nay, an accident, perchance as he fell he knocked his head?'

'Aye, because she attacked him. She has murdered one of your own, a priest! A man of God! Why do you protect her so?'

'Nay, it was the priest who, in a fit of madness, murdered! We have only just buried the infant he most brutally slew,' Father Paulus cried.

'That is for His Lordship the bishop, and his brother the count, to decide and not some scungy priest! The priest is dead and we have witnesses that say the wench from the wagon jumped to attack him.'

'Nay, to stop him! But too late!'

'Father, I grow impatient. Name this wench!' the captain said.

Reinhardt turned to me and said in an urgent whisper, 'Sylvia, I think we must away from here at once.'

'Nay, we cannot escape. Someone will point me out and they will run us down.'

'Sylvia, we must try, they will hang you for a murderer!'

'If they catch us escaping then they most surely will.'

'Sylvia, we have no tricks this time – rats and crows will not solve this problem! Come now, the woods are not far and they are on horseback – we have an even chance among the trees!' he whispered urgently, even though because of the noise the crowd was making his voice would not be heard by the horseman on the rock.

'Nay, I will not run from this!' I said. 'If God wishes me condemned then so be it. I did not kill the priest and if he died it was an accident. I will not be cut down with the sword without a word spoken, a common felon fleeing. That, ratcatcher, is what they would like! All my life I have run from something and now I must stay. If they would kill me then it must be for a cause and be seen by all.' But in my heart I felt a terrible despair, first my father and now a priest, both dead, killed by my own doing. Surely God has forsaken me and I am intended for the devil's child.

Reinhardt shook his head and said in a bitter voice, 'Jesus, Sylvia! Why are you stubborn unto death?'

'Do not blaspheme!' I shouted, close to tears and angry, though not at him but at life, at the sins that seemed always to engulf me so that my very shadow seemed possessed by the devil. But even yet I was not willing to die or be named a murderer except by God. I had almost reached the edge of the rock and while my heart was beating fiercely within my breast I was astonished at the little priest's courage and his defence of me. If he believed in me, then God was still with us and would protect our cause and perhaps me as well. I must place myself at His mercy. 'Don't go, Sylvia!' the children around me begged. Those closest were my healing angels and now they clutched at me in an attempt to stay me.

'We have no murderer in our midst, the maid is God's child and has been the subject of past miracles!' Father Paulus cried. 'The priest who died was possessed by the devil and killed an infant in front of witnesses. If he died from falling then the hand that smote him was the hand of God!'

'Perhaps the Virgin Mary's, eh?' the captain chortled. 'The hand of God cannot be a woman's!' The soldiers, having seen the crowd was not hostile, now returned to form a guard around the base of the rock. They all gave a dutiful laugh at their leader's clever jibe. This seemed to please the captain. In a voice now turned most reasonable and no longer shouting out the captain said, 'Come now, Father, be a good priest and declare this wicked wench amongst your flock of devil's urchins.' It was clear he was a man well-pleased with himself and not without wit.

'Eh?' Father Paulus said, cupping his ear, the horseman now speaking too softly for him to hear.

'Damn your eyes! Name this wench!' the captain shouted, losing his patience.

'Nay! I shall not! We have no murderer here!' Father Paulus again cried out defiantly.

I pushed past a surprised horseman and climbed up onto the rock. 'It is me that you seek, Captain. I ask only that I be judged fairly and in God's name!'

'Nay, Sylvia!' Father Paulus shouted. 'Do not let them take you!' He fell to his knees and started to pray for my protection.

'Ha! Sylvia, is it?'

'My name is Sylvia Honeyeater. What is it you want, Captain?' I asked, not knowing if my words were brave or foolish, but only that I wished to say them while I had courage left in my heart.

'Ah! It is as well you gave yourself up or we would have found you and put you to the sword and saved ourselves the trouble of the gallows!' the captain said. I could sense he was pleased that he remained well in command of the situation. The crowd below the rock, though loud with clamouring, did not surge forward towards the horses and remained calm.

'You may kill me now! Let all God's children see the way your bishop and your count serve out justice in the name of our heavenly Father!' I cried.

'You have a big mouth, Sylvia! I will be the one to hear it gargle as the rope tightens!'

'If you butcher me now or later place the knot about my neck, I remain God's child and I die in His name!' I shouted defiantly, though it was my voice that held me rigid, for my knees desired to collapse, and my furiously beating heart seemed to drown my cry so that I did not know with certainty if I had spoken or not.

'Pray that God might grant you life eternal.' He pointed to the west. 'For I doubt if you will see the sunset over yonder craggy hills, Sylvia Honeyeater.' And then I knew with an absolute certainty that he was bluffing. He had gone too far, enjoying the power at his command in front of this crowd. He had taken me for an ignorant peasant who would not know that no bishop's soldier could make such threats and carry them out. Though he might arrest me, I would be properly judged.

I knew a fair deal about the power of the Church from long discussions with Brother Dominic. No bishop could with impunity pronounce my death or cause me to be hanged or put to the flames. Even his brother, the count, who had the right to maintain the law within his lands, could not turn an obvious accident, clearly witnessed by a great many people, and name it murder at the behest of his brother in the Church. If he would do so he and his bishop brother would have to answer to Rome, and the bishop's career within the Church and his future wealth in land, rents and taxes could be severely curtailed.

I could hear Brother Dominic's voice clearly in my head. '*No bishop, archbishop, cardinal or even the Holy Father in Rome does God's work for the salvation of the people, but for the power and the money. There are rules prescribed that make it seem that they act with faith, love and charity and it is the priest and clerics who must be seen to demonstrate this for the people. Unless he has permission from Rome, no bishop may demand the death of even a heretic in the name of the Church. If he acts on his own there are many ways he may be punished, but the curtailment of entitlement is the usual way. The Church denies him land and rent and the ability to ask for taxes. Greed is the factor that will always stay a bishop's hand. The closer a Prince of the Church gets to the Pope, the more wealth he acquires. If he puts the Church in a poor light with arbitrary decisions concerning the life and death of common people, he denies the so-called charity and love of the Holy Roman Church. He spoils it for the other Princes and so he is removed from the largesse of the Pope. These are not men of God who seek to gather souls for Christ or live in the image of the Nazarene, but are greedy, ambitious and rapacious churchmen. Most are of noble birth, who care only for their own earthly gain and think that, in the end, their money will buy them salvation and a place in heaven.*'

Despite my distress I had not panicked, the pompous and puffed-up soldier serving to keep my mind clear. To this knowledge of the way the Church must behave, I added the power of the Children's Crusade. Even though the Church did not condone it, they knew that the common people believed this journey of children to Jerusalem to be a miracle and a result of God's command, and so they would not tolerate the hanging or burning of one of its leaders by a Prince of the Church. While I had not sought to be seen as such, this mantle of a leader had been thrust upon me. No bishop, even one as stupid as the Bishop of Cologne, would openly cause my death – that is why he and Master Nicodemus had planned the ambush of the wagon, knowing that he couldn't openly have me destroyed.

I took the few steps towards the now weeping priest. 'Father Paulus, I need you as a scribe and witness. Pull yourself together, we are not done yet.' The tearful priest stood up and I drew him to my side. Then I called for Nicholas and Reinhardt to stand with me. Both came quickly, Nicholas still in his woollen robes, and I thought how hot he must be for the mid-afternoon sun was scorching.

'What are you doing?' the captain cried out.

'If I am to be tried, then let the people hear me first, Captain. Let them bear witness!' I shouted this as loudly as I could, so that the children and the people gathered around would hear me, and there came a fair crying out, 'Let her speak to us!' from the mob below the rock.

'Nay! You are under arrest!' he shouted.

The cry from the mob came back louder. I turned to see Reinhardt whispering urgently to Nicholas who nodded and with his tau cross raised at the soldier shouted, 'Stay your hand! You are no Roman soldier and this is not Calvary!' The captain looked suddenly confused.

I am right, he is sent only to frighten us and has overplayed his hand, I thought. I stepped forward and addressed the crowd. 'Let the people decide who is guilty and then you may take their verdict to your bishop! We have six thousand children and it would seem most of your townsfolk – it is sufficient to judge this case.'

The captain, bewildered, shook his head as if to clear it, unable to comprehend what was going on.

'Have you seen the mad priest before?' I asked the crowd.

'Aye!' came the reply from below the rock.

'Has he molested your children?'

'Aye!' This time even louder.

'Did you see him murder the infant?'

Although only a few may have seen the murder, it now seemed they all had done so, a mighty roar of 'ayes' followed, to it added the thousands of children's voices.

Nicholas stepped forward. 'If you think Sylvia has committed a murder then raise your hands, if an accident, shout, nay!'

This time a great roar of 'nays' rent the air.

I then shouted, 'Let heaven itself and the very birds of the air witness that you have spoken my innocence!' I was aware that I was being overly dramatic and carried away as I began to call. But such was my relief that I had survived thus far and the people gathered had called out for me, that I thought to give them some small reward. Soon the birds began to fly from the surrounding woods, at first only a few and then in increasing numbers, until the air about my head was thick with their wings and the horses began to stamp and turn about and neigh in alarm. The cacophony all about made it impossible to speak, although the crowd could be heard roaring their approval. Then, as if God willed it, two ravens flew in and landed on the captain's shoulders and the crowd roared. This was a certain sign to them that he would suffer a terrible consequence if he tarried any longer. A look of terror appeared on the soldier's face as he beat at the ravens, knowing that their visitation meant a curse upon him. I then sent the birds away, the ravens the last to leave.

Then Reinhardt ran up to him taunting, 'The devil's birds have come for you, Captain! It is best that you and your men be gone! The crows come next to pick out the horse's eyes!'

The captain was plainly confounded, nay, terror-struck by what had just happened with the ravens. He crossed himself and looked at me and then at Father Paulus. 'I beg you lift this raven's curse from me, Fräulein Sylvia,' he cried. Then, looking at Father Paulus, 'I ask forgiveness before God!' he cried out, before he quickly led his horse down the side of the rock and called to his men to follow him.

The Pied Piper took up his pipe and played the opening to a hymn we all knew well and sang constantly on the crusade. As the crowd parted for the horsemen the children's voices rose to the glory of God.

I have often wondered what the captain said when he reported back to the bishop. But if we thought ourselves now freed of an openly disapproving Church, news of the incident at Koblenz must have preceded us, for trouble lay ahead when eventually we reached the city of Marbach.

Wherever we could we followed upstream the rivers that ran north, knowing that they flowed from the Alps and beyond that awesome barrier lay Italy. If all went tolerably well those first weeks, by mid-June the excessive heat and insufficient food was causing the weak to drop by the wayside. I was aware things were beginning to fall apart and that many of the children who had joined the crusade in Cologne had become disenchanted. At Mainz a large number had departed, some to return home and others, grown tired of the meagre and haphazard food supply, to seek work. But for as many children as deserted there were others that joined, so that our numbers were actually growing all the while with our difficulties increasing. Still we pressed on to the foothills of the Alps.

Our next major confrontation with the Church occurred at the monastery of Marbach on the upper Rhine, where there was a most concerted effort by the monks and the bishop to discredit us. This incident is well recorded so I will not dwell overmuch on it. It soon became apparent that they knew of the mad priest and his death and thought that we had escaped punishment. The story was now told with a heavy bias in favour of the dead priest, the accidental killing of the priest now a murder most foul, with the death of an unbaptised infant without a soul seen to be of little or no consequence.

However, if the Church thought to vilify us, here also was our faith eventually confirmed. Nicholas preached to the commonfolk a version of the sermon he had preached at Koblenz. At the same time he challenged the bishop to preach his sermon of denial on the same occasion by putting the Church's view to the people, but he would not appear, fearing perhaps the resentment of the common people. Instead the bishop sent the Augustinian prior to do his dirty work. But when the prior, a less fearful or perhaps less cautious man, named the Children's Crusade the work of the devil, even asserting that if it was created by a miracle then the devil could also work miracles, he was howled down by the simple folk. They believed, as we ourselves did, that we travelled through divine inspiration and not from any foolishness and they gave us generously of food and other necessities. A mob of our children had to escort the prior at my instructions back to the monastery for fear the townsfolk might beat him severely and so give the Church and its established authority another reason to call us the devil's disciples, a term repeatedly used by the prior.

Towards the end of June and into the second month of our journey, when we'd reached Ebersheim on a little island on the Ill River, our numbers were estimated at now near eight thousand. Despite the desertions and the dead we had doubled in number since leaving Cologne, and with the drought now having taken a grip upon the land, food was very scarce and daily the deaths reached a hundred children and on some days even more.

The children began to eat grass and weeds grown at the riverbank or, if they should find one floating by, the flesh from a drowned animal became a feast and they would race the crows for carrion. At night when we camped, the boys fished, but the river seldom proved generous. And each day Father Paulus performed the last rites to more dying children, and now each evening we said the Prayers for the Dead.

Father Paulus had long since ceased to surprise me. His loyalty and courage at Koblenz had even further earned my respect. Now, the more the local clergy seemed against us, the more inspired he seemed to become. He lost his stutter and spoke most forcibly to the gathered congregations so that they often gave more generously than we might have hoped. His love for the children was now overbrimming – this being a man who would once run from any contact with the young.

At Schlettstadt I found myself depressed and totally exhausted and grown weak from hunger, though Reinhardt, ever resourceful, would bring me a little food and watch over me as I ate, suspicious that I would take a small portion, then give the remainder to a starving child. 'Sylvia, if your strength fails we are all done for!' he would declare in his manner of over-exaggeration. What was true was that Nicholas had begun to falter and I could see he was going into one of his periods of isolation. Then Father Paulus suffered a severe bout of dysentery, a condition that was killing the younger children in increasing numbers.

After several days when Nicholas's sermons proved most lacklustre, he finally retired under the sacking cover we had made for the wagon. I knew that he could remain thus for a week or a month or more, and we could not remain where we were and must cross the Alps before the end of high summer. This, I knew, would be the most difficult part of our journey. Without Nicholas to lead us I feared that we must all perish. Increasingly it seemed only the children's faith in him kept us going. These small creatures, each day turning more skeletal in appearance, still persisted unwaveringly, chanting his name and his many litanies and constantly, though their bellies cramped with hunger, evoking God's love through him. In their eyes Nicholas was their saviour, as precious to them as if he was Jesus returned to earth to lead them.

Reinhardt had come to me and suggested that we desert, and instead of admonishing him I let him give tongue to his anxiety. 'Sylvia, we have made a big mistake and if we continue thus it may be the end of us. You and I can always make a living on the road. Your song and my flute will draw a generous crowd and we may roam wherever we wish.' He gave a semblance of his old grin. 'You often speak of meeting Francis of Assisi and telling him a thing or two about birds. We could do this in our own good time and eat well along the way. We are not like the city birds and cannot survive on crumbs. If we cross these mountains with this multitude, all will be certain to perish and you and me with them. How can this be God's will? How will your conscience carry this heavy load of the sick and the dying?'

We had tried most valiantly to keep up with the sick and injured, but as the weeks passed the task had become impossible – untreated blisters became sores and the sores ulcers and eventually a child would be crippled and unable to continue. We had tried to leave these children at the villages we passed through, knowing that it would be unlikely with the shortage of food that they'd be cared for, but they would at least be buried when they died. Many of the older girls who had been chaste and virgins had now grown emaciated yet bore the first telltale signs of pregnancy, and others came to us for herbs having spilled a foetus and found themselves still bleeding. We watched helplessly as the smaller children's stomachs distended from the effects of starvation. We could only stand by as they died like flies from dehydration or dysentery.

Every morning Father Paulus, with the help of a burial squad of older boys, would gather the corpses and pray over the little bodies. Often we'd be forced to leave those not yet dead with the sole comfort of the last rites, their accusing eyes staring at us, some begging us to save them, yet we knew that they would not survive another sunset. Our trail was becoming littered with the dead and dying. Their flesh was devoured by foxes or village dogs and their bones were picked clean by crow and raven before the peasants could cover them with a final shroud, a simple scoop of earth. Increasingly the bones remained uncovered, the flies the last to feast, until the scattered skeletons lay whitened in the sun. For years to come these would act as the signposts to indicate the passing of the Children's Crusade.

Now as we were poised at the foot of the Alps with Reinhardt exhorting me to leave this rapidly escalating disaster, I knew my faith to be sorely tested. How could this be God's will? Why was He allowing so many of His precious children to perish? They had not sinned. They had not blasphemed. They had no need of repentance. Their hearts were pure and their faith remained implicit. Yet He struck them down in increasing numbers each day. How could these starving children be God's wish? And then, deep within myself, I knew that I hungered for my own freedom and to be away from all this death and guilt and the despairing eyes of little children who cried out at night for their mothers. I began to sense that somehow the Miracle in St Martin's square had another translation or intention, that we had misinterpreted God's command, 'Our children in Jerusalem!' All along it had been, as Father Paulus had said at the archbishop's inquiry, a meaningless contagion among the women of Cologne.

'Nay, Reinhardt, I cannot forsake them now,' I said softly, and then started to weep.

CHAPTER FOURTEEN

The Silent Choir of God's Little Children

AND SO BEGAN THE last months of our journey by entering the Black Forest and the long and endless climb over the mountains into Italy. I have always loved trees and being alone in the woods, but I soon came to fear these deep dark forests of pine, beech, spruce and fir.

These were not the bright glades and swinging, breezy branches of the woodlands, but trees that sat with their roots tenaciously gripping the stone and gneiss like the talons of some bird of prey. Old trees have no humour or frivolity with their gnarled and twisted limbs weeping with moss and scarred by lichen, ragged giants that resent any presence but their own.

As we climbed higher the birds lost their cheerful busyness and took on the slow mournful caw of the crow or the high-pitched screech of the falcon, hawk and eagle, slow-winged carrion birds that lived on the dead or killed in a vortex of feathered fury. The daylight that filtered through the thick dark canopy of ancient pines had a gloom and a foreboding quality as if the tinted air was more accustomed to darkening the shadows than to dancing in sunlight.

At night came a stygian darkness and with it a slow wind, moaning and sighing through the thickness of the torpid, swaying foliage, and always there was the ghostlike hooting of the forest owl. These deep, dark forests were redolent of lost children and ugly, stumpy, big-nosed, evil-eyed, scaly-clawed creatures that lived in rock fissures, damp caves and holes in giant trees and who peopled fairytales and the nightmares of children who ate meat at night.

And in the towns the people spoke a difficult German, a dialect and accent with remnants of words derived in part from the Alemannian tribe converted to Christianity in the eighth century by St Boniface. They were the ancient people of these lower mountains and many of the words of these German folk derived from this time. Other words, equally strange to the ear, were borrowed from the Swabian and Franconian dialects. Talking with them was difficult and our children were placed at a great disadvantage when begging for alms as the locals either didn't, or pretended they didn't, understand. We soon learned that the people of the Black Forest were by nature tight-fisted, stoical and set in their ways and, like all complacent people, quick to judge and even quicker to condemn. Eight thousand barefooted, ragged, starving children did not seem to them to be the work of a merciful and indulgent God. Without Nicholas's charismatic preaching, begging food from a suspicious and careful people who lived by the proverb *Schaffen, sparen, haus bauen* (work, save and build a house) did not inspire generosity.

Now as we climbed higher the nights grew colder and the air thinner and the food even harder to find. Our children ate unripened fruit and berries they'd gathered in the forest as well as small rodents and other forest creatures, which the more enterprising among them managed to trap. Reinhardt was now piping for rats to feed them, but even these vile creatures were hard to find in these unforgiving mountains. I took to calling in the birds, betraying their trust to add to the meagre rations. Many children died from the cold, as even in summer the nights were freezing and the rags they carried on their backs were not sufficient to protect them. Criminals and madmen who lived in the forests raped the girls and robbed the children of what little they possessed. And every day more died from starvation, cold and disease, and the little ones, those who had miraculously managed to get this far, from despair. Soon we lost count of the dead. The ability to give them extreme unction was not always possible: some simply gave up and crept exhausted into the forest to die; some were too weak even to call out to the mothers they had forsaken. Often the scree and rock prevented the digging of graves and we simply piled the little bodies together and covered them with rocks and stones. Soon the carrion birds learned to follow us, and while we died of starvation they grew so fat some could not lift themselves into the air.

The two mules were skin and bone and it was increasingly difficult for them to find pasture, and a few days into the high mountains one of them died. One mule in a weakened state was unable to pull the wagon and so we slaughtered it, the two animals providing a meal for perhaps three hundred children who hungrily devoured the raw and half-cooked flesh – and many soon returned it, their stomachs unable to cope. Others rushed at this regurgitation and ate it as dogs do, dirt and all. I filled my Father John satchel with what few herbs and unguents we had left, and Reinhardt exchanged the wagon for ten bags of corn with a farmer greedy for a bargain and we kept going a little longer, each with a single ladle of gruel to last the day.

Now Nicholas travelled on foot with all of us, silent and withdrawn, a lone spectre in green monk's robes. He still piously carried the cross first forged in Antioch a hundred years before, where during the long siege of that city many in the First Crusade had starved as our children now did. Some, according to Brother Dominic, had eaten the flesh of humans to survive and many thousands perished, and yet in the end they had succeeded. If God had tested them yet in the end granted them Jerusalem, then perhaps He expected the same from us. We must somehow endure, though I despaired that without the blessed boy's preaching we would be unable to do so.

Nicholas's silent presence among the children was proving a blessing. He was no longer hidden from them under the wagon canopy and they gathered around him and seemed encouraged, if only by the sight of him. Not understanding his lost demeanour, they begged a hundred times each day that he should preach to them. I knew in my heart that if he would do so, showing the old Nicholas had returned to us, the hardships the children so stoically endured would lessen. The heart is a good friend when hope exists and a miserable companion when it is taken away.

I cannot take the credit for what happened next since it was the ratcatcher's idea, although I think it perhaps the most important reason why we eventually crossed the mountains with fewer dying than might have occurred. I had expected Reinhardt to leave us when he suggested we forsake the Children's Crusade but he had not done so. If that moment had been a low point in his usually optimistic mood, he had recovered, and it was his tongue and flute and rat-ridding and rat-finding and tireless encouragement that from that time kept us going. If Nicholas had forsaken us, then it was the Pied Piper who, with an ailing Father Paulus and the healing angels, saved us from complete despair.

Now seeing the children encouraged by Nicholas's presence the ratcatcher said to me one morning, 'Sylvia, we must preach again each night, the children must be given the hope they seemed to gain from Nicholas.'

I shrugged. 'Reinhardt, how I wish you could with that pipe of yours summon him back to us. Alas, this time he seems completely lost. Every day I ask him if he wants the magic mushroom, but he shakes his head and will not return from his dark place.'

'Nay, Sylvia, you must preach,' he said.

I looked at him astonished. 'It is not my gift! I do not have this message from God.'

Reinhardt laughed. 'But you have another gift worth just as much.'

'What?'

'Sylvia, you have a memory that never fails you. If I should ask you to repeat word for word every sermon Nicholas has given to the children or the townsfolk I know that you could do so.'

'So?'

'Well, you are also a gifted mimic, the best I've ever heard. I have seen you use Nicholas's voice in jest or when telling of something he has said and all present laugh, for it is as if he himself is speaking.'

'Ah, but I am not Nicholas! The children will not accept me as their leader,' I protested.

'How will they know?'

'Because I'm a woman, stupid. I have blonde hair and blue eyes and, in case you haven't noticed, two rather pronounced bumps upon my chest.'

He laughed. 'Nice but not so large that they may not easily be flattened by tying them tightly with a band of cloth.'

'Reinhardt, the children know me! We, the healing angels, have ministered to them from the first day. I work with Father Paulus and with you to bury the dead and comfort the dying. They have heard me sing a hundred times! What? Must I pretend that Nicholas has used me as his medium and speaks through me?'

'I hadn't thought of that. It might also work.'

'So, what are you suggesting?'

'At night, Sylvia. Preach to them at night, wearing Nicholas's robes, your face concealed deep within the cowl. You know every sermon and I'll vouch they cannot tell his voice from your version.'

I looked at him, astonished. 'Do you think it will work?'

'Of course!' he cried optimistically, then shrugged. 'How will we know if we don't try?'

'But if it fails?'

'Then we shall use you as a medium as you suggested. It is nearly as good and requires less deception.'

He looked at me and saw I was frowning, not sure. 'Sylvia, these children must be given some hope. You can do this, I know you can!'

'Perhaps the medium, eh? That way there is less chance of being caught.'

'Nay, please try the other first. If we can bring Nicholas back to lead them they will be much the stronger for it!' Reinhardt urged.

'What think you, Father?' I asked loudly, turning to Father Paulus.

'If we deceive we do so to God's glory and I am not troubled by this duplicity, but I think Reinhardt right, the presence of Nicholas himself will be much the stronger encouragement.'

We had reached the high mountains well above the tree line where bitter winds blew incessantly and the landscape consisted of scree, rock, coarse grasses and juniper bushes. The mountain passes were most dangerous to navigate, so that many children, weak with hunger and with their eyesight and their balance affected, plunged to their deaths in the chasms and roaring rapids below. We had been many days in the mountains and had reached the highest point and would soon start the descent into Italy. If we could but place a little more courage in each small heart we might save more from dying. And so the rumour was started that Nicholas would preach that night.

Earlier Reinhardt, Father Paulus and myself drew Nicholas aside and put the plan to him. Despite his despondency and to our chagrin he was opposed to it. 'They have only one leader and it is me! I am the only one who has the divine right!' he sulked.

'But, Nicholas, we accept this! We would not usurp your leadership, but instead show all the children that it persists,' Father Paulus explained.

'They will know it isn't me!' Nicholas said in a churlish voice.

'We will find out soon enough,' Reinhardt said brightly. 'If they do, we are not much worse off. If they don't, then they will take great heart from your reappearance.'

Nicholas looked at me despairingly. 'You know I cannot help this devil's time that comes upon me!'

'Aye, Nicholas, but the children are dying as much for lack of heart as of starvation. We must try.'

He seemed to be thinking, then at last looked up and addressed me again. 'This is a holy robe I wear. If you, a woman, should wear it, that would amount to sacrilege.' He shook his head slowly. 'I'm sorry, I cannot allow it!'

'Nay, Nicholas, that is not true!' Father Paulus said. 'Garments are only holy if worn by the Christ figure, the Virgin, the apostles, St Paul and various saints and martyrs, though not all.'

'What are you saying? That I am not among these?' Nicholas

demanded to know. We all looked at each other, too confounded to reply. Then he said, 'Am I not the one who had the vision of the angel who bore a message from our Lord Jesus that I should lead the children to Jerusalem? I do not see any other among you who can make this claim! Does this not entitle me? Are these robes I wear not sacred and blessed by God?' He pointed angrily at me. 'Now you would place them on the body of a *woman*!' He paused and shook his head vigorously as if trying to rid himself of an unpleasant thought. 'I'm sorry, Sylvia, I must be plain-spoken in this matter. I cannot allow you to commit such a terrible blasphemy!'

Father Paulus was the first to recover and to find his voice. 'Nicholas, it is not seemly that you speak of yourself as you do,' he chided, though gently. 'It is for God to decide and the Church to proclaim any beatification and this is done *after* your death. In truth, until that time, we all remain mere mortals and your robe is not yet holy and may well be worn by any other.'

'But by a woman!' Nicholas protested, plainly mortified. 'A woman who bleeds . . . down there!'

If Father Paulus was shocked by this profanity, he didn't show it. The old Father Paulus would have run for his life, completely mortified, but this was a different person, a priest who had been through a baptism of fire and knew God would test him even further. He wasn't to be waylaid by a silly sensibility. 'Aye, by Sylvia, who is your beloved friend. Our hope is that this small and harmless deception brings courage to the flock you lead. They are much in need of your encouragement and the sound of your voice. It is your voice and leadership that drives them onward and your honour and piety that is served.' Father Paulus, with the constant need to beg for food for his children, was also becoming an expert in persuasion.

Nicholas, confused by the compliment and forgetting his objection to me wearing his robe of but a moment or two ago, now looked at me, appealing. 'It's not my fault! Tell them, Sylvia, tell them it is not my fault! I cannot speak! My tongue is tied by the devil! I cannot! I cannot!

I must wait for Jesus to return!' His voice was now that of a small sobbing child trying to explain his hurt feelings to his mother.

I placed my arm about him and he began to sniff, then he said still in the choking little boy's voice, 'But if you take my monk's robe I shall be cold!'

'Nay, Nicholas, you shall have my sheepskin coat,' I comforted him.

I saw the expression on Reinhardt's face and gave him a quick cautionary look, restraining him from laughing at this transformation from would-be saint to frightened little boy. He had been converted by Nicholas's preaching, but when he saw him enter his dark place at a time he was most needed, Reinhardt had grown ever more impatient and seemed no longer taken in by the boy's power and mystique. 'He sulks, hunched up like a crow in the wagon and now, without it, walks as if we are forcing him against his will. He says nothing, does nothing and we must call him blessed and our leader!' he had railed.

'It is in his nature, either the one thing or the other. We must persist, the children will not go without him,' I had said lamely, knowing it seemed a poor excuse and that each day without him seemed to create more despair among the children.

Reinhardt had been the first to say it. 'Is this right? Is this God's will? All the dying?'

Because I knew that deep in my heart I was asking myself the same questions, I had grown suddenly angry. 'Go on . . . be gone! Get your arse out of here!' I had dismissed him with a backward wave of my hand. 'Piss off! We don't need you! You're nothing but a Jonah!' Then I had started to wail.

But Reinhardt had not deserted us and seemed always cheerful and hopeful, and but for the time he suggested we leave the crusade and when he'd expressed these doubts, I had not seen his spirits down. Without him I dare not think how we would have endured. Whatever might be said of his sexual proclivities, which, in the eyes of the Church, sent him to certain and eternal damnation, he was the most courageous, forbearing and loyal man I have ever known.

That night we camped in two craters to protect us from the wind; both proved to be natural amphitheatres. Nicholas, dressed in my rough peasant's gown and well wrapped in my precious sheepskin coat, his head covered and my stave beside him, stood among the choir of healing angels where the children would expect to see me. In the gloaming, my face in shadow from the cowl, I preached once in each of the craters, my voice echoing in the surrounding cliffs and carrying to reach several thousand excited children.

The reaction was astonishing. The huge crowd, all hungry, nay gripped by starvation, some near to death, stood to cheer and pray and sing as if a light from heaven had shone down upon them. It was plain that not one among them, other than the choir of the healing angels, knew that it wasn't Nicholas of Cologne who preached to them. We had found a way to sustain our faith and that night we slept knowing that while a great deal of suffering lay ahead of us, we would cross these terrible peaks and passes and survive the thundering, rushing gorges and reach Italy beyond.

I preached each night for the next few days, by the end of which time we had passed the highest point and had almost reached the long, sloping countryside leading into a vast valley with green fields that, it seemed from a distance, were not stricken by drought. Our path across the mountains was littered with the bodies of the dead and we estimated some one thousand tiny souls had perished coming over them. Near seven thousand children remained as we approached the fertile valley that had now become Italy and would eventually lead us to the sea. Then we would miraculously cross to Constantinople, held by the Venetians and the home of the Byzantine Christians where we hoped we might get a friendlier reception. From there we would enter the lands of the Saracens and then to Jerusalem. It all still seemed hopeful and attainable. The last night before entering the valley I preached a final time and used again Nicholas's sermon of our goodwill when the almond trees would blossom in the spring.

Nicholas, the morning of the night I preached this last sermon, had asked me for the magic mushrooms and by late that evening had come out of his trance, his eyes bright again and his demeanour eager to continue. Throughout our journey we had fed him first; what little we had he ate as his entitlement and though he was not plump he lacked the skeletal look the rest of us wore from months on the road. Throughout the journey he had seemed impervious to the suffering around him. Once when I had spoken of it, wondering why God would let His precious children suffer so, he had looked at me, completely lacking in sentience and as if I had suddenly blasphemed. 'It is their wickedness that kills them. Those who die are not worthy in God's eyes of attaining Jerusalem and the Holy Sepulchre. It is God's wish that they perish – they are the chaff that is winnowed from the good corn and you must not grieve for their souls, Sylvia.'

'But they are children, too young to carry such sin in their hearts and they have come with us believing!' I protested.

'We are all born in sin and only the pure in spirit will enter the Kingdom of God,' he said sanctimoniously, then added, 'or be with me to see Jerusalem and to pray at the Holy Shrine.'

'That is utter bullshit, Nicholas! They die for lack of food and care!' I cried out.

He'd shrugged. 'Whatever you say, Sylvia. I do not take responsibility for the dead. They are in God's merciful hands.'

'First they are sinners and slain by God, now they are in His merciful hands? Make up your mind!' I cried angrily. But Nicholas did not see this ambiguity. *He will make a good priest*, I thought angrily to myself, *grabbing every sanctimonious catch-cry without a thought for what he is saying, just a sentence mumbled, a hand touching a head like a fly alighting here and there and everywhere, its only purpose to buzz and land and move again.*

But if I begin to sound somewhat self-righteous, I have a confession to make. As I preached each night for the final days of our journey across the mountains I grew to enjoy the power it gave me. The adoring and worshipping children, despite their parlous condition, glued to my every word, were lifted, encouraged and strengthened by my (well, Nicholas's) sermons. While the voice I affected remained that of Nicholas, more and more the words were my own, my voice becoming bread and wine to the starving. I found myself carried away with my elucidation and the strength of my persuasive powers. I gloried in the ability I seemed to possess to make these children forget their misery for a few precious moments and to be transported to another, kinder world. It was exhilarating and I began to see how easily such arrogance and power over others could corrupt and how, like Nicholas, one might assume the mantle of the saints. I am ashamed to admit that the return of Jesus to once again possess the soul of Nicholas of Cologne left me jealous and resentful and I had need to ask Father Paulus to hear my confession.

I had grown to love the little priest with all my heart and soul and I watched in dismay as he grew weaker each day. My only hope was that when we reached Italy I might find a monastery with a hospice where they would treat him. As we reached the foothills he needed two of my healing angels, one at each side, to guide him as he was too weak to manage on his own. He would often lapse into a delirium and then he refused to eat what little we could find. In truth, his dysentery prevented him from gaining any strength or benefit from the thin gruel mixed with what weeds we could gather. We made him take water constantly and in the end we fashioned a stretcher made from strips of spruce bark with four of us taking turns to carry him.

We eventually left the main throng that was to continue with Nicholas, who with Jesus again at his side was once more our charismatic leader. Reinhardt had been sent ahead to see if he could negotiate a rat-ridding so that we might persuade the towns ahead to feed us. The four of us eventually reached a poor farm on the slopes, a stone cottage with a few fruit trees and a small rock-strewn garden of herbs, cabbage and turnips. A dozen hens scratched and clucked and a ewe, its dirty winter wool not yet shorn, stood tied to a stake driven into the ground. I could hear the snorting of two pigs in a sty behind the rude dwelling.

The sole occupant was an old crone, with hair growing from her chin, her shoulders so stooped that her head appeared to be at the centre of her chest. Thankfully, she spoke some German, but with a strange accent and with much pausing and searching for words that, when she found them, she spat out in bouts of sudden cackling, fast and furious, then long pauses ensued, then another burst of cackled and mangled German. She told us that there was a monastery three days journey away, and while she had never travelled that far she knew of its existence from her son, who with his wife had died in an avalanche two years previously. She lived in the cottage with her two grandchildren, small boys of six and eight or thereabouts, she said. They were away grazing their three sheep and a small herd of goats in the mountains and would not return that night, for they were sleeping in a cave.

She looked at the dying shape of Father Paulus, his cassock torn and ragged, his sandals broken and his freckled face gaunt with his sparse ginger hair matted with dirt. 'So this is what a priest looks like?' she cackled. Or words I took to mean this. 'I have never seen one.' She sniffed, her head nodding at the centre of her breast. 'Now I have, I think little of what I see.'

'He is very ill, frau. Not at his best.'

It seemed a silly thing to say of the dying Father Paulus, but there seemed no other reply in defence of this ragged and broken little priest. I begged that we might sojourn the night in the stable. She said they had no stable but the priest could stay in the cottage, as she could see he was too sick to harm her and was a priest, so she would trust him, although she had heard tell that not all holy men were to be trusted. She gave us a little food, coarse bread and some bitter greens, which was what she herself ate. With the three girls and myself to feed I could see it was all she had to give and I thanked her for sharing it with us.

'The hens will lay an egg, the ewe still gives a little milk and there are two cabbages plump enough and a turnip or two – I will manage well enough,' she cackled generously. Although this is, at best, a rough translation of what I thought she said, with hens, milk, cabbages and turnips being mentioned.

But Father Paulus could not eat even this poor fare and took only a few sips of water. As he lay on a straw pallet in the corner of the one-room cottage, I knew he was close to dying. I sat beside him praying that God might spare him long enough so that we could accomplish the journey to the monastery. But then I felt his hand reach out and touch me and I stopped praying and took his hand in my own. His eyes were over-bright and the freckled skin of his face seemed almost translucent. In the past months I had witnessed a great many children dying and with them the mothers of babies and adults sick before they left Cologne. I had learned that often with the dying there comes a few brief moments of profound lucidity and Father Paulus now licked his dry broken lips in an attempt to talk. What he said I tell only so that you may see in Father Paulus the richness of his spirit and the generosity of his heart and not so that I gain any praiseworthiness.

'Sylvia, I have much to thank you for,' he began.

'Nay, Father, it is I who shall be ever grateful to you,' I protested.

He held up his free hand to stay my voice. 'I have very few words left to spend and you must indulge me. Before you came into my life I wore a poor and worthless habit, a priest who didn't preach and, even if his shyness would allow it, one who had nothing whatsoever to say. The world about me seemed so filled with the calamity of humans, of babble and greed and cruelty and wickedness, death and destruction, that I often doubted the very existence of God. Everywhere I looked there was ignorance and stupidity, with the Holy Roman Church anxious to maintain this status quo so that its princes may grow ever more wealthy and powerful.

'The clamorous cries of hypocritical bishops and archbishops, cardinals and popes, princes and kings from their pulpits and thrones filled me with despair. They did not preach the message of salvation or heed the words of Jesus Christ the Saviour. Instead, they demanded that the common people must take up the sword against the Saracens in Spain and the Holy Land and now, of late, be granted a remission of their sins if they go to slaughter the Albigencians. This, so that the powerful of the Church may gain further riches and become even more powerful and gain more land and domination over others.'

The old crone in the far corner of the room began to snore and I gave Father Paulus a little more water to quench his parched lips. Then he continued.

'I spent my life as a humble scribe, scribbling the inanities of pompous bishops and writing down their lies and the duplicities they connived and contrived so that it might bring them closer to His Holiness in Rome and make them even richer and more powerful.' He sighed. 'Eventually I could bear it no longer and climbed into a tiny cell in the belltower of St Martin's so that I might ring the bells to drown out this constant cacophony of humans and the vainglorious mouthing of priests and Princes of the Church. I prayed that God might grant me deafness and the sanctification of silence.' Father Paulus paused and took a few drops of water from the cup I held to his lips.

'Hush now, Father, you upset yourself too much and must try to sleep,' I said gently.

'Nay, child, I have but only these words in me and then I have one last request, but please let me complete.' He took another sip of water. 'And then, Sylvia, you came into my life, your mind ever inquiring, as eager as a puppy to learn, already master of at least two languages and now craving to write Latin. You played me at chess and immediately beat me. You learned all I knew of Latin grammar and in a quarter of the time, nay even less, than it had taken me to learn the same.'

'And four times as long to master the goose quill,' I said quickly. '"Sylvia, when it comes to the quill, you are the goose!"' I laughed, reminding him of his witty remark.

He smiled weakly. 'And now you have brought me on this Children's Crusade where I have at last learned the true meaning of serving God and can count myself worthy as a priest. You have given me back my voice and allowed me to serve my God with the fullness of my being.' He smiled again. 'Even to preach with a conviction and to beg alms for my children, knowing God guides my tongue. Where I was once afraid of life, in all the death and calamity we have together witnessed, I have once again gained courage.' I barely felt his hand as he attempted to squeeze my own. 'And you have given me love and friendship so that I may die knowing that God has granted me every joy and sorrow that a soul may possess. But in the end it is my faith and the light of the Lord regained that you have allowed me to find and that lets me embrace death with my bosom filled with joy.'

'Don't die, Father, there is a monastery not far from here where they may heal you,' I cried, beginning to sob.

'Sylvia, cry later if you must, now you must help to give me extreme unction,' he said, his voice faded to near a whisper.

'Father, I may not, I am not a priest and cannot perform a last anointing,' I cried in despair.

He gave a weak smile. 'Then I ordain you, Sylvia. To me you are more, much more, than just a priest. Now repeat after me.'

'Father, I have heard the words a hundred times and many more from your lips. Do you wish me to repeat them as you say them or shall I take the priest's part and you the penitent?'

'Aye, in your own voice as priest, Sylvia. My last wish is that you take up this mantle. If you cannot find a priest to give a last anointing, you must give each child the comfort of a penitential psalm. God sees you as worthy as any priest to perform this final earthly task before a soul departs the sinful flesh and the travail of the mortal body.'

And so I committed his soul to God, not knowing if I blasphemed in doing so, but happy that it was what my tiny, loving friend wanted.

'Ah, Sylvia, I have no more words except that I would rather it is you than the Holy Father himself,' Father Paulus said, in little more than a whisper, all his words now finally spent.

'Sleep now, Father. I shall pray for your recovery,' I sobbed.

But I could not remain awake praying beside his bed and must have fallen asleep and when I woke at dawn to the cry of the old crone's rooster, Father Paulus was dead at my side. In my heart he will remain forever the priest in the truest image of Christ, more so than all the priests and bishops, archbishops and cardinals I would ever meet. I went outside and sang a requiem in that early misty morning long before the sunlight came, and my voice, caught up in the stillness, echoed against the great cliffs towering above me. I felt that it rose ever higher and higher into the sky beyond the cloud-covered mountains so that the words to the glory of God would help to transport the little freckled, ginger-headed priest to heaven, where a choir of angels waited to welcome him. A place where bells rang that could not deafen him.

And then a small thing, but for me a sign that God especially loved this humble priest and servant of salvation. We asked the old crone if we might bury him close by and where the rocky soil might be easiest to dig a grave.

'Where the fruit trees grow,' she replied. 'It is the softest and the deepest soil, the best is near the almond tree.'

And so his grave now lies beneath an almond tree that in the natural course of nature will come to blossom every spring with sprays of soft pink that turn to white to the glory of the Virgin and to all creation.

We again caught up with the throng, but now it seemed the people had no love for these ragged, barefoot beggars who were 'the German children'. We were not welcomed in Italy where, in our ignorance, we'd always thought they would be a pious people, closer to Rome, the earthly seat of God, who would, we thought, therefore embrace us. Instead they sent us away hungry, chastised us and attacked us, driving us from their towns. Every town we entered was worse than the one we'd left. Nicholas, who could not preach to them as he did not speak their language, had nothing to offer them except a ragged invasion of starving barefoot children.

The healing angels, those who had survived the ordeal to this point, had now become a most glorious-sounding choir where I sang the solo parts and, of course, Reinhardt played the flute. Now as we entered towns we would sing and when a good crowd was formed I'd summon the birds, a bewonderment that never failed to bring the townsfolk to a sense of piety. Then I would follow this with a catechism in Latin that all recognised and so could participate, then also a short familiar sermon such as usually followed mass, though again, knowing my words would not be understood. All this was done in the hope of softening their hearts to the plight of our children.

Sometimes it worked, but mostly not and Reinhardt would reluctantly persuade the town to undergo a rat-ridding in exchange for corn. This too did not always earn us the results we desired. The suspicious people of Lombardy and the Po Valley would not give us corn before the ridding took place, thinking we might be gulling them. Then when it was done and the rats marched into the river or an empty well, they would often halve the amount promised. We would barely have sufficient to get to the next destination and sometimes we'd go hungry for days on end, living on grass and weeds and water, with our children now forced to steal cabbages and turnips or anything they could find from the fields and from cackling barnyards, alas, Reinhardt having first stilled the dogs with his magic flute.

But it was never enough and soon our children began to despair. They had endured the Alps with the knowledge that the drought would be ended on the other side and that the folk would embrace them and fill their bellies to every content. Now they were harassed and chased away and the smaller ones beaten and kicked. It seemed that their dislike for us as Germans could not be contained and the children became objects they would use to vent their hatred on.

People constantly cried out the same words, and when we finally got the translation we discovered what they asked was, 'Where is your priest?'

'Mort!' we taught our children to shout back.

But without Father Paulus present the local priests were the first to chastise us, calling us the devil's urchins, German piglets and other terms of abuse we thankfully did not understand.

Many of the farm children, so they might eat, took work upon the land. I would later hear that most were harshly treated and some beaten to death. In every town we came to we left behind children to die in the streets and squares, too weak to continue. It became apparent that if we remained in one great multitude we had no chance of reaching the sea. So it was decided that we would break into groups of twenty or so, the better to scrounge and to beg and forage for food, taking various routes across the countryside so as not to overburden any district or town with the arrival of too many children.

Nicholas preached that the hand of God still guided us, that we must all reach Genoa towards the end of August. Those who arrived first would wait for the others and all would wait for the day when God told him to still the sea. He would create a pathway on the top of the waves so we might walk over it all the way to Constantinople without fear of drowning. Nicholas painted a pretty picture of this glorious path, frozen but not cold, that stretched like a silver ribbon across the ocean. On either side of the path, fish would swim to be scooped up from hand to lip, scaled and cooked by the angels who hovered in attendance over us. Well fed and vigorous of spirit, we would be welcomed by the Greek Christians and together give thanks to God. Whereupon, with salutations and speeches, banners blowing in the wind and the sounding of brass trumpets, we would make our departure. There would be flowers scattered over our heads and palm leaves strewn at our feet as we left the empire of the Byzantine and crossed into the lands of the Saracens. Then onwards, following the cross and going steadfastly in peace and love and understanding to Jerusalem to recover the Holy Sepulchre for Christianity.

Nicholas, who daily seemed to be jumping out of his skin, said he must be at the front with the strongest of the boys with their banners and brass trumpets, so that he could lead us to the sea. 'It is our most important occasion, the moment when we tread upon the sea. I must proclaim the Children's Crusade in the name of God and our precious Saviour Jesus Christ. I must be seen as the one inspired by our heavenly Father. The people must know that mine, and no other, is the hand that will receive the sacred keys to the Holy Sepulchre from the iniquitous Saracens!'

Since he had returned to us after we had traversed the Alps, he seemed less and less inclined to have me by his side. Reinhardt said it was clear that Nicholas resented my presence since the preaching in the mountains, thinking I was attempting to take over and rob him of the glory he was entitled to as leader.

I confess that on one occasion when I had suggested that we break his sermons, now growing too long and lugubrious for the weakened multitude of children, Nicholas had snapped at me. 'You try to steal the power of Jesus within me! My voice comes from God, yours from that silly screeching girl's choir!'

Suitably chastened I'd replied, perhaps a little angrily, 'Maybe you would prefer that we no longer sing? You have merely to say the word, Nicholas of Cologne.'

'Do not mock me, Sylvia!' he had cried. 'Ha! You steal my voice and now, when I am returned to Jesus, you would judge the voice of God too long and interrupt it with the shrieking of hymns!'

'No more singing,' I'd said, now truly angry, walking away from him. I had expected him to call me back, but he didn't and a little later he sent a message to say we should choose another route to Genoa, where he would wait for us.

We would choose one less arduous for the smaller children who increasingly gathered around the healing angels. Reinhardt and I gathered a group we hoped would be no more than twenty but ended as more than fifty. In all, there were fifty-six and that included the remaining healing angels. Half of the weak were girls who were under ten and the rest were boys even younger who, remarkably, still survived. These were the smallest and the weakest, the ones we deemed most needed our care, though, in truth, if such care might be given, every child who marched was in need of some. Death had become so familiar in my life that the last tears I had shed were for Father Paulus. If it may be said that God grants us only a certain number of tears to use in life's travail, then I had used my share. As we moved past the dead and dying children I could no longer cry.

'Please, Reinhardt, pray to God that we might find a road to the sea that does not carry the corpses of children,' I begged. But we never did find such a glorious path. All carried the reek of death and we could not avoid the sight of tiny ragged bodies cast aside as if they were carrion. Our nostrils were no longer assaulted by the stench and we had long since given up cursing the ravens, jackdaws, crows and hawks that feasted upon our dead. I would stop along the way to bring comfort and to recite a penitential psalm to any dying child we came across. Or when we reached the towns and villages, if there was a church I'd ask to see the priest and, speaking in Latin, beg him to give the dying children extreme unction. But they would invariably refuse and so I would try to bring these small souls some comfort.

I had attended so many last anointings of children with Father Paulus that I knew all seven penitential psalms off by heart. I had sometimes repeated them for the dying child while he anointed their heads with oil. He had given me permission to administer a penitential psalm to a dying child and assured me God would most surely approve, so I now gave this small and abiding comfort to them whenever I could. It was so very little, yet sometimes it could be seen to bring peace in death to a frightened child. It was because so many lay dying and in need of final comfort and this small preparation for the journey to heaven that our group moved the slowest of them all towards the sea.

Before we broke up into smaller groups I had prayed constantly that God should tell me what to do. We were now a ragged, desperate, starving mob. Nicholas seemed less in control and much of the fire was gone from his sermons to the children. I thought it as well that we now decided to break into groups so that the multitude did not see what I thought seemed like the waning of his powers.

Whereas Nicholas appeared as lively in his movement and enthusiasms as ever before, he now seemed puffed-up with self-importance. Previously he had seen himself simply following the instructions received from an angel sent by Jesus. Now he seemed to believe, not in the guiding hand of God's angel, but that he was the omnipotent, venerable and holy entity. Since the last deep, dark place – the longest he had ever experienced – he regarded his every decision and instruction as carrying the authority of the heavenly Father. He began to hint that he was himself the angel and that when he entered his dark place it was because his body remained behind while his spirit had been temporarily transported to heaven, where Jesus spoke to him directly and gave him his future directions.

In one of his sermons he told how, if the Saracens should attack us, where he walked the sand would be turned to gold dust and the infidels would grovel at his feet to scoop it up and so we would pass by safely. He spoke about how he intended to warn these heathens and devils that if any of his flock died by the infidels' spears and arrows, his footsteps would turn from gold to golden serpents that would strike them down.

As we crossed the lands of Italy his sermons became more and more exaggerated and bizarre and it astonished me that the four thousand or so children left in the crusade still believed. I confess myself grateful that we were separated for the last weeks on the road to the sea, that having endured near three months with the multitude I now need care only for the fifty-six children.

I still believed that Nicholas was blessed and that he was divinely inspired to lead us. But I did not believe, as the children did, that the surface of the sea would harden and that, in the manner of Christ on the Sea of Galilee, we would walk with dry feet across the water. Instead I thought it a figure of speech, that boats would transport us in God's name with the blessing of the Holy Father in Rome. This is sheer stupidity now when I think about it, for why would there be boats willing to transport four thousand ragged, penniless children for the glory of God as the boatmen's only compensation? But faith is a blind maiden and in God's precious name all things are possible. All I can say is I believed we would cross over the sea and eventually find ourselves in Jerusalem. I had no doubts whatsoever that this was God's wish and that we must obey Him through every hardship we might encounter.

The townspeople showed only animosity when we entered and would do all they could to make us feel unwanted. We had grown accustomed to them setting their dogs on us and their scowls and growls, the impatient shooing of the women as if we were a pestilence of persistent flies or a flock of parish pigeons underfoot. We had come to expect harsh and sometimes vile invective from the men and the spitting and punching of local youths as they beat our weakened, defenceless boys and grabbed gleefully at the breasts and crotches of the girls. Or if they came across one alone they were quick to rape her as if a yowling pack of dogs come across a carcass.

These people on the other side of the mountains had never wanted us in the first place. Unlike our own folk they did not believe in a Children's Crusade and their priests had warned them that ours was a false prophecy. With hundreds of small groups passing through their towns they had had their fill of desperate children falling to their knees, supplicating and sobbing while clutching their ankles and crying out piteously for food.

Many of the children were kicked aside or spat upon as they begged in what the locals thought the harsh guttural accents of a Teutonic people whom they despised. Any Christian charity they may have initially felt, they had long since abandoned in favour of denying compassion to these starving Child Crusaders. ('*If you feed them they'll only stay longer!*') They came to regard these German children, with their ragged banners depicting, of all things, a cross with a crow, as an invasion, no different to a plague of locusts come to steal their food and ravage their lands. The only certain cure for this infestation was to stamp it out as quickly as possible by refusing to give it food. The children who succumbed to starvation while in their towns were thrown into a communal pit and covered with quicklime before being buried in unconsecrated ground.

This was usually accomplished without a prayer, the local priest being too busy with God's important work to pray for the souls of this infestation of vermin.

Adding to all this was the lack of a common language. While still with the multitude I could sometimes communicate in Latin with the local priest or beg an audience with the bishop, though they would seldom accept an emissary from the Children's Crusade. Moreover we could not speak to the commonfolk. If Father Paulus had been with us, then at the very least we might have had access to the local priest; without him we lacked any credentials and were regarded as an invading mob.

The fact that we carried the cross of Christ and sang in praise of the same God seemed of little or no consequence. The sensibilities of the particular God who watched over these pious Italians were not to be compromised by the extra-territorial burdens unfairly imposed on Him by His cruder and more tempestuous German alter ego. Ours was a lesser God, if one at all, who guided the Children's Crusade. If I managed to see a priest or even, once or twice, have an audience with the local bishop, all we received were harsh words of admonishment and the demand that we return from whence we'd come.

A ragged, young *brunhilda* in broken boots, attired in the rough woollen garb of a peasant, her blonde hair denoting her Saxon beginnings, her face blistered from exposure to the sun, but one who spoke Latin with a fluency beyond the ability of the bishop, was not a welcome emissary. A mere female, who could quote the Bible chapter and verse with a greater facility than most priests and, if necessary, remind them of Christ's words about charity and little children, was a furtive stab to their ecclesiastical consciences and they resented me deeply.

Furthermore, I didn't make a fuss when I first came into their presence, but instead I played the pious and compliant maid and let them huff and puff and admonish me over our cause before parrying with arguments in the classical scholarly Latin of an educated cardinal. This Latin eloquence was, of course, due to Brother Dominic, who had taken great pains to remove all traces of the peasant German inflections from my Latin tongue and had taught me its syntax and grammar as spoken in the presence of the Pope.

In other words, I was no *dummkopf* whom a churchman could remove from their presence with a backward flip of a priestly hand, a priest who was more accustomed to blessing and head-patting and gesticulating while his tongue prattled inanities than he was in arguing the Holy Scriptures with a biblical scholar whom they'd completely underestimated.

However, I soon grew to realise that my intellectual acuity stood no chance of winning priest or bishop over to our side. In fact, it proved to be a hindrance. I was a young peasant woman of no possible influence or benefit to them, possessed of an argumentative manner better suited to an aging abbess. This, in one so young and unpropitious, was in itself a paradox and the Church, where men reign over God's earthly kingdom, does not like uncertainty and contradiction, especially coming from a woman. One Mother of God who is known to keep her mouth shut is sufficient for its needs.

And so, now that we were a small group at the tail-end of the marchers with the smallest and the weakest to look after, I asked the heavenly Father for His guidance to overcome these uncharitable people and their mean-spirited priests. I asked God to show me how we might survive these last weeks with these angry people on the far side of the mountains.

In asking God for guidance, unlike Nicholas or Father Hermann, I did not expect God to speak to me directly. But that night I dreamed of birds, every kind, in a chorus fluttering above my head. Standing with me was a choir of fifty-six children who sang with the voices of angels to open the hearts of all who heard them and who placed food in baskets at our feet. In the dream I heard a disembodied voice call, 'Hark! The Silent Choir of God's Little Children.'

Now I know, before declaring I had received a message from God, there may seem a simple enough explanation, as dreams are often only the ragged ends of the previous day's thinking. Besides, I dreamed often enough of birds and had done so since a child. We had fifty-six children in our group, among them the healing angels. Such a dream did not seem to contain any special quality – birds, children and the healing angels who sometimes sang as a choir being a simple enough explanation. Nevertheless I woke up quite sure the voice I had heard was from the heavenly Father and that the Silent Choir of God's Little Children was God's name and His will for us. If people refused to give us alms as a gesture of Christian charity they might feel better disposed towards us if we gave them something in return, and a children's choir was not a common experience. My only dilemma was the injunction to be 'silent', for how could a choir be silent? It seemed such an obvious contradiction. No choir may be silent.

I took God's instruction to Reinhardt, who laughed. 'A silent choir? Nay, Sylvia, not God's directive this one. Just a silly dream, eh?'

'NO!' I cried, surprised at the sound of my own vehemence. I shook my head vigorously. 'I prayed and the answer came – it must be a silent choir! I am certain of it.'

'But that's ridiculous. A silent choir?'

'I know.'

'Are you sure?'

'Aye!'

'Let me think.' He scratched his head. 'Let me think . . . Think, Reinhardt, think,' he said, urging himself and slapping his forehead in the exaggerated Pied-Piper-of-Hamelin manner he sometimes affected. Then suddenly, as only Reinhardt could, he cried, 'Aha! A *silent* choir!'

'What?'

'Got it!'

'Reinhardt, what?'

'Well, think how the children enter a town. They swarm in, using every mendacious trick in the book, some even beat themselves with willow rods to make their backs bleed and cry out that it is flagellation in the name of Jesus. But mostly the children beg, cry, sob, plead. They accept the kicks and blows they receive and come back for more until someone wears down and throws a scrap of food at them.'

I sighed. 'It is the only way.'

'Nay, but it's not! I have it now, the *silent* choir! The only time our voices are heard is when we sing. We never beg. In fact we never ask to be fed. No child speaks a single word, no matter what.' He danced around me and took up his flute and composed a funny little tune. Then withdrawing his pipe he called, 'Sing after me, Sylvia.'

Not a syllable spoken, never a squeak,
We love to sing but we never do speak.
Voices that charm birds from the trees
Sing praises to God on bended knees.

It was simple little rhyming couplets put to a happy little tune and the children loved it and repeated the rhyme, singing it constantly, though of course we had no idea if our silence would work. We plaited crude grass baskets to place at our feet when we stood to sing. We prayed that God would reward our efforts, and we practised two hours in the morning and then the same again in the afternoon for several days. The singing and instruction helped to take our minds off the state of constant hunger we endured and, as well, seemed to make the path to Genoa a little shorter.

I think God must have had His eyes on us because the children's voices proved, without a single exception, to be quite lovely. Some were more talented than others but none there were who couldn't sing or hold a note. Reinhardt proved an excellent teacher and, if I may be permitted to say so, I think I was a capable one as well. We worked together and surprisingly I proved better with the boys and the ratcatcher with the girls. Children, especially boys of around ten years old, have wonderful voices and if we could manage to fill their bellies, I knew they would sound better and try harder.

It seemed to work in the smaller towns and then the larger ones we passed through, where we soon developed a manner to attract a curious crowd. If we were lucky it would be market day with lots of peasants in from the surrounding countryside. We'd tarry outside the town and I'd enter alone and, as usual, seek out the priest and ask him formally to administer extreme unction to any dying children who had preceded us. There were always several I would pass on the way to the Church, but it was not until I received the priest's refusal that I would return to give them the final blessing of a penitential psalm. Then I would return to the waiting group and we would enter the town and make our way to the square that invariably fronted the church where I had recently visited the priest.

We'd enter a town to the usual jeers and shouts of abuse, with the dogs set upon us. Reinhardt would put his silent flute to his mouth and the dogs, as they did in the village on the evening of the first day we met, would drop to the road with their heads on their paws, tongues lolling. This almost immediately gained the attention of the townsfolk. Then as we climbed silently to stand on the steps of the church, it didn't take long for a look of bemusement to appear on the faces of the people in the square. It took enormous courage and discipline from the small children with empty stomachs to pass the market stalls, to remain silent in sight of the piled produce, loaves of bread, crisp apples and plump ripened peaches and apricots, cauldrons of steaming soup or rich stew they only dreamed they might eat just once before they died.

The ratcatcher waited until a curious crowd gathered. Some called for their dogs to return to them but the animals refused to move, even if severely beaten. This always added to the curiosity as the news spread among the folk that the dogs had been put under a spell. Then Reinhardt would play a few bright notes and hold up his hand for silence. Intrigued, people waited, quickly drawn to silence. 'Good people, we bring you the Silent Choir of God's Little Children!' he would announce. 'If we please you, then feed God's little flock. If we do not, then we shall trouble you no further.' We had managed to learn how to say these words in the regional tongue with the correct degree of pathos, though the description of the choir would usually bring a few titters from the more insensitive among the crowd who assumed the stupid Germans had mangled the local language by announcing a silent choir. Reinhardt started to play and there would be a gasp as the children's voices rose to the sky.

I would take four solo parts in the performance and two of the children, a ten-year-old boy Heinrich and an eleven-year-old girl Hilda, would each render a solo. Both had most remarkably pure and innocent voices, but Heinrich's was truly wonderful, and while he sang I would call out the various bird calls as if they were a part of the solo and the hymn. The birds would soon begin to arrive, to the astonishment of the crowd. Every bird of the air to be found in their region came to sit on the shoulders of the children or to land on their outstretched hands, adding their avian notes to Reinhardt's flute and the beautiful voice of little Heinrich. It was at this point, with Heinrich singing like a veritable angel, that people fell to their knees. The Silent Choir of God's Little Children had charmed the birds from the trees and they were certain that they'd witnessed a miracle.

It may seem immodest to say that we were good, very good, and that we quickly became outstanding. But nevertheless it was true. At the end of the performance there would be a great deal of applause and tears from the women in the crowd as we brought the town square to a standstill. When eventually the applause died down, in order to alter the sombre mood Reinhardt would do a few little dance steps in front of the first grass basket and play a little tune, then on to the next, a different melody for every basket, ten in all. The local folk would quickly get the idea and warmed with piety and goodwill would start to fill the baskets. As each brought something and placed it into a basket the choir, in perfect harmony, would sing the single word, 'Hallelujah!' As the baskets filled with more and more folk bringing something, it would soon become a continuous chorus: 'Hallelujah . . . hallelujah, hallelujah . . . haaaa . . . leee . . . luuu . . . jah, hallelujah!' until the square echoed with this single glorious word of praise to the Almighty God who so generously fed us that day.

Then, when the baskets burgeoned, we would silently gather them up and move on, our children smiling and nodding to the townsfolk but with never a word spoken. It was as if fifty-six mute children had marched into town, where they had been touched by the hand of God to sing His praise, then as silently as they came, departed, leaving the townsfolk feeling very good about themselves.

Always, as we were about to leave the square, someone would come running up shouting, 'The dogs! What about the dogs?' Whereupon Reinhardt, in his best exaggerated Pied-Piper-of-Hamelin manner, would smack his forehead and mime his abject apologies. Then he'd take up his flute and appear to blow, then look expectantly at the dogs, who hadn't moved, their jaws seeming locked to their forepaws. This was the sign for our children to sing out a single cry of concern in perfect harmony, 'Ooooh!' The ratcatcher would jump into a crouch with his hand cupped to his ear as if to test the pitch of the note they sang out. Then he'd replicate it on the flute pointing to the dogs, but with no better result than before. The choir would sing out again, 'Oooooh!' a single pitch higher, with the same failed result and performance from the ratcatcher. This would continue until the choir hit a pitch seemingly as high as their voices could reach.

Whereupon Reinhardt would jump from the crouched, cupped-ear position and into the air and do a ridiculous little dance, clapping the choir, then indicating with his forefinger held up that if they tried one more time he felt they'd find the answer for certain. But again he'd fail.

Reinhardt would examine his flute carefully and move his fingers over the holes looking quizzical as if he was trying to remember the right combination. Then he'd shake his head in an exaggerated gesture of concern and appeal silently to the crowd, spreading his hands and hunching his shoulders to indicate that he was unable to undo the spell. When looks of consternation began to appear on people's faces he would turn to the choir and fall to his knees and, clasping his hands in prayer, he'd silently beg them for a note just one pitch higher. This time it was the children's turn to shrug, lifting their chins by touching the underside and throwing back their little heads, in effect miming that they'd given him their best shot and could take their voices no higher.

Reinhardt would burst into tears (a remarkable trick involving real tears) whereupon he'd place his forehead in the dirt and bang the ground with his fist. After a few moments he'd rise up sadly into a sitting position and place the flute disconsolately to his lips, a dejected and defeated expression upon his face, appealing to the crowd for their sympathy.

'Our dogs! You can't go and leave our dogs to lie!' shouted the crowd.

The 'Oooooooooh!' suddenly emanating from the choir was so perfectly achieved and pitched so high that the people watching covered their ears in fright. In turn, the ratcatcher timed his flute for the silent note he blew to make it appear that the pitch the children had reached with their voices had released the canines from the spell.

The dogs jumped back to their feet, their tails wagging furiously, as if they too had much enjoyed the performance. To which the choir sang a beautifully rendered harmonious 'Ahhhhh!' as if a single grand note from a cathedral organ. The children loved this part and believed that it was they who had brought the dogs back to life. They would laugh (permitted) and clap as the dogs seemingly came back to life.

This became known as the Miracle of the Birds and the Dogs, and by the time we reached Piacenza, just five days journey from Genoa, our children were bright-eyed and putting on weight. The scattered groups that had gone ahead had been treated in the same harsh manner as had formerly been the case with us, and in Piacenza children lay dying in the streets and squares. As was my custom I went immediately to the parish priest and asked him in Latin to give them absolution. The church in Piacenza was a large one, not quite a cathedral but much bigger than usual. The priest also seemed a more educated type but no friendlier than any of the others. As usual he refused my request, but this time he claimed to have received strict orders from the bishop in nearby Cremona, forbidding the administration of last rites to the dying German children.

He produced a missive sent to the local clergy and began to read it aloud to me. '*This innumerable multitude of German boys, babes at the breasts, women and girls all hasten to the sea to fulfil the prophecy of an angel of God that they would recover the Holy Sepulchre from the hands of the iniquitous Saracens. This is a movement inspired by the devil. It is not God's will to allow His children to be sent on such a false errand or to die in the numbers that perish each day in our towns and villages. If not God, then who? We know whose dark spirit lies behind this. Do not administer the last anointing to these children from Cologne. You may not see their calloused feet as likened unto cloven hooves, but that is how they managed to scramble across the rocks and crags of the Alps to swarm down upon us as a pestilence visited upon our land!*' He shrugged, and looking me in the eye the priest said, 'Now I must ask you to leave my church!'

'God's house, Father,' I replied. Then looking directly at him I asked, 'Will you take my confession, please, Father?'

A look of shock was followed by one of real fear. 'Nay, get out, devil's child!' he admonished. Then visibly trembling he pointed a finger at me, then quickly withdrew it and made the sign of the cross. 'A peasant maid that speaks Latin! Get thee away from me, Satan!'

'I will pray for your bishop and for you, Father. "*Suffer little children to come unto me,*" saith the Lord.' With this I walked out of the church knowing I must contain my anger and that I had already said too much for my own good.

I began to say a penitential psalm to each of the dying children in the vicinity of the church, where many had come, too weak to continue but wanting to be as close to God as they might get. The church was always where most of the dying children would be found and it was here where we would invariably sing. If this sounds insensible, I can only say that we tried to make these dying children feel that their own kind was with them to the last and that the songs of praise the children sang would comfort their final hours on earth. Before we left we would leave food from our baskets for those of the dying we hoped might still take sustenance, and water to quench their parched lips. There was nothing more we could do and I had long since spent my allotment of tears on this earth.

I was kneeling beside a dying child trying to hear his murmurs when I felt a pair of strong arms clasped around me, pinning my arms to my side, and then a grunt as I was jerked backwards to my feet. I lashed out backwards with my feet and felt my heel land against a shin and then a cry of pain and a curse and then another huge black-bearded brute grabbed me around the legs. I sank my teeth down hard into the coarse hair that covered the arm of the male who held me but he continued to hold me in a vice-like grip, cursing the while. Then a cleric appeared and grabbed me by the hair and pulled viciously so that I was forced to release my grip on the arm of the man who held me, and a taste of blood entered my mouth. The cleric, still gripping me by the hair, brought his face right up to mine and began shouting in the local language so that I felt his warm spittle landing on my face.

The two brutes now held me parallel to the cobblestones, the back of my head and shoulders against the chest of one and my legs held under the locked arms of the other. The cleric, himself a big man, stood on my left gripping a fistful of my hair and pulled backwards so that I was restrained from biting my assailant. They carried me thus out of the sunshine that flooded the square into the dark interior of the church and down the centre aisle and into a room near the sacristy.

The priest who had earlier chased me from the church stood beside a very large wooden chair with a high back carved with two angels hovering on either side of a cross. The seat was large enough to accept a giant but, instead, seated in it was a tiny man in bishop's robes, his boots dangling so far above the flagstone floor that it seemed he must have been lifted into the chair. His tiny fingers were not large enough to curl around the edges of the chair's arms, and the chair back still allowed a full display of the hovering angels beyond the top of his head. His hair, a mixture of grey and the colour of red clay, was shaved close to his skull. His beard of the same colour grew no more than the width of a pinkie nail around his chin and seemed so fine that an orange light showed through it to give it a closer resemblance to fur than the coarsened hair on a grown man's cheeks and chin. His eyebrows were denser than his beard and of the same soft fur, and appeared to almost completely surround two bright little obsidian eyes that darted, monkey-like, everywhere at once. He looked to all intents and purposes like a small ape dressed in a bishop's robes.

'Put her down! Put her down!' he yelled in a high-pitched and plainly irritated voice that came from a tiny mouth displaying small, sharp, yellow teeth, each of which was separated slightly from the next.

The brute gripping my legs released them, allowing me to place them on the floor, while the one behind me pushed me upright before releasing me. 'Shoo! Be off with you!' the monkey bishop screeched with an irritated backward flick of his hand. The two men dropped briefly to their knees, then rose and left; the cleric who had pulled my hair remained behind. 'You too!' he screeched, pointing to the entrance and flicking his forefinger. Or rather, that is what I supposed he said, or something like it, his dismissive gestures making his meaning clear enough.

I dropped to my knees in front of the chair and moved my head forward so that I might kiss the ring that seemed a gold band too broad and a jewel much too large for so tiny a hand. But he quickly withdrew his hand from his lap. 'Nay! No blessing! No blessing at all!' he said in Latin. Then added, 'We have been watching you, you hear? Every movement! Why do you commit sacrilege?'

'Sacrilege, my Lord?'

'Extreme unction! Last anointings! You have sinned grievously! Sinned! Sinned! Sinned, you hear!'

'Nay, my Lord, it is not a sin to recite a penitential psalm,' I said, in little more than a whisper.

'What? What did you say? No sin! How dare you contradict me!' The bishop, grasping the arms of the large chair, pushed his torso forward and glared at me, his eyes momentarily ceasing from darting about.

Please guide my tongue, Brother Dominic, I thought desperately. 'There is scriptural instruction pertaining to the last anointing, my Lord. St

James, chapter five, verses fourteen and fifteen. But this does not forbid the saying of a penitential psalm. In the absence of a priest, a lay person may be permitted to give comfort to the dying by reciting such a psalm as a help and comfort to the dying.'

'Canon law! Canon law! You may not! You hear? Nay, nay, nay!'

'With the greatest respect, my Lord, the epistle from Pope Gregory to the First Crusade permitted any lay member of the Church, in the absence of a priest, to recite one of the seven psalms for the dying to repeat or, if unable, simply to hear.'

The bishop looked momentarily confused, then his monkey eyes lit up. 'Ha! That was a crusade! Thousands dying! Not enough priests! Infidels everywhere! Special circumstances, you hear?' he screeched.

'This be also a crusade, my Lord Bishop. The Children's Crusade. Alas, already thousands of children have perished and your priests, upon your instructions, refuse to give them extreme unction.' A sudden anger rose up in me that I seemed unable to control. I could feel the flush that burned on the surface of my face and neck. 'I have no choice, I have prayed and asked God's guidance. These are His little children and they have a right to the comfort of God's word as they leave this earthly hell and rise up to heaven. "*Suffer little children to come unto me,*" saith the Lord.'

The bishop's tiny simian face turned a deep scarlet and I thought his head must surely split open like an over-ripe melon. His sharp little eyes ceased their darting and fixed on me with a mixture of astonishment, anger and even, deep within, I sensed, a tincture of fear. He pointed a trembling finger at my feet. 'Take off your boots!' he demanded shrilly.

I removed my broken boots, knowing my feet to be sweaty from the heat and dirty from the black road dust entering where the leather had split from the soles. The monkey bishop wriggled his torso so that he sat on the edge of the chair where he peered down at my blackened feet.

'Ha! See how clever the devil!' he announced triumphantly.

The priest who was standing behind the chair had not uttered a word since I had been brought before the bishop. He now looked down and seeing only a pair of dirty feet, asked, 'What is it, my Lord Bishop?'

'Use your eyes! Can't you see, man! Satan has changed them back. Clever, eh?'

The priest grunted, obviously bemused, unable to understand. 'What see you, my Lord?

The bishop jabbed his ring finger at my toes, the red jewel catching the light. 'He thinks we are fooled! Ha! We have his measure! Every bit of it!' he yelled, his little yellow teeth clicking. Then a cackle escaped from his throat, followed by an abrupt hiccup.

'My Lord?' the priest asked, now completely confused.

'Hooves! Hooves, man! The devil thinks he can trick us. He's changed her cloven hooves back into feet!' The bishop stabbed repeatedly at my dirt-blackened feet with his bejewelled finger. 'See? They are still black!' He wriggled back into the enormous chair and his eyes now resumed their darting about. 'The devil's skin is black, black as pitch and can't be changed,' he declared gleefully. 'We have all the proof we need!' Then as suddenly he stopped and brought his hands together, his fingers touching as if he was about to enunciate a prayer. But instead he started to giggle in little bursts, as if he was trying to contain his mirth but with small spurts of inner merriment escaping. 'The flames . . . put her to the flames?' He shook his head, as if talking to himself. 'Pope's permission needed.' He thought again. 'Toenails . . . pull them out? Show them to be false, hiding cloven hooves.'

He seemed to quite like this idea until the priest cleared his throat. 'The people, my Lord. They would wish to see the Church punish this German pestilence inflicted upon us by the devil. This she-devil must be made an example for all to see. The people are very angry with these supplicating children and wish to see someone punished for their never-ending presence.'

'What, no toenails? What then, speak out, man!' the bishop chirped.

'A flogging, a public flogging with you as chief witness,' the priest suggested.

The bishop began to clap. '*Excellento!* The Church, the Holy Roman

Church, is seen to flog the devil in public!' He hugged himself. 'Oh, the archbishop will like this! Like this very much!' he said gleefully. But then as suddenly his expression changed and he looked stern. 'What about the toenails? The devil's toenails?'

The priest seemed to consider this, then said carefully, 'Maybe not, my Lord.'

'Why not?' the bishop demanded.

'The people may read into it wrongly, my Lord. The Scriptures tell us that Christ's feet bled when he carried the cross to Calvary and then later with the driving of the great iron spike into his crossed feet.'

'Good point!' the bishop replied. 'A good flogging then, eh? Plenty of blood!'

The priest nodded. It was quite clear that the monkey bishop was mad, but that none would say so, least of all the priest who, like Master Nicodemus, found himself the power behind the throne. I now realised that the priest was not in charge of the local church but was the bishop's assistant, the man who did his master's thinking for him. With perhaps the exception of the allusion to the cloven hooves and our scampering over the Alps like goats, the missive he had earlier read out to me had most likely been composed by him and not by the mad little monkey seated in front of me.

'I beg your mercy, my Lord. I am God's child!' I cried out.

'Ha! Of course you'd say that!' He turned to the priest. 'She'd say that, wouldn't she? Of course she would!' he said, nodding his head in agreement with himself.

The priest called out and the two brutes and the cleric, who must have been waiting for his call, returned. Both of the men now carried a length of rope and the cleric a strip of cloth. There was no escape and I had no defence, my precious stave lay outside, left beside the dying child. I backed into a corner and with my back against the wall I kicked and clawed at the two brutes. I could see the congealed blood where my teeth had bitten into the arm of one of them. I screamed and struggled and managed to bite one through the ear, the salty taste of blood again on my lips. They soon had me in their grasp, though not before the cleric holding the cloth to gag me came too close and with all my force I managed to kick him in the scrotum. He gave a loud groan and sank to the floor clutching his cassock between his legs. The two brutes turned me onto my stomach and tied my arms behind my back and my ankles. Blood dropped from the ear of one of them onto the back of my neck. Then the other one held my head while 'bleeding ear' bound the cloth tightly over my mouth to silence my angry screams. My last sight of the bishop was of him with his knees pulled against his chest and all of him squeezed back into the farthermost corner of the chair, a look of terror on his monkey face.

I was carried down into the crypt and thrown into a small cell with the blood from the brute with the torn ear dripping down and soaking the front of my gown. The two, having dropped me unceremoniously to the floor, paused momentarily, one cupping his ear in an attempt to stem the flow of blood. Then they leaned over me and spat into my face, cursing me in their own language before departing. I felt a small satisfaction that both men would forever wear a permanent scar by which to remember the German she-devil. Nor would I ever confess this as wilful behaviour nor confess the kick to the priest's unneeded manhood. I knew that if I'd had the opportunity I would have gouged an eye out or even worse. I was too angry to weep and managed somehow to pull myself up into the corner of the cell so that I could sit up in the dark.

Two hours or more passed, some of which I spent in prayer and some, I confess, silently cursing my tormentors in language I had heard as a peasant in the marketplace. I finally wept, though not for my parlous state but over the loss of my precious stave and Father John satchel. I felt sure the stave must be stolen and also the satchel, though of the two the stave was the most important to me. The stave was my talisman, sprinkled with holy water and blessed with the promise to guide me across the rocky paths of life. Father John had led me to believe, or perhaps I had simply come to believe on my own, that with it at my side, I would always be safe. Now it was gone and soon the flesh of my back would be flayed and I would be lucky to remain alive. Alas, my luck had deserted me.

It must have been towards noon when the cleric entered carrying a candle. With him came a lay sister who bore a clay pot and what looked like a crude brush, a stick with rags tied to its end, these no longer than the top joint of my finger. He placed the candle down close to my feet and, rising, placed his right leg over my body to straddle me with his broad backside facing me. He then lowered his fat arse down onto my thighs, wincing as he sat down. I could only hope that my kick would cause him to remember me for several weeks. Leaning forward he took hold of my legs just below my knees, pressing my shins hard against the flagstones so that I was unable to move them. Whereupon the lay sister proceeded to brush my feet with a wet substance, presumably from the jar, which I could feel but not see, brushing the contents onto the skin. Why, I wondered, would they wish to paint my feet? The lay sister soon completed this task and, taking the candle, rose, whereupon the cleric stood up and they hurried out of the cell so that the darkness returned and I was unable to see what she had done.

CHAPTER FIFTEEN

The Field of Forever Dreaming

LESS THAN AN HOUR passed from the time my feet had been mysteriously painted by the lay sister to when the bishop's assistant arrived carrying a lantern and accompanied by two strapping young monks, one of them a blackamoor. I had never seen a black man in a cassock and had always supposed that the black moors were infidels. I was also to learn the name of the bishop's assistant was Father Pietro, the same name as the priest who had baptised me. At least there seemed to be some symmetry – a Pietrus at the beginning and Pietro at the end of my life. Even more curiously, both Peters had pronounced me possessed by the devil.

If I appear reconciled to the almost certain prospect of death at the hands of the little monkey, this was not because I was without fear. I was mortally afraid, but not for my body, poor feeble corrupting flesh, but for my immortal soul. I had seen too much death and almost all of it among children. Emotionally I had become an old crone who, having witnessed the horror of life on earth, craves blackness, stillness, an absence of little children dying in the name of Jesus.

My despair was for what I had personally allowed to happen. I knew that my own blinding stupidity could not be expunged, wiped away with a confession and a penance even of the most arduous nature. I could not see how even the most generous and forgiving God could forgive me for what I had done. I had reached a point where the only thing I craved was eternal damnation. As a child, when my father took me to the pigsty I believed that his wanton actions had condemned me to hell and that I had no possibility of remission through no fault of my own. Now it was my own actions that condemned me. If I feared for my mortal soul it was because I knew I could expect no redemption for my sins.

I believed in the Miracle in St Martin's square with all my heart and soul. I had heard and been a part of the naked women's assiduous cries, 'Our children in Jerusalem!' These words had formed on my own lips and the subsequent confirmation given to Nicholas by an angel sent by Jesus to instruct him was all it took to seal my faith. I truly felt that I had been the recipient of a personal message from my Redeemer. I accepted that God, grown weary of the bloodshed and the slaughter committed in the name of the true cross, intended to show that the purity of a child's heart was the true requirement for a pilgrim if Christianity was to regain the Holy Sepulchre.

I had counted myself as one of the chosen by God to create this pilgrim's path to Jerusalem. I now knew, at the cost of countless tiny lives, that it was my own vanity and misbegotten faith that had brought about this terrible catastrophe known as the Children's Crusade. I prayed that the flogging ordered by the mad little monkey bishop would bring me the blessed release of death and allow me to suffer the eternal flames of hell I so completely deserved.

Father Pietro instructed the white monk to remove the gag. Interspersed with my cussing had been a rebuke that they hadn't even bothered to use a clean strip of cloth to gag me and this one had reeked of rotten fish. 'Will you walk or must we carry you?' Father Pietro asked sternly.

'Walk,' I replied through bruised lips. To be carried to the punishment for which I hungered was an insult to God. They had not carried Christ Jesus to the cross. He had not resisted the Roman soldiers but had only asked the heavenly Father why He had been forsaken. I had no reason to ask why I was being abandoned and led to my death. I already knew.

The black monk untied the rope about my ankles and the two of them helped me to my feet, though my hands remained bound behind my back. I was unable to stand by myself and the black man, who I now saw was a truly huge man, went down on his haunches and massaged my feet and ankles, my entire foot disappearing into his enormous hands. I soon felt the blood return and with the two monks again at my side I was able to hobble. Both were large men, but the black monk especially so – the top of my head reached no higher than his armpit. No doubt aware of the damage I had inflicted on the previous two brutes, Father Pietro was not prepared to take any chances with me and so had chosen the two biggest monks he could find in case there was need to subdue me. Now to my surprise, with Father Pietro out of earshot, the white monk said to me politely in German, 'Please do not try to run away, we have orders to beat you if you do, fräulein.'

'You are German?'

'My mother was German, I was raised in Genoa.'

'What will you do to me?' I asked, but received no answer except the single quiet admonishment, '*Stumm!*'

They led me up from the almost dark crypt into the main body of the church where my eyes slowly grew accustomed to the light, and it was here that I saw my feet. They had been painted jet black using an emulsion of soot, probably boot blacking, that had dried to a matt finish. Father Pietro was leaving nothing to chance and the people would have their evidence of the devil's cunning trick to hide the cloven hooves of a she-devil. The front of my peasant's shift was splattered with dried blood and I could feel the stiffness where it had dripped from the brute's ear onto the back of my neck and no doubt also my shift. My eyes, I felt sure, were red and swollen from weeping. I must have looked a frightful mess and every bit the demonic creature I was meant to be.

Gathered further up the centre aisle a group of priests, clerics and monks, perhaps thirty in all, waited. They stood in line, two by two, each carrying a wooden cross. Father Pietro walked ahead of us and came to stand at the head of the procession, signalling that we should fall in behind him. He started to move towards the open church doors, the priests behind us intoning a Gregorian chant, no doubt to give an appropriate church-sanctioned solemnity to the deliverance of Satan's child to the whipping post and waiting mob.

As we walked out of the semi-darkness into the blinding Italian sunlight I was forced to close my eyes, the sharp sting being too bright to endure. But from the sudden roar I knew that a large crowd had gathered. Then they began to chant, 'She Devil! She Devil! She Devil!', obviously previously primed for my arrival.

I kept catching flashes of the large crowd after each attempt to open my eyes until they eventually adjusted to the harsh light. I stood between the two monks on the topmost step of the church, looking down into the crowded square below. To my left sat the little monkey bishop, still in the giant's chair that had been moved onto the church steps for the occasion. He now wore his bishop's mitre and vestments, the mitre sufficiently high to conceal the carving of the angels and the cross behind him. Further to his left the priests, monks and clerics lined up in two rows and continued to chant. Father Pietro stood in his accustomed place beside the bishop's chair.

To my right a whipping frame that was used to punish thieves had been erected. We had seen these in the market squares of most of the towns we'd passed through. As though a silent warning to any miscreant, the timber was stained dark with crusted blood and always buzzing with swarms of flies. The frame, in the shape of an 'A', was fitted with a leather strap at each base of the 'A' and these were used for fastening the prisoner's spreadeagled legs at the ankles. The crossbar at the centre could be adjusted up or down to fit any body size and contained a rounded dent halfway along where the victim's chin rested. The apex held a second set of straps to bind the wrists, so that the felon's arms were tied high above the head exposing the naked back to the flailing whip.

For all my brave resolve to face my death calmly I began to tremble and turned to Father Pietro. 'Will you grant me extreme unction, Father?'

I asked loudly in Latin, as the chanting made speech difficult to hear. He did not reply but simply shook his head to deny me.

The tiny bishop reached out and tugged on the sleeve of Father Pietro's cassock and said something. Father Pietro cupped his ear, not hearing him because of the chanting. 'What, my Lord?' he shouted.

The bishop turned around to face the priests. 'Shut up!' he screeched furiously. 'Shut the hell up!' With the startled entourage silenced he turned back to his assistant. 'What does she want?' he demanded again.

'She wants a final anointing, my Lord!'

'Final anointing? The devil wants a final anointing? What new satanic trick is this? Tell her nay, nay, nay! I will not have it!'

'I have already done so, my Lord.'

'But not from me! You didn't tell her from me! The devil may trick a priest any day of the week including Sunday, but he can't trick a bishop. No, he can't, it's well-known he can't! Not even in a *month* of Sundays!' Then he glanced down at my feet. 'My goodness, would you look at that!' He clapped his hands gleefully. 'See, I told you, didn't I? The devil can't fool me! Not for a moment!' A tiny ringed finger pointed at my feet. 'Black as the hole into hell! Ha-ha! We have her now! Oh yes, yes!' He rubbed his palms together. 'No extreme unction! Lots of blood! Tell her! Tell her!' he screeched.

Father Pietro turned to me. 'No final anointing!' he growled.

'Now show the people her feet! Her black devil's feet!' the bishop cried excitedly. 'No, don't, I will do it myself.' With surprising alacrity he slipped over the edge of the giant chair, landed lightly on his feet and came to stand beside me. 'Lift your foot!' he commanded, pointing to my left foot.

'I will fall, my Lord,' I protested.

To my surprise he bent down and grasped my left ankle with both hands and yanked. I felt myself starting to lose my balance. While I cannot say I did so on purpose – but then, nor can I deny it – my foot shot out with some force so that the tiny bishop went flying backwards to lose his footing and tumble down twenty steps where he lay motionless.

Halfway down his mitre left his head and slid past him to land on the stone apron just four steps from the square.

The monk on my left attempted to stop me falling and grabbed at the neck and top of the sleeve of my shift. I felt it tear down the centre to the waist as I fell to my right and onto my bottom where I sat unable to rise, my hands still bound behind my back. My left breast was exposed where the top half of my shift had been torn away.

The black monk was the first to react to the bishop's tumble. 'Oh, my God!' I heard him cry, and then he leapt down the steps three at a time, the first to get to the tiny form of the inert bishop. An anguished shout rose up from the crowd and they surged forward. The monk, thinking they might crush the motionless bishop, scooped him up into his arms as if he was a small child and, turning quickly, ran back up the steps.

I cannot say if the bishop was dazed or unconscious when the blackamoor lifted him into his arms but now as he opened his eyes and looked directly into the huge black face he started to scream. 'Help! Help! The devil has come for me! Help!!!!' he cried in a terrified voice, and then he started to sob and beat at the black monk's chest, his tiny feet kicking out as he struggled wildly to be released, screaming. This was a very much alive and kicking ecclesiastical monkey with a cut eye and bleeding nose tightly held in Satan's arms. The monk, frightened by the bishop's desperate struggle to be free, showed the whites of his bulging eyes, which gave him even more the likeness of some imagined demon.

'Christ Jesus! Take him inside!' I heard Father Pietro shout. 'Quickly! Quickly!'

The black monk carried the kicking, scratching, screaming, sobbing bishop through the doors of the church with Father Pietro closely following, shouting at the hysterical bishop to be calm, though plainly close to hysteria himself. Then all the priests and monks and clerics, falling over each other in their haste, rushed after him into the church. That is, all except one, the white monk who spoke German and who had ripped my shift in an attempt to prevent me from falling. He was now on his knees beside me beseeching me to forgive him, the torn piece of my dress still clutched in his hand. 'Angel of mercy who carries the sign of our Lord Jesus Christ, forgive me for chastising thee!' he pleaded in German.

'You are forgiven!' I yelled impatiently. 'Get me to my feet!' Around me all hell seemed to have broken loose. In the square the crowd was running in every direction, beating at their legs, terrified screams of women and children coming from every corner of the square. Then I saw the ratcatcher emerge from the panicked crowd to appear at the foot of the church steps. He passed the bishop's fallen mitre and a moment later it was being trampled by dozens of rats. In fact, hundreds, nay thousands of rats were scurrying towards us from every possible direction. They bumped into the legs of the fleeing townsfolk, moving frantically, climbing and leaping over fallen bodies, biting at ankles, and all of them heading in a furious frenzy towards the church steps. It was the scene in the village all over again, although a hundred times worse, even worse than the bishop's palace.

The white monk now made as if to move from his knees, to do as I asked and pull me to my feet. 'No! Stay still! Do not move!' I countermanded urgently. He turned and looked and his eyes widened at the surprising sight of the rampaging rats. I could not resist the opportunity to assume the demeanour of the angel I was taken to be. 'Your bishop is the devil's child and the rats have come to claim him! God is very angry!' I announced in a stentorian voice, the way I thought an angel with an authority from heaven might remark to mortal flesh.

Reinhardt calmly climbed the steps up to the church, ignoring me, all the while blowing on what seemed a silent pipe. The rats now formed a seething mass behind him, some falling on the steps with others clambering over their furry bodies in their haste to get to the sound they could not resist. 'Still, sit very still,' I cautioned the terrified monk beside me. 'God will protect us from the devil's vermin, you are quite safe with me,' I said, relishing the role of angel, momentarily forgetting that I sat half-naked in the midday sunshine.

Reinhardt paused at the door of the church as he had done at the bishop's palace and allowed the rats to rush into the dark interior. I turned my back to the monk. 'Undo my wrists,' I commanded.

'Aye, blessed angel of God. What have we done to you!' he cried, his large and clumsy hands shaking as he grabbed frantically at the cords and untied them. 'The fish! The sign of the fish!' he kept exclaiming. The birthmark on my back had saved my life, and I knew this to be a sign to me that God did not wish me dead at the hands of the monkey bishop and that I might yet atone for my sins. Bright red welts showed where the rope had cut into the flesh and I was torn between massaging my wrists and hiding my naked breast by crossing my arms. The pain was better endured than the lack of modesty and I placed both my hands to cover my breast.

Moments later I heard the doors to the church bang and I looked over to see Reinhardt had closed them behind the rats. He quickly ran over to me. 'Are you harmed, Sylvia?' he asked, concerned, his hand placed on my naked shoulder.

'Nay,' I replied. 'My gown is torn, my bum is sore and I am half naked, nothing else.' I had long ago parted with my precious sheepskin coat; since coming down from the mountains it had been too hot to wear and I had exchanged it for food for the children.

Reinhardt looked down at the square where some of the townsfolk had stopped fleeing and were looking back, some even turning around to approach us. 'Do you think you can sing?' he asked suddenly.

'Sing? What, now?'

'Aye, we are not out of this pickle yet!' He pointed to the mayhem in the square. 'The townsfolk are still panicked but some have turned around and we do not know their mood. Our children are among them – we must get them up here or they may be harmed. Our singing will calm the crowd . . . I hope.' Without further ado he brought his flute to his lips and blew the opening notes to one of the hymns the children most liked to sing that began with a solo part from me. Somewhat tremulously I began the hymn and soon the children were running towards us to take up their customary positions on the steps, where they started to sing as I came to the end of the solo part.

The people, seeing the rats gone and the children's choir singing on the steps of the church, started to return in numbers. As we came to the end of the hymn there was sudden laughter among the crowd. We couldn't initially see what it was they laughed at, but soon the monkey bishop and his entourage of priests, monks and clerics hove into sight where they had emerged from the door of the sacristy at the side of the church. The black monk no longer held the bishop, who now lay prone on a church pew that was carried front and back by four monks. The entire entourage, heedless of anything in their way, were fleeing for their lives from the rats in the interior of the church.

'Go quickly,' I urged the German-speaking monk. 'Tell Father Pietro they will come to no harm if they return. Tell them that God forgives them.'

'They will not believe me!' he cried. 'What about the rats? The devil's rats?'

'Tell them I will ask, er . . . that is, the Angel of the Blessed Fish,' I corrected, inventing this title on the spur of the moment, 'will ask our heavenly Father to remove the scourge of rats.'

'And bring the birds,' Reinhardt whispered urgently.

'Oh, and as a sign of grace and love, the birds of the air will come to sing God's glorious praises. Now go, please. Hurry!' Then frowning, I added a further incentive: 'If they do not return I fear the rats may stay forever in the church!'

The German-speaking monk needed no further urging and ran down the steps into the crowd. I noticed that the bishop's mitre still lay near the bottom of the steps but seemed somewhat misshapen, flattened by the feet of a thousand marauding rats.

'He speaks German,' Reinhardt remarked.

'Aye, his mother was German,' I said absently. Then, 'There is always a small door at the back of the church. Can you remove the rats before the bishop returns?' I asked.

'And if he doesn't?'

'Then we'll invite the townsfolk into the church to see the miracle of the disappearing rats.'

'You seem very calm after your ordeal, Sylvia,' he laughed, plainly relieved.

'Aye, I thought I was going to die, but now I live and I feel certain I know what God wants us to do with the children. Better hurry, the crowd is returning.'

'No Jerusalem?' he asked hopefully.

'Hurry, ratcatcher!' I said, not wishing to, or having the time to, explain. Unthinking I turned to watch him enter the small side door to the main doors of the church, and in so doing I turned my back to the crowd that had begun to reassemble.

'The fish! On her back! Look, she carries the fish of Christ!' a man's voice cried. Then another called, 'A saint! An angel!' I turned to see the small crowd surging forward; some had already reached the flagstone apron where the bishop's mitre lay. Covering my left breast in the crook of my arm I held my right hand above my head. How or why I cannot say, but the voice of the abbot of the monastery of St Thomas, whose sermons I had so loved to mimic in my childhood, filled my head. '*Silentium!*' I thundered, the single Latin word resounding from my lips as if it had rushed up from deep within me and then, momentarily halted by my tongue, soon proved an irresistible force, brushing it aside to storm from my mouth.

To the crowd gathered at the base of the steps and now beginning to climb them, it may have seemed the voice of God coming from so slight a maid who had so recently sung a solo as a soprano. The forward line fell to their knees clasping their hands in prayer and almost immediately they were followed by those close behind.

I turned to the healing angel next to me. 'Maria, the chorus of hallelujahs, I will sing the *Tantum Ergo*, then the choir shall follow with the hallelujah canzona.' She nodded, and while the choir got ready I sang.

Then as I completed the hymn, 'HALLELUJAH!' the Silent Choir of God's Little Children responded, then 'Hallelujah, hallelujah, hallelujah . . . haaaa . . . leee . . . luuu . . . jah, hallelujah!' The rising words of praise used for the filling of the food baskets seemed to carry over, and even beyond, the church square as more and more people, some in the far distance, fell to their knees.

I signalled for the choir to bring the canzone to a close and with a great 'Haaaa . . . leee . . . luuu . . . jahhhhhhh!' they completed. I held up my hand again for silence. Then as the crowd watched, little Heinrich began to sing his glorious solo and I commenced to call the birds from the heavens.

God was with us on that glorious summer's day, for I don't believe I had ever seen such an avian response in all my previous bird beckoning. The sky started to fill with flocks of birds, and soon the church and the trees within the square and seemingly every available place they could perch were festooned with birds. I called the smaller birds to sit on the shoulders and heads of the children – the thrush, finch and robin to rest on their outstretched hands. The combined singing of the birds drowned out every other sound, so that the people simply looked upward and about, speechless and consumed in wonder.

It was then that we saw the bishop's procession returning but without the little monkey and being led by Father Pietro with the two monks, the black and the German speaker, on either side of him. I was surprised to see that the blackamoor carried my precious Father John stave and I saw it immediately as a sign from God that I would be safe.

The crowd had started to jeer at the priestly procession, the sound of their mocking only just audible amongst the birdsong. Reinhardt had not returned and I assumed he had taken the rats down to a nearby stream to drown them and so I would have to deal with the arrogant priest alone.

The procession, the priests, monks and clerics all holding their wooden crosses above their heads, reached the foot of the stairs and started to ascend, Father Pietro stopping briefly to pick up the bishop's mitre. The noise of the birds had now become almost unbearable and I sent out the signal for them to depart. A high-pitched crying-out and a sudden clap of my hands and they rose in a great cloud, the beating of their wings raising billows of dust in the square below.

Then something happened beyond my control and just as had occurred on the great rock in the little valley outside Koblenz to the captain of the bishop's troop. Two ravens came down to hover, screeching, their black wings flapping above the head of Father Pietro. Then one landed on each shoulder, to the horror of the two monks on either side of him. Father Pietro beat furiously at them but they rose up avoiding his blows and then attacked him again from the air, their claws briefly fastening to his neck as they pecked viciously at his head and face. He screamed and sank to his knees covering his head with his hands.

A sound I did not know I possessed rose in my throat and the two birds rose up and lifted into the air. The crowd watched in horror as they flew screeching upwards and landed on the church steeple where they seemed to be watching, waiting to be called again.

Then suddenly Reinhardt was at my side. 'Here, Sylvia, put this on,' he urged. 'It's all I could find in the church,' he explained hurriedly. He held the garment gathered up so that he could slip it over my head and allow my arms through the armholes. Then when it fell to cover me I realised that it was an alb, the white communion gown the priest would wear when conducting mass. Appliquéd on the front of the vestment was a large cross.

The two monks were helping a sobbing Father Pietro to his feet and I could see that he bled from the neck and on both sides of his face. The crowd was growing ugly, jeering and hooting at the clergy, some even spitting at their feet. The attack by the two birds of misfortune was interpreted by them as a clear sign that the priest was possessed by evil.

With both hands free at last, I held them up and once again called out in the abbot's voice, '*Silentium!*'

A hushed silence fell over the crowd. 'You have them in the palm of your hand, Sylvia,' Reinhardt, plainly awed, whispered.

'Yes, but what next?' I asked urgently.

'Call the monk who speaks German to come up and translate.' Reinhardt, as usual, was thinking clearly.

'Would the brother who speaks German please come up here to translate and the monk who carries my stave come also,' I called down in German, aware that not all clerics understood Latin other than the prayers they learned by rote.

The monk who spoke German turned to the black one and without seeking permission from the distraught Father Pietro they both ran up the steps. I reached out and took my stave and indicated that they should stand on either side of me as they had earlier done when I had been their prisoner, though I'm not sure that they were aware of the irony of the situation. 'What are your names?' I asked.

'I am Brother Bruno and this is Brother Aloysius.'

I turned to Brother Bruno. 'Ask Brother Aloysius how he came by my stave.'

The answer from the other monk seemed quite long. 'He says a child brought it to him, to the bishop's procession when they were, er . . . fleeing the rats. The child said he found it next to a dead German child and one of the other boys said it belonged to the angel and if the angel touched the child with the stave the dead boy would come alive again. The child said he was too frightened to return it himself.'

'Did the boy not also find a satchel?'

Brother Bruno translated and the other monk shook his head and said something in reply. 'He says no mention was made of a satchel.'

I thanked Brother Aloysius in the local tongue. 'Thank you' was one of the expressions I had inevitably picked up. Although I was saddened by the loss of my beautiful, though now much scratched, leather satchel, which I'd used to carry herbal unguents – though these had all but been used up – of the two Father John gifts the stave was by far the most precious. The thought of the lost satchel and the herbal remedies it contained brought my mind back to Father Pietro. The sharp pecks and scratches from the ravens could become infected and should be attended to as soon as possible. 'Is there a convent attached to the church?' I asked.

'Aye, we are Benedictine, they also.'

'Ask one of your monks to fetch the Sister Infirmaress to attend to Father Pietro. I greatly fear he is hurt.' Then, remembering my status as an angel, I added darkly, 'God is merciful, he is most fortunate not to have lost both his eyes.'

'Aye, thank you for saving him,' the monk said humbly. Then he called down for someone to fetch the sister from the convent that, presumably, was nearby.

'Please, Father Pietro, will you not come into the sanctuary of the church?' I called in Latin. Then turning to the monk, 'Tell them to bring Father Pietro and the other church officials into the church.'

'What about the rats?' he asked fearfully.

'Oh ye of little faith!' I admonished him. 'Did I not say that God would cleanse the church of rats and bring the birds to glorify him?'

'Aye, Angel of the Blessed Fish,' Brother Bruno replied, suitably chastened.

'No more of that blessed fish either! I am no angel and, as you see, quite mortal, and my name is Sylvia and that is sufficient burden.' I was suddenly tired of the pretence, thinking that it presented too many difficulties. I had trouble enough knowing all of Sylvia Honeyeater as it was, let alone taking on the demeanour of an angel. Two hours ago I was preparing for my certain death, content to go to hell everlasting for my sins. And now, surrounded by the Silent Choir of God's Little Children I had a sudden fierce desire to make sure they came to no further harm. My own emotions were difficult enough to contain, let alone the task of playing the role of an angel for which I was entirely unsuited. I had seen enough of Nicholas and the corruption that omnipotence brought, and even in the short time I had preached in his name I had felt the seduction of religious power. Better to stay with my two boot-blackened feet planted firmly on the ground. As Reinhardt had noted, we were not yet out of this pickle.

The monk translated the invitation to enter the church. Several of them called back in the local tongue, which brought a howl of laughter from the crowd. Brother Bruno grinned. 'They ask about the rats,' he explained. Then without pausing he started to speak, waving his arms and sounding quite liturgical. I who could speak four languages was becoming frustrated at not knowing this one. If I could have this monk by my side but a month I knew I would speak it tolerably well.

Brother Bruno now translated to me what he had said. 'Our heavenly Father has cleansed the church and it is now, as ever, consecrated to the worship of the Virgin and Christ Jesus! You may enter full-knowing that the hand of the precious Saviour guards you.' He was clearly pleased to be on my side and, perhaps a little self-importantly, took the liberty of adding some priestly rhetoric to the proceedings. One of the priests shouted something in the local language and Brother Bruno turned to me and shrugged. 'They want me to go and take a look inside,' he said.

'Trusting lot, aren't you?' I said tartly, feeling good about being back to myself and no longer a celestial being. 'Go then, take Brother Aloysius with you.'

The two monks took the still-bleeding Father Pietro by the arm and led him up the steps. The children stood to one side of the doors while Reinhardt and I stood on the other, thus to allow the bishop's former entourage to pass through into the church unimpeded.

'What do I say about the ravens?' I whispered to Reinhardt.

'Nought. Let it seem the will of God.'

'Ratcatcher, that's blasphemy!' I hissed.

'Are you sure it isn't?'

'Isn't what?'

'The will of God.'

Father Pietro had almost reached us and now stopped and turned towards me, shrugging free of the arms of the two monks. Then to my surprise he sank to his knees, his hands held in an attitude of prayer. 'Forgive me for my eyes were blinded by Satan,' he said, turning his bloodied face up at me with a pleading expression.

No longer the Angel of the Blessed Fish, I was unsure what to do. The only priest who had ever knelt in front of me was Father Paulus when he had first witnessed the blood on the virgin's rose. That had not been meant as obeisance to me, but to the blood-tinted petals of the pure white blossom. I did not consider Brother Dominic's prostration, since that was done while my back was turned. I sank to my knees in front of the supplicating priest. 'Nay, Father, it is not for me to forgive you. I am but a poor sinner much in need of confession.'

If he heard my protest he did not react to it, instead he closed his eyes and recited the *Actus Spei*: 'O Lord God, through Thy grace I hope to obtain remission of all my sins, and after this life eternal happiness, for Thou hast promised, who art all-powerful, faithful, kind and merciful. In this hope I stand to live and die. Amen.'

There seemed no reply I could safely make. So I sought quickly for a prayer of my own to recite so that I might at least show some initiative. The *Actus Caritatis* seemed the only one that might be appropriate: 'O my God! I love Thee above all things, with my whole heart and soul, because Thou art all-good and worthy of all love. I love my neighbour as myself for the love of Thee. I forgive all who have injured me, and ask pardon of all whom I have injured. Amen.'

'Amen,' I heard Reinhardt say beside me. Later he would laugh and say that of the two combative prayers mine had won.

I recall saying to him, 'Oo-ah, Ratcatcher! God is listening to all of this and some of the blasphemous things you say are written down in the Book of Life and you're going to be in *big* trouble when you get to heaven!'

He had sighed and looked a little woebegone and then said quietly, 'I don't think they accommodate my sort in heaven, Sylvia.'

After I completed my prayer, Father Pietro stood. 'If you wish to make confession we can do it now,' he said, indicating the church doors with a nod of his head.

'Father, you must attend to your face and neck. Any of the other priests may hear my confession.'

He shook his head. 'I would consider it a privilege, Sylvia. I have seen that you are truly blessed by our Lord.'

During the months on the road I had grown shameless and an expert at mendicancy, with all my senses tuned to seize any weakening of resolve. The priest's sudden softening towards us provided me with an ideal opportunity. 'Father, my children have not eaten and are hungry. We had intended to sing again for the townsfolk in the hope that they might provide a little sustenance.' I referred to them as *my* children so as to wring, to the very last drop, the newfound respect he seemed to possess for me. 'We are God's little children and do not beg,' I added, hoping he wouldn't see through this beggarly ploy.

It was at this moment that the Sister Infirmaress arrived and seeing his bleeding face and neck started tut-tutting, wincing and crying out her sympathy. 'Wait, sister, can't you see I am busy!' he remonstrated, brushing her aside. The newfound charity he had evinced but a moment before was a very thin crust and underneath it the same hard-nosed bishop's assistant lurked. For all his suddenly professed piety, this was a churlish man who must be carefully handled.

'Nay, Father, please enter the church where the good sister may attend to you.' I pointed to the crowd. 'They grow restless. We will sing for them and when you are ready perhaps you will come out again and thank them for coming and ask them if they will provide a little food for the choir?'

I had returned the initiative to him, allowing him on behalf of the Church to regain control of a crowd that clearly appeared to have lost respect for their local bishop and his churchmen. I could see that he quickly grasped this opportunity to reassert the Church's authority and be seen to make amends for the original purpose of the gathering.

'In thee I see a future saint, Sylvia,' he said clumsily. I could see he was pleased with the notion of regaining the authority, the advantages of my suggestion immediately clear. He indicated my priest's vestment. 'We will arrange for suitable raiment and perhaps you would like to wash at the convent?'

I looked down at my blackened feet and grinned. 'Perhaps I shall be named Saint Bootblack?' I said, thinking how frightful my general appearance must be and how far from the vision of a saintly personage I would seem. But judging from his slightly bemused expression my irony was lost on him. So I added quickly, 'Yes, thank you, Father, I would very much like to bathe and wash my hair.'

He turned to the nun beside him. 'See to it,' he instructed in Latin.

The nun looked confused and I realised, as he should have done, that she did not understand Latin other than the prayer rote and had not been following our conversation.

'She does not understand Latin, Father,' I said.

'Stupid woman!' he exclaimed, then spoke to her in the local tongue and I saw the nun nod. He must also then have instructed her to attend to his wounds because they both turned and entered the church.

'Father, if we may have Brother Bruno to translate?' I called after him and saw him nod.

'We will need to entertain the crowd if we are to eat today,' I said to Reinhardt.

'They have had more entertainment than they will receive in a lifetime, Sylvia. They will speak forever after of the Miracle of the Rats, then the birds, then God's wrath . . . er, the incident with the ravens and the priest. We have sung to them gloriously, what else?'

'The dogs? The trick with the choir?'

'Oh my God! I had forgotten them! They are all assembled beyond the square with their noses upon their paws. It is hot – they will be much in need of water.'

'Will they hear your pipe?' I asked.

'Aye.'

'And come?'

He looked surprised. 'They cannot resist the pipe.'

I nodded, confident that with the dog trick we could leave the crowd in a merry mood, enough so that they would be happy to feed us, though Reinhardt seemed confident that they would do almost anything we asked of them. 'First let us talk to these people,' I said.

At that moment Brother Bruno arrived and looked pleased to be with me again. I was surprised to see Brother Aloysius was at his side. I was later to learn that they were seldom separated and that Brother Bruno, who was four years older than the black monk, when they'd both been children in Genoa had rescued Brother Aloysius from a mob of boys who had attacked the dark-skinned child calling him an infidel and a Saracen. They were in the process of kicking him to death when Brother Bruno intervened, in fact, risking his own life. 'We are truly brothers in God's name and even as if we were born as kin,' he'd told me, smiling.

'Will you translate for us, please?' I asked him. 'Tell them we come in the name of God and will soon be gone. That we are the last of the Children's Crusade and after we have departed we wish them peace and happiness.'

Brother Bruno took a step forward and Brother Aloysius did the same, the two huge monks making an imposing sight. Brother Bruno held up his hand and called for silence from the crowd. But they had no sooner been hushed than a short fat man stepped forward and appeared to be asking him something in a loud voice. Brother Bruno turned to me and asked querulously, 'Dogs? He asks if you can bring the dogs back to life?'

'Aye, in God's name. But I will need twenty pails of water placed around the steps.'

He looked at me as if he didn't understand. 'Twenty pails of water?'

'Aye.'

He translated and several of the townspeople broke away, presumably to do as he'd asked.

'Shall we sing while we wait?' I asked Reinhardt.

'No more hymns, eh?' he said. 'The mood grows too sombre.' Taking up his flute he blew the first few notes of a folksong the children all loved. It was a most merry little tune and while the people wouldn't have understood the words it was intended as a jig and soon the people in the square were dancing. Reinhardt had once again correctly guessed their mood. We played two more songs until the pails of water were all positioned below the steps.

There was palpable tension in the air as I stepped from the ranks of the choir. Then, with my arms lifted and my head raised heavenward the crowd fell silent. I called out in Latin for the dogs to return. Beside me Reinhardt blew his special silent signal. Moments later there came a startled murmur from the crowd as several packs of dogs rushed barking into the square and made directly for the church steps where they lapped frantically at the water in the pails, three or four dogs to each pail. Then, as each dog or bitch had drunk sufficient from the pails, they moved about the mob quite peaceably looking for their owners.

I had not noticed that Father Pietro had now come out of the church and stood close. I felt sure he would not have seen or known about the dogs but had only seen them lapping from the pails. I knew somehow, just by looking at him, that he had undergone some sort of epiphany. 'I am deeply ashamed, Sylvia. You who have nothing think to provide water for our scavenging dogs while we, who have everything, refuse to provide your dying children with a final anointing. May the heavenly Father have mercy on us for we have sinned most terribly.'

I knew at once that I had seen a special moment in a man's life, that moment when God restores his faith. But I wasn't a priest and wasn't sure whether I should console him for his wicked past or congratulate him on his new redemption. 'Father, what has been done cannot be undone except by the grace of God.' It was all I could think to say.

'We will begin our repentance at once. I will send every priest from the monastery to find your dying children and we will give them extreme unction.'

His sudden and unexpected repentance and desire to make amends had quite the opposite effect on me to the subservient gratitude he might have expected. If I had spent my allotment of tears for one lifetime I had not used up my anger. I suddenly found myself consumed by a terrible fury and a bitterness that rose up in me and which I felt I could not contain a moment longer. My sensibility told me to bide my tongue, that my first duty was to the living, to finding food for our children. The thought of our beautiful children, their tiny broken bodies reduced to skin and bone, their arms and legs thin as twigs, covered in suppurating sores, thrown into a common pit and covered with quicklime without a prayer was too much to contain a moment longer. 'May God forgive me!' I shouted, then pointed to a small heap of rags that lay against the wall near the steps of the church. 'When your two brutes dragged me away this morning that precious child who belongs to God wished only to hear a few final words of comfort before passing from this earth. Now he is dead! He died alone under a blazing sun with no one to give him even a sip of water. Now he will be discarded like a lump of shit, thrown into a lime pit in unconsecrated ground. You and your fellow priests will answer for this on the final Day of Judgement! May your souls rot in hell!'

Father Pietro fell to his knees. 'Please, please, you must forgive us!' he begged.

I could feel the devil tugging further at my temper. The mob had never seen a priest go down on his knees in obeisance to a simple peasant maid. Or perhaps they thought I was an angel and he must bow down to me, and so they did the same, hearing only the Latin tones, the speech of heaven, contained in my furious voice. 'We will depart this vile place as hungry as we entered, but we shall not beg for your food, you can stick your charity up your arse!' To speak thus to a priest as a peasant might to his goatherd was nigh blasphemy, but I no longer cared. If my temper landed me in hell I knew I'd have the satisfaction of his company there and with him all the priests and monks and clerics and ugly little monkey bishops who had scorned God's children. I also knew I would continue there to scream my anger at these hypocritical sons of bitches, my voice rising above the moans and cries of the condemned and adding to the roaring flames of hell.

Father Pietro now lay prostrated on the flagstones, weeping like a child, with Brothers Bruno and Aloysius bending over him not knowing what to do. I must say he was making a proper job of his contrition but I remained too angry to care. 'Take the priest into the church, let him weep in front of the Virgin – maybe She will forgive him!' I said scornfully in German to Brother Bruno.

To my surprise he straightened up and turned to the crowd. 'Who among you will feed a hungry child?' he called out.

A hundred hands shot into the air and a roar of 'Ayes' followed. The townsfolk surged towards the steps beckoning our children to come to them. Reinhardt, as usual, took control. 'Go, eat!' The children, who throughout had not spoken a word except to sing, now gave a joyful shout. 'We will all meet here at Evensong, you may go,' he said dismissing them. The children could not contain their joy as they ran down the steps knowing that on this day their bellies would be satisfied.

The two monks lifted the sobbing Father Pietro and led him into the church. Reinhardt shook his head. 'Phew! At least our children will eat. Then we must be gone, Sylvia. I fear we have worn out our welcome.' He grinned. 'Every word a vituperative gem, well done!' He saw the sudden tears well in my eyes. 'No, don't cry – if I live a hundred years I will not hear a more justified and better chastisement.'

'What will they do to us?' I asked in a small voice, my anger replaced with concern.

But as if in reply Sister Infirmaress appeared, and Brother Bruno, returned from the church, translated. 'Come, we will bathe and feed you. May I call you Sylvia?' she asked kindly.

I turned to Reinhardt. 'What will you do?'

He laughed. 'Go, Sylvia, there are a hundred folk here who will feed me, they think me an angel's consort.'

'Sire, we would be honoured if you would take sustenance with us at the monastery,' Brother Bruno said.

The ratcatcher touched me on the arm. 'I think we're going to be all right,' he said.

And to my surprise we were. The nuns allowed me to bathe and I scrubbed until I felt as though I had removed the top layer of my skin, and when I sat in the sun to dry my hair the sisters came out to marvel at the colour. When I was given a brush to pull through the tangles my hair proved thin and came out in tufts and had quite lost its shine and vigour, yet they collected it as a keepsake, each a small handful as if it was a treasure to be coveted. I recalled the strong golden strands that had fallen so carelessly to the wet floor when Sister Angelica had gleefully hacked it off at the convent of Disibodenberg.

My stomach had grown unaccustomed to less than a handful of food per day and often not even this much, and despite the tut-tutting and clucking of the kitchen sister, I was able to eat only the smallest portion of the bread and fish she placed on my wooden platter. The wine I needed to water down considerably, yet it still made my poor head spin.

They clothed me in a nun's habit but without the wimple. My boots had been brought over from the church but they were pronounced unrepairable and I was given a new pair. How elegant and safe I felt in a new petticoat and my black linen habit and stout ankle boots with new wooden soles that would surely see us to Jerusalem, though I knew in my heart and soul that this destination was no longer possible unless a miracle should happen. Even then it would take a lot of persuasion to restore my faith in miracles or in messages from angels. I possessed but one desire and this was to save the lives of the Silent Choir of God's Little Children. I told myself I would keep my faith with Nicholas and go to meet him in Genoa, but that these children were no longer to be regarded as his responsibility – if ever he had thought they were. I was no longer willing to trust in the divinely received angel's message that I had come to realise I had helped to instigate with the use of Frau Sarah's magic mushrooms. If but one child had died as a result of his vision, it would have been one too many. But a thousand precious little souls had perished in our wake. As long as God permitted me to live, I knew I could not do the penance required to account for my role in this terrible disaster. I no longer believed that the blessed boy prophet could take us safely to the Holy Land.

Moreover, I knew that we must somehow seek to break the sacred *vota*, that is, our children must be released from the oath we had taken with Father Hermann to undertake a crusade to the Holy Land. I might have lost my faith in miracles but I knew that if we could achieve this end it would only be by a miracle, for the Pope in Rome was the only person in all of Christendom who could rescind the oath we had taken in the name of God. Brother Dominic had once said that the Pope was God's representative on earth but it was pointless trying to see him as he spoke only to his Master.

But if His Holiness was an ultimate challenge, I faced a more immediate one. I knew that I must eat humble pie and apologise to Father Pietro for my wicked temper and the way I had spoken to him. If he had had no cause to put me to the whipping post on the first occasion, on this one he had every right to do so. I could not believe that I had willingly used such foul language and knew that it was the devil that lurked within me that had brought it about. I had never in my entire life openly used such words, though it would be untrue to claim that I had not tested them often in my mind or said them in my thoughts. Sister Angelica and the abbess at the convent of Disibodenberg had been frequent but unknowing recipients. To use them openly and with malice at any time was deeply sinful. To use them in Latin against a priest was beyond any possible redemption. I knew that I must confess, beg God for forgiveness and with a glad heart accept any penance demanded of me. But first I must undergo the most difficult task of all. I must face this priest and apologise. Deep within me a small voice cried out that I had meant every word I'd said and given the same provocation would say them again. But I also knew that I must take the responsibility for my profanity and my wilful anger.

While he had prostrated himself in front of me, momentarily overcome by remorse, I wasn't so foolish that I did not know Father Pietro was a man and a priest, the bishop in everything but in name. He was arrogant and powerful and his epiphany on the steps of the church was likely to prove a temporary relapse into a piety of some distant youthful past. After I had bathed, received a change of raiment and eaten, I had been granted an interview with the abbess, Sophia of Piemonte, an educated woman who spoke Latin, and during our talk I had asked that she intercede and find out if I might see Father Pietro.

'He is, at his kindest, still a difficult man, Sylvia,' she sighed. 'When

I have need to petition the bishop, we all say a special prayer that God might grant Father Pietro an even temper on the day.' Then she added with a grin, 'I will send Sister Infirmaress and use the excuse that she has come to dress his wounds. She has no fear of anyone except perhaps the Pope and God, though I doubt even the former.'

How different this Abbess Sophia of Piemonte to the bitch . . . oops! I mean, of course, the abbess at the convent at Disibodenberg.

Sister Infirmaress returned shaking her head. 'He is not himself, Mother Superior. I think those ravens, for all the misfortune they bring a soul, seem to have pecked some courtesy into his stubborn head. He will see Sylvia with pleasure and at her convenience.'

'My goodness, he is most certainly sick!' the abbess exclaimed, first having politely translated the nun's remarks.

'Thank you, I will go immediately,' I said.

I was about to take my leave when the abbess said, pointing to my nun's habit, 'Sylvia, the nuns who brought you one of our gowns spoke of the sign of the fish, the sign of our precious Saviour on your back. Do you think? I mean, would it be possible to see it?'

'It is only a birthmark, Mother Superior.' I turned my back and dropped the top of the robe from my shoulders and back and heard the abbess gasp.

'Nay, Sylvia, it is more, much more. Then the Miracle of the Rats and the Birds is true, also the ravens!'

I adjusted the gown and turned to find her on her knees with her hands clasped in prayer. 'Please, please, I am just a humble maid. Do not think any more of me!' I cried. I had long since given up explaining the matter of the rats and the birds. The more I explained, the more doubtful people thought the explanation. People want miracles and when they are denied they become very upset. Just as the Abbess Sophia, despite being told the fish was a birthmark, would not accept this explanation, she would also not have accepted the explanation for the so-called miracles. Although, I confess, I had no idea why the ravens attacked Father Pietro and the troop captain of the Bishop of Koblenz.

She rose to her feet. 'We are truly blessed to have you with us, Sylvia,' she said, and I could see tears in her eyes as she smiled at me. 'I promise you, no pilgrim child will henceforth pass through this way without comfort and succour.' I did not tell her that we were the last, nor point out, as I had in no uncertain terms to Father Pietro, that charity should be given without thought of motive or gain, especially to hungry and dying children. *Don't get bitter, Sylvia,* I reproached myself.

Father Pietro welcomed me with a smile. He seemed in demeanour quite a different man from the scowling priest of only this morning, and thanked me profusely for what I'd done for him and the parish of Piacenza. I attempted to apologise for my remarks and in particular for my language. Seemingly completely mollified he said, 'We don't know what Christ said to the moneylenders when he drove them from the temple, but I feel sure he did not spare the whip the tongue becomes when anger is well justified.'

'It is most forgiving and gracious of you, Father,' I said humbly, unable to believe that this was the same priest who had first read out the indictment of the German children and the bishop's refusal to grant them a final anointing. 'How is His Lordship, the bishop?' I now asked tentatively.

'He has sprained his wrist, a few scratches and bruises, it is nothing,' Father Pietro said dismissively. He tapped his cheek and then his neck, indicating the raven pecks. 'Sometimes things happen to shake us from our lethargy and to restore our faith in God,' he said humbly. He cleared his throat. 'Sylvia, we cannot make amends for what has happened but I have done all I may to improve the situation. Our priest, clerics and monks are out in the town seeking any sick child from your pilgrimage. They will give those who are still alive the final anointing and those, alas, who are dead we will bury in consecrated ground. The church will create a special place, it shall be named "The Field of Forever Dreaming" and it will be where God's little children may lie and each shall be blessed with a stone cross. Henceforth, all the children who die in Piacenza will be buried with these precious pilgrims to the Holy Land, so they are forever honoured.'

'Thank you, Father, I am overwhelmed,' I said, for I truly was and also surprised at his poetical turn of phrase in naming the new children's cemetery.

'Will you and the children and the piper fellow stay a while in Piacenza so that we may restore their health and your own? Sister Infirmaress informs me that you are in need of rest and care, and the children are skin and bone and, she says, riddled with lice and many carry open sores.'

'It has been a bitter journey, but we are much better provided for since we became the Silent Choir of God's Little Children. Alas, Father, we thank you most graciously, but must be in Genoa in five days. We cannot tarry here even another day.'

He looked at me doubtfully, then asked, 'Hence you depart from Genoa to cross over the sea to the lands of the Saracens and some day reach the Holy Land?' He paused, seeming to be searching for the right words. 'I beg you, Sylvia, think carefully about this. We have seen your faith and your strength and all things are possible when we act with God's purpose, but you should pray most assiduously for further guidance.' I could see that his nature was now completely turned to compassion and that he was most concerned for our welfare.

'Nay, Father, we go to Genoa so that I might urge Nicholas of Cologne to abandon this Children's Crusade . . . this pilgrimage has seen enough death.'

He seemed hugely relieved to hear me say this. 'Can we not send a messenger? Five days is yet a goodly distance to travel and your children will suffer further.'

'Father, they are hard-set upon this destination. But if we might obtain a missive from the bishop that carries our safe passage and asks for the assistance of the church in each town we pass through, we would suffer little.' I smiled. 'We will sing for our supper and give good value,' I promised.

'Aye, you have the voice of an angel and the children are as cherubim. I vouch there are none as good in hymns of praise to our Lord from here to Rome. The letter shall be yours.'

'But has His Lordship not sprained his wrist?' I asked, remembering.

Father Pietro laughed. 'The only scripting His Lordship does is press his ring seal upon the wax and I have a spare ring for this purpose.' He looked at me and smiled. 'I have a suggestion.' Without waiting for me to ask what this might be, he continued. 'Will it not greatly help you with the local tongue if Brother Bruno goes with you and with him Brother Aloysius, for they are never parted and are as two peas in a pod. Both are ordained priests. What think you, Sylvia?'

I thanked him warmly. 'I would cherish the opportunity to learn to speak your language,' I said.

He looked at me doubtfully. 'In five days?'

'The beginnings. I will learn more on the way to Rome.'

'Rome? You go to Rome?'

'Aye, to have an audience with His Holiness, Father.'

He laughed, truly amused. 'Nay, Sylvia, you do not understand. You would more easily reach Jerusalem, or have the true cross returned to you by the infidel, than be granted an audience with the Pope.'

'But only he can rescind our sacred vows. We *must* see him!' I cried. 'Can the bishop give us a supplicating letter to His Holiness?'

Father Pietro sighed. 'Aye, but it is a waste of parchment, ink and wax, my child.'

'I am greatly in your debt, Father. I wish only that I could find a way to thank you.'

He hesitated, then said, 'There is one thing.'

'Aye, what is it, Father?'

'The curse.'

'Curse, Father?'

'Ravens, the curse of the ravens. Will you lift it?' His eyes left mine and looked down into his lap a little shamefully, then in a low voice he said, 'Please?'

I was glad that his eyes were downcast so they did not witness my astonishment. Here was a man of God, an educated priest and scribe, the bishop's assistant and likely some day to be a bishop himself, and he believed in witchcraft and in this peasant superstition of crows, ravens and jackdaws being the harbingers of misfortune. Hoping that he did not realise my surprise I knew that he had just presented me with an ideal opportunity to leave Piacenza without being seen to be beholden to the Church.

I had sworn to myself that I would not beg again, even if my life should depend on it. That our children would never again have to go onto their knees and, clutching the thick ankles of a peasant woman, kiss her dirty feet while pleading for a scrap of bread, only to be kicked aside in contempt, the crust denied with an impatient expletive. Then there was also the matter of learning the Italian tongue, a task that would take more than five days with Brother Bruno at my side. I would need some fluency if we were to survive in this heartless land.

'We will need to go outside where we may see the sky,' I said.

'Not in the square! Folk will see us,' he said quickly.

I smiled inwardly. *Ever the man, ever the priest.* 'Take me to the Field of Forever Dreaming, Father.' Our eyes met and I forced myself to have the boldness to hold his gaze. 'We will lift the curse in that soon-to-be consecrated place,' I said as seriously as I might.

We left the church and Father Pietro led me up a rise behind the convent, not quite a hill and certainly not a field but open woodland of scattered oak and elm, the summer grass beneath the trees still surprisingly green in the hot August sun. As a place to bury our children I liked it exceedingly, though I was not so foolish as not to guess that he had led me to the nearest open land adjacent to the church and had, in fact, named the place of child burials before deciding where it might be located.

'It is important that we choose this as the last place of rest for our children. This Field of Forever Dreaming must never be changed as I will cause it to be a sanctuary for birds and I will tell them it is consecrated ground chosen by God.' I turned to Father Pietro. 'Will you swear to commit this place to God's little children?'

'I swear to God I shall keep this promise, Sylvia.'

'Then I will call the birds to be witness to the lifting of the curse of the raven.' As I began to call I saw the look of alarm on his face.

'No ravens!'

'Aye, I must. They will be present with all the other birds so that they know I have, with God's help, lifted this disharmony from your soul.'

I resumed calling and already the birds had started to land, settling in the trees around us. When a host had gathered I beckoned the ravens, not knowing how many to expect. But to my surprise only two arrived and I wondered if they were the same pair who had earlier attacked the priest. I called them to sit upon my shoulders.

'Come closer, Father, stand directly in front of me.'

'What if they attack me again?' he cried, very frightened.

'God sees into your heart, Father. If there is no evil there, how may the birds attack you?'

'Are you sure?'

I stroked each of the ravens in turn and they tilted their heads and looked at the priest curiously. 'See, they bear you no malice,' I said. He now stood directly in front of me and I said, 'Touch each lightly on the head, Father.' His hand shook as he reached forward. The raven cocked its head and Father Pietro winced and quickly withdrew his hand. 'Nay, Father, they are most friendly.'

'Sylvia, I am sore afraid.'

All about us the birds were singing. 'See, all the birds laugh at you, Father.'

He tried a second time, this time with the second raven, but it too cocked its head. Ravens are ever curious birds. This time the priest jumped back frightened.

I had teased him enough. 'I will sing this matter to the birds, Father, they grow impatient to be gone. Their nestlings are almost grown by this time in summer and they have to work very hard at gleaning to feed them.'

I began to sing.

To all the birds of heaven
Know that the curse is spent,
Scattered to the four winds
On the wings of ravens sent!

Field of Forever Dreaming,
Here precious children lie.
If you listen in the stillness
You'll know they did not die.

Theirs is the New Jerusalem
Where children know no sin,
Their voices raised in glory
As God's precious cherubim.

We pray to our Lord in heaven
To make your suffering cease.
Small pilgrim, gone to paradise,
May your soul rest now in peace.

Hark! Hear you children singing?
Can you see their faces grave?
In the Field of Forever Dreaming
Where the oak and elm give shade.

When I completed singing the birds rose up in a great fluttering and with them the two crows. I looked to see that Father Pietro was on his knees and that tears ran down his cheeks.

At first I thought I must still be within the ambience of the little hymn I'd composed, that I had been caught up in the spell of this quiet and lovely place. But when he rose from his knees I became certain that what I was looking at was no illusion: there was no mark to be seen on his countenance, nor a single raven's peck upon his neck.

I contained my surprise and remained silent, the coming of the avenging ravens in Koblenz and now here in Piacenza was something I couldn't explain with my bird calling. God works in mysterious ways His wonders to perform and I had been grateful for His timely intervention and had thanked Him in my prayers. Besides, I'd just about had my fill of miracles. *Let him find out for himself. When he does, I feel sure there will be some advantage in it for us*, I decided.

Father Pietro was entirely overcome when he discovered the little miracle to his countenance and so was splendidly softened up for my proposition. In no time at all Brother Bruno and Brother Aloysius were granted permission to accompany us to Rome on a pilgrimage. With them they carried a missive to the priests we would meet on the way to give a last anointing to any pilgrim child in their town and to make sure we were fed and cared for. In Reinhardt's satchel was another to His Holiness, though Father Pietro had again stressed that there were delegates to the throne of St Peter who waited months to see the Holy Father and not to expect a veritable miracle.

In my head I could hear Master Israel's voice: '*If you are powerful, take a drum and beat it and the people will come to march behind you. But if you are weak, make music and the powerful will come to sit at your feet.*' It had been intended as a metaphor for the power of persuasion, but it could also be taken literally. I felt sure that the combined talents of Reinhardt and me could turn the Silent Choir of God's Little Children into a unique instrument of sacred music that would capture the attention of the Church and take us all the way to the throne of St Peter. Furthermore, if the Holy Father had been touched by the story of Francis of Assisi preaching to the birds, as I had been told he was, then we also had an avian trick or two up our sleeve. If we proved good enough, then the Holy Father would release us from our crusader's oath but would also want to keep us for his divine service and then our children would be safe forever.

Brother Dominic had once told me, 'Few of the Princes of the Church care much for God's laws, but all are careful to possess all the trappings of faith. The ceremony, not the conviction, that is what is important to them.' We would become trappings and a part of the ceremony. Reinhardt particularly liked the idea of trappings. 'Oh, we shall look beautiful, Sylvia. I shall design everything and then a gown for you and a uniform for me that will make the cardinals swoon with envy!'

Of the journey to Genoa there is little that is new to say, other than we travelled without a care, with sufficient to eat. Our singing, which seemed to get better and better as our shrunken stomachs began to accept more food, was marvelled at. People would say they had never heard voices so pure and sacred singing so beautiful. But I knew we could still improve and, by the time we reached Rome, be wondrously good.

Brother Bruno turned out to be a good and patient language teacher and in the five days on the road I had grasped the fundamentals of the local grammar, and with its many Latin roots I knew I would speak it tolerably well by the time we reached Rome.

The children adored Brother Aloysius who, by the way, possessed a beautiful baritone voice, and Reinhardt worked with him on the road to integrate him into the choir and also to give him a solo part. He became a deep contrast to the high soprano voices of the children and as a voice at the opposite end to my own.

Alas, Brother Bruno was tone-deaf, but made up for this by exhorting the crowd to be generous and was a born manager and a fusspot. The huge bulk and merry natures of the two surrogate brothers and brothers in Christ made for safe and joyful company.

However, our greatest pride, for which we daily gave thanks to our precious Saviour, was that all fifty-six children had survived the terrible journey from Cologne. If they looked like ragged little barefoot beggars, their sores were beginning to heal in response to regular food and an unguent made from calendula, a flowering plant from the marigold family. The Abbess Sophia of Piemonte had Sister Infirmaress prepare this for us. The good sister, known as 'the fearless one', was almost as good as Frau Sarah, and when she'd first seen Father Pietro's unblemished face she'd clapped and then clasped her hands together and cried out, 'Glory be to God! It must be the St John's wort I added to the mixture!'

I had been dreading the prospect of meeting up with Nicholas again and although I knew he no longer had any divine power to influence me, I also knew he had come to the end of his journey. Like King Canute, who had been persuaded by his sycophantic subjects that he could stem the tide, I knew in my deepest being that the sea would not still to the touch of Nicholas's feet. He had always been certain that this was to be the supreme gift to him from the angel, his own personal miracle. In the days before we'd parted he would increasingly proclaim, 'When I tread upon the sea to make a shining path, then all of Christendom will witness that I have become a living saint!' Without Father Paulus to pull him into line his vaingloriousness knew no bounds.

I simply couldn't imagine what might happen to him when he stepped into the harbour and sank up to his neck, as I felt certain he would. I had no idea if he could swim, but as he was born an urchin on the banks of the Rhine, I supposed he could.

We arrived in Genoa on the 25th of August in the year 1212 and made straight for the harbour. What a chaotic scene it proved to be, for near three thousand children had arrived and there was much singing and blaring of discordant trumpets and waving of ragged banners. The starving children clung to the ragged groups they'd formed and it was clear a great many of them had reached the end of their endurance and lay forlorn and abandoned on the dockside.

Many children called out to me. 'Sylvia! You have come. You have not forsaken us!' or 'Will you sing when the glorious path across the sea is shown to us?' or 'We are safe now that you and the piper are among us!' I felt a great lump in my throat and it was difficult not to cry out in despair at their misery and at the hope they still clung to. We had decided to sing, with Reinhardt and the two monks leading at the front.

But now I cried out that we must not, the energy of our own ragged urchins would be too obvious among the lethargic and broken children in our midst. We would be flaunting our good fortune.

Yet for all this, these child pilgrims still believed. My heart near broke when I thought how they might become when they saw no miracle, when the remorseless waves continued to lap onto the harbour front. They had put all their trust in Nicholas and had endured the impossible journey. The three thousand or so starvelings that remained still carried a burning faith for Jesus and the cross and they believed that they would reach Jerusalem to regain the Holy Sepulchre. What would happen when their faith was finally plundered, stolen forever from them? Would they turn on Nicholas? Many were in such a parlous state that I knew they would simply lie down and die; having abandoned all hope they would close their weary eyes and not have the strength or will to open them again.

Father Pietro had obtained (or so he said) permission from the monkey bishop to instruct the two monks in the final anointing and had carefully written down the procedure so they might learn it on the way to Genoa. I did not tell him that, sadly, I knew every word and could recite them in my sleep. When I wasn't taking language lessons from Brother Bruno I would rehearse them both. They would also help the parish priest to give the last sacrament to those children we found dying in the towns on the way. By the time we reached Genoa they were well versed in the catechism of death.

It wasn't difficult to find Nicholas. A great crowd of children milled around him on what must have been an open part of the foreshore. It was from here that the trumpets blared and from where snatches of the hymns sung on the crusade reached us. As we drew nearer I could see that he stood on the deck of a fishing boat drawn onto the beach so that he might be above the milling crowd. He wore his green monk's habit and carried his tau cross and it seemed from the excited children around him that he had just completed preaching. He was flushed of face and his eyes carried an unnatural brightness and I could see he was still glorying in the adulation he was receiving. He had become imbued with a sense of his own importance and power. Just by looking at him I knew that he still believed the waters would harden at the touch of his feet to create the miraculous pathway that, in his mind, would establish his qualities as a saint.

The two monks, almost obscene in their bulk and appearance of wellbeing, who towered over the skeletal children, pushed through the crowd so I was able to get close enough to Nicholas. 'Nicholas, we're here, we have arrived!' I called out. He had his back slightly turned to me and while I felt sure he must have heard me he gave no sign of having done so. 'Nicholas, it's Sylvia, Sylvia and Reinhardt!' I shouted again. He turned slowly. 'You're late!' he called down. 'We've been here two days!' His voice was edged with annoyance. I smiled, ignoring his rude rebuttal, and replied, 'Small children, short legs!'

He turned his back to me to face the bulk of the crowd and lifted the tau cross high. 'In two hours, at sunset we will commence to walk across the sea, along the shining path!' he announced, then added, 'Tell all to make ready, we will walk under a full moon God will send to light our way.'

'It's a new moon tonight,' Reinhardt laughed at my side.

A great roar rose up from the mob of children. Brass trumpets blared, tattered banners were hoisted and various groups broke into spontaneous song. Our own children and many others around us tasted the two beautiful words on their tongues – 'shining path,' they kept repeating.

I waited until I thought it possible for him to hear me. 'Nicholas, we *must* talk!' I called again.

'Not now, can't you see I'm busy!' he shouted back angrily.

I was not to be put off. 'When?' I shouted, trying to keep the annoyance from my voice.

He sighed visibly. 'Tonight, on the shining path!'

'Nay! I must see you now! It cannot wait!'

I could see the furious look on his face as he crossed the small deck to stand over me. 'Who do you think you are?' he screamed. 'I am Nicholas of Cologne and I must be obeyed! I am of a mind to forbid you to come with us! You seek only the glory! You wish to take it from me! I will not have it! It is me who heard the voice of the angel, Jesus speaks only to me! You hear? I am his spokesman!' he shouted, wagging his finger at me, and then he stamped his foot like a small boy.

I might well have lost my temper were it not for this last childish action. Nicholas, I could see, was close to breaking point.

'Nicholas, I am not coming with you. Please listen, there will be no shining path across the sea!'

'What? What did you say?' He had yet to address me by my name.

'It won't happen. Can't you see what we have done is wrong? Come with me to Rome. It is only a month's journey. We will ask the Pope to cancel the *vota* and declare the Children's Crusade over.' As if to emphasise my despair I added, 'Too many children have died, too many still suffer, you cannot go on with this.'

He drew back as if I had struck him across the face. 'Blasphemer!' he yelled, backing away and pointing at me. 'Blasphemer! Blasphemer!' he repeated. Then he went down on his knees with one forearm shielding his eyes, the other still pointing at me. 'Satan, get thee away from me!' he screamed, and then collapsed to the deck weeping.

A dozen bigger boys forced their way towards us. I would later learn that they were his bodyguards, the ones who ate first of whatever was available. They were referred to fearfully by the other children as 'The First Biters' and several of the young females claimed to have been raped by them. There were said to be fifty of these young bullies who hadn't been present when we had broken into groups.

One of the larger specimens now came up to me and stood with his snotty face so close to me I could smell his rancid breath. He sniffed a glob of mucus back into his nostril and jabbed a dirty finger into my chest. 'Bugger off!' he growled. Then he grabbed my habit at the neckline to further threaten me or perhaps to throw me off my feet. But my knee smashed into his groin first and he let out a yelp, like a dog suddenly struck, then collapsed into a foetal position, groaning and clutching at his pubescent manhood.

I felt a pair of strong arms embrace me from the back and was about to struggle and bite when I realised they were black. 'Come, Sylvia, it is time to go now,' Brother Aloysius said gently into my ear. My language lessons were coming along nicely – I understood every word and unhappily withdrew with the two huge monks on either side of me. A nervous Reinhardt, piping for our children to follow us, looked exceedingly relieved to be away from the scene.

Poor, poor Nicholas. He had lost his way completely and there seemed nothing we could do but wait for Evensong to observe his ultimate destruction. My greatest concern was for the disillusionment of the pilgrim children. It was obvious that, despite the terrible suffering and hardship and the deaths they had witnessed all around them, those that remained *still* believed that on this very night they would begin the second half of their journey along the shining path to the Holy Land, that the glorious Redeemer would supply a full moon on a near moonless night to light the way across the sea and all the way to the gates of Jerusalem.

We spent the rest of the afternoon giving dying children the final unction. They had managed to get this far and in their minds they believed they had almost reached Jerusalem. Those who still had the strength begged to be saved so that they might complete the journey. Brothers Bruno and Aloysius were strong men, but many times that afternoon they broke down in tears at the pathetic little bundle of bones they were sending on their way to heaven.

The bells of the Holy Cross Church that looked over the harbour pealed Evensong and we made our way back to where Nicholas was preparing to preach. Children, most of them barefoot and all of them in rags, parted respectfully at our approach, many calling out the glad tiding of their imminent departure and asking if I would sing. The tide had come in and the fishing boat now floated in about an arm's length of water, still sufficiently close to the shore for Nicholas to preach to the children.

Nicholas stood on the deck in his green monk's habit with the hood pulled over his head so that his face was in shadow, behind him a magnificent Genoese sunset splashed across the western sky, the harbour surface burnished with gold. A child trumpeter of considerable expertise, who I had not previously heard, stood beside him and blew a series of beautiful notes to bring the excited children to silence. Then the child jumped into the water up to his waist and waded to the shore. This was the water that all the children present, except perhaps for the healing angels in our own little group, expected would soon become a shining path where they would walk with dry feet across the surface of the sea.

Nicholas began to preach, repeating the sermon he had given on our departure from Cologne where God parted the Red Sea for the escaping Israelites. He had lost none of his power and soon captured the imagination of the enraptured children, who for a short while seemed to forget their hunger and suffering, enchanted with his wonderful words. They groaned as the Egyptians approached, closer and closer to Moses and his fleeing Israelites, some of the smaller children fearfully covering their eyes with dirty little hands as if they couldn't bear to witness what might happen next. They cheered when God's hand emerged from the clouds to touch the towering waves and cause them to resume in a crash of thunder and foam down onto the hapless Egyptian chariots. They wept at the escape of the crippled shepherd boy. This was a story that was about to involve the same God acting on behalf of the Children's Crusade, though this time Nicholas, their Moses, promised that the giant forefinger of the Creator would draw a line across the ocean to make a path for them. They gazed enraptured up into the golden heavens expecting the miracle of God's forefinger at any moment.

Nicholas came to the end of his sermon by which time the sun had almost set and, indeed, a path of gold where its rays focused down on the opening to the harbour appeared to make a clean and perfect shining path across the sea. A single shaft of light carried from the dying sun into the golden shine of water became in their minds the finger of God. To these children, who had never seen the sun set over a shoreless expanse of ocean, the miracle seemed intact. They watched, shouting and weeping to the glory of God, as Nicholas stepped from the deck of the boat and dropped with a loud splash into the harbour.

That was the last time I was to see Nicholas. We tried in vain to get to him, but the crush of weeping and wailing children was impossible to navigate. They bumped and ran into each other and into our own terrified children, some tore the rags from their emaciated bodies, others fell onto the sand pushing handfuls into their mouths, some were screaming and clawing at their eyes and scratching open the festering sores on their arms and legs. Children around us threw fits or simply perished, their hearts failing from the shock. It became impossible to get near to where Nicholas of Cologne had ended the Children's Crusade in a splash of dirty harbour water. Almost as he'd entered the water the setting sun dipped behind the rim of the ocean and the shining path disappeared. To those children who may have been watching it must have seemed as if God had changed His mind and cancelled the Children's Crusade.

In all the mayhem and despair that followed, our own children needed to be protected. They too had been carried away by Nicholas's charismatic preaching and, despite being told that there would be no shining path across the sea, most had believed Nicholas to the very end.

So we made our departure from the harbour with many of the smaller members of the Silent Choir of God's Little Children weeping and greatly distressed. We walked into the gathering dark and then on into the moonless night, until our children could go no further. We stopped beside a field of cabbages on the outskirts of the city where the children fell almost where they stood and slept the sleep of the dead.

I made my way still further into the dark field until I knew I was beyond earshot. Then I sat among the cabbages and wailed and wailed, but no tears would come. Although my heart had been broken, I knew I had long since spent my lifetime allotment of tears. I am ashamed to say that at one stage I removed the dagger from Father John's stave and thought to use it on myself. But I heard his voice clearly in my mind, although it seemed a hundred years ago since I'd walked to the Monastery of St Thomas and traded my hens to the mean-spirited kitchen monk and my father's carpentry tools to the lovely Father John. '*Each time you use it, when you place it back, you must pray to our Saviour and thank Him for protecting your life.*' He had blessed this knife with holy water and so I knew it would be committing a terrible blasphemy to use it to end my own life. 'You don't even have permission to kill yourself!' I wailed, then I stabbed a cabbage again and again and when I'd killed it several times by stabbing it in the heart, I went onto my knees and started to pray. I begged God to punish me, knowing that I could never, in what remained of my worthless life, do sufficient penance for the untold misery I had helped to bring about. Then in the cold dawn light I promised my precious Lord and Saviour that I would spend my life protecting His little children.

As the glorious sun rose, and still on my knees, I finally had the courage and the temerity to ask Him for a miracle of my own, a miracle that I could never doubt was from the Father of Heaven Himself. I asked Him to increase my allotment of tears.

It was here that Reinhardt found me and lifted me to my feet. I was cramped and sore from kneeling. 'Look at you, Sylvia Honeyeater! Your knees are caked with mud and your nice nun's habit soiled, there's mud on your boots and, if you'll excuse my French, your eyes, my dear, look like piss holes in the snow!'

I laughed, despite myself. He'd taken a battering on the road and his many-coloured tunic was faded and torn, his hose possessed more holes than yarn and his broken boots clung to his feet as if by some magic trick. His once splendid cap flopped forlornly over one ear but, as if by some miracle, the ridiculous peacock feather remained almost pristine, the morning sunlight catching its brilliant colours. I kissed him on the cheek. 'I love you, ratcatcher,' I said quietly.

He touched his cheek where I'd kissed him. 'Goodness! My goodness!' I could see he was close to tears. 'Come, Sylvia, we must hasten to Rome. The Pope mustn't be kept waiting to hear the finest children's choir in the world, not to mention the glorious lead singer and, of course, the flautist, a truly exceptional talent.' His eyes suddenly shot open in surprise. 'Sylvia, what on earth did you do to that poor cabbage?'

It would not be normal practice in the twelfth century to permit a lay person to sing in church or during mass. If Sylvia's voice was exceptional she may have received a special dispensation from the archbishop, and I have assumed this to be the case. Furthermore, this is a work of fiction and, while it is woven around known events and people, it may contain inaccuracies regarding church practices and life in the twelfth century. In writing this story I have attempted to capture the essence of what we now know as 'medieval times'.

Bryce Courtenay

Acknowledgements

At the conclusion of a new book I often wish that, like the characters in a novel, I could allow my reader to know more about the people who help to make a story happen. The author's mind is the engine, but each chapter is a carriage and each carriage is filled with what other people know and generously allow the engine driver to use. To each of you who helped me write *Sylvia*, some in small ways, others hugely, my heartfelt thanks.

First in line are Jessica Wynands and Clare Rowan who acted as my main researchers. Jessica wrote her Honours thesis on the Children's Crusade at Macquarie University and Clare is Adjunct Professor in the Department of Modern History at Macquarie University. They were unrelenting, patient and diligent, as well as exceedingly scholarly, allowing nothing to be written they hadn't authorised – often with pursed lips and a *'Let me check that first.'*

However, the history of the Children's Crusade is a difficult and obscure subject and most of the scraps of information that make this remarkable and true story lie buried in short and sometimes contradictory Latin texts. I take full responsibility for those translations I chose to use.

Other scholars who assisted are Adjunct Professor John Walmsley, Department of Modern History, Macquarie University; Dr Andrew

Gillett, Department of Ancient History (Division of Humanities), Macquarie University; Professor Alana Nobbs, Head of the Department of Ancient History, Macquarie University; Father David Ranson, Department of Spiritual and Pastoral Theology, Catholic Institute of Sydney.

Then there are the other indispensables, my editor and publisher, Lee White and Clare Forster. Without a good editor a writer is an often hapless wordsmith wandering in the dark. Lee fulfils every criterion for a great professional and all-round nice person. I am very fortunate to have had her at my side and on my side. Clare, as publisher, is the one who encourages and questions, though always gently (*'Perhaps, Bryce, you may wish to look at this section again?'*). I thank you both. You never failed me and never compromised your own high standards.

My gratitude to my beloved partner, Christine Gee, who sustained me, helped in a thousand ways, coordinated everything and never failed to encourage me.

Now in alphabetical order those others who so generously helped: John Adamson for his tireless help with music and, in alphabetical order, John Atkin, Adam Courtenay, Benita Courtenay, Gina Courtenay, Kate da Costa, John Forsyth, Bruce Gee, Dr Ross Hayes, Alex Hamill, Graeme Inchley, Alan Jacobs, Peter Kalina, Dr Irwin Light, Christine Lenton, Fiona McIntosh, Hugh Mackay, Kate Maclaren, Robbee Spadafora, Simon (Naturopath – Macro Wholefoods), Robert Swan, Duncan Thomas, David and Pia Voigt, Annie Williams, Greg and Lorraine Woon.

Finally, those in the engine room, my publishing family at Penguin Books. They were as usual patient, long suffering, refused to panic, trusted me to the end and were always encouraging. Bob Sessions, as Publishing Director, honest, forthright, always encouraging and greatly respected and loved as the boss of publishing. Anne Rogan who, hands on, literally made my book happen. Then all those who help up until the day when my novel appears in a bookshop and I commence a media and book tour: Carmen de la Rue, David Altheim, Deborah Brash, Cathy

Larsen, Tony Palmer, Julie Gibbs, Frances Bruce, Jessica Crouch, Mary Balestriere, Ian Sibley, Rachel Scully, Beverley Waldron, Peter Blake, Louise Ryan, Dan Ruffino, Sally Bateman, Gabrielle Coyne, Peg McColl. I thank you all.

Finally, my thanks for spending the lonely hours with me. Tim Courtenay, who wagged encouragement when awake and never left my side throughout the writing, mostly snoring at my feet. Also, to Princess Cardamon, our beautiful Burmese cat, who deigned to comment occasionally, adding to the narrative by walking across the keyboard before settling in a pool of late afternoon sun on the far corner of my desk.